*Four terrific, talented authors bring you
four fun-filled, sexy romances
to help make your summer a*

Perfect
Summer

You can stroll through the Pacific surf in
Northern California with one of Hollywood's rising
stars, spend your holiday on Lake Mead with a
gorgeous tycoon, revel in the heat of Arizona with a
sexy fire-fighter or visit steamy Atlanta and make a
usually cool, controlled lawyer all hot and bothered!

Could a woman ask for anything more?

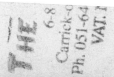

GW00693484

THE
6-8
Carrick-o
Ph. 051-64
VAT.

ABOUT THE AUTHORS

Vicki Lewis Thompson

Vicki Lewis Thompson was a journalist before she became a Mills and Boon® author. She went up in a plane with skydivers, interviewed a witch and took photos of a man who who milked rattlesnakes for their venom. But when her husband Larry bought some romantic novels for her to read, she knew she'd found her niche.

JoAnn Ross

The bestselling author of over fifty novels, JoAnn Ross wrote her first story—a romance about two star-crossed mallard ducks—when she was just seven years old. JoAnn married her high school sweetheart—twice—and makes her home in Arizona.

Janice Kaiser

Janice Kaiser has written over thirty books for several series including Mills and Boon Temptation®. Her stories range from romantic adventures to mysteries to emotional dramas. Janice lives in Northern California with her husband, who is also a bestselling author.

Stephanie Bond

Stephanie Bond's friends, family and fellow computer programmers are usually surprised when they discover she writes romantic comedy. After all, computer nerd and comedienne is a strange combination. When Stephanie isn't in front of her computer, she's usually boating with her husband Chris or at home near Atlanta.

Perfect Summer

VICKI LEWIS THOMPSON
JOANN ROSS
JANICE KAISER
STEPHANIE BOND

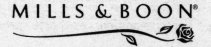

MILLS & BOON®

DID YOU PURCHASE THIS BOOK WITHOUT A COVER?
If you did, you should be aware it is **stolen property** as it was reported
unsold and destroyed by a retailer. Neither the author nor the publisher
has received any payment for this book.

*All the characters in this book have no existence outside the imagination
of the author, and have no relation whatsoever to anyone bearing the same
name or names. They are not even distantly inspired by any individual
known or unknown to the author, and all the incidents are pure invention.*

*All Rights Reserved including the right of reproduction in whole or in part in
any form. This edition is published by arrangement with Harlequin
Enterprises II B.V. The text of this publication or any part thereof may not be
reproduced or transmitted in any form or by any means, electronic or
mechanical, including photocopying, recording, storage in an information
retrieval system, or otherwise, without the written permission of the publisher.*

*This book is sold subject to the condition that it shall not, by way of trade
or otherwise, be lent, resold, hired out or otherwise circulated without the
prior consent of the publisher in any form of binding or cover other than
that in which it is published and without a similar condition including this
condition being imposed on the subsequent purchaser.*

*MILLS & BOON and MILLS & BOON with the Rose Device
are registered trademarks of the publisher.*

*First published in Great Britain 1999 by
Harlequin Mills & Boon Limited,
Eton House, 18-24 Paradise Road,
Richmond, Surrey, TW9 1SR*

PERFECT SUMMER © Harlequin Books S.A. 1999

The publisher acknowledges the copyright holders of the
individual work as follows:

GOING OVERBOARD © Vicki Lewis Thompson 1997
I DO, I DO...FOR NOW © JoAnn Ross 1996
JUST THE WAY YOU ARE © Belles Lettres, Inc. 1996
IRRESISTIBLE? © Stephanie Hauck 1997

ISBN 0 263 81769 5
49-9906

*Printed and bound in Great Britain
by Caledonian Book Manufacturing Ltd, Glasgow*

Going Overboard

VICKI LEWIS THOMPSON

A funny thing happened…

As research for this book, three inexperienced friends and I spent some time on a houseboat not too long ago. It wasn't pretty. I was the genius who suggested renting the biggest houseboat on the lake. After all, bigger is better, isn't it? I had visions of Cleopatra's barge—the reality was closer to the *Titanic*. The four of us survived the trip, but as for the boat, let's just say it was fortunate we decided to take out propeller insurance.

—Vicki Lewis Thompson

Dedication

To my three shipmates on the Houseboat from Hell. As long as you're prompt with your cheques, your identities will remain our little secret.

1

"I'M WORRIED ABOUT how the stripper will go over."
Andi Lombard expertly popped the cork from the champagne bottle and poured the bubbly into the crystal punch bowl being refilled at her elbow. "With the exception of my little sis, Nicole, those women in your living room seem kind of..."

"Repressed?" Ginger Thorson grinned as she added the punch mix.

"No kidding! All the nightgowns Nicole has opened so far must've come from the Vestal Virgin Boutique."

"I'll bet the one you bought isn't like that."

Andi winked. "No, ma'am. Nicole will have to hose Bowie down after she models it for him." She put the empty champagne bottle on the counter. "We need to do something, Ging. How many more of these bottles do you have?"

"That's the last one I have chilled, but there's more in the cupboard. I just thought—"

"Chill 'em. And let's bring out the salty snacks to get them thirsty. If these uptight matrons don't start slugging back the champagne punch, my stripper is going to bomb."

"You want to get them smashed?"

"The way I see it, I'm removing their inhibitions so they'll get the most out of the experience."

"Including your sister's future mother-in-law?"

"That woman is a pain, Ginger. Did you notice how she acted when we met?"

"A little snobbish, I'll admit."

"A little?" Andi drew herself up, adjusted an imaginary set of glasses and stared disapprovingly down her nose as Ginger began to giggle. "Good evening, my dear," Andi mimicked. "You must be Andi. Nicole tells me you live in *Las Vegas.*" Andi looked as if she'd smelled something bad as she pronounced the name of the city. "But then, I suppose everyone has to live *somewhere.*"

"You're right. She is a pain," Ginger said, laughing.

"Admit it, you'd like to see her ripped."

"I would." Ginger opened a cupboard and pulled out chips and pretzels. "Forget the petits fours. We'll serve these." She dumped the snacks into bowls and took a handful of chips. "I like this stuff better, anyway. You can be on punch patrol."

"And let's take a break from opening presents and get some games going. Do you have Pin the Penis On the Man?"

Ginger nearly choked on her mouthful of chips.

"I guess you don't," Andi said, patting her friend on the back. She dipped a cup in the punch and handed it to her. "Sorry about that."

Ginger took a gulp of the punch and cleared her throat. "Andi, these women would pass out if they heard the word *penis* spoken aloud."

"Okay, then how about Twister? That's fun."

"They expect sedate paper-and-pencil games."

Andi groaned.

"As long as they're sitting down, they'll be able to drink more," Ginger told her.

"Then let's get to it. I'm afraid pouring punch down them is the only way we're gonna save this evening."

"Andi Lombard, you are a wicked, wicked lady." Ginger picked up the punch bowl. "And thank God you showed up."

She wouldn't have dreamed of *not* showing up, Andi thought as she followed Ginger into the living room with the chips and pretzels. After all, her baby sister was getting married, and they'd always been there for each other. As globe-trotting military brats, they'd faced new base housing, new schools and new playmates with a united front. Andi had shared with her sister the friends she made so easily, and Nicole had kept Andi from flunking out.

Then Andi had watched with pride and a touch of envy as little Nicole graduated from college and landed an accounting job at prestigious Jefferson Sporting Goods of Chicago. Meanwhile, Andi had decided to abandon her search for the perfect major at the University of Nevada, and in the past few years had turned her hand to everything from dealing blackjack to selling jet-skis. Nothing held her interest for long.

In two days Nicole would marry Bowie Jefferson, younger brother of Chauncey M. Jefferson the Fourth, the man who ran the sporting goods company. Andi hadn't met this latest in the line of Roman-numeral Chaunceys, a guy who liked to be called *Chance*. Nicole had told her that he was cute, but strictly a type A who thought only about business. Bowie, thank the Lord, was a barrel of laughs. And although Andi was thrilled for her sister, she couldn't quiet the nagging voice telling her that Nicole was making a life, while she—Andi—was making a mess.

She walked into the living room toward her sister and picked up Nicole's camera from an end table, although there had been precious few Kodak moments at this shower. If it weren't for her faith in Bowie to make Nicole's life interesting, she'd kidnap her sister and haul her fanny out of here before she became as boring as this crowd.

A glance at Nicole's punch cup told her the guest of honor hadn't taken time to taste any of the first batch. She leaned toward her sister. "Drink up. Wine is about to flow in torrents around here."

Laughter twinkled in Nicole's clear blue eyes. "And what plot have you and Ginger been hatching in the kitchen, as if I couldn't guess?"

"Trust me, your shower will become much more interesting if you're three sheets to the wind," Andi said under her breath. Then she turned to the assembled women. "Anyone for charades?"

Nicole's muffled laugh was the only thing filling the silence as all the women stared at Andi.

Ginger quickly put down the punch bowl and picked up a stack of small notepads from a lamp table. "There's a new guessing game I thought would be fun."

"Guessing games!" Andi smiled. "I have a great idea. Everyone can guess the size of Bowie's pe—um, schlong."

Eyes widened, and a few titters circled the room.

Mrs. Chauncey M. Jefferson the Third, ensconced in a corner wing chair like a monarch on a throne, got red in the face. "I don't think we're going to—"

"We'll all guess the number of children Nicole's going to have," Ginger said quickly. "Then once we've guessed, we shuffle a deck of cards…"

Andi zoned out on the explanation of the dweeby game. Maybe she'd have to kidnap Nicole, after all, along with Bowie, and take them out to Nevada, where they could let loose and have a good time. The tentacles of the Jefferson Sporting Goods money and prestige just might choke the life out of them here in the suburbs of Chicago.

As everyone else played the games Ginger orchestrated, Andi made the rounds, quietly refilling punch cups. She emptied and refilled the punch bowl twice. Nicole still didn't seem to be drinking the punch, but Andi wasn't worried about her sister. In the right atmosphere, Nicole could party with the best of them, even stone-cold sober. Andi liked what she saw happening to the group, however, as laughter grew raucous and postures became more uninhibited.

Then Ginger glanced at her watch and suggested they open the last few gifts. Figuring the punch had done its work, Andi returned to her station beside Nicole and handed her another package wrapped in tasteful white paper with a virginal white bow.

Nicole held up a flannel granny gown and exclaimed over how warm it would keep her.

"Wozy and carm," said a women in a conservative brown suit. "Whoops, I mean *warmy and coze*." She giggled. "Goodness, what *do* I mean?"

Andi glanced up at Ginger, who was pressing her lips together in what seemed like a desperate attempt not to laugh.

"You're trying to say *warm and cozy,* Edna," said Mrs. Chauncey M. Jefferson the Third. "You shimply got your tongue twishted around your eyeteeth."

"Dolores Jefferson, you sound a little tipsy!" exclaimed a woman sitting demurely on a love seat. Then she began slipping down into the cushions. "And so do I. What fun! I haven't been tipsy in years."

"Nonshense," said Mrs. Chauncey M. "Nobody's tipshy around here. Sit up straight, Mary."

As Mary tried unsuccessfully to right herself on the

love seat, Nicole gripped Andi's shoulder. "Andi, I think they're all—"

"Time for my gift!" Andi said, grabbing the black box decorated with a large red ribbon.

"It's time for coffee," Nicole muttered.

"First open this." Andi plopped the box into Nicole's lap.

"What naughty wrapping!" said a woman whose upswept hairdo seemed to be coming unraveled. "Naughty, naughty, naughty." She started laughing, as if she'd made a wonderful joke.

"Here goes nothing." Nicole tucked a blond curl behind her ear and lifted the lid of the box as if afraid something might jump out. "Oh…my…God." She slammed down the lid.

"Let us see," said Mrs. Chauncey M. with a wave of her punch cup. "You think we were born yeshterday?"

"Show us," called out another woman.

"Show us," chorused two others, and soon a chant had begun, complete with clapping. *Show us, show us, show us.*

Ginger sat on the floor next to Andi and elbowed her in the ribs. "How's this?"

"Perfectamundo." Andi grinned as she surveyed the results of her handiwork. "The ladies are tight as ticks." She leaned over toward Ginger. "And our little stripper is due any minute." Then she aimed the camera as Nicole slowly opened the box and held up a crotchless black teddy.

Ginger whooped her approval. "You go, girl!"

"I have *always* wanted to see one of those," said Mrs. Chauncey M. "Pass it over, Nicole, *deary*."

"Me, first," cried Mary, trying to struggle up from the love seat. "You always get to be first, Dolores, *deary*."

"I want to see it, too," said Edna of the brown suit.

As Andi clicked the camera, the women staggered to their feet and clumped together in a laughing, joking circle around Mrs. Chauncey M., who had lunged forward and snatched the sexy lingerie before Mary could get it.

Nicole shook her head slowly. "Unbelievable. My sister comes to town, and within hours my very proper mother-in-law-to-be is examining a crotchless teddy, slurring her speech and calling me *deary.*"

Andi lowered the camera. "Enjoy it, Nic. Life just doesn't get much better than this."

"But it will, right?" Ginger nudged her and tipped her head toward the door.

"Let's hope so." Andi glanced at her watch. "It's getting kinda late. I—"

The doorbell rang, and she shot to her feet, the camera in her hand. "Bingo."

"Andi," her sister called after her. "My heart can't take much more. What are you up to now?"

Andi twirled back to her. "The usual. Try some of that punch, sis!" Excitement pumped through her veins as she hurried to the foyer and squinted through the peephole at the visitor on the other side of the door.

Sure enough, a gorgeous specimen stood in the apartment hallway. He'd assumed the guise of a quintessential businessman—beneath an unbuttoned wool topcoat, he wore a navy pinstriped suit and a pale blue dress shirt. He was probably wearing burgundy wingtips that would pass her military father's spit-shine test with flying colors.

As he stood waiting for her to answer the door, he lightly mussed his dark, close-cropped hair, unfastened the top button of his shirt and loosened his red and navy power tie. She would have enjoyed performing those little tasks for him. Even if the women in the room behind her didn't have a good time with this hunk, she would.

His deliciously square-cut jaw had just a hint of five-o'clock shadow, making him look exactly like an executive who'd just spent a long day at the office. He held a briefcase that probably contained a compact sound system. If he performed as beautifully as he'd presented himself, he'd earn a big tip.

Andi unlatched the door.

CHANCE JEFFERSON hated to interrupt Nicole's bridal shower, but he needed her signature on an insurance policy and she kept forgetting to come by his office and take care of it. Once her parents arrived from Germany tomorrow, she'd be completely occupied until the wedding, and he thought it would be worse dealing with insurance policies at the wedding reception. He wasn't letting his new sister-in-law leave on her honeymoon without being properly insured.

God, he was tired. Sighing, he unbuttoned his collar and loosened his tie. Although pleased his brother had found Nicole, Chance felt the heaviness of yet another weight settling on his shoulders. Bowie would never think of things like life insurance, so once again Chance had to remember what responsibilities his father would have assumed had he been alive. Those responsibilities seemed to come thick and fast these days. Bowie's new wife, wonderful as she was, would contribute another one.

A tall blonde in a miniskirt opened the door and gave him an enthusiastic smile. Some of his fatigue evaporated. He took note of spectacular legs and a tight black sweater that stirred his hormonal urges. Her hair was about the same shade as Nicole's, although she wore it longer and more flyaway than Nicole, and there was a similarity to the eyes, although this woman's were hazel, not blue like

Nicole's. At the moment those hazel eyes were full of mischief.

Chance didn't feel in much of a party mood, but he summoned up a smile and held out his hand. "You must be Andi."

"Yes, and you're late!" She took his hand and pulled him through the doorway.

Caught off guard, he allowed himself to be yanked inside. "I wasn't—"

"Never mind giving me excuses. We're wasting time. Let me have your briefcase." She grabbed it out of his hand.

He grabbed it back. "I'll handle this, if you don't mind."

She took hold of the handle again. "You can't do everything! I'll take care of this part. I know how these things work."

"Really?" Fascinated, he let her have the briefcase. He couldn't believe she was planning to handle Nicole's insurance needs, especially after Nicole had described her sister as a lovable, impractical nut.

"Any idiot can operate a tape player. Let's get your coat off." She started working him out of his coat, brushing her body against him in the process, filling his senses with her heady perfume.

"What tape player?" He wondered if he was so tired he was hallucinating.

She paused with the coat half removed. "You don't have one?"

"Well, sure, but not—"

She abandoned her task, leaving his coat dangling from one arm, and came around to stand in front of him, hands on hips. "Look, you're not on anything, are you?"

He took his coat the rest of the way off and tossed it

on the hall table. "I don't know what you're talking about."

"The hell you don't. Let's take a look." In another totally unexpected move, she put both hands on his shoulders and pulled him forward to peer into his eyes.

He caught his breath, too entranced by this close-up view to protest. Looking into those hazel eyes of hers, he could think of nothing but what it would be like to kiss her. He couldn't understand it. He'd been sane before she opened the door, but now he wouldn't testify to having any brain cells working.

"Your pupils don't look dilated, but I swear, if you've come here doped up, I'll report you."

He gazed down at her and detected a flicker of sensual awareness in her eyes. "Who're you going to tell?" he asked softly.

She released him just as quickly as she'd grabbed him and pushed him toward the living room. "Never mind who I'll tell. Just get in there."

He stood his ground. No matter how sexy she was, he wouldn't be ordered around. "I'll need my briefcase."

"I told you that I'd take care of that part."

"I don't think so." He made a grab for the briefcase, but she jerked it out of reach.

"I'll do it! Will you *please* get into that room and start stripping before those women sober up?"

He stared at her, unable to process the whole sentence at once. First he had to digest the part about her wanting him to strip in front of a group of women including his mother. He had just about worked his way around that and was heading for the *sober up* part, when the doorbell rang.

She grimaced. "Oh, for heaven's sake. Wait a second. I don't want you starting without me."

"Not on your life."

She strode back to the door and jerked it open.

A guy in a police uniform stood there, grinning at her. "Somebody called about a loud party up here."

"Sorry, Officer, we'll keep it down," Andi said, and started to close the door.

He stuck out his hand and held the door open. "Just a second. You'd better get me Andi Lombard."

She opened the door wider. "I'm Andi."

"Hello, Andi. I'm your stripper."

Chance folded his arms and waited. He told himself not to feel the least bit sorry for her. She'd hired a stripper for a party that included wives of major stockholders. That included his *mother*, for God's sake. She'd also apparently gotten them all blotto. She deserved this little moment.

He felt sorry for her, anyway.

She stood motionless, her back to him. Finally she spoke, her voice high and squeaky. "Would you both excuse me for a minute?" Then she walked out the door, past the confused stripper.

Chance followed her out the door. "Stay right there. Don't do anything," he said to the man.

"I'm paid by the job, not the hour. I can wait."

He found her several feet down the apartment hall, her face the color of a stoplight, her eyes squeezed shut as she pumped her fists up and down in an obvious effort not to scream.

"Andi, listen, I—"

She went immediately still but kept her eyes shut. "A kind person would just shoot me."

God, she was cute with her color high like that. Too cute for his own good. "I'll leave the papers for Nicole on the hall table," he said. "Have her sign where I indicated and get them back to me tomorrow."

She nodded, still not opening her eyes.

He started to say something else, something to ease her embarrassment, but thought better of it. His position didn't allow him to condone this kind of behavior, even if the perpetrator was the most adorable screwup he'd met in years.

He walked back to the apartment, took the papers out of his briefcase and left them where she'd see them. Then he picked up his topcoat and walked out. As he passed the stripper still standing outside the doorway, he paused. ''Just remember that most of the women in that room have only seen one naked man in their lives. Go easy on them.''

2

SEVEN LONG MONTHS since she'd seen Nicole, Andi thought as she paced the gate area of the Las Vegas airport, waiting for her sister and Bowie to walk through the jetway. This houseboat trip on Lake Mead, just the three of them, was a great idea, and she had Nicole to thank for it. For one thing, she'd get to see Nicole before the baby was born in two months, and for the other, Nicole would be able to give her some guidance as she struggled, at long last, to get some direction in her life.

The prospect of becoming an aunt had trained a spotlight on her own unsettled lifestyle and made her yearn for more stability. Maybe she'd found something worth pursuing in her latest venture of teaching yoga, but she wasn't quite sure, and desperately wanted some validation from Nicole. It was, she thought with a smile, sort of like running to Nicole with her unfinished term paper, the way she'd done so many times when they were younger. Nicole would know what to do.

Andi had been having similar thoughts for quite a while, even before the wedding, but that hadn't been a time for long talks with Nicole. After the disaster with Chance Jefferson at the bridal shower, Andi had tried to keep a low profile. In fact, she'd specifically been trying to avoid him when she'd toppled over backward into the hotel fountain during the reception. She was certain he thought she'd had too much to drink, when actually she'd stayed away from the trays of champagne flutes. She didn't want to get tipsy and embarrass herself.

And it *really* wasn't her fault that two of those waiters had been so busy watching her climb out of the fountain they'd run into each other. Could she help it if Chance had been right in the line of fire when the champagne trays went flying? Thank God she wouldn't have to spend much time in Chance's company. Between being attracted to his good looks and intimidated by his efficiency, she became a basket case every time he showed up.

She concentrated on the flow of people from the black tunnel of the jetway, and finally spied Nicole. With a shriek of welcome, she hurried forward, arms outstretched. "Come here, you pudgy woman!"

"I am not pudgy!" Nicole hugged her fiercely. "I'm just smuggling a small watermelon."

"You look darling carrying a watermelon."

"Doesn't she?" Bowie came up behind her, holding a duffel bag. His good-natured face beneath a thatch of sandy hair had filled out a little, probably due to Nicole's cooking, Andi figured.

Andi released her sister and turned to give him a hug. "Hey, what do you mean, knocking up my sister?"

"It's what guys do," he said. "I can see we need to have a talk about the facts of life. How've you been? Fallen in any fountains lately?"

Andi pulled his head down and whispered in his ear, "That's a dangerous thing to say when we'll be on a houseboat together for a week. Accidents happen, you know."

"Andi," Nicole said, a tremulous quality to her voice, "we have the best surprise."

Andi turned toward her sister. "Twins?"

"No." She glanced behind her.

For the first time, Andi's field of vision lengthened to take in more than her sister and brother-in-law, and when she saw who was standing behind them, suited up as if for Michigan Avenue, briefcase in hand, she gulped.

"Look who agreed to come on the trip," Nicole said. "The four of us will have a ball, don't you think?"

As Andi looked into Chance Jefferson's blue eyes, she saw her own astonishment mirrored there.

He glanced at Bowie. "Andi's going, too?"

HE'D BEEN SET UP. And so had Andi, judging from the look on her face when she'd first seen him. As they headed toward baggage claim, Andi and Nicole walked ahead, lost in conversation. Chance hoped it was about bassinets and crib mobiles; he feared it was about him. Andi had her arm around her sister. At first, Chance had wondered if she'd back out, knowing he was part of the package, but apparently she was willing to suffer through a week in his company to be with Nicole.

Chance grabbed Bowie's arm and dropped back a few paces.

Bowie sighed. "Okay, so I should have told you."

"And *her*. Did you see the look on her face when she first saw me? She doesn't want me on this trip."

"Nicole wanted to tell both of you, but I was afraid at least one of you would cancel if you knew. Nicole and I cut cards to settle the argument about telling or not, and I won."

Chance kept his voice low. "So what's the deal? Is this some plot to create family harmony between Andi and me?"

Bowie glanced at him. "Something like that."

Chance didn't trust the gleam in Bowie's eyes. "Oh, no, you don't."

"Just get to know her, Chance."

"Hey, I'm not interested in—"

"She's a great gal. You two got off to a rocky start, but—"

"Are you insane? I can't believe you're seriously trying to fix me up with your wife's sister. There's, conservatively, a million-to-one chance of it working out, and that leaves a hell of a lot of room for total chaos. This is a terrible idea, Bowie."

Bowie set his jaw. "Is it? I saw the way you looked at her when she climbed out of the fountain, like somebody hit you between the eyes with a two-by-four."

"Which is about what I expected to happen next! Whenever she's around it's like being in a disaster movie. Coming this summer, to theaters near you—*Andi*."

"You looked that way when you went bonkers over Myra Oglethorpe in tenth grade," Bowie persisted.

"You can't possibly remember how I looked at Myra Oglethorpe."

"Wanna bet? I was the kid brother. You were like a god to me. I remember the orchid corsage you bought her for the Christmas dance. I remember the burgundy cummerbund you didn't want to wear until Mom told you it made you look like Tom Selleck. You were so nervous you passed out ten minutes before you were supposed to leave with Dad to pick her up."

Chance's eyes narrowed as he looked at his brother. "And you threatened to tell her all about it at the bus stop on Monday unless I gave you twenty bucks."

Bowie shrugged. "So I was into blackmail. A guy has to supplement his allowance somehow."

"Now I know why I came on this trip. So you could remind me of all those golden memories. Dammit, Bowie, I think I'll snag my luggage and take it back upstairs to the ticket counter. I have a ton of work to do, and Andi would love to see me disappear. I'd save us all a lot of trouble.''

"I wish you wouldn't.''

"Look, if you're trying to get something started between Andi and me, I might as well leave. I can see it's a mistake, even if you can't.''

"It's not just that.''

"So what else?''

"This is supposed to be my birthday trip, right? The one Dad always took us on a week or two after our birthdays.''

The role he'd been shoved into so abruptly began wrapping its tentacles around him. "Yeah, but—''

"When you said we could take this trip together, I felt like…'' Bowie looked away. "Well, like we were keeping something important going.''

Hell. Chance knew a killer argument when he heard one. Bowie had instinctively appealed to his sense of tradition and responsibility. As much as he might want to fly back to Chicago, as much as Andi might want him to, he was stuck here.

"Okay, I'll stay," he said quietly. "But this matchmaking thing is not happening, Bowie. I—'' He was distracted by the beeping of a cart whisking passengers to a gate. It bore down on Andi and Nicole, their heads together in serious discussion, oblivious to the world around them.

"Nicole! Watch out!'' he called, sprinting forward.

Andi looked up first and pushed Nicole out of the way, but the cart had to swerve to avoid Andi. It sideswiped a gift-shop display, which launched glittering souvenir visors and fanny packs out into the terminal. The smooth soles of Chance's dress shoes found a slick spot on the floor and he landed on his butt amid the scattered merchandise. Fortunately, a fanny pack cushioned his briefcase as it slammed to the floor. And so it continues, he thought. *Andi, The Movie.*

ANDI WOULD WALK through hell for her sister, and hell it would be this week, she thought as she drove her van toward Lake Mead. They'd all bought visors and fanny packs from the disrupted gift stand as a peace gesture, and everyone wore a visor except Chance, who'd stuck his in his briefcase. Andi supposed it didn't go with his suit, but he should have put it on just to demonstrate solidarity, in her opinion. Not that he gave a damn about her opinion.

Before the latest incident, Nicole had been explaining that Chance desperately needed a break from his crushing responsibilities and besides that, he and Bowie needed time to bond. She'd been laying the blame on Bowie for not notifying Andi about this little surprise appearance, when the courtesy cart had nearly taken them both out. Andi figured she might as well get used to that sort of pandemonium. It never failed to happen when she was around Chance.

For the moment, she concentrated very hard on her driving, which wasn't simple considering that Chance sat in the passenger seat next to her. It was a logical arrangement, along with assigning Bowie and Nicole to the middle seat. The rest of the van was stuffed with luggage and the gear she'd brought. Bowie had packed an extra sleeping bag for Chance, and brought an extra fishing pole. As long as they caught fish, the groceries Andi had bought would probably stretch to four people. Logistically, Chance's presence wouldn't cause a problem. Emotionally—well, she'd just have to try to ignore him.

Ha. What red-blooded woman would be able to ignore

a man who looked like Chance? Too bad he hadn't turned out to be a stripper. So far today he'd taken off his suit coat and tie after experiencing Las Vegas in the middle of an August heat wave, but that was the extent of his disrobing. A faint scent of expensive men's cologne drifted across to Andi as he shifted in his seat to say a few words to Bowie.

In the midst of the conversation, a phone rang.

Andi glanced around before realizing the noise came from the briefcase at Chance's feet. "Your briefcase is ringing," she said.

"Yeah. Excuse me." He pulled it onto his lap, flipped it open and took out a cellular phone.

While Nicole pointed out landmarks to Bowie, Chance spoke at length with the person on the phone and made notes on a pad he pulled out of a briefcase pocket. He looked as if he were sitting in his office back on Michigan Avenue. If he kept this up, there would be precious little bonding going on, Andi thought.

"Look at that lake, Nic," Bowie said as Andi took the road leading around it toward the marina. "Smooth as glass."

"I've been looking. I'm dying to get into the water and cool off."

"Me, too," Andi said.

"Control yourself," Bowie said. "I know how you like to fling yourself into the first body of water you come to."

"Sometimes it's more fun to fling someone else into the first body of water I come to," Andi retorted. Although Bowie's teasing helped keep her from obsessing about Chance's being around, her brother-in-law was partly to blame for her having to deal with Chance in the first place. She just might push Bowie overboard. She'd push Nicole overboard, too, except she had to think of the baby.

Chance put the phone back in his briefcase and continued to make notes on the pad.

"Who was that?" Bowie asked.

"Eikelhorn." Chance kept writing.

"You know," Bowie said, "I wonder if he's steering us wrong about that ad agency. I've seen a couple of their ads, and they seem pretty pedestrian to me."

"Mmm." Chance's attention remained on his notes.

"There are a couple of other agencies that might be able to do a better job for us, if you'd like me to check them out."

"Eikelhorn has it under control." Chance underlined something and tapped the end of his pen against the paper. It was obvious he wasn't really listening to what Bowie had said.

"Yeah, well, it was just a thought." Bowie sounded disappointed but resigned.

Andi glanced in the rearview mirror just as Nicole put a comforting hand on Bowie's knee. Then she looked over at Chance, who was still engrossed in the notes he was making, apparently unaware that he'd cavalierly sliced and diced his brother's suggestion. Anger boiled in her. Bowie was a great guy, and he sure as hell didn't deserve to be dismissed like that. Chance might be gorgeous. He might be skilled and efficient at business matters. But he didn't know squat about how to treat his brother.

Andi suddenly didn't feel so intimidated by the man. Chance Jefferson wasn't perfect, after all. In fact, he needed to be taught a thing or two. Apparently, Nicole hadn't made any progress in that department, but then, she'd always been shy about such matters. Time for the second team to take the field.

CHANCE MADE SEVERAL calls on his cellular phone before they reached the marina and, in the process, he concluded that concentrating on business this week would help him keep his mind off Andi. She'd met them at the airport in very short shorts, a skinny little neon-green shirt and high-tops. He could tell she enjoyed flamboyance, although she probably considered him immune to it. He wasn't. Bowie was right about his reaction to her. Despite the disasters that swirled around her, he was fascinated. Come to think of it, the emotions she stirred in him weren't so different from the way he'd felt when he'd fallen for Myra Ogle-thorpe.

But he wasn't in tenth grade anymore, even though there were days he wished he were, days when he'd give anything to abandon the prestige and money in favor of freedom. It wasn't an option.

"Well, gang, here we are." Andi parked the van next to the marina. "I'll get the paperwork taken care of if you'll load everything into those wheeled carts down by the dock." Then she hopped out of the van, grabbed a folder of papers and started toward the registration office.

Chance watched the hypnotizing motion of her bottom for about two seconds too long and Bowie caught him at it. "Well, what are we waiting for?" he asked briskly, ignoring Bowie's grin as he stepped into the blast furnace of a Nevada summer day. The growl of outboard motors filled the air and the acrid scent of diesel fuel triggered memories of his uncle's boat and lazy Wisconsin sum-mers. Back then he'd been impatient to grow up, with no clue how precious those carefree days had been.

"Nicole, you just relax your pregnant self," Bowie said. "Chance and I, in an incredibly manly gesture, will load up those carts."

Nicole spread her arms wide. "Ah, vacation."

"Of course, we expect you women to do all the cooking," Bowie added.

Nicole laughed. "I'll be willing to cook whatever you manly men catch, but you'd better not let Andi hear you talking like that. She'll roast you on a spit over the campfire in no time."

Chance didn't doubt that for a minute. In fact, at the wedding reception, prior to the fountain debacle, they'd spent their obligatory dance together as maid of honor and best man arguing about her decision to hire a stripper for Nicole's party. Chance had initiated the argument on purpose once he realized how potently she affected him at close range. She'd obliged his need for conflict by taking the offensive and reminding him that men had hired strippers for bachelor parties for generations. She happened to know, she said, that there had been a stripper at Bowie's party. Chance thought it was the better part of valor not to admit who'd hired her.

"I'll go get us a couple of those carts." Chance headed for the dock, where people dressed in Day-Glo-bright bathing suits or T-shirts and tattered shorts moved leisurely around on rubber thongs. The water looked like heaven, and he had the urge to fling himself into it, suit pants, silk shirt, shoes and all. But that was more of an Andi Lombard thing to do, not a Chance Jefferson move.

He restrained himself and grabbed two carts, which he started pushing toward the van. He also needed to put in a call to Annalise, his secretary, before leaving the marina, to impress upon her that she shouldn't hesitate to call him in an emergency. He wished the Ping Golf representatives hadn't been so irritated when he'd postponed a meeting with them until next week.

He wondered again how his dad had been able to manage the birthday trips that had become such a tradition.

Maybe he'd felt more relaxed because he'd built the business. Chance had the daunting task of keeping it going and making it even better.

He wheeled the carts up to the back of the van, where Bowie stood.

"Brings back memories, doesn't it, bro?" Bowie said with a grin.

"Yeah, it does." He'd only seen Bowie this excited twice in the past year—on his wedding day and when he told Chance about the baby.

Bowie heaved a sleeping bag into one of the carts. "I hope you're not gonna tie yourself to that cell phone the whole week."

"I can't just cut off communication with the office." Chance lifted a full cooler out of the back.

"Dad did."

"Well, I'm not Dad."

Bowie unloaded bags of groceries. "I hope to hell you're not. Dead at fifty-six. That's too young."

"He never got any exercise." Chance put four fishing poles into the cart. By now his shirt was sticking to his back. Damn, but it was hot. "I go to the gym three times a week."

"Even that seems to be a job for you. Be honest, what do you do for fun?"

Chance gave him a smile. "I go on houseboat trips with my brother."

"Ah." Bowie stopped to wipe his sweaty forehead. "So, are we having fun yet?"

"Well, boys, I just signed our life away," Andi said, coming up with the folder of papers, swelled by a few extra documents, in one hand. "We're now the temporary occupants of a ten-person houseboat sitting in slip number ten, A dock."

Chance blinked. "Did you say *ten*-person?"

"Yeah," Bowie put in. "Remember? I told you that the only thing available on short notice was a cancellation from a church party, and they'd rented the biggest boat they had, so we got it."

Chance figured he hadn't been listening carefully when Bowie told him that, because the houseboat plans hadn't been high on his list of priorities. "Just how big is a ten-person boat?" he asked.

Andi thumbed through her papers. "I have the dimensions right here. Aha. Forty-seven by fourteen."

"Feet?" Chance asked.

She looked at him with a deadpan expression. "No, inches. All four of us should fit nicely on a boogie board, don't you think?"

"Hey, so what if it's a big boat?" Bowie said. "More room to party!"

"What's all the commotion about?" Nicole asked, climbing out of the van and coming around to the back.

"Chance seems to think the boat's too big," Andi said.

"No, he doesn't," Bowie said.

"Yes, he does," Chance said.

"Look, as I told Bowie when we made the arrangements," Andi said, "it was the same price as a smaller boat, because they had this last-minute cancellation, and they gave us a special deal. So if you're worried that it's costing us too much money—"

"No, it's not the money. That's just a damn big boat."

"So?" Andi asked.

"So it probably takes more than one motor to run it."

"Well, of course it does," Andi said. "It has—" she paused to consult her papers "—twin screws, according to this. I guess that means two sets of propellers. When I signed up they heckled me about getting propeller insurance, but I said we didn't need that because we had two experienced houseboat pilots in the party."

"One for each screw," Bowie said with a grin.

Chance scratched the back of his head and looked at Bowie. "Twin screws. Wasn't Uncle Trevor's a single screw?"

"Twin screws, single screw, what difference does it make?" Bowie said. "A houseboat's a houseboat. A motor's a motor. One for you, one for me. Come on, let's get under way."

Andi looked from Chance to Bowie and back to Chance again. "You two are beginning to sound a lot like Laurel and Hardy, and that makes me nervous. You do know what you're doing, right? Neither of you crewed on the *Exxon Valdez* or anything?"

"Very funny," Bowie said.

"'Cause I can always go back and get propeller insurance. They had an example of a pretty ugly shredding job on display, just so you can see what happens if either of you Jacques Cousteaus back that sucker into a pile of rocks."

"I'm sure that won't happen," Nicole said, "considering all the time they spent on their uncle's houseboat."

"Exactly," Bowie said. "Chance and I aren't about to back this baby into the rocks, are we, bro? Propeller insurance. What a joke."

Chance longed for that insurance, but he didn't want to argue with Bowie about it. "We'll do fine. No worries."

Andi gazed at him. "So said the captain of the *Titanic,* I hear."

That finally got his back up. He wasn't used to being questioned. "Trust me, we can handle this. Now, let's stop standing around in the heat, and get aboard our bargain boat."

With Chance pushing one cart and Bowie the other, they started toward the dock. After a brief stop for ice at the general store, where Chance also put in a quick call to Annalise, they continued toward the mooring slip. Andi and Nicole walked ahead of them, showing the way toward slip number ten.

Chance lowered his voice as he leaned toward Bowie. "I take it Uncle Trevor let you run that boat of his?"

"Are you kidding?"

Chance looked at him in alarm. "You didn't ever drive it?"

"Hell, no," Bowie murmured. "Uncle Trev thought I was a complete screwup and wouldn't let me touch the controls, but I figure you have enough experience for both of us."

"And what makes you think I was allowed to operate that boat?"

"Because you were always considered the responsible one, and I—" Bowie brought his cart to an abrupt stop. "Oh my God. He didn't let you, either?"

Chance shook his head.

"Holy Houseboats, Batman. What do we do now?"

"We stay cool." Chance started pushing the cart down the dock and Bowie continued beside him. "We've both seen the ads for these vacations, and nobody mentions having to be experts at boating, right?"

"Right."

"We haven't operated a houseboat, but we've both driven motorboats."

"Yeah," Bowie responded with a little less confidence. "A few times, anyway."

"And there's got to be some sort of manual."

"And we can both read! Hey, I'm liking this plan.

We're smart. Or at least you're smart. We'll figure this out.''

"I just wish we didn't have such a big boat," Chance said.

"Maybe forty-seven by fourteen isn't as big as you think. Maybe—"

Andi spun around to face them and gestured dramatically toward her left. "Here we are! Home sweet home!"

Bowie turned and gulped. "My God, it's an aircraft carrier."

Speechless, Chance stared at the monster tied up to slip number ten. He'd seen ranch homes in the Chicago suburbs smaller than this.

Andi and Nicole seemed as thrilled by the size of the boat as he was dismayed. They swung open the railing gate and hurried aboard, chattering happily about the spacious accommodations.

"It's spacious, all right," Bowie said in a subdued voice. "I'll bet the church group was gonna hold a revival in there."

"Hell, you could take this across the friggin' Atlantic Ocean."

Bowie rubbed the back of his neck. "Here's an idea. We just stay right here. People do that in Seattle, right? Smart people, those Seattlites, living on houseboats that are permanently tied up to the dock. Never worry about sailing anywhere, those folks. We could—"

"Nope. We're going to take this tub out of here, Bowie. Our manhood is at stake."

"Hey, you guys, get a move on," Nicole called from the deck. "If you don't hurry up, Andi's liable to get sick of waiting around and start up those motors herself."

"We're coming!" Chance and Bowie shouted together as they nearly collided in their effort to get aboard.

3

ANDI FELL IN LOVE with all the little nooks and crannies of the houseboat. As she and the others stowed their gear, she kept finding interesting cubbies for stashing stuff. She'd also discovered something else. Chance wasn't as immune to her as she'd imagined. He probably hated the fact that he reacted to her, but react he did. A slight flush and a quicksilver gleam in his blue eyes gave away his X-rated thoughts about her. It could prove useful. She could teach him a lesson about all work and no play—and perhaps teach him to better appreciate his brother.

At last the four of them gathered in the living-room area of the houseboat. Bowie and Nicole's sleeping bags lay in a back double bunk and Chance had chosen a fold-out bed in the living room. Andi would sleep in the middle of the boat on the top bunk of a single set of bunks.

Nicole dusted her hands together. "That's it for the housekeeping chores. Anchors aweigh."

"You bet," Bowie said, grabbing the thick operations manual from the shelf beside the captain's chair.

Chance took the book out of his brother's hands before he'd even opened it. Frowning, he started flipping pages as Bowie peered over his shoulder.

Andi watched the interaction with some impatience, although she had to admit that air of command could be attractive. Chance had rolled up the sleeves of his dress shirt and his arms had a nice flex to the muscle as he turned the pages. A man as disciplined as Chance probably worked out on a regular basis. But how long had it been since he'd thrown a Frisbee or cannonballed into a swimming pool? Probably years.

"So which one of you is taking us out?" she asked.

"He is," they said in unison, pointing to each other.

"Oh, this is good," Andi said, folding her arms.

Bowie gestured toward Chance. "Just deferring to your age and experience, buddy."

Chance sent him a long look before walking into the pilothouse and slowly taking his seat at the controls. "Right." He flexed his shoulders and studied the panel.

"You're both quite sure you can handle this?" Andi asked.

They responded with a flurry of assurances that left her feeling not the least bit reassured.

Chance ran his fingers over the buttons and stood up again. "I'm going aft to take a look at the motors and figure out the best trajectory when we back out."

"Good idea. I'll go with you." As Bowie followed Chance, he said over his shoulder "*Aft* means the rear of the ship."

"Thank you, Captain Ahab," Andi called after him. She turned to Nicole, who was sitting on one of the bench seats. "What do you think, sis? Do they know what they're doing?"

"I'm not sure about Bowie, but I'm under the impression Chance always knows what he's doing."

"He is pretty damn sure of himself. Does it bother you the way he discounts Bowie's contributions?"

"Drives me nuts. But from what I understand, their father treated Bowie the same way. I'm hoping that maybe on this trip…well, we'll see."

"That's assuming we ever get out on the lake."

"Oh, we will," Nicole said. "You and I both know people who've taken houseboat trips with no boating experience at all. These guys at least have some idea of the process, and I'm sure we can manage it. Plus, I *really* need this break, Andi. I didn't realize bearing the first Jefferson heir was going to be such a big deal."

"Is Mrs. Chauncey M. giving you a hard time?"

Nicole gave her a weary smile. "You know those language tapes you're supposed to play while the baby's still in the womb, so the kid is born already programmed to be bilingual?"

"She bought you some of those?"

"No, she hired a French teacher to come over three times a week and talk to my belly."

"No!" Andi started to giggle. "What does Bowie think of this?"

"He doesn't know. It's supposed to be a surprise for him."

"And when is this surprise going to be unveiled? When little whozit sails onto the delivery table shouting *bonjour?*"

Nicole grinned. "I have no idea."

"What does this French person say to your belly?"

"How should I know? I don't speak French."

"Me, neither, but I gotta try this." Still chuckling, she walked over and got down on her knees in front of Nicole. *"Parlez-vous français?"* she murmured, patting Nicole's belly. "Hey, she kicked back! That must mean she understood me!"

"Oh, I'm sure."

Andi searched her memory for French phrases. "Darling, *je vous aime beaucoup.* Let's see—what else? Oh, that little cartoon skunk." She leaned closer to Nicole's belly. *"Pepe le Peu."*

"Oh, do go on," Nicole said, laughing.

"That's all the French I know. No, wait. Food. French food." Between giggles, she leaned forward again. *"Filet mignon,"* she crooned. *"Pâté de foie gras. Croissants.* Come on, Nic. You cook more than I do. Help me communicate with this kid."

Nicole laughed harder. *"Coq au vin."*

"Coq au vin," Andi repeated. She pushed her lips out in a Gallic pout. *"Château...briand. Vichyssoise. Oui, oui, oui,* all zee way home, my little radish."

Nicole laughed until tears ran down her face.

"Will you look at that, Chance?" Bowie said, coming through the hallway. "We leave them for five minutes and all hell breaks loose. What's up, Nic?"

Nicole just shook her head, helpless with laughter.

"It's a surprise," Andi said, getting to her feet. "But I'll give you a hint. Start practicing 'Frère Jacques' in the shower."

Bowie stared at her before turning toward Chance. "You make any sense of this?"

Chance stood gazing at Andi with a bemused expression on his face. He seemed totally absorbed by the playful scene he and Bowie had interrupted, absorbed by Andi, for that matter. Andi looked into his eyes and saw an emotion she hadn't associated with him before—delight. She was encouraged.

"Chance?" Bowie prompted.

Chance snapped out of his reverie and broke eye contact with Andi. "Uh, sorry. What was that?"

"Never mind. You ready to start the motors?" Bowie asked, exchanging a glance with Nicole.

"Yeah, the motors." He walked quickly to the captain's chair and sat down. Then he consulted the control panel a few seconds more before he started flicking

switches. Soon the boat hummed and throbbed as the twin
engines chugged to life.

Andi watched the mantle of responsibility settle on his
shoulders again. Tension tightened his jaw and narrowed
his eyes. The boy inside him had been banished, at least
for the time being. Andi wondered if she'd be able to coax
that boy out again during this trip...and if she dared get
close enough to try.

HEAVEN HELP HIM, Chance thought, if he allowed Andi
to become a distraction. As he listened for an irregularity
in the chug of the engines, he thought about the ease with
which Andi clowned around with Nicole. Her sheer freedom of spirit mesmerized him. For that brief moment he'd
forgotten everything but Andi, and it had been exhilarating. It had also been embarrassing to have Bowie catch
him at it, yet again.

If Andi could capture his attention so completely when
she wasn't even focusing on him, what would happen to
his concentration if she turned that happy-go-lucky charm
on him full force? He'd have to be damn careful this
week.

Chance turned to Bowie. "You'd better go aft and tell
me how I'm doing. When you give me the signal, I'll
start backing."

Bowie paused. "Uh, Chance?"

"What?" Chance looked up impatiently.

"We're still tied to the dock."

Chance grimaced.

"I'll take care of it," Bowie said, heading toward the
front deck.

Another lesson, Chance thought. He'd been so engrossed in thoughts of Andi he'd almost pulled half of the

Echo Bay dock out into the lake. God knows, the boat was big enough to do it.

"I think I'll go help him untie us," Andi said, following Bowie out onto the deck.

Chance watched her sashay through the door. The light played with her golden hair as she crouched to help Bowie with the thick ropes securing them to the dock. Just looking at her lifted his heart. And addled his brain.

"She's amazing," Nicole said, almost as if she could read the direction of his thoughts. "It's impossible to be depressed around her. She always searches out the fun side of life."

Chance looked over at Nicole. "I thought it was the younger one who was supposed to be wild and crazy."

Nicole laughed and waved a hand toward the front deck. "Tell that to her."

Chance looked outside again. Andi was swinging a rope like a lasso and threatening to hog-tie Bowie, who was pawing the ground and using his forefingers as horns.

"Don't underestimate her because she likes to kid around," Nicole said. "She'd go to the wall for the people she loves."

"Like Bowie."

"Yeah." Nicole smiled. "I recognized right away how alike they were. I'm sure that's what attracted me to him."

"I just wish he enjoyed his work at Jefferson more."

"Well, maybe if you could—" Nicole cut herself off as Andi and Bowie came back inside, flushed and laughing.

Chance felt an overwhelming urge to take Andi in his arms and kiss that laughing mouth. What a huge mistake that would be. "All set?" he asked.

Bowie snapped him a salute. ''All secure and remarkably tight, Captain.''

''Then get back there and protect my ass, Bowie.''

''Aye, aye, Captain.''

Nicole stood. ''I'll go with you and help direct.''

Bowie leered at her. ''Trying to get me alone so you
can have your way with me, aren't you?''

''Of course.''

''Hot-diggity.'' Bowie guided Nicole down the pas-
sageway to the rear of the boat. ''We'll be in the back
making out, if you need us, Captain.''

''Just don't embarrass the family,'' Chance called after
them. He wished Andi had volunteered to go with Bowie
instead of Nicole. That meant smart-mouthed Andi would
be staying up front with him and be a witness to the disaster if he miscalculated and drove this barge into something. From the way she'd reacted to everything so far,
he'd probably never live it down, either. He wiped his
sweaty palms on his pants.

''Don't worry. You'll do fine,'' Andi said.

He glanced at her in surprise. Whatever he'd expected
from her while he attempted this feat, it hadn't been moral
support. ''Thanks.''

''I mean, what's the worst that could happen? You
could wreck the boat, which is worth about a gabbillion
dollars, by backing into someone else's boat, also worth
about a gabbillion dollars, and both boats would sink in
the middle of the harbor, making it impossible for anybody else to get in or out, and we'd all have to swim to
the dock while crowds of people threw rotten food at us.''

He chuckled. ''Thanks for the encouraging words.''

''Anytime.'' She smiled back.

He reached for his sunglasses and put them on, feeling

a little like Tom Cruise in *Top Gun*. He could by damn do this.

Bowie yelled the first command, and he put the boat in reverse. Funny thing, but his palms weren't sweating anymore.

SHE'D DONE IT, Andi thought as she sat on a bench seat where she could watch Chance at the wheel of the boat. She'd made him see the funny side of the situation and a little of the tension was gone from his jaw. And there were signs, small but significant, that he was loosening up. He hadn't acknowledged that Bowie had saved them from pulling off a section of the dock, though.

Slowly the boat slid out of the mooring slip, and when it had cleared, Chance muscled it around to the left with the help of instructions coming from Bowie in the back.

"You're clear. Punch it!" Bowie shouted.

The engines roared as Chance thrust the boat forward before it could drift toward the dock again. Bowie let out a rebel yell as the houseboat moved smoothly out of the marina.

"See?" Andi said. "Piece of cake."

He glanced at her. "Want to drive it?"

She was taken aback. "You mean that?"

"Sure, why not? Getting in and out of the marina has to be the worst of it. Just steer it along the shoreline. It's probably not much different than driving your van."

She stood and walked over to the captain's chair. As he began to explain the control panel to her, she caught another whiff of his cologne and her stomach did that funny little twisting trick again. *Face it, you're attracted to him.* She'd always been a sucker for a man with a nicely sculpted mouth and strong chin. That slight five-o'clock shadow she remembered from that first night in

Ginger's hallway was making its appearance again. Coupled with his flyboy sunglasses, it gave him a roguish air.

"Got it?"

She hadn't heard a word he'd been saying. "Got it."

"Then it's all yours," he said, sliding out of the chair and releasing the wheel.

She quickly took his place and put both hands on the wheel. The lake sparkled in front of her and the rocky coastline slipped by on her right. She adjusted to the motion of steering the boat. "Don't leave."

"I won't." He stood right behind her. "Ease over to the left. That outcropping looks like it extends into the water a ways. It sure helps that the water's so clear. You can see all the obstacles really easy."

"Too bad life isn't like that, huh?"

He sighed. "Yep."

That heartfelt sigh stirred her compassion. She was beginning to imagine what life might be like for the son of a dead business tycoon and a woman who sent a French teacher to instruct her unborn grandchild. Bowie had reacted by accepting the role of the reckless screwup, so nobody expected much of him, but Chance was just gritting it out, trying to carry the load for everyone.

Even through the engine noise she could pick out the sound of his breathing, and the steady rhythm gave her goose bumps. She fantasized what it would be like if they were on this boat by themselves, instead of sharing it with her sister and brother-in-law. She imagined Chance putting his arms around her and helping her steer as they navigated along the rocky shore. "How'm I doing?"

"Just fine." His voice sounded deeper than usual.

What a kick if he'd been having some of the same fantasies, she thought.

"Think you can handle it by yourself now?"

Her rosy fantasy collapsed. "I guess so. Got an important meeting to go to?"

"In a way. I want to change clothes, and I do have some calls to make while clients are still in their offices in New York. Plus, I want to see what the stock market did today."

"Couldn't you let it go for now? It's such a glorious afternoon."

"Can't."

"What's the worst that could happen? I'll bet the clients will still be around tomorrow, and if the stock market crashed, you might as well enjoy your evening, because you're in deep doo-doo, no matter what calls you make."

"First of all, the clients may not be around tomorrow. They might interpret my delay as lack of interest and do business with another company that's more enthusiastic. And the stock-market prices will affect what I say to my broker first thing in the morning, and I have tonight to consider my next move."

"It sounds exhausting. Don't you ever wish you could swim with the minnows for a change?"

"Did I hear somebody up here mention swimming?" Bowie said, coming into the living area. "Nicole's changing into her suit and mourning her lost figure, so I thought I'd—well, shiver me timbers, look who's driving the boat! Hey, Chance, want me to climb up to the roof and put out the distress flag to warn people out of our path?"

"She's doing fine," Chance said.

Andi warmed to the praise. "Watch your tongue, sailor," she said, "or the captain, who is yours truly at the moment, will order you flogged for insubordination."

"Cool. S and M," Bowie said.

Chance laughed.

"Hark!" Bowie said. "A strange sound fills the air.

Could it be? Is the Grand Pooh-Bah of Jefferson Sporting Goods—be still my heart—chortling?''

"I've never chortled in my life," Chance said, still laughing.

"Oh, yes. Chortling. In fact, there was the Great Chortle of 1975, when we snuck those turkeys into—"

"Nicole's out of the bathroom," Chance said, smoothly interrupting. "I'm changing clothes and making those calls."

"You just don't want Bowie to tell about the turkeys and spoil your image as a buttoned-down executive," Andi accused.

"That was a long time ago," he said. "You both will have to excuse me, but I have some work to do."

Andi waited until he left before she spoke. "He should have thanked you for remembering the ropes."

"What ropes? Oh, you mean untying us from the dock? That was no big deal."

"It would have been if you hadn't remembered."

"He probably didn't thank me because he's embarrassed that he forgot. He doesn't think he can afford a mistake, especially since Dad died. Once upon a time the guy knew how to have fun, but lately he's been nothing but old sobersides."

"Look, Bowie, I know you've engineered this trip partly to encourage him to relax, but he might not. Will you be okay with that?"

Bowie stared at the light dancing on the water. "I guess I won't have a choice," he said, his voice low. "But Andi, if he can't loosen up in a place like this, he's more of a mess than I thought."

"There's no such thing as an attractive maternity swimsuit," Nicole wailed as she came down the hallway and walked to the front of the boat so Andi could see her.

"Look at this, sis. I'm afraid if I go in the water somebody will try to harpoon me!"

Bowie rushed to her side and threw a protective arm in front of her. "I would *never* allow that, my love."

"Aw, Nic, you're very cute," Andi said. The loose-fitting white suit made Nicole look like an egg on stilts, but the effect was very endearing, especially when Andi considered that soon Nicole would have a baby girl for her troubles. Vanity didn't seem much of a price to pay for that. She wished their mother could have lived closer to take part in this pregnancy—she suspected Nicole missed that. "Motherhood looks good on you," she added, meaning every word.

"I absolutely agree," Bowie said gallantly, giving her a quick kiss.

"And it will all be worth it in two months," Andi said.

"You're right," Nicole said. "I haven't a complaint in the world, except that right now I would kill to get into that cool, clear water."

"Your wish is my command, love," Bowie said. He shaded his eyes and swept himself into a one-legged stance while he gazed off toward the continuous shoreline. "Land ho!"

"All ashore who's going ashore!" Andi decided it was time to take charge of the fun around here. "Sailor, go tell His Stuff-shirtedness that he's needed on the bridge. He can go commune with his laptop after we beach this sucker. It's time to party!"

4

TWO HOURS LATER, Andi, Bowie and Nicole sat on the rear deck in plastic deck chairs, their feet propped on the railing, and fishing poles dangling over the end of the boat. The prow was wedged firmly into the sand of a secluded little beach, and stout iron stakes held the mooring ropes for extra stability. Chance had taken the helm to run the boat aground and had helped Bowie drive the stakes into the sand and tie the mooring ropes. Soon afterward, he'd claimed he had reports to type and had disappeared inside the boat while the rest of them took a swim.

"We shoulda bought some live bait," Andi said, taking another sip of her beer. She and Bowie were indulging, while Nicole, the pregnant lady, had to settle for a soft drink.

"I agree," Nicole said. "These lures may be from Jefferson's finest stock, but the Lake Mead fish are not impressed."

"I want to try something," Bowie said, handing his fishing pole to Nicole. "Mind the line for me a little while. I'll be back."

"No problem. Nothing's biting anyway," Nicole said.

Andi was glad for the moment of privacy with her sister. She was determined to get Nicole's opinion about her latest career plan, but she didn't want Bowie or Chance, *especially* not Chance, throwing in their two cents worth.

"Listen, before he comes back, I want to talk about this idea I have."

"Please tell me this isn't about artificial insemination."

"What?"

"Don't do it, Andi. I've seen that longing look on your face, and that usually means you're about to try something crazy. I know this baby stuff looks like fun, but you don't have a steady income, and raising a kid alone would be hard enough if you had a lot of money, so—"

"Time out, Nic!" Andi braced her pole between her thighs and made a T with her hands. "The thought never crossed my mind."

"Never?"

"Well, okay, one time after we'd talked on the phone, and you were so excited about what color to paint the baby's room, and you'd just bought her first teddy bear, I *fleetingly* considered the possibility."

"Aha!"

"But I came to the same conclusions you just listed. I have to put my life together before I can think about bringing another life into the world. And I'd like to find a nice guy, too. Easier on me, easier on the kid." She smiled triumphantly at Nicole. "So there. Do I get points for that?"

Nicole wet her finger and drew three stripes on Andi's shoulder. "Well done, soldier."

"God, I remember how Dad used to do that. Remember when he started awarding us ranks?"

"Yeah, and you hated it because I usually outranked you."

"I think when he started assigning us ranks, I decided never to be that regimented. But...there comes a time... Don't laugh, but I'm thinking of expanding on yoga instruction and opening a school of my own, Nic."

"I'm not laughing. Would it take much capital?"

Andi gazed at her. "Spoken like the Nicole I know. Not *what a terrific idea,* but *would it take much capital?*"

"Isn't that why you're asking me, so I'll point out these things?"

Andi sighed. "I guess. And no, it wouldn't take much capital. I could build slowly, use creative ways to advertise. This is scary, but I'm actually thinking about a career, an honest-to-goodness vocation."

"My first reaction is that it sounds perfect for you. You're definitely the self-employment type."

"Thanks. I think so, too."

"And Mom will be *très* relieved to know you're not headed for the sperm bank."

"Mom thought I was about to get inseminated, too?"

Nicole adjusted her souvenir visor and looked at her. "She has some idea that you like to horn in on what I'm doing."

"I do not horn in."

"Remember the guppies?"

"The guppies weren't my fault!"

"Ha! Who dumped Jaws into the tank when I wasn't home? Maybe he was the hit man who wiped out Myrtle, Harry, Genevieve and Bernie, but you hired him."

"I thought an angel fish was a lot prettier than those dumb guppies. I just thought he'd show them up a little. I didn't know he'd eat them."

"Speaking of eating fish, I'm hoping to do that on this trip," Bowie said, plopping into the chair next to Nicole. "And I'm hoping we can catch something bigger than a guppy. So which one of you wants to help me try my new lure?" He held up two iridescent clusters of feathers and beads.

Nicole glanced at him. "Oh, Bowie, don't use those. I

promise to wear them really soon. They just take some getting used to.''

Andi gazed at the dazzle of colors. ''Those are earrings? Fantastic!''

Bowie shrugged. ''It was just an idea I had, so I made a pair for Nicole, but she really doesn't like them. She's more the pearl-and-diamond type.''

''Not me,'' Andi said. ''I think they're perfect, and you'll put them in the water over my dead body. Give them here.''

Bowie handed them across Nicole with a smile of delight. ''They're all yours.''

Andi took out the red hoops in her ears and replaced them with the lure earrings. ''What do you think?''

''They're you,'' Nicole said.

''Do you mean that in a good way or a bad way?''

''A good way.'' Nicole squeezed her knee. ''After all, I trundled all the way out here just to get my Andi fix. The phone's okay, but I wanted a face-to-face.''

''You miss not having Mom and Dad around, huh?''

Nicole nodded, and her eyes grew a little moist.

''Damn, we're so spread out. I wish you two lived out here.''

Bowie leaned back in his chair. ''I could deal with living like this.''

''I guess Chance can't,'' Andi said. ''Is he still hunched over his laptop in there?''

''Sad but true,'' Bowie said.

Andi took another sip of her cold beer. ''I can't imagine how he can stay inside, working on that stupid laptop when it's so gorgeous out here.''

''To be honest, I didn't think he would, either. He used to love to fish,'' Bowie said. ''It's almost as if he's deliberately avoiding being around us.''

"That's weird."

"Yeah." Nicole gave Andi a speculative look. "Unless…"

"What? Why are you looking at me like that?"

"That red suit is dynamite on you."

"You're changing the subject."

"No, I'm not. You put that suit on while the guys were out staking the boat to the sand, remember?"

"Well, duh. It was the obvious chance to get naked without embarrassing anyone, so I grabbed it. We're not exactly loaded with privacy around here, in case you hadn't noticed. You'd think they'd put a few more doors on this thing."

"Yeah, I noticed. I also noticed Chance's reaction when you appeared in that swimsuit. The guy was salivating."

"He was?" Bowie said. "Hey, cool."

"I don't believe you," Andi said as a flush crept over her skin.

"Look at the facts," Nicole said. "It was right after you came out in the suit that he made some excuse about not feeling like a swim and went inside to work on those reports that suddenly became so important."

"They probably *were* really important, as far as he was concerned. The guy's driven," Andi said, but excitement stirred in her.

"I like the looks of this situation," Bowie said. "Day one, and we already have progress."

FEROCIOUS HUNGER PANGS and the aroma of grilling steak proved irresistible to Chance, and he stood and stretched, sniffing appreciatively. Switching off the laptop, he leaned down to peer outside. The sun glowed from behind a bank of clouds stretched across the horizon. A spectacular western sunset could be in the offing.

A sunset and a steak fry on the beach…with Andi. Now that he wasn't concentrating on his reports, he could hear laughter and a tape of some tropical-sounding music. He sighed. For the first time in years he had no idea what he was supposed to do. Oh, he knew very well what he wanted to do—become much better friends with the beauty in the red swimsuit. Yet despite his bachelor status, he didn't feel the least bit free. Jefferson Sporting Goods claimed his first loyalty, and the company was a jealous mistress.

Sometimes he could almost hear his father's voice. *The stockholders expect us to show a profit and still maintain stability, son. Take risks, but not foolish risks. Watch out for Bowie. He doesn't understand the difference.* There had been a heady joy in being the chosen one, the heir to the throne, but there was also a weight that seemed to get heavier every day. He'd never thought the day would come when he'd feel twinges of envy when he looked at Bowie's situation. He'd been wrong.

Watch out for Bowie. And although his father had never met Andi, no doubt he would have warned Chance to watch out for her, too. Still, he couldn't hold himself aloof for an entire week on this houseboat, just to avoid becoming involved with Andi. That would be boorish and rude. And he'd also starve to death.

He walked out the front sliding door and glanced at the beach. They'd taken four deck chairs down to the sand, and the empty fourth chair touched him. This afternoon they'd left him alone to do his work, but they obviously hoped he'd show up for dinner. He was so used to people wanting his company because of his position with Jefferson Sporting Goods that it was a revelation knowing someone wanted to spend time with him because they liked him.

They had the chairs arranged in a semicircle around a bed of embers where they were cooking the steaks. The chairs faced the sunset, which was just starting to pink up. They hadn't noticed him yet. Bowie still had on his trunks, but he'd added an unbuttoned shirt. Nicole got up to take a picture of him sitting in his chair, his beer can raised in a toast. Probably because she was self-conscious about her protruding belly, she'd put a filmy cover-up over her bathing suit. Bowie and Nicole looked relaxed and happy, and his heart swelled with love for them.

A more potent emotion hit him as he studied Andi in her red suit and sarong-type skirt. She crossed her legs and the flowered skirt fell away, revealing her smooth thighs. Chance swallowed. Well, it wasn't going to get any easier, so he might as well go down. He took off his deck shoes, opened the metal gate at the prow of the boat and leaped the short distance to the sand.

"Ahoy and avast, matey!" Bowie called, raising his can of beer again. "The grog isn't half-bad in these climes."

"The company's not so bad, either," Nicole said.

"The fishing sucks," Andi said, "but the grog and the company make up for it."

"I figured the fishing wasn't working out when I smelled steak," Chance said, walking through the sand to the available chair, which was right next to Andi's.

Bowie pulled a beer out of a cooler and tossed it to him. "Andi picked out the brewskies, and let me tell you, the woman knows her beer."

"A highly sought-after talent," Andi said.

Chance popped the top and took a drink. "Good stuff." He glanced at Andi, then looked closer. She'd swept her hair up on top of her head, and dangling from both ears were what looked like fishing lures. "Are those hooks in your ears on purpose, or are you the victim of Bowie's lousy casting skills?"

"Hey," Bowie said. "Just because I happened to hook a woman's cheek once, which really wasn't—"

"Ew, Bowie!" Nicole made a face. "How awful! You could have blinded her!"

"It wasn't her face," Chance said. "And she was wearing a string bikini at the time."

"Oh," Nicole said. "Still, that makes me wince, Bowie. I hope now you're more careful when you cast."

"That's just it. I wasn't casting. We were out on a charter fishing boat, and everybody else was in shorts and shirts except this Bo Derek clone. I think she was after bigger fish than the ones in the water, if you get my drift. I was bringing in my line, and here she comes, wiggling along listening to *Bolero* on her headset, I suppose. I got a little discombobulated, and next thing I know, my hook's in her butt."

"Oh." Nicole glanced at him. "That does sound kind of stupid on her part. Who was this bimbo?"

"Chance's date."

"Ooo-wee!" Andi threw back her head and laughed. "He got you back, Chance." Then she flashed him a look that heated his blood. "Better not mess with the Bowie-man."

"Good advice." Chance took a long swallow of his beer, which quenched at least one thirst he was feeling. He remembered that woman he'd asked out on the fishing trip. He hadn't known her very well. Matter of fact, that was the problem with most of the women he'd dated recently. To get to know someone, you needed to spend time with them, and he hadn't had that kind of time.

"To answer your question about the decorations in my earlobes, they're earrings Bowie made. Take a look." She leaned toward him, bringing her coconut-oil scent close enough to make him dizzy.

He wanted to nibble on her ear instead of examining her earring. "That's not an actual lure, is it?" Even as he said it, he realized it was a lure of a different kind, dancing feathers and beads capable of hooking him, but good.

"Nah, it's not the real thing," Bowie said. "I just put together stuff I thought looked pretty. Nicole wasn't wild about them. But Andi loves 'em, so I gave them to her."

"I do love them." Andi settled back in her chair and raised her beer can to her full lips. "Hey, everybody, sunset alert. The sky's on fire."

"Wow," Nicole said. "I'd forgotten how spectacular the sunsets are around here."

Chance sipped his beer and listened to the sound of steel drums coming from the tape deck. Red and gold unfurled in the sky, spilling over the mountains and into the water.

"It's like looking through rose-colored glasses, isn't it?" Andi said in a voice so soft only he would have been able to hear.

He glanced over at Bowie and Nicole. They were holding hands and leaning close, caught up in their own private love fest. "It's also like watching a giant fingerpainting being made," he said.

"I like that," Andi said, giving him a smile. "I used to love fingerpaints."

"Me, too."

She was silent for a while as the colors slowly faded to brick and a few stars winked on. "When was the last time you fingerpainted?" she asked finally.

"Thirty years ago." Funny how he could still remem-

ber the claylike scent of the paint and the cool squish of
the colors beneath his hands. He'd used his palms, his
knuckles, even his wrists to make designs.

"I wish I'd bought some to bring on this trip."

"I think our niece is still a little young, don't you?"
He'd meant it as a joke, but the minute he said the *our
niece* part he got a tingle of awareness. Uncle Chance.
Aunt Andi. They'd be linked together even more closely
once this child was born. He felt himself sinking deeper
into inevitability.

"I meant fingerpaints for us," Andi said. "It would've
been a fun thing to do this week."

"Yeah, I can picture you and Bowie getting into that."

"I wasn't picturing Bowie. I was picturing you."

He grew uneasy. "Oh, yeah, right," he said sarcastically.

"Why not?"

"Because it's too childish for me now." He winced at
how crude his response had sounded. "Sorry. That didn't
come out right. I meant that—"

"You meant exactly what you said. But the thing is,
I'm not insulted at all. As a matter of fact, I feel sorry for
you."

That brought him out of his chair. "*Sorry* for me?" He
faced her. "What in hell do you mean by that crack?"

"Chance, watch out," she said.

"Ah, the peaceful tranquillity of twilight," Bowie said.
"The call of a nightbird. The indignant shout of my
brother."

"She feels sorry for me because I don't want to fingerpaint!" Chance said, backing up.

Andi started to get out of her chair. "Chance, don't—"
Her skirt caught on the arm of her chair, pulling the chair
over and knocking her off balance, toward him.

As he stumbled backward in the process of trying to catch her and stay upright at the same time, he tripped over some rocks and figured they'd both land on the ground. Miracle of miracles, he staggered but stayed vertical, and so did she. Maybe his luck was changing. He released her with a sigh of relief at another disaster averted. "She feels sorry for me," he said to Bowie and Nicole. "Can you beat that?"

"Sure," Bowie said, standing. "I feel sorry for all of us. You just backed into the grill. Our steaks are in the coals."

"Oh, hell." Chance turned to the fire. Instinctively he reached to grab a sizzling piece of meat and singed his fingers. "Dammit!" He stuck his fingers in his mouth. So much for changed luck.

"Here's a barbecue fork," Andi said, waving the pronged instrument dangerously close to him.

"Keep your distance, woman!" Chance held up both hands. "Next thing I know, I'll be impaled on that thing."

"I was trying to warn you about the fire! Do you need first aid?"

"Mustard's the best thing to put on it," Nicole said, getting out of her chair with a small groan. "I'll—"

"No, I'll get it," Bowie said. "After two beers I'd need a crane to help me hoist you back on the barge, sweetheart."

"Bowie Jefferson, you take that back!"

"Yeah, Bowie," Andi said. "You try smuggling a watermelon and see how spry you are."

"My apologies, ladies." Bowie swept them a bow and went over to kiss his wife on the cheek. She glared at him. "Chance, buddy, I think we might want to retreat to the boat, get your fingers taken care of, and return with more libations and the salad while these gorgeous, *petite,* talented women pull our steaks from the fire. Maybe if we're lucky, they'll find it in their hearts to let us eat dinner by the time we get back.''

''Don't count on it,'' Nicole called after them as they trudged through the sand.

Chance followed Bowie toward the boat. ''Hey, I'm sorry I knocked the steaks into—'' Sharp pain interrupted his apology as his toe collided with a piece of driftwood. ''Dammit!''

''What?''

''Stubbed my toe.''

''I guess it's been a long time since you've walked barefoot on the beach, huh, buddy? You gotta watch where you're going.''

''Bowie, right now I feel as if I'm standing in the middle of a damn minefield.''

''Just relax, buddy. You're among friends.''

''And some are more dangerous than others,'' Chance muttered.

5

ANDI WAS SO HUNGRY that she didn't even care that the steak tasted like charcoal on the outside. Everyone balanced their plates on their lap. After attempts to cut the steak with a knife and fork nearly tipped her plate upside down in the sand, Andi picked up the piece of meat in her fingers. "If it was good enough for my ancestors, it's good enough for me," she said, biting into the steak.

"Fine for those of you who have working fingers," Chance said. Bowie had wrapped three of his with gauze.

"I happen to know you can drive with one hand," Bowie said. "I'll bet you can eat one-handed, too."

"Ah, yes," Nicole said. "The old one-handed driving technique. The left hand for the steering wheel, the right hand for taking liberties with us, your dates. I remember it well."

"And they always thought they were being so subtle," Andi said. "They'd be staring straight ahead, like they didn't even know you were there in the car. But the hand would come creeping over like Thing in 'The Addams Family.'"

"You wanted us to *look* at you?" Chance said. "We're not about to take our eyes off the road and risk wrapping our pride and joy around a telephone pole."

"Yeah," Andi said, laughing, "and you might wreck the car, too." She noticed that Chance was on his second beer, and it was having a good effect. He was definitely loosening up. If she could just avoid another mishap, she could build on that. "I'm going down to the lake to wash my hands. Anybody else need to do that?"

"I'll just lick my fingers," Chance said.

"If I play my cards right, I can get Nicole to lick my fingers," Bowie said.

"In your dreams, Romeo," Nicole said. "Andi, would you bring me back a wet napkin? I don't think I can move from this spot."

"Anything for you, toots." Andi grabbed a couple of napkins and stood.

"You're tired, my little cabbage?" Bowie asked Nicole.

"Exhausted. Don't forget, it's two hours later, Chicago time. It's been a long day for a pregnant lady."

"Then I guess dancing wild and barefoot on the sand is out," Bowie said.

"Get Andi to dance with you," Nicole said as Andi started down toward the lake.

"What about Chance?" Bowie asked.

"Get him to dance with you, too. Just let me sit and digest that charred steak in peace."

Andi hadn't considered the prospect of dancing on the beach. Would Chance finally abandon his sedate corporate image, or would he let Bowie be the life of the party, as usual? This night could get very interesting indeed.

She walked to the edge of the lake, the sand cool under her feet near the waterline, and discovered that the lake was filled with stars.

Fascinated, she rippled the water with her fingers and watched the stars become streaks of light, like a thousand comets dashing across the liquid surface. Then she looked up and found that she was standing under a bowl of stars reaching all the way to the horizon. Overcome with the beauty of it, she reached her arms up to the sky. "Hallelujah!"

"Amen, sister!" Bowie called back.

"Have you chowhounds looked up from your plates long enough to notice all these stars?" Andi asked.

"They're gorgeous, Andi," Nicole said.

"But nothing compared to you, my sweet Nicole," Bowie said.

"Cool it, Bowie. I'm not dancing with you, and that's that."

"It's as if Liberace swirled his cape over the sky," Andi said, staring upward until her neck hurt.

"Let me know if you see Elvis walking across the lake," Bowie said. "In the meantime, I'm putting on a dance tape. Despite my heavy-lidded wifelet, the Lake Mead Jefferson Houseboat Party is just getting started."

As Andi dipped napkins in the lake, the sound of marimbas and guitars filled the air. She smiled as she listened to Bowie trying to get Nicole to dance with him.

"Aw, come on, Nic. One little turn around the sand," Bowie coaxed.

"Forget it, Fred Astaire. Head on down the line."

Andi turned just as Bowie gyrated rhythmically over to where Chance sat.

"May I have this dance?" he asked, still holding his beer in one hand.

To Andi's amazement, Chance got to his feet. Taking occasional swigs of his beer, he started executing a credible cha-cha with his brother.

"Ooh, have we got style!" Bowie cried. "Have we got rhythm!"

"Have you drunk way too much beer!" Nicole said, laughing.

Andi stood, the wet napkins dripping on her bare feet,

almost afraid to move for fear the spell Chance was under would break and he'd make some excuse to go type reports again.

"Come on, Andi!" Bowie called, whirling in her direction and snatching the wet napkins. "Cut in."

Breathless and smiling, she entered the dance in Bowie's place. All she could see of Chance's face in the dim light was the white flash of his grin as he matched his steps to hers. They didn't touch, yet they seemed to know when to pivot, when to turn in time with each other, as if they'd been dancing this way for years.

The small space between their bodies crackled and snapped in time to the rhythm. Andi forgot everything but the music and the sensuous movements of the man across from her. His transformation, no matter how temporary, had completely captured her imagination.

Then the music changed to something slower and more languorous.

Vaguely she heard Bowie's plea and Nicole's weary agreement to dance the slow number with him. One dance.

For a heart-stopping moment, neither Chance nor Andi moved. Then he stepped forward and drew her slowly into his arms, the empty beer can cradled against the small of her back as he wrapped both arms around her in the casual dance position of lovers. She wound her arms around his neck and breathed in the tangy scent of beer mixed with his sexy aftershave.

Their bodies moved with the lazy rhythm of the music, but she could feel the rapid tattoo of his heart against her breast, and her own heart was racing out of control. Of course, they'd just been doing a very athletic cha-cha. Of course, that was the reason. Not.

She lifted her head to look up at him. He gazed down

at her. She could barely see his shadowed eyes, yet she knew he was looking intently into her face. All that intensity he'd focused on his business was now trained on her like a laser, and she had trouble breathing. The twist of desire in her stomach grew stronger with each moment she spent swaying in his arms.

His head dipped lower. Her lips parted in anticipation. She closed her eyes.

Then another set of arms enfolded both of them. "Just carry on," Bowie said, one arm around each of them as he swayed with the dance rhythm. "Nicole's really dead on her feet. We're turning in."

The magic between Chance and Andi shattered like starlight on the lake when a pebble was tossed in.

"Good idea," Chance said, backing away from Andi as Bowie and Nicole headed for the boat.

"Yeah, we've all had a big day," Andi said. She could have cheerfully killed Bowie with her bare hands. "You guys all go ahead. We have to take turns in the bathroom, anyway. I'll stay out here and do a few yoga routines. Can't abandon my practice, you know."

Chance paused. "Is that right?"

"Well, sure. You have to stay toned, stay flexible, especially if you're a role model for other people."

He gazed at her as if the concept hadn't occurred to him.

She felt slightly insulted. "You're not the only one who has to think about work sometimes."

"I guess not. Well, good night." He turned and headed for the boat where Nicole was trying to hoist herself up to the deck with Bowie's help. "Hey, newlyweds. Let Uncle Chance help." He leaped to the deck in one smooth motion and lifted Nicole from above while Bowie steadied her from below.

"I *hate* being so awkward," Nicole complained.

"Bowie and I consider it a privilege to help you," Chance said as he drew her up beside him.

"You're sweet." She patted his cheek. "Why don't you go back and dance with Andi some more? I didn't mean to break up the party."

Andi held her breath. The music still played on the tape deck.

"I think it's time we all turned in," Chance said.

Andi walked over and shut off the music.

CLOSE CALL, Chance thought as he switched on his laptop and tried to concentrate on some spreadsheets while Bowie and Nicole got ready for bed. If Bowie hadn't interrupted him, he'd have kissed Andi. It would have been so easy. Bowie would have been thrilled with that, dog-gone his matchmaking hide.

Watch out for Bowie. No kidding, Chance thought. Here he was doing his damnedest to keep a level head, and Bowie springs Andi on him. Just thinking about the warmth and softness of her body moving rhythmically against his made him ache. He wouldn't think about it, or he was liable to go back out there.

The beer had probably lowered his resistance. He'd give it up for this week. He'd totally underestimated the power of her attraction, and the unconscious—or maybe conscious—provocation of her movements. When she'd stood down by the lake, her womanly figure silhouetted by stars, he'd begun to want her with a fierceness that swept aside all reservation.

And when she'd come willingly into his arms for a slow dance...when she'd lifted her mouth so invitingly...

The laptop beeped and the spreadsheet disappeared from the screen. Chance straightened on the bench seat and pressed a few buttons, but the spreadsheet was no longer on the menu. In his clumsiness with the gauze bandages and his preoccupation with Andi, he'd deleted it.

"Dammit!" He exited the program before he could do any more damage.

"What's wrong?" Bowie said, coming out of the bathroom with a toothbrush in one hand.

Chance grimaced. "Nothing a brain transplant wouldn't solve."

"Is it a problem with Jefferson?"

"Yeah. Chauncey M. Jefferson the Fourth, to be specific."

Bowie came over and sat opposite him. "I screwed up big-time by interrupting your dance with Andi."

"Even matchmakers miscalculate, thank God."

"Damn. We should have just quietly slipped away."

"Oh, right. You should have silently hoisted Nicole four feet off the ground and heaved her onto the boat without either of you making a peep."

"She is getting to be a load, isn't she? And still two months to go. It's going to be a giant kid."

"We should always use two of us to get her in and out of the boat, so nobody gets hurt."

"Keep your voice down. She still hasn't forgiven me for saying essentially the same thing."

"Not quite. You mentioned the need for a crane. Women get touchy at a time like this."

"So speaketh the expert on pregnant ladies. Is there anything you're not an expert on?"

"A few things." Chance glanced out into the night, where Andi still presented a huge temptation.

"Go back out there. Turn on the music. Andi's a great gal, and I think it would do you a world of good to spend some time alone with her."

Chance eyed his brother. "Forget it. I had a momentary lapse. It won't happen again."

"I know I'm not imagining things. You're attracted to her. Go with it."

"Doesn't matter. If you took the time to think it through, you'd see what a mistake it would be for all of us if I get involved with her. She belongs out here, in the wild and woolly west. I'm tied to Chicago, so the relationship couldn't go anywhere. The most likely scenario is that we'd have a fling and split, which would make the family dynamics even worse than before."

"I don't know. Andi might relocate to Chicago. She misses Nicole a lot, and with their parents always on the move, the two of them really depend on each other."

Chance refused to allow himself a smidgen of hope. "If Andi wanted to be closer to Nicole, she would have moved by now. It's not as if she has a skyrocketing career going here in Nevada. My guess is she likes the weather and the lifestyle."

"Dammit, Chance, this seems like a good shot at having a relationship. Dad wouldn't have expected you to become a monk."

"No, but he sure as hell would expect me to find somebody who'd genuinely want to be a corporate wife. That's not Andi."

Bowie frowned. "Unfortunately, you might have a point there."

"And that's why I'm not going back down to the beach. Not tonight or any night this week."

"I still think you're making assumptions that might not be true." Bowie stood to leave. "Sleep tight, buddy." He started to walk away and turned back. "Like I have to remind you." He went into the bathroom and closed the door.

Chance sighed. Bowie was still Bowie, spouting his favorite philosophy—live for the moment and never face the facts. He walked over to the seat where Bowie had been sitting and unfolded it. For the first time he noticed how quiet the night was without traffic noise and the scream of sirens. Somewhere in the bushes at the edge of the beach a cricket chirped, but that was the extent of the excitement. He hoped to God he'd be able to sleep.

A half hour later he lay in the dark, listening to the same damn cricket. A musician it wasn't. Same monotonous tune over and over.

He couldn't blame the cricket for his insomnia, though. He'd realized after turning out the light that Andi would have to walk right past him when she came in. He needed to remind her to lock the door after her. Yeah, that was why he was still awake. She might forget.

No, that wasn't it. He might as well admit that he worried about the door lock because it was a safe topic. Worrying about whether he'd speak to her, whether he'd reach for her, whether he'd pull her down to this bed and kiss those full lips—that wasn't safe. He got up and put his shorts back on, as if they'd act as some sort of chastity belt.

Then he heard an unfamiliar noise. He sat up. There it was again, and it was no cricket. He knew that yoga involved chanting, but this was no chant, either. More like an obnoxious drunk braying at the moon. Andi was out there, vulnerable to whatever lunatic might be prowling the beach.

His feet hit the floor and he barked his shin on the edge of the bed. Swearing under his breath, he grabbed the barbecue fork from the table and barreled out the front door onto the deck. "Andi?"

She was sitting cross-legged in the sand, facing the bushes. She turned and glanced up at him. "Shh."

For one wild moment he wondered if she'd made the noise herself, as part of some mystic pagan ritual, but then it came again, from the direction of the bushes.

Andi might think safety lay in silence, but hiding from danger wasn't Chance's style. Wielding the fork, he leaped to the sand. "Who's out there?" he shouted. "Show yourselves or get the hell out of here!"

There was a snort and the clatter of hooves. *Hooves?* Damn drunks must have been riding horses.

"Hey!" Andi protested, getting to her feet. "You scared them."

"That was the idea." He was breathing hard and his heart pounded from the adrenaline rush. "You'd better come over here, closer to me, in case they circle around and come back."

"They wouldn't hurt us."

He stared at her. "What's that, some New Age trust in your fellow humans? Some drunken bastards riding around the lake on horses don't sound like the kind of company we want around here. This isn't the Old West, y'know, where you invite any passing saddle tramp to share your campfire."

She began to smile. "They were burros."

"Okay, drunks riding burros. That doesn't make them any less suspicious, in my opinion. You saw how they took off, acting guilty as hell. They were up to something."

"Nobody was riding the burros," she said, her smile widening. "They're wild. The sound you heard was them braying."

He mentally replayed the noise he'd heard. "I thought donkeys went hee-haw."

Her shoulders shook and she covered her mouth with one hand. "It's not quite that neat a sound." She cleared her throat. "It's more like *eeagh-haugh!*"

"You do that very well."

"Thank you." She continued to grin at him. "I guess you've never heard a real one."

"No." He glanced down at the fork he still clutched in his hand. It was tough to imagine how he could have made a bigger fool of himself than by charging out of the houseboat ready to battle wild burros with a barbecue fork.

"It was really sweet of you to be so ready to defend me, though."

He grimaced and walked over to toss the fork back up on the deck. "From fuzzy little burros."

"You thought it was a band of drunken desperadoes, and you were ready to take them on with a barbecue fork. That's pretty gallant."

He turned back to her. "Oh, I'm a regular Lone Ranger."

She walked up to him. "I think you are, at that. All the cares of the world rest on those Armani-covered shoulders, don't they, Chance?"

He shrugged, trying to remain calm. She was dangerously close, and the adrenaline rush seemed to be meshing with a different kind of jolt to his system. He'd be wise to end this little conversation before things got out of hand. "Somebody has to be the grown-up."

"Twenty-four hours a day?" Her bathing-suit-covered breasts lightly nudged his bare chest as she moved closer still.

"You can't just turn it on and off."

She slid a cool hand behind his neck. "Isn't there an override switch somewhere?"

He closed his eyes. Her touch was like velvet against

his suddenly hot skin. She spread her fingers and ran them lightly up through his hair. He drew in a breath.

Then she applied subtle pressure to the back of his head, urging him down. "Kiss me, Chance. Trip that override switch."

6

ANDI HAD ALREADY hot-wired his override switch, Chance thought, winding his arms around her and opening his eyes long enough to make sure his mouth would connect solidly with hers. He felt her lips part beneath his hungry assault, and the muffled groan that filled his throat sounded the death knell of his restraint.

She took the first thrust of his tongue with an urgency that sent the blood pounding straight to his groin. He pulled her closer, wanting her to feel the pressure of his erection. The coconut scent of her suntan oil mingled with the scent of arousal, his and hers. Finally he accepted the truth—he'd wanted this from the first moment he saw her seven months ago. Maybe she'd wanted the same thing.

She tasted forbidden and lush. The sensual movement of her hips told him she was ready for anything he had in mind, and his mind raced with images of hands stroking, mouths exploring, bodies joining in pulsing completion.

His lips sought the honey from her warm mouth as he wedged his pelvis firmly between her thighs. She moaned and pushed against him, blotting out all reason.

He reached for the shoulder strap of the red suit that had tantalized him for hours. The strap offered no obstacle as it slipped down her smooth shoulder. Pushing his throbbing erection against the cradle of her thighs, he abandoned her lips to seek the pulse at her throat. His heart hammered as he worked the bathing suit down and finally cupped her breast in his hand.

She arched her back, pushing up against his palm. She was matching him desire for desire, and he'd never felt so excited by a woman in his life. She moaned as he leaned down and took her nipple into his mouth. He rolled the sensitive tip against his tongue and felt her shudder. Ah, this was going to be good. Very, very good.

He pulled the other strap down so he had access to both breasts as she writhed and whimpered against him. He felt her warm breath on the back of his leg. Dimly he realized that would be difficult, given their upright position. He paused.

Someone, or some*thing,* was breathing on him. He lifted his mouth from her breast.

Andi grew still in his arms. ''Chance.'' Her voice held a warning.

The warm air traveled up the back of his legs. Every hair on his body stood erect. ''What's breathing on me?'' he whispered.

''A burro.''

''*Shi—*''

She clamped her arms tight around his shoulders. ''Don't make any sudden moves.''

He leaned his forehead against hers and tried to stay calm. At least he wasn't naked. ''Do they bite?''

''I don't know.''

''That's not the right answer.''

''Just stand still.''

''Easy for you to say,'' he muttered. ''It's not licking your leg.''

''Licking?''

''Yeah. Probably for the salt, but God, it tickles.''

"I'm going to try something. Stay still." She leaned around him. "Shoo!"

He stared down at her. "Shoo?"

"You got anything better?"

"Yeah. I'm going to turn around really fast and yell at him. Stay behind me."

"I don't know if that's a good idea."

"I do. He's started nibbling on my shorts."

"Then it must be a female."

"Ha, ha. Okay, on three. One, two, three, *now!*" He whirled and shoved her behind him. His eyes widened as he gazed at not one, but *four* burros. "Go home!" he yelled, waving one arm as he kept the other behind him, protecting Andi.

The burros trotted away a couple of yards and stood looking at him.

Andi started to laugh.

"What's so funny?"

"They *are* home. We're the trespassers."

"Oh. Okay, then go...somewhere else!" he yelled again, waving his arm some more.

Andi whipped off her sarong and stepped out from behind him. "Shoo!" she said, waving the skirt at them.

The flapping cloth seemed to do the trick. They spooked and took off into the bushes.

Chance stared after them, shaking his head. "Burros."

"Now that they know interesting stuff is here, they might come back."

He glanced at her. She was sliding her arms into the straps of her swimsuit.

The burros had broken the spell that had caused him to forget everything except the need to make love to her, but sanity had returned, and he was flabbergasted at his behavior. What had he been thinking? "Do you realize what almost happened?"

She smiled at him. "I think so. I watched all the films in junior-high health class."

"Exactly. And in those films, do you remember that little matter of taking precautions?"

She paused and gave him a long look. "You don't have anything with you?"

"No. Why would I have anything? This was supposed to be a family vacation. I didn't even know you were coming along, and I wouldn't have brought birth control even if I had known. Our last meeting wasn't exactly romantic."

"But I thought guys always carried something."

"Well, they don't. And even if I had something, what kind of guy would have grabbed a condom on his way out to save you?"

"One who expected me to be very grateful?"

He laughed in spite of himself and shook his head. "Oh, boy."

"So you would have made love to me without using anything?"

"Looks like it, doesn't it?"

"Hmm." She gave him a slow smile.

"What's that supposed to mean?"

"It's nice to know Chance Jefferson isn't quite as buttoned-down as he pretends."

He rubbed the back of his neck. He didn't like being at a disadvantage, and he always seemed to get in that position with Andi. "I'd appreciate it if you'd keep this little incident just between us."

"Of course."

"Thanks."

"What shall we do now?" she asked.

"Go to bed—separately."

"Well, that's pretty obvious, but what about the rest of the week?"

"Andi, we're on a houseboat with two other people. I went crazy enough to want to make love out here on the sand, but obviously that has certain…hazards. And I don't know about you, but even if we had birth control, I wouldn't feel very comfortable getting wild and crazy inside the houseboat, with Nicole and Bowie just down the hall. The only doors on this barge are for closets and the bathroom. Neither place seems appropriate, so I think it's a moot point."

"That stinks."

"To be honest, it probably saves us from making a terrible mistake."

"It didn't feel like a terrible mistake a little while ago. If you're so intent on being honest, why don't you admit it felt damn good, Chance?"

And it still would, he thought, watching her standing there, her breasts thrust forward in defiance. He remembered how the blood had raced in his veins when she'd arched into his caress. "I want you, Andi," he said quietly. "After this, I can't very well pretend not to. But our lives don't fit together, and all we can do is hurt each other. That's not going to promote family harmony, and I don't think either of us wants to make difficulties for Bowie and Nicole."

"Ah, I see, the reasonable, responsible Chance is back in control."

"Barely."

"Well, that's something." She turned and hoisted herself up on deck. "Good night, Chance."

He watched her go, and then he swore under his breath. For the first time in his life, he truly resented the wealth and position life had settled on him. Had he been the only one to consider, he would have figured a way around all the obstacles. He would have made love to Andi Lombard.

"HEY, the stock market rebounded last night!"

Chance's enthusiastic announcement from somewhere in the front of the boat woke Andi up.

"Bully," she muttered. "Better than an orgasm anytime, right, Chance, old boy?" She'd gone to sleep frustrated and had awakened in the same condition, although the smell of bacon and coffee coming from the kitchen helped mollify her. From the sound of things, everybody was up except her. Waves slapped the side of the boat and a breeze blew through the tiny window over her bunk. She peered out at a cloudy day and choppy gray water.

Hopping down from the top bunk, she located her duffel bag in the stash of supplies on the bottom bunk and went into the bathroom to change into her spare bathing suit. Acting so impulsively with Chance had been a stupid move, she thought as she took off her nightie and put on the suit. Recently, she'd vowed to start looking before she leaped into romantic encounters. Maybe then she'd find herself kissing Mr. Right instead of the usual Mr. Wrong.

The black tank-style suit might be a tad provocative, she thought as she glanced in the bathroom mirror. A lace insert down the front and each side didn't leave much to the imagination. But what woman deliberately bought a suit that made her look sexless? Mother Teresa, maybe. Not Andi Lombard. Chance would just have to deal with his hormones, she decided, walking out into the kitchen.

Bowie looked up from the bacon he was turning with a familiar-looking barbecue fork. "He-ere's Andi!"

"Morning. Did every—"

"Oh, God!" Chance wailed from the table which had become his temporary office. "Quick, throw me a towel, somebody."

Andi grabbed a towel from the kitchen counter and threw it at his head with a certain amount of relish. He caught it and started mopping his keyboard.

Nicole slid down from her perch on the captain's chair and went over to watch. "What happened, Chance?"

"Spilled my coffee."

Bowie paused with the fork in midair. Then he turned to give Andi the once-over. "Uh-huh. Wonder what came over him? Any ideas, Andi, sweetheart?" He winked at her. "Nice suit, by the way."

Nicole looked over at Andi and back at Chance. She grinned. "It is a nice suit, don't you think, Chance?"

"Didn't notice," he mumbled.

Bowie leaned closer to Andi. "He didn't notice," he said in a stage whisper. "It was pure coincidence that the minute you came into the room, he started pouring his coffee into his computer."

"I guess I'll just have to let it dry out and hope it still works." Chance picked up the open laptop as if it were an injured animal and carried it out to the front deck.

Nicole clapped her hands together. "I *love* it. I haven't seen him this rattled since he got showered with champagne at our reception. I wish I'd seen his face when you first walked in just now. I'll bet his jaw was on the floor."

Andi looked down at the black suit. "Is it too much? I'm beginning to get a complex. Every time I'm around, something crazy happens to Chance."

"It's time a few crazy things happened to Chance," Bowie said. "The guy needs to have his chain rattled. Now, if anyone cares to scramble up a few eggs, the bacon's about ready."

"I'll do it," Nicole said.

"Nope. I will. You relax." Andi opened the refrigerator and took out a carton of eggs. "How did you sleep last night?"

"Unfortunately, your niece kicked most of the night, so I didn't sleep a lot."

Andi paused in the midst of closing the refrigerator door. "That's too bad." She wondered if Nicole had heard what had gone on in the sand outside the boat the night before.

Chance came back in. "I put the laptop on a deck chair outside, but turned it away from the sun. I think it'll dry quicker that way than leaving it in here."

"I wouldn't know," Nicole said, "but it sounds logical. I'd offer you a hair dryer, but I didn't bring one. Did you, Andi?"

"Nope." She stood next to Bowie and cracked eggs into a bowl while butter melted in a frying pan "I figured I wasn't on this trip to be gorgeous."

Bowie lowered his voice. "Just sexy as hell."

She answered out of the corner of her mouth as she whipped the eggs. "These are the suits I happen to have, okay?" She poured the eggs into the frying pan.

"Very okay. He's a basket case."

"By the way, I heard those crazy wild burros braying last night," Nicole said. "And you tearing out to save Andi, Chance."

Andi froze. Sound tended to carry in such an open area. How much else had Nicole heard? Not that there had been much talking. Moaning and gasping, but not much conversation.

She turned, a spatula in her hand. "Yeah, it was very sweet, Nic. He'd never heard what real burros sound like, and he thought some drunks were out there having a party.

I explained it, and that was that. It's nice to know chivalry isn't dead.'' She didn't look at Chance.

"It's nice to know my brother isn't, either,'' Bowie said.

Andi kicked him. "Eggs are ready.''

During breakfast they plotted the cruising for the day. Andi sat across from Chance. She couldn't help noticing that he seemed intent on keeping his gaze on her face whenever he looked in her direction. Even then, there was a banked heat in his blue eyes that made her stomach flutter every time she saw it. His hormones were definitely giving him problems. But then, so were hers.

"I hope the weather doesn't deteriorate,'' Nicole said, glancing at the cloudy sky outside the windows as they cleared away the dishes.

"It's not supposed to rain this week,'' Andi said. "But we might have wind.''

"Then we'll just find a sheltered little cove and wait it out,'' Bowie said. "Before we break up camp, though, I want Andi to teach me a couple of yoga moves.''

"Seriously?''

"I'm a man of many facets,'' Bowie said. "And yoga's always intrigued me. Maybe after we finish the dishes, we can—''

"I'll do the dishes,'' Chance said. "You two go ahead.''

"And what am I supposed to do?'' Nicole asked.

"Be pregnant,'' Andi said, giving her a hug. "Go lie down in the back for a little while. If you didn't sleep much last night, you probably could use some more rest.''

Nicole looked relieved. "Thanks. Maybe I will, at that.''

After she left, Chance turned to Bowie. "Is she okay?''

"She says she's fine. The baby's just being especially

active, that's all. I told her we'd cut the trip short anytime she wanted to, but she wouldn't hear of it."

"She's really looked forward to this week," Andi said. "It would be a huge disappointment if we had to go home early, but we have to think about her health, too."

"We won't go far from the marina today, just in case," Chance said. "And don't forget, I have the cell phone if we have an emergency."

"Let's hope the stock market isn't closing when we need to use it," Bowie said.

Chance gave him a lazy smile in response. "Have I increased your personal investments in the last six months or haven't I?"

"Yeah, but I'm a little worried about that ticker tape that's started coming out of your ear every morning." Bowie's smile was just as lazy, but there was an edge to it.

"I'm surprised you noticed. The laugh track that runs constantly in your brain must drown out everything else."

"Boys, boys." Feeling like a dorm mother, Andi stepped between them. Her father would have suggested these two put on the gloves and go a few rounds to work out their frustrations with each other. He'd even tried that technique a couple of times when she and Nicole had been bickering, until their mother had protested that he was raising a couple of brawlers. "Come on, Bowie. I'll teach you the salute to the sun."

"What sun? It's cloudy."

"So maybe we'll coax it out." She gave him a steely stare. "And do not *ever* question the master, grasshopper. Always remember, you are but a speck of bug dung on the windshield of humanity."

"You're not the first person to offer that opinion."

Andi had been kidding, but she wished she could pull

the joke back. No doubt when his father had told him something similar, he'd been deadly serious. And Chance wasn't improving Bowie's self-esteem. She really needed to knock him off his almighty perch. Nobody ever deserved it more.

CHANCE WASN'T PREPARED for the sight of Andi demonstrating yoga moves in the bathing suit that had made him dump coffee on his keyboard.

He tried not to watch. The sink was at right angles to the deck, and if he faced straight ahead while he washed dishes, he only caught flickers of the activity out of the corner of his eye. But, sure as the world, before long he'd be standing like an idiot, his hands motionless in the soapy water while he stared outside at Andi executing her salute to the sun.

She and Bowie faced east, which made a great deal of sense if you were saluting the sun, but that meant presenting her cute little backside to Chance, and that was not helpful, not helpful at all. Several of the moves involved bending over, which gave him a heart-stopping view of her firm and very inviting behind. When she placed both her feet and her palms on the deck and lifted her hips high in the air, he nearly broke a glass as it slipped from his fingers and clattered into the sink.

His only relief from surges of sexual arousal came from watching Bowie, who was definitely yoga-challenged. Chance didn't kid himself that he'd be any better at it than Bowie, but still, his brother's uncoordinated efforts made him chuckle. He was a little surprised that Andi didn't kid Bowie about his performance.

He regretted the exchange he'd just had with Bowie, but after the effort he put into making sure all the family investments stayed solid, it rankled to have Bowie accuse him of being preoccupied with money. As if he kept track of the stock market for his own benefit. He had little use for money, but his mother needed a strong retirement account, and Bowie needed funds for the baby's security. Everybody expected him to take care of that.

He continued to watch Andi work with Bowie, and his admiration grew. Bowie's request for a lesson had been sincere, and Andi was doing her earnest best to teach him. Good teachers didn't ridicule their students, and Andi was obviously a very good teacher. Maybe she'd finally found her niche. From what Nicole had said, Andi had been searching for the right career for years. Chance wondered if she realized just how talented an instructor she was, and if she was capitalizing on that talent.

Then, suddenly, the lesson was over, and as they turned to come back inside, Chance started washing furiously to make up for lost time.

"That was great," Bowie said. "Let's do that every morning. I've always wanted to be more flexible, and this beats ballet lessons."

"You were going to take ballet?" Chance asked. He risked looking up, and realized he shouldn't have. The exertion had left Andi's face flushed and her hair a little mussed, just as it might be if she'd been making love. God, how he ached.

"They say it's great for flexibility and rhythm, both of which I ain't got," Bowie said.

"Yoga won't be much help with rhythm," Andi said, "but you don't have a problem with that, judging from the way you danced last night."

"I've practiced a lot. Chance here picked it up naturally. Played drums in a garage band during high school."

"Really?" She gave Chance one of those looks that

fried his circuits. "I've heard drummers are the craziest members of the band."

"I was the exception." Chance returned his attention to the dishes.

"Don't believe him," Bowie said. "He had the makings of a wild man, but Dad convinced him of the error of his ways and brought him into line. I guess Dad decided I was hopeless and left me alone. Unfortunately, I had absolutely no talent for drums, so the band folded."

"I see." Andi walked over to the counter and took a dish towel off the rack. "You're not very far along on this chore, drummer boy. I'll dry."

"That's okay. You helped cook. I'll do it." The close-up scent of her brought back those heady moments from the night before, and he was having trouble breathing normally.

"I feel as if I ought to do something," she said, grabbing a dish from the strainer.

Put on more clothes, Chance thought. "I guess we should pick up everything from the beach, if we're going to leave."

"I'll do that," Bowie said. "You guys finish up the dishes." In a flash he was out the door, leaving them standing alone together at the sink.

Chance searched for something to say. He cleared his throat. "Thanks for covering for me with Nicole." He set a glass in the strainer and miraculously didn't break it in the process. His hands were shaking.

"I said I would. She may know more than she's saying, though."

"They both do." He took a deep breath and leaned both hands on the edge of the sink to steady himself. "Andi, if you have any compassion in your soul, you'll put on something extremely shapeless and ugly over that suit.''

"Bothers you, huh?"

He didn't look at her. Didn't dare. "Yeah."

"Bowie thinks you need to have your chain rattled."

Chance bowed his head. "Bowie's clueless about the kind of pressures I'm under. He has no idea what would happen to Jefferson Sporting Goods if I threw caution to the wind, like he does."

"Or maybe he cares more about you than about that precious business."

He stared at her.

"New concept, isn't it? Bowie watching out for you for a change. Well, drummer boy, I'm not covering up. Just remember, it's for your own good. I think I'll go check on Nicole." She ran a fingernail down his backbone and sauntered toward the hallway. Just before she turned the corner, she looked back at him, raised her hand to her lips and blew him a kiss.

He groaned and closed his eyes.

"That's done," Bowie said, coming in through the front sliding door. "Aren't you finished with those dishes yet? You are the slowest dishwasher in the world, bro. Where's Andi?"

Under my skin. "Checking on Nicole."

"Good. Think I'll do the same. And by the way, you're working too hard at that dishwashing job."

"What do you mean?"

"You've been scrubbing that same plate since I walked in the door, and it looked clean when you picked it up." He headed down the hallway in the same direction Andi had gone.

7

As Chance was finally rinsing the last dish, Bowie and Andi came back.

"She's got a slight backache," Bowie said. "And of course she's not supposed to take painkillers or anything. We forgot to bring the thing she uses for it, one of those gel packs you heat in the microwave. She thinks this is a stupid idea, but I'd like to go back to the marina and see if the general store has anything like that."

"Let's do it," Chance said. His pulse quickened. Oh, God, he'd have a chance to buy—no, he wouldn't think about that now. He had to concentrate on Nicole. "You're sure she's okay?"

"She seems fine," Andi said, "but those microwaveable packs are great. I recommend them to my yoga students all the time. If the general store doesn't have any, there's a little town not too far down the road. I'll volunteer to go. Then we'll have the heat pack for the whole trip. I'll bet she'd sleep better with it, too."

"Great," Bowie said. "Come on, Chance, let's get those stakes pulled up and take this sucker back in."

Chance followed his brother out to the front deck, battling his thoughts the entire time. All the reasons for not getting involved with Andi still existed. Without birth control he might be able to avoid making a stupid mistake. Not buying it would serve as a built-in brake to his runaway libido. So why was he even considering it? Because he was going insane, that's why. His famous discipline was crumbling in the face of temptation. He couldn't guarantee he wouldn't grab her in a moment of lust and say to hell with precautions. It had almost happened the night before. He wished he'd receive some sort of sign, some indication of what he should do.

"Chance?" Andi called after him.

"Yeah?" He turned around just before he was ready to leap to the sand.

"Want me to bring in the laptop?"

The laptop. It had been the furthest thing from his mind. Had it stayed balanced on the deck chair, which it would have if she hadn't reminded him, one good roll of the boat in the choppy water could have sent it into the lake. "Thanks," he said, gazing at her.

"You're welcome." She smiled at him, without a trace of sarcasm. "I know how much it means to you."

As signs went, it wasn't much. But it was a small indication that she understood the demons that plagued him, that he might, just might, be able to trust her. That when he lost his head, she might keep hers. That she wasn't trying to ambush him. Hell, he'd known all along what he wanted to do when he got to that general store. He would have taken just about anything as a sign to do it.

ALL THINGS CONSIDERED, Andi thought Chance did an admirable job of docking the houseboat. True, he brought it in a little fast and banged the prow against the dock, causing the cupboards to fly open and a few things to topple out, but nothing broke. The wind made it difficult to stay the boat's course, and he'd needed the greater speed to avoid drifting into one of the other boats as he came in.

He and Bowie headed off to the general store to try

their luck, with Nicole protesting all the while that the effort was totally unnecessary.

"Let them pamper you," Andi said as they sat on the foredeck and watched the marina activities around them. "They love it. It's not every day they get to take care of a pregnant lady."

"They do seem to be getting a kick out of this. On the plane ride out here, Chance told me about the time he and a fraternity friend helped deliver a baby when a couple got stuck in a snowstorm on the way to the hospital. I could tell it made a huge impression on him. He's pretty awed by the whole process."

"No kidding! I'm sure we'd all remember something like that. The poor woman must have been panic-stricken."

"I'm sure. I'm glad this baby will be born before the snow hits Chicago." Nicole arched her back and put her hand to the base of her spine.

"Boy, am I out of it," Andi said, getting up. "I have the perfect exercise to help you with your backache, and I haven't even shown you." She pushed aside her chair and lay down on the deck. "Come on down here beside me."

Nicole laughed. "Shouldn't we go inside and do this?"

"No, the deck floor is warmer. It'll feel good. Come on."

"You are the most uninhibited person I know. Okay, but I refuse to do that inverted vee thing where you stick your butt in the air."

"You won't have to." Andi waited until her sister was lying beside her on the deck. "Now, bring your knees up as far as your tummy will allow, and wrap your arms around them as best you can."

"Which isn't much."

"That's good enough. Now just gently rock back and forth on the small of your back, like this."

Nicole followed her directions. "Oh, Andi, that does feel good. It's like giving myself a massage."

"Told you." Andi rocked in a synchronized motion with her sister. "Close your eyes. That'll focus you on the massage and it'll feel even better."

"Oh, God, yes. That's it."

Bowie's voice came from somewhere above them. "I swear, Chance, we can't leave these women alone for a minute. Now they're in the fetal position having a religious experience on the deck."

"Don't knock it until you've tried it, Bowie Jefferson," Nicole said.

Andi opened her eyes and looked up at the two men standing over them. Bowie held a plastic bag that probably contained Nicole's gel pack. Chance had something smaller wrapped in concealing plastic clutched in his large hand. Her pulse rate picked up. The purchase she'd hoped Chance might make would come in a package about that size. She wondered if Bowie had any idea what his brother had bought at the general store.

"We were in luck, sweetheart," Bowie said. "Got just what we needed, right, Chance?"

"Right." With his aviator shades on, it was nearly impossible to read his expression, but he seemed to be looking at her. "Everybody ready to set sail?"

Andi got to her feet as Bowie helped Nicole up. Andi had the feeling Chance had been thoroughly enjoying the view of her lying on her back, knees pulled to her chest, in her revealing black suit. The game had become a little less playful and a lot more erotic. There wouldn't be burros on the beach every night. She swallowed. "Sure. Let's go for it."

ALTHOUGH ANDI campaigned for Bowie to take the boat out of the slip this time, Chance ended up at the wheel, after all. Andi told herself that she just didn't have enough leverage yet. Before the week was over, Chance would have new respect for his brother's abilities, or her name wasn't Andi Lombard.

"How about sailing down toward Hoover Dam?" she suggested as she heated the gel pack in the microwave. She'd noticed that the small package he'd had in his hand when he'd returned with Bowie had disappeared somewhere, and he'd never mentioned buying anything at the general store. Her certainty about the contents of the package grew.

"Sounds like a good idea," Bowie said. "Nic, is that okay?"

"Just fine."

"Try this on your back." Andi brought the fabric-covered gel pack to where her sister sat.

Nicole placed it at the small of her back. "Heaven. I know it was a bother to go back for this thing, but I appreciate the effort, you guys."

"Glad to do it," Chance said.

"It was important," Bowie agreed.

Andi tried to tell from their expressions if there was any double meaning to their comments. Andi had seen the general store. It wasn't large. For Chance to buy the condoms without Bowie knowing would have been difficult. Yet there were no exchanged winks or clearing of throats to indicate the brothers were giving each other invisible nudges in the ribs. If they were colluding in this effort, they were better at it than she'd have given them credit for.

The prospect that Chance would be looking for an opportunity to make love to her totally changed the way she viewed him. She became fascinated by the curve of his fingers on the wheel, the flex of his shoulders, the shift of his hips on the captain's seat, the angle of his foot. Fascinated and aroused. She hoped to hell his little package wasn't a couple of packs of chewing gum.

"Bowie, want to take the wheel for a while?" Chance asked.

"Sure," Bowie said.

"Good. I've checked my laptop, and it seems to be working okay. I'll go in the back, place some calls and make a few notes."

So his mind wasn't similarly occupied, she thought. He could plan a seduction, then efficiently continue going about his business. She was irritated that he wasn't as focused on their relationship as she was. He had a lot to learn, and she was just the woman to wake him up. "Give my regards to Wall Street," she said.

"Be glad to." He gave her a totally bland look as he turned the captain's chair over to Bowie.

Chewing gum, she thought. The jerk had probably bought himself a supply of tutti-frutti and had no intention of following through on last night's impulse. Which would save her from making the mistake of getting involved with Mr. Business-Comes-First.

Chance picked up his laptop and walked down the hallway without giving Andi another glance.

"Hey, Nic, I'll play you a game of gin," Andi said, mentally sticking out her tongue at Chance's retreating back.

Sometime later, the cards began sliding across the table of their own accord as the boat pitched from side to side. Nicole was looking a little green, and Andi turned to Bowie. "A little bumpy out there, huh, Captain?"

"Yeah." He adjusted his visor. "We talked about pulling into a sheltered cove and waiting it out if the wind picked up. What do you say we moor this tub, at least for lunch?''

''Good idea.'' Andi got a nod of approval from Nicole, who had her hand over her mouth and wasn't looking too chipper.

''I'm gonna have some of that canned chili, cut up some onions, maybe shred some cheese,'' Bowie said. ''How does that sound, Nic, honey?'' He looked over at her. ''A little woozy, babe?''

Nicole nodded.

He smiled. ''Then you don't have to fix my chili.''

''I just may fix your chili, buddy-boy.'' Andi scowled at him as she stood and gazed at the shoreline. ''Hey, up ahead, see that spot with outcroppings on both sides of the beach? We'll slip in there, tie up and be protected from the wind. Are you ready for that, sis?''

Nicole nodded again.

''Okay, I'll take us over there.'' Bowie eased the boat to the right. ''Man, can you feel the boat hydroplaning?''

Andi walked over to put a hand on his shoulder. ''Maybe it's time to have a silent cockpit.'' She rolled her eyes in Nicole's direction. ''Want me to go get Chance?''

''If I know him, he's on his way down the hall.''

''We're bobbing around like a damn cork,'' Chance said as he walked into the room.

''What'd I tell you?'' Bowie said under his breath.

''Good thing we don't have anybody who gets seasick in this group,'' Chance said, setting his laptop on the table. ''Rocking back and forth like this would sure bring on the upchucks if we did.''

Nicole bolted from her seat and rushed past him toward the bathroom.

He stared after her. "What's the matter with Nicole?"

"Way to go, Einstein," Andi said as she started down the hall.

"God, I'm sorry. I had no idea." Chance sounded contrite.

"Nic hates people to pay attention to her when she gets like this," Bowie called after Andi.

"I know," Andi said, but she continued anyway. "Nic?" She tapped on the door. "Let me help you, hon."

"I'm okay," came a muffled response.

Andi stood there, unsure how much to push. Bowie was right—Nicole hated having anyone see her in embarrassing circumstances. "I'll check back in a minute," Andi said finally.

By the time she returned, Bowie was heading the boat into the inlet. Jagged, narrow rock walls rose on either side.

"Not much maneuverability in here," Chance said.

"Yeah, but the rock walls on either side will protect us from the wind," Bowie said.

"Still, I'm not—"

"No use debating. We have to moor," Andi said. "Nicole needs to get off this boat for a little while and let her stomach settle down."

"You're right." Chance stood behind Bowie. "Looks like there's a channel there we can use to get in. There's not a whole lot of clearance, but we can make it."

"Andi," Bowie said, "go back to the bathroom and warn Nic when we're ready to hit the beach. I don't want her losing any teeth."

"Okay." Andi started toward the bathroom.

"And brace yourself," Chance said. "With this much wind, we need to really dig into that sand."

"Right." She looked into his eyes and drew comfort

from the confidence she saw there. A little wind on the lake wasn't going to panic a man like Chance Jefferson. She held on to that thought as she went to the bathroom door. "Nic? Hold on, kid. We're going up on the beach, and we're going in fast and hard."

"Okay," came the weak response.

"Want me in there with you?"

"Nope."

"Here we go," called Chance from the front of the boat.

Andi grabbed the doorjamb and flexed her knees. Whomp! She nearly lost her grip as the force of the impact threw her forward. She recovered herself and pressed her ear to the bathroom door. "Nic?"

The door opened, and a pale Nicole stood patting a washcloth over her face. "Good thing you warned me," she said with a little smile. "Otherwise I would have beaned myself on the toilet lid, and Lord knows how I would have explained that to my mother-in-law. She was very much against my coming on this trip. She thought Bowie and Chance should go alone. Which made me all the more determined to be here, of course."

"Of course. That's the Lombard spirit coming through. And the meddling battle-ax will never have to hear a thing about this." Andi put her arm around Nicole. "How about a glass of water?"

"Fine."

Andi walked her slowly into the kitchen, got her the water and waited while she sipped it.

"Ready to get off this tub for a while?"

"Sure."

As they walked to the front of the boat, the ringing sound of sledgehammers against iron stakes told Andi that the brothers were already mooring the boat.

"Oooh, Bowie, let's rent a houseboat," Nicole said, mimicking herself. "It'll be so cool. We'll lie around in the sun, fish, and feel the gentle rock of the waves. Ha."

"We did that yesterday," Andi said, giving her a hug. "You wanted two days of that? Greedy woman."

"I'm sorry I barfed, Andi. How gross."

"I'm sorry, too, but only for your sake." She walked Nicole out on deck. "Nobody minds. Are you okay?"

"Feeling better every minute. But I can hardly wait to put my feet on solid ground."

"Solid ground, coming up." Andi called to the men, who immediately came over and helped Nicole to the sand. Andi handed down chairs and towels so they could establish a little camp.

"Are you coming down?" Nicole asked.

"In a minute. I'll rustle up some beer and chips for our gallant lads first. Want anything?"

Nicole swallowed. "Not yet."

"I'll be there in a minute." Andi walked inside and almost tripped over Chance's laptop lying on the floor. She stooped to pick it up from where it had apparently fallen when the boat hit the beach. He must have been so concerned about getting the boat firmly anchored and Nicole on steady footing that he hadn't even noticed.

As much as she resented the darn thing, she didn't want it to be broken and all the information in it lost. She set it on the table and snapped it open. Everything looked fine, but she'd been around computers enough to know that looks were deceiving. The thing could be deader than a doornail. She flipped the switch and the screen began to glow. So far, so good.

The operating program came up, but that didn't always mean anything, either. She clicked the mouse and opened his list of files. If one of the files opened okay, then the laptop was probably okay. She glanced over the cryptic list and picked one with the initials AL, just for the heck of it. She expected a report on Athletes and Litigation, or Assets and Liabilities. Chance wouldn't have a file on her in his precious laptop, for heaven's sake.

But he did.

Andi gasped, and then her eyes narrowed. Oh, he would pay for this. Nobody listed the pros and cons of making love to her on some *spreadsheet* and got away with it. He made an emotional choice sound like some sort of corporate decision.

Andi skimmed down the pro side and read sentences like: *She excites me more than any woman I've known* and *Touching her would give me intense pleasure.* Now, that was sort of nice, even listed coldly in columns. It made her tingle. A lot. But there were less complimentary phrases on the con side such as: *She'll destroy my concentration* and *Her wacky view of life spells trouble.*

"Oh, I'm going to spell trouble, all right. And you won't need a spell-checker to know when it's arrived," she muttered. After typing *Who cares?* next to the sentence about destroying concentration, she highlighted the *wacky view* sentence and switched it to the pro side. Then she changed *wacky* to *unique* and *spells trouble* to *fascinates me.*

Apparently Chance was confused. He'd written, *Her kiss blots out all reason* in both columns. Andi deleted it from the con side. Kisses were *supposed* to blot out all reason. Otherwise there was no point in kissing. Boy, did he have a lot to learn. For good measure, she added another sentence to the pro side. *She's the most beautiful woman I've ever known* looked very nice on the screen. It looked so good, she added another: *Her intelligence is matched by her sweetness and charm.*

"Hey, Andi!" Bowie called from the beach. "Are you brewing the beer yourself?"

She jumped. "Be right there!" She'd forgotten all about her errand. Quickly she saved the information on the screen, closed the file and turned off the computer.

As she pulled beer from the refrigerator, she considered what Chance would do when he opened the file and discovered her changes. Then she smiled. He wouldn't be likely to make a public scene, now, would he? She had him. And at least she knew he'd been writing about her instead of doing his work. That almost made up for his stupidity in thinking that she could be reduced to a list on a computer screen.

CHANCE DIDN'T LIKE the quality of the sand holding the mooring stakes. The night before there had been a more solid feel to the way the stakes went into the ground, and he'd never doubted they'd hold, even in a wind. The sand was more loosely packed here, but they had to do the best they could to secure the boat. Even if Nicole wasn't seasick, he couldn't imagine how they'd back out of this narrow spot with the wind blowing the way it was. He would have preferred a different mooring inlet, but this was the one they had, and they'd make the best of it. To anchor the stakes more securely, he and Bowie piled large rocks around them.

They decided to have a picnic on the beach. Although gusts of wind blew sand into their food during the meal, nobody suggested going back on the boat. At least two-thirds of the hull remained in the water, and there was too much motion to consider moving the picnic inside and risking a relapse for Nicole. Chance kept an eye on the stakes, which seemed to be holding.

After lunch, Bowie and Nicole walked to the edge of

the water to rinse the dishes. Chance pretended to doze on a beach towel, but he soon became completely absorbed watching Andi throw potato chips to a pair of ravens. Bigger and glossier than the crows he'd seen in the Midwest, they would glide down from the rock ledges where they apparently lived, seize the morsels she threw and retreat again.

Andi's blond hair danced and became tangled in the wind, making her look like a wild thing herself as she called to the birds, coaxing them nearer. His eyes hidden behind shades, he was able to study the lace-covered strips of bare skin revealed by her black suit, and how the lace shifted as she leaned down to get more chips and toss them gracefully to the birds.

He allowed himself to imagine kissing his way down those lace strips before he slowly peeled them away. Much as he loved his brother and sister-in-law, he wished they could beam themselves somewhere else for about two hours. Knowing they'd trudge back up the beach any minute, he turned over on his stomach to hide the evidence of his thoughts. The warm sand shifted a little beneath his erection, but it wasn't nearly the sensation he had in mind.

The potato-chip bag was within reach. He pulled it over just as Andi turned and came back for more chips.

She walked toward him and dropped to her knees in front of him. "You have my chips."

He propped his head on one hand and looked up at her. "Want some?"

She held out her hand.

He reached into the bag, took out one chip and put it in her outstretched hand.

Her gray-green eyes were covered by sunglasses, but

the corners of her full mouth tilted up. "You're flirting with me, right?"

"Right."

"So, did you go shopping this morning, too?" she asked.

"Would it make any difference to you if I did?"

"Possibly."

"Then it's possible I went shopping."

"Oh my God!" Bowie shouted. "Chance! The stakes!"

Chance surged to his feet at the sound of Bowie's shout. One set of stakes had pulled out, and the huge boat was blowing sideways. If somebody didn't turn the craft, it would wedge itself on the beach, the motors out of the water. They'd be marooned.

8

CHANCE SPLASHED into the water and grabbed the mooring stakes just as Bowie leaped in beside him and took hold of the ropes. Pulling together they battled the wind that pushed relentlessly against the side of the houseboat.

Andi joined them, latching on to a section of rope. "Problem?"

"Hell, no," Chance said. "We're just showing off."

"Glad to hear it. I hate problems." She started pulling with him.

Nicole appeared beside Bowie and put her hands on the taut rope.

"No, Nicole!" Bowie said, his voice a stern command.

"But—"

"You might hurt yourself. No."

Chance had never heard his usually laid-back brother take such charge of a situation. He was impressed. "Nic, go stand on the beach and guide us," he said, breathing heavily. "Andi, climb in the boat and turn on the motors. If we get it headed in straight again, gun it." He prayed this highly independent woman wouldn't question him.

She didn't. "Right." She started running toward the prow of the boat. Then she turned. "What if the stakes on the other side pull out, too?"

Chance managed a grim smile. "Don't leave without us."

"Right." She took off.

Bowie strained at the ropes. "Maybe we'll rent something a little smaller next time?"

Chance gritted his teeth and planted his feet. His arms began to ache. "A canoe."

"A boogie board."

Chance snorted. "Nic, are we moving it at all?"

"A little."

The engines roared to life.

"Now," Bowie said, "if we can just pull it around so it's straight, Andi can ram it back up on the beach."

"Yep." Chance gasped for breath as he renewed his efforts. Unfortunately the wind seemed to do the same, blowing harder than ever. "Just straighten it out. No problem."

Bowie pulled until the muscles bulged in his arms, but he staggered farther into the water as the boat continued to swing in the wrong direction. "Anytime, Chance."

"I was waiting for you." Chance felt the water lick the bottom of his shorts, and the sandy bottom had given way to slippery rocks. "Didn't want to show you up in front of Nicole."

"You're losing ground!" Nicole called.

"You know, I didn't notice," Bowie muttered breathlessly to Chance. He stood up to his waist in water. "Did you notice?"

"I can't get my footing on these damn rocks." *Rocks.* "Nic, how much clearance does Andi have for the propellers?" he yelled.

"I'll see!"

Almost immediately came the sound of giant ice cubes being crushed in a blender the size of…the houseboat. Then the motors stopped.

"Not much clearance," Nicole said. "In fact, I think she hit 'em."

Chance gazed at Bowie. "Gee, do you think?"

"Could be. Plus, my shoulder's about to be dislocated."

"Mine, too," Chance said tightly.

"Ever moved a houseboat that's stuck sideways on the beach?"

"Bet it would be easier once the wind's died down."

"Let 'er go, Chance. This houseboat's bigger than both of us."

"This houseboat's bigger than Detroit."

"We're letting go!" Bowie called to Andi and Nicole. "The boat will just drift sideways up on the beach."

"Won't that be a problem?" Nicole called back.

"Nothing we can't handle!" Chance shouted.

Bowie laughed. "And if they believe that, we've been playing our cards way too close to our chest."

"On three," Chance said. "One, two, *three.*"

The brothers released the stakes and ropes. Slowly the boat turned until it was broadside to the buffeting wind. Then it edged toward the shore until the side crunched into the sand. Wedged tight.

Once the inevitable had happened, the adrenaline rush subsided and Chance had time for remorse. "This is my fault," he said as they waded out of the water. "I knew the sand wasn't stable enough. I should have paid more attention."

"I knew it wasn't stable, too. Why isn't it my fault?"

"Because I'm—"

"Older? Wiser? The biggest martyr the world has ever known? Come on, look on the bright side," Bowie said. "From this angle we'll be able to get a premiere view of those completely uninsured propellers."

Chance grimaced. "Don't remind me. That's the other

thing I should have thought of. I knew we didn't have much clearance.''

''Oh, lighten up. Stuff happens.''

''That's pretty much your attitude about life, isn't it? I hate to think what would happen if I started thinking like that.''

''You *might* start acting like a normal human being instead of a superhero.''

Chance's jaw tightened. ''I can't afford mistakes.''

''I'll tell you what you can't afford, man.'' Bowie paused to face him. ''You can't afford this need to be perfect.''

''I don't need to be perfect!''

''The hell you don't! You're so petrified of making a mistake that you work night and day, supposedly for the good of the ones you care about. But what kind of caring is that, when you never spend any time with us because you're so damn busy?'' A flush spread across Bowie's face and he looked away. But he didn't retract a word.

Chance stared at him, his heart thudding painfully in his chest. ''That's what you used to say about Dad.''

''Yeah, well, he would have been real proud of you. You've turned out just like he expected. And so have I.'' Bowie glanced at him. ''For a minute there, when we were working together to get this boat straightened out, I had the feeling we were a team. We'd worked as a team to screw things up, and we'd take the blame together and try to work it out together. But apparently you want all the blame, and when the time comes, all the glory. Well, take it away, bro. It's all yours.'' He continued toward the beach.

ANDI COULD HEAR Chance and Bowie arguing as they came out of the water together. This was no time for dissension in the ranks. She walked out on the deck. "Hey, guys!"

They both looked up at her.

"Is it time to use Chance's cell phone to call the Coast Guard?"

"The *Coast Guard?*" Bowie said.

"Yeah. Somebody who knows something about getting boats unstuck."

Bowie turned to Chance, as if waiting for whatever command would come next.

Chance cleared his throat. "We let it get stuck on purpose," he said. "That was the plan."

Bowie stared at him for a few seconds. "Exactly," he said at last. "For a windbreak. You women need some protection from the wind."

"I see." She glanced at Nicole, who'd walked down to meet the guys. "They say they did this on purpose, for a windbreak."

Nicole looked doubtful. "Really."

Andi folded her arms. "And how did you two geniuses plan to get us unstuck again, wait for the tide to come in?"

"Well, we—" Bowie turned to Chance. "Tell the women the plan, Chance."

"Why don't you tell it?" Chance said, gazing at his brother.

"Okay. We, uh, we figured when the wind dies down, we can pull on the ropes from one side, and push from the other side, and—"

"I'm calling 911," Andi said. "You two don't have a clue, but like typical males, you'd rather sit here forever wedged into the sand than ask for backup and look stupid." She turned around.

"Wait!" Chance called. "Let's not rush into this."

"Do they even have a Coast Guard station around here?" Bowie asked Chance in a tone so low Andi almost missed the comment.

She turned back in time to see Chance shrug. Clueless, both of them. "How long do you want me to wait?" she asked.

"Just a little while," Chance said. "See if the wind dies down. I'm sure Bowie and I can use leverage on this puppy as long as we're not fighting the wind."

"What about the propellers?" Nicole asked.

Bowie clasped his hands in front of him. "Well, by golly, we were just on our way to take a look, weren't we, Chance?"

"We were, as a matter of fact."

"Before you head around that way, would one of you gentlemen help me down?" Andi asked. "There seems to be a lake where the sand used to be."

"Oh. Right." Chance turned toward Bowie and Nicole. "You guys go ahead. We'll be along."

Chance waded out to the back of the boat. "Just hold on to my shoulders and I'll lift you down."

"Are you and Bowie having a problem?" she asked in a low voice.

"Nothing that a miracle couldn't fix."

"Chance—"

"Never mind. Bowie's had his say and I have some thinking to do. Come on down and we'll go see what shape the propeller's in."

She got to her knees at the opening in the railing and followed his directions. Touching his smooth, sweat-dampened skin started to blur her thinking, right when she needed to keep her mind clear to evaluate the situation.

"That's it. Just lean into me," he said. He reached up and placed his hands firmly around her waist.

If touching him was disorienting, having him touch her was worse, setting loose disturbing little tremors throughout her body. "I think we need to call for help, Chance," she said. "I think that would be the wise thing to do."

"You may be right, but I'd like to avoid it if we can." He started lifting her down.

"To preserve your pride? Because—"

"It's a little more complicated than that."

"Well, I just want you to know that I—" She lost her place in the sentence as he eased her down, causing her to slide against him in the process.

"That you what?" He set her gently into the shallow water, but he didn't take his hands from her waist.

She looked up at him. For some reason her hands still rested on his shoulders, and she was reluctant to move them. In fact, she'd begun unconsciously kneading the muscles beneath her fingers, and her heartbeat just kept getting faster. "That I..."

He reached up to take off his sunglasses. "Yeah, me, too," he murmured as he lowered his head.

Her eyes drifted closed as he took unquestioning possession of her mouth. She was lost. If she ever wrote out a pros and cons list for Chance, the pro side would have several entries about his kiss. She'd list how he managed to exert the most exquisite pressure, urgent but never bruising, that brought about her complete surrender. As he wrapped his arms tightly around her, she molded herself to him with a soft moan of pleasure.

He lifted his mouth a fraction from hers, but he continued to hold her very close. "I don't want anybody towing us out of this cove and back to the marina if we can help it," he said softly as his lips brushed hers. "For several reasons. This is just one of them."

She had trouble getting her breath. "I'm beginning...to understand."

"Good." He deepened the kiss, and his tongue boldly claimed her in a way that left no doubt as to his intentions. Then he slowly released her. "But no matter what I want or don't want," he said, his voice husky, "we have to find out how Nicole's doing and make a decision based on that."

She took a long, steadying breath. "Of course."

"If she's not feeling well, then we'll call for help and if necessary, get towed out of here and back to the marina."

"Right."

"But if she's feeling okay, we'll get the boat unstuck when the wind dies down, which might not be until morning." His gaze moved over her, as if he was anticipating what might happen between them before dawn.

"Yes."

Passion flared in his eyes. Then he put his sunglasses back on. "Let's go look at those propellers and talk to Nicole."

She gazed up at him in dreamy contentment. "I'm sure at least one set is mangled beyond belief."

"I'm sure you're right." He smiled down at her. "Funny, but I don't seem to give a damn."

THAT WAS A GOOD THING, Andi thought a little later as she looked at the mess that she'd help create by running the motors as the boat swung into a bed of rocks.

"I'm guessing what we have now," Bowie said, "is a single screw."

"On a boat designed for a twin-screw," Chance added, wading out in the water to examine the bent propeller. "But airplanes can fly with an engine out, so I'm sure

this boat can do fine, once it's not battling a killer wind."
He turned to Nicole. "But there are no guarantees. How
are you feeling, Nicole?"

"Fine, now that I'm not rocking and rolling on that
boat."

"The wind might keep up until tomorrow, and we'd be
stuck on this beach until then. If we call somebody now,
we can get towed out of here."

"Towed?" Bowie grimaced. "Aw, Chance."

Nicole smiled at her husband. "Poor manly man. Don't
worry, sweetheart. As long as it's still windy, I have no
desire to get on the boat, whether we're under our own
steam or being towed. In fact, if it's windy for the rest of
the week, this might be right where I'd vote to stay."

"Then I guess—" Chance paused and glanced at
Bowie. "What do you think?"

"I think we should wait for the wind to die down and
see what we can do with this barn. We have plenty of
supplies, so that's not a problem."

Chance turned to Andi. "What's your vote?"

"If Nicole wants to stay, that's fine with me."

"Then it's settled," Chance said. "Anybody for a
swim?"

"You all go ahead," Nicole said. "I want to park a
deck chair in the shade of this windbreak you've created
and read a romance novel."

"I'll sit beside you and feed you grapes," Bowie said,
putting his arm around her.

"You just want to read the juicy parts over my shoulder," Nicole said.

Andi could see where this was heading. The couples
were dividing up. Then she remembered she had yet to
see Chance in a bathing suit. "I'll swim with you," she
said.

"Great." He waded out of the water and headed toward the back of the boat. "I'll go put on my suit."

Andi thought offering to help him might be a little obvious. "Toss down a few deck chairs and we'll get Nicole set up. She needs an extra one for her feet, too."

"Sure." Chance heaved himself out of the shallow water and onto the deck.

"Oh, and maybe you should warm up that microwave thing for her back," Bowie said. "And her book's on the shelf above our bed, if you could get that, too."

"Hey, guys," Nicole said. "Don't treat me like an invalid. I barfed. I had a slight backache. No big deal. I came on this trip to have fun with all of you and enjoy my last few weeks of freedom, but I didn't come to be fussed over."

Chance leaned over the railing and smiled down at her. "In that case, would you mind straightening this boat out? It seems to be stuck and none of us can do a damn thing about it."

"And after that, you can give me a rubdown and a beer," Bowie said.

"And gather firewood and rocks for a fire circle," Andi added. "Oh, and if you could—"

"Hey, all right! I get the point! Fussing's good. I like fussing."

"That's better," Chance said. "Deck chairs, coming down."

Nicole glanced up at him. "And a bowl of ice cream?"

"Okay."

"With some of that fudge sauce Andi brought?"

"You're sure you don't want me to whip up some baked Alaska? I'll be in the kitchen anyway."

Nicole smiled sweetly at him. "Not right this minute. I'll let you know."

After Chance passed down the deck chairs, along with a cooler full of beer and Nicole's gel pack, book and ice cream, he disappeared inside to change into his suit. As Nicole exclaimed over the wonders of Andi's fudge sauce, Bowie came over and gave Andi a smacking kiss on the cheek.

"What was that for?" she asked.

"Whatever you said to Chance while he was helping you off the boat."

"Believe me, I didn't say anything."

"Okay, then, whatever you did. And I'm not asking. But it's had a good effect, whatever it was. He actually asked for our opinions for a change."

Andi blushed. "Maybe he's finally starting to get the message that he's not God."

"Looks like. He even condescended to go swimming."

Nicole looked up from her bowl of ice cream. "You have to remember, though, that he may well slip right back into his old ways after this trip."

"Yeah, that's true," Bowie said. "But it's a start. And I think Andi's been a good influence."

"Now *that* would be a first," Andi said. Then her attention was thoroughly captured by the man who walked out on deck in sexy black trunks. "Last one in is a rotten egg," she called to him, and without seeing whether he'd heard her or not, she ran down to the water.

Splashing her way around the end of the boat until she was waist-deep in the lake, she looked up just in time to see Chance execute a shallow dive off the side and disappear under the surface. The wind ruffled the water, making it impossible for her to see beneath it.

Launching herself into the coolness, she swam to the area where she'd seen him disappear. Fear clutched at her stomach at the thought that he might have hit his head on a submerged rock. Men were so foolish. They always had to do one of those macho dives when they had no idea what was under the waves.

A hand closed around her ankle, and a moment later she was under the water, in his arms. Holding her tight, he kicked to the surface and grabbed one of the loose mooring ropes that dangled from the lake side of the boat.

"You scared me," she said, gasping. "You shouldn't be diving into water you can't see under."

"That was the channel we came in through." He worked his way up the rope so they drew nearer the boat and shallow water. "I knew it was okay."

"Then why did you have to stay under and scare me like that?"

"It's part of the coed swimming game," he said, grinning at her. "You say, 'Last one in's a rotten egg,' which is me, so I have to get back by grabbing you from under the water. I thought you said you went to junior high?"

"I did, but it's hard to picture you there."

"Oh, I was there. That's where I learned to take off a bra with one flick of my fingers." His chest muscles flexed, creating a sensuous friction against her breasts as he eased along the length of the rope.

His nearness and the conversation were heating her up, and fast. "Tell me," she asked. "Do guys steal their sister's bras and practice that technique by fastening them around the back of a chair?"

"Maybe, but I didn't have a sister, so I had to practice on the real thing."

"Gee, that must have been tough."

"Sheer hell." He let go of the rope when they were within a short distance of the boat. "Can your feet touch here?"

She wiggled her toes toward the bottom. "No."

''That's okay. I can. Wrap your legs around me, Andi.''

She did, and immediately realized how aroused he was. Glancing up into his fevered gaze, made even more intense by the moisture spiking his dark lashes, she decided there was nothing sexier than a gray-flannel-suit type who was, even temporarily, unplugged. As her attention drifted to his mouth, she noticed the glistening drop clinging to his full lower lip. She slowly wiped it away. ''Aren't we going to swim?'' she murmured.

''Not if I can help it.''

9

THE PRIVACY CREATED by the shelter of the boat made Andi bold. "Then I guess you'd better kiss me."

Chance smiled. "Where?"

She placed a finger against her lips. "You can start here."

And start he did, with an inborn talent that soon had the blood pounding through her veins.

After several seconds he drew back very slowly. "Where else?" he murmured in a husky voice.

Mouth tingling, her whole body coursing with need, she leaned back in his arms and tilted her head as she traced a circle on her exposed throat. "Here."

He licked and nibbled as she ran her finger along her shoulder. Taking her bathing-suit strap in his teeth, he pulled it down before nuzzling her shoulder. "Now where?"

Andi slipped her arm out of the strap and cradled her breast just above the cool lap of the water. "Here."

"Devil woman." He eased down into the water and took her nipple into his mouth.

Fierce desire tightened the womanly core deep within her as he suckled and licked. Whimpering softly, she wrapped her legs closer around him, pressing herself against his erection. She was going slowly crazy. "Stop," she whispered, easing away from the delicious feel of his mouth on her breast. "I can't take this. Now without being able to…"

He cupped her face in one hand and pressed his lips gently over her damp face. "I can help you if you'll loosen up."

"That's the problem. I'm so loose all I can think of is having you make love to me."

"Which I want to do." He slid his hand down to her inner thigh. "I meant loosen up here."

She held his gaze and relaxed the grip of her thighs around his torso. The elastic of her suit gave way before the questing probe of his fingers. As he found the pulse that was throbbing so desperately for release, she gasped.

"There?" he murmured.

She could barely breathe. "Yes."

His voice was a low rumble of restrained desire as he stroked her. "I would kiss you there, too, but I might drown."

She closed her eyes, transported on a wave of pleasure. "Who…cares?"

The next thing she knew, he'd slid beneath the water, pulled the fabric aside and pressed his mouth against her flash point. She wriggled free and sank down to take him firmly by the shoulders. As she urged him to the surface, he brought her up with him and they clung together, breathing hard.

"I was kidding," she said, gasping. "I don't want you to drown."

His chest heaved as he drew in several gulps of air. "Some things are worth drowning for. I would have died a happy man."

She wound her arms around his neck. "You're absolutely insane."

"And it's your fault." He kissed her again, thrusting his tongue deep until she moaned in frustration.

He lifted his lips from hers a fraction. "Let's try something." He turned her slowly in the water until her back was to him and the water sloshed just above her collarbone. Then he pulled her in tight with one hand around her waist. "That's better." He nuzzled her neck as he pushed the other strap down. "Lean into me, Andi. It feels so good when you do."

She hooked her feet behind his knees and locked herself against his arousal. "Somebody's a little worked up," she murmured.

"Somebody's a lot worked up," he said, his mouth close to her ear. "It's a small price I pay for touching you like this." Beneath the concealing water he pushed her suit to her waist and cupped her breast in his hand, stroking his thumb across her nipple until she quivered in his embrace. He leaned close to her ear. "I've wanted to strip this suit off from the first minute I saw you in it."

Her breathing was ragged. "Is that why you spilled your coffee?"

"Yes, that's why I spilled my coffee." He nipped her earlobe. "And then you just had to go out on the deck and wave that tempting bottom of yours in the air, didn't you? Did you know how I'd react?"

"I had hopes."

"You've been driving me crazy all day. You're the reason I wasn't paying attention when the stakes pulled out, and why I'm here right now, loving you instead of making calls and writing memos."

She leaned her head against his strong shoulder and arched into his touch. "Good."

"Yes, it is," he murmured against her ear. "And it's about to get better." He shifted his hold, wrapping his arm beneath her breasts as he slipped his free hand inside the front panel of her suit.

She drew in her breath as he teased his way down through her wet curls and pushed into the moist channel that ached for him.

"Better?" he whispered, stroking her.

"Mmm." She shuddered as the tension began to build to an almost unbearable level.

"It's risky," he said into her ear. "If you cry out, we might have company."

As he lightly caressed the nub of her passion, holding her on a maddening plateau of desire, all she wanted was release, whatever the cost. "I…won't. Please, Chance."

His touch grew firmer and more rhythmic as he held her tight against his body.

So close. So very close. She whimpered and pressed the back of her hand to her mouth.

"Shh. Now." He pushed deep and pressed upward.

Her world exploded, and she rammed her fist into her mouth to stop the cry that rose from her throat as she convulsed in his strong grip.

He turned her around and gathered her close, kissing her face, her hair, her throat as she clung to him limply and tried to catch her breath. Gently he repositioned the straps of her suit.

As her sanity slowly returned, she gave him a long, sensuous kiss. Then she eased away from him, held up both arms and slipped under the cool water. She allowed herself to sink until she was even with his hips. Figuring he needed a surprise as well as some pleasure, she hooked her thumbs in his suit and pulled it down in one lightning move that freed his manhood. She had a split second to admire his impressive dimensions before he hauled her to the surface.

"And what are you doing, devil woman?" he asked, crushing her against him.

"I figured I could die happy."

"I'm not letting you drown, either."

"But I'll bet you'll let me do this." She reached down and grasped his shaft firmly.

He gasped. "I...might."

She stroked him, paying special attention to the sensitive tip, as she gazed into his eyes.

The blue of his irises grew dark and a muscle tensed in his jaw.

"This is risky," she murmured. "If you cry out, we might have company."

He said nothing, but his breathing quickened.

"Ah, no promises from you, I see. No begging, either. I'll bet I could make you beg, but as mellow as I'm feeling, I won't." She caressed him deliberately, relentlessly, as he trembled and grabbed at the rope to steady himself.

At last he shuddered, wrapped both arms around her and pulled her down under the water, where they melded together in a slow-motion dance until he captured her mouth in a gentle kiss as they drifted slowly back to the surface. All this unbelievable pleasure, she thought, and they hadn't even made it to the main event. She was beginning to wonder if by tempting the likes of Chauncey M. Jefferson the Fourth, she'd bitten off more than she could chew.

CHANCE HAD HOPED the interlude in the water would give him some relief from his obsession with Andi, but no such luck. After they returned to the beach, she pulled up a deck chair next to Nicole's and they started reading sexy passages aloud from Nicole's novel. Chance joined Bowie in the bawdy discussion that followed each reading, but beneath his lighthearted laughter desire boiled and flowed like lava.

Behind the protection of his sunglasses, he followed Andi's every gesture, traced the contours of her laughing mouth, focused on the curve of her breast and the tilt of her thigh. Although it was obvious Andi and Nicole had shared books like this aloud before, Chance figured Andi had initiated the activity now just to taunt him and keep him at a fever pitch. If total conquest was her goal, she was waging one helluva campaign.

"How are real guys supposed to compete with the heroes of those books?" Bowie asked.

"Sweetheart, you stack up just fine against them," Nicole said.

He adjusted his visor. "Well, I knew that. But I meant ordinary guys, like Chance, here."

"It's a struggle." Chance looked at Andi. "The dragons just aren't out there waiting to be slain like they used to be."

"That's what you think," Andi said.

"So you have dragons that need slaying, lady?"

She gave him a little smile. "Every day."

"Tell me about it," Nicole said. "There's the dragon of the leaking brake line, and the dragon of the frayed lamp cord, and the dragon of the tight jar lid, and the dragon of the plain old blues."

Bowie raised his fist. "And I slew them, every one."

"My hero." Nicole smiled at him.

The exchange had the most curious effect on Chance. He longed to play the same role for a woman, a woman like…Andi. The only times he could claim to be a hero on a white horse involved Jefferson Sporting Goods. And a company couldn't smile at you with love the way Nicole

was smiling at Bowie. He was—hard as it was to believe—jealous of Bowie's life.

The sun was beginning to sink behind the mountains,
and he wished he had the power to personally shove it
below the horizon. He wanted the cover of night so he
could be alone with Andi again, alone to make love and
to explore the unusual feelings this vacation had offered
him.

"Well, this hero is ready to eat dinner," Bowie said.
"Time to form our little supply line again, build a fire,
all that hero stuff. Ready, Chance?"

Chance sent Andi a look. "Yes."

ANDI WAS WORRIED about Nicole. She didn't think either
of the men had noticed, but Nicole was in pain. Maybe
only another woman would notice the little hitch in her
laughter, or the way she twisted in her seat and pressed
her hand low on her belly when she thought nobody was
watching. Andi was watching.

As the men gathered rocks and driftwood to build a
fire, Andi leaned toward Nicole. "What is it?"

"What's what?"

"Don't pretend with me. Something's bothering you."

"It's nothing. Just little…twinges."

"The baby?"

Nicole chuckled. "Yeah. She probably wants to join
the discussion."

"In French."

"Right."

"How long have these twinges been going on?"

"Not long." Nicole put her hand on Andi's arm.
"Please don't make a big deal of it. I've talked to lots of
women who've had babies, and you get all sorts of things
like this. Nothing to worry about."

"Not if you're sitting at home, right next to a phone and blocks from a hospital. This is a little different. The houseboat's not even sailable right now, and even if it were, it doesn't have running lights. The manual says very plainly not to go out on the lake at night with it."

"I don't need to go anywhere." Nicole's grip tightened on Andi's arm. "This has been so good for me, Andi. I'm not letting anything spoil it."

"But—"

"Bowie's great, but I've missed being with you, especially at a time like this. And I can't tell you how grateful I am that he and Chance are talking again."

"Even if it leads to arguments?"

"Arguments are better than no discussion at all. Chance was well on his way to being just like his father, but I see signs that he could still be saved."

"Such as?"

"Take a look." Nicole glanced over toward the cliffs.

Andi watched as the brothers dueled with sticks. Chance's stick kept breaking, until he was dueling with a piece about five inches long. As he continued to thrust and parry, laughing all the while, the setting sun gave his skin a ruddy glow, and he looked very hero-like indeed. A telltale emotion twisted her heart. It felt like…no. She didn't want to start building castles in the sky.

"I'd be in heaven if those two became friends again," Nicole said.

Andi glanced at her. "That's all well and good, but you have to promise to tell me if the twinges get worse. We have Chance's cell phone. We'll do something."

Nicole patted her arm. "That isn't going to be necessary. Besides, you know how I hate drama like that, especially if I'm in the middle of it."

AN HOUR LATER, shortly after dinner, Andi was wondering how long before she and Chance could steal off into the shadows for some serious necking, when Nicole cried out.

They all rushed to her side.

"I think I'd better...go back to the boat," she said. "I—oh, dammit!" She doubled over.

"You're in labor!" Andi cried.

Nicole lifted her face, her expression defiant. "I am *not*. It's just gas. I'll be—*augh!*"

Bowie squatted in front of her. "If that's gas, we're gonna have to give you an antacid the size of a manhole cover."

"Don't make me laugh. It hurts."

Chance gazed at her. "Childbirth does, I hear."

"Childbirth?" Bowie sounded frantic. "But it's only seven months! The baby's not done yet!"

"It's...a little more than seven months," Nicole said.

Bowie stared at her. "You were pregnant before the wedding?"

"A little."

Andi gasped. "Omigod. How pregnant?"

"Six weeks."

"And you didn't tell me?" Bowie shouted.

"I didn't want your mother to know!"

"I wouldn't have told my friggin' mother!"

"I wasn't sure!"

"Oh, Nic," Andi said, her heart aching that her sister hadn't felt free to confide in her. "You could have told me."

Nicole looked miserable. "I was afraid to tell anyone. I didn't want anything to spoil the wedding...or this vacation."

"But your doctor," Andi said. "Surely she knew. I can't believe she let you come on—"

"I didn't exactly tell her about it."

"Nic!" Bowie yelled, his face red.

"I had to be here! We all did! And first babies are supposed to be late!"

Chance drew a deep breath. "None of this matters now, guys. The main thing is to get her inside."

"You're right," Andi said, drawing strength from his calm voice. "Let's go."

As the men helped Nicole to her feet, fluid rushed down her bare legs.

"Oh my God," Bowie said. "Now she's leaking."

"It's okay, Bowie," Chance said, his voice amazingly gentle. "That's part of it. She'll be fine."

"Easy for you to say." Nicole doubled over with another pain.

"Aw, geez," Bowie said. "We didn't finish that birthing class, either."

"You're about to get a crash course," Chance said. "Let's go."

It took all three of them to lift Nicole, who kept convulsing with pain, up to the deck of the houseboat, but they eventually accomplished it.

"My bed," Chance said. "Hold her right there and I'll open it up."

Andi and Bowie supported Nicole until Chance returned. Nicole looked pale, but Bowie looked white as the plastic deck chairs.

"Bowie and I will get her into bed," Chance said to Andi. "My briefcase is on the back top bunk. Take my cell phone out of my briefcase and call 911."

"And what do we want, a boat?" she asked.

Nicole moaned. "No boat."

"A chopper, then." Chance said. "That'll be quicker, anyway."

Andi shook her head. "I doubt they could land on our minisize beach."

"Then they'll have to land on our maxisize roof." Chance's smile was grim. "The size of this monster has to come in handy for something."

Andi found Chance's briefcase and decided to stay in the back to make the call so she wouldn't alarm Nicole by whatever she discussed with the operator. Several frustrating minutes later she replaced the phone and hurried down the hallway.

"Are they on their way?" Bowie called out as she walked into the kitchen.

"Not quite." She stopped in her tracks. "What the hell's this?" She stared at Chance stretched out unconscious on the bed and Nicole sitting in a deck chair beside the bed.

"He passed out," Bowie said as he rubbed Nicole's back. "And Nic says she feels better sitting up than lying down."

"Passed out? Is he okay?"

"Sure. He did the same thing in the tenth grade before his big date with Myra Oglethorpe. Intense stress affects him like that sometimes, I guess. He'll come around in a few minutes."

"So he does have a weakness," Andi murmured.

"Yeah, and he's going to hate that this happened to him right now."

Andi turned to Nicole. "You really feel better sitting?"

Nicole nodded. "I think Chance hated seeing me in pain. He—*ah!*" She gripped the arms of the deck chair as another contraction grabbed her.

"By the way," Bowie said, continuing to massage Nicole's back. "What did you mean *not quite* with the chopper? I don't like the sound of *not quite*."

"Our timing's not great. There were several car pileups during a sandstorm on the freeway, and medical helicopters are in short supply. I gave them our approximate location, told them to look for the houseboat wedged sideways on the beach. They said that should make it easy to find us. They'll show up when they can."

"And in the meantime?"

"They asked if we had anyone here with experience delivering babies, and I said yes."

"Unconscious, but experienced," Bowie said.

"I didn't know that he'd passed out. We can hope he comes around, but in the meantime, you'd better go scrub up."

Bowie's gaze locked with hers and she watched the uncertainty fade and the determination grow. She decided she would wake Chance up, if only to witness his brother taking charge of a situation.

While Bowie tried his best to sterilize his hands and arms at the kitchen sink, Andi moved Chance's laptop to the floor, unscrewed the tabletop and converted the second set of benches into a double bed. She kept up a conversation with Nicole as she worked and checked her every few seconds. The pains were very close together.

"I'll get every pillow on the boat, so we can prop you up," she told Nicole. "But I'd feel better if you'd move this program to the bed. Otherwise Fifi's liable to land on the floor, and it's not very clean."

"Fifi?" Nicole managed a weak smile between pains.

"Or Gigi. I figured you'd want to go with something French to please your mother-in-law."

"Oh, Andi." Nicole's eyes rounded in horror. "She's gonna *kill* me for this. She wanted to videotape the birth."

"With subtitles, of course."

Nicole started to giggle. "Andi, thank God you're—oh, sh—" She clapped her hand over her mouth before the swearword came out.

"I'd advise you to go ahead and swear," Andi said. "Trust me, the baby won't pick it up, despite Mrs. Chauncey M.'s theories."

"What theories?" Bowie came around the counter holding his hands in the air.

"Tell you later. You're on duty. I'm going to get pillows. I'll be right back."

"Get my camera!" Nicole called after her as Andi raced down the hall.

10

WHEN ANDI RETURNED with pillows and towels in her arms and the camera shoved down the front of her suit, she found Bowie kneeling in front of Nicole. He was talking to her softly, his hands still in the air to keep them clean, while Nicole dug her fingers into his shoulders.

"Just hang on until it's over," he murmured. "That's it. Quick little breaths."

"I must be hurting you," she gasped out.

"Not at all. Just hold on."

"There." Nicole hung her head and relaxed her grip. "That one's past."

"I'll fix the bed," Andi said, "and then I'll try to wake Sleeping Beauty."

"Yeah, I'd feel better if he was in on this," Bowie said.

Andi walked around them and made a backrest of the pillows as she listened to Bowie help Nicole through another pain. "If you didn't finish the childbirth classes, how do you know the breathing techniques?"

"Watching 'ER,'" he said.

"Thank God for television." Andi set the camera on a nearby shelf, where it would be handy, before crouching in front of Nicole. "I'm going to help you over to the bed now, okay?"

"Okay." Nicole gripped her hand tight when another pain hit.

Wondering if Nicole had the strength to break the bones in her hand, Andi held on until the contraction passed, and then she finally got Nicole settled on the bed. ''We'll have to get that bathing suit off, Nic.''

''But what if Chance wakes up?''

''Hey, sweetheart, this is no time to be—''

''Let's get her a sheet if it'll make her feel better,'' Bowie said. ''That's how they do it in the hospital, anyway.''

''Bowie, I love you,'' Nicole said, her eyes teary. ''Don't you just love him, Andi?''

''Yeah, I'm crazy about him. You got yourself a winner, there, sis.'' Andi leaned down and kissed Nicole on the cheek. ''Sit tight. I'll get you a sheet.''

She returned quickly, helped Nicole out of her bathing suit and draped the sheet over her, forming a tent over her bent knees. None too soon, apparently. Just as Andi was adjusting the sheet, Nicole let loose with a swearword Andi had never heard her use before.

Bowie looked startled. ''Nic? You okay, babe?''

''Don't you *babe* me,'' Nicole said, panting. ''And wake up that worthless brother of yours. It's showtime.''

Andi stifled a chuckle as she looked at Bowie. ''Guess I'd better rouse Marcus Welby. Watch over her.''

Nicole took one look at her husband, gave a loud groan and started swearing again. ''I hate men!'' she cried, breathing hard. ''Every one of you can take a leap off the Sears Tower, as far as I'm concerned. And take your pride and joy with you!''

Bowie patted her knee. ''We will, I promise. Right after we bring another delightful little girl into the world.''

''I'm never letting her have sex,'' Nicole said darkly.

''She'll be a nun,'' Andi promised as she dampened a kitchen towel at the sink and walked back to the unconscious Chance. She wiped his forehead until he stirred and moaned.

Nicole continued to swear a blue streak during each contraction.

Andi figured her sister must be getting close to zero hour. "Let me know if you need me over there," she said over her shoulder as she applied the damp towel to Chance's face.

"I may need an interpreter," Bowie said.

Andi grinned. "She learned to swear in Italian when Dad was stationed in Sicily. She just told you and Chance where to shove your precious houseboat."

Chance slowly opened his eyes and looked up at her with a dazed expression. "Is that Nicole yelling?"

"Yeah. The paramedics couldn't make it so we're delivering this baby ourselves. We could use your help."

Chance squeezed his eyes shut. "I passed out. Dammit."

"Think you're up to helping us out?"

"Yep." With a grim set to his mouth, he heaved himself to his feet.

"Steady," Andi said as he staggered slightly. She grabbed the chair Nicole had vacated and shoved it under him.

He sat down heavily. "Hi, Nic. How're you doing?"

"Oh, so now I get to deal with two of you Jefferson sleazeballs."

Bowie peered around her tented knees. "But hon, I'm your hero, remember?"

"I'm never letting you hero me again, you slimebucket. Oh, God!"

Chance swallowed and turned pale.

Bowie was concentrating on the task at hand and

seemed not to notice his brother's condition. "What should I do, Chance?" he asked.

"Tell her to push," Chance said, his voice strained. Sweat popped out on his forehead.

"Push," Bowie said, excitement lacing his voice.

Nicole swore some more.

"Push, sweetheart! That's it. She's coming!"

Andi noticed Chance didn't look too good, but she didn't have time to tend to him. She grabbed the camera and stationed herself at the end of the bed. Kneeling down, she looked through the viewfinder as Nicole gave one more colorful curse and Bowie gently eased his daughter into the world. She forgot to click the shutter, and tears blurred her view. The tiny baby began to cry, and so did Bowie.

Andi lowered the camera. Some things just couldn't be captured on film. Bowie lifted the baby, umbilical cord still attached, and laid her against Nicole's breast. Then he leaned down and kissed his wife on the forehead, just as the whir of helicopter blades sounded in the distance and Chance moaned and slipped off the chair onto the floor.

WHEN CHANCE CAME TO he was looking into the face of a paramedic. Dammit, he'd passed out again. Major disgrace. He struggled to sit up.

"Take it easy," the guy said. "Don't move too fast. Fathers pass out all the time during deliveries."

"I'm not the father. I'm the uncle."

"So you're the sensitive type. No reason to be embarrassed about that."

Chance clenched his jaw. "I'm not the sensitive type." He got to his feet and shook his head to clear it. The houseboat was a rush of sound and motion as the medical team worked in its practical and efficient manner to clean up mother and baby and prepare them for the flight to a Las Vegas hospital. Everyone exclaimed over the healthy baby. Nicole wasn't in pain anymore and smiled at everyone who came within her field of vision. Chance felt his strength returning.

It really was a miracle, he thought, catching the contagious spirit of goodwill that touched everyone on board. Bowie ran around slapping the medical-team members on the back and promising to mail them all cigars. His little brother had delivered a baby, Chance thought, while he had been worse than no help. He'd been in the way. All in all, it had been an extremely humbling day.

He watched Andi rush around gathering belongings for Bowie and Nicole to take with them. Then she handed Bowie the key to her apartment so he'd have a place to stay in Las Vegas while Nicole and the baby were in the hospital. Everyone had a duty, a responsibility, except him. He couldn't remember ever feeling quite so useless. Or quite so relieved.

"That does it, then," the woman in charge said, surveying Nicole bundled on a stretcher and the baby tucked into a plastic bassinet. "We'll transport mother, baby and father to the hospital. Here's the phone number." She handed a card to Andi. "I can radio someone to fly in and take you two off tonight, or the marina can send a boat here tomorrow morning. Your choice."

Andi flicked a quick look at Chance. "Are you okay until tomorrow?"

"I'm fine." And he was. With every passing minute he felt stronger...and more foolish. The least he could do to redeem himself was figure out a way to get this boat off the sand. "We can call in the morning if we need help," he added.

"But you're stuck here."

"I may be able to do something about that tomorrow," he said. "I'd like to try."

"Just the two of you, with this huge boat?"

Andi glanced at him. "We'll use leverage," she said.

The woman looked at them with a resigned expression, as if she knew better than to argue with tourists. "Okey-dokey. I guess that's why God made cell phones. Let's go, gang."

"Bowie," Chance said.

His brother turned.

"Hell of a job, Bowie," he said. And for the first time in years, Chance embraced his brother. "Take care of those two."

"With my life," Bowie said, his voice hoarse as he stepped back. Then he hugged Andi as the medics picked up Nicole's stretcher.

"Just a minute," Chance said. "Let me say goodbye to my niece." He hurried over and leaned down toward the tiny child tucked in the bassinet. Andi came up beside him, and he slipped his hand around her waist and drew her in close.

"See you soon, whatever your name is," Chance said, touching his finger to the baby's soft cheek.

"*Au revoir,* Colette," Andi said, flashing a grin at her sister.

"*Colette?*" Bowie said, elbowing nearer. "Where did that come from, Nic? You know I was holding out for Bowina."

"*Bowina?*" Chance stared at his brother.

"I made it up, but it's supposed to be the feminine version of—"

"It's the feminine version of blockhead! You can't name this gorgeous little girl *Bowina*. Not while I'm—"

''Okay, folks,'' the paramedic said. ''You can name her Fred, for all I care, but you'll have to do it on your own time. We're outa here.''

Despite his faith in the paramedics, Chance followed them out to the rear deck and watched, the wind from the rotors whipping his hair, as they lifted Nicole and the baby up to the roof and got them safely inside the helicopter.

''I'll call Mom from Las Vegas!'' Bowie yelled over his shoulder as he climbed the ladder to the roof of the houseboat.

''And my parents!'' Andi cried out as she came to stand beside Chance.

''I'll call everybody!'' Bowie called over his shoulder.

As he got into the helicopter, he turned to wave. ''Bowina rules!'' he shouted, laughing.

''Dream on, idiot!'' Chance yelled back.

''You don't have to worry,'' Andi said from beside him. ''Nicole would never let him get away with naming her that.''

''To hell with what Nicole would let him do. *I'm* not letting him name her that.''

Andi chuckled as the helicopter lifted off over the water, creating a small tidal wave on the surface. ''You may not get a vote.''

''I may not, at that. Some help I was.'' He watched the blinking lights of the helicopter as it carried the little family up into the night sky. ''Thank God you and Bowie came through.''

''I think it all worked out absolutely perfectly.''

He continued to gaze after the departing helicopter. ''Perfectly? With me passed out most of the time?''

''You bet. With you out of the picture, Bowie got to shine. It may have been his finest moment. If you'd been in charge, as usual, he wouldn't know that he had the strength to handle a crisis like this. Now he does.''

Chance mulled that one over. The implication was pretty clear—he had been one of the obstacles to Bowie taking on his fair share of responsibility. How could he have, when Chance had always grabbed it away from him?

He couldn't see the lights of the helicopter anymore. ''Bowie will be a good father,'' he said. A picture of Bowie cradling the little girl in his arms hit him like a sucker punch in the gut. He wanted what Bowie had. Wanted it bad.

Andi was silent for several seconds as the helicopter lights grew smaller. ''Do you wish you were on that helicopter going with them?'' She sounded subdued.

Her comment took a minute to register. Their situation took a moment longer. Bowie, Nicole and the baby were on their way to Las Vegas, and he and Andi were…

Alone. A quiver of anticipation ran through him as he turned to her. She could ease this empty feeling. She might be the only person in the world who could. Her hair was tangled from the wind created by the helicopter blades, but now only a faint breeze stirred around them. ''No, I wouldn't want to be on that helicopter.''

''You wouldn't?'' She lifted her eyebrows.

Memories of the afternoon came rushing back to heat his blood and tighten his groin. Those thoughts, combined with the need to hold and be held, created a desire so strong it took his breath away. An answering need flashed in her eyes and suddenly they were locked in each other's arms, their mouths seeking, their hands searching, unfastening, stroking.

''I could take you right here,'' he said, gasping. ''Right on this damn deck.''

She pushed her hand inside his shorts. "We have ten beds—oh, yes, touch me there—ten beds, inside."

No. He didn't want to make love inside that crazy place where so much had just happened, where he'd been so weak he'd passed out in the middle of the action. With superhuman effort, he wrenched away. "The roof. Go on up. I'll get what I need."

She stared at him as she struggled for breath. "The roof? Why on earth do you want to go up on the roof?"

He gazed at her as an image of making love under a canopy of stars fueled his imagination. "I have my reasons."

"Name one."

God, she was saucy. And he loved it. Needed that spirit to lift him up. "I want to see your naked body caressed by starlight as you lie beneath me."

"Oh." Excitement flared in her eyes. "Well, okay, but we could—"

"I want to hear your moans echo between the rock walls of this inlet."

She sighed. He'd pulled her bathing suit half-off and her breasts quivered as she took a deep breath and gazed up at him. "Oh."

"And I want you to be able to look up and see the whole universe while I'm deep inside you."

Her lips parted, but no exclamation came out this time.

He smiled. Finally, he'd made her speechless. It was worth slowing down the action, just for that. "Cat got your tongue, Andi? Better find it. I also want to feel the lick of your tongue, and the press of your lips, on every inch of—"

"Go," she said in a breathless whisper. "I'll be waiting."

"On the roof?"

"I can't think of a place I'd rather be."

Neither could he, he thought moments later as he climbed the ladder carrying their sleeping bags. The contents of his general-store purchase rested in the pocket of his shorts.

But the roof was empty.

He tossed down the sleeping bags and looked around. "Andi?"

"I want to stroke my hands over your starlit, naked body," she said.

"Where are you?"

"And then I want to flick my tongue over every delicious inch of you," she said, her voice drifting up from somewhere below him.

"Then you'll have to get the hell up on the roof, which is where I am, woman."

"And I want your moan to echo between the rock walls when I finally put my mouth over your—"

"Andi!" His cry echoed back to him. He was going wild.

Slowly she appeared, coming up the ladder. She'd changed out of her swimsuit and put on the sexiest underwear he'd ever seen—wispy bits of black lace that barely covered her nipples and the vee between her thighs. And she was carrying an open jar of something. "Gotcha," she whispered.

"You had to do some sneaking to get behind me like that." But he had trouble being angry when he was so damn aroused.

"Oh, I'm very good at sneaking." She reached between her breasts and unfastened a catch that allowed the skimpy bra to fall away. She shrugged out of it and it fell in her wake. "And I should also tell you, before we get too involved and you might forget, that I'm terrible at taking orders, and I hate letting someone else get the upper hand.''

He gazed at her, off balance as he usually was when this woman was around. ''What's in the jar?''

''Fingerpaints.''

He peered closer. ''Looks like fudge sauce to me.''

''Does it?'' She dipped her fingers into the jar as she came toward him. ''Does that mean we don't get to paint? You said you liked doing that.'' Her breasts swayed provocatively as she approached.

He ached for her. ''We may not have time.''

''I'll let you paint, too.'' She stopped in front of him and smeared sauce around his nipple. Then she tilted her head to one side. ''Nice design, but I can improve on it.'' She started making swirling patterns, kneading his skin with her fingers.

He couldn't believe what the sensation did to him, how his loins began to pound as she played with her design. And then she began to lick him clean, murmuring her appreciation as if she were enjoying a piece of Godiva.

His breathing grew labored. ''Andi…''

She lifted her head and held up the jar. ''Sorry,'' she said, her tone low and sultry as she slowly sucked the chocolate from her fingers. ''Didn't mean to hog all the fun. Your turn.''

He took the jar. He couldn't remember ever touching fudge sauce with his fingers, and it felt creamy and sinful as he scooped some out.

She shook her hair back over her shoulders and cupped her breasts with both hands. ''Your canvas.''

He set the jar at his feet. Then he straightened and began painting the sauce on as if she were wearing a fudge bikini top. Her nipples tightened as he swirled and smoothed the sauce, and the visual and tactile pleasure of smearing the fudge over her breasts drove him crazy. She'd lured him into creating the sweetest treat he could ever imagine taking into his mouth. Finally he could wait no longer. Easing her supporting hands away, he cradled one chocolate-covered breast in his hand and began to taste his handiwork.

"Good?" she murmured, arching upward.

"Mmm." He licked and suckled and went slowly out of his mind. "Mmm-mmm."

He wasn't exactly clear how they got there, but somehow they'd ended up on their knees as he continued to feast on her breasts. He was so engrossed he barely noticed when she unfastened his shorts and pulled down his briefs. Then she demanded another turn, and he found himself stretched out flat, the stars above him, the roof of the houseboat under him. He had the first fudge-covered erection of his life.

And indeed, his moans did echo against the canyon walls as she enjoyed her chocolate-coated treat, comparing him favorably to every candy bar she'd ever known. Through the unbelievable bliss of her nibbling forays, he fought to keep some kind of control.

"Snack time's over," he said finally, gasping as he drew her away and brought her up to plunder her mouth with his lips and tongue. "You are outrageous."

"Is that good?" she murmured, nibbling on his lower lip.

"Good doesn't even begin to cover it." He rolled her gently to her back. "But I don't want to fingerpaint anymore."

"Time for a new game?"

"The oldest game of all." He slipped his hand beneath the black lace of her panties as he licked some lingering smears of fudge from her breasts. "Even better than chocolate."

"You'll have to prove it to me."

"Love to." He drew in a breath as he slid two fingers deep into her moistness and felt the tremor go through her. He nuzzled her ear as he created a subtle friction with his fingers and another tremor shook her. "I don't think it'll take long to prove," he whispered.

"Ha. I'm cool...as a cucumber." Her breathing grew uneven. "If you can last forever, so can I."

"I have a reason to last forever." There it was again. She pulsed against his fingers. Soon. "You don't."

"Pride," she whispered. "Oh, Chance, that's...I don't want you to think...ohhh...to think I'm a...pushover."

"Never." He settled his lips over her mouth and drank in her cries as he propelled her over the edge. Then, as she gradually returned to earth, he eased her panties off and reached behind him to find the shorts she'd stripped away during the fingerpainting session.

"My pride is gone," she murmured as he sheathed himself. "I still want you."

"I was hoping you would." Cradling her head on his arm, he moved over her and eased between her sleek thighs. His heart hammered frantically in anticipation of burying himself within her heat at last. He gazed into her eyes, those wise, funny, passionate eyes. "I'm very glad you still want me."

"I do." She grasped his hips and drew him down. "Show me the universe, Chance."

He pushed deep, and he thought his heart might stop altogether from the sweet ecstasy of the moment. He looked down at her, and she seemed as awestruck as he, but the shadows hid her expression from him. "I wish I could see your face better," he murmured.

She swallowed and took a shaky breath. "You can't because it's dark."

"Thank you, Einstein," he said softly, leaning down to kiss her. "Oh, well. Tomorrow we'll have sunlight." He eased back and buried himself again, and as he did, she lifted her hips and welcomed him with an undulating motion that made him gasp with delight. It was the most sensuous joining he'd ever known.

"Tomorrow we…have to move…the boat," she said between ragged breaths.

"Who gives a damn about the boat?" He abandoned himself to the exquisite pleasure of matching her rhythm and discovering which movements brought forth her lusty moans.

Vaguely he realized he'd just turned away from responsibility once again, and that doing so was becoming a dangerous habit. Then she tightened around him and began crooning his name, and he no longer cared. The drive for satisfaction crowded out all rational thought, until at last the sounds of their joyous completion careened off the surrounding canyon walls and floated up into the star-sprinkled night.

11

WRAPPED IN Chance's arms, satiated by his lovemaking, Andi drifted into a light sleep beneath the glow of a million stars. A gentle rocking motion only increased her sense of well-being as the stars gradually faded and the sky lightened to the color of antique pearls.

"Oh, dammit!"

Andi came fully awake with a start. "Chance?"

He was on all fours staring around him. "Un-frigging-believable."

"What?"

He crawled over to where the unused sleeping bags lay in a heap, grabbed one and threw it at her. "Wrap up. We're in the middle of the lake."

"No!" She pulled the sleeping bag around her and sat up. Sure enough, water stretched on all sides of the boat. The shore seemed very far away, and the pattern of rocks and mountains was unfamiliar. "What happened?"

He struggled into his discarded shorts. "Maybe the helicopter setting down dislodged us."

"Or maybe you did." She smiled. "You were pretty enthusiastic there at the end, Romeo."

He zipped his shorts and glanced at her. "You weren't exactly passive yourself, Juliet."

"I *knew* we could get the boat unstuck. See how things have a way of working out?"

"Yeah, this is just peachy." Chance squinted in all directions. "We just have to hope the remaining propeller works, and that we have enough gas to cruise around and figure out which little dimple in that shoreline is the cove where we left half our stuff. We're in terrific shape."

"You worry too much." Andi refused to let a little glitch spoil her contentment. The lake was calm, the footing on the houseboat roof good. Deciding to celebrate her newfound joy in the fresh light of dawn, she tossed aside the sleeping bag, stood and spread her arms. "Hey, world, *qué pasa?*"

Chance gazed at her. "We also have to hope that the guys in the fishing boat coming up behind us don't have binoculars."

Andi dropped like a stone, scrambled for the sleeping bag and crawled completely under it. She lifted up a corner and glared out at him. "You might have warned me, Chance Jefferson."

He grinned. "I would have, if I'd had any idea you were planning your own special salute to the sun."

She poked her head out. "Are they coming closer?"

"Yeah, they are, as a matter of fact."

She pulled the sleeping bag over her head with a groan. "Wave them off," she said through the layers of the bag.

He lifted a section to peer at her. "What?"

"Wave them off! And stop talking to me! I don't want them to know I'm under here."

"Hell, I'm waving them in. I want to ask which way the marina is from here so I can orient myself."

"Chance Jefferson, don't you dare call those fishermen over here while I'm lying naked under this sleeping bag."

He pulled the edge of the bag up again. "What did you say? I can't hear you through all that down filling."

"Scat! Vamoose!" She grabbed the edge of the sleeping bag from his hand and jerked it over her head. The soft growl of the fishing boat's motor drew nearer.

He patted her bottom. "Relax. You worry too much."

"Oooh! Wait'll I get my hands on you!"

"That sounds promising." He squeezed her through the sleeping bag.

"Don't touch me!" Grasping the sleeping bag in both hands, she crawled on her belly away from him like a paratrooper.

"Subtle, Andi," he said. "Nobody will ever guess you're under there dragging that thing all over the roof. They'll just think I bought myself a motorized sleeping bag."

The sound of the approaching boat changed from a steady drone to the putt, putt of an idling engine. "Yo, buddy!" called an unfamiliar male voice. "You got problems?"

Andi scrunched her eyes closed and prayed the conversation would be brief.

It wasn't. She lay under the increasingly hot sleeping bag for what seemed like hours as the men laughed and joked. A sneeze tortured her for several minutes before she beat down the urge. She couldn't hear what the men were saying, and the hotter and more cramped she became, the more certain she was that they were laughing and joking about her. As time dragged on, she planned elaborate tortures for Chauncey M. Jefferson the Fourth.

After an eternity the idling motor roared to life and the fishermen left.

The edge of the sleeping bag lifted. "They're gone," Chance whispered.

She threw back the suffocating material and sat up, her patience frayed. "You were making fun of me hiding under here, weren't you?"

"No, we—"

"I'll just bet. I'll bet you all had a good laugh about the bimbo under the blanket."

He crouched and smiled as he tried to gather her close. "You look so cute and ruffled. Honest, I wouldn't—"

She shoved him away. "Then why did you take so long?"

"Because." He reached for her again. "Come here."

"Because you didn't care if I was under there, did you? Because you get a kick out of all these scrapes I get myself into."

"I do, but—" He lost his balance and reached for her all in one movement, so that she toppled onto him as he rolled to his back. His arms tightened around her. "Stop struggling or we'll both flip over this little six-inch railing into the water. Knowing you, it's a miracle it hasn't happened already."

She stopped struggling. Falling into the lake from the top of the houseboat would not be a good way to start the day. "See, you think I'm a brainless klutz."

"Not brainless."

"But a klutz." She supported her chin on her hand so she could look at him. His eyes were warm and full of humor, and despite her irritation, the brush of his chest hair against her bare breasts felt very good.

He smiled. "An adorable klutz. And don't forget you're talking to the guy who passed out when he was supposed to help deliver a baby."

"Twice."

"I see I won't have to worry about you forgetting. You'll probably blackmail me with it."

"Thanks for the idea." She laid her cheek over his heart and listened to its steady beat. "So you weren't joking about me with those guys?"

"Of course not." He rolled them both over gently, so they weren't so close to the rail and he was propped above her. "There. That makes me a little less nervous. It's a damn good thing neither of us stumbled around in the middle of the night looking for the bathroom."

"If you weren't talking about me, what took you so long while those fishermen were here? I was beginning to think you'd discovered a couple of fraternity brothers."

"Just playing the good ol' boy game." He stroked her hair back from her face. "I had to let them carry on about me floating in the middle of the lake all alone on a ten-person houseboat."

"They really thought you were alone?"

"Yep." He kissed her on the nose. "I pretended my buddies were back on the beach, clueless that the boat had drifted during the night with me on the roof. I implied there was a lot of beer involved. Yeah, they thought I was alone. I didn't see any sign of binoculars in their boat, either." He gazed down at her. "Looks like the dawn flasher was only seen by me."

"Thank you for checking on the binocular situation. That makes me feel better."

"Me, too. I'm a little proprietary about my Lady Godiva." He stroked her breast. "You're still sticky."

"We need a swim or something."

"Or something." He leaned down to give her a few swipes of his tongue as he continued to talk, and the stubble of his beard prickled tantalizingly against her skin. "I also described the cove to them, and they gave me directions how to get back. I figured if I brushed them off too fast, they'd start wondering if I had a dead body under the sleeping bag. If anyone took the time to notice, you were a strange-looking bundle under there."

"A strange-looking bundle. How flattering."

He eased his hips between her thighs. "Ah, but you're also the prettiest bundle I've ever found naked under a sleeping bag." Beneath the cotton of his shorts, his arousal was evident.

"Chance, I really think we should—"

"Funny how the same thing keeps happening whenever I'm near you like this."

"Hysterical. Shouldn't we be testing the motors or something?"

"I'm testing yours." He raised up enough to unzip his shorts, although he left the waistband buttoned.

"Chance! Another boat could come along, and it's almost broad daylight."

"I'll listen for boats." He pulled a condom from his pocket.

"Oh, sure you will. Let's go below." She found herself growing moist and ready, despite her misgivings about his latest plan.

"If we're inside the boat I really wouldn't see anyone coming. This way I'll know if we're alone out here or not." He handed her the condom. "Open this for me."

"You're really serious!"

"Did you doubt it?"

"Of course I doubted it!"

"Where's that wild spirit of yours, Andi?"

"You really plan to make love on top of a houseboat in the middle of a lake in broad daylight?" But the idea excited her tremendously.

"Yeah, if I can get some cooperation. Open the condom and help me put it on."

She did. The open zipper of his shorts brushed against her thigh as he slipped deep inside her.

"You're beyond crazy," she murmured.

He eased back and thrust forward again. "That's how you make me, fudge woman, beyond crazy."

Her body welcomed him, rising to meet his thrust even as her mind said she should make him stop. "I can't believe we're doing this."

As he gazed into her eyes, he settled into the insistent rhythm that had carried her away so completely the night before. "And I can't believe you're still talking."

"I just think...mmm." She quivered as he made firm contact with her most sensitive spot.

"Yes?"

"Never mind," she whispered as he continued his deep, deliberate strokes. "Just keep doing that."

"I thought I might."

As the tension mounted within her, she held his gaze. The tenderness in his eyes revealed that this joining was about more than pleasure, although the pleasure was incredible. A rush of joy surged through her, heightening her response.

"Oh, Andi," he murmured, lowering his mouth to hers.

Her name had never sounded so sweet. No kiss had ever touched her soul like this one. He slowed the pace, as if to draw out the last moments, and then, in response to one mighty thrust, she surrendered to a shattering climax. He caught her cries against his mouth and mingled them with his own as his release shuddered through him.

FALLING IN LOVE with Andi wasn't a great idea, but Chance didn't seem to be able to stop himself. At the beginning of this trip, he'd thought he could avoid becoming involved with her sexually. Then, once that stronghold had fallen before the onslaught of her incredible appeal, he'd thought he could avoid becoming involved with her emotionally.

Yet, as he piloted the boat in the direction of the little cove and Andi busied herself clearing away the confusion from the night before, he kept catching her hand as she went past him and pulling her over for a kiss. The kisses weren't so much for sexual stimulation, although they definitely gave him that, but for the joy of connecting with her and feeling that surge of electricity between them.

They had decided on an agenda—moor at the cove, call the hospital to check on Nicole and the baby, then load everything they'd left on the sand, assuming it was all still there. Beyond that, they'd made no plan. Logically they should take the boat into the marina and drive into Vegas to see Nicole. Logically they should end the vacation today. He'd agreed to the trip in order to fulfill Bowie's birthday wish. Bowie wasn't even here anymore.

But Chance didn't want to turn the boat in. It seemed to be running fine even with one propeller pretty well chewed up. He'd hauled in the trailing mooring lines and miraculously the stakes had still been tied to them. The wind had died down, there was food in the refrigerator, and ten beds. He felt the urge to try them all.

He spied the little cove up ahead. "Land, ho!" he called out to Andi, who was putting away pillows in the back.

"Is anybody there on our beach?"

"Nope." *Our beach.* He'd like to make it that. The cove was secluded and there certainly wasn't room for another houseboat to moor, which meant they'd have a lot of privacy. But Andi probably wanted to go visit Nicole and the baby. Although he'd seen a soft light in her eyes this morning when they'd made love on the roof, he wasn't sure how to interpret it.

She came up beside him. "There's our stuff! The deck

chairs, and the fire circle, and the cooler and beach towels. Everything's there, thank goodness.''

''I figured it would be. We haven't been gone that long.''

''I know, but it seems like years since we sat down on that beach and read excerpts from Nicole's book.''

''Yeah, it does.'' He'd been falling in love with her then, but he hadn't wanted to admit it to himself. Sharing the birth of the baby, knowing she accepted the vulnerability he'd shown through the crisis, and then making incredible love, twice, pretty much clinched it for him. And everything would be terrific—as long as they stayed on this houseboat for the rest of their lives. That's where the problem lay. He couldn't picture her in Chicago putting up with his stress-filled schedule and he sure as hell wasn't moving to Nevada.

''Hang on,'' he said. ''I'm going to ram it up on the beach.''

''And I bet you love doing that, too. What a thrill, sitting at the controls of this long, massive boat, and then shoving it deep into that soft, yielding sand. What a macho power trip.''

She sure had a way with words. He lost all interest in beaching the boat in favor of the act it symbolized. But the job had to be done. He grinned at her. ''Just to prove that I don't need this macho power trip, I'm going to let you ram it up on the beach.''

''Yeah? Cool.''

''Get over here, and bring your testosterone.''

She popped into the seat the minute he vacated it. ''How fast?''

''I'll let you decide. But don't be tentative. You don't want us sliding back out.''

''God, no.'' She chuckled. ''Nothing worse than that.''

He watched her settle into the task, her expression intent.

"Give me a little direction, at least," she said.

"Okay. The technique I've used is to go in slow and make sure your aim is good, and then, just before you hit the beach, gun it. You should end up nice and tight."

"Oh, I bet. I love it when you talk dirty."

"You started this. I was only beaching the boat."

"Sure."

He had a feeling that the longer he hung around Andi, the more he'd adopt her sexy, playful view of the world, and the tougher it would be to concentrate on the serious business of running a huge company. He couldn't pay attention during a stockholders' meeting if he found himself daydreaming in sexual metaphors.

"Here we go," she said, her voice humming with excitement.

He gripped the console as the motors roared, the boat hit the beach and the prow dug firmly into the sand.

She let out a whoop of triumph.

"That's great! Shut 'er down. Let's moor this puppy."

"Are you gonna drive those long stakes into the ground?" Her smile twinkled at him.

He threw his arm around her shoulders and treated himself to a fast, hard kiss. "What do you have, a one-track mind?"

"Don't you?"

He gazed at her. She'd put on a T-shirt and shorts for the trip into the cove. There was nothing particularly sexy about the outfit, but all he had to do was concentrate on her for two minutes and he was hard and aching. "At the moment, yes," he said.

12

ANDI HELD THE STAKES while Chance swung the sledge-hammer. One glancing blow and he could have broken one of her fingers, but she never feared that he might miss and hit her hand.

She helped him wind the mooring ropes around the stakes, and then she dusted off her hands. "Should we start loading, or call the hospital first?"

Chance took off his sunglasses and wiped his arm over his sweaty forehead. Then he replaced his glasses. "Before we do either one, let's talk about a few things."

Andi panicked. They were coming to the end of the trip. They'd load up the stuff, call the hospital and take the boat back to the marina. Despite the look he'd had in his eyes when they'd made love this morning, when push came to shove, he wasn't interested in a yoga teacher from Las Vegas. He probably wanted to make sure she understood that although he'd had a great time, everything would end when he left Nevada, because he had a business to run. She'd told herself to expect this, yet she'd forgotten in the excitement of loving Chance.

She remembered what he'd said a moment ago, when she'd asked him if he had a one-track mind. *At the moment, yes.* The moment had come to an end.

She decided to preempt him and salvage her pride. She walked over to the semicircle of chairs and sat down in a deliberately nonchalant pose. "You know, this has been great fun, but when you get right down to it, totally out of the realm of reality.''

''That's true.'' He looked at her with some wariness.

She leaned back in the chair and forced a small laugh. ''We're two adults, and should be able to have a little flirtation without turning it into a federal case.''

''I guess so.''

''Well, just so you know, there's no pressure from my side of this equation. It's been great, but hardly enough to build a future on. We're too different. I mean, you have a company to run and I have…my own crazy life to live, right?''

''Mmm.'' He turned to look out over the water. ''I can't argue with your logic.''

''I didn't expect you to.'' She swallowed the lump in her throat. What had she imagined, that he'd drop to his knees and pledge his undying love? That he'd abandon his megamillion-dollar company and sell shoes in Las Vegas, just to be with her?

''The only thing is—''

''What?'' she asked too quickly.

He turned to look at her. ''The boat's rented for a week.''

She told herself not to grasp at straws. ''Are you worried about whether we'll get a refund if we return it early?''

''No, I'm not, dammit. After all we've been through, do you still think I'm that focused on the bottom line?''

''Well, I—''

''Don't answer that. I'm trying to find out if you have any interest in…keeping the houseboat a little longer.''

She grasped at a whole handful of straws. ''With you on it?''

He grinned. ''No, all by yourself.'' He walked over to

her chair and leaned his hands on the arms, which brought him very close. "You and a ten-person houseboat. Of course with me on it, you nut!"

A reprieve. A person with any self-respect would reject a few more days, knowing the ending would be exactly the same. But as he leaned over her, his very kissable mouth inches from hers, all she wanted to do was gobble him up. "I would be very interested in that."

"Good. So would I."

She couldn't keep the big smile off her face. By the end of the week she might be in tears, but in the meantime, she would party hearty.

"There's the matter of Nicole and the baby," he said, pushing himself upright again. "If she needs us there for any reason, or if you want to drive into Vegas and see them, we could dock at the marina for a day or so."

"I guess we could. If she needs us." If she didn't, Andi knew she'd rather stay here with Chance. That's how far gone she was. "If she doesn't need us, I was planning to spend a week in Chicago with her after the baby was born, anyway, so it's not like I won't have the opportunity to play aunt."

"And once I'm back in Chicago, I'll have plenty of opportunities to play uncle."

"But not much time to play houseboat," Andi said.

"No." He smiled gently. "This is it."

"Then I guess we'd better make the most of it, huh? We could drive all over this lake, take in all the sights, and—"

"Or we could stay right here for the next three days." Taking off his sunglasses, he pulled her out of the chair and drew her into his arms. "I like these sights just fine."

She gazed up at him, her heart pounding. "You realize

that means no more ramming the boat into the sand and no more driving the stakes into the ground.''

"Yeah.'' He cupped her bottom and held her tight as his manhood stirred against her. "I'll have to find other outlets for my testosterone surges.''

"Oh.''

He gave her a lingering kiss that left her throbbing. "But first we need to call the hospital.'' He released her and headed for the boat. "I'll get the cell phone.'' He turned and walked backward, twirling his sunglasses in one hand as he continued talking to her. "The paramedic gave you a card with the number on it. Where is it?''

"It's—Chance, look out!''

Too late. He flipped backward as the taut mooring rope caught him behind the knees and he landed with a crunch on the sand.

She hurried to his side. "Are you okay?''

He got to his feet and glanced down at the mangled sunglasses he'd just sat on. "Yeah, but I doubt if my shades will pull through.''

"I'll bet they were expensive.''

He took her by the shoulders. "Will you stop implying I give a damn about money? The only time I care about the cost of things is when it negatively affects the business or my family. How come nobody *gets* that?''

"Maybe because you're so busy playing with figures, you don't take the time to tell them.''

"They should *know*. But maybe you're right. I'll try to remember to say it, too.''

"But in order for them to really believe you, you'll have to stop playing with figures all the time. Actions speak louder, and all that stuff.''

"But if I don't handle those things, nobody else will!''

Andi gazed at him silently for a moment and wondered

if he'd already forgotten Bowie's heroics during the baby's birth. "Are you absolutely sure of that?"

Uncertainty flickered in his eyes.

"I didn't think so," she said.

"Well, something weird is happening, at any rate. I'm not in the habit of knocking food into the fire and flipping backward over mooring ropes. Not to mention finding myself in the middle of the lake without a clue."

"It's probably all my fault." She sincerely hoped that was true. Maybe he was turning into a klutz around her for the same reason she became one around him.

"No, I just need to stop acting like an idiot. Where did you say that card was?"

She sighed. No revelation yet. "It's on the kitchen counter, I think."

He stooped to pick up the broken glasses. "I'll be right back. And after we call the hospital, I need to call the office."

"Okay, you do that." So he thought he could settle right back into his old role, did he? Not while she had something to say about it. Until proven otherwise, she'd assume he was becoming disaster-prone because she distracted the hell out of him. And if she had any influence over him, she damn well wasn't going to spend three days watching a man work on his laptop.

Moments later he hopped down from the boat and came toward the chair where she'd gone to await his return. He held the cell phone in one hand and two pop-top cans of orange juice in the other. Barefoot and dressed only in his shorts, he didn't look much like a man dedicated to business pursuits, she thought. With his well-sculpted pecs and rakish stubble, he looked like an international playboy.

He tossed her a can of juice. "Breakfast."

"Thanks. Maybe I should have warned you earlier that Nicole's the domestic goddess, not me. With her gone I can't promise we'll have a well-balanced menu."

"Don't be so modest." He handed her the phone and the card with the number on it before plopping onto a deck chair next to hers. "I happen to know you're a regular Julia Child with fudge sauce." He opened his juice can and took a long swallow.

"I didn't say I wasn't creative." She glanced at him, enjoying the sexy ripple of his throat as he tipped his head back and closed his eyes to drink the juice. "Just not well-balanced."

He finished the juice and crumpled the can. "I'll take creative over well-balanced any day," he said, giving her a very suggestive smile.

She absorbed the implications of that smile and decided that she was definitely capable of keeping him from disappearing into his corporate fog, at least most of the time.

"Make your call," he prompted gently.

"Right." She peered at the card the paramedic had given them and punched in the number. Within a few seconds she was connected with Nicole, who answered the phone with gusto.

"Hey, Nic! Wow, you sound great," Andi said.

"I feel great. The doctor said it was because I didn't take any kind of drugs during delivery. It was a little rough at the time, though, and I guess I swore a tiny bit, huh?"

Andi couldn't resist. "Why do you suppose Chance passed out again?"

"No, really? Did I use the F-word?"

"Are you kidding? That was one of the milder ones. It's all Chance and I have been talking about ever since."

"Oh, God! I'm so embarrassed. Tell Chance I don't usually do that, please!"

"I told him he'd finally seen the real you."

"You didn't! Andi Lombard, so help me, if I weren't in this hospital bed, I'd—"

"Oh, relax," Andi said, laughing. "Seeing you let loose like that was one of the highlights of the evening. And Chance hasn't commented on it once. I don't know if he even noticed, as woozy as he was the whole time."

"You are a rat. I'm telling Mom."

"No, you're not, because then you'll have to admit to all that swearing. Just think what it would have been like if Mom or Mrs. Chauncey M. had been around with a video camera. And sound."

"It would have been completely different because I would have asked for about a million drugs. But I'm sorta glad I couldn't have them, because I don't have any side effects. Chandi's bright and alert, too."

Andi sat up straighter. *"Who?"*

"Chandi. Your niece. My daughter."

"Chandi?" Andi stared at Chance, who was shaking his head frantically and turning both thumbs down.

"Don't you love it? Bowie and I came up with it during the helicopter ride."

"Because they started giving you drugs on the helicopter, right?"

"No! Bowie and I were completely serious."

"That's one opinion. Listen, it's not written down or anything, yet, is it? Like on a birth certificate."

"It most certainly is. Signed, sealed, witnessed. Chandi Bowina Jefferson."

"Oh, God." Andi was torn between horror and hysterics. "Forget all those childbirth courses they offer. There should be mandatory classes in how to name a baby. You and Bowie shouldn't have been turned loose on that birth certificate without supervision.''

Nicole laughed. ''Give yourself time to get used to it. After all, you and Chance are going to be the godparents, so a combination of your names is exactly what Bowie and I wanted. And I'm not crazy about the middle name, but Bowie loves it, and she won't have to use it much. Trust me, it's a great name.''

''For a first-round draft pick of the Chicago Bulls, maybe. Did you ask poor Chandi Bowina how she feels?'' Andi heard a crash and looked over to see Chance on the sand, his chair tipped over backward.

''Chandi *Bowina?*'' he said, scrambling to his feet. ''Give me that phone.''

''Oh, Uncle Chance has a few words to say.'' She handed him the phone, holding her palm over the speaker. ''Don't get too carried away now. Remember, she's a new mommy,'' she murmured.

''Oh, like you didn't tease the devil out of her about the swearing.'' He took the phone. ''Nicole? What the hell is this Chandi Bowina nonsense?''

''That was subtle,'' Andi said.

Chance scowled at her, and then, as he listened to Nicole, his mouth dropped open. ''You're kidding.'' He rolled his eyes. ''Engraved, huh? Yeah, she likes to do that kind of thing.''

He covered the mouthpiece. ''My mother loves the name,'' he murmured to Andi. ''She's already had a silver cup engraved with it.''

Andi shook her head in disbelief.

He cradled the phone against his shoulder and picked up the deck chair he'd tipped over in his agitation. ''Well, if she likes it, and you like it, I guess I like it.'' He covered the mouthpiece again. "Mom thinks the name sounds French."

Andi smothered a laugh.

"Yeah, I suppose we'll all get used to it by the time she's, say, thirty-two." Chance paused and nodded. "Sure. Listen, Nic, do you need us to drive in there and help out with anything?" He glanced at Andi.

She held up her crossed fingers.

"Yeah, we got the boat unstuck." He rocked back on his heels and stared up at the cloudless sky. "Actually, it came loose pretty easy. I think the chopper affected it."

Andi grinned at him.

"Well, if you don't need us for anything, we were considering just finishing out the week with the boat." He listened for a moment. "You're sure? Then I guess we will."

Andi leaped up and started doing her version of an end-zone victory dance.

Chance smiled at her. "But we can certainly drive in if you need us to," he added, giving Andi the thumbs-up sign. "Yeah, Andi said she was planning to fly to Chicago for a visit pretty soon." His smile faded as he continued to listen. Then he sighed. "Yeah, I know that, Nic. Okay, here she is."

Andi took the phone back. "You're sure you don't need us?"

"First tell me how it's going with His Stuffed-Shirtedness," Nicole said.

"Okay."

"I can tell he wants to stay, but do you?"

Andi blew out a breath. "Yeah, I do."

"Look, I certainly don't need you to run in here. In fact, we may try to book a flight out the day after tomorrow. But I worry about you. Bowie says this is the perfect thing, you two being stranded alone together like "Gilligan's Island" or something, but I'm not so sure. I wanted to be around to referee."

"Nicole Lombard Jefferson! I wondered if you'd planned this."

"Not the part where I gave birth on a houseboat. But Bowie and I did think that maybe, if you and Chance got to know each other…"

"Forget it, Nic. Bad plan."

"But you're going to finish out the week with him. That must mean that things are progressing."

"Only to a point. I'm not stupid."

"Well, if that idiot doesn't beg you to marry him, he is extremely stupid. Whoops, they're ready to bring Chandi in for another feeding, so I'd better go. Can you call back tonight? I should know by then when we're leaving."

"Sure, we'll do that."

"Take care of yourself, Andi."

"I will. Bye." She clicked off the phone and handed it to Chance, who was watching her intently. "You said something about checking in at the office, I think."

He set the phone on his chair and came over to rest both hands on her shoulders as he gazed into her eyes. "Is staying with me for the next three days going to be a problem for you?"

She took a deep breath "No. I want to."

"Nicole wanted to make sure I wouldn't hurt you by leading you on with no intention of—"

"That's ridiculous." Andi lifted her chin. "Sometimes Nicole makes the mistake of thinking everyone wants what she wants."

"You mean, a husband and a baby."

"Yeah."

His gaze searched hers. "But you don't want those things?"

The truth hit her like a blow. She wanted a husband and baby more than anything in the world, and in the past few hours she'd even settled on an unlikely candidate to provide both. But she certainly couldn't tell him that. "Maybe someday, but not now, when there's so much fun and adventure to be enjoyed." The lie made her heart ache, but telling it was the only way to keep her pride intact at the end of the week.

"I guess it would take somebody quite unusual to make you give up the freedom you love so much."

"Yes, I guess it would." *And here you are.*

He looked deep into her eyes, and for a moment it seemed as if he might say something more. Instead, he released her and stepped back. "I need to call the office. They're going to wonder what happened to me."

"Tell them you were kidnapped by gypsies," Andi said, and started over toward the boat. "I'm going to make coffee and rustle us up something to eat."

THE GYPSY EXPLANATION wouldn't be far wrong, Chance thought as Andi walked over to the boat and hoisted herself back up on deck. Andi was definitely a free spirit with no desire to be tied down. That was perfect, because she'd never fit into his life anyway. At least, that's what he was busy telling himself as he stared at the cell phone without dialing.

No, it wasn't perfect at all. He sighed and leaned back in the deck chair, closing his eyes so he could think. What he wanted, if he were brutally honest with himself, was to have Andi come to live in Chicago, whether she'd distract him from his work or not. He had a feeling his obsession with her was going to distract him even if he didn't have her physically there. So what was he thinking? Marriage? Ha. She'd just announced that she wasn't interested.

Maybe, if he continued to satisfy her sexually, she'd consider becoming his mistress. That would be better than nothing, but he had a growing conviction it wouldn't be nearly enough. And it wouldn't sit well with Bowie and Nicole, either. No doubt about it, they'd push for a wedding ceremony. The idea intrigued him more than a little. Too bad it intrigued her not at all.

He could smell coffee brewing, and he opened his eyes and sat up straight. He wasn't getting anywhere running around this mental squirrel cage, anyhow, so he might as well make that call to the office. With a sigh he punched in the number and put the phone to his ear. The office phone had just started to ring when Andi reappeared on deck with a broom, and dressed in the red suit she'd worn the first day. She swept the deck vigorously.

"Chance Jefferson's office. Can you hold, please?" Annalise said on the other end.

"Sure." As he listened to canned music, he continued to watch Andi, and damned if she didn't lie down on the deck and start doing her yoga exercises. Through the open railing gate he could see the whole performance as she twisted and turned that luscious body. Oh, God. He disconnected the phone.

13

ANDI HAD HOPED her ploy of yoga exercises on the deck would shorten Chance's business call. She hadn't meant to prevent him from calling altogether. She didn't discover what had happened until after they'd made love on Chance's bed and polished off a breakfast of scrambled eggs, coffee and toast.

"How are they surviving at the office without you?" she asked as they cleared away the dishes.

"I don't know." Chance set the dishes on the counter and got out the dish soap. "I hung up before I talked to anybody."

She almost dropped the carafe of coffee. "You hung up? Why?"

He set the bottle of soap on the counter and turned to her, his glance roving from her head to her toes. His eyes glinted with appreciation. "I think it was the inverted-vee position that did it."

"You didn't even talk to your secretary?"

"Nope." He turned back to the sink and started filling it with warm water and soapsuds.

"Well, now I feel guilty."

He chuckled. "I wondered if you were deliberately trying to sabotage me."

Whoops. "Uh, not exactly. I mean, I do like to start the day with yoga exercises, and the deck has the most space."

"It's okay, Andi." He dumped the breakfast dishes in the soapy water and looked over at her. "Do your damnedest. If I don't have the willpower to ignore you, that's my problem. I have a couple of projects to finish on the laptop before I go back to Chicago, and I plan to spend some time on them today. Trust me, when I'm really concentrating, you could dance naked in front of me and I wouldn't notice."

"I see." Her eyes narrowed. This ol' boy didn't know her all that well, she thought. If he did, he wouldn't have thrown down such a rhinestone-studded gauntlet. Dance naked to get his attention? Hell's bells, she was a damn sight more creative than that.

THREE HOURS LATER, Chance sat on the rear deck. The platform covering the boat's generator served as a desk for his computer, and he had his phone to his ear. He'd been working ever since they'd finished the dishes. Andi had figured she'd be reasonable and give him some time. After all, he did have a trunkload of awesome obligations. But considering the magnificent surroundings and the delicious isolation, three hours glued to a laptop and cell phone was bordering on excessive.

Time for diversionary action—for his own good, of course.

"Think I'll go for a swim," she said, walking past him.

"Mmm. Have fun." He didn't even look up.

She could have dived right off the side and splashed him, but that was too juvenile. She used the ladder to climb down into the water. She even swam for a little while, to lull him into complacency.

Chance continued to type away on his laptop, the phone clamped between his shoulder and his ear. He could get a permanent neck condition from doing that, she thought.

He needed her to save him from those kinds of compulsive work habits, at least for the next three days. Treading water, she worked her way out of the red suit.

Her aim needed to be perfect for the next part. Too close and she'd soak him, which wasn't her goal. Too far away and it wouldn't have the same effect. She tossed the suit and it landed with a soft plop on the railing about two feet from where he sat.

He glanced up quickly, obviously startled. Then he looked at the suit hanging there, a brilliant statement on the dark blue railing. As she watched him, Andi thought of a bull staring at the matador's red cape. She was hoping for a similar effect.

When he turned his head toward the water, she dived under the surface. When she came up for air, she had to clamp her hand over her mouth to keep from laughing out loud. He was still working on the laptop, but he'd repositioned his chair so he was closer to the railing and had a better view of the water.

A lesser woman might have faked a leg cramp, Andi thought, but she wanted Chance in the water out of desire, not responsibility. He had enough responsibility in his life, as it was.

Thanking her lucky stars that she'd chosen water ballet for her physical-education requirement in college, Andi changed her swimming style from the standard strokes to the more graceful movements she'd learned in the class. Floating on her back and sculling with her hands, she lifted one leg, toes pointed, and slowly allowed herself to sink until at last her toes disappeared under the water.

Breaking the surface, she caught a quick glimpse of Chance before making a dolphin-like forward dive that hid her smile and displayed her bare bottom. He was no longer typing and he'd put down the phone. When she came up again, he was already starting to unfasten his shorts. He was halfway out of them as she began her next move. Arching her back, she propelled herself into a slow backward dive that lifted her breasts above the water, then her hips.

The movement finished with her toes pointing at the sky, her leg muscles firm and...cramping! She gasped and swallowed a mouthful of lake. Oh, God, major cramp. She flailed to the surface, her calf muscle screaming. Her cry for help came out a gurgle. Still thrashing, she looked through a glaze of pain toward the houseboat.

"I'm coming!" Chance shouted, stumbling half-in, half-out of his shorts.

In his panic, his hand shot out toward the generator cover to steady himself and his fist bounced against the laptop, a lightweight piece of technology that skimmed across the fiberglass surface like a hockey puck and flipped over the railing.

Chance made no effort to save it. As the computer landed with a splash and sank beneath the waves, he dived into the lake and started toward her, his powerful stroke cleaving the water with grim purpose.

CHANCE HAD ALWAYS prided himself on his ability to stay calm in a crisis. But when Andi screamed for help, panic grabbed him and shook him until his teeth rattled. Putting the shorts on again would take too long. Desperate to rid himself of them, he became clumsy. Vaguely, he realized he'd knocked the laptop into the water, but he spared it no thought as he tore the seams of his shorts in his frustration, threw them aside and vaulted the railing. Double-checking Andi's position, he dived into the lake and swam harder than he had in his entire life.

He reached her quickly, hooked his arm around her and towed her back to the boat.

"Your laptop," she gasped as they reached the boat and she clung to the ladder.

"I don't give a damn about the laptop." He held on to her as he grasped the other side of the ladder. "What happened?"

"Leg cramp."

"Which one?"

"Left calf."

He managed to hoist her on his knee and reach down with his free hand to massage her leg.

"Chance, never mind me. Get your computer."

"To hell with the computer. You could have drowned out there." His heart beat wildly. He'd never been so scared. Never.

"Because of my own stupidity. That's better, Chance. Go get that laptop, please." She eased her leg out of his grasp.

"You should probably get back in the boat. I'll—"

"No, I think the water's better for it. Will you get that darned thing?"

"Okay. Just stay right here."

"I will. I promise."

Giving her one last glance, he swam to the spot where the laptop had disappeared and dived down. Scooping it off the bottom, he sculled his way to the surface and over to Andi. Using the ladder for support, he lifted the computer, water streaming from every crack, to the deck.

"Oh, Chance!" Andi stared at it, her eyes huge. "Is there any hope?"

"Who cares?"

"I'll...I'll pay to replace it," she said, looking miserable. "But I know that's not the point. You've lost all the stuff you had on there.'' She sniffed. ''I should never have tried to distract you.''

He realized with a shock that not all the moisture on her face was lake water. She was crying. Crying because of what he'd lost. Crying because of a dumb piece of office equipment.

Reaching across the ladder, he closed his hand around her arm. ''Hey,'' he murmured. ''Come here.''

She allowed him to draw her close, but she averted her face. ''I think I'm so smart, so clever. *I'll get him away from that laptop,* I said. Well, I sure managed that, didn't I? What a gal.''

He caught her face and turned it toward him. ''Don't ever apologize for being yourself. I told you to do your damnedest. It was a dare, and I can imagine how you react to dares. And I knocked the stupid thing into the lake, not you.''

Her eyes brimmed with tears that spilled over her wet lashes. ''Because I was teasing you, trying to get you to lose your cool! And then I got a cramp, because I'm not used to pointing my toes like that.''

He smiled tenderly at her. ''It was a good show while it lasted.''

''I was dumb to try it. Now everything's ruined—your spreadsheets, your reports, your list of pros and cons. All gone.''

He was becoming increasingly aware of her naked body cuddled next to him in the water. ''You know what? I don't really give a—'' He paused as he registered what she'd just said. He tilted her face up so he was looking directly into her regret-filled eyes. ''And what list of pros and cons would that be?''

Her eyes widened just like those of a little kid caught climbing on the counter in search of the cookie jar. ''Oh, um, well, I just threw that in. I've heard busy executives often keep—''

''Bull, Andi.'' He grinned at her. ''You were in my files.''

''I just wanted to make sure the laptop was working after it fell on the floor.''

''You could have determined that without snooping.''

She went on the offensive. ''And it's a good thing I did! You had that list in a mess.''

''I did?''

''A complete mess! What do you mean by referring to my *wacky* view of life?''

Watching emotions blaze in her eyes was an incredibly exhilarating experience. Feeling her slipping and sliding against him in the gentle current was even more exhilarating. ''I can't imagine what I was thinking.''

''Damn straight. That's why I changed it around.''

''You *what?*''

''I rearranged a few things so it's more accurate.''

He was nuts about this woman. ''You edited my list?''

''It needed some work. Now it looks better.'' She looked pleased with herself, but then her mouth drooped again. ''Or it did. Now it sleeps with the fishes.''

He started to laugh. He should have been outraged that she'd messed around with his computer, and furious with himself for dumping it overboard. But the strangest thing had happened. Once he'd accepted that the laptop was unusable, a huge weight had lifted, one he hadn't even known he was carrying. He couldn't work. He physically couldn't work. My God, but he felt liberated.

''Chance,'' she said, ''maybe we should try to dry it out again, like we did after you poured coffee into it. You never know. Miracles do happen.''

"Yeah, you're right. Miracles happen all the time. Hang on to the ladder for a minute. I'll get it."

She followed his instructions, moving away from his supporting arm.

When his hand was free, he reached up and took the computer off the deck. Then he held it out over the water…and let go.

Andi shrieked and started after it, but he grabbed her before she could dive under the water.

"What are you doing?" she cried. "There's no way it'll work now!"

"That's right." He pulled her close. "When we're ready to leave, I'll go get it. In the meantime, pucker up those lips and kiss me. We have three hours to make up for."

ANDI COULDN'T BELIEVE the transformation in Chance with the laptop six feet under the surface of the lake. Apparently it had been the anchor weighing him down, reminding him of his obligations. Without it, he seemed reborn. He stripped off his bathing suit and they cavorted in the water like children, chasing and splashing around the cove until they were panting from the exertion.

But beneath the playfulness ran the sensuality that held them both in its passionate grip, and eventually Chance led her back to the boat and made love to her until the sun dipped below the horizon. They called Nicole and found out that she, Bowie and Chandi were flying back to Chicago the next day, which left Andi and Chance free to finish their vacation as they pleased. In celebration, they cooked dinner on the beach, spread out beach towels and made love again.

And it was love they were making. Andi couldn't kid herself that physical pleasure was all she felt when he touched her, when he moved within her. She'd promised Nicole she wouldn't let down her guard, wouldn't let herself get hurt. Maybe if he hadn't knocked his laptop into the lake, she would have managed not to fall so completely in love with him, but this unhampered Chance was impossible to resist.

As they retreated to the boat for the night and Andi snuggled into his arms, she tried not to think of how little time they had left.

HE WOKE HER at dawn with little nibbling kisses. The aroma of coffee drifted from the kitchen, and she turned toward him, thinking she knew what he wanted before his morning coffee.

"Time to get up," he whispered. "Time to fish."

"Fish?"

"It's the very best time. Come on. The coffee's almost done. I have the poles ready."

She reached for him. "I had a very different pole in mind."

He backed away and grinned at her. "Thanks for the compliment. Hey, don't close your eyes again." He leaned down and pried her lids open. "Come out to the rear deck. I set up two chairs. It's more fun with two."

"So's my idea."

"We'll do that later. Now it's time to catch some fish. Fish for breakfast. Yum."

"Doughnuts for breakfast. Yum squared." She swung her legs to the floor. "I remember Bowie saying you loved to fish, but I thought you must have outgrown it."

"Luckily I didn't."

"Luckily." She peered at him. He really did look all excited, as if getting up before the sun was the greatest idea in the world. "Chance, it's barely light out there. Fish don't have alarm clocks. They won't be up yet."

"Fish get up *very* early."

She loved most of the changes in him since he'd dumped the laptop overboard, but she wasn't sure this fishing thing qualified as a positive sign.

"Here, wrap the sleeping bag around you." He draped it over her shoulders. "You're going to love this."

"Oh, yeah." She stumbled down the hall, trailing the sleeping bag like a down-filled bridal train.

He settled her in a deck chair, cast her line for her and put a cup of coffee in her hand. "Isn't this great?"

"Outstanding."

An hour and another pot of coffee later, she turned to him. "So when does the excitement start?"

"Well, they're not biting on the lures we have."

"That's because we should have bought live bait. I told Bowie that we—"

"Your earrings."

"Excuse me?"

"What have we got to lose? Let's try your earrings and see if they go for those."

"You may not have anything to lose, but I have a lovely pair of earrings, a memento from my darling brother-in-law, to lose."

"He can make you another pair. He'd love to. Please, Andi. I really want to catch a fish for breakfast, don't you?"

"You bet," she muttered.

"You don't sound very enthusiastic."

She couldn't bear to squash his excitement, even if she didn't understand it one single bit. "I am. I really am. I'll go get the earrings, one for each of us. Maybe we'll catch two fish!"

"Hey, yeah!"

Turning away, she rolled her eyes and went in search of the earrings.

A half hour later, Andi begged Chance to stop catching fish because they had more than they could eat for breakfast, lunch and dinner.

"You could take some home and freeze them," he said hopefully as they stood on the rear deck with a cooler full of fish.

"Sorry. I have an understanding with my freezer. I don't put dead fish in there and it gives me an endless supply of Fudge Ripple Delight."

"Did you see the way your earrings worked, though?" He held the feathered creation, a little the worse for wear, in one hand. "I've never seen anything like it. Jefferson Sporting Goods needs to get this lure on the market."

Andi looked at him. "Gonna give Bowie a bonus?"

He glanced up, startled. "Yeah, I suppose I should, huh?"

"You know, this may work as a fishing lure, but the idea of earrings isn't bad, either."

"Yeah, if you don't lean too far over the boat while you're wearing them."

Andi laughed. "Hey, cross-promotion! Catch a guy or catch a fish, whichever you're in the mood for."

"I don't know, Andi. Jefferson's always been a pretty conservative company. That sounds kind of goofy, considering our image."

"Too bad you're so restricted. It would be fun to see what would happen if you turned Bowie loose on a campaign for marketing his lure earrings. In fact, if I were you, I'd turn him loose, period. Let him be in charge of new ventures for the company. His creativity is pretty much wasted in sales."

"I'm not sure he has the discipline to carry through if I didn't have him in some structured position."

That did it. "Better erase that old tape, Chance. That's your dad talking, not today's reality. Think about what you've seen on this trip. Think about the night little Chandi was born. When you were sidelined, Bowie picked up the ball without missing a beat."

"It was his wife, his daughter."

"It's his business, too! He's a Jefferson, although he hasn't been given much opportunity to prove it. You have no idea what would happen if you cherished his free spirit instead of scoffing at it, like your dad did all his life."

"I don't scoff."

"Don't you?" She was determined that this time they'd finally get to the end of the argument.

"I get a kick out of Bowie. He's a fun guy."

"Yeah, but fun has its place, right? There's a time for it, and then there's a time to get down to business and be serious."

"Well, of course." He stared at her as if he couldn't believe she'd even bother stating the obvious.

"You don't trust Bowie's ability to get down to business and be serious when the situation demands it. Even though you've had some powerful evidence recently that he's not the fluff-brain you think he is."

He seemed uncomfortable. "I don't know if what happened the other night would translate into business situations."

"The hell it wouldn't! A crisis is a crisis. And in this particular one, you folded. You hate that, don't you? You'd like to forget it, and return to the old days, when you could handle anything and Bowie couldn't be trusted to tie his own shoes without direction."

Chance's gaze grew flinty. "This isn't about me, it's

about him. You haven't lived with him for twenty-seven years. I have. If I gave Bowie the kind of freedom you're talking about, he'd be all over the map. He'd flit from one thing to another, never settling on anything long enough to make a success of it.''

''Well, I'm no different. Does that make us so bad?''

He didn't say anything, but the answer was there in his eyes.

She'd guessed that was his opinion of her. She just hadn't wanted to think about it. ''Bowie and I are fun to have around once in a while, but don't count on us for the long haul, because we don't have that kind of stamina, right?''

He took her by both arms. ''Let's take Bowie out of this for a minute. You have tremendous potential, Andi. I'm not so blinded by lust that I can't see how capable you are. When you were working with Bowie on yoga, I realized that you're a natural teacher. If you'd just grab hold of something, maybe open your own yoga school, for example, you could be ''

''Like you?'' Had he not made this comment, she would have taken great satisfaction in having him learn from Nicole that she'd gone into business for herself. Now he'd suppose it was his idea, not hers, which took the incentive right out of it. ''You want me to drive myself day and night to achieve some goal someone else set for me? No, thanks.''

He released her and turned away. ''I suppose you think I should just abandon Jefferson Sporting Goods to Bowie and run away with you to some desert isle where we can live on love.''

Tears of frustration filled her eyes, but she blinked them back. ''Bring Bowie's fishing lure and you have a deal.''

He bowed his head. ''I can't, Andi.''

Her throat hurt from the effort not to cry. She'd set herself up for this, after all. "Can't or won't?"

He turned, his eyes filled with agony. "Won't, then. Good or bad, I'm the way life has made me. I can't imagine turning the company over to Bowie, no matter what I've seen on this trip. And I can't image life without the challenge and the competition I'm used to. I'd go crazy on a desert island."

"And all that you love about your life would drive me crazy."

He swallowed. "I've been asking myself if there was any way you could come to Chicago, any way we could work out some arrangement."

She closed her eyes against the pain and took a long, shaky breath before she dared speak. "What we've found here is too fragile, Chance." She forced herself to look at him while she finished. "We'd kill that special feeling in a week."

He gazed at her in silence. Finally he spoke, his voice husky. "Please tell me we didn't just kill it this morning."

If the ache in her heart was any indication, she still loved him, stubborn type-A behavior and all, with a fierceness that promised to give her a great deal of misery in the future. "Is your laptop still in the lake?"

"Unless you hooked it with one of your wild casts."

"Would you expect me to cast any other way?"

"No."

She held out her arms and gave a seductive little shimmy. "Then let the good times roll."

14

CHANCE MARVELED at Andi's generosity of spirit as she threw herself into their last full day as if there were no tomorrow. He'd never encountered that kind of resilience and he was both awestruck and fascinated.

In the morning she made love to him with gusto, and in the afternoon she taught him water ballet until she nearly drowned herself laughing as he gracefully pointed his toes in the air. Most women he'd known would have spent hours in hurt silence after a conversation like the one he'd had with Andi on the rear deck of the boat. But as the sun set behind the cliffs, ushering in their last night together, Andi was standing on the beach, instructing him on the finer points of the macarena.

The only problem was, he couldn't imagine who he'd be dancing with once Andi was no longer a part of his life. But they'd come to an impasse. She apparently expected him to become some sort of beach bum, which was out of the question. As for transplanting her to Chicago, he'd pretty much given up that idea. She was probably right—their carefree relationship wouldn't survive once he returned to the world of big-city business.

"You have a decent sense of rhythm, Jefferson," she said, bobbing in time with him as they undulated through the moves of the dance, she in her black swimsuit and he in his bathing trunks.

"You should have seen my rendition of the hokey-
pokey in kindergarten. I put them all in the shade."

"I'll bet. You know what this dance would be good
for?"

He kept up the rhythm. "Yeah. Slapping mosquitoes.
Just got one."

"I was thinking of people who work at computers all
day. See how I'm moving my arms around?"

"I love watching you move your arms around. I love
watching you move your everything around."

"But think of it. If you called a macarena break every
hour or so, they might not get that thing they get, you
know—carpal tunnel syndrome."

"Or how about a yoga break?" He stopped dancing
and gazed at her.

"Well, I suppose." Her glance was wary.

Despite what he'd vowed to himself, the idea was too
good to ignore. "Come to Chicago, Andi. There are carpal
tunnel sufferers in every office on Michigan Avenue. With
your talent and charisma, you could build up a business
in no time."

She closed the distance between them and took his face
in her hands. "And you? What would you be doing while
I ran up and down Michigan Avenue in my tights and
leotard?"

"Carrying your yoga mat."

"Never kid a kidder, Chance." She stood on tiptoe and
kissed him gently. "You'd be working those fourteen-
hour days Nicole's told me about. I'd be lucky to catch a
glimpse of the tailored sleeve of your Armani suit jacket
as you whipped by."

He wound his arms around her and almost groaned
aloud at the pleasure of pulling her close. "Wrong. I'd
go without sleep before I gave up making love to you."

"Did you hear what you just said?" she admonished, and kissed him again, slipping her tongue into his mouth before drawing away again.

"Yeah, I asked you to keep French-kissing me for about a hundred years, give or take a decade."

"You offered to give up sleep. Not work. Sleep. No, my workaholic lover. I'm not adding myself to your packed schedule."

"Then I'll just have to kidnap you." He delved into her lush mouth and tried to forget that tomorrow at this time he wouldn't be able to kiss her. He wouldn't be able to run his hand over her smooth back and cup her firm behind. He wouldn't be able to pull down the straps of her swimsuit and kiss her warm breasts.

And he wouldn't have to try to remember where he'd thrown the box of condoms when he'd brought them down to the beach. During these last few hours, he'd considered stringing the box around his neck so he'd never be without, just in case she started doing what she was doing right this minute. She'd reached inside his swimsuit to caress him in ways that meant he'd better find that box, and fast.

"Wait," he said, gasping as she fondled him with the exquisite talent he'd learned to associate with Andi. "Let me get the—" He glanced toward the towel where he remembered leaving the box of condoms. A raven was pecking at the box. "Hey! Scram!"

He ran, or more accurately, considering his aroused state, he lurched toward the towel. The raven took the box in its beak and flapped skyward. "Oh, no, you don't, bird-brain!" He leaped like a star pass receiver and grabbed the box, wrenching it from the bird's claws. Then he did a belly flop into the sand. It knocked the wind from him, but it wasn't hitting his belly that caused him to grimace in pain.

"Chance?" She hurried over to him and crouched beside him. "Are you okay?"

"I think…I broke…my…pride and joy."

"Turn over and let me look."

He spit out some sand and struggled to draw a breath. "You're laughing, aren't you?"

There was a muffled sound, and then she cleared her throat. "I wouldn't laugh about a thing like this. Come on, roll over."

He did, drawing another tortured breath in the process.

"Poor baby." She brushed the sand from his heaving chest. "Knocked the breath right out of you."

"Damn wildlife."

"Let's see if I can inflate you again." She eased his swimsuit down. "Why lookee here! It's a valve!"

Laughing made his chest hurt, but he couldn't help it. "I think I squashed it."

"Oh, I'll bet it still works."

Darned if she wasn't right. Not long after she put her mouth there, he felt ready to explode. "Easy, Andi. Easy, sweetheart."

She kissed her way up his chest and smiled down at him. "Time to put the cap on," she said, taking the condom box from his unresisting fingers. She pulled out a cellophane-wrapped package. "Uh-oh. Beak holes."

Chance groaned. "I don't want to hear this. If that featherbrain ruined all of them…"

"Uh-oh. More beak holes."

Chance struggled to a sitting position. "Let's see."

"I have a better idea." She grabbed the box and raced down to the water. "We'll test them and find out if they leak."

He eased his trunks over his erection and slowly got up to follow her. As he started toward the lake, he cursed the bird kingdom in general and ravens in particular. "Andi, I don't know if—" Whap! A water-filled condom hit him in the face. "Hey!"

"It had a leak, but I hated to waste such a perfect water balloon," she said, laughing.

"Water balloons," he mumbled, heading toward her again. Bam! Another bulging condom hit him on the chin.

"Another leaker," she called out gaily.

He was dripping. "I'm trying to make love to one of the Marx Brothers," he muttered to himself. Another water-swollen condom sailed toward him, but he ducked and caught it. It didn't break. Good. He needed some ammunition.

"Leak city," she sang out, busy with her experiment at the edge of the water.

"I'm beginning to think you don't want that valve job, after all," he said, approaching her. He held the filled condom behind his back.

"I do." She glanced up at him, her expression impish. "I just don't want any surprises, if you know what I mean."

He dropped to his knees in the shallow water and grabbed her. "Too bad." He broke the water-filled condom over her head, soaking her hair.

She shrieked and struggled in his grip as water dripped down her face. "No fair!"

"You're a fine one to talk. Now kiss me, and make it quick."

She stopped struggling and turned her face up to his, her expression seductive.

"That's better." He started to kiss her just as a condom of water broke over his head. "Ah!" He lifted his head and shook the water from his eyes as she giggled. "Okay, that does it." He scooped her up.

"Wait!" She struggled and kicked. "Put me down! No fair using superior strength."

"If you can be sneaky, I can be macho." He waded out until the water licked his thighs. Then he dropped her with a splash. "Whoops."

She floundered around and finally staggered upright, sputtering, her hair streaming in her eyes. Then she pushed him. He was laughing so hard he couldn't keep his balance, and he went under.

As he came up, he grabbed her and tugged her in with him as she squirmed and flailed in his arms. "Were any of those damn things any good?"

"One!" she said, gasping and trying to get away from him.

"Where is it?"

"In my—oh, no, there it goes!"

"Where?"

"I tucked it in the front of my suit. It's floating away!"

"Where?" Chance lunged through the dancing, star-flecked water. Several times he imagined he saw the floating condom, but nothing was there.

"It's over there!" Andi pointed to her left.

"I don't see it. Oh, God, where did it go?"

"Here. I found it."

"Where is it?"

She stuck out her tongue. The condom was on it. And he was pretty sure it had never floated away in the first place.

"Oh, you're asking for it." He advanced on her.

She pulled the condom off her tongue and backed up, grinning all the while. "Just a little joke."

"Uh-huh. And now it's my turn."

She chuckled as she continued to back toward shore. "You should have seen yourself looking for it."

"I'm sure I was a riot." He stalked her patiently as his blood heated.

"Actually, there's more than one."

"Now *that's* hilarious. I was killing myself and it wasn't even the last one."

"I left a couple in the box."

"I'm only interested in the one in your hand."

"This one?" Smiling, she held it up.

"That one." He launched himself at her and grabbed the condom as they both tumbled down in the shallow water. He was on her in a second, peeling her suit off as she squirmed in the wet sand. She was no match for him, and he soon tossed the suit up on the beach.

"Chance!" she said, panting, "I'll get sand in my hair!"

Holding her with his upper body, he wrenched away his suit and snapped the condom on. "When this is over, I'll wash it for you, strand by strand. But by God, we're doing this right here, right now." And as the water lapped at their bodies, he buried himself in her.

This could be the last time. The sudden thought pierced the red haze of his passion. Everything in him rebelled at the idea of never loving her again.

"I need you, Andi," he murmured into her ear.

"You have me."

"When you come to visit Nicole—"

"No. I won't spoil this with scattered, stolen moments."

"Andi." Her name had become a plea.

"Make love with me, Chance." She began to rock gently against him. "Because I need you, too."

15

For the first few days after Andi said goodbye to Chance at the airport, she invited friends to the movies until her friends grew weary of the routine and she'd seen every comedy playing at least twice. If a comedian was booked on The Strip, she was there, no matter the cost of the ticket. Then she recorded all the "I Love Lucy" episodes she could find in the television guide so she'd have something to watch when she couldn't sleep.

Sometimes her raucous laughter threatened to turn into tears, and then she'd put on loud rock music until the feeling passed or the neighbors pounded on the walls of her apartment. She beat back her tears with Dave Barry columns, "Beavis and Butthead" and David Letterman.

By God, Chance would not make her cry.

She talked to Nicole often and downplayed the significance of the time she'd spent alone with Chance. Nicole said she'd barely seen Chance since he'd come back. He seemed to have lost himself in his work. So he wasn't pining away for her, Andi thought. But the satisfaction of knowing she'd made the right decision didn't help as much as she'd hoped it would.

Andi's parents spent two weeks in Chicago soon after Nicole and the baby arrived home, so Andi decided to save her week with Nicole for Chandi's first Christmas. Besides, the longer she put off seeing Chance at some family function, the better.

As the weeks went by, she realized there weren't

enough comedies in the world to keep her mind off Chance. His idea of arranging yoga classes for computer operators in large businesses rustled around in her head until, desperate for the distraction, she finally called a couple of Las Vegas's bigger corporations. The response was encouraging. Before she quite realized what was happening, she'd set up a schedule that kept her going five days a week and caused her to cancel the small classes she had been teaching for a local yoga school. She was forced to print up her own business cards. The irony of it didn't escape her.

She was so busy, in fact, that she rarely stayed home. Looking forward to a quiet Friday night for the first time in weeks, she'd even decided against stopping by the video store on her way home, which had been her recent pattern whenever she anticipated being alone for the weekend.

Juggling her mail from the box in the hall downstairs and an order of Chinese takeout, she opened the door and promptly threw everything up in the air. Fried rice, almond chicken and advertising circulars rained down as she stared in disbelief at the man sitting in her living room, a duffel bag beside him on the couch.

Chance stood and came toward her. He was dressed casually in a T-shirt and jeans. Weekend wear.

He glanced at the food scattered over the carpet. "It's not exactly fudge sauce, but I guess we can work with it."

She backed away from him. "Oh, no, you don't! You're not showing up now. I didn't even have to rent videos tonight! I suppose that means nothing to you, but—"

"You're right, it means absolutely nothing to me." He stared blankly at her. "What videos?"

"Never mind. The point is, they're not here."

"Good." He came closer. "I don't want to watch videos, anyway."

"I know what you want to do, and we're not doing it." Her heart was pounding so loud she could barely hear herself speak. "No, sir. I'm aware that Las Vegas is an airline hub."

"Andi, this is a strange conversation."

"It makes perfect sense to me! You may think you can drop by whenever you're in the neighborhood and stop over for a quickie, but that's not how it works, Mister Sex-on-Your-Mind. I may be easy, but I'm not consistently easy."

He grinned. "Couldn't prove it by me. Your apartment key is floating all over the place." He dangled a key he pulled from his pocket.

Oh, that smile. It melted something she'd been trying to freeze for weeks. But she was fighting for her sanity, and she took a deep breath and plunged on. "That's another thing! What do you mean, barging in here uninvited...what do you mean, my key's floating everywhere?"

"A few weeks ago, I went to see Bowie and Nicole when your folks were in town, and I asked if anybody could loan me a key to your apartment. They all had keys."

"Well, of course they did. They're family." She held out her hand. "But you don't get one. Give it here."

"I'm family."

"Only in a very general way."

He took her hand and placed a kiss on her palm. "I'm here to make it more specific."

She jerked her hand away. That touch set her on fire. She couldn't allow it. "I'll just bet. The key, Jefferson. You are not invited for the weekend, if that's what you had in mind. I see you even brought luggage. I made our terms very clear and you're violating our agreement.''

He seemed to be having a hard time keeping a straight face. ''I want to negotiate new terms.''

''I should have known. You probably want another little valve job, right? Sorry, but the warranty has expired. You men are so predictable.''

''Okay, let's start with this. I love you.''

She rolled her eyes. ''Oh, yeah, like nobody's ever tried *that* line to get what they want from their little hotsie-totsie.''

''Then let's try this, Miss Hotsie-Totsie. Will you marry me?''

''I suppose next you'll—'' She stared at him. ''What did you say?''

''Marry me, Andi. Please. I'm going out of my mind.''

All the fight went out of her. ''Oh, Chance. You don't know what you're asking.''

''I think I do. I'm reasonably bright—I took phonics in school, and the sentence only has four words in it. Will…you…marry…me?''

She gazed at him as she struggled with her answer. She'd missed him horribly in the past few weeks. How she longed to fling herself into his arms and agree to anything he wanted. But what would they do to each other, living under the pressure of his frantic life? She'd go into the marriage knowing she wanted to change him, and that wasn't fair.

Taking a deep breath, she looked him right in the eye. ''No.''

''Why not?''

''Because I love you.''

''Well, now we're getting somewhere.'' He closed the distance between them, fried rice mashing under the soles of his running shoes, and pulled her into his arms.

"Chance, don't." She tried to push him away, but not very hard. A girl had only so much willpower. "Getting physically involved again will only make us more miserable, in the long run."

"Not if we get married." He ducked his head and tried to kiss her.

She twisted away. "I just told you—"

"That you won't marry me because you love me." He captured her chin and made her look at him. "Have I got that straight?"

She was drowning in his blue, blue eyes. "I know it sounds backward, but it's true."

"It sounds fine to me. I'm becoming an expert in Andi-think. All I had to know was that you love me. The rest is details."

"The rest is the whole point!"

"No." He combed his fingers through her hair and cradled her head in his hand. "I used to think so, too. I thought the obstacle was my job, but finally it occurred to me that the only real obstacle was whether or not you loved me—whether I was the kind of guy who could coax you into giving up your freedom."

"Of course you are, but *you* aren't free, Chance."

He smiled. "Oh, yes, I am."

She looked into his eyes and saw something she'd never seen there before—a gleam of sheer exuberance. "Okay, what have you done?"

"Taken back my life. Come share it with me."

"You quit?" Her pulse raced. "Because of me?"

"No. I had to do this for myself. I might have come here tonight and discovered you didn't love me, after all. Those days on the houseboat might have been just a fling for you."

"Oh, no." A joyous song was wending its way through her heart, building in volume the longer she gazed into his eyes. She'd probably still have to live in the big-city atmosphere of Chicago, but that was a small compromise. "It was never just a fling. You have no idea how miserable I've been since you left."

He sighed. "Good."

"Good?" She pushed at his chest. "That's not nice, hoping I've been miserable. I was hoping you were doing just fine."

"Liar." He glanced down at the spot where she'd pushed him, released her and walked back to the duffel bag sitting on the couch.

"Chance?" Oh, God, she'd offended him. "I didn't really mean to shove you away. I was kidding. You know me. Always joking around."

"Don't worry." He shot her a rakish smile. "You won't get rid of me that easy." He zipped open his duffel and pulled out another T-shirt. "When you pushed at my chest, I suddenly remembered your present." He tossed the shirt at her. "It may not look like much now, but once you put it on and wet it down, I'm sure it'll be outstanding."

She held up the T-shirt and realized it was identical to his. She'd been too preoccupied to pay attention to what was printed on the front. Now she looked more closely, and glanced up at him. *"Bowie and Chance's Bait and Tackle?"*

He looked so proud of himself he almost preened. "Yeah. We're partners. It was his idea to try this, and after all that you said finally sunk into my stubborn brain, I realized his solution was brilliant."

"Is it connected to Jefferson Sporting Goods?"

"Nope. Mom may insist we get a discount on merchandise, but it's an independent operation."

"Your mother?" Andi felt as if her brain was shorting out from the overload of information.

"She's running Jefferson Sporting Goods now. Remember when I said nobody would handle things if I didn't, and you warned me not to be so sure?"

"I remember."

"Well, when Bowie and I left for a week, she started dropping by the office, just to check on things. Turns out she loves the business and always had a secret desire to be in charge. I never knew. She's learning all the ropes and becoming really great at it."

"Amazing."

"So." He focused on her, his gaze like a laser. "Do you really like the shirt?"

"I really do."

"Do you like it a lot?" he prompted.

"Well, sure." She held it out in front of her. "The crossed fishing poles make a good logo, and you have Bowie's name first, which was generous." She studied the shirt, looking for more things to praise. That was when she saw the small lettering beneath the logo. *Lake Mead, Nevada*. Her glance came up to lock with his, and she couldn't keep the grin from her face. "Here?"

"It's where Bowie's lure works." He crossed the room. "And if you'd been stubborn about marrying me, I'd planned to move in next door and lay siege."

"Oh, Chance!" She flung herself into his arms. "You can start anytime."

He caught her and held on tight. "Start what?"

"Laying siege."

"But you've already said yes."

She gave him a hot, wet and very suggestive kiss. "No, I haven't. I just admitted to loving you. You're gonna have to work to win my hand, Chance Jefferson. You're gonna have to lay seige, just like you said. And I can hardly wait."

I Do, I Do...For Now

JOANN ROSS

Author's note

Whenever I'm asked if my stories are based on real life, I usually answer that I make them all up. In this case, however, that's not entirely true. Many years ago the neighbour's nasty dog chased my kitten up a tree. Although everyone assured me Fang would come down when he was ready, I wasn't convinced. Hours later, when I couldn't resist his plaintive, terrified cries any longer, I decided to take matters into my own hands. But I needed bait to lure him down. My husband arrived home that evening just in time to see his very pregnant wife climbing down from the tree, the salmon I'd planned to bake for dinner under one arm, and a howling, squirming kitten under the other. So, when my fireman hero needed to rescue a kitten from a tree, I resurrected my plot. Fortunately, my return to earth was a great deal easier than Mitch's.

—JoAnn Ross

Dedication

To Jay,
who can always make me laugh

1

MITCH CUDAHY was a genuine all-American hero. Although he'd be the first to tell folks that he'd only been doing his job, the twenty-seven-year-old Phoenix fire fighter had a medal from the mayor, a certificate of commendation from the fire chief, and most impressive of all, he'd even received a letter from the President, written on official White House stationery. It hung on the station wall, right beside the crayon drawings from Mrs. Bingham's first grade class, which were a thank-you to Ladder Company No. 13 for a tour of the firehouse.

In the weeks following his death-defying dash into a burning apartment building to rescue twin infant girls from the flames, Mitch had appeared on "Good Morning America," "The Today Show," "Nightline," "Ricki Lake," and had even been interviewed by Regis and Kathie Lee, making his very proud mother the star of her neighborhood.

So with all that going for him, what the hell was he doing up a tree, juggling an open can of tuna fish while trying to keep from falling on his butt?

"You're not high enough," the aggravated female voice complained from the ground. "You'll never reach Buffy from there."

"I'm doing my best, darlin'," Mitch said through clenched teeth.

He'd just reached for a neighboring limb when the one beneath his feet cracked. There was a chorus of gasps from the crowd gathered below him as he managed to grab onto a branch above his head. As he hung there, dangling high above the desert floor, Mitch didn't feel much like a hero. He was also extremely grateful that Kathie Lee wasn't here to see this.

"Now look what you did," the seven-year-old girl scolded. "You dropped the tuna fish."

Tempted to suggest the smart-mouthed little kid rescue her own damn cat, Mitch reminded himself that all-American heroes were not allowed to cuss at kids. But that didn't stop him from cursing beneath his breath—ripe, pungent expletives directed at Buffy the adventurous Siamese, the damn bureaucratic animal control guys who'd decided that rescuing treed cats wasn't in their job description and yes, even sexy, blond Meredith Roberts of KSAZ, for showing up with her TV cameraman to capture his indignity on videotape.

Yet even as irritated as he was at most of the western world at that moment, Mitch saved his harshest condemnation for himself.

Hero?

How about chump?

The muscles in his arms were about to give out and his hands were sweating. With a mighty effort, he managed to pull himself up on to the limb. Straddling it, he found himself staring straight into the oblique blue eyes of a seal point kitten.

"You realize, of course, that you've caused a lot of people a great deal of trouble," Mitch said to the terrified kitten. The cat's tail, fluffed up to three times its normal size, was twitching back and forth like a pendulum. "But it's okay now. We're going to get all four paws back on solid ground."

When he reached for the kitten, it backed up, arched its back and began hissing like a burst radiator hose.

"Come on, cat." He was unable to keep the edge of frustration from his coaxing tone. "Look, there's a little girl down there who's got a can of tuna fish with your name on it."

Inching forward, Mitch forced down his irritation and began talking to the reluctant animal in the same rational, calm tone he'd used on more than one occasion to convince a frightened civilian to jump from a third-story window into the net below.

"And not just any ordinary old cat chow stuff," he crooned. "This is genuine, water-packed white albacore we're talking about, Buffy. The caviar of canned tuna."

The closer Mitch got, the louder the cat's howling became—a grating, particularly Siamese complaint that affected Mitch's already touchy nerve endings like fingernails scraping across a chalkboard.

"That's my girl." The kitten was inches away. Pasting a huge, false smile on his face, Mitch made a grab for it.

Unfortunately, the cat was quicker. It leapt deftly out of his grasp and as he struggled to regain his balance, it landed, razor-sharp claws extended, smack in the middle of his back.

"Dammit!"

It was a roar, a bellow of fury mixed with pain that only made the howling kitten dig in deeper. Tempted to peel the cat off and fling it into the neighboring county, Mitch remembered—just in time—the television crew filming from the ground.

"You're just damn lucky we've got witnesses, you miserable, mangy fur bag." Grinding his teeth against the needle-sharp pain, he gingerly made his way back down the tree, the kitten's strident complaints ringing in his ear.

About ten feet from the ground, the cat bailed out, abandoning the relative safety of Mitch's back like a teenage dragster peeling away from a red light.

Buffy the Flying Kitten took a patch of Mitch's skin with her, and his bellowed curse made that scene unsuitable for the TV station's family audience. Unfortunately, the shot of all-American hero Mitch Cudahy's three-point landing in a spreading cholla did made the evening news.

Mitch's mother, always eager to see her famous son on television, was thrilled.

WHILE MITCH was playing the reluctant hero, Sasha Mikhailova, recent émigré to the United States, sat in a government office across the city, scared to death. She was also determined not to show it. Especially to the man who'd been a constant source of aggravation for the past month. Just as Superman had Lex Luthor and Batman had The Riddler, Sasha had been cursed with Mr. Donald O.—for obnoxious, she thought—Potter.

Deported.

"You can't possibly be serious," she said, but she knew he was. The word tolled in her mind like a death knell. Her lips began to tremble; she managed, just barely, to control them as she looked around the cramped office that offered not a single clue to the man seated across the government-issue black metal desk. There were no family photos, no newspaper cartoons taped to the side of the desktop computer, no personal mementoes of any kind.

"The government doesn't make jokes, Ms. Mikhailova," he said, his voice as stiff as his manner.

As she looked across the unrelentingly neat desktop at her nemesis, she couldn't help thinking what her employer—and friend—had recently called him when he'd first shown up at the diner during the lunch rush hour. *Squinty-eyed weasel.*

The term, she decided, definitely fit. In all her twenty-four years, she'd never met a more mean-spirited individual. And considering all the bureaucrats she'd had to deal with to get to this country in the first place, that was really saying something.

"A lack of humor seems to be a universal trait where governments are concerned." Although her nerves were humming, Sasha lifted her chin fearlessly. "However, your government has made a mistake." She decided, for discretion's sake, not to mention that the mistake was mostly his. "You cannot deport me."

He arched a pale blond brow, licked the tip of his index finger and began flipping through the thick pages of her immigration file.

"It states here that when you first requested a visitor's visa, you declared yourself to be a nurse—"

"I worked as a surgical nurse. In St. Petersburg." She'd planned to attend nursing school here in the United States, to earn her license to practice, as soon as she'd settled down. Unfortunately that plan, like so many others, had turned out to be impossible, given the fact that she'd moved around like a Ukrainian gypsy since her arrival in New York one year ago.

"And then you were an English teacher?" His voice was thick with disbelief.

"Only part-time."

They'd gone over the same things the half-dozen other times she'd been summoned downtown to his office. He had all the information in her file. So why was he torturing her this way? Sasha decided he enjoyed toying with her emotions the same way a fat cat enjoyed tormenting a cornered mouse.

"My mother was a translator for the U.S. consulate in Leningrad. She taught me English from the time I was a very young child, so I was able earn the additional money necessary to come to this country by tutoring students after my shift at the hospital."

She was not surprised when he ignored her explanation as he had so many times before. "And now you're a waitress."

The amount of scorn he heaped on her current occupation made her temper flare. Counting to ten, first in her native Russian, then in her adopted English, she overcame her irritation and met his derisive gaze with a defiant look.

"Waitressing is good, honest work."

"Point taken," he said, surprising her by agreeing with her. Too late, Sasha realized she'd been set up. "That being the case, you certainly shouldn't have any trouble finding a job waiting tables back home."

His thin lips curved into a sneer. "Especially now that McDonald's has opened up shop in Russia."

Sasha tossed her dark head, sending the lush waves bouncing. She refused to let him bait her. Not when so much was at stake. "You cannot deport me."

The nasty smile reached his eyes, confirming her suspicions that he was thoroughly enjoying himself at her expense. "Want to bet?"

She'd studied the immigration laws carefully before coming to this country. When she'd arrived in New York, she'd gone to an attorney who'd taken her money and assured her that she was on firm legal ground. Two days later, he'd moved out of the storefront office and left no forwarding address.

He'd been only the first in a very long line to steal her nest egg. But that was no longer a problem because she'd spent the last of her hard-earned funds on the Greyhound bus ticket that had brought her from Springfield, Missouri, here to Phoenix.

"My father…" Embarrassed when her voice cracked, she felt the hot sting of furious, frustrated tears at the backs of her eyelids.

No. She would not cry! Sasha Mikhailova had the blood of czars running through her veins, along with that of a U.S. Confederate major, who'd reportedly done the O'Brien family proud fighting alongside Stonewall Jackson at the first Battle of Manassas.

Her Russian ancestors were hot-tempered, emotional aristocrats; her Irish ancestors were hot-tempered Celtic rebels who'd escaped County Cork one step ahead of the British sheriff. She would not give this sadistic little bureaucrat—this squinty-eyed weasel!—the satisfaction of making her weep in public.

She hitched in a deep breath and prayed for calm as she resolved not to crumble. "My father is an American."

He eyed her uncompassionately over the metal frame of his reading glasses. "Do you have any idea, Ms. Mikhailova, how many people, on any given day, tell me that same thing?"

"In my case, Mr. Potter, it is true."

"That's what they all say." He briskly stamped the manila file that represented a world of hope. A lifetime of dreams. "You have until Wednesday at 10:00 a.m. to compile the documents necessary to prove your case. If you can't, a deportation hearing will be scheduled for the following day. And then, Ms. Mikhailova, you will be put on the next plane back to Russia."

After making a notation on his desk calendar, he closed the file and placed it in a metal basket on the filing cabinet behind his desk.

Case closed.

Her life ruined.

Just like that.

"You would schedule this hearing so soon?"

He sighed, took off the glasses and gave her a stern look. "We've been through this before. You were granted a temporary visa in order to locate your alleged father—"

"He is not alleged!" Her flare of temper, which she could no longer restrain, brought much needed color into her pale cheeks.

She tilted her chin in a way that dared him to argue this all-important point. "All my life, while I was growing up, my mother told me stories about my father." Exciting, wonderful stories that had made the dashing American reporter who'd swept her mother off her feet and kept her warm during that frigid Leningrad winter seem larger than life.

"That's undoubtedly all they were," he sniffed. "Stories."

It was not the first time the horrid immigration officer had suggested such a possibility. The other times, in an attempt to prevent annoying him—and getting into more trouble—Sasha had dared not challenge his remarks. This time she decided she had nothing to lose.

"My mother, Mr. Potter, was not a liar." Maya Mikhailova had been the most honest, kindest woman Sasha had ever known. Since her mother's death eighteen months ago, there had not been a day that Sasha hadn't missed her wise advice, her warmth, her love.

"We're getting off the point." Frustration edged his voice and he waved his hand, brushing off her argument as he might a pesky insect. "The point I am attempting to make, Ms. Mikhailova, is that during your past year in this country, you have not resided at the same location—or for that matter, in the same city—for more than ninety days at a time—''

''It was important to keep searching.''

He frowned at the interruption. ''Perhaps it was important to hide your tracks.'' The accusation was, of course, preposterous. It was also one she'd heard from him before.

''I wanted to hide nothing.''

''That's what you say. But I believe differently.'' He gave her a smug look over the tent of his fingers. ''And unfortunately for you, the U.S. government tends to take the word of a sworn immigration officer over an alien who is attempting to circumvent the laws of this land by disappearing into the general—legal—population.''

His evil, superior smirk made Sasha squeeze her damp hands tightly together in her lap to keep from giving in to the very strong temptation to slap the smile off his face. She had no doubt that he'd have not a single qualm about calling the police, which would, of course, result in her immediate deportation. Which would undoubtedly give Mr. Donald O. Potter vast pleasure.

He stood behind the desk, signaling that the interview was over. Sasha couldn't help wondering if his less-than-average stature explained his seeming need to push people around so cruelly.

''Ten o'clock next Wednesday,'' he reminded her. ''You are, of course, entitled to legal counsel.''

This was Friday, which gave her only four more days. Sasha's mind whirled. How was she going to find her father in so short a time when she hadn't been able to locate him in the past twelve months? And where was she to find the money for yet another lawyer?

She felt as if an iron fist was clutching at her heart as she left the cold, sterile government office. Determined not to reveal her pain to all the clerks who were buzzing around

like busy worker bees, Sasha held her sable head regally
high. Her back was straight as an arrow and as she marched
past the other grim-faced resident aliens waiting to learn
their individual fates, she was reminded of her long ago
royal Russian ancestors.

Granted, this was not a fatal verdict. Still, as Sasha
waited for the elevator to arrive, she thought she knew
something of what her mother's relatives had felt as they'd
prepared to face the Red Army's firing squads. As the metal
elevator doors closed behind her, she found herself alone
with a dark-suited man who reeked of some no doubt expensive but suffocating cologne. And adding to her discomfort, instead of watching the lighted numbers above the
door as everyone else did while riding in an elevator, he
couldn't seem to stop looking at her breasts.

Sasha had known it was a mistake to wear the snug uniform, especially when she would have preferred her single
good black suit. But she knew from experience that she'd
be kept waiting hours past her appointment time, which
would not give her time to stop by the rooming house to
change her clothes before work.

She kept her eyes straight ahead as she exited the elevator ahead of the other passenger, but she felt his preda-
tory gaze all the way out of the building. Then she stood
outside the towering black-glass office building, frustration
escalating to the boiling point as she watched the city bus
pull away from the curb. It would be at least ten minutes
before another one arrived.

Which would, unfortunately, make her late to work.

Which meant she'd miss Mitch Cudahy when he picked
up dinner for the firemen of Ladder Company No. 13. Although Sasha knew that the chances of an American hero
looking twice at a mere waitress, let alone one who was
shorter, darker, and far less stylish than the willowy blondes

she knew he favored, ever since Mitch had arrived, sirens wailing, to put out a fire she'd accidentally started in the diner's kitchen, her heart had steadfastly refused to listen to her head.

After dousing the flames, he'd amazed her by apologizing for the three inches of water on the green-and-white checkered linoleum floor. Sasha had gazed into the depths of his eyes—their crystal blue absolutely riveting in his handsome, soot-smudged face—and against every bit of pragmatism she possessed, had fallen hopelessly, head over heels in love.

After that fateful day, whenever he came into the diner, with his cocky masculine stride, his compact body looking so wonderfully fit in the navy blue T-shirt and jeans favored by the city firemen, Sasha would feel light-headed and giddy.

The thought of having to leave Phoenix, to leave America, to never see Mitch again, was one more depressing thing in an already ghastly day.

She sighed, looking up at the clear blue sky. The morning rain had stopped. That, at least, was something.

She waited at the bus stop, her mind whirling, tossing up problems without solutions, dilemmas without answers. For a fleeting moment she considered running away, like the dreadful immigration officer had suggested she might be planning to do.

But where would she go? And how long could she hide before the government discovered her and sent her back to St. Petersburg in disgrace?

Her thoughts on the logistics of pulling off such an admittedly risky—not to mention highly illegal—plan, Sasha didn't see the pizza delivery truck speeding down the street until it shot through a puddle in front of her, splashing a wave of muddy water that drenched the front of her bubblegum-pink uniform.

2

It was more than forty-five minutes before the bus finally showed up.

"It took you long enough to get here," the elderly woman in front of Sasha complained.

"Hey, don't blame me." The driver, who looked more like a roadie for a heavy metal band than a city employee, shrugged uncaringly. "The scheduled bus broke down."

"What about the one after that?"

"Do I look like Dan freaking Rather?" he retorted as he punched her card. "How should I know?"

"Young man, I have been riding this route every day for twenty-five years." The woman snatched her card back and jammed it into her already overstuffed shopping bag. "And never, in all that time, have I experienced such rudeness. I've a good mind to report you to your supervisor."

"You've got me trembling in my boots," he snarled in return.

As the woman stomped down the aisle, the driver leered at Sasha. "Well, hello." His eyes, hidden behind a pair of purple sunglasses, slid over her, taking in the muddied uniform. "Looks like you've had a rough day, sugar."

Although she certainly did not approve of the way he'd spoken to the previous passenger, Sasha was in no mood to enter into a confrontation with yet another government employee.

"I have had better." She held out her card.

"Well," he said, "this is my last run for the day. You need any help getting out of that wet outfit, just let me know."

The lewd suggestion was every bit as annoying as the immigration officer's earlier derision. "I do not think that will be necessary."

"If you're through insulting old ladies and trying to pick up waitresses, do you think we could get this show on the road?" an irritated blue-suited Yuppie type behind Sasha inquired.

"Hold your water, man." The driver punched Sasha's card, purposefully brushing his fingers over hers as she took it back.

Assuring herself that this had to be the low spot of her day, that things could not possibly get any worse, Sasha sank onto a hard seat midway down the aisle.

Although she hated the idea of being late for work, Sasha couldn't help feeling somewhat grateful for the delay. Because, as much as she looked forward to seeing Mitch Cudahy, she couldn't bear the idea of his seeing her looking so disheveled. Once again, she compared herself with his latest lover, a sleek, blond television news reporter, and once again Sasha realized that her fantasies of a life with the sexy fireman were exactly that—fantasies.

In front of her, two teenagers sat, heads together as they exchanged warm looks and soft murmurs and light kisses. Their hands were never still, stroking each other's hair, arms, faces all the way up Central Avenue.

Although no one could pay her to relive her own tumultuous teenage years, Sasha couldn't help being just a little envious. And when the boy bent his head and gave the girl a hot, lingering kiss that was obviously a prelude to many more before the night was over, she felt the ache all the way to her toes.

She'd never, in all her twenty-four years, had any man look at her that way. She'd never had any man kiss her that way. And until Mitch, she'd never met a man she'd even wanted to kiss her with such passion.

She closed her eyes and rubbed her temples where the Potter-caused headache throbbed painfully. With a six-hour shift yet to get through, Sasha could only hope that tonight would be a light one.

As the bus pulled up to the curbside stop on busy Camelback Road, Sasha viewed the shiny red fire truck parked outside the diner and groaned. Apparently she wasn't the only one who was late today.

She debated staying on the bus, riding to the next stop, then walking back. But she was already late for work; it would be wrong to leave Glory Seeger to pick up the slack simply because she was uncomfortable having the man of her dreams witness her looking like some homeless person.

"He never notices you anyway," she told herself as she exited the bus with the teenagers who were so besotted with each other. Reminding herself that she had far more problems to worry about than the lack of a lover, Sasha squared her shoulders, took a deep breath, pushed open the diner door and immediately found herself face-to-face with Mitch, who was on his way out.

CONTRARY to what she believed, Mitch had definitely noticed Sasha. He'd noticed her thick, wavy sable hair, her flashing dark eyes that revealed every emotion and the full rosy lips she was always forgetting to paint.

Since he was male, and human, he'd certainly noticed that her uniform fit a bit too snugly over her lush curves and that although she wasn't tall, her legs were long and firm, with an attractive fullness at the back of her calves.

He'd also noticed, over the aroma of hickory smoke from

Glory's famed barbecued ribs, that the painfully shy waitress smelled damn good.

There had been a time, during a two-day lull between women, that he'd considered asking her out. But then Meredith Roberts had shown up at the fire station to interview him and one thing had led to another, and by the time the cameraman had packed up his videocam and equipment, Mitch had accepted her offer to take in the Cardinals football game from the television station's executive box.

They'd been dating for about three weeks now. And although he thoroughly enjoyed his single life and had no intention of ever settling down with any one woman for any extended length of time, he did tend toward serial monogamy. Which meant that he'd never gotten around to asking Sasha out as intended. But he'd continued to look.

Today, however, the sight was anything but appealing. She looked as if she'd gone through a car wash. Without the car.

''What the hell happened to you?''

It was then that Sasha burst into tears.

Terrific. This was all he needed, Mitch thought as the question he'd unthinkingly blurted sent Sasha into a torment of noisy weeping that had the fireman behind him looking at him as if he were an ax murderer.

This was just one more lousy thing in an already rotten day. After falling out of the tree, he'd spent an hour having cactus needles picked out of his flesh. He figured that he had more holes in him than a damn sieve and had arrived at the diner in a filthy mood.

''What the hell did you say to the poor girl, Cudahy?'' Jake Brown growled. Jake was his brother-in-law and also his best friend. But the look he was giving Mitch right now was anything but friendly.

"I only asked what happened to her," Mitch retorted, his mood worsening by the moment.

"Mitchel Cudahy!" The booming voice coming from behind the chipped Formica-topped counter reminded him of his uncle Dan Cudahy, who worked as a logger in southern Oregon. With her wide shoulders and arms the circumference of Virginia hams, Glory Seeger even looked a bit like his uncle Dan. But without the mustache. "What are you doing, making my best waitress cry?"

"I didn't do anything!" Mitch turned to Sasha for confirmation.

Lord, the lady was really pitiful. Unlike the women he was used to, who could weep genteelly on occasion to gain their own way, Sasha was bawling like a baby. Her dark gypsy hair was a wild tangle over shoulders that were shaking like the L.A. Coliseum during an earthquake. Tears were streaming down her face like the Niagara over the falls, and her nose was as red as Rudolph's. There was an enormous wet brown stain covering the front of her Pepto-Bismol-pink skirt.

Even as he told himself that he hadn't done anything to cause this outburst, that he owed the sweet-smelling, Russian-born waitress nothing but a tip whenever she served him a cup of coffee and a piece of Glory's incomparable pecan pie, Mitch felt the familiar, unbidden sense of responsibility raise its nagging head.

It was the damn cat all over again. Sasha was a grown woman. The fact that she'd managed to make it out of Russia and come to the U.S. in the first place proved that she was more than a little capable of taking care of herself. Besides, whatever her problem, it had nothing to do with him.

He'd done his good deed for the day.

So why couldn't he just leave well enough alone?

Mitch wanted desperately just to walk past her and get back to work. Instead he sighed, set the foam containers he was carrying on a wobbly white wooden table close by, then took hold of her quaking shoulders. "Hey, Sasha." His smile was friendly and encouraging, not unlike the one he'd first given that ungrateful kitten. "Whatever it is, darlin', it can't be all that bad."

Darlin'. It was a word Mitch used indiscriminately with women in general. Today he'd already tossed it at the cat's seven-year-old owner and Meredith—even though he'd been ticked off about her bringing along a cameraman to record his indignity. He'd also used it on the pretty blond nurse who'd wielded those treacherous tweezers at Good Samaritan Hospital, and who, after plucking the cactus needles from his bare ass had given him her telephone number.

It was an all-purpose, friendly endearment. It didn't mean anything. Not really.

But when Sasha heard that drawled "darlin'," that same tender term she'd dreamed about so many times over the past weeks, her yearning heart turned a series of dizzying somersaults. For a fleeting, wonderful moment, hope sang its clear sweet song through her veins.

Then she made the mistake of looking up into Mitchel's thickly lashed eyes. The pity she saw in those crystal blue depths stimulated a fresh torrent of hot tears.

"Christ." Mitch wondered what he'd done now. He turned to Glory, who was watching the little drama, meaty arms folded over her abundant chest, her expression every bit as daunting as the meat cleaver she was holding.

"Would you please do something?" Mitch demanded with overt frustration. He'd had his fill of other people's problems today.

"You're the one who made the poor little girl cry."

Glory's broad face reminded him of a threatening dark thunderhead. "*You* do something."

Mitch turned to Sasha, who'd turned her back and had buried her face in her hands. Her life was none of his business, he reminded himself yet again. It had nothing to do with him.

Aw, hell....

"You know, darlin'," he said soothingly, "if you don't turn off the waterworks, you're liable to flood this place worse than I did when I put out the grease fire in your kitchen."

At the reminder of that fateful day when she'd fallen so totally, helplessly, in love with this man who was now witnessing her humiliation, Sasha's response was to sob louder.

Mitch threw up his hands. "I give up." The lady was about as volatile as an open can of gasoline next to a lit match. Having already used up his daily store of patience even before he'd arrived at the diner, Mitch sought assistance from his brother-in-law.

"You're used to dealing with hysterical females. Talk to her." The way Mitch figured it, any man who could handle Katie Cudahy Brown's PMS-induced tantrums could undoubtedly calm this sobbing, near-hysterical woman down.

"Ain't that just like a man," Glory broke in before Jake could answer. "Breaking a woman's heart, then leaving someone else to clean up his mess."

"Mess?" Mitch couldn't believe this. "What mess? What are you talking about?"

"I'm talking about whatever you did to Sasha." If looks could kill, the diner owner's glower would have put Mitch six feet under. "So help me, God, Mitchel Cudahy, hotshot hero or not, if you dared to get this poor, sweet, innocent girl in the family way—"

"What?" Mitch immediately went beyond disbelief to horror. He might not be a monk, but he was definitely not the irresponsible bastard Glory had just accused him of being. Hell, he'd practiced safe sex before it had gotten popular. "I didn't… I never… Whatever gave you the idea—"

"Mitch?" Jake finally entered into the discussion. His expression, Mitch noted with consternation, was suddenly as serious as Glory's.

"Dammit!" He took hold of Sasha's shoulders again and spun her around. "Tell them," he demanded as she lowered her hands from her face and stared up at him through glistening dark eyes, "tell them we've barely said two words to each other the entire time you've worked here."

"That doesn't prove a thing," Glory insisted. "My first three husbands never said all that much, either. In bed or out. Which is one of the reasons I divorced them. But that didn't stop the jerks from leaving me with five babies to raise."

"Sasha." Although it took a herculean effort, Mitch managed to draw in a deep breath that allowed him to inject a note of almost reasonable calm into his tone. "We both know that whatever is bothering you has nothing to do with me."

He gave her an encouraging smile and ran his palm down her dark hair, then jerked his hand away when he saw Glory's eyes narrow even more and realized the caress, meant to soothe, might, under the circumstances, look like something far more intimate.

"So why don't you do me a great big favor and get me off the hook by telling Glory and Jake that I'm just an innocent bystander here."

That wasn't true. Not really. The fact of the matter was that Mitch was, if not the cause, at least the trigger for her tears. But seeing the naked distress written all over his handsome face, and honestly appalled at how Jake and Glory had misunderstood the situation, Sasha dragged in a deep, shuddering breath that had the unfortunate side effect of drawing Mitch's rebellious eyes to her breasts, a movement that did not go unnoticed by Jake, who continued to frown at his brother-in-law.

"M-Mitch is r-right." She forced the ragged words through trembling lips. "He did nothing." She felt the strong fingers on her shoulders relax ever so slightly.

"See?" He shot the skeptical pair an I-told-you-so look over his shoulder.

"I don't know," Glory mused grumpily. "Maybe she's just covering up for you."

When his fingers tightened again, digging painfully into her shoulders, Sasha shook her head. "No." She hitched in another deep breath that threatened to pop a button. "It's not Mitch's fault. And I apologize for upsetting everyone."

Sasha tried to force a wobbly smile and failed miserably. "It is nothing," she insisted. Her lips began to tremble again. "Really."

Although Mitch was ready to leave, relieved to escape the uncomfortable emotional female scene, Jake wasn't about to let the matter go so easily.

"Obviously it's something." He added the foam cartons he was still holding to the ones Mitch had left on the table and pulled out a chair covered in cracked red plastic. "So why don't you sit down and tell us all about it, honey?"

"You are very kind, Jake." Sasha rubbed at her shining, red-rimmed eyes with the backs of her hands, reminding Mitch of how that unhappy little cat owner had looked when he'd first arrived on the scene. "But it is not necessary." She looked past the two firemen to Glory. "I was late today. It is past time I began working."

"You see any customers around here?" Glory asked.

Her eyes swept the small storefront diner, taking in the empty tables and the row of red booths along a wall decorated with brightly colored posters touting Louisiana hot sauce. "Sit down, girl. And spill the damn beans before they get you all choked up again. Besides," she added, when she got the impression Sasha was about to continue arguing, "a bawling waitress tends to spoil customers' appetites."

She turned to Mitch. "Get the poor girl a drink of water."

After the way Glory had attacked him without provocation, Mitch was tempted to suggest that, since she owned the place and he was merely a customer, it was her damn responsibility to get her crazy, overwrought waitress a drink.

However, ever since the fire, a grateful Glory had insisted on supplying the meals whenever it was his turn to cook for the crew of the fire station located down the street. Since Mitch's culinary repertoire consisted of hot dogs, hamburgers and a very pedestrian spaghetti utilizing canned sauce, both he and the rest of the fire fighters were more than a little grateful for the meat loaf, barbecue chicken and ribs Glory provided. That being the case, he held his tongue.

He crossed the room, went behind the counter and poured ice water from the pitcher into a green plastic glass. When he returned and held the glass out to Sasha, the blatant appreciation in her dark brown eyes reminded him uncomfortably of a cocker spaniel he'd had as a kid.

"Thank you, Mitch." When she felt her cheeks burn with embarrassment, she looked away and concentrated on the steady flow of traffic out the window.

Embarrassed at receiving such a degree of gratitude for such a simple gesture, Mitch merely shrugged in response.

But as he watched her lift the glass to her mouth, he found himself wondering, not for the first time since Glory had hired her, if those lush, rosy lips were as succulent as they looked.

All too aware of Mitch watching her as she took a sip of the icy water, Sasha dragged her attention back to her less-than-ideal situation.

Glory, Mitch and Jake knew that she was searching for her father, but she hated the thought of having to tell them more of her private family problems. Glory, however, had treated Sasha more like a daughter than an employee, and knowing that her employer would just keep after her until she revealed what had her so upset, Sasha slowly, painfully, related the details of her afternoon interview with the horrid Mr. Donald O. Potter.

"That damn weasel," Glory said, right on cue.

"That's not fair," Jake said. "Sending you back to Russia just because you haven't been able to find your father."

"Unfortunately, laws are not always fair," Sasha murmured.

It was a lesson she'd learned early in life. Which was another reason that the stories her mother had told her about life in America—where supposedly the people themselves made the laws—had seemed almost like fairy tales. She lifted the cool glass to her temple, where a headache was pounding with unrelenting force, and sighed.

"Well, it's obvious that we can't let them send you back," Jake declared.

He was such a nice man, Sasha considered. Always ready with a smile for her, always asking about her day, showing her new photos of his baby daughter. He routinely overtipped and whenever she'd complain that he'd left far too much beside the empty white coffee cup, he'd invariably wink and tell her to put the money into her search fund.

Still, as nice as Jake was, Sasha knew he did not possess the power to solve this dilemma.

"I don't think I have a choice."

"Hell, girl, everyone has a choice," Glory insisted. "That's what America is all about."

The loyalty of these people she'd known only a few weeks moved Sasha tremendously. As she thought about how much she would miss them, once she was deported, she felt a renewed threat of tears. Not wanting Mitch to think her a complete idiot, she managed to keep the floodgates closed this time.

She twisted her hands together in her lap. "I was thinking of running away," she admitted in a voice that was little more than a whisper. Still, hearing the words out loud made them suddenly seem almost possible.

Her mind began to whirl, considering the possibilities. She'd heard Seattle was nice. And, of course, there was Los Angeles. In a city so large it should not be difficult to disappear.

Perhaps Montana. She could get a job on a ranch, far away from civilization, cooking for cowboys. Upset as she was, Sasha conveniently overlooked the fact that she was a terrible cook.

"Running away is never the answer," Jake said, interrupting her agitated thoughts. He shook his head. "Especially in this case. You'd have broken the law and immigration would eventually catch up with you."

"Which would mean immediate deportation," Glory pointed out. "You can't give that squinty-eyed, chinless weasel the satisfaction of getting rid of you that easily."

Mitch, Sasha noticed, had not joined in the conversation. He was standing there, absently rubbing his jaw as he stared out the front window of the diner, his thoughts seemingly a million miles away.

"The law is the law." She repeated what Mr. Donald O. Potter had told her. "I have four days to find my father. If I cannot locate him in that time, I will be sent back to Russia."

"We could hire a private detective," Jake suggested. "Granted, four days isn't all that much time, but—"

"I've already hired many investigators," Sasha interrupted glumly. That was how she'd ended up in Phoenix. It had cost her one-hundred and fifty-five dollars to learn that her father had supposedly moved from Springfield, Missouri, to the desert town to work on a suburban weekly newspaper. Unfortunately, the lead had proven to be a dead end. One more in a very long string.

"Besides, I don't have the money necessary—"

"Don't worry about that," Jake said. "We'll take up a collection at the station. All the guys will be glad to pitch in."

"A P.I. isn't the answer," Mitch said suddenly, breaking into the conversation for the first time.

"You don't know that," Glory snapped. "That detective I hired last year to track down my second ex managed to get me five years back child support."

"It also took two months," Mitch reminded her. "And you had your ex-husband's social security number, which made it a helluva lot easier." He shook his head. "Unfortunately, Sasha's right. There's not enough time."

Glory's face was a stony mask. "We can't let them send her back. Her mother's dead. She doesn't have any family there anymore. She'll be all alone."

"I wasn't talking about letting her be deported."

Although Sasha was mildly annoyed that they'd begun talking about her as if she were no longer in the diner, she couldn't help being curious.

She slowly lifted her eyes to his. "I don't understand."

"The answer's obvious. And simple."

Glory lifted a dark brow. "So why don't you share it with us, hotshot?" she said, calling him by the name that had appeared in all those newspaper headlines.

"Sasha needs to marry a U.S. citizen. That way, she'll get her green card."

Sasha's hopes, which had soared when Mitch had suggested he had the solution to her dilemma, plummeted. Her shoulders sagged. He might as well have suggested she discover the Lost Dutchman's gold mine that was supposedly hidden somewhere in the nearby Superstition mountains while she was at it.

"As much as I appreciate your suggestion," she said with a tired sigh, "there is one little problem. I do not know anyone who would marry me."

"Of course you do."

Mitch heard the fatal words come out of his mouth and knew he was sunk. Although he'd tried to resist the idea as he'd listened to Sasha's painfully told story, he could feel himself about to take yet another headlong plunge into trouble.

Mitch wondered what deep-seated inner flaw he possessed that made it impossible for him to resist putting on his tarnished suit of armor.

He remembered a serial killer a few years back who wrote letters to newspapers all around the country that always began "Stop me before I kill again."

Perhaps he should have little cards printed to hand out at times like this; cards that read "Stop me before I help again."

Knowing he was about to make the biggest mistake of his life, but unable to resist, Mitch flashed the smile that had graced the cover of *Newsweek* and had so charmed

Kathie Lee—the cocky male grin that had the power to melt Sasha's heart.

Leaning down, he rubbed his fingertips lightly along the lines furrowing her brow, a gesture Sasha found wonderful and unnervingly intimate at the same time. ''You know me,'' he said.

3

SASHA COULDN'T SPEAK, couldn't think. She was certain that what she'd heard was a joke. Or a wild hallucination born of stress and her subconscious desires.

"Well?" Mitch said when she didn't immediately answer. "What do you say?"

Sasha stared at him. Hope fluttered its delicate hummingbird wings in her breast, even as her mind assured her she must have misunderstood.

"I don't understand," she said, looking desperately at Jake and Glory for assistance.

Jake shrugged and continued to stare at his wife's brother, while Glory burst out laughing. "It may not have been the most romantic proposal in the world, Sasha, honey, but I do believe hotshot here just asked you to marry him."

"Marry?" She turned back to him, her eyes wide and disbelieving. "This is true, Mitch? You wish to marry me?"

"It wouldn't be a real marriage," he said quickly, ignoring Glory's easily heard muttered grunt of disapproval. "It would only be a legal maneuver to buy time for you to find your father."

"Now that's being real gentlemanly." Jake shook his head in disgust.

Mitch turned on him. "At least I came up with a solution. Which is more than you managed to do."

"Gotta point there," Jake agreed. "Of course, gettin' married to your sister kinda took me out of the matrimonial sweepstakes." The laughter left his eyes as he looked from Mitch to Sasha, then back to Mitch. "You know," he murmured, rubbing his square chin, "it could work, I suppose."

His gaze was warm and encouraging as it moved slowly over Sasha's tearstained face. "The hardest part, the way I see it, would be living under the same roof with you, hotshot." He winked at Sasha. "Not many women consider Jockey briefs hanging on the doorknob a decorating plus."

Sasha was more confused than ever. If she'd understood correctly, and she believed she had, Mitch was suggesting nothing more than a legal ploy to keep the nasty immigration officer at bay until she could find her father and prove her citizenship.

These things were done all the time. She knew of girls from St. Petersburg who had entered into similar agreements with men from Europe and the United States. Such marriages had nothing to do with romance. Or with love.

"We would live together?"

"No!" Mitch shouted.

"Yes!" Glory said at exactly the same moment.

Jake chuckled, seeming to enjoy his brother-in-law's discomfort and said nothing.

"If you two kids do try to pull this off, you're going to have to make it look like a real marriage," Glory warned. "I saw a report on '20/20' a couple weeks ago, showing how, because of the upcoming election and all the illegal alien arguments, the government is starting to crack down on green card marriages.

"That weasel Potter down at immigration isn't going to be satisfied with any convenient piece of paper signed by some Phoenix justice of the peace. He's going to want to make sure you two are actually living as man and wife.''

Hell, she was right. Mitch had seen the same report himself. He'd been over at Meredith's, and although it certainly wasn't the way he'd planned to spend an intimate Friday night with the sexy reporter, she'd appeared briefly in the segment anchored by John Stossel, so of course they'd both had to watch.

Meredith. Mitch cursed inwardly as he wondered what Meredith was going to say when she discovered her man of the moment had run off and gotten married. If only he'd taken the time to run the errant thought through his brain before letting it come out of his damn mouth. But, no. Once again, he'd gone charging into the breach, the same way he'd rushed into that burning building and ended up a media hero.

One of these days, Mitch told himself glumly, he really was going to have to learn self-restraint.

Sasha had never seen Mitch do anything but smile. Even after fighting a blazing, four-alarm fire in the blistering desert heat, when he was covered with soot and sweat, he could still flash her a devastating grin designed to turn any woman to butter.

But at this moment his handsome face was grim, telling her that he was already having regrets. In fact, she thought, he looked a great deal like a Siberian wolf who'd just stumbled into a trap and would be willing to chew his leg off, if necessary, to escape.

That being the case, although she desperately longed to say yes, if only to forestall her deportation to Russia, Sasha knew what she must do. Mitch had done a gracious and generous thing, a heroic thing, by asking her to marry him. Now she must be equally as honorable and refuse.

She swallowed her disappointment and tried to keep her

lips from trembling. "As much as I appreciate your offer, Mitch, I can't allow you to ruin your life for me."

There it was, Mitch told himself. The escape hatch. All he had to do was walk through it and he'd be home free.

But then Sasha would be on her way back to a homeland where she had no home.

"I wouldn't be ruining my life." *Terrific, Cudahy,* he blasted himself. *Why don't you just dig the hole even deeper?* She was willing to let him off the hook, so why couldn't he just wiggle free? Like any sensible, sane person would do?

"Sure, marriage might prove a bit inconvenient, but it isn't going to last all that long. Just until we locate your father and you can prove your claim of citizenship."

Sasha turned toward the others, seeking advice. "Jake—Glory? What do you think of Mitch's idea?"

"I think you should do it," they said together.

She bit her lip and stared out the window again at the shiny red fire truck, remembering how wonderfully dashing Mitch had looked leaping down from the back of the truck with that lethal-looking ax in his strong dark hands, come to save her by stopping the diner from going up in flames.

To be married to this man would be a dream come true. Even if it wasn't a real marriage, what could it hurt to pretend? Just a little.

And it would definitely solve her problem with Potter. When the image of the sour-faced government official popped into her mind, Sasha made her decision.

"All right, Mitch." She turned back toward him, her expression as grave as her thoughts. "I will marry you."

Although Mitch knew it was his imagination, he was sure he could hear a door close and the lock click behind him.

After a brief discussion, they scheduled the wedding for Saturday night after Mitch's shift ended. At his suggestion, it was decided that they'd drive to Laughlin, Nevada, a small gambling town situated on the banks of the Colorado River across the border from Arizona.

"We can get the deed done there," Mitch promised, "then be home before lunchtime Sunday."

It would be, he assured her, quick and efficient. It also did not escape Sasha's notice that he didn't suggest that anyone else in his family be present for the ceremony.

There was a reason for that. Knowing how his mother wanted him to "find a nice girl and settle down," Mitch purposely decided not to tell her about the plan. Although he'd hoped that Katie and Jake's new baby would take the heat off him for a while, she was continually informing him that it was his responsibility to ensure the Cudahy name be carried on into another generation. He definitely didn't want to get her hopes up with this fake wedding.

MITCH WAS three hours late arriving at her rooming house the night they were to get married.

Sasha had given notice that she would be moving out, had packed her meager belongings and then had waited worriedly, afraid he'd changed his mind.

"Sorry," he said, "there was a fire in a warehouse. I couldn't get away."

"I was worried."

"That I wasn't going to come?"

"No." As he watched the soft color bloom in her cheeks, Mitch tried to remember the last time he'd been with a woman capable of blushing. "Well, maybe I did worry for just a little while that you'd changed your mind," she confessed. "But mostly I was worried about you. When I heard about the fire on the radio, I feared you would be hurt."

"Never happen," he said with the same bravado that

allowed him to eat smoke for a living. "Well, I suppose we may as well get this show on the road."

Conversation on the drive to Nevada was stilted. And the mood was decidedly less than upbeat. In fact, Sasha had seen a movie where an old Western outlaw had gone to his hanging with more enthusiasm than Mitch showed for his upcoming marriage.

Like most little girls the world over, Sasha had dreamed of her wedding day. And although that dream had changed as she'd left her childhood behind her, the one thing that had remained constant was the fact that her groom would be handsome. And that he would love her.

Absolutely.

Forever.

Well, Sasha considered, giving a soft, rippling little sigh, at least one of those things would be true. Although Mitch didn't love her, he would certainly make a handsome groom. Even better than any of her romantic fantasies.

Once in Laughlin, the proceedings moved fast and efficiently, just as Mitch had promised.

"So far, so good," he said with feigned enthusiasm as they filled out the paperwork. Sasha had seemed down in the dumps since he'd shown up at her apartment and he doubted she'd said two words during the drive from Phoenix.

Her sad little frown kept her from looking much like a glowing bride-to-be. Conveniently forgetting that he'd been the one to insist this wasn't going to be a real marriage, Mitch figured the lady could at least try to appear a little enthusiastic about the idea.

Didn't she realize more than one woman in Phoenix would be tickled pink to receive a proposal from all-American hero Mitch Cudahy? Hell, after appearing on "Good Morning America" and "Ricki Lake," he'd gotten marriage proposals from interested females as far away as Anchorage, Alaska. He'd even received a candygram—accompanied by her centerfold photo—from a former *Playboy* Miss July.

Mitch handed over his Visa card to the clerk. They waited while the charges were run through the machine, then carried the forms next door to the Chapel of Love.

It was then things got interesting.

"I don't believe this!" Mitch stared in horror at the overweight man wearing a white jumpsuit.

"Mitch?" Sasha's eyes widened. It was just like her favorite American film! "This is an Elvis person, yes? Like in the movie, *Honeymoon in Vegas*."

"That's right, honeybun," the rotund man answered boisterously before Mitch had a chance to respond. He had to raise his voice to be heard over an enthusiastic rendition of "All Shook Up" coming from the oversize speakers hanging on all four walls of the room.

"I'm Elvis Presley." He flashed a bold, confident grin as he held out a fleshy hand weighted down with diamond rings. "Had my name legally changed for my profession."

"You thought it would help your ministerial business to be named after a dead singer?" Mitch asked.

"Not just any old run-of-the-mill singer, boy. The King." He gave Sasha a broad smile. "I'm an Elvis impersonator, all right, little lady. Just like in that nifty movie, only I'm too old and too chicken to go jumping out of airplanes. And aren't you the prettiest little bride I've married all day?"

Mitch had been regretting his decision to propose since he'd first heard the words coming out of his mouth. There was no way he was going to go through with a farce like this.

"We're getting out of here." He grabbed hold of Sasha's hand and began to pull her out the door.

To his surprise, she dug in her high heels.

"Sasha?" Impatience surged as she held her ground. "What's wrong now?"

"Nothing is wrong, Mitch." The way she was looking at the ridiculously clad minister reminded him of the way Dane, the six-year-old boy assigned to him in the Big Brother program, looked at the latest Power Ranger action figure in the toy store window. "This is wonderful!"

"It's ridiculous, is what it is," he corrected gruffly, immensely relieved that none of the guys from Ladder Company No. 13 were here to witness this debacle. "Let's go. There's gotta be another minister somewhere in town."

"But, Mitch—"

"The little lady seems real happy right where she is," the minister observed in a deep Tennessee drawl.

"When you suggested coming to Laughlin, I never expected anything like this, Mitch," Sasha said.

"That makes two of us."

"It is so exciting. And romantic," she wheedled prettily. "We would never have anything so wonderful like this back in Russia. Ever since I was a little girl, I have dreamed of such a wedding."

"You dreamed of getting married by an old fat Elvis?" Realizing that he'd just insulted the minister, he said, "Sorry. I didn't mean that personally."

"No offense taken," the man said cheerfully as the Muzak system segued into "Don't Be Cruel." "And, hell, I know I'm old and fat. But the original Elvis was carrying a few extra pounds, too, at the end. So the way I figure it, if it was good enough for the King, it's good enough for me."

"Please, Mitch." Sasha removed her hand from his iron

grip and placed it on his arm. "We've already paid for the license. This nice man is ready to marry us—"

"Nothin' I'd like better than to unite you two lovebirds in holy matrimony," the minister broke in.

"See." She pressed her case. "Doesn't it make sense to exchange our vows here? Instead of driving all over town looking for a substitute minister? Or perhaps having to go all the way to Las Vegas?"

"Aw, hell." He wondered what kind of man that unyielding immigration officer was to be able to refuse this woman anything. Obviously Donald O. Potter had a heart of stone. "Okay. Here's the deal… If I agree to go along with this ridiculous circus, you have to promise never to tell Jake, or Glory, or anyone else we know."

"I promise." Her slender fingers squeezed his forearm with surprising strength. "It will be our secret. But, Mitch, it would make me so very, very happy."

Mitch didn't know which one of them was crazier. The old guy in the rhinestone-covered polyester jumpsuit with about a quart of Valvoline in his hair; Sasha for wanting to get married by an Elvis impersonator—and not a very good one, at that, or himself for even considering going along with the cockeyed scheme.

Looking down into her warm, brown, hopeful eyes, he felt himself giving in again. "All right," he agreed with a deep, resigned sigh. "If it's really what you want."

"Oh, thank you!" Excitedly, she flung her arms around his neck and kissed him.

At the first touch of her mouth, Mitch experienced a momentary surprise. Then, as her silky lips melded into his and her wondrous breasts pressed enticingly against his chest, he decided not to think of all the reasons why this was a big mistake and dove headlong into the kiss.

Her generous mouth was as soft as it looked. But much,

much, warmer. Mitch had given the matter a great deal of thought since that fatal day when, after putting out the fire in the diner, he'd looked up to see her standing in the doorway, pale as a wraith and trembling. Her lips had quivered in a way that practically begged for a man to kiss away her fears, and Mitch had suspected that Sasha's mouth would be sweet. And innocent.

Innocent, it definitely was. From the way she kept her lips pressed tightly together, he suspected she had not been kissed very often. Or very well. And yet even with her obvious lack of experience, her kiss was far more potent than even he, who'd certainly known more than his share of women, could have imagined.

The dark, rich taste of her seeped into his mouth, into his blood, causing it to burn. When he caught her full lower lip between his teeth, her resultant shudder sent all that heated blood shooting south, below his belt.

Even knowing that such a scenario was impossible, Sasha had dreamed of this moment innumerable times over the past weeks. But never could she have imagined the power of Mitch's kiss. Her head filled with sounds like the roaring winds of a hurricane, and her body began to glow as if somehow the sun had fallen from the sky and entered her bloodstream through Mitch's hot, hungry mouth.

And then, just like that, it was over.

The strong, dark hands that had created such heat as they'd roamed up and down her back, settled at her waist as Mitch put her away from him. He was looking down at her, but his shuttered gaze gave Sasha no inkling of what he was thinking.

"Well, we've wasted enough time," he said. He had no way of knowing how his brusque words stung Sasha who was still caught up in the glory of that wondrous kiss.

"I'd say so," the minister said with a bold laugh that

made his belly shake and the rhinestones flash. "Because if there was ever a couple ready for a honeymoon, I'd say it was you two."

At the mention of a honeymoon, Sasha blushed. As Mitch's body continued to throb, on cue, the King began belting out "A Big Hunk O' Love."

"So, you two kids got a ring?"

Mitch cursed. "I forgot all about a ring."

"It's all right," Sasha said quickly. Her brave little smile only served to make him more irritated at the entire situation. And even more, at himself. "I do not need a ring."

"Maybe you don't. But I'll bet Potter will."

"Oh." She sighed as she envisioned the grim immigration officer. "I suppose you're right."

Elvis rubbed his beefy hands together with robust satisfaction. "You're in luck. Because I just happen to have a real nice selection right here."

He pulled a black velvet tray out of a drawer beneath the counter. The rings ranged from a simple silver band to a sparkling diamond the size of Vermont.

Mitch scanned the tray, his gaze settling on a gleaming woven gold ring boasting a small but good quality diamond. "How about this one?"

"That's a dandy choice," Elvis agreed. "It's one of my most popular styles."

"Sasha?" He held the ring out to her. "What do you think?"

What did she think? She thought the delicate gold mesh was the loveliest thing she'd ever seen. And the diamond glittered like a midnight star! She also worried he couldn't afford such a glorious piece of jewelry on his modest civil servant's salary.

"It's very pretty." With effort, she dragged her eyes

back to the tray. "But this one will be fine." She pointed to a thin, plain silver band.

"That'd be nice, too," Elvis said agreeably. But with less gusto, Mitch noticed. And for good reason. The silver ring practically shouted "Cheapskate budget special."

"I like this one." Telling himself that he had a reputation to protect, that he didn't want his new bride returning to Phoenix and showing off that miserably mediocre excuse for a wedding band, he held his ground. "Let's try it on."

Sasha obediently held out her hand, embarrassed by the way it was trembling.

"Don't worry about the shakes, honeybun," Elvis said reassuringly. "I've done over a thousand marriages and, believe me, every one of those brides-to-be had prewedding nerves."

Sasha thought that could well be true. But, of course, she was not really a bride. So why was she so nervous?

"It fits!" The ring slid onto her finger so easily it could have been made with her in mind. She held it out, admiring the gleam of the yellow gold, the flash of the diamond.

"Okay, that's it, then." Mitch dug his billfold out of his jeans and again handed over his Visa card.

"How about flowers?" Elvis asked.

An instantaneous flash of pleasure lit Sasha's dark eyes. When it was just as quickly extinguished, Mitch realized that she was trying to be frugal on his account.

"Can't get married without flowers," he said.

As he watched Sasha dip her head and breathe in the sweet scent of carnations, Mitch remembered the elaborate preparations for his sister's wedding to Jake. Katie had driven everyone crazy, insisting the formal ceremony live up to the one she'd always dreamed of.

Although at the time he'd found her behavior incomprehensible, now he began to realize that wedding fantasies were apparently one thing all females—from Phoenix to St. Petersburg—had in common.

"Is that it?" His irritation at himself for being miserly at a time like this made his voice harsher than he'd meant it to be.

Sasha jumped, dropping the edge of the lovely short white lace veil she'd been fingering. "You have already bought more than enough, Mitch. Truly."

"Fine." He turned to the minister. "Let's do it."

"You got it, young fella. Soon as I call my wife, Annie, so she can be a witness." He tapped on a small bell and a door behind him opened and out came a tall, curvaceous redhead.

"Don't tell me," Mitch groaned as he recognized the woman's uncanny resemblance to Ann Margaret. *"Viva Las Vegas."*

"Got it on the first try." Elvis grinned conspiratorially.

If he ever got married again—which he had no intention of doing—Mitch vowed he was going to insist on a civil ceremony at the Phoenix courthouse.

Mitch and Sasha followed Elvis and his wife into an adjoining room where an ivory satin runner led to a small altar set up in front of a white satin curtain. On the altar, a vase in the shape of the young Elvis holding a guitar, held a fragrant assortment of fresh gladioli.

"Sorry, little lady," Elvis said, "I can understand how you probably hate to part with it, but I'm going to have to ask you to give me that ring. Just for a few minutes."

Sasha took the diamond ring from her finger, experiencing a sense of loss as she handed it over.

"All right," he said with robust satisfaction, "it's time for the show! Sasha, honey, you start at the door and walk toward your fella, while Annie and I sing your wedding march."

"Is that really necessary?" Mitch asked.

This was already dragging on a lot longer than planned. And, although he kept telling himself that it wasn't real, despite the surrealistic aspect of the ceremony, it still felt too much like a wedding for comfort.

"All brides dream of walking up the aisle, don't they, honey?" the older woman said to Sasha.

"I would like that very much," she agreed, casting a hesitant glance Mitch's way. "But if Mitch would rather just begin, that would be all right with me, as well."

Damn. She'd gotten that whipped cocker spaniel look in her eyes again. "We're wasting time arguing," Mitch said. "Why don't you just walk up the aisle?"

"Thank you, Mitch!"

Once again that warm pleasure flooded her eyes, making him feel like the grinch who'd tried to steal Sasha's wedding.

Holding the overpriced flowers in her hands, she walked slowly up the white satin runner toward him, while Elvis and Annie sang a medley of "Love Me Tender," which Mitch had to admit wasn't half bad.

As Mitch watched her approach, he realized that somehow, even in her ugly-as-sin severe black suit and starched white blouse, Sasha was still lovely.

When she reached Mitch's side, Elvis pulled a white satin cord. The curtain behind the altar opened, revealing a large-screen television. A moment later the wedding scene from *Blue Hawaii* flashed onto the oversize screen and the deep tones of the King crooning "The Hawaiian Wedding Song" filled the room.

"Oh, Mitch, isn't it romantic!" Sasha clapped her hands in pleasure.

Immensely grateful that Jake wasn't there, Mitch shook

his head and imagined his brother-in-law telling this story at the firehouse. Hell, he'd never be able to live it down.

"Dearly beloved," Elvis began, raising his voice to be heard over the ballad.

The images on the television screen began to shimmer. As the music swelled, the vaguely familiar words of the wedding ceremony began to sound like a dull roar in Mitch's ears.

Sweat beaded on his forehead and above his upper lip. As he heard Sasha promise to take him as her lawfully wedded husband, his legs began to shake. But not from fear, Mitch assured himself, stiffening his knees as he managed to shove the ring onto her outstretched finger.

He was a smoke eater. A hero. Guys like him lived on the edge; they weren't afraid of anything.

Elvis turned toward him. "And do you, Mitchel Dylan Cudahy, take this woman, Sasha Mikhailova, for your lawfully wedded wife?"

Her face, as she looked up at him, appeared concerned. Mitch straightened his spine and took a deep breath.

"To love and to honor." Little white spots began to dance in front of his eyes. "For richer or poorer." Blinded by the sweat pouring from his brow, Mitch wiped his forehead with a quick swipe with the back of his hand. "In sickness and in health. For as long as you both shall live."

"I do," Mitch managed.

He'd barely croaked out the response before he pitched forward, landing facedown at Sasha's feet.

"Mitch!" As the King wrapped up the song to his movie bride, Sasha sank to her knees beside her groom. Heedless of the blood that was pouring from his nose, darkening his shirt, she gathered Mitch into her arms.

Annie, apparently accustomed to nervous grooms passing out, calmly plucked the gladioli out of the vase, then tossed the water into Mitch's face.

Mitch sputtered, shaking his head like the ladder company's Dalmatian who'd just had a fire hose turned on him.

As he regained consciousness, he heard Elvis boomingly proclaim, "By the power invested in me by the State of Nevada—and the King of Rock and Roll—I now pronounce you husband and wife!"

4

"ARE YOU SURE you're all right?" Sasha asked with concern as they walked out into the blinding sun.

"I'm fine," Mitch snapped from between clenched teeth. "Why wouldn't I be? I was up nearly the whole damn night fighting a two-alarm blaze, I drove halfway across the damn desert, I practically maxed out my credit card to get married by some fat old Elvis impersonator and his crazy redheaded wife, and then, to top if off, I passed out and broke my nose."

"The doctor Elvis called to the chapel said it is not broken," she reminded him quietly. Sasha had never seen Mitch so angry. Obviously he was already regretting this false marriage.

"The guy was probably a quack," Mitch growled as he opened the passenger door of the Mustang.

Not wanting to risk angering him further by arguing that the doctor had seemed quite competent, Sasha didn't answer. Every atom in his body was radiating with irritation as he came around the front of the red convertible, yanked open the door and flung himself into the bucket seat beside her.

Tears stung behind her lids. Refusing to humiliate herself by crying again in front of him, Sasha bit her lip.

He jammed the key into the ignition and turned it.

Instead of the familiar purr of the engine coming to life, there was only a faint click.

Mitch cursed.

Then twisted the key again.

Again, nothing.

"Dammit!" He hit the steering wheel with the heel of his hand. "This will definitely go down in history as the worst damn day of my life!"

That did it!

Sasha had tried to stay cheerful during the long drive to the desert gambling town, even when Mitch hadn't bothered to say more than two gruff words to her.

She'd ignored his less-than-enthusiastic response to a wedding, that while not exactly a fairy-tale dream ceremony, was at least more colorful than the dreary civil procedure she'd been expecting.

She hadn't even complained about his blood stains all over her only decent suit.

But to have him behave as if he was blaming her for his car not starting was the final straw!

Bursting into the furious tears she'd tried to forestall, she flung open the passenger door and went marching off across the parking lot.

"Aw, hell." Mitch lowered his forehead to the steering wheel, ignoring the painful lump that was forming there. He closed his eyes and took a deep breath. Then, calling himself every kind of bastard, he took off after his bride.

Despite her head start, Mitch quickly caught up with her and grabbed hold of her arm. "Dammit, Sasha—"

"Let go of me!" She shook free and kept on walking.

"Look, I'm sorry."

No answer.

"It's just that it's been a lousy few days," he tried again.

"You think you have had bad days?" She spun around, her eyes shooting furious sparks. "Let me tell you, Mitch

Cudahy—'' she began, shoving her finger in his chest, then went off on a furious stream of Russian.

Although he couldn't understand a word she was shouting at him, Mitch suspected that she wasn't being complimentary.

''Would you mind very much speaking English so I at least understand you?''

She glared at him. ''This has not exactly been wonderful for me, either! I have been threatened with deportation by a dreadful man who would like nothing more than to send me back to Russia, made to believe that I'd been stood up at the altar when you did not arrive at the time you promised—''

''I explained about that,'' Mitch reminded her. ''It wasn't my fault that warehouse caught on fire ten minutes before the end of my shift. What was I supposed to do? Tell the captain that I was sorry, but I couldn't climb on the damn truck because I had to get married?''

She raised her chin haughtily. ''I would appreciate it very much if you did not continually interrupt while I am speaking.''

''I was just trying to make a point. And you're not exactly speaking, sweetheart, you're shouting.''

Knowing he did not mean the word sweetheart as an endearment, Sasha let loose with another heated barrage of Russian.

''And I am not shouting!'' she finished in heavily accented English.

Of course she was. Sasha paused and took a deep, calming breath.

Watching her shoulders begin to shake, Mitch readied himself for another onslaught of feminine tears.

''I am not shouting,'' she said with a surprising giggle that lit up her eyes and moved something very elemental—

and disconcerting—inside him. "I am a calm person. I never shout."

Mitch felt his own lips curving into a reluctant smile. "Of course you don't. Just like I'm never in a bad mood."

Their individual anger cooled like flames hit with a stream of water from one of Mitch's fire hoses. This time when he took hold of her hand, she did not pull away.

"I'm sorry, Sasha. I overreacted."

"No," she sighed, unhappy that she'd created such a scene when all he'd been trying to do was help, "it is I who should apologize. After all, you were kind enough to offer to marry me."

Mitch didn't want to be reminded of his unfortunate tendency to rush into situations where any self-respecting angel would hesitate to tread.

"How about we just start over?"

"You want to go back and do our Elvis wedding again?"

Her eyes twinkled with laughter, her smiling lips were full and inviting, suddenly reminding Mitch that by passing out, he'd missed the traditional ending to the wedding ceremony.

Unfortunately, as memories of their earlier shared kiss flashed hotly through his mind, he decided kissing Sasha in a public parking lot was more of a risk than he was willing to take. Even in a town built on gambling.

"We might as well get a hotel room," he said. "Then I'll call the auto club."

"A hotel room? But I thought you wanted to return to Phoenix right after the wedding."

"We can't go anywhere until we get a new starter. It's Sunday. There won't be any place open that can put one in until tomorrow. Looks like we're stuck here for the night."

"Oh." The idea of spending the night in a hotel room

with Mitch was as terrifying as it was thrilling. "This will cost more money, yes?"

"Don't worry about it."

With their fingers laced together, they walked back to the car, retrieved their things and walked to the hotel next door.

"What do you mean, you're all booked up?" Mitch asked incredulously.

"Exactly that." The man behind the registration desk shrugged. "All our rooms are taken."

"Fine. We'll just go to another hotel."

"Don't think you'll have much luck anywhere else," the clerk said laconically. "There's an international Shriner's convention this weekend. And a championship boxing match at the Flamingo."

"Don't worry," Mitch assured Sasha as they walked out of the gilt and marble lobby into the blinding Nevada sunshine, "there's got to be something available."

Thirty minutes later he was ready to concede defeat. "I'll give you whatever you want if you will only find us a room," he said, staggering up to the reception desk of the sixth hotel they'd tried.

Sasha's luggage, which had not seemed heavy in the beginning, now felt like a ton of bricks. "All my money, my credit cards, my firstborn child. Anything you ask for. It's yours."

The sleek blonde behind the desk eyed Mitch with unsuppressed amusement. "You're in luck. We've just had a cancellation."

"Bless you." If the counter hadn't been between them, Mitch would have kissed her. Right on her glossy pink lips.

"A couple from Wichita booked the honeymoon suite six weeks ago," the reservations clerk revealed. "Then apparently, they got in a fight over which Elvis song to play at the ceremony, and the bride stormed out of the chapel and took a cab to the airport. The groom just called to cancel the room.''

Mitch exchanged a look with Sasha, who was struggling to keep a straight face. ''They should have gone with 'The Hawaiian Wedding Song.'''

''It worked for me and my husband when Elvis married us last year,'' the clerk agreed cheerfully. ''But apparently when the groom-to-be insisted on 'Jailhouse Rock,' the bride took that as a metaphor for how he viewed their marriage, and blew up.''

She began tapping on the computer keyboard. ''The suite's all ready. Will you be paying with a credit card?''

''Why not?'' Mitch said, pulling out the gold card yet again.

Five minutes later they were alone in a vast suite that appeared to have been designed by a crazed cupid and cost him nearly two week's pay. Mitch decided that whoever had said two could live as cheaply as one obviously hadn't eloped to Laughlin, Nevada, during a Shriner's convention.

''Goodness,'' Sasha said, staring at the round bed set on a burgundy fabric-covered platform, surrounded by gilded pillars, covered with a pink and velvet spread and strewn with pillows. ''I had no idea they made waterbeds so large. Even in America.'' In some of the apartments she'd been in St. Petersburg, entire families would undoubtedly be expected to share such an expansive bed.

She glanced up at the ceiling. ''And what a strange place for a mirror.''

She looked a mess, Sasha decided regretfully. Her hair was windblown, her makeup had melted, she'd chewed her lipstick off and the blood on the front of her white blouse had dried to an unattractive rust color. At least she wouldn't have to worry about Mitch kissing her again. Because, looking as rumpled as she did, she was definitely not the least bit appealing.

"Not so strange," Mitch said, putting her suitcases beside the bed. "Given the fact that this is the honeymoon suite."

"I still do not understand…oh." Color flooded into her face as comprehension dawned.

"Oh," he mimicked with a quick grin, once again enjoying that soft pink color brightening her cheeks. She was so damn pretty. Her hair was a dark froth around her shoulders, and although she'd chewed off her lipstick, her lips were a rich rosy hue that, even though he knew it would be playing with fire, made him want to kiss her senseless. "I guess it's a good thing that this wedding of ours isn't real."

He tamped down an errant image of Sasha, lying nude on satin sheets, her hair spread out on the pillow, as she held her arms out to her lover, her husband.

"A very good thing," she agreed, having to force the words past the lump that had suddenly taken residence in her throat.

Unbidden, a mental picture flashed though her mind, of Mitch's muscular back and firm buttocks reflected in the overhead mirror as his lips blazed a hot trail down her naked body.

Their eyes met in the mirror and held. Silence settled over them as each was unwillingly drawn into a sensual fantasy to which neither was prepared to admit.

"Well." Mitch cleared his throat and dragged his gaze away to the gilded dresser that looked like it could have come straight from Versailles. Atop the dresser, on a silver tray, was a bottle of champagne and a box of Belgian chocolates wrapped in gold foil paper and tied with a red satin ribbon.

"I'd better call the auto club and arrange for someone to come out first thing tomorrow morning."

It was not Mitch's first choice. What he wanted to do was to pop that cork, ply his bride with champagne and spend the rest of the day feeding her chocolates and making love.

"Yes." It was barely a whisper.

"If you want, you can freshen up. Then we'll see about getting something to eat. We can go out, if you'd like. Or maybe you'd rather call room service."

"They will bring our dinner to our room?"

"All you have to do is ask." *And pay through the nose,* Mitch thought but didn't say. He'd already gone so far over budget, he wasn't about to start quibbling about extra costs now.

"That sounds very nice." Sasha thought about the temptations of staying here so close to this ridiculously sensual bed with a man who'd played a starring role in her fantasies since she'd first seen him.

"But, perhaps, if you don't mind, we could go out?" she suggested. "I saw a coffee shop next to the lobby."

"Good idea." Relief and regret flooded through Mitch; relief that she'd suggested getting them out of this gilded love nest, away from temptation, regret that he wouldn't be making love to her on the terrifically sexy bed.

Sasha might be able to resist the oversize waterbed, but the pink-tiled, heart-shaped Jacuzzi bathtub was another matter. Seemingly as deep as a lake, and nearly large enough to swim laps in, she decided American plumbing was one of the seven wonders of the world.

"Mitch?" she called out through the open bathroom door, "would you mind very much if I took the time for a bath?"

"Suit yourself," he answered as the recorded message

assured him that his call was important and thanked him for his patience. "I have the feeling I'm going to be on hold for a long time."

When she spotted the crystal jars of bath salts lining the pink rim of the enormous tub, Sasha considered that if the angry bride had known what she was passing up, perhaps she wouldn't have been so quick to reject her groom's choice of music.

Thirty minutes later, the perfumed, bubbling water had soothed Sasha's exhaustion and her nerves. As she wrapped the thick, terry bath sheet around her body, she couldn't remember ever feeling so relaxed.

Although she suspected dining in such a splendid hotel would require something equally dazzling, her luggage did not offer a plethora of chic outfits. That being the case, she opted for a short denim skirt and a red cotton blouse with handstitched embroidery along the peasant neckline, hoping she wouldn't embarrass Mitch too badly.

Then she brushed her hair in an attempt to subdue her wild waves. She was, as usual, unsuccessful. Her thick hair remained as unruly as ever, making Sasha envy the sleek blond bobs favored by Mitch's usual women.

Reminding herself that she was not one of Mitch's women—nor was she likely to ever be one—she left the bedroom.

Having spent the previous night fighting a fire had obviously caught up with Mitch. He was sprawled on his back on the sofa, sound asleep, giving Sasha the opportunity to study him undetected. Her gaze drank in the thick curly eyelashes that seemed such a waste on a man, the slightly pug nose, the full, firmly cut lips, the square, pugnacious chin.

His chest rose and fell with each slow breath and as she remembered how it had felt against her breasts, hard as marble but so much warmer, a disturbing heat flowed through her. Her eyes continued their stolen tour, taking in his lean hips, his long legs.

When she found herself wanting to lie down beside him, Sasha knew it was time to leave.

Not wanting him to think she'd run away again, she took the time to write a note on the hotel stationery. Then she quickly left the honeymoon suite.

She was on the way to the coffee shop when the noise from an adjoining room made her realize she was passing the casino. Curious, she glanced inside. It was exactly like *Honeymoon in Vegas!*

Hand-cut prisms on the crystal chandeliers sparkled from the ceiling, murals had been painted on the walls between gilded pillars, the carpet underfoot was burgundy and gold. Slot machines clattered and conversation hummed, punctuated periodically by shouts of excitement and cries of despair.

Sasha found it all enthralling. So enthralling, in fact, she couldn't resist venturing inside.

"Here you go, little lady." A man wearing a fez stood up and handed her a large silver coin. "I've been sitting on this stool for the past hour and haven't won a blessed thing. Perhaps you'll have better luck."

"Luck?" Sasha glanced down at the coin. She had been in America a year and had never seen such a denomination. "I do not understand."

"At the slots." His dark eyes narrowed as he studied her closer. "You're not from around here."

"No. I am from Phoenix, Arizona."

"Before that."

"Oh." She nodded. "I came to America from St. Petersburg, Russia."

It was his turn to nod. "That's why you sound like Natasha."

"Natasha is a common name in Russia," she said with another brief nod. "But I am called Sasha."

"Now isn't that a right pretty name, too?" he said. "But I was talking about Natasha from the TV show. You know, the Saturday morning cartoons? Bullwinkle? Rocky? Moose and Squirrel?"

He could have been speaking Transylvanian. She stared mutely at him, trying to decode the unfamiliar references.

"Never mind," he said. "It's not important. So, Sasha, you want to try your luck?"

"I'm afraid my luck has not been very good lately," she admitted with a soft little sigh.

"Mine, either. Perhaps we can be each other's good luck charm. My name's Ben Houston, by the way. From Dallas, Texas, which doesn't make a lot of sense, I know, but I couldn't help where my pappy decided to settle. Old Sam Houston was a kin of mine."

Not understanding this reference, either, Sasha gave Ben Houston another longer, more judicial look. He was in his mid-fifties, with silver hair beneath the red-tasseled fez and friendly blue eyes. She could see nothing dangerous in his smiling gaze.

Besides, she reminded herself, it wasn't as if they were alone. The room was filled with people, all of whom seemed to be having a wonderfully carefree time. There was an energy here like nothing she'd ever felt.

It had been so long since Sasha had truly enjoyed herself, she found it impossible to resist the offer to do so now.

"I'm afraid you will have to teach me what to do. I have never gambled before."

"Sure you have. Life's a gamble. We risk getting run over by a bus every morning when we leave the house.

And, hell, do you have any idea how many people are struck by lightning every year?''

"No."

"Neither do I. But it's a lot. The thing is, Sasha, honey, most days, we manage to beat the odds. Take my pap for instance. When he graduated from Texas A&M on the G.I. bill after World War Two, he was just another dirt-poor wildcatter with a degree in geology and a yen to get rich. Drilled twelve dusters before he hit lucky number thirteen. And never looked back.''

Sasha was Russian enough to find such fatalism appealing. "I think I would like to try my luck, Mr. Houston,'' she decided.

"That's the girl! And the name's, Ben, honey. My daddy's Mr. Houston. Now let's get rid of this last unlucky damn dollar, then we'll decide what to play next.''

Sasha put the coin in the slot he indicated, then pulled the lever beside the machine. The reels in the center of the machine spun around, too fast for her to follow the spinning pictures.

Then the first one stopped on number seven. The second one stopped on a seven, as well. Then the third.

Before Sasha could ask the man what happened, bells began to ring, the lights on the machine began flashing and her companion started slapping her on the back!

"Hot damn, sugar!'' he whooped. "You won the jackpot!''

"The jackpot?'' She had to shout to be heard over the deafening racket as coins started pouring into the tray. "The machine is broken, yes?'' she asked as more and more silver dollars flowed into the tray.

"The machine is perfect, yes!'' Ben corrected. "You won, Sasha. This is all yours! Hot damn, I knew a pretty little thing like you would change my luck!''

A crowd had gathered around her, applauding, shouting out encouragement as the money continued to flow from the machine like a sparkling silver waterfall. When it began flowing over the tray, someone handed her a foam cup. And then another. And another, and still the money continued to pour forth, almost faster than she could scoop it up.

A woman clad in a tuxedo shirt, very tight shorts and black mesh panty hose appeared with a tall green bottle and two tulip-shaped glasses.

"For you," she said, holding one of the glasses out to Sasha. "A gift from the management, with our congratulations."

Still confused, her hands filled with coins, Sasha looked over at her companion for guidance.

"It's champagne," Ben told her.

"Ah." She nodded. "*Shampahnskaye.* I know of this wine. But I have never tasted any." In Russia, the exorbitant cost had made it a drink only high party officials and government diplomats could afford.

"Now that's a real shame. Because pretty girls should always drink champagne." Ben took the glass and held it up to her mouth. "Drink up, honeybunch," he said encouragingly. "It's celebration time."

The shimmering gold wine was like nothing she'd ever tasted. It tickled her nose, even as it slid smoothly down her throat. "It tastes like laughter."

"You called that one right," Ben agreed, laughing heartily as he downed the contents of the other glass in one long swallow. "Come on, Sasha, let's go count your winnings."

She couldn't believe it. This couldn't be happening to her! Not even in America. Why, it hadn't even happened to Nicholas Cage in *Honeymoon in Vegas.* In that movie, she remembered, he'd lost all his money.

"Four thousand dollars?" she asked after the calculations had been completed.

"Four thousand, seven hundred and forty-eight dollars," Ben corrected.

"This is real?"

"About as real as you can get."

Sasha thought about what she could do with so much money. She could reimburse Mitch for all he'd spent on her behalf today—the ring, the flowers, the license, the wedding and the luxurious suite. She could pay it all back and still have money left over to hire another private detective to track down her father.

There was only one small problem.

She turned to Ben, who'd poured them both another glass of champagne. "This money belongs to you, Ben."

Startled, he choked on the champagne. After giving her a long look, he said, "You know, I think you mean that."

"Of course I do. It was your dollar I put into the machine. So this is rightfully your jackpot."

There was a murmur from the gathered crowd, as if everyone else was as surprised by her response as Ben was.

"That's not the way it works," he insisted. "I'd already given up on that fool machine when I gave you the dollar. You won it, Sasha. Fair and square. All four thousand, seven hundred and forty dollars of it."

"Forty-eight," she corrected absently. Her head was swimming from the sight of all that money, the excitement and the champagne.

"Forty-eight," he agreed with a rough, hearty bark of a laugh.

As generous as he seemed to be, Sasha could not help feeling guilty at the way his act of kindness was turning out. "Perhaps we could share."

"Honey, so long as the black gold keeps flowing back

home, I've got so much money that my wife can't even break me with her damn daily shopping trips to Neiman Marcus,'' he assured her. ''Gambling's best when it's done for fun, and I'm having more fun watching you win than I've had in a long time.'' He gave her another of those bold friendly grins that had her smiling back.

''So, you want to stop now? Or see if we can make this pile grow even higher?''

This was all new to Sasha, but even so, she knew that a sensible woman would stop now. She'd take her winnings and go back upstairs. Before she ended up like Nicholas Cage, broke and desperate.

But then another part of her, the part of her that had left her homeland and crossed an ocean to find a father everyone told her did not exist, the side of her that had married a man she barely knew, pushed aside the practical, careful Sasha.

''I think I would like to try to make it higher,'' she said recklessly.

As the onlookers cheered their approval, she allowed Ben to lead her over to a long table covered with green felt. There were numbers on the felt. And colors. And a black wheel. As she watched, a man in a tuxedo spun the wheel, causing a metal ball to bounce.

''This here is roulette,'' Ben said. ''You'd have better chances with blackjack, but this'll be easier for you to understand.''

The wheel stopped. A pile of colorful plastic chips was placed in front of her.

She looked up at Ben. ''Now what?''

''Choose a number.''

She shook her head as she stared at the wheel, suddenly all too aware that she was risking real money. ''There are too many.''

"No problem. Let's start with a color. Red or black."

"Oh, that is easy. Red." The color of Mitch's shiny fire truck and his racy Mustang convertible.

She placed a chip on the spot Ben indicated, then held her breath as the banker spun the wheel and the ball started bouncing again.

Time seemed to pass in slow motion. Just when she thought she couldn't stand the suspense any longer, the wheel stopped and the ball bounced into the number ten slot.

"It is red!" she cried, clapping her hands. "This means I won, yes?"

"It means you won, yes," Ben agreed as the banker shoved her chip plus another one toward her. "Didn't I tell you we'd bring each other luck? Want to go again?"

"Yes." She put both chips on red again.

Ben followed her example, putting an enormous stack of his own plastic chips beside hers.

Feeling more daring than she'd ever felt before in her life, Sasha quickly took a smaller stack of her own chips and placed them on red, as well.

Then held her breath again as she waited for the spinning wheel to stop.

5

_____

MITCH'S FIRST thought when he woke up to silence was that Sasha must have fallen asleep in the tub. A check of his watch revealed that he'd been out for two hours. If she was still in the water after all this time, she'd be as wrinkled as a prune.

Perhaps, he decided, she was taking a nap on that ridiculously sexy waterbed.

He pushed himself off the glove-soft leather sofa, finger combed his hair, ran his tongue over his teeth and wished he'd thought to at least pack a toothbrush. "Sasha?"

There was no answer. The only sound was the pounding beat of music drifting up from the floor below. It seemed that their expensive honeymoon suite in the exclusive tower area of the hotel was situated over a cocktail lounge. Terrific, he thought with disgust.

He went over to the closed bedroom door and knocked softly.

Then again.

And a third time.

Lord, she must sleep like a rock, Mitch thought as he gingerly opened the door.

The bed had not been slept in.

"Sasha?" A prickle of fear had the hair on the nape of his neck standing up. "Are you still in the bath?"

When he received no answer, he crossed the room in three long strides. The bathroom door was open and he was vastly relieved to see that the tub was empty. For a fleeting, terrifying moment he'd pictured her lying beneath the water, having fallen unconscious while he'd been sacked out in the living room.

"Damn!"

Frustration kept him from appreciating the fragrant pink surroundings, although the thought did cross his mind that most honeymooners sharing this suite would undoubtedly discover that the huge tub held vast erotic possibilities.

Her luggage was still in the bedroom, which Mitch took as a good sign. Unfortunately, the sight of her suit draped over the back of a pink velvet chair revealed that she'd changed her clothes. He hoped it wouldn't be necessary to give the police a description of what she was wearing.

The police? He dragged his hand through his hair and asked himself what the hell he was thinking of. Obviously, she'd simply gotten tired of waiting for him to wake up, and had gone downstairs to have lunch by herself.

The note, which he finally found in the living room propped up on the coffee table, where he'd obviously been meant to see it as soon as he woke up, said exactly that. Mitch didn't think he'd ever felt so relieved, not even when he'd escaped that burning house with a twin baby beneath each arm.

The problem was, Sasha was too damn naive. Too trusting. Hell, he could imagine her opening the door to anyone. If anything had happened to her, Mitch knew he'd have never forgiven himself. And then there was the little matter of what Glory and Jake would have done to him.

As he rode the elevator down to the first floor where the coffee shop was located just off the lobby, Mitch assured himself that the only reason he was actually looking forward to having lunch with his bride was that it had been too many hours since he'd eaten.

"Are you certain you haven't seen her?" Mitch asked the statuesque forty-something hostess who had the look of a former showgirl. "She's about this tall—" he held his hand up to his shoulder "—long, dark, wavy hair, dark brown eyes, about one-hundred-and-five pounds—"

"I told you, honey, I haven't seen her. But you're welcome to look around."

"I've looked around. Hell, I've been through this restaurant three times. And I tell you, she isn't here!"

"If you'd been paying attention, you'd realize that there aren't any women in here, period. Just a bunch of Shriners wearing hats with red tassels. These are guys who like to have a good time. And a single girl as young and good-looking as the one you've described would definitely classify as a good time. Believe me, if she had been here, everyone would have noticed."

"She's not single," he snapped without thinking. "She's married. As of two hours ago."

The woman lifted an auburn brow. "And you lost her already? That's not a real encouraging start to a marriage."

When a couple of Shriners waiting to be seated laughed at her teasing remark, Mitch began grinding his teeth. "Not that it's any of your business, but I fell asleep. When I woke up she was gone."

"Can't say as I blame her." The hostess picked up same menus. "So, you want to sit down and hope she shows up?"

The note Sasha had written said she was coming down here. But if she hadn't arrived yet, obviously something had happened to change her plans. Mitch only hoped she hadn't been waylaid by a bunch of drunk conventioneers. Although he knew their reputation for good works, Shriners were also renowned for their wild conventions.

"Where can I find the head of security?"

She shook her head. "You're overreacting, hotshot. She'll be back when she decides she's punished you enough."

"Sasha isn't the type to play those kinds of games." Even though he hardly knew her, instinct told Mitch that his bride didn't have a deceitful bone in her body.

"Every woman plays games," the hostess corrected flippantly. "It's the only way we can stay ahead of you men." With that closing remark, she led the waiting conventioneers to a table that had just been cleared.

Frustrated, Mitch left the coffee shop and was contemplating whether to check out the hotel's other restaurants first, or to go straight to security, when the sound of familiar laughter coming from the adjacent casino caught his attention.

It was there he found her, seated at a blackjack table. The combination of the tall chair and the short denim skirt she was wearing revealed a distracting bit of firm thigh.

Not surprisingly, she was surrounded by a group of boisterous males, all wearing the familiar Shriner fez. Although most of the men appeared old enough to be her father, something that felt remarkably, uncomfortably like jealousy, stirred in his gut.

"What the hell do you think you're doing?"

She looked up at him in surprise. Then smiled in a way that could have melted all the ice over the North Pole. "Hi, Mitch! Did you have a nice nap?"

Mitch wasn't in the mood for small talk. "Why aren't you in the coffee shop? Where you belong?"

"Oh." She flashed him another beneficent smile, even more dazzling than the first. Her eyes were bright and gleamed like onyx. "I was on my way there, when I noticed this room. So I came in, thinking I would watch for just a moment, when Ben gave me a dollar to play in the slot machine.''

"Ben?'' Dammit, it was jealousy, Mitch realized with astonishment. And it had claws.

"Ben Houston,'' a deep voice with a Texas twang boomed. A hand the size of a catcher's mitt was thrust toward Mitch. "From Dallas, Texas. You must be the Mitch we've all been hearing so much about. This little girl does go on and on about you.''

"I'm Mitch Cudahy.'' Mitch's tone was hard. "And Sasha's not a little girl. She's my wife.''

"She told us all about your wedding,'' Ben said, ignoring the warning edge to Mitch's voice. "Congratulations. You've got yourself one sweet peach of a bride.''

There was a wave of enthusiastic approval from the other Shriners gathered around her chair. As he watched more than one pair of greedy male eyes practically eating Sasha up, Mitch's hands curled into fists at his side.

"I thought you were hungry.''

"Oh.'' Her eyes widened in surprise. "I was.'' When she shrugged, the blouse slid off one shoulder revealing a creamy bit of flesh. "But I have been having so much fun, I forgot.''

"Well, I could use something to eat.'' Mitch knew he sounded stiff, almost stodgy, and he hated himself for it. And hated her for making him feel like something he wasn't.

"Oh.'' She frowned. "I'm sorry, Mitch. I should have thought of that.''

When the dealer cleared his throat, Sasha treated him to a smile almost as warm and wonderful as the one she'd greeted Mitch with. "I guess I had better stop playing now.''

"You've been gambling? All this time?'' That idea had

never occurred to Mitch. He'd figured she was just keeping this Houston guy company.

Mitch knew she didn't have any money of her own. Surely, he thought wildly, the house manager wouldn't have given her credit? But then again, the hotel did have his credit card number. What if she'd used it to get an advance? As his wife, she'd probably be entitled to.

"It didn't seem so very long," Sasha explained. "The time went by very fast."

Terrific. She'd undoubtedly bankrupted him. "So, how much have you lost?"

"Hell, Cudahy," Ben Houston's voice boomed again, "your little lady didn't lose. She's been beating the socks off the house for the past two hours. From the slots to roulette to blackjack."

"Ben taught me how to play blackjack." Sasha grinned up at the oilman standing beside her. "I like it very much."

"That's cause you're damn good at it, sweetheart," Ben said. He winked at Mitch. "I'll bet you didn't know you'd married a gal with a near photographic memory. If she was any better, the management would throw her out of here for card counting."

"You've been winning?"

"Yes!" She waved her hand, drawing his attention to the towering stacks of red, white and black plastic chips in front of her. It was then Mitch also noticed the half-empty champagne flute. "I have been very lucky, Mitch. Ben says I'm his good luck charm."

Mitch stared at Sasha, then down at the chips, then his eyes moved questioningly back to his bride. "How much do all those chips represent?"

"I don't know. When we left the roulette wheel I had eight thousand dollars. But we've been winning more over here, and as Ben taught me, the odds are better, so—"

"Eight thousand?" His voice cracked. "You've won eight thousand?"

"More than that," she reminded him.

"I'd say she's around twelve, give or take a few hundred," Ben offered.

"Twelve thousand dollars?"

"Not peanuts, boy," Ben said, slapping him on the back. "And although we hate like the dickens to give our little Sasha up, I suppose you'd kinda like to have her to yourself for a while." His lips curved in a masculine grin. "Considerin' that this is your honeymoon and all."

"Yes, I would definitely like some time alone with my wife." Mitch was still having trouble taking it all in. "Where did you get the money in the first place?"

"Ben gave me a dollar." She smiled up at the man, who grinned back, annoying Mitch even more. "Then I won the jackpot. And a very nice woman brought me some champagne." Her smile softened. "Have you ever had champagne, Mitch?"

"Sure."

"This was my first time." She sighed happily. "I think it is my very favorite drink." She smiled at him over the rim of the glass before polishing it off. "Can we have some more with lunch?"

"Why not," he agreed absently, his attention drawn back to that amazing stack of chips. "It appears you can afford it."

"I won them for you, Mitch," she said earnestly as she slid down from the chair. "To pay you back for the wedding and the ring, and…"

Before she could finish her sentence, her legs suddenly folded. If Mitch hadn't caught her, she would have fallen onto the crimson-and-gold carpeting.

"I do not understand." She gave a silvery little giggle.

"My legs seem to have fallen asleep." She was holding on to him, her arms wrapped around his neck, her body against his, her breath coming in soft puffs against his throat.

For the first time Mitch realized that her words were faintly slurred. "How much of that champagne have you drunk?"

She tilted her head back and looked into his suddenly narrowed eyes, which was difficult to do the way he kept going in and out of focus. Sasha blinked to clear her vision. "I do not know, exactly." When she began to sway, his hands settled more firmly at her waist, literally holding her up. "Every time I won, the waitress brought me more." He was so fuzzy! Sasha blinked again. "Did you know that it is free?"

"So I've heard. I also know you're smashed."

"Smashed?"

"Drunk." Last year a group of Russian firemen had toured the U.S. to learn modern fire-fighting techniques. When they'd arrived in Phoenix, Mitch had been assigned to show them around. The experience, which had included visits to all of Phoenix's popular watering holes, proved helpful now as he recalled one of the few Russian words he'd learned. *"Pyahnyj."*

"Oh." She considered that for a moment as she continued to cling to him. Then she giggled. "I think, Mitch, that you are right."

Her musical laughter set the others off, as well. For his part, Mitch found little humor in the fact that his bride of two hours had gotten drunk with a bunch of Shriners in a casino.

"I'd better get you upstairs to bed."

When that suggestion earned a roar of appreciative laughter, Mitch experienced a hot urge to slam a well-placed fist into a few grinning faces. But since Sasha obviously wasn't the only one who'd had too much to drink, and the last thing he needed was to start a drunken brawl, he managed to rein in his uncharacteristic anger. "Let's get out of here."

This was easier said than done. When he released her to scoop up the chips, she began to crumble bonelessly to the floor again. Fortunately, once again, he caught her just in time.

While he tried to figure out what to do, a dark-haired man appeared at his elbow. "I'm Quenton Vaughn, manager of the casino," he told Mitch. The slim gold badge on his lapel confirmed his words. "Why don't you let me cash in your wife's winnings for you, Mr. Cudahy? And I'll have a cashier's check delivered to your suite."

"That's so wunnerfully nice of you," Sasha said before Mitch could answer. She tilted her head back, and smiled blurrily up at Mitch. "Isn't that nice, Mitch?"

"Yeah." Her arched back succeeded in pressing her hips closer against his, which did nothing to soothe his discomfort. "Real nice."

He started to sling her over his shoulder fireman style, then, remembering the brevity of her denim miniskirt, cradled her in his arms instead. He left the casino followed by waves of laughter and applause.

Although her brain was strangely fogged, it gradually occurred to Sasha that Mitch had not smiled once since he'd entered the casino.

"Mitch?"

"What?" The elevator walls were mirrored, allowing a disconcerting view of lace-trimmed panties. The skirt really was indecent, he decided.

"You are mad at me, yes?"

Sighing, he looked down into her lovely face, where a

watery sheen brightened her eyes. Fearing a crying jag, he said, ''I'm not mad at you, Sasha.''

''But you are not happy.''

''Of course I'm happy,'' he retorted. ''Why shouldn't I be happy? I go to sleep after a hellish night trying to keep Phoenix from burning to the damn ground, then I wake up and find my bride of two hours has deserted me in order to play roulette with a bunch of drunk Shriners. And gotten smashed, besides. What man wouldn't be thrilled?''

''I did not mean to get smashed,'' she said earnestly. ''But when I began winning—''

''You've explained all that.''

His tone was sharp. And final. She fell silent and bit her lip to keep from embarrassing them both by crying again.

As the elevator continued its climb up to the tower suite, neither Mitch nor Sasha said a word.

''Mitch?'' she asked as the mirrored doors finally opened on their floor.

''Yeah?''

''I did not think you would be angry.'' Her voice was thickening. He could hear the tears. ''I left you a note.''

''I wasn't angry, dammit. Not in the beginning. Not until I got scared something had happened to you.''

She thought about that, struggling to clear the cobwebs from her head as he marched down the hallway. ''You were worried about me?''

''Of course.'' He had to juggle her in his arms as he dug into his jeans for the coded card key to the room.

That was nice, Sasha decided. Surely a man would not be concerned if he didn't care, just a little.

His next words dashed her faint hope. ''I'm a fireman. Worrying about people comes with the territory.''

It was true. But what Mitch was not prepared to admit, even to himself, was that the cold fear he'd experienced when Sasha wasn't in the coffee shop was like none he'd ever before felt.

He carried her into the bedroom, and tossed her unceremoniously onto the bed, creating waves. "You'd better try to sleep some of that champagne off. I'll call room service."

His tone was flat and uncaring. Sasha sighed, trying to recapture a bit of the pleasure she'd experienced before Mitch's arrival in the casino.

"Mitch?"

"What now?"

Although it was difficult, she managed to push herself up to her knees, wrap her arms around his waist and press her cheek to his chest. "I am truly sorry that I upset you. Especially after you were so kind to marry me."

Hell. He reached out, intending to put his hands on her shoulders to push her away. Instead they found their way into her hair. "Sasha—"

"Please, Mitch." She held on tighter. "Do not tell me you would do it for anyone. Even if it is the truth."

The anger and frustration drained out of him and was replaced by something far more dangerous. "That wasn't what I was going to say." He buried his face in her lush, fragrant hair and felt himself slipping deeper and deeper into hot water.

They stayed that way for a long, silent time, holding on to each other. The air between them grew thick with unspoken thoughts.

She could feel his heart pounding beneath her cheek, hard and fast. Her need for him was so powerful, so staggering, that it made her tremble. Something deep and secret inside her was struggling for release. Something that could no longer be denied.

"Back in the chapel," she murmured against his chest, "before you fainted—"

"Thanks for bringing that up," he muttered.

"I was just wondering something."

"What's that?" Mitch asked distractedly. Her hair felt like silk and smelled like flowers.

"Is our marriage official? If you did not kiss me as the minister instructed?"

The dangerous words vibrated against his chest, seeping into his bloodstream. Did she know what she was doing? Did all Russian women foolishly play with fire this way? Or was Sasha Mikhailova—Sasha Cudahy, he reminded himself—unique?

When she pressed her lips against his shirt, the last of his good intentions fled. He tangled a fist in her hair and tugged, pulling her head back.

"You're right. It's high time I kissed my bride."

His mouth took hers quickly. Stunningly. She hadn't expected it to be so hot, or so hungry. Kissing Mitch was glorious. And terrifying.

"You're supposed to close your eyes," he murmured against her champagne-sweet mouth.

"If I close my eyes, I will not be able to look at you." Her fingers climbed up his neck to cup the back of his head. "I like looking at you, Mitch."

"Not as much as I like looking at you." He tilted his head, changing the angle of the kiss. "But I want to kiss you properly. So, close your eyes, sweetheart." He pressed his lips against her lids, encouraging them to flutter shut.

As his mouth took a slow, sensual journey over her face, she felt the scrape of his afternoon beard against her cheek and the pleasure of it, dark and dangerous, lanced through her.

"Lord, you are sweet." His hands pushed her blouse off

her shoulders, allowing his lips access to silken perfumed flesh. "And warm."

When his hot, wicked mouth left a trail of sparks on the way back up to her tingling lips, Sasha heard a ragged sob and realized through her swimming senses that it was coming from her own burning throat.

The little sounds she was making, along with the way she was moving her lush feminine body against his, made Mitch feel about to burst. It was not something he was accustomed to feeling from a mere kiss.

To prove to himself that he'd not lost control, Mitch decided to court danger a little further.

"Open your mouth for me, sweetheart." His thumb tugged at her rosy lips. "Let me kiss you the way a woman like you should be kissed."

A woman like her. He made her sound special. Desirable. Loved. Melting against him, Sasha did as instructed, accepting his plundering tongue as she longed to accept his heart.

It was only a kiss, Mitch reminded himself. He could end it anytime. His hands roved down her body, brushing the sides of her breasts, before settling on the shapeliest little butt he'd ever felt. He pulled her tight against him, so close he could feel their hearts beating in the same wild rhythm.

He wanted her. Here. Now. He wanted to drag her down on to the wildly rocking mattress, strip off her clothes and taste every ounce of her warm flesh. He wanted to bury himself deep inside her, so deep and so hard the heat of their bodies would raise the water in the bed to boiling point.

It was when he realized that he was on the verge of doing exactly that, Mitch became vividly aware of how close he'd come to a line he dared not cross.

"Mitch?" She swayed when he abruptly released her, her hands reached for him, her eyes were wide and confused. And laced with a passion he could still taste.

"You'd better get some sleep, Sasha." She was as pale as milk. Not wanting her to fall off the bed onto her face, he took hold of her bare shoulders and lowered her gently but firmly to the mattress. "You're going to have one helluva hangover."

"I do not understand. I thought you wanted me."

Her accent had thickened. Mitch could hear the hurt in her voice. See it in her eyes. "Any man would want you, Sasha. You're beautiful and sexy as hell. But that's all it is. Animal attraction. It happens."

"Perhaps to you." The vast quantity of champagne she'd drunk allowed her to say something that under any other circumstances she would have wisely kept to herself. "But nothing even close to this has ever happened to me, Mitch." Her teeth nervously began worrying her ravished bottom lip. "No one has ever made me feel the way you do."

As he felt himself being inexorably drawn into Sasha's warm, doe-brown eyes, Mitch felt something move through him that was more complex than lust, more dangerous than desire.

"It's the champagne." Knowing it could be fatal to touch her, but unable to resist, he ran his palm down the tousled silk of her hair. "Go to sleep, Sasha. You'll feel differently after the buzz wears off."

With those less than encouraging words ringing in her ears, Mitch left the room. A moment later she heard him making a telephone call on the other side of the closed door.

Reminding herself that she was a survivor, Sasha vowed that she wasn't going to let Mitch Cudahy break her heart.

If he wanted to claim that the heated kiss meant nothing to him, that was fine with her. Because she didn't care. She wouldn't let herself care.

Sasha's last thought, as she drifted off into an alcohol-induced sleep, was to wonder when she'd become such a liar.

Mitch ate a solitary dinner, and as evening gave way to night, he sprawled on the couch, staring out the undraped windows at the lights of the gambling city. And thought about Sasha, warm and oh, so very willing, just on the other side of the door.

He could have had her. And if the kisses they'd shared were any indication of the passion lurking inside her, it would have been incomparable.

But then what? Although the license on the coffee table declared them to be man and wife, they'd gone into this agreeing that it was only a marriage of convenience, designed to get immigration off her back.

If he were to make love to his bride, which he had every legal right to do, he reminded himself, he'd be taking advantage of her sweet and generous emotions. And Sasha was the kind of woman who deserved more than a passionate one-night tumble on a waterbed. She deserved a real marriage, with a husband who'd mow the lawn and take out the trash because he adored her, and a passel of gorgeous, dark-eyed kids who looked just like her.

What she deserved was the happy-ever-after ending that was a staple of Russian fairy tales. And unfortunately, since he had no intention of tying himself down to one woman for the rest of his life, he was not the man to give it to her.

That being the case, it was important that he maintain some physical—and emotional—distance.

Which was going to be a helluva lot easier said than done.

Just thinking about Sasha made his body ache in a way it hadn't since his hormone-driven teenage days. As he lay in the dark, trying to keep erotic fantasies about his bride at bay, the sounds of yet another Elvis impersonator singing drifted up from the cocktail lounge on the floor below.

When the baritone voice began singing ''Are You Lonesome Tonight?'' Mitch cursed.

Timing, he thought with an agonized groan, was indeed, everything.

6

NEITHER MITCH nor Sasha mentioned the kiss the following morning. Nor was it brought up during the long and silent drive back to Phoenix after a new starter had been installed in the Mustang.

But they both were thinking about it. A lot.

"I'm afraid Jake was right about the place being a mess," Mitch mumbled as he carried Sasha's suitcases up the outside stairs leading to his second-story apartment. His voice sounded rusty from all the hours of disuse. He cleared his throat. "But, all this happened so quickly—"

"You don't have to apologize to me, Mitch," Sasha said quickly. Too quickly, Mitch thought, which revealed her own nervousness about the situation.

He opened the door and stared. Obviously some fairy godmother had waved her magic feather duster over the place while he'd been away getting married in Laughlin.

"It's very nice," Sasha said, her own surprise evident. It also occurred to her that if Mitch considered this Spartan example of housekeeping excellence a mess, he was going to be less than pleased with her housekeeping skills. She could literally see her reflection in the gleaming cherry end table. "And very clean."

Mitch ran his finger over the top of the television, which, when he'd gone to work four days ago, had looked as if it had been frosted with a layer of snow. "It is that," he agreed absently.

It was more than the fact that a guy could go blind from the sun streaming through the polished windows and reflecting off the shining furniture that had the apartment looking so unfamiliar. There was also the little fact that the furniture was not the same.

The cherry end table and the candlestick lamp, for example. And what the hell had happened to his couch? All right, so it might have had a few broken springs. And perhaps the stuffing was coming through the cracks in the burgundy red leather. But it had been huge. And if a guy spilled some salsa or beer on it while watching a football game on the tube, nobody cared.

Unfortunately, he could not say that for the new blue-checked cotton sofa that had taken its place. What kind of people broke into a place, took your stuff and replaced it with new?

"Oh, look," Sasha called from the adjoining kitchen, "fresh flowers!"

The minute he saw the handwriting on the white envelope stuck in the bouquet of perky yellow-faced daisies, tiger lilies, carnations and star asters, Mitch had his answer.

"They're from my mother." He skimmed the lines of familiar handwriting. "She wants to welcome us home."

The congratulatory note had him wondering what, exactly, Jake had revealed about the hastily planned wedding. It also explained the furniture, which, now that he thought about it, Mitch realized belonged to his grandmother Cudahy. His mother had stashed it away in her basement when his grandmother had moved into that condo on the San Diego coast.

"There's a casserole in the refrigerator we can heat up in the microwave," he continued reading. "And a bottle of champagne in the refrigerator, if you'd like a glass."

Sasha put her hand to her head, which, while not throbbing as badly as it had when she woke up this morning, still felt as if someone had hit her with a very sharp rock. "I think I've had enough champagne for one weekend."

"Hangovers are the pits."

He'd watched her obvious suffering all day and although he'd experienced random urges to offer her sympathy and aspirin, he'd resisted both. There was something about Sasha that encouraged a man to want to protect her, to take care of her. And, dammit, to care for her.

And that definitely wasn't the plan, he reminded himself as a ball of ice formed in his stomach.

Get married, get that bureaucratic weasel Potter off her back, help her get a green card and move on. That was the plan. And so long as they both stuck to it, everything would be okay.

She looked at him with interest. "You have felt this way?"

He laughed. "Sweetheart, more times than I care to count."

There it was again, that easy endearment that made her heart turn somersaults. Sasha reminded herself that the only reason she was standing here, in Mitch's spotless sun-warmed kitchen that smelled of lemon cleanser and spring flowers was to trick the U.S. government.

Mitch had been chivalrous enough to come up with the marriage ruse in the first place. It was not his fault she loved him. It was not his fault that she'd lain awake last night, fantasizing about a real wedding night.

If her heart was suffering, the pain, like her pounding headache, would pass. And in the meantime, she'd just have to keep reminding herself that thinking too much about Mitch—especially thinking about tomorrows with Mitch—would be a very grave mistake.

They stood there, on either side of the kitchen table, the

wicker basket of flowers between them, looking at each other, attempting to hide their feelings.

As he felt himself being pulled into the velvety warmth of her eyes, the icy knot in his stomach pulled even tighter and Mitch realized that if he didn't get out of here now, he'd be in danger of suffocating.

"Why don't you unpack?" he suggested, waving his hand in the general vicinity of the single bedroom. "I've got some errands to run."

It was more than a little obvious that he was desperate to escape. Sasha lowered her eyes and began toying nervously with the flowers, rubbing the ruffled edges of a white carnation between her thumb and index finger. "Will you be back for dinner?" The words were no sooner out of her mouth than she wished she could retrieve them.

Hell, she was already starting to sound like a wife. That's all he needed. Deciding to establish the parameters of this mock marriage now, before things got entirely out of hand, Mitch shrugged. "I don't know. But it'd probably be better if you didn't wait for me."

His voice was more distant than she'd ever heard it. Deciding she liked him better when he was yelling at her, and refusing to allow him to see that his cold dismissal stung so cruelly, she lifted her chin and gave him a look of icy aloofness that one of her czarist ancestors might have used to demoralize a recalcitrant servant.

"Fine. I am accustomed to eating alone. And I was not attempting to control your behavior."

"Good. Because, just for the record, others have tried. But no one has succeeded."

Now they were even sniping at each other like an old married couple. Deciding that this must've been the shortest honeymoon on record, Mitch clenched his teeth and met her cool, level gaze. "Use whatever drawers and closet space you need."

With that he was gone. Almost, but not quite, slamming the door behind him.

Sasha sank down onto one of the Windsor kitchen chairs and sighed. But having already cried more in the last few days than she had in her entire twenty-four years, her eyes remained resolutely dry.

"DARLING!" Meredith smiled in welcome when she opened the door to her townhouse and saw him standing on her front porch. "I didn't expect you."

"We need to talk."

"This sounds serious."

"Not really. Well, I guess it is, in a way." Mitch dragged his hand through his hair. "Can I just come in, so we don't have to have this conversation in front of an audience?"

Meredith glanced past him toward the elderly woman walking the ancient Schnauzer, as she did each afternoon, rain or shine. "Of course." She moved aside to let him in, and waved to her neighbor.

"Good evening, Mrs. Lansky," she called out in those perfectly modulated tones that always reminded critics of Diane Sawyer. "How is Petey tonight?"

"His arthritis seems to be easing up," the elderly woman answered. "In fact, he hasn't had so much spring in his step since he was a pup. I think it's the new dog food I switched him to after your consumer report last month."

"I'm glad to hear that." Meredith's smile could have melted butter. "I have a life-style segment tonight that might interest you—it's about a gourmet restaurant catering to dogs."

"That does sound interesting." The elderly woman nodded her snowy head. "Petey and I never miss a broadcast." That said, owner and dog continued down the walk.

"Stroking your public again?" Mitch asked as he threw himself down on the white silk sofa. The first time he'd entered Meredith's house, he'd felt as if he'd stumbled into a blizzard. Or a hospital emergency room. Everything— floor, walls, furniture, silk flowers—was as white as snow.

"Laugh all you want to, Mitch, darling. But my Q-ratings are the highest in the Rocky Mountain region."

"I always thought that was because of your legs." Despite the seriousness of his mission, his gaze drifted down to the long legs attractively showcased by the short emerald silk robe.

"Anyone ever tell you that you're a terrible chauvinist, Cudahy?"

"All the time." In spite of the seriousness of his mission, he grinned. "Personally, I've always taken it as a badge of honor."

"You would." She sighed dramatically. "Although I have to admit that if there's one man who can get away with it, it may be you." She leaned down and planted a kiss on his mouth. It was hot and long and involved a lot of the clever tongue action she did so well. "I missed you the other night," she said when the kiss ended.

"I was out of town."

"That's what Jake told me when I called the station. So, does this sudden need to get away have anything to do with your reason for coming here?"

"What makes you think that?"

"From your grim expression, darling, I have the impression that you haven't dropped in for a quickie before I leave for the 6:00 p.m. newscast."

"No."

"I didn't think so." She sighed and glanced down at her

watch. "We don't have a lot of time. Why don't you come talk to me while I redo my makeup?"

He followed her into the bedroom, which, like the living room, was a sea of white, suggesting the same Grace Kelly restraint she wore like a second skin in public. Having discovered firsthand exactly how unrestrained the newscaster could be while tumbling around in those white satin sheets, Mitch knew the cool outward appearance was deceiving.

Which was, he reminded himself, what his wedding to Sasha was all about. Deception.

"I don't want you to start throwing things," he warned as he watched her smooth moisturizer into her skin with her fingertips, "until you hear the entire story."

"Gracious." She met his eyes in her mirror. "This does sound serious."

At least he had her full attention. Sometime between explaining who exactly Sasha Mikhailova was, and ending with yesterday's wedding ceremony—leaving out the fact that he'd fainted and the part about Elvis and Sasha's incredible streak of luck at the tables—Mitch was aware of Meredith abandoning her tubes and pots.

"Well," she said when he finally finished, "that's quite a story." She turned around on the little white satin stool and began sponging on her foundation.

Mitch warily watched her, waiting for the explosion he figured would eventually come. The silence was beginning to drive him crazy.

"Since the wedding wasn't real, there really isn't any reason for us to stop seeing one another," he said reassuringly.

"Don't you mean sleeping together?" she asked, moving on to rose-tinted blusher.

"Well, yeah." He knew he was mumbling and hated himself for it. "I guess that's what I mean."

She accented her eyes with a smudge of kohl at the corners, and applied three coats of mascara. "May I ask a few questions?" she asked finally, after outlining her lips with a vermillion pencil.

"I'd say you're entitled, given the circumstances."

"Did you happen to tell your new bride you were coming here?"

"Not exactly."

"Why not? If this is simply a marriage of convenience, why should she care what you do? Or with whom you do it?"

"It's more complicated than that."

"Most marriages are," Meredith said sagely. Since she'd already made three trips to the altar before the age of twenty-eight, Mitch figured she knew more about such things than he did.

"But it's still just a green card marriage," he insisted.

"So you said." She filled in the vermillion line with a bright crimson, pressed her lips against a tissue, then turned to face him.

Here we go, thought Mitch as he steeled himself for the fireworks.

"But I don't have time to get sidetracked with personal discussions right now," Meredith said calmly, "not when we have something far more important to discuss."

Mitch, who'd been balanced on the balls of his feet prepared to duck flying tubes, jars and bottles, released his guard somewhat. But Meredith's next statement had the effect of a fist to his midriff, leaving him breathless.

"Mitch," she said sweetly, "I want you to get me an exclusive interview with your bride."

"I DON'T GET THIS," Jake said as he dribbled the basketball. "Are you telling me that you're ticked off because your lover isn't mad at you for getting married?''

''The least Meredith could've done was act a little put out,'' Mitch complained, anticipating Jake's move to the right. After leaving Meredith's, he'd dropped by the station, hoping to find his brother-in-law working out on the court. They'd been playing one-on-one for the past half hour, he was having the damn pants beat off him, and after thirty minutes of sweating and running, he was still as frustrated as he'd been when he'd arrived. ''And it isn't a real marriage.'' He switched to the left.

''Who are you trying to convince? Me? Or yourself?'' Jake feigned right, moved left, and sank a nice easy jump shot. ''He shoots. He scores! And the crowd goes wild.''

''You traveled,'' Mitch complained as he took Jake's pass and began dribbling the ball. ''And you also sound just like Meredith.''

''She didn't buy the marriage-of-convenience story, either?''

''No.'' Mitch swore as Jake deftly stole the ball and shot another quick two points from the perimeter. ''How the hell do you expect me to concentrate on my game when you keep bringing up my damn marriage?''

Jake tossed him another pass. ''Sorry. I thought you came here to talk.''

''Well, you're wrong.'' Mitch cursed again as he threw up a brick that missed the rim by a mile. The ball went rolling off the court, and came to a stop against the wheel of a fire truck. ''I came here because I don't have anywhere else to go.''

Jake eyed the ball and shrugged, deciding to let it go, for now. ''How about home?''

''Which home? The comfortable, messy one I used to live in? The one with the leather couch? The one that didn't smell like a lemon orchard and look like an explosion at a rose parade?''

''Ah.'' Jake nodded sagely. ''I told Katie I thought that was a mistake.''

''Obviously she didn't listen,'' Mitch muttered.

''When you've been married a bit longer, you'll realize that women never listen when it comes to decorating or matchmaking.''

''I don't intend to be married all that much longer. And I want my couch back.'' Mitch raked his hand through his hair and glared at the late rush-hour traffic streaming by the station. ''Hell, I want my life back.''

''Let me see if I've got this right. You're ticked off at your mom and Katie for getting rid of your couch, so you're going to take it out on Sasha by leaving her alone her first night as a married woman.''

''It's not her first night.''

''That's right.'' Jake leaned against the backboard post, folded his arms across his broad chest and eyed Mitch with amusement. ''You two had an unexpected honeymoon in Laughlin. So, how did it go?''

''It didn't.'' Although he didn't elaborate, Mitch's scowl spoke volumes.

''Sounds as if you wish otherwise.''

''And you sound like some damn radio talk show shrink!'' Mitch's outburst caused a trio of pigeons perched on the roof to flap their wings and fly off to the top of a nearby palm tree.

''You probably just need to get laid,'' Jake said, laughing. ''Which, I figure, probably makes sense. I doubt if there are many guys who could spend the night with Sasha and not want to jump her lush little Russian bones.''

Mitch's hands curled unconsciously into fists at his side. ''Keep that up and I'll have to kill you.''

Humor was mixed with the open speculation in Jake's gaze. "Now you sound like a husband."

Mitch's muttered curse was ripe and vulgar. "It's just that she's a nice woman."

"The best," Jake agreed. "And the little fact that she's in love with you probably makes this marriage thing stickier."

"She's not in love with me," Mitch snapped. The idea was as ridiculous as it was horrifying.

"She's been bonkers over you since you showed up at the diner like Sir Galahad in a yellow coat and helmet." The laughter left his eyes as his gaze turned serious. "Which is why you're going to have to tread carefully, pal. Because if you break that little girl's heart, there'll be a whole bunch of people standing in line waiting to kick out your lung."

"Beginning with you?"

"Nah." Jake shook his head as his natural humor returned. "Glory will be first. But I'll be right behind her. Followed, I'll bet, by your mom and sister." He nodded in the direction of the station house. "Then the rest of the crew. Then Glory's regular customers, then—"

"I get the idea." Mitch's shoulders drooped as he realized exactly how deep a mess he'd gotten himself into this time. Compared to this phony marriage gambit, rushing into blazing buildings seemed like a lead pipe cinch.

"You want to play some more?" Jake asked. "Or go get drunk?"

"You'll just keep beating me if we play," Mitch grumbled. "So I guess the only thing left to do is get drunk."

"You could go home."

"No." Mitch shook his head. "That's not an option."

It was Jake's turn to curse as he shook his head. "I'll drive. Just let me call Katie." A smile twitched. "Some of us have learned the wisdom of letting the little woman know we'll be late.''

As Jake went into the station to make his call, Mitch's mind wandered to Sasha, alone in his apartment, eating her solitary dinner. Sympathy stirred, guilt clawed treacherously at his gut.

''Ready?'' Jake asked when he returned.

Reminding himself that Sasha was a big girl and had understood the rules going into this fake marriage, Mitch forced down the sympathy and tried to ignore the guilt.

''Ready.'' He climbed into the passenger seat of the new minivan Jake had traded his Corvette in for when the baby had been born, and told himself that this married man's car was just one more reason he had every intention of regaining his single status as soon as possible.

Marriage meant sedate wheels and exchanging Saturday night poker games with the guys for driving the baby-sitter home after an early movie. Marriage meant spending Sundays mowing lawns instead of playing softball and watching ESPN until your eyes glazed over.

Marriage meant doing dishes and changing diapers, buying life insurance, worrying about orthodontists' bills and college tuition and pretending to be interested by paint and fabric swatches.

Marriage was okay, Mitch supposed, for guys like Jake. Guys who actually seemed to enjoy their tranquil, predictable lives of suffocating domesticity.

And although Mitch was truly glad his sister had found such a paragon of a husband, he vowed that there was no way he was going to spend the rest of his life in captivity.

7

———

IT WAS TWO in the morning when Mitch poured himself out of the minivan and managed to stagger up the stairs. His head was swimming with a combination of Mexican beer and tequila chasers and he knew he was going to hate himself in the morning. But right now, he felt just fine.

It took him three tries before he managed to unlock the door. Then, leaving a trail of clothes across the living room carpet, he managed to make his way into the bedroom, where he threw himself facedown onto the bed, pinning Sasha with an arm thrown across her chest. And then he began to snore. Loudly.

His breath was like a warm breeze in Sasha's ear—a beer-scented breeze. When she tried to shift away, he mumbled and pulled her closer. As he held her against his chest, Sasha realized he wasn't wearing a stitch of clothing. His body was hard and warm. And undeniably inviting.

Assuring herself that she was only worried about waking him if she tried to pull away, she decided to stay right where she was. As she finally drifted off to sleep, Sasha was smiling.

Mitch dreamed he was in the islands, making love to a beautiful woman on a sun-drenched, deserted beach. Somewhere in the distance, a deep voice was crooning ''Blue Hawaii.'' The woman fit against him perfectly. Her smooth, oiled skin carried the scent of tropical flowers. As he covered her mouth with his, her lips trembled apart on a sigh as soft as the island tradewinds. She was every bit as delicious as he'd known she would be. Her mouth tasted like ripe fruit. Kissing her was like dining on paradise.

Wanting more, he ran his hands down her body, stroking her smooth curves and taut muscles with a smooth, practiced touch that quickened her breath and drew low murmurs from between her succulent lips that in turn set off a series of fiery eruptions deep inside Mitch. He slid his knee between her thighs and dragged his mouth down her throat to her breast.

Caught up in the wonder and heat of her own erotic dream, Sasha combed her hands through Mitch's hair and murmured her pleasure in her native Russian.

The unfamiliar words had the effect of a bucket of icy water. Mitch froze, then slowly, gingerly, opened his eyes.

The bedroom was draped in deep purple shadows. But it was not so dark that Mitch couldn't see the awareness slowly flooding into Sasha's sleepy eyes.

"Aw, hell." He withdrew his hand from beneath her white cotton nightgown. "I can't believe…I never…"

With a muffled sound that was part moan and part curse, he rolled onto his back and covered his eyes with his forearm. "I didn't know," he said, his husky voice strained. "Why the hell didn't you stop me?"

"You were not the only one who was sleeping."

He took his arm away, his expression anything but encouraging. "You weren't awake?"

She gnawed a bit on her lower lip, trying to decide how much to tell him. It was true that she'd been asleep when she'd first felt his lips brush her temple. But by the time his wicked, wonderful hands had begun moving over her body, seeking out pleasure points she'd never even known she possessed, Sasha had been fully, blissfully awake.

In the end, she opted for a half-truth. "I was dreaming."

She looked so lovely, with the rosy hue of passion still blooming in her cheeks. Her eyes held a lingering vestige of desire and passion that he found almost impossible to resist. If she were any other woman, Mitch knew, now that they were both awake, they wouldn't be wasting time talking.

"That must have been some dream."

"It was quite pleasant." She tugged the rumpled sheet up nearly to her chin. "As yours must have been, as well."

Mitch felt a twinge of disappointment when she covered up those wondrous breasts that were enticingly visible beneath the thin white cotton, but reluctantly decided it was the prudent thing to do.

"I haven't woken up so horny since I was seventeen."

The word was unfamiliar. But Sasha did not need a Russian/English dictionary to understand its meaning. "I have never before woken up feeling like that," she admitted.

He'd suspected as much. "I should have sacked out on the couch. But by the time I crawled home, I'd forgotten you'd be here."

Although she knew he hadn't meant the words as an insult, they stung nonetheless. "I should not have taken your bed."

"Don't be silly. You're a guest. You get the bed."

"But—"

"I said, you get the damn bed." Frustration sharpened his tone. "Don't argue with me on this one, Sasha. Not while a sadistic maniac is pounding away inside my head with a jackhammer."

She knew the feeling. Intimately. "You have a hangover?"

"Not a hangover," he corrected, groaning as he sat up. "The grandpappy of all hangovers." He blinked his eyes and wondered if someone had glued sandpaper to the insides of his lids after he'd passed out. It was just the kind of sick practical joke Jake would have enjoyed.

"I'm sorry."

"It's not your fault. You didn't pour those tequila chasers down my throat."

"No. But if you hadn't been trying to stay away from me, you would have come home earlier."

He opened his mouth to lie and knew he wouldn't be able to pull it off. What she'd said was the truth. And they both knew it.

"I'd better brush my teeth." He pushed aside the sheet on his side of the double bed. "I think a badger must've died in my mouth while I was sleeping."

She watched him walk into the bathroom with the casual air of a man comfortable with nudity. Which, she considered, made sense. What man wouldn't enjoy showing off such a perfect body?

She heard the sound of water running, and the flush of the toilet. And then she heard him turn on the shower. When her unruly mind pictured Mitch standing beneath the stream of hot water, she closed her eyes, tight, trying to block the provocative image. But it didn't work.

It was still with her, lingering in her mind as she dressed for their meeting with Mr. Donald O. Potter.

Sasha had never seen Mitch in a suit. As she entered the kitchen after her own shower, she thought he looked even more handsome than he did in his usual polo shirt and jeans. And the blue tie exactly matched his eyes.

She stifled a sigh, wishing he really was her husband.

"You look very nice," she murmured as she took out a carton of orange juice out of the fridge.

"I feel like a man on the verge of death." He took the carton from her and poured the juice. The way her hands were shaking, he was afraid she'd pour it all over the counter, herself and the tile floor his mother and sister had gleaming with a mirrorlike sheen.

He took a look at her unadorned white blouse, navy skirt and flats. Although the plain-Jane clothes weren't any more appealing than the suit she'd worn for their wedding, he decided that Sasha was a woman who would probably look gorgeous in a gunny sack.

"You look pretty." It was the truth. "But a little pale." That, too, was the truth. His eyes narrowed as they moved over her face. "Wait here."

He left the room and returned with a tube of cream blush. He unscrewed the cap, squeezed a dot onto the end of his finger, then smoothed the soft rose cream along the slanted line of first one cheekbone, then the other. His fingers created an enervating warmth that nearly made her knees buckle.

He stepped back to study the results. "That's better."

"You have many talents," she murmured, wondering how he'd acquired such cosmetic skills.

Mitch shrugged. "I grew up sharing a bathroom with my sister." He saw no point in revealing that years spent watching other women playing with their pots and brushes had taught him a lot. "A guy's bound to pick up a few things." He glanced at his watch, then gulped down the mug of cooling coffee he'd left on the counter. "Well, I guess it's time to face the inquisition."

The chill started at the top of her head and worked its way downward. Watching the renewed color leave her face, Mitch felt a stir of pity. She was trembling like a willow in a hurricane. Touching her was asking for trouble, he looped his arms around her waist and pressed his lips against her hair. There was no passion in either his embrace or his light kiss, only tenderness.

"It's going to be all right."

She closed her eyes and allowed herself to draw from his strength. When she felt she wouldn't humiliate herself by weeping, she tilted her head back and looked up at him.

"What if it isn't?" she asked in a soft, fractured voice that once again pulled at something elemental inside him. "What if Mr. Donald O. Potter gets his way? And I'm deported?"

"That won't happen."

"How can you be so sure?"

"Because any immigration bureaucrat who even tries to deport you is going to have to go through me, first."

He winked. "Come on, sweetheart. Let's go break the happy news of your marriage to the weasel. Then we can deposit that cashier's check from the casino in your bank account."

Sasha reminded herself that this was America, the land of promise and limitless possibilities. As she left the apartment with her new husband, she felt almost confident.

Unfortunately, that feeling was not to last long.

Sasha was not surprised when they were kept waiting. This was, after all, standard operating procedure for her nemesis. Mitch, however, did not bother to conceal his growing impatience.

"I don't get it," he growled as they waited on the hard plastic chairs in the overcrowded waiting room. "Our appointment was two hours ago. We haven't seen anyone else go in there. So what the hell is the guy doing? Pulling wings off flies?"

"He is a government employee," Sasha explained for the umpteenth time. Having experienced a lifetime of Russian bureaucratic red tape, she was more able to take the immigration officer's stalling tactics in stride.

"So am I," Mitch noted pointedly as he popped two more aspirin into his mouth and swallowed them dry. "But

I wonder how Potter would like it if his damn house caught fire and I showed up two hours late to put it out.''

''That is different.''

''It shouldn't be.''

She thought about that. ''I suppose you're right. But it doesn't change things.'' All too aware of the aggravation surrounding Mitch like a red-hot aura, she said, ''You won't say anything that will make him angry?''

''Nah.'' Her relief was short-lived. ''I think I'll just punch his lights out.''

''Mitch!''

The absolute terror in her wide eyes could not be feigned. Realizing how seriously she was taking this, Mitch instantly regretted his flippant tone.

''Sasha. Sweetheart. I was just joking.'' He patted her hand just as the office door opened.

''Mr. Potter can see you now, Ms. Mikhailova,'' the secretary, clad in a severely cut gray suit that did nothing for her scrawny figure, announced. Her expression, beneath the sixties beehive was grim.

''It's about time. And the name is Mrs. Cudahy,'' he said as they walked past the woman. ''You might want to make a note of that in your records.''

It was not, Mitch discovered, going to be easy. Although he'd not doubted Glory's statement about immigration cracking down on arranged marriages, neither had he expected to be treated like Public Enemy Number One.

From the moment he learned of their hasty marriage, Potter didn't mince words. ''If you think this is going to forestall deportation proceedings against you, Ms. Mikhailova—''

''Cudahy,'' Mitch broke in.

''Excuse me?''

''Sasha's name is Mrs. Cudahy now.''

"Yes." He pinched his thin lips together, making them practically disappear. "The timing of the marriage is quite convenient. Considering that Ms. Mik—"

"Cudahy," Mitch reminded him.

Potter gave him a long look, then shrugged, as if deciding he could afford to concede this point. After all, he had the power of the United States government behind him. What chance did these two have?

"It strikes me as very suspicious," he continued stiffly, "that Mrs. Cudahy—" he glanced at Mitch, who nodded his satisfaction "—did not mention your engagement at Friday's appointment."

"That's simple." Mitch took Sasha's cold hand in his, lacing their fingers together in an easy, familiar husbandly gesture. "She didn't know I was going to propose."

"Do you really expect me to believe that you coincidentally popped the question at the same time the government was preparing to deport your wife, Mr. Cudahy?"

Although Mitch had been insisting to everyone—including himself—that this was not a real marriage, the way the squinty-eyed little weasel had heaped an extra helping of scorn on the word "wife" made his temper flare.

Reminding himself that leaning over the spotless metal desk and planting his fist in the jerk's supercilious face would not help Sasha's cause, he reined in his anger.

"I'm not going to lie to you," he said, deciding to go with a half-truth. "Sasha's meeting with you did have something to do with my asking her to marry me." When Sasha's hand turned even icier, he squeezed it reassuringly.

"Aha!" Potter looked as if he'd just won the lottery. Once again Mitch was tempted to punch him. Once again he managed, just barely, to resist.

"It was when I realized that I could actually lose her—"

he gave Sasha a fond, loving look ''—that I realized I loved her. And wanted us to spend the rest of our lives together.''

''That's a lovely story, Mr. Cudahy. Unfortunately, it's not the least bit original.'' Potter took an ominous stack of forms from the filing cabinet behind the desk. ''In light of your new status, I'll need to interview you separately.''

''What kind of interview?'' Mitch asked. He'd figured that he'd put on the blue suit he'd bought to wear to his sister's wedding, go downtown with Sasha, explain he was her husband and walk out with her new green card in hand. An interview with the weasel hadn't been in the plan.

''For starters, we need to ensure that you're actually living together.''

''Of course we are. We're married.''

''Yes. So you say.'' Skepticism dripped from the acid tone. ''Well, your wife will have to wait in the outer office. I'll question you first. Then it will be Mrs. Cudahy's turn.''

Listening to the thick disbelief in the man's voice, Mitch thought that he should have just knocked the guy through his office window while he'd had the chance.

As Sasha prepared to leave the room, her lovely face more miserable than he'd ever seen it, Mitch took her chin between his fingers. ''It's going to be okay,'' he assured her quietly. Then he captured her lips in a quick kiss.

''Sorry about that,'' he told a frowning Potter, ''I couldn't help myself. You know how newlyweds are.'' With a rakish wink, he walked Sasha the few feet to the closed door, then gave her a proprietary, husbandly pat on the rear.

Sasha's head was still reeling as she sank down onto one of the chairs in the waiting room. A baby being bounced on the lap of a woman next to her screamed its discontent and nearby a husband and wife squabbled loudly. But still stunned by Mitch's hot kiss, Sasha didn't notice them.

When it was finally her turn, Sasha tried her best to answer the questions, but there were so many, and they were so intimate! Thanks to her conversations with Jake, she managed to correctly name Mitch's mother and sister and new baby niece. And from his dinner orders for the firehouse, she knew he preferred ribs over chicken, and steak to everything else. He didn't like apple pie, but warm cherry pie topped with vanilla ice cream was his favorite dessert.

These things she knew. Almost everything else—including his favorite television programs and the last book he'd read—drew a blank.

"Why don't you go on down and wait for me in the car, sweetheart?" Mitch suggested when she was finally allowed to escape the inquisition. She was as pale as a wraith. "I have something I need to do. It won't take long."

There was something in his tone, something unsettling. A dark and dangerous edge she'd never heard before. Quite honestly, it frightened her.

"Mitch?"

He ran his hand down her hair. "Don't you worry that pretty little head about a thing," he said loud enough for the avidly watching secretary to hear. "Everything's going to be okay."

Sasha, too, was aware of the secretary's interest. Not wanting to do anything that might get reported back to her enemy, she sighed, nodded, then left the office.

Mitch waited until he heard the ding of the elevator door opening. Then he marched back into Potter's office.

The immigration officer was making notations in a manila file even thicker than Sasha's. From the satisfied smirk on his face, Mitch decided the bastard must be ruining someone else's life.

He glanced up and frowned at Mitch. "I believe our interview was over, Mr. Cudahy."

"That's what you think." Mitch put both hands on the black metal desk and glared down at the man, mayhem threatening in his stance and his eyes. "I want you to listen to me, Potter. And I want you to listen good."

"What you want is none of my concern."

"Now that's where you're wrong."

Potter took one look at the thundercloud on Mitch's face and reached for the phone. "I'm going to call security."

Mitch snatched the receiver out of the man's hand. "If you don't want to end up picking your teeth off the floor, I'd suggest you listen to what I have to say."

"Are you threatening me?"

"You bet your wingtips I am." Mitch hung up the phone. "The same way you threatened my wife."

"That Russian émigré is not your wife."

"Now there you go," Mitch said with an exaggerated sigh, "questioning my veracity again. I don't really give a flying fig what you think, Potter, because I happen to have a piece of paper stating that according to the laws of Nevada—and the United States of America—Sasha is my lawfully wedded wife. My spouse. My woman. And call me oversensitive, but I don't like autocratic little jerks who make my woman cry." His fingers curled around the wrinkled brown tie as he pulled Potter toward him across the top of the desk. "If you ever so much as look crossways at Sasha again, you'll have to answer to me. And believe me, it won't be an enjoyable experience."

Potter's Adam's apple bobbed as he swallowed. "It's against the law to threaten a federal government official," he said, his attempt at bluster belied by the sickly ash color of his face.

"It'll be your word against mine," Mitch reminded him.

"And who do you think the cops will believe? A squinty-eyed little weasel with yesterday's lunch on his tie? Or a genuine American hero?"

He released the tie and Potter fell back into his chair with a force that sent it rolling dangerously toward the window. Mitch was vaguely disappointed when it stopped a few inches away.

He left the office, pausing in the doorway. "Leave my wife alone."

As he took the elevator downstairs, Mitch was smiling.

Unfortunately his feeling of goodwill was short-lived. As he left the office building, he saw Sasha, not waiting in the car as he'd instructed, but standing on the sidewalk gazing into the window of the jewelry store next door.

At that same instant, a kid with baggy shorts, a purple-and-orange Phoenix Suns T-shirt and high-top sneakers grabbed her purse and took off running.

8

SASHA COULDN'T BELIEVE what was happening!

One minute she was soothing her jangled nerves by drinking in the lovely sight of diamonds and rubies in the jewelry store window. Then, in less time that it took to blink, her purse—with her valuable gambling winnings inside—had been ripped from her shoulder.

She cried out in dismay.

At the same time, she saw Mitch sprinting off after the thief.

The part of her that was desperate for the money that would help her find her father was immensely relieved that Mitch had appeared on the scene. Another, stronger part, feared he could get hurt.

Refusing to let him risk his life alone, she began running.

Mitch was proud of the way he'd kept himself fit. His work, after all, depended on his being in shape. He damned his suit and dress shoes, but vowed that there was no way this punk was going to get away with the crime.

The kid ran across the street, dodging between a city bus and a delivery truck. On his heels Mitch followed, ignoring the strident angry blast of the truck horn.

An elderly woman with pewter curls came out of a coffee shop. The thief pushed her aside, almost knocking her down, and kept running. Cursing, Mitch slowed to ensure that she was all right. He picked up her red pocketbook, handed it back to her, then rushed on.

Neither of them noticed Sasha, half a block behind, struggling to keep up.

Adrenaline was racing through Mitch's veins, pounding in his ears like the beat of a drum. He could hear his own labored breathing, feel the burning in his lungs.

The signal at the intersection said Don't Walk. The thief ignored it, shoved aside a city maintenance crew barricade, leapt over an open manhole and raced into traffic. Brakes squealed as Mitch followed.

By the time they cut across the basketball arena's outdoor courtyard, Mitch had gained on the thief. The kid might be younger, but as Mitch forced his legs to keep up their pistonlike motion, he reminded himself that he was a hero, dammit. Savior of women and children and kittens.

There was no way he was going to allow himself to be a failure in Sasha's eyes.

Even if he had to take on the entire immigration service.

Even if this ridiculous race gave him a frigging heart attack.

A bicyclist shot out of an alley between them. The purse snatcher put on an extra burst of speed just as Mitch slammed headlong into the bike, sending himself and the rider sprawling into the gutter.

His knee hit the ground with a painful cracking sound, then he skidded across the pavement, picking up gravel, making his palms feel as if they were suddenly on fire.

"Hey, man," the bicyclist complained, struggling to his feet, helmet askew, "what the hell do you think you're doing?"

"Sorry." Ignoring his aching knee and burning hands, Mitch pushed himself to his feet and took off running again.

Sasha, who'd waited impatiently at the red pedestrian signal was horrified when she saw Mitch crash into the bicycle. Her cry of alarm drew the attention of a passing motorcycle cop, who immediately pulled over to the curb.

"Something wrong, ma'am?"

"My husband!" She pointed toward Mitch. "He's trying to catch the thief who stole my handbag!"

The cop took one look at the situation, hit his siren and lights, gunned the motorcycle and took off, leaving her to watch helplessly as Mitch chased the teenager across the Civic Center plaza. Just as he reached out again, the kid put on another burst of speed.

"Dammit! That's enough!" With a low flying tackle, Mitch managed to pull the purse snatcher down.

Sasha's heart caught in her throat as she watched Mitch become airborne. He and the thief careened into the fountain and began splashing around, throwing punches while water poured down on them as if from a cloudburst.

Seconds later, the cop caught up with them.

By the time Sasha arrived on the scene, the perpetrator had been handed over to the cop. Mitch was bent over, his hands on his knees, his breathing labored. He was also soaked to the skin.

"Mitch!" She flung herself at him, almost knocking them both over in her enthusiasm. "Are you all right?"

He caught her around the waist, steadying her as he steadied himself. "I'm…fine." He dragged in a huge draft of air as he handed her the purse. "I saved…your money."

"The money is not important. Not compared to you!" She'd never made a more truthful statement. "When I saw you fall…"

"It wasn't anything." He drew in another breath that didn't hurt nearly as badly, making him think he might live, after all.

"You could have been hurt," she scolded. Now that she

was no longer terrified, Sasha was angry. "Such reckless, dangerous behavior should be left to the police."

After what he'd just been through for her, Sasha's criticism stung. "In case you didn't notice, sweetheart, there weren't any police around when you decided to go window shopping with every cent to your name in your purse so every gangbanger and crook in the city could steal it!"

"I was waiting for you!"

"I told you to wait in the damn car," Mitch shouted. He dragged his hand through his wet hair in frustration and cursed the flaw that had made him chase the kid in the first place. It wasn't his job. The cops didn't fight fires—so why should he fight crime?

"Oh, Mitch!" Sasha's temper deflated like air leaving a balloon as she observed the blood smear on his temple. "You have hurt yourself." She grabbed hold of his hand and turned it over, gasping as she viewed the asphalt imbedded in his skin.

"I told you, it's nothing. A little soap and water and I'll be fine."

"Excuse me, ma'am." A third voice entered the conversation.

Sasha turned toward the motorcycle officer. The thief, she noticed, was now in the custody of a second policeman who'd been cruising by in his patrol car.

"I assume you and your husband want to press charges."

"Yes," Mitch said.

"No," Sasha said at the same time.

"What?" Mitch stared at her, unable to believe what he was hearing. "After I nearly break my neck—"

"You said it was only a little fall," she reminded him.

"After I nearly break my neck," he repeated from between clenched teeth, "chasing the little creep, what do you mean, you're not going to press charges?"

"It's not necessary," she insisted.

"The hell it isn't." He turned to the cop who was looking bored, as if he'd heard all this before. "If she doesn't want to file a complaint, I will."

"Mitch!" Sasha frowned at him, then forced a shaky smile at the policeman. "Will you excuse us, please? I would like to speak with my husband."

The cop shrugged as he pulled his leather gloves back on. "Make it quick. We can't stand around here all day."

Mitch took her arm and pulled her a few feet away. "Okay. Shoot."

"Shoot?" She glanced nervously back at the 9 mm pistol the patrolman was wearing.

"Talk to me."

"Oh." Relieved, she said, "If we press charges, we'll have to go to the police station. And sign papers, yes?"

"Sure." It was Mitch's turn to shrug. "So?"

"So, then I'll have a police file. And I'll be automatically deported."

Comprehension flickered. "Sasha, you won't have a record, the kid will. Hell, he probably already does. You'll be doing society a favor if you get him put away. Or would you rather have him steal someone else's purse? Like that little old lady he nearly knocked down?"

She knew he was right. But still…

"In Russia, having the police know your name is not such a good thing," she argued weakly.

With that single statement, she made all the news reports and magazine articles he'd read about life behind the former Iron Curtain come crashing home.

She looked so serious, so distressed, Mitch had a sudden urge to take her in his arms and kiss that worried frown off her face. Instead he reached out and touched her cheek with a roughened fingertip.

"This isn't Russia, sweetheart. In America you're considered a good citizen for reporting a crime."

"I have seen such things on 'Crime Stoppers,'" she admitted hesitantly. "And 'America's Most Wanted,' but—"

"But nothing. We'll go to the station, press charges, then take your money to the bank. Before anything else happens."

He could practically see the wheels turning in her head as she looked over at the waiting patrolman. "I suppose it is the right thing to do."

"Of course it is." He rewarded her with the warm smile that she knew would continue to have the power to thrill her long after this mock marriage had ended. "You've got to learn to trust your husband, Sasha."

"I do." Even though she knew he was joking, the idea was a pleasant one. It continued to comfort her during their time in the police station. And while they deposited the gambling check in her meager savings account.

"I'm so sorry about your suit," she murmured as they drove back to the apartment.

Mitch shrugged off her concern. "I don't have that many occasions to wear one, anyway."

"But you looked so handsome in it. I suppose the cleaner could dry it, but I'm afraid your trousers are ruined."

He glanced down at the long tear over his knee. "Next time, I'll have to remember to just run the perp down with my Batmobile."

Sasha smiled at the image. "You are talking about Batman, right? The American movie superhero."

He smiled back. "Got it on the first try."

Not wanting to embarrass him, Sasha refrained from adding that she considered Mitch her very personal superhero.

A comfortable silence settled over them. Mitch was the

first to break it. "I think we did okay with Potter. Though I sure wasn't expecting a pop quiz."

"Neither was I." Sasha's tone turned gloomy at the memory.

"I felt like a contestant on 'The Newlywed Game.' With a lot more at stake than a side-by-side refrigerator. At least I could answer what side of the bed each of us sleeps on."

"I sleep on the right side," she said promptly. "You sleep on the left."

"That's what I said," he agreed.

She exhaled a sigh of relief. "So, we got one right."

"How about favorite movie?" Mitch asked.

"That's easy." Despite the seriousness of their situation, Sasha grinned.

"Honeymoon in Vegas," they both said together.

"Favorite song?" Mitch asked.

"'Blue Hawaii.'" It hadn't been. But after last night's dream…

"Three for three," Mitch said as he stopped for a red light. "We're on a roll." It was then he made the mistake of glancing over at her. Their eyes held, each remembering the sensual dream. And their slumberous response to it. "I guess we didn't do so badly, after all."

"I guess not." Her voice was soft and throaty and strummed innumerable emotional chords. "At least we managed to stall the final decision until Mr. Donald O. Potter's home visit."

"Won't that just be a barrel of laughs." Mitch would rather invite Ghengis Khan to the apartment than let Potter cross his threshold. He idly considered digging a moat and filling it with bureaucrat-eating alligators.

"I don't suppose we could bar the doors and windows and pour boiling oil down on him?" Sasha suggested.

Mitch laughed. Pleased they were thinking along the

same lines, he reached out and ruffled her hair in a casual, friendly gesture. "Sweetheart, I do like your style."

The light turned green. But the mood had been lightened enough that Mitch regained his confidence about pulling off the marriage charade.

Working together, they could fool Potter. And any other obnoxious bureaucrats the government might send their way. But as he approached the apartment building and viewed the familiar car parked at the curb, he realized that he and Sasha were about to undergo a test far more rigid than anything the United States government could come up with.

"What's wrong?" she asked, hearing his muttered curse.

"Better brace yourself, Sasha, darlin'," Mitch said with a long sigh as he pulled into his parking space, "because you're about to meet your new mother-in-law."

The moment she saw Margaret Cudahy, Sasha knew where Mitch had gotten his good looks.

Vivid blue eyes that were twins of her son's swept over him, from the top of his wet head down to his soaked shoes. "Mitchel Cudahy, what on earth have you gotten into now?"

"It's a long story. And not very interesting."

"That's what you said while the ER nurse was pulling cactus needles out of your rear end last week," she retorted. "Lord, if it weren't for Lady Clairol, my hair would be as white as snow. However, you may be right. I'm probably better off not knowing."

She shook her head with maternal chagrin, then changed the subject. "I was about to scold you for eloping without telling your mother. However—" she gave Sasha a genuine warm smile and a quick hug "—I'm so happy to have a new daughter that I can't work up all that much irritation."

"Mom, this is Sasha." To Sasha's surprise, her all-

American hero began shuffling his foot in the pile of the carpet. "Sasha, this is my mother."

"Hello, Mrs. Cudahy," Sasha said. She began to extend her hand, but decided the gesture was too formal after that hug. "It is nice to meet you."

"It's a delight to meet you, Sasha." Her warm smile seconded her words. "And please, you must call me Margaret. Or, perhaps when we become closer, you might want to call me Mom."

It was, Sasha thought, a wonderfully American word. "I think I would like that."

Her mother's death had left a terrible void in her life. And although she knew that getting emotionally close to this open-hearted woman would be a huge mistake, Sasha found the idea of friendship with Mitch's mother undeniably appealing.

"So would I." The smile flashed again, warmer and wider, revealing a dimple high on Margaret's tanned cheek. "Jake has told me so many wonderful things about you, dear."

"Jake is a very nice man."

"He is, isn't he?" Margaret nodded. "He's been a wonderful husband to Katie." She smiled at Mitch. "It seems both my children have married well."

Mitch felt as if he'd just stepped into quicksand and was in danger of getting sucked in up to his neck. "That's probably because you and Pop set such a good example," he said, cringing inwardly as he wondered what his mother would say when she discovered the details of his marriage to Sasha.

"Your father was a wonderful husband," Margaret said. Her blue eyes became reminiscent. "It's too bad you didn't have a chance to meet him, Sasha. He would have been so happy to see his son happily married."

"He was a fireman, yes?" Sasha remembered Jake having mentioned that.

"That's right. We met after he was brought into the hospital for smoke inhalation." She sighed. "Although I could barely see his face through all the soot, it was love at first sight."

"I didn't know you were a nurse," Sasha said.

"I've worked the past thirty-three years in the emergency room at St. Joseph's," Margaret revealed proudly. "These days, of course, it's been upgraded to a trauma center."

Sasha liked knowing that she and Margaret had something in common besides Mitch. "I was a surgical nurse. In Russia," she revealed.

"I didn't know that." Mitch looked at Sasha with surprise. He'd assumed she'd waited tables in her native country.

Margaret's intelligent eyes narrowed at her son's unexpected comment. Sasha and Mitch both breathed a sigh of relief when she did not comment. "How are your licensing efforts coming along?" she asked Sasha.

"It's been difficult, because I've been moving around so much."

"Yes." Margaret nodded. "Jake also told me about your father. I'm sorry you're having such a troublesome time."

"I won a great deal of money while we were in Laughlin. Enough to hire a new detective."

"Well, isn't that lucky? And what a good omen for your marriage." She smiled at Mitch, who felt the guilty color rising from his collar.

"Meanwhile, why don't I see what I can do about getting you enrolled in a licensing school? I belong to several professional groups. I'm sure we can facilitate getting your papers processed. In fact, classes are beginning next week, I believe."

Mitch's mother's words made Sasha's heart soar. To be doing what she loved again, to be caring for people and helping them get well, was a glorious prospect!

"That would be very nice of you. But I wouldn't want to take advantage—"

"Nonsense, dear," Margaret said with that same brisk, cheerful attitude that made her such an excellent charge nurse, "that's what family's for."

Feeling horribly guilty about the charade they were perpetuating on this warmhearted woman, Sasha looked away. When her gaze met Mitch's, she could tell she was not the only one experiencing more than a twinge of conscience.

"Did you stop by for a reason, Mom?" Mitch asked as silence settled over the trio.

"Well, of course I wanted to meet your bride. And to invite you both to dinner Friday night. I'd dearly love to have you sooner, but there's been an outbreak of flu among the staff, so I'm working double shifts the next couple of days."

If there was one thing Mitch didn't want to do it was spend an entire evening being cross-examined by his mother. As much as he dearly loved her, Margaret Katherine Cudahy could be like a pit bull terrier with a bone. She'd want to know everything about Sasha and his courtship. And since he wasn't prepared to tell her the unvarnished truth, Mitch decided avoiding the issue was the prudent thing to do.

"Sorry, but I'm due back at work tomorrow. Which means I'll be on duty until midnight Friday night."

"You're returning to work so soon?" Margaret arched a chestnut brow. "I suppose I can understand your elopement," she said in a tone that suggested just the opposite, "but surely you're planning to take some sort of honeymoon? Something longer than a single night in Laughlin."

"Of course," Mitch said quickly.

Too quickly, he realized an instant later as his mother gave him one of those pointed looks he remembered too well from childhood: an omniscient mother stare that made a guy realize he'd never get away with a thing—no matter how old he might be.

"But everything was so unexpected, there wasn't time to rearrange the schedule."

"I suppose that makes sense."

"It's true," Mitch and Sasha said at the same time. They exchanged faint, conspiratory smiles, acknowledging that once again they were on the same wavelength. A smile that did not go unnoticed by the third member of the family.

"Well, all the more reason for Sasha to come to dinner," Margaret decided briskly. "You can't leave your bride all alone so soon after the wedding, Mitchel. In fact, a wonderful idea just occurred to me."

Mitch realized that he was not the only liar in the Cudahy family. His mother was one of those people who never began a day without a detailed list. Although she could shift gears with the best of them in her beloved ER, it was not like her to make a suggestion off the top of her head.

"What idea is that, Mom?"

"Katie and I can throw Sasha a bridal shower Friday night."

"A shower?" Mitch and Sasha asked at the same time. Her expression displayed a lack of understanding; his revealed something close to horror.

"It's a party most girls get before their wedding," Margaret explained to Sasha. "But by rushing you off to Laughlin, Mitch cheated you out of a traditional American experience. So, what time do you get off work?"

Sasha ignored the vibrations radiating from Mitch, who she realized wanted her to reject the idea. But his mother was so nice, and it had been so long since she'd been to any kind of party, she said, "I always work until closing on Friday. Which is usually a little after ten o'clock."

"Fine. Fortunately, Katie's baby is still at the age she's able to sleep anytime, anywhere." She walked toward the door, then turned and looked thoughtfully at Sasha. "It will be late in the evening when you finish work and I live quite a distance from the diner. Perhaps it would be more convenient for you if we have the shower here?" She looked questioningly at Mitch and Sasha, but did not wait for an answer.

"It's settled, then." She rubbed her hands with satisfaction. "We'll take care of all the preparations, dear, so all you have to do is show up. And have a good time."

9

THE PHONE RANG just as his mother left the apartment. It seemed one of the crew had called in sick, Mitch told Sasha. He was needed as a replacement.

Although she smiled and pretended to understand, she could not miss his relief at having an excuse to escape. A little afraid that he'd lied to spare her feelings, that he was really intending to visit his lover, Sasha sighed and reminded herself that she'd gone into this relationship with her eyes wide open.

Trying to make herself useful, she decided to do the wash. Mitch had told her that he sent his laundry out, something she considered a terrible waste. "Besides," she told herself as she gathered up the soiled clothes from the bathroom hamper and put them in the laundry bag, "if I save him money and show him how useful I can be, perhaps he will not regret his decision so much."

Sasha found the apartment complex laundry room without any trouble. She poured in the detergent and, following instructions, started the washing machine.

Afraid to leave the clothes unguarded, she sat in the uncomfortable plastic chair, pleased to discover someone had left behind a glossy woman's magazine. She picked it up and immediately became immersed in the joys of cooking for the man you love.

It wasn't until she realized that her feet were wet that Sasha looked up from the pages of the magazine.

"Oh, no!"

She jumped up, staring at the machine that was belching soapsuds. It looked like an erupting volcano spewing foamy white lava. When she opened the lid to peer inside, more suds drooled thickly over the porcelain rim, down the sides and over the floor. Slamming it shut, Sasha felt a surge of panic.

She yanked the plug, stopping the machine in mid cycle. Then, slowly, tentatively, peeked beneath the lid again.

"Hello?" a woman's voice called from the door of the laundry room. "Is anyone in there?" Sasha heard the sound of high heels tapping on the vinyl floor, then a surprised gasp.

"Good heavens," Meredith Roberts exclaimed. "What on earth happened?"

"I was doing a wash," Sasha inwardly groaned at the idea of Mitch's lover—former lover, she hoped—catching her in such an undignified situation. "I don't understand what went wrong…"

"Well, here's your problem." Meredith picked up the box of detergent. "It's super-concentrated. You used too much."

"Oh." Sasha's spirits sagged. "I didn't know."

Meredith shrugged shoulders clad in an expensive and very stylish fuchsia and turquoise silk jacket. "I imagine things are a bit different in Russia."

"How do you know I'm Russian?"

"Well, even if Mitch hadn't told me all about you, your accent is a sure giveaway. You sound just like Natasha."

It was the same thing Ben Houston had told her. "That's a cartoon, right?"

"A very good one," Meredith agreed. "Although I'm not certain you'd find it all that flattering. I'm Meredith Roberts, by the way."

"I know. I've seen you on television. And in the diner."

"After the fire," Meredith agreed. "I remember wanting to interview you, but the owner didn't want the negative publicity."

"She was trying to protect me. Since I'm the one who started the fire."

"I got the impression that's what she was doing." Meredith surprised Sasha by taking off her pumps and stockings and wading barefoot through the suds. "Let's get your wash into another machine to finish it," she suggested. "Then I'd like to talk with you for a while."

Worried that Meredith was going to demand her right to Mitch's attention, Sasha didn't answer, but watched unhappily as the chic woman opened the washer.

"Uh-oh."

"What now?"

"I don't recall Mitch owning pink underwear."

Sasha viewed the bright pink cotton briefs Meredith was holding up—briefs that had been white when she'd put them into the washer—then groaned as she sank down onto the chair again.

"I must have accidently mixed my red blouse in with the whites. Mitch will be furious."

"It's no big deal." Meredith sat down beside her. "Just buy him some more. He'll never know."

"I do not want to lie to my husband. A marriage should be based on honesty."

Meredith gave her a puzzled look. "Mitch told me this marriage was a green card scam."

"Mitch has talked with you? About our marriage?"

"Of course. He came by my place to explain the situation the day you two got back from your little trip to Laughlin." When she realized that her words seemed to cause

Sasha even more misery, she sighed. "Oh, hell." She gave
Sasha a long look. "You're in love with him, aren't you?"

Sasha opened her mouth to lie, but she couldn't. Not
about this. "Yes," she admitted.

"Well." Meredith reached into her purse, pulled out a
pack of cigarettes and, ignoring the No Smoking sign on
the wall, lit up. "Imagine that."

Since she had no answer to that enigmatic statement,
Sasha said nothing.

"You know, that explains a lot," Meredith said finally.

"What do you mean?"

"He seemed edgy after your elopement."

"I imagine it was difficult for him. Explaining why he
hadn't told you his plans ahead of time."

"Mitch and I never had any claims on one another,"
Meredith assured her. "I was surprised, but not particularly
upset. Although he seemed to be."

Sasha had to ask. "Perhaps he loves you?"

Meredith laughed at that. "Honey, what Mitch and I
shared had absolutely nothing to do with love." Realizing
what she'd said, and to whom, her grin was replaced by a
frown. "I'm sorry. I was out of line."

"No." It was Sasha's turn to smile. "To be truthful, I'm
relieved to hear that the relationship between you and Mitch
wasn't serious." She sighed. "Unfortunately, that doesn't
mean his relationship with me is."

Meredith exhaled a long stream of blue smoke. "I
wouldn't bet on that."

"I am not the kind of wife a man like Mitch needs."

The newswoman lifted a brow. "And what kind is that?"

"A woman who knows how to cook his meals. A woman
who would not turn his underwear pink."

This time Meredith's laugh was loud and long. "Sweetheart," she said, tossing the word off with the same casu-

alness Mitch was accustomed to using, "the domestic goddess route of catching a husband went out of style the day men discovered sex."

She stubbed out the cigarette in a foam cup left behind by an earlier visitor to the laundry room, crossed her legs, and said, "Let's talk about your search for your father. There's no telling how much help some free publicity might be. Then we can discuss ways to save your marriage."

If anyone had told her she'd been seeking romance advice from her husband's lover, Sasha would have said they were crazy. Yet somehow it seemed strangely right.

Reminding herself that her marriage had been unconventional from the start, she sat back in the chair, ignored the melting soapsuds and began to talk.

"YOU KNOW, HONEY, you didn't have to come into work today," Glory said when Sasha arrived at the diner that afternoon.

"I'm grateful to have something to occupy my mind."

"Having second thoughts, are you?"

Sasha thought about her father; about how far she'd already come; about how she refused to return to Russia without at least having met this man who'd contributed half of everything she was. And so much of what her children someday would be.

"Mitch was right. Marriage was the only practical solution to my problem."

"It's not going to be easy," the older woman warned.

"Convincing Mr. Donald O. Potter that our marriage is real?"

"No." Glory's eyes warmed with sympathy. "Convincing yourself that it isn't."

As usual, Glory was right.

Trusting her friend's judgment, Sasha showed the cook

a recipe from the laundry room magazine and explained her plan to win him over with gourmet fare.

"I don't know," Glory muttered as she studied the instructions for flambéing chicken breasts with warmed apricot brandy. "Mitch has always been pretty much a steak-and-potatoes man from what I can tell."

"But this dinner looked very good in the pictures."

"I'm sure it did. But in case you've forgotten, honey, you weren't exactly born with a white thumb. Last time you tried frying a few pieces of bacon, you managed to set my kitchen on fire."

"There isn't any bacon in this recipe."

"Well, that may be, but believe me, Sasha, a woman with all you've got going for you doesn't have to worry about slaving away in the kitchen. Not when your husband would rather have you in the bedroom."

Sasha blushed as her friend and employer unknowingly echoed Meredith Roberts's words. "That is too easy, for Mitch. He doesn't have any trouble getting women into his bed. I want to show him I have more to offer."

"I'm still not sure it's a good plan," Glory said worriedly. "How about I help out and cook it for you?"

"That would be cheating. I want to do it myself."

Glory shook her head. "Since it doesn't look as if I can change your mind, why don't you go on home right now? Then you can surprise Mitch with your fancy dinner at the station."

"But you need me for the dinner shift."

"No problem. You know my niece Amber?"

"The one who was in here last week to talk with you? The pretty one who just graduated from high school?"

"That's her. She's putting herself through college and can always use a few extra bucks. I'll call and have her

come down to fill in for you.'' The older woman gave
Sasha a hug. ''Now, scoot.''

Sasha returned to the apartment loaded down with plastic
grocery bags. Although her shallots and mushrooms did not
end up possessing the same geometric perfection as the
magazine photographs, Sasha was relieved when she managed to get them cut into pieces without slicing off a finger.

She browned them in the extra-virgin olive oil, as instructed, keeping the heat turned low.

So far, so good.

She was transferring the mushrooms and shallots from
the frying pan to a plate for safekeeping, when the mixture,
helped along by its oil coating, slid off the plate onto the
floor.

''Damn.'' Sasha cursed first in Russian, then English.

Glancing around, as if looking for spies, she picked up
the spilled pieces and put them back on the plate. After all,
the floor was clean. And she didn't want to return to the
store where she would be faced with another dizzying array
of American consumer goods.

Although her boned chicken breasts did not look anything like the perfect, almost heart-shaped ones depicted in
the magazine, she managed to cook them to a lovely golden
brown shade without any further problems. Meanwhile, she
had the brandy warming in a saucepan on a nearby burner,
just as instructed.

After returning the mushrooms and shallots to the cop-
per-bottomed frying pan, she poured the heated apricot
brandy over the mixture, struck a match and lit it.

There was a roar, sounding like a rushing wind, and an
explosion. Sasha cried out as blue flames shot up to the
ceiling, engulfing the frying pan and its carefully prepared
contents.

MITCH WAS IN the station exercise room, punching the lights out of the canvas weight bag he imagined as Donald O. Potter's face when the shrill sound of the alarm shattered the lazy afternoon silence.

As the familiar adrenaline shot through him, he yanked off the padded leather gloves and raced toward the truck, pulling on his protective gear as he ran.

Emergency lights flashing, the truck tore through the streets, dodging traffic, slowing at intersections, picking up speed to career around corners. Despite the seriousness of his work, riding on the back of the truck, leaning into the curves, the siren blaring in his ears, was a high that always left Mitch grinning.

By the time the red truck pulled up in front of his apartment building, Mitch was no longer smiling. When he realized that the smoke was pouring out the window of his apartment, his blood chilled.

"Dammit!" he shouted to Jake as he jumped down from the truck. "Sasha could be in there!"

Before anyone could remind him that he was going against procedure, he ran up the outside stairs, his heart pounding in his throat, terrified at what horror might await him.

Whatever he'd been expecting, it was definitely not what he found.

Sasha was standing in the middle of the small kitchen. Everything around her—the cupboards, the countertops, the floor, as well as herself—was covered with foam. The ceiling was charred, though most of the smoke had dissipated. She was frozen, like a marble statue, the large red fire extinguisher still held out in front of her like a shield.

"Sasha?" Lingering fear made his voice little more than a croak. "What the hell happened here?"

"Mitch?" She turned toward him, her face as white as

the foam, her wide brown eyes dominating her pale face. "Oh, Mitch!"

Relieved to see him, looking wonderfully like that glorious hero she'd first fallen in love with, Sasha dropped the extinguisher and hurled herself into his arms.

"I was s-so frightened! It happened so fast. One minute everything was fine, then the next minute, wh-whoosh! And then the room filled up with smoke and the smoke d-detector started blaring and I didn't know what to do, so I called 911, because I was afraid I was going to b-burn down the building.

"But then I remembered the fire extinguisher beneath the sink and I tried to spray it on the pan, but it was very hard to hold steady with all that foam spraying out of it, and now I've made the most horrible mess of your lovely clean kitchen!" She finished on a wail.

If she hadn't been so damn upset, Mitch would have laughed. He rubbed away some dissolving foam so he could press his lips against her temple. "You know, sweetheart, we really have to stop meeting like this."

In answer, she wrapped her arms around him tighter and buried her face in his heavy coat. From the way her shoulders were shaking, and the strangled sounds she was making, Mitch realized that his words, which had been meant as a joke, had instead made her cry.

"Honey, I'm sorry. I didn't mean to hurt your feelings." He ran his hand, which suddenly felt too large and clumsy, down her foam-slick hair in an ineffectual attempt to soothe.

"Please don't cry," he begged as he felt her hitch in another of those deep, shuddering breaths. "It's going to be all right. I promise."

"Oh, Mitch." She lifted her face, which was streaked with soot and tears. "I truly am sorry." Her words dissolved on a breathless little giggle that amazed him. "I was trying to cook a dinner to bring to you. But instead my dinner brought you to me!"

She wiped at the moisture streaming down her blackened cheeks with the backs of her hands. "Do you have any idea how funny you looked, charging in to rescue me?"

It was a direct hit to his ego. Mitch was not accustomed to women laughing at him. But as he thought back on how he had played hotshot, leaving the rest of the crew and kicking in his own door, he could see the humor in their situation.

"Funny? I looked funny?" His smile took the objection from his words.

"Funny," she agreed. "But also very dashing."

"That's better." He put a palm against her cheek. "You are," he said with a deep, low chuckle, "the only woman I have ever known who uses a smoke alarm as a cooking timer."

Her laughter reminded him of sunshine. Champagne. Music. "I wanted to surprise you."

His chuckle deepened as he dove his hands into her hair and tilted her grinning smoke-stained face up to his. "Well, darlin', if that was your goal, you sure as hell succeeded."

They were both laughing as their lips met and clung.

"Sorry," Jake drawled as he entered the kitchen, "looks as if you two newlyweds don't need any help here."

Immersed in their blissful, smoky kiss, neither Mitch nor Sasha answered.

Neither did they notice the man who'd entered the kitchen behind Jake.

"What the hell is going on here?" the all-too-familiar voice demanded.

Sasha and Mitch turned, observed a rigidly angry Donald O. Potter standing amid the foam covering the floor, and burst out laughing.

10

AFTER MITCH HAD LEFT with the firemen, and Potter had returned to whatever rock he spent his time away from the office lurking beneath, Sasha got busy with buckets and mops and sponges and cleaned up the mess she'd made.

Although the task was not the least bit pleasant, she couldn't stop smiling. The sweet kiss she and Mitch had shared lingered in her mind and on her lips. Even Mr. Donald O. Potter's unexpected arrival could not dampen the happiness that lighthearted moment had instilled.

After muttering something about the government not having a policy about inviting firebugs into the country, Potter had stomped off in a snit. At the time, Mitch claimed he was undoubtedly angry about having stumbled into their lives at a particularly romantic moment. Now he'd have difficulty reporting back to his superiors that their marriage was a scam.

Which, of course, it was. But the more Sasha thought about it, the more she knew that they belonged together. She could make Mitch happy.

''So long as I do not burn down his house first,'' she amended as she stood beneath the streaming shower, washing the foam and soot down the drain.

By the time she finally crawled into bed, she was exhausted. Hugging Mitch's pillow, which carried his scent, she drifted off into a deep sleep resplendent with romantic dreams of her dashing husband.

ALTHOUGH SASHA'S BRIDAL shower might be after the fact, and the only guests were Mitch's mother and sister and Glory, who closed the diner early for the festivities—she'd never had a more wonderful time.

The conversation flowed easily and unsurprisingly centered mostly around men. As the night grew later and the champagne continued to flow, the stories grew more intimate and the jokes more bawdy, making Sasha feel as if she must be the only twenty-four-year-old virgin left in the world.

"Are you sure it was the right thing to do?" she asked Margaret for the umpteenth time that evening. "Agreeing to tell my story on television?"

"It couldn't hurt," Margaret assured her. "And who knows, perhaps someone who sees the newscast will know your father."

Since her quest had been fruitless so far, Sasha wasn't holding out a lot of hope for this latest effort. "I should have asked Mitch." Ever since Meredith had left with her cameraman, Sasha's doubts had grown like billowing smoke from a forest fire.

"I don't know how marriages work in Russia," Katie said, "but here in America, women don't need to get permission from their husbands for every little thing they do."

Sasha had liked Mitch's sister on first sight. Part of that, she realized, was due to the woman's striking resemblance to her brother, but mostly she liked her because she was warm and outgoing. And seemed genuinely interested in Sasha's dilemma.

"Appearing on television is more than a little thing," Sasha argued. Especially since…" Her worried voice drifted off as she realized she'd been about to reveal the status of their marriage.

"Especially since your marriage to my son is supposed

to be only one of convenience?'' Margaret asked, slanting her a sideways glance as she cut the white-tiered wedding cake Sasha had been deprived of by eloping.

Sasha could feel the damning color flooding into her face. ''You know about that?''

''It wasn't that difficult to figure out,'' Katie said. ''My brother has specialized in hit-and-run relationships since he was fifteen. Then he suddenly runs off and gets married to a woman who just happens to be embroiled in immigration problems. And we're expected to buy that story?''

''That's the same thing Mr. Donald O. Potter said,'' Sasha admitted. ''You must think I'm a terrible person to be part of such a deceitful scheme.''

''Of course we don't think you're a terrible person,'' Margaret said.

''But that may be because we also know something that hateful Mr. Potter doesn't,'' Katie added.

''What is that?''

''That Mitch is in love with you, of course,'' Margaret answered mildly.

If only that were true! Sasha sighed and decided she must be totally honest with this kindhearted woman. ''I am afraid you're mistaken.''

''Not according to Jake,'' Katie said, rising from the couch when the baby, Megan, started whimpering in the bedroom. ''He says he's never seen Mitch so distracted as he's been since you two got back from Laughlin.''

Sasha was surprised. And pleased. ''I distract Mitch?'' she asked when Katie returned with Mitch's two-month-old niece.

''I think his exact words were 'bothered and bewildered.''' Katie grinned as she unbuttoned her blouse and put her daughter to her breast.

As she watched the infant's rosebud mouth begin to

suckle, Sasha felt an unexpected maternal tug deep inside her.

"That's the same way I feel about Mitch."

"There, you see?" Margaret began passing out the pieces of cake. "You're made for each other. Because believe me, Sasha, my son has never let any woman get under his skin. Or into his heart, until you."

Sasha thought about that a moment. "He says it is just physical attraction."

"That's what he'd like to believe," Katie said with an amused laugh that shook her chest and made the baby complain for a moment. "And although I love my brother to pieces, for a bright guy, when it comes to love and romance, he's as dense as every other male on the planet. So, it's going to be up to you to prove him wrong."

The idea was enormously appealing. "How do I do that?"

"Seduce him," the other three women in the room said at the same time. They laughed at Sasha's expression, which was equal parts shock, embarrassment and interest.

"Mitch's father was a confirmed bachelor," Margaret revealed. "But the moment I met him, I knew he was the man for me. Poor Garrett didn't know what hit him." Mitch's mother's smile was warmly reminiscent. "We were married two weeks after we met."

"I tried the same thing with Jake," Katie said. "Of course, either he was more resistant than Pops, or I was more impatient. Because after three months, when he still hadn't caved in, I proposed to him."

"You asked Jake to marry you?"

Katie shrugged off Sasha's incredulous response. "I loved him. He loved me. Marriage seemed the next logical step."

"My son may have gotten the order a bit reversed,

Sasha," Margaret allowed, "by getting married, then falling in love. But that doesn't change the fact that Mitch is in love with you, dear. Anyone can tell by the way he looks at you and by the way his voice changes when he talks to you. Or about you."

"And the way he threatened to beat up Jake for suggesting that any other man might want you," Katie added.

"Mitch threatened to hit Jake? Because of me?"

"After he mentioned wanting to personally murder a bunch of Shriners."

The idea was incredible. And wonderful.

"There is one problem," Sasha said reluctantly.

"What's that?" Margaret asked.

"I don't have any idea how to seduce a man. Especially one as experienced as Mitch."

"Don't worry about that," Katie said. "You've put yourself in the hands of experts."

"And the first thing any woman needs going into battle," Glory said with a deep, knowing chuckle as she handed Sasha the box wrapped in white paper embossed with silver bows, "is the appropriate artillery."

It seemed that all the women had had the same idea. Every one of the gifts were frothy bits of satin and lace designed to appeal to a man's sexual fantasies.

"I don't think I have the nerve to wear this," Sasha murmured, taking a sheer black lace catsuit from a layer of tissue paper wrapping.

"Sure you do," Katie assured her. "Just make certain you have a lot of protection handy. It's because of an outfit just like that one that Jake and I have Megan."

Once again Sasha blushed as the others laughed. Despite the raised voices, after being burped, little Megan fell back to sleep, happily satiated.

A short time later, a few minutes after midnight, a knock

came on the door. Sasha opened the door and was terrified to see a uniformed policeman standing there.

"Sorry, ma'am," he said, his stern expression reminding her of every policeman she'd ever feared back in Russia, "but we've received a complaint of noise coming from this apartment."

"I'm sorry," she managed to get out through lips that had gone as dry as dust. "We did not mean to be too loud. I promise we will be more quiet." Although the other day's encounter with the police had not been unpleasant she didn't think she would ever outgrow the instinctive fear such a uniform instilled.

"I'm afraid that's not good enough, ma'am," he said, stepping past her into the apartment. The others watched expectantly as he crossed the room to the stereo. Sasha was surprised when he turned the volume even louder.

She was flabbergasted when he suddenly ripped off his uniform, revealing an amazingly tanned and toned body clad only in a skimpy pair of underwear adorned with a gleaming badge in a most inappropriate place. As he began to gyrate his hips, the women—Margaret Cudahy included—roared at Sasha's shocked expression and began to clap in time to the driving beat of the music.

AT FIRST, a night on the town after his shift ended had seemed like a good idea. After all, Mitch assured himself, since Sasha was having her own party, she wouldn't be expecting him home anytime soon. Besides, the idea of facing his mother, sister and Glory—who'd be watching him like a wiggling bug stuck to a corkboard with a pin, to ensure he was treating his new bride properly—was enough to make him want to run off and join the French foreign legion the way Gary Cooper had in *Beau Geste,* which still showed up on late night cable every once in a while.

Even if his and Sasha's marriage wasn't real, a bachelor party was a time-honored American tradition. That being the case, who was he to deprive the guys at the firehouse of an opportunity to party?

The only problem, Mitch realized as he sat at a table at the French Cabaret—a Club for Gentlemen—nursing his first beer of the night was that he wasn't having a good time. The platinum-blond stripper lying on her back on the stage peeling black mesh stockings down her long, long legs was undeniably gorgeous. And her remarkable breast enhancement alone must have paid for some local plastic surgeon's new boat.

Although she was doing her best to entertain, with sultry looks, bold smiles and saucy tosses of her long spiral curls, he couldn't help thinking about how sexy Sasha had looked, sitting at the roulette table in that ridiculously short denim skirt. And how her breasts, beneath the virginal white cotton nightgown had felt so soft, so inviting.

The stripper's seductive smile didn't fade in the slightest when a drunk down at the end of the bar began shouting raucous suggestions as she dispensed with the second stocking. But when she stood up again, she moved a little bit closer to the table occupied by Mitch, Jake, and three other firemen from Ladder Company No. 13.

Unfortunately, when she leaned forward, meeting Mitch's eyes, and licked her glossy crimson lips with her tongue, it was Sasha's mouth Mitch immediately imagined tasting. It was Sasha's kiss he found himself fantasizing about yet again.

"Damn."

Jake shot him a look. "So, which is it? Are you regretting the fact that you shouldn't go home with the luscious

Miss April Luv? Or are you were wishing you were home with your bride?''

''She's not my bride,'' Mitch muttered as one of the fire fighters, rising to the sensual invitation in those heavily lashed, kohl-lined eyes, slipped a five dollar bill in the woman's sequined G-string. Mitch took a long pull on the brown beer bottle. ''Not really.''

Before Jake could argue, the stripper leaned down toward him. ''How about you, bachelor boy?'' she cooed, revealing that she'd overheard the earlier table conversation about the impromptu party. Although he'd like to think she found him irresistible, Mitch figured April Luv's real interest was that such occasions were undoubtedly good for a big tip.

She gave her silicone marvels an enthusiastic shimmy that sent her tassels swirling. ''How about your own private table dance?'' She was so close he could detect the faint odor of perspiration underlying the cloyingly sweet perfume. Her breasts were waving in his face like Old Glory on the Fourth of July. ''So you'll have something to remember when you've settled into safe, boring domesticity.''

As unpalatable as he found the idea of settling down, Mitch still found himself unmoved by Miss April's charms. He was just about to hand over the dough and forego the private attention, when the obnoxious drunk suddenly pushed his way between Mitch and the stripper to grab fistfuls of those voluptuous, offered breasts.

April Luv let loose with a stream of swear words that could have made a longshoreman blush. The drunk, angered by the invective tried to climb onto the stage while the stripper attempted to discourage him by stomping on his hairy-backed hands with her high heels.

Mitch quickly glanced around looking for the bouncer who'd been standing guard at the door when they'd arrived.

Unfortunately the muscle-bound giant was nowhere to be seen.

Which left Mitch no other choice. Acting on instinct, cursing ripely, he leapt up, tipping over his wooden chair, and threw himself onto the drunken assailant's back.

The cretin's buddies staggered to their feet, fists flailing, and naturally, the other members of Ladder Company No. 13 rose to the challenge.

It took less than thirty seconds for the attraction between the drunk, the stripper and Mitch to turn into a full-fledged brawl. By the time Mitch heard the familiar sound of sirens, four chairs had been broken, six noses bloodied and the drunk who had started all the fun lay on the floor below the stage, the victim of a well-placed punch, a shimmering tassel clutched in one fist.

11

MITCH ARRIVED HOME with a rapidly swelling eye, in a rotten mood from having had to talk his way out of being arrested. He was not at all pleased to discover Sasha handcuffed to a buffed-up guy with a tanning salon bronzed body who was the male equivalent of Miss April Luv.

Fortunately, his mother efficiently herded everyone from the apartment, leaving Mitch and Sasha alone.

"Well," Mitch said finally, "I guess your party, at least, was a success."

"I had a very good time." Her worried gaze swept over his face, lingering on the horrid discoloration circling his right eye. "It seems you did not."

"No." That, he decided, had to be the understatement of the year. "I didn't."

"Did you get hurt fighting a fire?"

"No." His answer was brusque, discouraging further discussion.

Sasha waited for Mitch to elaborate. When he didn't, she glanced down at his hands and said, "We must tend to your wounds."

Amazingly, the discomfort of facing his mother, sister and wife with the evidence of the brawl on his face and hands had made Mitch forget all about his scraped knuckles. "It's no big deal."

"Mitch." Her tone was soft, but surprisingly firm. "I am

a nurse. I'm also your wife. It is my duty to take care of your injuries.''

The issue settled as far as she was concerned, Sasha headed toward the bathroom where she'd seen a bottle of hydrogen peroxide in the medicine chest.

Mitch shrugged, then followed her. He leaned against the doorjamb and watched as she lined up the bottle, some soap and a stack of gauze squares with an intensity that suggested she was preparing to perform open heart surgery right on that faux marble countertop.

''I've never heard you talk like that.''

''Like what?''

''I don't know.'' He hesitated. ''Kind of bossy, I guess.''

''I'm sorry if you don't like it, but—''

''Actually, I think I do.''

''Really?''

''Yeah.'' The more he thought about it, the more he found this new aspect of Sasha's personality interesting. ''I guess I've been thinking of you as poor, beleaguered little Sasha for so long, I never considered the fact that you might have had a different sort of life in Russia.''

The portrait he painted was far from flattering. And regrettably true. Sasha decided that it was time she stopped behaving like a victim. She'd graduated at the head of her class and had been a highly respected surgical nurse. She'd overcome miles of red tape to come to this country. As nice as it was to have Mitch coming to her rescue every time she turned around, it was time for her to begin fighting her own battles.

''Different,'' she agreed mildly, ''but not necessarily better. Although I do miss nursing. Which is why I'll be very grateful to your mother for anything she can do to facilitate my licensing.'' She gestured toward the closed commode. ''Sit down and I'll take care of your cuts.''

"Yes, ma'am." With a ghost of a smile playing at the corners of his lips, Mitch did as instructed.

Briskly and efficiently she washed the scraped skin with soap, trying to ignore the scents of cigarette smoke, beer and perfume that clung to his hair and clothing.

"It's not what you think," he said, noticing the faint wrinkling of her nose.

"I wasn't thinking anything."

"Sure you were. You think I've been brawling in some bar."

"Were you?" Drunken behavior was nothing new to Sasha. Since many men in Russia suffered from alcoholism, she'd witnessed the dangers of such overindulgence when they showed up injured at the hospital.

"Not exactly."

"I see," she said mildly as she rinsed his right hand beneath the faucet.

Surprised she wasn't going to push him for an explanation, Mitch felt the need to explain anyway. "Some of the guys wanted to take me out for a bachelor party. Kind of a male version of your bridal shower."

"How nice for you." She rinsed the left hand.

"Well, it should have been. But there was this drunk and he was bothering Miss April Luv, and—"

"You rushed in to rescue her." Sasha reminded herself that it was only Mitch's nature. It didn't mean that he had any romantic feelings for the woman with the sensual name.

Besides, she wasn't all that innocent herself, she admitted, thinking about how attractive she'd found the sexy pretend policeman. Even if he didn't stir her blood the way Mitch could with a single glance, or a warm smile.

"Someone had to do it," Mitch said grumpily. "Unfortunately, the bouncer was outside having a heart-to-heart conversation with a couple of bikers.''

She had no idea what a bouncer was, did not know why he would feel the need to leave his post to talk with bicycle riders, but she did understand exactly how Mitch had received his injuries.

''She was fortunate you were there.''

''The lucky thing was that one of the responding cops was Jake's cousin,'' he muttered, ''or I'd be spending the night in jail.''

''Don't be silly. They do not put heroes in jail.''

He frowned as he remembered the stripper's enthusiastic kisses and her breathy declarations that he'd always be her knight in shining armor. ''Believe me, Sasha, there's nothing the least bit heroic about bar fights.''

''I believe Miss April Luv would see things differently.'' Sasha swabbed on the hydrogen peroxide with the sterile gauze.

''Does that hurt?'' she asked when Mitch flinched.

''Not at all,'' he lied.

Knowing he was not telling the truth, she lifted his hand and blew softly on the stinging wounds.

Her breath was as soft as thistledown, as warm as summer sunshine. And it stirred emotions that Mitch knew were better left alone. But he'd never been one to stick to the safe or prudent path in life.

''I lied,'' he admitted.

''I know. But that's all right, Mitch.'' She blew on the other hand. ''Many men have difficulty admitting to pain.''

''I'm not talking about that. Well, maybe I did fudge the truth a little about how my hands felt, but I was referring to what I said earlier. About only seeing you as beleaguered and all that.''

''Oh. You don't see me this way?''

"Actually, I do. I mean, I guess I did. But there was more I didn't say."

"Oh." She looked down at him. She saw the heat in his eyes, and with a shocked intake of breath tried to release his hand, but he stopped her by deftly lacing their fingers together.

"Don't you want to know what else I was thinking?" He lifted their joined hands to his lips and pressed a kiss against the inside of her wrist, causing her pulse to leap.

"Mitch…" Sasha was suddenly honestly afraid. Afraid of him. Afraid of herself. And terrified of having her heart broken.

Reminding herself of her new resolution to take charge of her life, she tried to tug her hand free. "I don't think this is a very good idea."

"What's wrong, Sasha?" His eyes were on hers as his wicked lips forged a fiery trail of sparks up her arm. "How can a husband telling his wife that he thinks she's about the sexiest, most desirable woman he's ever seen be a bad idea?"

Sexy? Desirable? Her heart soared at the long-awaited words.

"We're not really husband and wife."

"That's funny." When his tongue touched the crook of her elbow, desire pooled hotly between her legs. "I have a paper tucked away in my underwear drawer that says we are." He spread his legs and pulled her closer.

Heaven help her, she did not resist. Instead, Sasha found herself staring down at the buttons on his blood-stained shirt, struck with a sudden, almost overwhelming impulse to rip them all away.

"Our marriage is in name only," she protested. "That was what you proposed."

"True enough." Her skin was as soft as silk. Mitch

wanted to touch her all over. Taste her all over. "But there's really nothing to prevent us from changing the terms of the deal, is there?"

Never had Sasha been so tempted. Never had she wanted a man so badly. And never had she loved anyone so deeply. Which was why, she warned herself, she must tread very carefully where Mitch Cudahy was concerned.

"There is one reason."

Her voice was so soft Mitch could barely hear her. "What's that, sweetheart?" he murmured, pulling her closer still so he could nuzzle his head against her abdomen.

It was that throwaway word that he tossed so casually to every woman he met that assured Sasha she was right to be cautious.

"You do not know me." It was the hardest decision she'd ever made. Sasha could only pray it was the right one. "And I do not know you."

"Hell, sweetheart," he argued, unwittingly driving another nail into the ragged wound he was making in her heart, "we know more about each other than a lot of people who tumble into bed together."

Unfortunately, Sasha realized that he was speaking from experience. "I realize many of the women you know take lovemaking lightly. But I am not most women, Mitch."

That firmness was back. In her voice and, as he looked up at her, in her steady brown gaze. Mitch sighed and reminded himself that bedding Sasha probably would have been a mistake, anyway. Every instinct he possessed told him this situation could get emotionally sticky.

"You're right." He released her, but the warmth of his touch, his gaze, continued to linger in her breast. "I'm sorry. I had no right to try to take advantage of you that way. No right to try to talk you into doing something you don't want to do.''

Sasha experienced a moment of panic. This was not what she wanted! She'd only intended to stall long enough for them to get to know one another better. To give Mitch time to fall in love with her. So that when they ultimately did make love, he'd understand that they belonged together.

The one thing she didn't want to do was to encourage him to give up on her entirely!

She took a deep breath and, having no experience in how to maneuver in such tight emotional quarters, decided to follow her instincts and hope they'd lead her in the right direction.

''But I do want to make love to you, Mitch.'' There, she'd said it. ''But it's more complicated than that.''

''I don't understand. We're legally married. The mutual attraction—the chemistry—has been obvious from the beginning, Sasha. I want you and you want me. What's so complicated about that?''

Because I love you. And you don't love me. ''I told you,'' she said, ''I do not take sex lightly.''

He nodded his approval. ''That's wise. Especially in this day and age.''

''Yes.'' She twisted her fingers together and tried again. ''It's just that all this has happened so fast, Mitch. You and I, and our marriage. And winning all that money, and then the meeting with that horrid Mr. Donald O. Potter, and the purse stealer, and your mother…''

''All right.'' His lips quirked with a small smile and humor brightened his eyes as he held up his wounded hand. ''I get the point, sweetheart. I don't need a blow-by-blow replay.''

''Fine.'' Reminding herself once again that she was not the pitiful little wretch he thought he'd married, she tilted her chin and forced her runaway pulse to something resembling normalcy.

"We'll take our time," Mitch agreed. "And get to know one another." Personally, he'd always felt like bed was a dandy place to get to know a woman. But never having had to push, let alone coax a female between his sheets, he had no intention of beginning with Sasha.

"Thank you," she said. "And while we're being honest, may I request a favor?"

"Sure."

This time she managed to ignore the warmth of his smile. "I would appreciate it if you would stop calling me sweetheart."

That finally said, she swept from the room with a regal air that reminded Mitch of royalty. For a moment he was irked at being dismissed so coolly, then he threw back his head and laughed.

"So, WHAT DID YOU expect?" Jake asked the next day. He was spotting for Mitch, who was working off his frustration by lifting weights in the workout room at the station. "That just because you married the girl, she'd show her undying gratitude by leaping naked into your bed?"

"I wasn't looking for gratitude." Mitch grunted as he hefted the bar over his head. "I was looking for sex."

"Makes sense to me. I told you most men would love a chance to roll around in the hay with our little Sasha Mikhailova."

"She's Sasha Cudahy. At least for the time being. And I told you I don't want to hear about most men!" Mitch dropped the bar back down with a curse.

"Whooee." Jake grinned and held his hands up in a gesture of defeat. "Sounds like you've got it bad."

"That's ridiculous. I'm just horny." Mitch pushed the

bar up again, irritation providing an extra burst of power. "You would be, too, if you'd gone a week without getting laid."

"Yeah. Like that never happens to the rest of us," Jake said dryly. "Wait until you've got a wife in the eighth month of pregnancy, pal. Our water bill went through the roof from all the cold showers I was taking."

"Since I'm leaving the responsibility of providing Mom with grandkids to you and Katie, I have no intention of ever experiencing that aspect of marriage," Mitch insisted. "And if I'd wanted a life of celibacy I would have joined an order of trappist monks instead of the fire department."

Jake added more weight to both ends of the bar. "Katie was telling me something about some home visit by Glory's squinty-eyed weasel. So, when is it scheduled?"

"I don't know. Apparently they surprise you. Like fire drills." The first one, when Potter had discovered them kissing in the kitchen, had been a bonus. Mitch didn't expect subsequent visits to go as smoothly.

"Oh." Jake rubbed his chin. "So you and your bride have to continue to live as normal newlyweds as much as possible, just in case the immigration police stop by in the middle of the night?"

"That's pretty much it," Mitch muttered, shoving the heavier bar up with a force born of frustration.

"Tough break." Jake steadied the barbell as Mitch's inner turmoil set it shaking. "Well, at least once the visit is over with, and Sasha has her green card, you can get on with your separate lives."

"Yeah. And let me tell you, I can't wait."

Mitch sat up, wiped his hand against his sweat-stained shirt and wondered when he'd become such a damn liar.

GLORY WAS WAITING with a question when Sasha arrived the next day at work. "How come you didn't tell me about

Mitch's mother's offer to get you enrolled in a licensing school?'' she demanded with a frown.

Sasha hadn't known how to break the news that she'd be leaving to her friend. ''I was going to tell you about that.''

''That sounds like a terrific deal,'' Glory said after Sasha had explained. ''And I know how much you've missed working in the operating room. So what's the problem?''

''For one thing, I don't want to leave you without a waitress. Not after you were so nice to hire me.''

At that Glory broke out laughing. ''Honey, I think it's time for me to come clean with you. The reason my sister's girl Amber stopped by last week was to ask for a job. I told you she's putting herself through Phoenix College.''

Sasha nodded.

''The problem is, I had to turn her down because I knew how badly you needed work. But now that you're married and your mother-in-law is going to get you into school—''

''But what if Mitch doesn't want to stay married?'' Sasha asked. ''Even if I didn't want to keep working, which I do, once we get our annulment, it will be necessary to support myself.''

''By then you'll have your nursing license,'' Glory observed. ''But I'll bet you dollars to doughnuts that Mitch won't want that annulment.''

Sasha hoped that would be true.

THE NEXT WEEK went by smoothly enough. Which Mitch decided was probably due to Sasha's being at school on the days he was home, and his being at the station for three of those days and nights.

The first morning they actually shared together was Friday, a week after Sasha's bridal shower and Mitch's stripper-club brawl.

They were just finishing breakfast when Margaret dropped by.

"Good morning, dears," she said, studiously ignoring the black eye that was still evident on Mitch's face. After declining Sasha's offer of coffee, she said, "I was planning my day off when I realized that Sasha probably doesn't have a proper dress for tomorrow night."

"Tomorrow night?" Sasha turned toward him. "Mitch?"

Hell. With all he'd had on his mind lately, he'd forgotten all about the upcoming governor's awards banquet.

"I don't know if I'm going to go to that dinner, Mom," he hedged.

"Well, of course you are." Margaret waved his words away. "The governor," she told Sasha with maternal pride, "is going to give Mitchel a medal. And name him Arizona hero of the year."

"Really?" Sasha's face was glowing with something that horrifyingly appeared to be wifely pride as she turned toward him. "This is true, Mitch?"

"It's no big thing," he mumbled as he began tearing apart a paper napkin.

"On the contrary," Margaret corrected, "it is a very big deal. Your father won the same award, Mitch. You owe it to his memory to show up. Besides," she said, her friendly gaze returning to Sasha, "you'll be sitting up on the dais with the governor. What better opportunity to show off your new bride?"

As he mumbled something that sounded like agreement, Mitch could feel the quicksand closing in over his head.

12

"I CAN'T AFFORD to do much shopping," Sasha said as she drove to the mall with Margaret and Katie. "I should save my money to use to find my father."

"Of course you should," Katie said. "But you're a married woman now."

"And I know my son would want to spend whatever is necessary for you to look your best Saturday night," Margaret added as extra inducement.

Remembering how Mitch had sighed as he had handed over his credit card in Laughlin, Sasha wasn't as certain that he would approve of this shopping trip.

Ten minutes later, she was standing in front of a three-way mirror, staring in stunned disbelief at her reflection.

"Didn't I tell you?" Katie, who'd found the glittery lamé cocktail dress in the chichi boutique, crowed. "As seduction artillery goes, that dress is decidedly lethal."

"It is definitely short," Sasha murmured. She'd lived with her legs for twenty-four years without realizing how long they were! The knife-pleated, baby-doll style dress, held up with thin glittery straps, ended a great deal closer to her waist than her knees. "And bright."

"Red is perfect for a fireman's wife," Katie argued. "And the color is dynamite with your dark hair."

The contrast was appealing, Sasha admitted secretly. Still, she didn't think she'd have the nerve to leave the house in such a skimpy, sexy dress.

She turned to Margaret, hoping the older woman would suggest something more prudent. "What do you think?"

Mitch's mother's judicial gaze swept over the brief cocktail dress. "I think my son's a goner." She held out a pair of dangling crystal earrings. "Try these. They'll be perfect."

Outvoted and more than a little overwhelmed, Sasha did not resist as the pair dragged her from store to store, seemingly determined to push the limit on Mitch's credit card.

By the end of the day, when she returned to the apartment laden down with packages, Sasha decided she knew exactly how Cinderella must have felt when her fairy godmother had shown up with that sparkling new ball gown and pumpkin coach.

The transformation the two women had wrought had been nothing short of miraculous. Anticipation bubbled like sparkling champagne in her veins as Sasha contemplated seducing her husband.

MITCH WAS LATE and not in the best of moods when he arrived home Saturday night from the station.

Although he'd left with time to spare to stop at the rental shop and pick up his tux, a three-car accident, while not serious, had tied up traffic, leaving him with a scant fifteen minutes to shower and change before leaving for the awards banquet.

"Sasha?" he called as he entered the apartment. "I'm sorry I'm late, but this damn hay truck got caught under a freeway underpass, then a guy in a pickup swerved to miss hitting the bales of hay that fell off, and—"

His words stuck in his throat and his jaw dropped as he caught sight of the stranger standing in his bedroom. "Sasha?"

The glamorous woman behind the makeup counter at

Saks who had, at Margaret's prompting, sold Sasha enough cosmetics to open her own salon, had helpfully drawn the application instructions on the sketch of a face. Sasha had followed the instructions carefully, and after numerous failed attempts, thought she'd succeeded. But the way Mitch was staring at her—as if he'd never seen her before—made her worry that she'd overdone the makeover.

"Is something wrong?" It was the eyeliner! She'd known it was a mistake!

He opened his mouth to answer, but his stunned mind could not come up with the appropriate words. All he could do was shake his head.

He'd known she was pretty. Even, on occasion, beautiful, in a sweet, natural sort of way. But never in a million years could Mitch have imagined that Sasha could be so breathtakingly sexy.

The kohl liner made her smoldering eyes look even larger and darker than usual. A deep slash of color accented her chiseled Russian cheekbones, and her lips, glistening with gloss, made him think of ripe, succulent berries.

As for that skimpy excuse of a dress…it was both strangely innocent and outrageously alluring. As the dangling crystal earrings drew his attention to her bare shoulders, he felt a sudden, almost irresistible urge to sink his teeth into that gleaming skin.

"You do not like my new dress?" Her wet, ruby-red, eat-me-up mouth turned downward. Her hands ran over the sparkling scarlet fabric in an unconscious caress that made his mouth go dry. "I can change, if you'd like."

"No!" The word came out on an explosion of pent-up breath. "No," he repeated as his stomach muscles tightened into treacherous knots. "Don't change a thing. I was just surprised, that's all." He cleared his throat. "I wasn't expecting, I didn't know…aw, hell."

He dragged his hands through his hair as he continued to stare at her, wondering what, if anything, she was wearing beneath that sparkly, fire-engine-red, baby-doll dress.

It was working! Giddy with newfound feminine power, Sasha held out her arms and slowly turned on the dangerously spindly high heels. "Your sister picked it out."

"Remind me to thank her."

"I will do that." She smiled at him over her bare shoulder, a slow, seductive siren's smile that promised untold erotic delights. "Tomorrow morning." She glanced down her bare back at her legs. "Oh, dear," she sighed prettily, "I told Katie these stockings would prove a challenge."

The damn stockings in question had seams, Mitch realized, slender black ones that lured a guy's eyes all the way from her trim little ankles to where the dark lines disappeared beneath that scandalously short skirt. As she bent over to ostensibly straighten the right seam, blood rushed hotly from his head, flooding straight to his groin.

"Lord, lady." His deep voice was strained and husky with hunger.

"Is something wrong?" she asked innocently.

He shook his head. "Not a thing."

"I'm glad. This is your special night, Mitch. Everything should be perfect." Satisfied, she straightened. "How is that? Are they straight now?"

Knowing how a suicidal man felt when looking over the ledge atop a skyscraper, Mitch made himself take a longer look at those amazing legs. "Perfect." Lord, perfect didn't even begin to describe it.

He wanted to run his hands all the way up that glistening dark silk; he wanted to roll those stockings down, centimeter by centimeter, tasting each bit of warm ivory flesh. He wanted to lick her, bite her, eat her up. He wanted her in a way he'd never—ever—wanted a woman before.

He tossed the tux in its plastic bag onto the bed, then crossed the few feet separating them and ran his hands down her arms.

"Mrs. Cudahy, I do think you're trying to seduce me."

His eyes were dark and dangerous. Sasha was thrilled by the desire in those stormy blue depths. "Why, whatever made you think such a thing?" she asked with blatantly feigned innocence.

"Let's just say it was an educated guess." He smiled, enjoying the moment. "I have an idea."

"Last time you had an idea, I ended up getting married." She laughed and tossed her head, causing a frothy ebony cloud of hair to drift over her naked shoulders. "I'm almost afraid to ask what you've come up with this time."

The stunning metamorphosis went beyond the change in clothing and makeup, Mitch realized. Her entire personality had changed, as if someone had broken into the apartment while he'd been at the station, kidnapped his sweet, shy little bride and left this sexy vixen in her place.

"You really want to know what I've come up with?" He took her slender, beringed hand in his and pressed her palm against the front of his jeans. "How's this for starters?"

Beneath the denim barrier, he was hard as a boulder. And seemingly as large. Even as she feared she'd never be able to take all of him inside her, Sasha felt herself growing warm and wet between her thighs.

"That's a very good start." Obviously Katie had been right about her new outfit being dangerous ammunition. It appeared Mitch was more than ready to surrender the seduction battle. "But don't you think you should be getting ready to leave for your awards ceremony? As you said, you were late getting home and we don't have much time."

"How about we just stay home? Like an old married couple?"

"I would like that." She sighed dramatically, drawing attention to her perfumed breasts. "But unfortunately, it wouldn't be fair to disappoint so many people. After all, the dinner is in your honor. And it's for charity."

Her caressing fingers caused desire to pool and throb. If she kept it up, there would be no way he'd be able to walk into that ballroom without wearing his fireman's jacket to hide his aching arousal.

He lifted her treacherous hand to his lips and touched the tip of his tongue against the slender blue vein on the inside of her wrist. "I guess you're right." He looked at her over their linked fingers. "I suppose, if I were to kiss you, I'd mess up your lipstick."

"I think, Mitch," she said honestly, "that if you were to kiss me, we would never get to the banquet."

"True." His sigh was rougher and deeper than hers had been.

"I suppose it was unfair of me to wear such a revealing dress when you are trying so hard to be a gentleman." There was not a scintilla of apology in either her tone or her expression.

"A gentleman wouldn't be thinking the thoughts that flimsy excuse of a dress inspires. And I'll admit that I couldn't breathe when I first walked in the door and saw you wearing it. But it's more than that, Sasha.

"Whatever I'm feeling for you is a helluva lot more complicated than animal lust caused by a skimpy red dress and hooker heels." His gaze skimmed down her legs. "Although they are pretty terrific."

Despite the seriousness of the topic, Sasha laughed. "The shoes were your mother's contribution. I've been worrying all day that I won't be able to walk in them."

''Don't worry your gorgeous head about that little problem. I think it's my husbandly duty to hold you up.''

He rocked forward on the balls of his feet, as if intending to kiss her on the mouth. At the last minute he changed course and touched his lips to her powdered cheek instead. ''Since we have to go to this shindig, I'd better go shower and get dressed.''

An unpalatable thought occurred to her. While she'd spent a long luxurious time bathing in the perfumed water, contemplating her seduction plans, she'd completely forgotten that Mitch would be needing a shower, as well. ''I hope I left you enough hot water.''

He laughed at that. ''Darlin', that's the least of my worries.''

He went into the bathroom and stripped off his clothes, trying to prevent ruining his chances for a future family while gingerly unzipping his too-tight jeans.

As he stepped beneath the purposefully icy water that did nothing to lessen his desire for his stunningly alluring wife, Mitch told himself that it was going to be a very long evening.

THE AWARDS DINNER was held in a resort ballroom overlooking formal gardens and a golf course. To Mitch's delight, amazement, and physical discomfort, Sasha tormented him all during dinner.

Under the long, white damask cloth covering the head table she slipped one foot out of her high-heeled shoe and ran her stocking-clad toes up his calf beneath his trouser leg, while her free hand stroked his thigh.

During dessert, while the introductory speaker droned on and on, she slanted him a coy glance from beneath the dark fringe of her lashes as she slowly, deliberately, licked a bit of whipped cream from her top lip. Watching her, Mitch felt his blood pressure soar through the high gilt ceiling.

"You realize," he murmured, his own hand delving beneath the tablecloth to squeeze her smooth leg, "that you're playing with fire."

"Ah, but you're a fireman, Mitch," she responded in a lush, silky voice he'd never heard from her before. "Surely you're capable of handling a few flames."

"I like to think so." His fingers were making slow, melting circles against the sensitive skin on the inside of her thighs. "The challenge is going to be, not to put the fire out too soon."

Before she could respond, Mitch realized that the speaker had finally called his name, drawing applause from the gathered crowd below the dais.

"Later," he murmured in Sasha's ear as he tossed his napkin onto the table and stood.

"Promises, promises," she murmured with a dangerous siren's smile that momentarily wiped his mind as clean as glass.

It took Mitch a moment to recover. Then, as he looked out over the audience and saw his mother and sister seated at a front table, he remembered what he'd wanted to say.

"I want to thank the governor, the mayor, and everyone on the citizens' council who voted me this honor," he said. "And it is an honor. But the truth is, I don't deserve it." Ignoring the unified intake of breath that rippled across the room, he continued. "At least no more than any of the other fire fighters—and cops—who put their lives on the line every day.

"People have this romantic notion that we fight fires and bad guys because of some strong inner urge to help people. And that's true. But most of all, we do it because there's nothing—well, almost nothing—" he amended, with a quick grin toward Sasha that caused a few chuckles "—that gives a greater high than the job.

"Thirty years ago my father received this same award for rescuing three of his fellow smoke eaters from a department store after the roof had fallen in on them."

He held the plaque in his hand and looked down at it, as if imagining that day. "I wasn't born yet, but I was lucky enough to witness many more acts of heroism. Such as the day he showed up at the ballpark, still sooty and drenched in sweat from fighting a desert grass fire, in time to watch me pitch in a Little League playoff game.

"Or when my sister Katie had an attack of appendicitis while we were camping and he drove like a maniac while assuring us all the way down from the mountains that she was going to be okay. And we knew she would be. Because Pops promised."

He paused again, his warm gaze sweeping over his mother—who surreptitiously wiped a tear away with the back of her finger—and his sister, who smiled back at him through moisture-bright eyes.

"Garrett Cudahy was a generous, faithful husband, a strict but loving father, and yes, a man who chose to fight fires as his life's work because he truly loved people.

"If I can ever become half the man my father was then, and only then, will I even begin to consider myself a hero. Like my pop."

He descended the few stairs to the floor to a standing ovation, handed the plaque to Margaret, kissed her on her wet cheek, accepted a kiss from Katie and a handshake from Jake, then returned to his seat.

"That was wonderful," Sasha said, her own eyes bright with tears. And then, because it had been too long since she'd kissed her husband, she brought his mouth to hers, causing another thunderous burst of applause.

"That reminds me," the governor said as he stood up again to officially end the awards portion of the evening. "It may come as a disappointment to any single ladies out there, but Mitch has recently gotten himself hitched." He smiled at Sasha, who'd reluctantly surrendered Mitch's lips. "Cudahy, you are not only a hero, you are a very lucky man."

There was more laughter. Then, on cue, the band began playing, inviting couples onto the dance floor.

When Mitch held out his hand to Sasha, she didn't hesitate. And when he gathered her into his arms and they began swaying slowly to the music, she knew that she'd never been happier.

"That was a very nice thing to do," she murmured. "Talking about your father like that."

"It was true." Mitch pressed his lips against the top of her head. "Pops was the best." He trailed his hand down her back and, unable to resist the lure of all that creamy bare skin, bent his head and kissed her neck, her shoulder.

Sasha sighed and closed her eyes as she allowed her own hands to play in his hair.

"I wish I could have met him."

"You would have liked him." He pulled her closer, enjoying the feel of her soft breasts pressed against his chest. As her smooth thighs brushed against his legs, he felt a resurgence of the desire he'd managed, just barely, to bank long enough to give his brief acceptance speech. "And he would have liked you."

It was the truth. Although at first he'd mistakenly considered Sasha a victim—a poor little Russian waif in need of rescuing—he'd come to realize that the lady had a helluva lot of guts to leave her country and the only life she'd ever known, to cross an ocean, seeking a father who could turn out to be nothing but a fanciful story told by a mother who wanted her daughter to grow up believing she'd been conceived in love.

Sasha opened her eyes and tilted her head back to look up at him. "Do you really think so?"

"Absolutely." He smiled and brushed the back of his hand up the side of her face, pleased by the soft drift of pale pink color that bloomed beneath his caressing touch. "He'd say you had gumption."

She sighed her pleasure, wondering what it would do to Mitch's heroic reputation to have his wife melt into a little puddle of need right in the middle of a public dance floor.

"This is good? This gumption?"

"The best."

She thought about that, and smiled. "Mitch?"

"Mmm?" He gave her earlobe a playful nip.

A mist of arousal was drifting over her mind, wrapping her in a silvery haze of pleasure. "Did it upset you? When the governor told everyone you were married?"

Mitch smiled, amazed by the change Sasha had wrought in his life in such a short time. "Actually, if you want to know the absolute truth, I was proud."

"Really?"

Looking down into her exquisite face, Mitch felt the hunger he always experienced when he was around Sasha meld with an easy affection he had never expected to feel for her.

"Really. Watching every male in the room lusting after a woman and knowing she's going home with you arouses some very primal feelings."

"Primal?" She smiled up at him. "Although your English is admittedly better than mine, Mitch, I believe the word you are looking for is possessive."

Mitch grinned. Enjoying the evening. Enjoying her. "Guilty." He cupped her chin between his fingers and bent his head. His lips hovered a breath above hers, nearly close enough for tasting. "How would you like to take a little stroll out on the golf course with your husband?"

Smiling, she touched the tip of her tongue against her top lip. Then, daringly, against his. "I thought you would never ask."

A full moon rode in a clear desert sky, shining its soft silver light over the velvety dark lawn. The perfume of bougainvillaea, hibiscus and roses drifted on the warm air from the nearby gardens. Fingers linked, Mitch pulled Sasha away from the ballroom terrace, across the greens, into a grove of pyramid-shaped silk oak trees.

"Alone at last," he breathed, then lowered his mouth to hers.

Sasha had expected passion. And fire. And lightning. Instead, she was being treated to a pleasure so sweet, so sublime, it nearly made her weep. Images tumbled seductively through her mind—flickering yellow candlelight, lush red roses, she and Mitch entwined on white satin sheets.

Even as his strong hands played in her hair, she longed for them to touch her everywhere. Even as his firm lips plucked enticingly at hers, drawing her deeper and deeper into a warm, fluid passion, she wished to feel his mouth against every inch of her heated flesh.

Although urgency rose, Mitch kept the pace slow, pleasuring himself, pleasuring her. His lips took a leisurely journey over her face, brushing heat against her temples, before moving on to her closed lids.

"You're trembling," he murmured as he tasted the fragrant flesh behind her ear.

"I know." His warm breath, his tender kisses, were making her knees weak. "I can't help it."

He pulled back and smiled into her eyes. Those wide, wonderful, expressive eyes. "Believe me, darlin', I know the feeling.'' Still smiling, he slowly and deliberately took her mouth again.

Tension twisted in his gut as he deepened the kiss, degree by devastating degree. Mitch had kissed more women than he could count, but never had a mere kiss made him ache. And never had kissing any other woman made him tremble.

She was so sweet. So soft. And she was his!

As Mitch reveled in that thought, the part of his brain that was still functioning rationally took note of a distant, familiar sound.

''Aw, hell,'' he groaned just as the golf course sprinklers turned on, shooting a fountain of water into the air, drenching them both.

13

"OH, NO!" Sasha shrieked. And then let loose with a torrent of passionate Russian.

"I suppose we could have used some cooling off," he admitted, raining short, laughing kisses over her wet face. "But this is ridiculous."

She was laughing, as well, as she kissed him back. "No matter what Ben Houston said, I do not think I am your good luck charm, Mitch. In fact, I am beginning to worry that I bring you bad luck."

"Never." He stopped laughing long enough to frame her face between his palms and hold her smiling gaze to his. "Although I was too dense to realize it at the time, Sasha Mikhailova Cudahy, I'm beginning to think the day we got married may just have been the luckiest day of my life."

Oblivious to the water streaming over them, soaking her carefully created hairstyle, melting the makeup she'd spent so much time on, ruining her new, ridiculously expensive dress, Sasha was suddenly frozen to the spot. Her wide eyes, still laced with lingering desire and laughter, swept over his handsome face, studying him intently.

"I believe you mean that," she said finally.

"You believe right." He traced her parted lips with his thumb, remembering their taste, and imagined what they would feel like skimming their way all over his naked body. "And although I've tried to play by the rules of our agreement, sometime between when I walked into the bedroom and saw you looking like every male's midnight fantasy and when those damn sprinklers went off, I realized that I can't do it.

"I want to make mad, passionate love to my wife."

She flung her arms around his neck and clung to him. "Oh, yes!"

LATER, WHEN SHE TRIED to recreate the evening, wanting to tuck every golden moment of it away in her mind the way a teenage girl might save an orchid prom corsage or a bride might preserve her lace-and-satin wedding dress, Sasha would realize that she had absolutely no memory of leaving the resort and driving back home to Mitch's apartment.

But somehow they must have managed it, because the next thing she knew, he was scooping her up into his arms, the same wonderful way he had in the casino, and was carrying her through the front door.

"I only had one glass of wine with dinner," she said, afraid he might think her uncharacteristically sexy behavior was due to too much alcohol. "I am not drunk. Like in Laughlin."

"I know." He looked down into her soft, lovely face and saw not the ruined makeup she'd so painstakingly applied, but her tenderness, her love.

My woman. The thought ricocheted through his mind as he kicked the door shut behind him, managing somehow to latch the chain lock. "But it's an old American tradition for a groom to carry his bride across the threshold."

He kissed her, a long, deep, moist kiss that left her head spinning even more than it had after all the champagne in the casino.

"I think I like this tradition," she managed when the blissful kiss ended. "Very much."

"You and me both, darlin'." Taking her mouth again, he carried her into the bedroom. They fell on the bed together, rolling over the mattress, arms and legs tangled, hands lighting flames on anxious bodies that had waited too long for fulfillment.

"I have dreamed of this," she managed, her mouth feasting on his as hungrily as he was eating into hers.

Even as she confessed her erotic secret, Sasha knew that it wasn't the same. Because as thrilling as those sensual dreams had been, they didn't come close to this aching reality.

Somehow, Mitch managed to yank the wet dress over her head without tearing it, then, with greedy hands ripped the brief strapless bra away as well. When he took her breast in his mouth, a surge of fire shot through Sasha like a flaming brand. The wooden bed frame groaned as she bucked upward, raking her hands in his hair, pressing him deeper into her burning, yielding flesh.

She cried out in wonder when Mitch's teeth captured a rigid tip, biting down in a way that sent the first wave crashing through her. Desperate to touch him as he was touching her, she tugged his shirt out of his slacks and began fumbling with the front of his pleated and starched shirtfront.

"I can't..." Her voice trembling, she swore in Russian when it looked as if the unfamiliar jet studs were going to defeat her.

"Here." The single word exploded on a torment of shared frustration. "Let me." Heedless of the rental cost, Mitch tore the shirt open, sending studs flying across the room. Then he pulled her against him, crushing her breasts against his chest, their mouths feeding ravenously again as they rolled over the bed, kicking off shoes, ripping at clothes, demanding, offering, taking.

Pillows tumbled to the carpet and went unnoticed. Mitch swore as they tangled in the bedspread, managed to rip it from beneath her and throw it in the direction of a nearby chair.

Here was the fire he'd warned her about playing with earlier. The glorious conflagration she'd been longing to experience. His hard, taut body was like a furnace, the flames licking higher and higher, and he pressed her deeper and deeper into the mattress, making her glow from the inside out. His mouth burned into hers, sending tongues of flame flickering across her damp flesh, heating her degree by treacherous degree.

My woman. The refrain repeated over and over again in his mind, like a bridge from a never sung yet strangely familiar song. Mitch had promised himself that he'd be gentle; had vowed to be tender. But as the waves of fire scorched through his mind and the billowing smoke blinded him, for the first time in his life he felt the need to conquer. To possess. To claim his bride for his own, for all time.

The heat was unbearable. When he pressed his palm against that secret place between her legs where damp warmth flowed, she gathered up handfuls of crumpled sheet.

"Oh, please," she gasped as his mouth replaced his hand, sending white-hot flames licking through her blood. Another wave of ecstasy swept outward from that ultrasensitive core like wildfire, leaving her gasping and panting. And, unbelievably, wanting more.

"I need you, Mitch." If begging was what was necessary to end this torment, Sasha would beg. She would crawl. Or scream. Whatever it took. She couldn't wait any longer.

Calling out his name, she dragged his mouth back to her hot avid one and wrapped her legs around his hips in a viselike grip. "I need you," she repeated raggedly. "Now."

Filled with a fierceness that frightened him, Mitch braced himself on his elbows and looked down at her, his blue eyes dark and savage. "Sweet heaven, I need you, too." He moved his hips forward, pressing against her, rekindling hot glowing coals that he had no intention of allowing to cool. "And that scares the hell out of me."

Before she could answer, before she could tell him that the enormity of her love for him was frightening to her, as well, he plunged into her with a force just this side of violence. Her body shuddered as he broke through the virginal barrier, taking her innocence while bringing her a pleasure that overwhelmed any fleeting pain. Loving him as she'd never dreamed of loving any man, Sasha twined her arms around his neck and opened for him—lips, mind, body, heart.

It was like being enveloped in molten satin. Hot and smooth and unbearably erotic. Mitch began to move, slowly at first, then faster, his strokes harder, deeper as he drove her, drove them both, into the inferno.

She cried out his name on a gasp of pleasure an instant before his own ragged shout tore from his burning throat.

My wife. With that last coherent thought, Mitch flooded into her.

They lay together, arms and legs entwined, Mitch's mouth buried into the fragrant flesh of her neck, enjoying the soothing afterglow of passion. As impossible as it seemed, every nerve ending in Sasha's body was still tingling, making her feel more alive than she'd ever felt in her life.

"I'm sorry." His words vibrated against her damp skin.

"Sorry?" The odd tone in his voice made her look up

at him with curiosity. "What could you possibly be sorry about?"

"You were a virgin." He'd known that, but his need for her had scorched the knowledge from his mind.

"Yes. But surely you knew that."

"Of course I did. Which is why I should have taken you with more finesse."

Finesse. Such a pretty word. Such a polite, civilized word. For something that had been in no way even remotely civilized.

"I think it was perfect. Just the way it was." She took his hand in hers and pressed it against her still-pulsating body. "Feel what you have done."

Inner eruptions exploded against his palm. "I did that?"

"I do not see anyone else in this bed." She was bathed in a golden glow that made her smile. "That was the most special thing that has ever happened to me."

He combed his fingers idly through the dark curls between her thighs, loving the way her jet pupils were already expanding with renewed desire.

"To me, too." Although her body's instinctively sensual response to his stroking touch was making him hard again, Mitch was afraid that to take her again, so soon, might cause her pain. So he managed, just barely, to restrain himself. For now.

He ran his hand down her side, from her breasts to her thighs. "Did I mention that I love those stockings?"

"Not in words."

She cuddled against him, thinking that as wondrous as his lovemaking had been, this settling down, talking period afterward was nearly as enjoyable.

"But I could tell you found them appealing," she said, feeling that delicious desire building all over again.

"What was your first clue?" He toyed with the elastic

band holding them up. ''The fact that I looked as if I was on the verge of exploding when you pulled that seam-straightening stunt.''

She giggled softly. ''I suppose that was unfair. But I wanted you to think of me as a sexy woman.''

''If that was your intention, sweetheart, it sure worked.'' He slipped his fingers between the stocking and her warm flesh. ''But it was also unnecessary, since I'd already decided that you were pretty damn sexy the first time I saw you in that bubblegum-pink uniform.''

She laughed again, a soft shimmer of sound that slipped silkily into his blood. ''That was such an ugly dress.''

He wasn't going to argue the point. It was, after all, true. ''Which is why it's so amazing you could look so good in it.'' He smoothed the stocking back up her thigh with both hands, then sat back on his haunches, enjoying the contrast between her smooth ivory thighs and those long dark stockings.

''How did you manage to wear these with that short skirt, anyway?''

''Katie taught me a trick.'' She was totally vulnerable, lying there, naked, her legs spread, open to his gaze. She would have expected to feel embarrassed, but as his fingers trailed seductive little circles on the sensitive flesh on the inside of her thighs, she experienced instead feminine pride that her husband would find her so appealing.

''She said that if I bought the larger size…'' His stroking touch was causing renewed desire to pool inside her. ''If I bought the larger size they would go up higher on my leg… Mitch!'' She began to tremble as he touched his lips against that still-tingling flesh. ''How do you expect me to answer you if you keep distracting me?''

''Sorry.'' His rakish grin, as he looked up at her, said just the opposite. ''Am I a distraction?''

"You know you are."

"Serves you right." When his teeth nipped at that ultra-sensitive nub, a ragged moan slipped from between her ravished lips. "After the way you tried to seduce me."

"I did not try." She grabbed him by the hair and lifted his head again and gave him a blatantly female, unmistakably satisfied look. "I succeeded."

He laughed, as he was meant to. "Touché." He rocked forward and brushed his mouth against hers. Sweetly. Tenderly. As if they had all the time in the world. "There's an old American saying," he murmured. "What's sauce for the goose is sauce for the gander."

"I do not think I know that one."

"It means—" his fingers slipped smoothly into her slick heat "—I think it's only fair that this time I seduce you."

Her lips curved beneath his. "I am so happy that I married such a fair-minded man."

Twining her arms around his neck, Sasha invited her husband to take her back into the mists.

Which he did. Again and again. All night long.

WHILE MITCH MANAGED to catch some much needed sleep, Sasha crept quietly into the kitchen, determined make him a proper American breakfast. "What could be more American than waffles?" she asked herself as she took the box from the freezer.

There was just one little problem. She'd ruined the toaster last week by filling it with foam. Never one to let small obstacles defeat her, she turned on the oven and put the frozen squares onto a cookie sheet.

She'd just put the cookie sheet on the oven rack when the phone rang. Before she could answer it, she heard Mitch's voice coming from the bedroom.

"Yeah?" he grumbled, irritated by having been roused

out of a dream where he was making love to Sasha beneath a waterfall.

"Mitch? Did I wake you?"

Mitch tensed at the familiar voice. "Actually, you did." He glanced up at Sasha, who was standing in the bedroom doorway, clad in a froth of silk and ivory lace, looking downright delectable.

"This isn't a real good time." When she entered the bedroom, a beam of sunlight rendered the sheer gown nearly invisible. Mitch sucked in a sharp breath. "How about I call you back later?"

"Actually, I wanted to talk with Sasha, anyway."

"What about?" Mitch asked suspiciously.

Meredith laughed at that, a low, sultry laugh that didn't affect him nearly as much as Sasha's light, musical one. "Don't worry, darling, I'm not going to share female war stories with your bride. I just want to talk to her about our interview."

"Interview? What interview?"

"Oh, dear. I take it you don't know." She paused. "Well, if your wife hasn't discussed it with you, I'm certainly not going to say a thing. Could you just put her on the phone?"

He held the receiver toward Sasha. "It's Meredith Roberts. Something about an interview."

"Oh, yes!" She took the phone and sat down on the edge of the bed. "Hello, Meredith. Your station is running it?"

"Monday and Tuesday nights. In segments at six and ten o'clock."

"That is very good news! I appreciate this very much, Meredith."

"I told you, it's a good story. The kind of touchy-feely

thing people want. Thanks for giving me the exclusive.'' Her message delivered, the reporter hung up.

"I didn't know you'd given Meredith an interview," Mitch said.

"I was going to tell you—" Sasha handed him back the receiver "—but I didn't know if the station would run the story, so I waited. Besides, you were at work so much last week, and I was at the school, and then I made the decision to tell you after the banquet, but—"

"Afterward, I was distracted."

"Yes." Sasha watched the desire rise in his eyes and felt a similar heat begin to glow inside her. "Meredith says there's a chance the networks might pick up my story."

"That could be a help." He ran his hand down her tousled hair, over her bare shoulders. "Maybe someone will see it who knows your father."

"That's what Meredith said," she agreed breathlessly as his caressing touch made her feel as if she was going to melt.

It was amazing. Mitch had thought his obsession for this woman was born of sexual frustration. But he'd taken care of that little problem last night. And each time they'd made love, he'd been left wanting more. As he still did this morning.

"I missed you," he said, pulling her against him.

"You were sleeping."

"Ah, but I knew you weren't beside me. Where you belonged."

He touched his mouth to her silky skin. "I take it this is one of your shower presents?"

"Yes. Do you like it?"

"Sweetheart, like doesn't even begin to come close." He untied the satin ribbon lacing the front of the gown together. "It's just too bad I'm going to have to take it off you."

As he nuzzled his face between her silky breasts, Sasha combed her hands though his thick hair and fell back against the pillows as that delicious, enervating heat began to spread through her bloodstream.

"You're making my head spin," she complained on a long, shuddering sigh.

"Good." He cut a wet swath up her throat to her mouth with his tongue. "Let's see if we can make the rest of you spin."

Of course, he could. And, in turn, Sasha did the same to him. Bathed in the benevolent golden glow of a desert morning, they spent a long leisurely time pleasuring each other, pledging vows with words and bodies and hearts. And it was glorious.

He could spend the rest of his life right here, Mitch decided much, much later as he lay steeped in this woman who'd come to mean so much to him in so short a time. She was lying in his arms, her head nestled against his shoulder. From her slow, soft breathing, he realized she'd fallen asleep.

He could use some more sleep, as well. But his mind wouldn't rest. It was too filled with Sasha—her scent, her feel, her taste.

Mitch had never been much for introspection. He'd always lived for the moment, which for the first twenty-seven years of his life, had suited him just fine. But now he realized that falling in love was even more dangerous—and more exhilarating—than running into a burning building.

He pressed his lips against her hair. When she smiled, and stirred and wrapped her arms tighter around him, he felt a sense of rightness he'd never felt before. Closing his eyes, he drifted back to sleep.

MITCH WAS AWAKENED by a siren's blare echoing through the room. He was out of the bed like a shot, reaching automatically for the clothes he always kept within arm's reach, and cursed when they weren't there.

"Oh, no!" As he watched Sasha leap from the bed and go racing into the kitchen, Mitch's first thought was to wonder what his wife—his naked wife!—was doing at the station. A second later, comprehension dawned and he realized where he was. And what was making that godawful air raid sound.

Following her into the kitchen, he waded through the billowing gray smoke and watched as she pulled a cookie sheet from the oven.

"Am I allowed to ask what those were?" he inquired as she threw the black squares into the sink and proceeded to drown them beneath the faucet. He reached up and reset the smoke detector, silencing it.

"I'm sorry! I wanted to make you a nice breakfast, like a good American wife…"

"That was breakfast?"

"Waffles." She shook her head. "I'm such a failure!"

"So you can't cook." He crossed the room and gathered her into his arms, gently tilting her chin up to meet his reassuring gaze. "You can learn. Or I can learn. Or we both can." He traced her quivering lips with his thumb. "Or we can eat all our meals out." He touched his mouth to hers. "Or, better yet, live on love."

"We would waste away."

He pulled her even closer and deepened the kiss, literally stealing her breath. "But what a way to go," he said when they finally came up for air.

Reluctantly he released her, and began opening windows.

14

AFTER THEY'D FINISHED the breakfast Mitch picked up for them at Glory's, he suggested spending the night at a French country inn in Sedona.

Sasha found the magnificent red rock country of Oak Creek Canyon awe-inspiring. "I can't remember ever being so relaxed. Or so happy."

"Neither can I." They were sitting on a wrought-iron bench beneath the spreading green canopy of an oak tree.

They'd spent the Sunday drive up from Phoenix talking. Mitch had told Sasha things he'd never told any other person—not even his mother, whom he dearly loved.

He admitted the pain and debilitating sense of loss he'd experienced in those days following the fire that had taken his father's life and how he'd felt he could never live up to Garrett Cudahy's hero image. And how he believed that his father still watched over him, and hopefully approved of how he'd chosen to live his own life.

In turn, Sasha shared much of her life with him—a hard life filled with struggles and loneliness, which confirmed what he'd already figured out for himself.

And now, as they sat beside the crystal stream, she told him stories her mother had told her, romanticized tales of how their life would be when they reached America.

"My father was going to buy a house with many flowers. And a wide, covered front porch with a swing. The house would be blue with white shutters. And there would be clay

pots overflowing with bright red geraniums on the porch."
She smiled. "Mama always called it their red, white and
blue American house."

"It sounds nice."

"Yes," she sighed, "it does."

Hearing the faint sadness creeping back into her tone,
Mitch caught her downcast chin in his fingers and turned
her head toward him. "We'll find him," he promised.

Mitch was a hero. Her hero. But he was not a miracle
worker. After a year of failure after failure, Sasha no longer
held out a great deal of hope. But not wanting to ruin this
exquisite afternoon, she reminded herself how lucky she
was to have found such a kind and loving man.

"Yes." She wrapped her arms around him, tight.
"Mitch?"

"Mmm?" He buried his lips in her hair and breathed in
her light, flowery scent.

"I am suddenly very tired. Do you think we have time
for a short nap before dinner?"

"Darlin'—" he stood and lifted her into his arms
"—I'm suddenly overcome with an attack of exhaustion
myself."

Laughing, Sasha pressed her lips to his as he carried her
back across the lawn to their cottage.

THE INTERVIEW AIRED, as promised, on Monday and Tuesday of the following week. It was also, Sasha had been
excited to learn, picked up by the network.

On Wednesday morning, a woman in a taupe suit and
carrying a briefcase arrived at the apartment door.

"Mrs. Cudahy?" She greeted Sasha with a friendly
smile.

"Yes. I am Mrs. Cudahy." Sasha thought it both strange

and wonderful how she'd grown accustomed to answering to Mitch's last name.

"I'm Mrs. Kensington. From the U.S. Immigration Service. May I come in?"

"Of course!" Sasha stepped aside, glancing past the woman, half expecting to see her nemesis lurking nearby.

"I've been assigned your case, Mrs. Cudahy," the woman said, answering Sasha's unspoken question.

Mitch chose that moment to wander in from the bedroom, clad in jeans and bare feet. He was buttoning a blue chambray shirt. "What happened to the weasel?" The possessive way he put his arm around Sasha's too-rigid shoulders did not escape the immigration officer's professionally trained eyes.

"I assume you're referring to Mr. Potter." A hint of a smile tugged at her lips. "He was reassigned yesterday."

"Reassigned?" Sasha asked.

"Actually, I believe a more accurate word is demoted." The satisfaction in the woman's eyes suggested to Mitch that Potter had made life as uncomfortable for his fellow workers as for Sasha and all the other poor immigrants unlucky enough to have him assigned to their cases. "Our regional director was not exactly pleased with how your network interview made our office look."

As he felt Sasha begin to relax, Mitch decided to send Meredith a dozen roses for having solved one of Sasha's problems so neatly.

"So," he said, squeezing Sasha's shoulder reassuringly, "I suppose you're here for the home visit."

"Yes." The woman glanced down at her watch. "But since my caseload has more than doubled since inheriting Mr. Potter's files, I'd better be on my way."

"That's it?" Even Mitch was surprised.

"That's it," the woman agreed.

"Did we pass?" Sasha risked asking.

"With flying colors." She glanced at the two cups and two cereal bowls still on the kitchen table. "It's obvious you're living as man and wife. It's also obvious that you care for one another. And, after such a remarkably sympathetic network appearance relating your attempts to locate your father, we'd look like Scrooge if we tried to deport you," she assured Sasha with a warm smile.

"It will take a few weeks for the paperwork to clear." She held out her hand. "In the meantime, welcome to America."

As she shook the woman's hand, Sasha felt the tears begin to overflow. But this time they were tears of joy.

TWO DAYS LATER, after Mitch had left for the station, Meredith telephoned.

"I just received a call," the reporter said. "From your father. He wants to meet you."

"Really?" Although Sasha's suddenly frantically beating heart wanted to believe that this was the happy ending she'd been searching for, her head reminded her of all the other times she'd been disappointed.

"Really. Actually, he wants you to come live with him."

"Live with him?"

"In Big Sur. South of San Francisco. Seems he's got a huge house—one of those glass and redwood things—overlooking the beach. Looks as if you struck it rich, Sasha.

"Of course we'll want to film your reunion. It'll make a dynamite Cinderella story—how the penniless little immigrant waif discovers the streets in America really are paved with gold."

The knowledge that her father wanted her after all these years, should have given Sasha pleasure. Instead she felt a shadow move over her heart. Her mind went numb as she wrote down the information.

MITCH WAS GLAD when the day turned out to be one emergency after another. It kept him from thinking of Sasha. Of how much he missed her.

He was grinning as the truck headed back to the station after putting out a car fire. For the first time, he understood why Jake had traded his sportscar for a minivan. There wasn't anything he wouldn't do for Sasha. Because somehow, when he wasn't looking, he'd fallen in love with his wife.

With that amazing, yet highly satisfying thought in his mind, Mitch idly glanced around at the neighborhood they were passing through. It was an older neighborhood, the kind with deep front lawns and mature trees, and small, but well-built houses sporting wide front porches that harkened back to days when an evening's entertainment meant sitting outside with a glass of ice-cold lemonade, watching your neighbors.

"Hey!" he shouted, pounding on the side of the truck. "Tell Jake to stop!"

The word filtered forward, fireman to fireman, to the cab of the truck where Jake was behind the wheel. He pulled over to the curb and leaned out the driver's window. "What's wrong?"

"I gotta check on something," Mitch said. "I'll be right back." He jogged back down the street to the information box attached to a white wooden For Sale sign surrounded by bright flowers.

This was it! Sasha's dream house. Right down to the blue siding, bright white shutters and the swing. All right, perhaps the red flowers were petunias instead of geraniums, but with that single exception, it could have been drawn straight from her mother's description.

He plucked a brochure from the box, tucked it into his jacket and returned to the truck.

"Thinking of doing a little nest building?" Jake asked with a knowing grin.

"Just drive," Mitch said, his own grin taking the edge off his words. "I want to get back to the station. I have a call to make."

He looked back at the house and pictured Sasha standing on the front steps, looking pert and sexy in her white nurse's uniform, welcoming him home with open arms while their baby slept in an old-fashioned blue buggy on the old-fashioned shaded porch.

The idea was more than a little appealing.

After talking with the real estate agent on the phone, Mitch was even more enthusiastic. The house sounded perfect. And what's more, he'd socked away enough to easily make the down payment.

Next on his agenda was to see the inside and make an offer before the house was snatched up.

"Hey, Jake," he asked his brother-in-law, whose three-day shift was just ending. "How'd you like to do me a big favor?"

"Like stick around while you take your bride to see her new home?"

One thing about so many guys living so close together was that privacy became a rare commodity. Mitch grinned. "Yeah."

Jake grinned back. "Since Katie would kill me if I screwed up a chance to make Sasha happy, it doesn't look as if I have much choice. So go play real estate magnate. And have fun."

"Thanks." Needing to wash the lingering smell of

smoke from his hair, Mitch took a quick shower. When he came out of the communal bathroom, there were hoots of amusement.

"Nice undies, Mitchie," one of the firemen called out.

"Pink is definitely your color," another one pitched in.

"This is what marriage does to a guy," a third drawled. "Softens him up. Next thing you know, he'll be measuring the station windows for gingham curtains."

Mitch flashed them a good-natured middle finger and proceeded to finish dressing. So what if Sasha had messed up the wash? So what if she couldn't cook? He loved her. Just the way she was.

He was just about to call her, to tell her he was on the way home to pick her up for a surprise, when Jake called out, "Sasha's on the phone."

He took the receiver. "Hi, darlin'. Your timing's perfect. I was just getting ready to call you."

"I heard from my father," Sasha blurted out.

"What?" Mitch shook his head, certain he must have misunderstood her.

"I said, my father called me. Just a few minutes ago."

He still didn't understand. "How—"

"He saw Meredith's report on the network broadcast and called her. She gave him my number."

"I see." Wondering how this was going to affect their marriage, Mitch paused and let out a long breath. "Well, this is what you've been wanting."

"Yes." She did not sound all that enthusiastic.

"So. How did it go?"

"Very well, actually." It was her turn to let out a breath. "He wants me to come live with him, Mitch. In Big Sur."

Mitch waited for her to say that of course she'd told him that was impossible. That she already had a home—and a life—in Phoenix, with her husband.

Nothing. Just dead air coming from the other end of the telephone line.

"Big Sur, huh? Sounds like he's done okay for himself."

"He wrote a book on journalism that's required reading in most colleges. And some novels. Meredith said he's very rich."

"Looks as if you've hit the jackpot."

"That's what Meredith said."

The pause this time was longer. And deadlier.

"Congratulations," Mitch said finally. "I hope he's everything you wanted him to be. Look, Sasha, I'd love to talk some more, but I've got a fire to go to."

He hung up before he resorted to begging. Then slammed his fist into the wall.

SITTING on the edge of the bed, Sasha stared down at the telephone receiver. He'd hung up on her. Just like that. And she knew he was lying. If there'd been a fire, she would have heard the alarm.

She'd done everything but beg him to ask her to stay. Couldn't he tell she didn't want to leave him to run off to Big Sur? Didn't he know how much she loved him? As she raised her hand to replace the receiver, the flash of her gold wedding band drew her attention to her reflection in the dresser mirror.

They were married. In front of Elvis they had promised to love and honor each other, for better or worse, for richer or poorer, in sickness and in health—forever. And although the marriage may have been fraudulent in the beginning, Mitch himself had pointed out that the rules had changed.

She was his wife. Mitch was her husband. That being the case, she wasn't going anywhere.

Except, Sasha amended, to the store. To buy a cookbook.

MITCH WAS LYING on his back on his bunk staring up at the ceiling. Although he knew how badly Sasha wanted to find her father, he also knew damn well that she loved him. And he loved her. That being the case, they belonged together. Forever.

They were married. And, if he had anything to say about it, they were going to stay married. "Hey, Jake…"

"I figured you'd change your mind," his brother-in-law drawled. "That's why I stuck around."

Before Mitch could thank him, the alarm blasted through the building. "Hey, Mitch," the dispatcher called out, "it's your apartment complex."

He cursed. Sasha must have been in the kitchen again. At least, he thought as he climbed onto the back of the truck, she hadn't been packing.

Mitch's mild irritation turned to terror when the truck rounded the corner and he could see that the building was engulfed in flames. Two other trucks from nearby stations had already arrived on the scene and the firemen were busy pouring water on the raging inferno.

"What the hell happened?" Mitch asked, grabbing the arm of the first fireman he saw.

"Nobody knows for sure." The man pointed the stream of water directly at Mitch's apartment. "But one of the neighbors says there's a kid living in the end apartment who thinks he's Mr. Wizard. Always fooling around with chemicals and stuff. He could have made a bad mix."

Mitch knew the kid. He should. His parents were his next-door neighbors. "What about the people inside?"

"Everyone's accounted for except some woman in the apartment next to the end one." The fireman raised his voice to be heard over the roar of the fire as it ate away a section of wooden roof shakes. "It's too hot to get up there and see."

His apartment! Mitch watched horrified as an explosion blew out the arcadia doors leading to his balcony. This time there was no way up the outside stairway. However, if he could make it to the roof of the adjoining units…

"Don't even think it," a voice shouted in his ear. Mitch turned and glared at Jake, who, officially off duty, had followed in his minivan.

"Sasha could be in there!"

"And she might not be," Jake said. "And I'm not about to explain to a pretty young bride that I let her husband kill himself with some damn fool stunt."

"She's my wife, dammit." When Jake grabbed his jacket, he reacted on instinct and swung.

Jake dodged the fist. "Sorry, hotshot." He landed a blow on Mitch's jaw, sending him sprawling into a pile of fire hoses.

That was how Sasha found them, rolling on the wet ground, arms flailing, fists flying, while all around them the firemen continued to fight the blaze, ignoring the fact that two of their own were engaged in a brawl.

"Mitch! Jake!" She dropped the plastic book bag, ran over to them, and began pulling them apart. "What are you doing?"

Adrenaline was pumping through Mitch's blood and fear had its icy grip on his mind, distorting his thinking process. It took him a minute to figure out that it was really Sasha who'd thrown herself on his back and was trying to grab hold of his hands.

"Mitch!" she shouted in his ear. "You must stop this! Now!"

"Yeah, Mitch!" Jake yelled. "Knock it off!"

Realization finally sank in. Mitch twisted around and stared up at her. "Sasha? You're safe?"

"Yes." She pressed a kiss against his mouth. "I am safe."

The breath went out of him in a deep, relieved whoosh. "I was so worried."

"I am sorry." She glanced up at the building that was engulfed in a cloud of steam as the fire hoses doused the flames. "I promise, Mitch. I was not cooking."

Her expression was so earnest, Mitch had to laugh. "Sweetheart, I wouldn't care if you had started it. So long as you're safe, that's all that matters."

Jake pushed himself to his feet. "Since you two love-birds don't need any company, I think I'll go see about getting some ice for my eye. You pack one helluva punch."

"Sorry about that," Mitch said, not bothering to point out that Jake had gotten a few good licks of his own in.

"Hey, you were worried about your bride." Jake shrugged. "I would've behaved the same way if I'd thought Katie was up there."

When he was gone, Mitch said, "We need to talk."

Sasha nodded, and opened her mouth to respond when a sudden burst of water from a misdirected fire hose sent them skidding across the lawn. When they came to a stop, Mitch was lying on top of her. And they were both laughing.

"How come I always end up getting wet when I'm with you?"

"You're not the only one," she mused, grinning up at him.

"True." He tenderly pushed strands of wet hair away from her face and said, "I love you. And I don't want you to go to Big Sur."

His heart plummeted as tears flooded into her eyes. "I mean, to live," he said quickly. "Of course you want to visit your dad. But I want you to stay here with me."

''Oh, Mitch, I love you, too. And I wasn't going to leave you. Ever! You're stuck with me. For better or worse.''

The way she was looking up at him made Mitch feel ten feet tall. He also decided that perhaps it wasn't so bad being a hero after all. As long as he could always be Sasha's hero.

''I found your house, Sasha. Your dream house. It's ours if we—you—want it.''

Sasha stared up at him. It was too much. Her father, a husband, her American citizenship, and her dream house. *Their* dream house, she reminded herself. Hers and Mitch's. All in one glorious day!

Surely no woman had ever been luckier. Or happier. She laughed as she threw her arms around her husband. ''My hero.''

Just The Way You Are

JANICE KAISER

Dedication

For Jack and Susan Pfeiffer

Prologue

————◆————

Britt Kingsley stood in the tired old lobby of the Roxy Theater and stared out at Main Street. Her father, the Reverend Thomas Kingsley, was nearby, chatting with Norm Williams who'd buttonholed him just as they were about to leave. Both men were speaking earnestly about church business, but Britt wasn't paying close attention. Instead, she was thinking how strange it was to be back in Indiana, and how true the old saw was that you couldn't go home again.

Los Angeles seemed a million miles away. Still, if nothing else, the past few days had convinced her that L.A. was home now. Britt loved her father and appreciated the happy childhood he and her late mother had given her. Yet this visit had confirmed that win, lose or draw, her future lay elsewhere and there was no turning back.

After she'd fixed her father a big Caesar salad and seafood pasta to give him a taste of the California cuisine she'd come to love, she'd suggested they take in a movie. *Code Red,* a hot new thriller, was playing at the Roxy. On the plane coming from L.A. she'd read an article in *Variety* about the film and its director, Derek Redmond. It was a highly favorable piece, praising both. She'd told her father she just had to see it.

"I'm afraid all the shooting and explosions and car chases aren't my cup of tea, honey," he'd said. "Especially not during Christmas week. This is the time of year to see *It's A Wonderful Life*."

"I know that, Daddy, but it'll cost seven or eight bucks to see *Code Red* in Los Angeles and it's only four-fifty here. Can't pass up a bargain like that."

The Reverend Thomas Kingsley had tapped his daughter on the nose and jokingly said, "Another good reason to come home, Britt. Hays Crossing might be boring compared to California, but life's affordable here. And safe."

In the end, they'd compromised. He'd agreed to go with her to the movie theater—something he hadn't done in years—and she promised to rent *It's A Wonderful Life* and watch it with him on TV.

As Norm droned on, Britt wandered over to have a look at the latest movie posters. The tangy smell of buttered popcorn filled the air, evoking a thousand memories. She'd seen her first film ever at the Roxy. And this was where she and Tommy Bender had come for their first date in junior high. She didn't recall what film they'd seen, but they'd sat in the balcony and held hands the entire time.

That had been eleven or twelve years earlier, but in a way it seemed like forever. Yet the Roxy remained unchanged. The worn ruby red carpeting looked exactly the same as it had back then. Only the face of the kid behind the refreshment counter and the names of the films advertised on the posters were different.

Now that she thought about it, her father and Hays Crossing were sort of like the Roxy—they hadn't changed very much, either. The town had gotten a new Burger King. A farm-implements dealership had opened and a there was a new wing on the community hospital. Still, the essential nature of both her father and the town was the same. *She* was the one who was different.

Britt glanced back at her father, who was listening patiently to Norm's lament. She'd forgotten how trying a clergyman's life could be. Her mother had complained about that often while Britt was growing up, although she wouldn't have changed her husband for the world. Thomas Kingsley was a decent man, a man who gave unstintingly of himself whenever he was needed. That made being his child both easier and more difficult.

Britt wandered back to him. "Excuse me, Daddy," she said, touching his arm, "I'll wait out front while you finish your conversation. I want to get some air."

"Sorry to interrupt your evening, Britt," Norm Williams said.

"No problem, Norm," she told him. "I want to enjoy a little of this crisp Midwestern air."

"Guess it's a change from the palm trees and beaches out in California," he replied.

"True."

"Bet you don't miss having to shovel sidewalks, though."

"No, but I do miss the seasons," she said, turning for the door. "Finish your conversation."

"I'll be there in a few minutes," her father called after her.

Britt stepped onto the icy sidewalk that had been cleared of snow and sanded for better footing. The cold air stung her eyes. She turned up the collar of the bright pink parka she'd worn as a teenager and had left in the closet of her old room for just this sort of visit. Then she looked up and down the nearly deserted street. It was festooned with Christmas decorations and twinkling lights.

Main Street, like the old two-story brick house where she'd grown up, seemed smaller than she remembered. Smaller even than it had on her last trip back to Indiana. Its main appeal now, besides the comfort of familiarity, was that it was safe. L.A. was sparkling and glittery but it was a jungle, and living there was an adventure. Southern California was a place where people went to chase their dreams. That's why she'd gone there, and had been struggling so hard to make her dreams come true.

Britt stepped over to the glass case where the movie poster for *Code Red* was being displayed. How many times had she looked into that very case as a girl and imagined her own name and face on a poster for the world to see—her thick honey hair just brushing her shoulders, her firm jaw and the even features that the camera loved. A year and a half ago she had left Indiana with stars in her eyes, determined to make a name for herself as an actress, become famous.

Britt knew she was pretty by most standards, blond with the good looks of the girl next door. "Meg Ryanish" was the way her agent had billed her—girlish and womanly at the same time. And she was a good actress—not the most fabulous ever to hit Hollywood, but good enough to make it to the big screen. Talent was only the starting point, though. Everybody knew that. You needed luck and something else—a drive to succeed, a determination not to accept failure.

If there was an explanation for why she hadn't made it, that was it. She hadn't wanted it enough. She hadn't been willing to keep at it, no matter what. But she'd stuck it out for a year as she'd promised herself, getting a few bit parts along the way and a number of propositions having more to do with her sex appeal than her acting talent.

If her struggle had proved anything more than the fact that she wasn't meant to be an actress, it was that she had another love besides acting—a love that *was* powerful and consuming. She'd discovered it almost by accident. She had been reading a screenplay to prepare for an audition when she realized it wasn't well written. At least, not by her standards.

She had carefully analyzed the script, deciding she'd change the motivation here and the characterization there. Before she knew what was happening, she'd gotten out the old computer she'd used in college and started tinkering, and in the process had become a writer.

While she was in college her mother had died and left her a small inheritance, which she'd used to finance her trial year in Hollywood. There hadn't been enough money to stay there after she'd finally given up on an acting career, so she'd taken a job as a temp to pay the rent while she pounded away on her computer at night, churning out screenplays and honing her craft.

It was clear from the start that she'd discovered her life's work. She had a burning passion, an uncompromising determination to succeed—no matter the consequences. There had been no greater joy than the night she'd finished her first screenplay. It was at three o'clock in the morning on a balmy August night. She was alone in her apartment. In five hours she had to be at work, but she couldn't have felt more exhilarated. It had been a wonderful, miraculous moment.

Even though she hadn't been able to get an agent to take on that project, she had gotten some words of encouragement. Others recognized she had talent, and that was all she'd needed to keep her hooked. She wanted to see the world of her imagination come to life on the screen.

For the past few months she'd lived for that. And for the past few months she'd been learning how difficult it was to get a script read by someone who mattered. But she remained undaunted. By day she typed forms, answered phones and ran copy machines. At night she came alive, living in her imaginary world.

On Thanksgiving Day her father had phoned and invited her home for Christmas. She couldn't afford the price of a plane ticket, but promised that next year she'd find a way. A few days later a ticket arrived in the mail with a note from her dad, saying that both he and Hays Crossing deserved to see her. That made Britt realize she couldn't turn her back on the people she loved simply because she'd become obsessed.

Just then a flatbed truck piled high with bales of hay and carolers came up Main Street to the strains of "Jingle Bells." When it got opposite the Roxy, the truck stopped momentarily and the singers went into full voice, serenading her.

Britt recalled doing the very same thing not so many years before—riding through the streets of Hays Crossing, full of the holiday spirit, singing joyfully and having a good time. After thirty seconds, the truck moved on up the street. The carolers waved and Britt waved back, a sentimental tear coming to her eye. It wasn't the sort of thing one saw in L.A. It was no longer a part of her life, and she felt sad about that.

She watched the truck turn the corner and disappear from sight. For a moment or two she could hear the singing, but it soon grew faint and Main Street was quiet again.

The door opened behind her and her father stepped out onto the sidewalk. "Sorry, honey. Norm's been concerned about the shortfall in the budget and wanted to speak with me before the board meeting tomorrow night."

Thomas Kingsley was a slight man with refined features and an aesthetic, sensitive face. His once-sandy hair was now mostly white. He was quietly stately, a caring person. His greatest virtue as far as Britt was concerned, was that with her he could step out of the minister role and be a father first and foremost. She liked him as a person and considered him a friend.

"I understand," she said, taking his arm. "Don't forget, Daddy, I'm a veteran of lots of nights at home alone with Mama while you were attending meetings and calling on the sick or grieving."

They started up the sidewalk, headed for home. At Britt's insistence they'd walked the six blocks from the house to the movie theater.

"One of my biggest regrets is that I didn't fully appreciate how much I neglected you and your mother all those years," her father said.

"Don't be silly, Daddy. We knew you had important work to do. And we didn't consider ourselves neglected. Mama said she knew what she was getting into when she married a minister, and she never regretted it for one minute."

He patted her gloved hand. "You have the same generous spirit as your mother, sweetheart. I can't tell you how much I miss you both."

"Not being able to see you regularly is my only regret about leaving Indiana," she said.

"You really love it out there in California, don't you, honey?"

"I love writing. I can't tell you how much satisfaction it gives me. My regret is I'm not a bit more successful. But you know, the funny thing is that it doesn't matter. Not really. I'll keep on writing even if I never sell a screenplay."

"Strangely enough, I understand that. I feel the same way about my work."

"I'm a chip off the old block, I guess."

"The block you're a chip off is your mother, Britt. You're fortunate to be so much like her. I suppose that's why I feel so much more possessive of you than I should. It's also why I keep telling myself you have your own life to lead, and that I should be supportive but not domineering. But if I should slip now and then, I hope you'll understand."

Britt leaned over and kissed him on the cheek. "I couldn't ask for a better father."

He beamed happily.

They stopped at the corner and looked in the brightly lit window of Swig's Hobby and Toy Shop. It had been the origin of many of Britt's Christmas presents growing up. They watched the model train making its way around the snowy mountain.

"Funny how I never noticed that Santa always brought me the very thing that had delighted me most when you and Mama brought me down to Swig's to browse."

"We're all attached to our dreams, sweetheart, and none of us wants to let them go. Your mother and I always wanted to make your dreams come true when you were a child, and I want your dreams to come true now."

Britt wondered if he was making a subtle reference to her dream of being a screenwriter. "What are you trying to say, Dad? Tell me the truth. Do you think I'm chasing an empty dream by wanting to write?" she asked.

They waited for a car to turn the corner at Maple and then crossed the street, continuing on their way.

"I think you should do what makes you happy, Britt."

"Writing makes me happy. This isn't like when I wanted to act. I know it probably seems like it is to you, but it's not. This is…different. I feel it in my gut. And besides, I'm sure I have talent."

"You were a good actress, too, Britt. The trouble was, you picked a challenging and difficult field. It's shattered lots of hopes and dreams."

"I know you think I should pursue a more practical career, and you may be right, but this is something I just *have* to do. There's no other way to explain it."

"It's your life, honey, and you have to live it as you see fit. My only word of advice is to consider all your options, not just the work you do."

Britt knew he was referring to her personal life. One of his greatest concerns from the first had been about the people she would associate with in show business, especially the men. Her father had always had confidence in her judgment. He knew she was levelheaded. But his fear was that she wouldn't meet the sort of man she'd want to settle down with in a place like Hollywood.

She'd tried explaining that nice as many of the young men were in Hays Crossing, she simply didn't have anything in common with them—and never would. The men she'd met thus far in L.A. were a lot more interesting, but they had their limitations, too. And their dangers.

Her first morning home her father had mentioned that her high school boyfriend, Tim Ragsdale, had opened his own insurance agency and that he and his wife now had a second child. Britt's first reaction was that she was glad Tim had married Ellen Cross, not her. And yet, she liked Tim a lot. It was too bad she couldn't find someone with his character and decency, but who also shared her dreams.

The thought made her smile. Now *that* was a pipe dream if ever there was one.

They were soon beyond the business district. They walked past homes festooned with Christmas lights, painted wooden Santas on the roofs, snowmen on the lawns and glittering trees in the front windows. It was all so warm and familiar, and yet in an odd way vaguely sad. They both had been silent for a while.

"Tell me, Daddy, what did you think of *Code Red?*"

He thought for a moment, then replied, "I could have done with a little less shooting, but I was surprised how good it was, actually."

"That's because we cared about the characters and their problems. The most powerful drama is the human drama."

"Do you write that way, Britt?" her father asked.

"I try. I'm just a beginner, Daddy, but I'm learning."

"Well, tell me this. Was the script for *Code Red* significantly better than what you've done?"

"I'm sure it was, though I can't be objective about

my own work. I'm determined to do something *as* good down the line, though. It may take a while, but I'll do it someday.''

He patted her hand again. ''I admire your spirit, honey.''

They turned the corner and headed up their street. Britt squeezed her father's arm as the night chill started getting to her.

''The interesting thing about film is that it's a collaborative effort,'' she said. ''The script is important, of course, but what the director and actors do with it is equally important. *Code Red* was brilliantly directed, in my opinion. He's awfully good.''

''I didn't even notice who the director was.''

''A man named Derek Redmond.''

''Do you know him?''

Britt laughed. ''Would that I did. He's one of the up-and-coming directors in Hollywood.''

''Then he's young.''

''I'd say early thirties.''

''Believe me, Britt, from my perspective, that's young.''

''*Code Red* was his first big commercial film. He's done a few smaller, low-budget flicks. This one put him on the map.''

''Why don't you send him one of your screenplays?''

Britt sighed. ''If only it was that easy. When you're a nobody, it's hard to get people to actually read anything you've written. In fact, it's hard to get a script into their hands in the first place. And even if you have an agent—which I don't—selling a script is tough. Only one out of a hundred screenplays ever gets made.''

They'd come to her father's home and turned up the walk.

''And this is what you want to do as your life's work?'' he asked.

She chuckled. ''I know it sounds crazy, Daddy, but I'm determined. No matter what it takes, I'm going to find a way to make it as a writer. You'll see.''

1

Britt kept glancing at Harry Winslow's door, dreading the moment it would open. She didn't like going on job interviews any more than the next person, but that wasn't what was bothering her. This anxiety was different. Her moral integrity was on the line. She was about to do something she'd never thought she'd do—she was try to get a job under false pretenses.

The door opened and a short chubby man with thick glasses appeared. He looked to be in his early thirties and had an air of self-importance. Without even speaking to him, Britt decided he was bad news.

"Britt Kingsley?" he said.

Britt got to her feet and walked toward him. He checked her out in an obvious, unapologetic way, a smug grin on his face.

"I'm Harry Winslow," he said, offering her his hand. He was the personnel director of Continental Artists, the second-largest talent agency in Hollywood, and the man she had to get past in order to get the job.

"How do you do, Mr. Winslow?" she said, taking his clammy hand.

"I do fine," he said, twitching his brow provocatively. "Come right in."

Harry touched her waist as she passed by and Britt groaned inwardly. She hoped this wasn't going to be a casting-couch-type interview. Lord knew, she'd experienced more than her fair share of those. It had taken her a while, but she'd eventually learned that once she made up her mind not to be used that way, she could deal with the situation, though it had nearly always cost her the job. That had been okay when she'd been working as an actress, but getting on the inside of Continental Artists was essential to her plan—the plan to help promote her writing career.

Winslow gestured toward the visitor's chair, then took his place behind his desk. He folded his hands and leaned toward her, giving Britt a penetrating look, although the intimidating effect he evidently strived for was diminished somewhat by his weak chin.

"Look, Miss Kingsley," he said, "let me be blunt. There's a big red flag on your résumé from my standpoint. We might as well discuss it now, because there's no point continuing if we're not on the same page."

"What seems to be the problem, Mr. Winslow?"

"You're an actress and we can't have people working here with the intention of using the agency to further their acting career. C.A. has a firm policy against employees promoting their own interests with clients. Anybody caught doing it is summarily dismissed. No ifs, ands or buts about it."

"Mr. Winslow," she said firmly, "I am not an actress. I'm a *former* actress. There's a difference."

"How can I be sure what you say is true?"

"I don't know. I suppose you'll have to trust me." Even though that was true, Britt's words sent a stab of guilt through her.

Trust, honesty, integrity. Those had been the ideals she'd grown up with—the ones her parents had instilled in her. Britt wanted desperately not to lie. Yet she knew all too well that Hollywood was a place where fact and fiction often blurred. The town made its living on illusion. Everyone here tried their best to be what others wanted them to be. For a minister's kid from Indiana, squaring that with her core beliefs had not always been easy.

"A nice sentiment," Harry Winslow said, "but I'd rather make my decisions on the basis of cold, hard fact. When was the last time you read for a part?"

"It's been more than a year," she answered honestly. "As you can see from my résumé, I've been working as a temp with People Power for over a year now."

"Yes, but we all know that aspiring actors have to feed themselves. You could have squeezed in casting calls and small acting jobs."

"You could check with the Screen Actors Guild, Mr. Winslow."

"I will, but I thought I'd save myself the trouble if you had something you wanted to say." He grinned. "You see, I've been down this road before. More than once."

"I admit I wanted to be an actress once, but that's behind me. I haven't read for any parts or registered with any talent agents since I signed as a temp. And in the two or three months before that, I scarcely left my apartment."

"Going through withdrawal, were you?"

"Yes," Britt replied. "That's exactly what it was."

Harry Winslow scrutinized her. Britt did her best to stare him down. So far, at least, every word she had uttered was true. What ate at her was what she wasn't saying—that she wanted so badly to become a successful writer that she would scheme and hustle and manipulate and do whatever it took to get her work in front of the people who counted.

The simple fact was, Continental Artists and agencies like it were essentially dating services for the movers and shakers in the film business. Anyone on the inside of a place like C.A. had access to those people. The trick would be figuring out how to promote herself without alienating the people who mattered. That wouldn't be easy, but she'd deal with it when the time came. For now, the problem was getting her foot in the door.

She'd tried everything she could think of to get her stuff read. Nothing had worked. Now she'd been reduced to trickery. Playing the Hollywood game—that's how she'd rationalized her scheme. It had helped some, to think of it in those terms, but not a lot.

There was one other factor in the equation, as well. Britt needed to survive, and Continental Artists was an excellent place to work. The pay was good and the people were interesting. Who wouldn't want to be in the same room with Keanu Reeves or Brad Pitt? Even if it was only to serve them coffee?

Britt had been fleshing out her plan with Allison O'Donnell, her good friend who lived in the apartment across the hall from her. "Think of it this way," Allison had said, "Even if you never get one of your screenplays sold, you'll still have to eat, buy shampoo and go to a movie now and then. You could work in worse places than C.A."

Britt had reluctantly embraced Allison's logic. But the one thing she hadn't done was call her father for advice. She didn't have to. She knew what he'd say.

Harry Winslow leaned back in his chair, clasping his hands behind his head. He was checking her out again, measuring her sex appeal, perhaps speculating on his chances with her. Not that big blue eyes and thick honey hair were all that unusual in Hollywood, but Britt could tell he fancied himself the Louis B. Mayer of personnel. She'd become an expert on spotting that sort of thing.

There were times when she lamented the fact that Hollywood was so image-oriented. Everybody had to look good. Style was everything and substance hardly mattered. She'd played the game. She wore her skirts short and got sixty-dollar haircuts when she could afford them, and sometimes when she couldn't. She flirted, too, because in L.A. people flirted as routinely as they chatted about the weather at home in Indiana.

"All right," Harry said after a few moments of reflection, "let's assume you've kicked the acting habit and gotten it out of your blood. Why do you want to work for C.A.? Do you expect to get some kind of vicarious pleasure from being around people who have made it?''

Britt drew a long breath. ''I'm looking for a position with career possibilities and I just didn't have that at People Power. I see that sort of opportunity here.'' She looked him in the eye, but that didn't prevent another pang of conscience.

''Why a talent agency? There are careers to be had in law firms, brokerage houses, whatever.''

Britt shifted uncomfortably, recrossing her legs. Harry watched her every move, probably thinking he'd backed her into a corner. Britt knew she had to play this very carefully.

''Having been an actress briefly, I know the business,'' she said. ''I can't say that about law or investments. It seems to me I'd be more effective working in a field in which I've had at least some experience.''

Harry Winslow leaned back in his chair, rubbing his chin. He did his best to look unconvinced. ''Let's say I'm your best friend. Tell me about your goals. Assuming we hire you, where do you see yourself in five years?''

''Occupying one of those offices out there. I see myself making people stars and contributing to their success.''

''You want to be an agent.''

''Yes,'' she said, elevating her chin to signal determination. Britt was acting now. ''I don't want to be a secretary forever,'' she went on. ''I'm willing do a damned fine job of it for however long it takes to learn the business. I know I've got to pay my dues. But sooner or later I'll be ready for more.''

The skepticism on his face had been transformed into glowing pride. Britt sensed that she'd convinced him. He'd decided she was all right, perhaps even an unpolished gem. That, after all, was his mission in life. She could almost hear him gloating to his associates. ''I've found a real firecracker. Dedication, ambition, drive, T&A—a girl that's got it all.''

''Very impressive,'' he said aloud. ''You sounded like you meant that. Couldn't be you gave up on your acting career too quickly, could it?'' He gave her a wink.

Britt wanted to slug him, but she kept her poise, knowing he was baiting her. ''I'm a hard worker,'' she said simply. ''All my references will vouch for that.''

''They already have,'' he replied, grinning smugly. ''You check out. I just had that question about your real motives. I had to satisfy myself you were on the up and up.'' He let his eyes roll down her, signaling his satisfaction.

Britt's first reaction was to ask him to get on with it, but she told herself that she had to let him do his thing. Once she was hired, Harry Winslow wouldn't matter. But right now he still stood between her and access to some of the leading producers and directors in Hollywood.

Harry suddenly swung his chair around and stared out the window at the smog. All Britt could see over the back of the chair was the top of his head with its tangerine-size bald spot. "Tell you what I'm going to do," he said. "I'm going to send you down to Miranda Maxwell. The position we've been talking about reports to her. Miranda's our newest partner, a real go-getter. She's asked for someone with initiative, a fast learner. This is your chance to prove yourself to her. What happens from here on out is up to you." He turned his chair back around to face her. He was steepling his fingers. "Remember, at C.A. we view former actresses with skepticism. Don't think this is the way to the silver screen, because it isn't."

"No, I understand."

He reached for the phone, letting his eyes flicker over her. "I'll let Miranda know you're on the way down."

"So, Britt, did you have a nice little chat with our Mr. Winslow?"

Miranda Maxwell was thirty-five, English, darkly attractive with pale, pale skin, smooth as porcelain— the sort that was as common in the British Isles as raindrops. Britt's Grandmother Kingsley, who'd been born in Wales, had told her that.

"He's...unusual," Britt said in response to Miranda's question.

"Good job, you're a diplomat. Heaven knows, it doesn't hurt in this line of work," Miranda Maxwell said. "Don't repeat this, but Harry's our stalking horse. If an applicant survives half an hour with him, we know she's got grit. From this point forward it's qualifications and chemistry.'' Miranda looked down at the résumé on her desk and contemplated it for a moment.

Britt felt better already. It was nice to know Miranda had a sense of humor, and a sense of proportion. Harry Winslow had made her wonder if coming to work at C.A. would be such a good idea, after all.

The real problem—the dilemma that wouldn't seem to go away—was that to get the job she had to keep her true agenda hidden. Her determination to succeed as a writer at all costs was so fierce that she was no longer sure in her heart what was right and what was wrong. The desperation that had been building over the past several months had blurred everything.

It was October now. Another year had passed. She had six screenplays in her drawer and not a single offer to show for all her effort. If she'd learned anything this past year, it was that nobody in Hollywood gave you something for nothing. You had to fight for every break, every opportunity. But did it mean she had the moral right to engineer her own breaks? That was the question.

While Miranda Maxwell studied her application, Britt checked out the office. It had a certain panache even though it was not very large. The decor was eclectic. There were several framed prints, mostly nineteenth-century theater scenes. A fine antique mahogany desk. Lots of books. And photos of family and celebrities. Miranda in evening clothes with Sir John Gielgud and Sir Anthony Hopkins. Miranda, looking much younger, with Vanessa Redgrave. Miranda in the fatherly embrace of Sir Richard Attenborough. Miranda standing between Kenneth Branagh and Emma Thompson, everyone smiling, especially Miranda.

Britt wanted to ask if she really knew all those people, or if she just happened to get photographed with them. Miranda was either well connected, or she had a knack for getting invited to parties. A bouquet of mixed flowers sat on the corner of the desk. Britt savored the perfume of it.

"No doubt Harry gave you his speech about forswearing screen and stage to work here," Miranda said, looking up.

"Yes."

Miranda studied her. "You've got the looks and a definite presence. What kept you from making it?"

"I guess I didn't have the burning desire. Not deep down."

"That usually is key. Some are luckier than others, but in this business a determination to succeed is essential."

Britt nodded, knowing that Miranda was describing her as a screenwriter, not an actress.

"No regrets?" Miranda asked.

Britt knew that although more subtle, Miranda was asking the same question Harry Winslow had. "My acting phase is over," she said.

"I don't mind a person 'having done,'" Miranda said. "To be truthful, I consider it an advantage. Always helps to know what it's like to be on the other side."

Britt nodded, pleased that her past didn't constitute a black mark. Of course, that still left the problem of her present ambitions.

"All the same," Miranda went on, "I can't have staff mucking with my clients. There'll be no self-promotion. When a star or director is with their agent, it's like visiting Mother. This environment must be safe, supportive and salubrious. The three *S*s, I call them. We're looking out for *them,* not for ourselves."

The admonition made Britt feel sick. Promoting herself was *exactly* what she had in mind and Miranda had put the moral issue squarely on her shoulders. What should she do? Her mind raced. She could say she'd changed her mind and walk out. But then she would be without a job—and she did need to eat. Perhaps there was a way she could be honest with Miranda and still take the position. After all, fledgling screenwriters needed daytime work, too.

"I trust you can live with that," Miranda said.

"Yes, Miss Maxwell."

"Miranda, by all means. Good heavens." She smiled faintly. "I only *look* this old," she said, making Britt laugh. Miranda glanced at the résumé again. "And you are…twenty-six, I see. Just the right age for a younger sister."

Britt smiled, liking the woman, although in a way that only made things worse.

Miranda placed a well-manicured finger against her cheek, assessing her. She was in a plain white blouse and dark wool skirt. Understated earrings. Thin gold watch. No rings. Safe, supportive, salubrious. The words went through Britt's head.

"Tell me about yourself, love," Miranda said. "It's a ruddy bore, I know, but we are our pasts, aren't we?"

Britt shifted uneasily. She felt like such a phony. "Well, let's see…"

"You can skip the parts the law won't allow me to question," Miranda said. "Your rules about employment in this country are too bloody confusing for me to keep straight."

Britt smiled. "I don't have any dark secrets in my past. I grew up in Indiana. Majored in theatrical arts at the University of Michigan. After graduation I returned to my hometown and took a job in the local recreation department, teaching theater arts to children. Then I did a stint in regional theater, doing some acting, but mostly behind-the-scenes work. Everything from scenery, props and lighting to typing letters and reading scripts.

"Finally, I decided if I was ever going to get anywhere I'd have to head for L.A. So I came here a couple of years ago with stars in my eyes."

"I know the story well," Miranda said. "But now your dream is to be an agent. Harry's made a note to that effect."

Britt was sorry now she'd come up with that story, but if she hadn't said something when Harry had pressed her, she'd have found herself in the parking lot five minutes later, headed for her next job interview. "I admit to being ambitious," she said, waffling.

"Enough about that," Miranda replied. "Let's discuss this position. I should tell you how I work and how you'll be expected to fit in. No point in going on if it doesn't appeal to you."

Miranda gave her a rundown of her client list, discussing the way she liked to work. She also spoke of the individuality of each of her clients.

Fifteen minutes of rapport-building passed before Miranda leaned back in her chair and said, "I've got a good feeling about you, Britt. I think we'd make a good team. I want you to be my administrative assistant."

Britt was elated. The door had finally opened. She'd be on the inside! It might take weeks or months, but sooner or later she'd find a chance to talk to someone about her screenplays—someone who might help her get her work read…or optioned…or, please God, produced.

The hell of it was, in order to do that she'd have to live a lie. She'd done her best to rationalize that, though. She had no intention of hurting anyone and until the time came when she did have a chance to put her work in the hands of someone who might appreciate it, she'd work her tail off, do the job to the best of her ability.

"Well, ducks," Miranda said, "what do you say?"

Britt had to pull herself together. "I'm speechless," she finally managed. "But I couldn't be happier."

"Super!" Miranda Maxwell seemed genuinely

pleased. "I'm sure we'll get on fabulously. I must warn you, though, there's loads of work. In a week I'm off to London for a fortnight, so I'm glad to see you can start immediately. It's essential I have you in place and trained in the basics before I'm off. I'm not keen on going just now, but it can't be helped. Family business. But never mind, we'll be talking daily while I'm gone. You'll be my lifeline to my clients, Britt, so you'll have to be up to speed, as we say."

"I'll certainly do my best."

Miranda beamed. "The hectic pace of life at C.A. can be a bloody nuisance, but of course I wouldn't trade it for anything. Let's hope you feel the same."

"I'm sure I will, Miss Maxwell—Miranda, I mean."

Miranda picked up the phone. "I'll just give Harry a ring and tell him to start the paperwork on you." She spoke briefly, saying that Britt would be down to see him presently, then put down the phone and sighed. "That's done, though I'm afraid you'll have to humor Harry a bit more. Forms, you know."

Britt nodded. She looked at Miranda and had a tremendous urge to blurt out the truth, to tell her that she was really an aspiring screenwriter, a woman who desperately wanted to get her work into the hands of the right people.

"What is it, dear?" Miranda asked, fingering her necklace. "You look distraught. Surely the prospect of seeing Harry's not that horrific."

"No, I'm just letting it all sink in."

Miranda nodded and got to her feet. So did Britt.

Then Miranda came around her desk and shook Britt's hand. "Off you go. Half an hour or so with Harry and you're free till tomorrow at eight-thirty, sharp. Come prepared, ducks. Before I leave for London, you're going to know my clients as well as I!"

2

"So, a week on the job and already you're in charge." Sally Farland was at the door, cheerful and pleasantly plump in another of her short leather skirts and boots. She grinned as she peered into Britt's office.

"In charge of answering the phone and relaying messages to London," Britt said. "I haven't had to make any earthshaking decisions so far."

"Never fear, Miranda will keep you hopping," Sally said. She touched her unruly brown curls. "She's ambitious, that one. Smart lady. And a good boss."

Sally was Gordon Mallik's assistant. Gordon, an affable, balding man of forty-five with apple cheeks, had several actor clients, including two or three of Hollywood's biggest names. During Britt's third day on the job, Carrie Hunter had visited him.

Britt couldn't help staring when the actress had passed her in the hall. Since her Oscar nomination, Carrie Hunter was one of the hottest names in the business. She'd dropped by to talk scripts with Gordon as Sally had run around frantically, bringing them Evian water, or getting somebody or other on the phone. The energy level in the place always went up, Britt discovered, when a big star was visiting.

Work at C.A. was stimulating, and Miranda's list of director clients looked absolutely mouthwatering to a budding screenwriter. The biggest name among her clients was Oliver Wheatley. He'd had one Oscar nomination and was a contender for a second. Like many of Miranda's clients, he was British. Miranda had explained that her goal now was to increase the number of Americans on her list. She'd been working hard to cultivate the younger, up-and-coming American directors. "Get them early," she'd told Britt. "That's my philosophy."

Britt gave Sally a woebegone look. "A week isn't much preparation time to be left alone. I hope I'm ready for this."

"You'll be fine. Gordon and I will help if you need anything. He promised Miranda he'd watch over you."

"She didn't seem too concerned when she left. But there's so much to remember—who I can say what to, and what not to say to certain people. There are the ones to be businesslike with, and the ones to kiss and hug."

"Fear not. My extension is your panic button," Sally assured.

Sally had been helpful from day one. They'd gone to lunch twice and Sally hadn't been shy about giving her the skinny on the office, from the "working slob's perspective," as she called it.

"I'll do my best," Britt said.

"Piece of cake," Sally said, giving her a thumbs-up. "Got to get back to my desk. By the end of the week you'll be loving it. Trust me."

Alone at her desk, Britt checked her list of things to do. Miranda wanted her to call Ian Harbury's L.A. publicist and reiterate that under no circumstances could Westley Asquith agree to an interview with Joyce Wilson. According to Miranda, Joyce had tried to crucify Oliver Wheatley in a recent interview.

"Joyce Wilson may still be fighting the Revolutionary War, as you call it," Miranda had explained, "but my clients are not, and I won't have them treated in such a shoddy manner. Westley simply can't be allowed to speak with the woman."

Britt couldn't make the call until midafternoon. Nothing else had to be done just then so she pulled out the client list, comparing the names with her notes. Miranda had discussed some of the clients' career goals with her, but the thing Britt cared about most—which of them might be interested in her own work—was not something she could easily bring up without raising suspicion. And besides, except for Oliver Wheatley, Britt didn't know enough about any of them to judge whether or not they were likely to be interested in one of her scripts. She'd have to bide her time and watch for an opportunity.

The phone rang and Britt jumped to answer it. It was Tiffany, the receptionist. "Britt, Derek Redmond is on line three for Miranda."

Britt's mouth dropped open. Derek Redmond! Ever

since she'd seen *Code Red* with her father the previous December she'd been fascinated by the director and his work. His next film was due to be released by TriStar soon and she couldn't wait to see it. In fact, Derek Redmond had been on her mind a great deal during the past ten months.

It seemed pieces on him kept turning up in newspapers and periodicals. At the dentist's office she'd picked up a copy of *People* Magazine only to find a picture of him and a short article. And then a few months later there was a blurb on him in Walter Scott's "Personality Parade" column in *Parade*. A reader had asked for particulars on his personal life. Scott had said Redmond led a very private life, avoiding the Hollywood social whirl. There was no particular lady in his life, although he'd been seen in public with several different young women, none of them celebrities. Scott had used the word "charismatic" to describe Derek Redmond, which fit perfectly with Britt's perception of him. Ever since seeing *Code Red* she'd had a crush on him.

He was the first director to whom she'd sent the script of her thriller, *Flash Point*. She'd been certain he would love it, but the envelope had been returned unopened with a note saying that he didn't read unsolicited manuscripts when sent through agents.

Now Derek Redmond was on the telephone, waiting to speak with her! She couldn't believe it.

"Tiffany..." Britt said, feeling a sudden panic.

"Yes?"

"Did you tell him Miranda's in London?"

"No, I didn't say a thing, except that I'd put him through to her office. You'll have to tell him whatever she wants. Got to go, kid. Got another call."

Britt looked at the flashing light on her console. Her hand shaking, she picked up the receiver. "Miranda Maxwell's office," she croaked, her insides quavering.

"Hi, this is Derek Redmond," he said easily. "Is Miranda in, please?"

"No...no, I'm sorry she isn't, Mr. Redmond. She won't be back for...at least...uh—"

"Well, I don't actually need to talk to her. Are you her assistant?"

"Yes, sir."

"I'll bet you have a name," he gently chided.

"Yes, it's Britt," she replied.

"Britt, huh? But you aren't a Brit yourself by the sound of your voice."

"No, sir."

He chuckled. "Well, it wasn't very funny, was it? Not even a very good pun. Sorry."

It was only then that she realized he was trying to be humorous. She flushed, not knowing what to say.

"Maybe you could give Miranda a message for me, Britt," he said.

"Certainly."

"Last week I did breakfast with Oliver Wheatley. We were comparing notes on the business and I told him the hardest part was finding a good script. I really admired *Go Fish*. It wasn't hackneyed. When I asked Oliver how he found the script, he said Miranda had put him onto it. Claimed she had a wonderful eye, a real sense for the director's artistic impulses.

"Which is the long way of saying that I wanted to know if Miranda's seen anything that might be good for me. Ask her to give it some thought, if you would, then maybe she and I could talk."

"Yes, I will, Mr. Redmond." Britt's brain was reeling. Dear God, was this the opportunity she'd been waiting for? If so, she had to say something. Fast. *Carpe diem.* Seize the moment. "Uh…I'm sure Miranda will want to know what it is you're looking for, exactly."

"That's the problem. I'm not sure. Not another thriller, I don't want to get typecast. That happens with a short résumé, I know, and if I want to be regarded as diverse, I might as well start branching out now. From what Oliver said, Miranda's perfectly in tune with that."

"I'm sure she is. I know she's a fan of yours."

"Oh, really?"

"Yes. We were talking about *Code Red* the other day. Miranda thinks you have a lively, fresh style. In my opinion, *Code Red* was everything a good thriller should be. It had heart as well as thrills."

"What a nice compliment, Britt. Thank you. I'd like to take full credit for the success of the film, but I was working with a good screenwriter and some very talented actors. It's nice to know that people appreciate the things you strive to accomplish, though."

"You have millions of fans, I'm sure."

"You seem to be knowledgeable about filmmaking," he said.

"I try to keep up."

"Miranda's fortunate to have you working for her."

"Thank you."

She felt equal measures of elation and terror. Derek Redmond sounded like a nice person, somebody she could talk to about the things she cared about. The fantasy image of him in her mind was apparently more accurate than she could possibly have imagined.

"I've got to run, Britt," he said. "It's been very nice talking to you. Have Miranda give me a buzz, will you? Let me give you my number."

Britt jotted it down, her heart pounding like crazy. For a solid year she'd been reduced to considering ploys like throwing a brick with a script tied to it over some producer's garden wall or lying down in front of a director's limo—anything to put her work into the hands of somebody who mattered. And now, who was at her fingertips but Derek Redmond! Fate had to have done this for a reason.

"Mr. Redmond," she said quickly before he could hang up, "have you given much thought to romantic comedy?"

There was a short pause. "What do you mean? Nora Ephrom-type stuff?"

"Yeah, but maybe a little more down-home. Not so New York."

There was a hesitation on the line. Britt felt her stomach knot.

"Why?" he asked. "Does Miranda have something along those lines she's shopping for?"

Britt swallowed hard. "Well...I heard her talking about a script the other day, saying it had tremendous possibilities, but that it needed the right director."

"Hmm," Derek said. "Who's the writer?"

Panic seized her. "Oh, an unknown. Miranda came across it purely by chance." Britt felt her cheeks burn. She closed her eyes and the sexy photo of Derek Redmond in *People* came to mind.

"Does the screenplay have a title?" he asked.

She bit her lip, hesitating. Then she plunged ahead and said, *"Dream Girl."*

"Hmm. Well, you've piqued my curiosity, Britt. Never can tell what gem might by lying around waiting to be snatched up, can you?"

"No, that's certainly true." She almost forgot to breathe.

"Listen," he said, "tell Miranda I'd be interested in seeing *Dream Girl.* Maybe when she calls we can discuss it."

Britt was so excited, she thought she'd expire on the spot. "I'll tell her, Mr. Redmond."

"Great. I'll be looking forward to her call."

Redmond said goodbye but it took Britt a few seconds after he'd hung up for her to have the presence of mind to put down the phone. What had she done? How on earth could she have Miranda call Derek Redmond from London and talk about a script she knew nothing about? Dare she tell her boss the truth? No, to Miranda it would look like she was feathering her own nest—which she was. Even if Britt's script was the best she'd read in ten years, Miranda would be furious.

Britt stared at the number Derek Redmond had given her. Maybe she could call him back and say she'd been mistaken. On the other hand, what if she sent her script over to him and he loved it? What if he actually wanted to do it?

If that happened, she wouldn't need this job. On second thought, maybe she would. Even if he optioned *Dream Girl,* it did not guarantee that the film would get produced—and that was when the writer made serious money; when the movie was actually shot.

Britt put her fingers to her fiery cheeks. This was insane. Absolutely crazy. Yet she was sure it was the golden opportunity she'd been waiting for. This was her chance to put her script in the hands of a director with a guarantee that it would be given serious attention.

But the fly in the ointment was that he wanted to talk to Miranda. How could she handle that? Send the script over with a cheery note saying that Miranda was headed for London and would chat with him when she returned? If he decided to phone her in England, the jig would be up. No, she had to figure out something else. But what?

Britt looked at her telephone for the millionth time in less than an hour. Never had she felt so torn. In fact, she couldn't remember ever feeling this indecisive. It had been awfully hard telling her father she'd decided to move to L.A., but that wasn't because she was unsure about what she wanted to do—it was because she loved him and knew he'd be disappointed. This was a horrible quandary. A voice in the back of her mind kept saying, "Pick up the phone, do it!" But still she hesitated.

Her basic plan was good—if she could pull it off. The problem was she hadn't practiced the accent. Still, she'd been around Miranda long enough to know how she talked, and she had a darned good ear. Her drama teachers had agreed that her accents were her greatest talent. In class skits she'd done Edith Bunker, both Scarlett O'Hara and Prissy from *Gone With the Wind,* and even Marlon Brando as the Godfather. The real question now was whether she'd be able to do a serious businesswoman talking about serious business. And even if she could, did she dare?

She wrung her hands, torn, uncertain, sure one moment that her whole life had been leading up to this point, positive the next that God would strike her dead for her perfidy and deceit. She told herself that this was why she'd come to work for C.A. It was all part of the plan. But now that the moment of truth had come, instead of rushing ahead she was asking herself how anything so necessary could be wrong. Surely courage would be rewarded. Fear and guilt could only lead to defeat.

Finally, riding the crest of a wave of fierce determination, she stepped into Miranda's office and closed the door. When she shut her eyes Britt could hear Miranda's voice, her crisp British middle-class accent. Educated, but not too educated. Sophisticated, but not too sophisticated.

"You'll love it here, ducks," she intoned, testing her voice. "But you'll earn every penny, I promise you that. No rest for the wicked." Britt had to laugh. How prophetic *that* remark had been.

She sat down in Miranda's chair, took a deep breath, and dialed the number Derek Redmond had given her. He answered himself.

"Derek," she said in her best BBC voice, "this is Miranda Maxwell over at C.A. My young lady tells me you rang me this morning."

"Yes, Miranda, thanks for calling back. I'm sure Britt told you I was looking for a special script, something fresh, and that she'd brought *Dream Girl* to my attention. I'm intrigued by the notion of a romantic comedy. So the question is, can I entice you to let me have a peek?"

"Oh, my."

"Is something wrong?"

"Derek, dear, you aren't supposed to know about that script. It's not something I'm officially representing, which means it doesn't exist." She paused a heartbeat. "I'll have to talk to Britt about her loose lips."

"You mean it's unavailable?"

"Well, I didn't exactly say that, now, did I? You see, I always have something interesting in hand, love, but I try to direct the best projects toward my clients. You understand, surely."

"Well, certainly. But Britt made it sound like this might not be appropriate for your regular clients."

"She did, did she?" Britt's Miranda showed a touch of indignation.

"I might have made some unwarranted assumptions," he quickly said. "Don't blame her. In fact, I kind of forced her to tell me what she knew. She was doing her best to look out for your interests, Miranda, believe me."

Britt put her hand over the mouthpiece. She couldn't help a little giggle. He was being sweet, protecting her from Miranda's wrath. What a decent thing to do. It was endearing and made her heart reach out to him. "This is Hollywood," she said, pulling herself together and getting back in character. "Which means we're all selling something, aren't we, love?"

"Thanks for being understanding."

"Continental Artists is in business to serve, Derek."

"Would you tell me a little about *Dream Girl?*" he asked.

"There's no harm in that, I should think. Well, let's see.... Innocent but clever country girl—say, Winona Ryder—meets hip young man from the city—say, Brad Pitt—and they have a romance. Gordon described it as a Generation X *Bridges of Madison County.*"

"I get the picture. I want to see it."

"Hmm. You've put me on the spot now, haven't you?"

"If I'm out of line, just say so," he said.

Britt felt a rush of power—power as she'd never

known it before. Here she was, with one of the brightest young directors in Hollywood practically begging
her to send him her script. But then she realized that
her power was false. The instant she was discovered,
she'd go down like the *Hindenburg*.

"Are you quite sure you want to see it, Derek? It's
good, but it has absolutely nothing in common with
Code Red."

"That's exactly what I want, Miranda. Something
completely different."

"I see." Britt allowed a pregnant pause, almost
bursting with excitement. She was on a roll, but on
terribly thin ice. She couldn't lose sight of that.

"You didn't have somebody else in mind for it, did
you?" Derek asked.

"No, love. I don't officially have control of the
project, but of course that's a technicality. I could have
a word with the writer and fix things up in the blink
of an eye, but..."

"But what?"

Britt didn't know where her words were coming
from. It was almost as though she was sitting at her
computer and the dialogue was spilling out. "Well, to
be bloody frank about it," she said with uncanny assurance, "an associate of mine promised Ron Howard
a look, or at least I think he did. Gordon was the one
who first brought the script to my attention, you see."

"When will you know?"

"If you're that eager, I suppose I could give him a
tinkle now. Do you prefer to hold or should I ring you
back?"

"I'll hold."

Britt pushed the Hold button and all but bounced in her chair. "Bloody hell!" she said excitedly. "Miranda couldn't have done better herself." She spun the chair around, whooping with laughter. "What do you think, Gordon, love? Shall we let the poor sod have a wee peek at Britt Kingsley's masterpiece?"

She stared at the flashing light, hoping Derek Redmond's heart was pounding as furiously as hers. God, she wished she could see his face.

And then a curious feeling came over her. In the midst of her excitement she thought of his kindness, his consideration. They'd only had a couple of conversations, yet she was beginning to get a strong sense of him. And what she'd seen, she liked.

But was that good? After all, it wasn't a relationship she was striving for—not a personal relationship, anyway. This was business. She had to think of Derek Redmond as a professional opportunity.

Britt turned her attention to the phone. She stared at the flashing light, counted to twelve, then pushed the button. "You may have it, if you wish, Derek," she announced airily. "But only for a few days. Will that do?"

"Fine. Courier it to me?"

"Tomorrow."

"Sold," he said.

"You're an easy man to deal with, Derek Redmond."

"However this turns out, Miranda, we'll do lunch soon."

"That would be lovely, but I'm booked for London in a few days' time. We might have to do it later."

"I never forget a kindness," Derek said. "Oliver told me you walked on water, and now I believe it."

"You aren't sweet-talking me, are you, dear boy?"

"Yes."

"I admire your candor," she said.

"And I like your style, Miranda. We'll have to talk about the future, regardless how things turn out with *Dream Girl*."

"Delighted, of course."

"I look forward to getting the script. *Ciao*."

Britt let the receiver fall gently into the cradle, then leaned back heavily in Miranda's chair. The sober reality of it all hit her like the proverbial ton of bricks. "Dear God," she murmured, "what have I done?"

3

Britt lived on the third floor of a fifty-year-old apartment building in West Hollywood, off Sunset Boulevard. She parked her ancient Toyota up the street from it and walked back toward her complex, her mind going a mile a minute. Derek Redmond actually wanted to see *Dream Girl!* In fact, he'd practically *begged* to read it!

This was a red-letter day. Yet with her euphoria was a nagging sense of guilt she couldn't shake off. All afternoon she'd struggled to rationalize her duplicity, telling herself that in Hollywood, *everyone* was on the make; everyone hustled everyone else. True, once you had fame and status, you played the game with less desperation, but you still played it. Self-promotion was what Hollywood was all about. But no matter how hard Britt tried to convince herself that was the way the business worked, she still felt uneasy.

Arriving at the entrance to her building, she opened her mailbox and removed a utility bill, a credit-card statement and some advertising flyers. The problem was, she was a minister's daughter at heart and her conscience simply wouldn't let her enjoy her triumph.

Annoyed with herself, Britt started trudging up the stairs. The stairwell had a distinctive musty smell, overlaid with the scent of cleaning solvent. For some reason it triggered a rare sensation of homesickness—recollections of her parents' home. She could almost see herself sitting in her father's study when she was nine, listening to the regulator clock ticking as he read the letter from her teacher saying that she'd allowed a classmate to copy her homework assignments. Thomas Kingsley had mournfully removed his reading glasses, then asked what had happened. She'd only gotten half a sentence out before bursting into tears.

It wasn't only the shame, it was the mortification of having let her father down, of having failed in his eyes. To this day, his words rang in her ears. "Good intentions aren't all that matter, Britt. It's whether what you do is right. First, to thine own self be true. Remember that. You'll never be sorry."

So what did the moral principle she'd learned that autumn day in Indiana so long ago tell her about the way to deal with Derek Redmond now? Did she call him up and confess that it was all a hoax? Should she try to explain that she really wanted to succeed because of the merit of her work, not because of a phony story or false endorsement? Did she tell him she was a wannabe like hundreds of others, scratching and clawing to get their work read at any cost? Should she suggest he ought to read her screenplay anyway? Fat chance. He'd laugh in her face.

Britt had climbed to the third-floor landing when the door to Allison O'Donnell's apartment opened.

Her friend, who worked as a property manager at Paramount, smiled at her.

"Hi, kiddo," Allison said cheerfully. "Discover any new stars today?"

"Yeah, one."

"Good for you! Keep it up and you'll be a partner before your boss gets back from England."

"Dream on, Allison," Britt said as she fumbled in her purse for her key. "I'll be happy if I still have a job when Miranda gets back."

"Don't despair. The first month on a new job is always stressful," Allison said. "But I sympathize. I really do." She put her hand on Britt's arm.

Allison was tall, lean and gangly—not homely, but not pretty. She had a long narrow face and big brown eyes behind her glasses. Her thick, dark brown hair was her best feature. Britt liked her because she was always upbeat. Allison was also kind and generous, a great person to have as a friend.

"I was just on my way down to the supermarket," Allison said. "Anything I can get for you while I'm there?"

"Yeah, a bottle of cyanide—or truth serum—whichever's on sale." Britt put her key in the lock and turned the dead bolt.

"Hey, Britt, what's wrong? I thought you were sort of down at first, but you sound really upset."

She turned to face her friend. "Why should I be upset? Derek Redmond asked to see my script today. He's all excited about it."

Allison blinked. "So what's the problem?"

Britt groaned and rolled her eyes. "You'd never believe me, if I told you."

"Maybe you should tell me anyway," Allison replied, her tone growing more serious. "Shall I invite myself in, or are you going to?"

"I thought you were headed for the store."

"That can wait. I don't want to return and find the paramedics carrying you out of here on a stretcher."

Britt gestured for Allison to come in. The apartment was a tiny one-bedroom, furnished mostly with rented pieces. Britt had hoped to replace the rental stuff with things of her own, but she hadn't worked steadily enough to be able to afford much.

Her most valuable possession was her computer. It sat on the small desk against one wall. The decor consisted mostly of movie posters, candles, dried flowers and her books. She'd always been a reader and had dragged her collection around everywhere, putting her beloved books on shelves made with bricks and boards covered with contact paper. The life of an aspiring writer was not much different from that of a student. Sometimes Britt felt as though she hadn't grown up.

"I'm sure I'm blowing things out of proportion," she said. "I guess it's guilt." She tossed her purse on a chair and headed for the kitchen.

"Guilt?" Allison followed her to the kitchen and stood at the door.

"How about a glass of wine?" Britt asked, taking two glasses down from the cupboard and getting the jug of white wine from the refrigerator.

"Sounds like it might be a good idea."

They sat at the tiny kitchen table as Britt began relating what had happened that day. After she'd finished telling the story, Allison leaned back in her chair, pondering her.

"I don't see why you're so down in the dumps. I think what you did is clever." She beamed. "A damned good marketing ploy. It's even sort of funny."

"At the time I was halfway pleased with myself, I admit, though the other half of me was scared to death." Britt took a slug of wine. "But now that I'm able to get a little perspective on what I've done, I can see how dishonest it was."

"Maybe you're having second thoughts because you're afraid."

"Afraid of what?"

"Failure. You're afraid Derek Redmond won't like your screenplay."

"Allison, that's ridiculous. I want him to read *Dream Girl* more than anything."

"Really? Are you sure that deep down the thought of rejection doesn't terrify you?"

"Of course, I'm nervous. But I want my screenplay read. Look at the lengths I've gone to."

"Then why are you having second thoughts?"

Britt grimaced. "Well, I don't like the fact that I've had to lie and cheat to set things up."

"And so you're thinking of not sending the script."

"Well..." Britt agonized. "Do *you* think I should send it?"

"Of course I do."

"Why?"

"Come on, Britt, let's be honest," Allison said. "All any director cares about is getting good material. What does it really matter how it gets into his hands? You found a clever gimmick to promote yourself, that's all. In my opinion, you should be congratulated for your ingenuity."

Allison's words of reassurance made her feel better. The cloud that had been slowly gathering all day seemed momentarily to lift. "I suppose if nobody's hurt, my posing as Miranda isn't the end of the world."

"Heavens, no. It was just a way of getting your foot in the door. Besides, if Redmond doesn't like your screenplay, he'll send it back and all will be forgotten."

Britt tapped her wineglass absently with her fingernail. "But what if he *does* like it?"

"Isn't that the kind of problem you'd like to have?"

Britt smiled. "You're the devil incarnate, Allison O'Donnell. You realize, don't you, that you're counseling a life of crime?"

"Hell, when you're a famous screenwriter, pulling down a million a script, I'll be able to say with satisfaction, '*I* made that woman. But for me, Britt Kingsley would still be answering phones at C.A.'"

"Yeah, but will you feel the same pride, bailing me out of jail?"

"Fear," Allison said, pointing her finger at her. "Fear."

Britt smiled. "You're probably right. This is a town of con artists and hucksters who happen to wear fifteen-hundred-dollar suits. Why should I worry if I play a little loose with the facts?''

Allison picked up her wineglass and clinked it against Britt's. ''That's the spirit! Success at any price!''

They both began to laugh.

Arriving at the office the next morning, Britt prepared her script for the courier. Since she'd told Derek Redmond her name, she had to put a pseudonym on the byline. It occurred to her to use Allison's, at least for the time being. After all, her friend was virtually her partner in crime.

Once she'd typed a new title page and had the script packaged and ready to go, she took it down to the mail room with instructions to courier it to Derek Redmond's office in Westwood. Then she returned to her office to agonize. *Dream Girl* was out of her hands now. Everything was up to fate.

The phone started ringing. It seemed all Miranda's clients wanted something at the same time. For three hours they had her running. She was glad. At least it got her mind off *Dream Girl* and Derek Redmond.

Then, just before lunch, Miranda herself called from London. ''Keeping the home fires burning, love?''

''I haven't let the house burn down,'' Britt replied, feeling a surge of guilt at the sound of her boss's voice. ''At least, not yet.''

''What's up?''

Britt went through the list of things that had happened. For the most part Miranda was pleased with what she'd done and had a few suggestions for follow-up. There were two clients she would call herself from London.

As Miranda rattled on, Britt had another brief urge to confess all, but then she remembered what Allison had said. Fear. She shouldn't be afraid of success. Allison had also been right when she'd argued that if Derek Redmond ended up not liking *Dream Girl,* her worries would have been for nothing. And if he did like her screenplay, well, she'd just cross that bridge when she came to it.

"I'll be visiting friends in the country for a few days," Miranda said. "Let me give you the number so you can reach me in an emergency."

Britt jotted down the number, glad that Miranda would be incommunicado for a while. That way her charade was less likely to be exposed.

They ended the conversation with Miranda assuring her that she should feel free to ring up at any time, day or night, if there was an emergency. Britt hung up, relieved that she'd gotten over another hurdle without being exposed.

A few minutes later, Sally Farland stuck her head in the door and asked if Britt wanted to go to lunch. She accepted at once. Getting away from the office would be great. Of course, lunch would be even better if she could talk about her doubts and fears with Sally, but she didn't know her well enough for that. They were friendly, but not that friendly.

Over sandwiches at the deli up the street, Britt listened to Sally lament her trials and tribulations with her boyfriend. It was a conventional tale as boyfriend stories went, but Britt did her best to be a good listener even as her mind kept turning to her own saga with Derek Redmond.

Their lunch over, Britt and Sally returned to the glass-and-steel high rise on Santa Monica Boulevard where C.A. was located. As they walked in the front door, Tiffany, a slender blonde with an affection for chewing gum, waved a message slip at Britt.

"Derek Redmond called three times while you were at lunch," the girl said. "He left messages in your voice mail but insisted I tackle you the moment you walked in. He desperately has to speak to Miranda."

Britt's heart leaped. He must have loved the script. But then she wondered what Tiffany had told him. "Did you say she was in England?"

"No, Britt, I never say anything unless I'm instructed to. All I do is connect people to the office they want and take an occasional message."

Sally took Britt's arm. "We've been caught with our pants down too often," she said as they headed for the elevator. "The assistants are the only ones besides the agents who can pass on information or answer questions. It's standard procedure."

Britt's heart was pounding as they waited for a car.

"Sounds like you've had some success," Sally said. "What's with Derek Redmond?"

"Miranda wanted me to get some information to him," Britt said nervously. "That's all." She winced, not thrilled about telling another lie. She tried to focus instead on the fact that Derek Redmond had called three times. It had to be because he loved *Dream Girl.*

Bidding Sally goodbye, Britt ran to her phone to listen to the messages Derek had left. They were brief and to the point. Tiffany was right. He urgently wanted to talk to Miranda.

Britt went into Miranda's private office, closed the door, and settled into the big leather desk chair. She shut her eyes, conjured up Miranda's voice, and took a few moments to get into character. Then she picked up the phone and dialed.

"Miranda, I want that script!" he said right out of the chute. "It's just what I've been looking for."

It took all of Britt's willpower to keep from jumping to her feet and shouting with glee. "Lovely, Derek," she managed, bouncing in her chair.

"Can we talk deal?" he asked. "You can get control of the material, can't you?"

"Well, yes, of course I can. It's just that I…er…should talk to my client a bit first. Formalities, you know." It only then occurred to her that she didn't have the slightest idea what to do next. Did she—that is, C.A.—draw up a contract, or did Derek Redmond? Clearly she wasn't prepared.

"This Allison O'Donnell has real talent," Derek went on. "I'm eager to meet her."

"Uh…yes, she's…a lovely girl."

"I don't care what she looks like, Miranda. I don't even care about her disposition. She writes a damned good script and that's all that matters."

"Right you are, Derek." Britt couldn't help tittering, but it was more from nerves than anything else. "Shall I prepare the…uh, usual formalities?" she ventured, not knowing what else to say.

"Let's don't worry about that yet," he said. "The first thing I want to do is meet with your client. There are a few things in the script I'd like to discuss."

"What sort of things?"

"Just some ideas I have, possibly some changes to consider."

"I see." Britt felt her euphoria falter.

"Nothing big," he hastily added. "But I like to run my ideas past the writer. I don't believe anything worthy can be written by committee. Collaboration is the name of the game."

"Quite right," Britt said, fumbling.

"Since you and I haven't met, why don't the three of us get together? We could do lunch tomorrow, or better yet, breakfast. I like to get an early start."

Britt's mind started spinning. There was no way she could meet with him! Good heavens, what had she gotten herself into? "Uh…that would be delightful…" she stammered, struggling to focus her thoughts. "But I do need to talk to Allison. Can I ring you back, love?"

"Sure, Miranda. I'm doing lunch today with a friend, but I'll be in my office from three on."

"Okay, well, talk to you soon, then, Derek, love." Britt hung up the phone and let her head drop right down on the desk. "Lord," she mumbled. "Just strike me with a lightning bolt and get it over with."

4

---◆---

Derek Redmond left his office in Westwood and drove east on Wilshire until he came to Santa Monica Boulevard. He pulled into the Peninsula Beverly Hills Hotel, left his Porsche 911 with the valet parking attendant, and went inside. He breezed through the lobby.

"Mr. Redmond," a voice called from the direction of the reception desk.

He glanced over as an assistant manager made his way toward him, smiling.

"Good to see you," the man, a young sophisticated European, said in a cordial tone. "Will we be serving you in the Belvedere this afternoon?"

"I'm meeting Oliver Wheatley for lunch."

"Oh, yes, sir, of course. Mr. Wheatley's poolside. I'll have you shown to his cabana." The assistant manager signaled for a bellhop, who promptly joined them and was told to take Derek to Oliver Wheatley's cabana.

They took the elevator to the rooftop pool, which had become the latest deal-making meeting place for Hollywood moguls. Derek was more into making pictures than doing the Hollywood scene, but a certain amount of schmoozing was unavoidable. That meant putting in time at places like this. One modest hit under his belt and another in the can and ready to be released had not exactly made him a power to be reckoned with, but he no longer had to sit in outer offices by the hour, waiting to see someone with juice. He'd done breakfast or lunch in the Peninsula's Club Bar a couple of times, but this was his first trip to the rooftop pool.

Oliver had told Derek on the phone that morning that he was working on putting together a three-picture package and was up to his ears in lawyers and accountants, but he'd be taking a break around lunchtime and would enjoy seeing him. Derek had been glad to accept.

Like a lot of Brits who'd come to California to make films, Oliver didn't fit the typical Hollywood tycoon mold, either, but his successes of the last few years had, by his own reckoning, "sucked him into the game." For reasons Derek wasn't entirely sure about, Oliver had taken him under his wing and acted as a mentor. In fact, he'd been helpful in getting the package together for *Code Red*.

They arrived at the hotel rooftop and Derek looked out at the pool area, squinting in the bright sunshine. Then he slipped his sunglasses down from where he'd pushed them into his dark hair, so that he could take in the scene.

There was the usual assortment of bikini-clad girls sunning themselves in deck chairs or wading in the pool. There were also a few young bronze studs, but it was quickly obvious that all the important action was taking place in the canvas cabanas surrounding the pool. As he strode past them, Derek could hear the clatter of fax machines and the sound of cellular phones ringing. It was a circuslike atmosphere, but instead of greasepaint the performers were wearing jeans, polo shirts, Carrera sunglasses, and fifteen-thousand-dollar gold watches.

As he came to Oliver's cabana, Derek found him in a lounge chair, a cellular phone to his ear and Meg, his dark-haired, middle-aged secretary, beside him with a laptop computer nearby. Oliver, in his mid-forties, was wearing Bermuda shorts and a short-sleeved silk shirt. Noticing Derek, he gave him a wave and beckoned him to enter. Derek handed the bellhop a couple of bucks and stepped into the cabana's shady interior. Meg smiled up at him.

Oliver, who was a bit on the portly side and had very pink skin, finished up his call and extended his hand. "You made it, old bean. Come sit down. I'm ready to take a break from this insanity." He turned to the secretary. "Meg, why don't you go have some lunch? We'll start again in an hour's time."

"Yes, sir."

"Oh, and send a waiter over so Derek and I can order something to eat, if you would, please."

She nodded and left. Derek took the chair she'd vacated. Oliver lay back in the lounge chair, his hands clasped behind his head as he surveyed the panorama of pool and sky. Two young women in bikinis paraded by. Derek watched Oliver follow their progress.

"Incredible, isn't it?" Oliver said, smiling. "Sometimes I'm embarrassed to admit I've been seduced by it."

"Everything's relative," Derek said.

"Relative to what?"

"No matter what kind of life a person leads, now and then you have to stop and ask yourself what it's all about."

"Oh, gawd, a philosopher. I didn't know there were any in this country."

Derek chuckled. "I guess what I'm saying, Oliver, is I try not to get too caught up in all this. The biggest mistake people in this town make is taking themselves too seriously."

"You don't, evidently."

"I'm into my work. Or at least I like to think so."

"That's not taking yourself seriously?"

Derek stared abstractedly. "I suppose it is, in a way. But I don't regard this as the real world," he said, waving his hand toward the scene before them.

Oliver didn't say anything for a while. "Maybe I don't, either, Derek. When I'm home in England, this place seems more like a dream. And when I'm here I feel like I'm on holiday, a great long one."

A long-legged blond beauty in a thong bikini climbed from the pool right in front of them. She smiled in their direction before padding off.

"There's something to be said for living out one's fantasies, however," Oliver said with a laugh.

The waiter came and took their orders for lunch. After he'd left, Derek said, "I owe you thanks, by the way."

"How's that?" Oliver asked, draining the last of a fruit drink that had been sitting on the table beside him.

"Miranda Maxwell was kind enough to put me onto a wonderful script by an unknown screenwriter. It's a bit rough but there's a real freshness to the writing."

"Miranda has judgment," Oliver said. "It's her best quality, in my opinion."

"How is she to deal with? Pretty straight?"

"Oh, Miranda's a straight shooter, all right. She won't make any promises she can't keep or representations she can't back up. She's a love."

"I'm looking forward to dealing with her," Derek said. "She's trying to set up a meeting for tomorrow with her client. Hopefully the three of us will get together for breakfast and hammer things out."

"Breakfast? Has the Concorde started flying to L.A. without me knowing about it?"

"What do you mean?"

"Miranda's in London. Has been for a week."

Derek looked at him, perplexed. "Oliver, what are you saying? I've talked to Miranda in her office several times over the past couple of days."

Oliver shook his head. "Couldn't have, old man. Miranda's in London. Trust me. I've spoken with her twice this morning. Conference calls. Had trouble hooking up the London link. The operator had to go through the business three or four times to get it right.

Miranda said it was probably the bloody fog. Said the whole town was swimming in the stuff. She must have rung you up and you assumed she was in L.A. Happened to me once. Talked to a bleeding lawyer for half an hour, thinking he was across town. Turned out the sod was in Rome with his mistress, probably eating grapes from her navel while talking to me.'' Oliver laughed.

Derek scratched his head. He tried to recall the circumstances of his conversations with Miranda. He was certain he'd dialed C.A. and had been put right through to her. Or could her assistant have patched him through to London? No, that made no sense. When he'd proposed breakfast, Miranda would have said she was in London and couldn't meet with him. He wondered what the hell was going on. Something was fishy.

''Oliver, is it possible Miranda spoke with me from London, but didn't want me to know that's where she was?''

''Whatever for?''

Derek stroked his chin, considering the situation as the waiter arrived with the fresh order of fruit drinks. The man went off and Oliver raised his glass.

''Cheers.''

Derek ruminated. ''Somebody's smoking something, Oliver. Could it be one of us, or is it Miranda?''

''Ah, a philosopher *and* a skeptic. What say we ring Miranda up in London and ask her what gives?''

''No, don't bother her. I'm sure it's a misunderstanding.''

"Balderdash! You've got me curious." Oliver reached for his cellular phone, holding it up for Derek to see as he dialed. "Note the international code." Then he sat back and waited. "Hello," he said airily, "Oliver Wheatley here. Miss Maxwell, please....Oh? She's not in, then? She wouldn't have gone off to America, would she?...The country, you say. Has she been gone long?...Left an hour ago? I see. You're the housekeeper, are you?...And what's your name, love?...Priscilla? Smashing. We've a wee problem, Priscilla. I'm a client of Miranda's and ringing up from California. I've a gentleman here with me from the FBI. That's the American Scotland Yard. We're investigating a case of mistaken identity and we'd like to confirm where Miss Maxwell's been for the past few days. Would you be kind enough to tell Mr. Ness where Miss Maxwell has been, say, the last few days?...That's a love." Grinning, Oliver handed the phone to Derek.

"Hello," he said in his best Kevin Costner voice, "this is Elliot Ness. Sorry to trouble you, Priscilla, but if you could just verify that Miss Maxwell has been in London the past few days."

"Oh, yes, sir," the woman assured. "She would have been here at her town house Monday a week. But an hour ago she did leave for the country, sir. If it's urgent, I can give you the number there and you can ring her. You might wish to allow an hour or two, though. The traffic's bad on the M-5 and, well, she'd likely have stopped for her supper on the way."

"Oh, that won't be necessary," he said. "This is just a routine inquiry."

"Are you certain, sir?"

"Quite sure. You don't have to trouble Miss Maxwell with this. Everything is quite satisfactory. Thank you very much." Derek pushed the Off button, then handed the phone back to Oliver, who was beaming.

"Are you the one who's been smoking, laddie?" Oliver asked.

"Could be a suspect as yet unnamed," Derek replied. "I should be having some interesting phone calls this afternoon."

"Be certain to let me know what's happening, Mr. Ness. Sounds like you have a very interesting case on your hands."

Derek Redmond picked up his glass and took a swig of juice. "Let me put it this way. Breakfast tomorrow could prove to be very interesting."

Britt closed the last of the client files on her desk and returned the stack to the file cabinet in Miranda's office. She checked her watch and decided it was time to call Derek Redmond. Closing the door and taking her place at Miranda's desk, she took a deep breath and slowly exhaled as she conjured up Miranda in her mind. When she was satisfied she was fixed on the right character, she dialed the number to Derek's office. After a brief delay he came onto the line.

"Miranda," he said cheerily, "were you able to talk to your client?"

"Yes, Allison would be pleased to meet you for breakfast, Derek. She's terribly excited."

"Terrific. Will you be joining us?"

"I would, love, but I've got other commitments. Early-morning powwow over at Disney."

"What a shame. I was really hoping we could get together. I find it much easier talking to someone after meeting face-to-face. But I guess it won't hurt if Allison and I meet first."

"Not in the least, Derek. She'd be delighted, believe me."

"Can you have her at the Polo Lounge at, say, eight tomorrow morning?"

"She'll be there with bells on her toes. I promise."

"Terrific," he said. "I'm looking forward to it. I'll give you a jingle after Allison and I talk."

"I'll be eager to hear how it goes," she said.

"Yes, it seems to me you said something about having to go to London soon. When do you plan on leaving?"

Britt gulped, thinking quickly. "Uh...not for a few days, anyway. I've a couple of things to finish up before I'm off. One of which, if all goes well, will be doing a deal with you, Derek."

"I'm sure we'll have the pleasure. I can't tell you how much I'm looking forward to it."

"*Ciao,* love." Britt hung up the phone, clenching her fist in triumph. It was easier than she'd thought. "Bloody hell!" she exclaimed and spun the desk chair around, giggling gleefully.

There was a light rap on the door, bringing her celebration to an abrupt halt. She got out of Miranda's chair and went to see who was there. It was Sally, with an inquisitive look on her face.

"Everything all right?" she asked. "You weren't at your desk and I saw the door closed. I...uh...thought maybe—"

"Oh, I was on the phone," Britt said. "I wanted a little privacy because..." She hesitated, feeling another lie forming on her lips. She tried to find a way to avoid it, but couldn't come up with anything truthful, yet safe. "Because, uh, I was talking to my doctor," she finally blurted.

"Oh. Aren't you feeling well?"

Britt swallowed hard. "I'm okay," she said, "but tomorrow morning I have a doctor's appointment. He wanted me to come in. I'll be late for work."

"No problem," Sally replied. "I'll have Miranda's calls routed to my phone. I'll cover for you until you get in."

"That would be great," Britt said. "I don't think I'll be too late."

"Well, the reason I dropped by," Sally continued, "is that Joyce Wilson is on the warpath again about the British getting special treatment in Hollywood. Gordon ran into her last night at Spago and she had a few choice barbs for Miranda. She blames her for sabotaging her interview with Westley Asquith."

"Rightly so," Britt said.

"Yes, well, Gordon thought you ought to be on your toes and aware."

"Thanks, I'll give Westley's publicist another call.

I'm sure that's what Miranda would do. And the next time I talk to her, I'll mention what Gordon said.''

Sally patted Britt on the arm. ''You're getting the hang of the business real fast.''

Britt smiled, but felt like a terrible hypocrite. She liked C.A. and she was uncomfortable about having used Miranda, although she wouldn't allow her boss to be hurt. On the contrary, once she became one of the leading screenwriters in Hollywood, she'd want Miranda to represent her—assuming she was willing.

Of course, that was a bit premature. Right now her most pressing concern was her meeting with Derek Redmond. It still hadn't sunk in completely, but one of Hollywood's up-and-coming directors loved her script! Maybe, at long last, her time had come!

5

A few minutes before eight the next morning Britt turned off Sunset Boulevard and drove up the palm-lined drive of the Beverly Hills Hotel—the ''Pink Palace,'' as the locals called it. She had passed by the place many times, and had often wondered if she'd ever be inside, wheeling and dealing with the big boys. Now her chance had come and she was thrilled.

The Polo Lounge was one of the primo meeting places of the Hollywood moguls and had been for over fifty years. She figured that Derek Redmond had probably picked it to impress her, which was fine by her. Negotiating her first deal under the watchful eye of the ghosts of Darryl Zanuck, Spencer Tracy, Walt Disney and all the other old polo players who haunted the place was as good a way to begin as any.

Ignoring the valets, Britt drove past the entrance and went on to the parking lot. Aspiring screenwriters in six-year-old Toyotas couldn't throw money around like a celebrity. Besides, this wasn't her turf. She was a guest, and glad for once to be able to behave like the humble person she was.

Of course, it was unfortunate that she'd be meeting

Derek Redmond under an assumed identity, but Britt was relieved that she wouldn't be playing a role, as well—like she had on the phone when she'd pretended to be Miranda. For this meeting, she could answer questions honestly and be candid when discussing her craft. She'd be herself—in all but her true name, of course.

Britt got out of her car and locked it. She smoothed her lightweight navy knit dress that nicely showed her curves. Her heels made her legs look great. Her honey-colored hair hung straight to her shoulders. Her only jewelry was a pair of chunky fake gold earrings. No rings, bracelets or necklaces. The overall effect was attractive without being flashy.

She'd considered dressing down to minimize her sex appeal but she liked flattering clothes and always bought the best that she could afford, although her budget was modest. Besides, she knew she had a good figure and great legs. Still, this was an extraordinary situation and she wanted to project the right image. Maybe she should have made an exception and gone really conservative, but it was too late now.

Walking toward the entrance of the hotel, Britt was nervous. This was the worst case of stage fright she'd ever had. How many times did someone like her, a real unknown, get an opportunity like this? She knew she had to stay focused, ignore things like the way the valets were eyeing her.

Britt stepped inside the hotel and glanced about the lobby, immediately noticing the entrance to the Polo Lounge. Several middle-aged men and one woman were waiting near the maître d's podium, but none of them looked familiar. Derek Redmond's dark good looks from the pictures she'd seen of him were emblazoned on her brain, although the image may have been embellished some by her fantasies of him. She hoped she would like him, that he would be a nice man. But all that really mattered was that he wanted to turn her screenplay into a movie.

Standing at the rear of the small crowd, she waited for her turn. When the leader of the group completed his conversation with the hostess, the people moved to the side and Britt stepped forward.

"May I help you?" the stately woman behind the podium asked.

"I'm meeting Derek Redmond," Britt replied.

"Oh, yes, Miss O'Donnell. Mr. Redmond is waiting for you in the Loggia. This way, please."

They went through the Green room with the telephone-equipped booths, many of them in use. There was a low buzz of activity. Gray-haired men in Italian suits and younger men with sunglasses pushed up in their hair glanced at her as she passed by, if they weren't too engrossed in conversation.

Judging by the looks she was getting, people were wondering whose bimbo she might be. That had to be their conclusion. She didn't have a famous face and she was too young to be one of the industry's female movers and shakers. In Hollywood, that left only one category.

Never mind, Britt told herself. One day she'd be

known by the insiders as a great writing talent. She'd be recognized for her ability and achievements.

The hostess took her into the quiet inner sanctum of the Loggia where, according to Allison, the really big mucky-mucks did their megamillion wheeling and dealing, especially during breakfast. Britt felt a swell of pride. It was the first time since she'd been in L.A. that didn't feel like an outsider with her nose to the glass, looking in.

She glanced at the sober-faced, affluent people occupying the booths. She could smell the money and power, but didn't recognize anyone. Allison had told her the crowd would be mostly the less well-known, but terribly powerful money people and industry execs. "The stars don't get up that early, kiddo, so don't expect to see Tom Cruise."

Britt was shown to one of the lesser booths in the corner, where Derek Redmond sat waiting.

"Miss O'Donnell has arrived, Mr. Redmond," the hostess said pleasantly as she stepped aside, smiling at each of them in turn.

Britt, covering her awe as best she could, watched him as he checked her out. Then Derek slid from the booth and extended his hand before she could say a word. He looked like his pictures, but the flesh-and-blood presence was even better looking than she'd anticipated. She was actually a bit stunned, not expecting him to have the effect on her that he did.

He was lean and muscular, with longish straight black hair and clear green eyes. He had a sensitive face, and yet there was a manliness about him, too.

He was wearing an open-necked shirt under a sports coat and round wire-rimmed glasses that gave him an almost-intellectual look, although he had an easy, casual manner.

"Allison," he said, "it's an honor to meet you. I'm a big fan, if Miranda hasn't already told you."

She left her hand resting in his as she looked into his green eyes. "Thank you. I'm a fan of yours, as well, Mr. Redmond."

"Derek," he said warmly, still holding her hand.

He had an engaging smile and a warm, charming manner that seemed genuine. The line between self-confidence and arrogance was narrow. First impressions put him on the right side of it. At one level she'd been prepared for him, though not quite the way she found him. She realized that she was reacting to him as a man, which was not at all what she'd had in mind.

"Well, come sit down," he said, taking her arm.

Britt slipped into the booth on the side opposite where he'd been sitting. "I hope I'm not too late," she said.

"Not at all. You're right on time." He took his place.

They looked at each other for what seemed like a very long time. Britt was feeling something—an awareness—that she knew she shouldn't. Derek Redmond seemed to be peering right inside her as though he were searching for something. She knew her hands were trembling, but she didn't dare look down at them to confirm it.

"I loved your screenplay, Allison," he said.

His words thrilled her. "I'm glad you liked it."

He went on, discussing what he liked about her writing and the kinds of scripts he liked to direct.

Britt listened, mesmerized. She couldn't recall ever having felt such a deep and compelling rapport with someone so quickly. Usually it took hours of conversation—hours of feeling someone out—before common links were discovered.

"Why did you decide to do a screenplay? Why not a novel?" he asked, curious.

"I suppose because I'm visual and my background—limited though it is—is acting. I visualize raw material for actors and actresses to do their thing."

"And directors," he said.

"Yes, directors of course—foremost, I suppose."

Derek stared at her mouth, taking her in as his eyes moved over her. It was an appreciative appraisal, but not a salacious one. He might have been evaluating her for a lighting effect or a camera angle. Whatever was going on in his mind, she read admiration on his face.

"I've a confession to make," he said. "Not many directors like to admit this, but there are scripts that almost direct themselves. When you read the script and it's good, you're able to visualize the whole thing as though the film has already been made and you're simply watching it. That's what happened to me when I read *Dream Girl*."

"That's a very nice thing to say, but you're discounting your importance."

"You're saying even a good script can be bungled."

"I'm saying there's a big step from script to the screen. Michelangelo believed his sculptures were already fully formed in the block of marble and his task was to liberate the figure from the stone. But I'm not willing to give the marble that much credit," she added with a laugh.

"Your script is a good deal more to me than a block of stone is to a sculptor, Allison. But the comparison is flattering. Thank you."

Britt beamed, incredibly happy.

"You know," he said, "*Dream Girl* is the sort of script I've tried to describe. It works in my mind. I really want to make it into a film."

"I hope you do."

He reached across the table and took her hand. "I fully intend to, believe me."

She glanced down at the hand that unconsciously caressed hers as he gazed at her with intensity. The affection, unconscious or not, flustered her. "Miranda said you wanted some changes, though."

Derek gave her hand a final squeeze before removing his. "There are always little things, sequences or transitions you see a bit differently than what's in the script. It's almost an editing function."

"Miranda gave me the impression it might be more than that."

He shrugged. "I want to play with the ending. I haven't decided how I feel about it, exactly, but it's something we can talk about."

Britt shrugged. "Sure."

"There were two principal writers on *Code Red* and before it was over, I was practically a member of the writing team. While I like to work closely with writers on changes, I don't see this film going the same way. Thrillers are a different kettle of fish."

Britt wasn't sure if he saw a problem and was trying to play it down, or if he was assuring her that his concerns were minor. For the first time she began to sense he was giving her a sales pitch and that made her wonder.

"So, what's the bottom line?" she asked.

"If I do the film, I'd like to have you as a member of the team—helping me to fine-tune it. The actors will be critical, as well."

"That sounds good to me."

"And what if our visions diverge?"

Britt studied him. "You're asking if I can be a good soldier."

"I'm asking if you can be a team player."

"And recognize who's in command," she added.

"I wouldn't put it that way, exactly."

She pondered his point. "I'm a rookie, I know," she said, "but I'm familiar enough with the business to know a writer has to let go at a certain point."

"Good. I wanted us to be clear, to get everything on the table up front. The fewer surprises, the better."

"I appreciate that," she said. "I really do."

Derek nodded as though he'd heard what he wanted. "I like the feel of this," he said, gesturing back and forth between them. "Do you?"

Britt knew he was talking about their collaboration on *Dream Girl,* but she couldn't help considering the question another way, too. They were two people who'd been finding common ground over something they both felt passionate about. She'd never experienced that before.

Britt didn't realize it, but she was staring at him, her mouth slightly agape. All kinds of crazy and wonderful notions streamed through her mind, thoughts and feelings she'd never experienced before, a quiet excitement that was new to her.

"Allison?"

"Huh?"

"Is this feeling good?"

She blinked. "Oh…uh…yes. I like your philosophy."

"Can you live with it?"

She shrugged. "Sure."

She wasn't going to tell him, but he probably could have made chaining her to the wall and facing a cat-o'-nine-tails part of the deal. Derek probably knew it, too, but it said something about him that he could refrain from being pushy.

"Good," he said, beaming. "That gets us over the first hurdle." He signaled the waiter. "And now, how about some breakfast?"

Britt was feeling so amenable that he could have said, "And now, how about a dip in the pool?" and she would have agreed.

"Sounds good," she said.

Derek recommended the Dutch apple pancakes for

which the Polo Lounge was famous, and although a glass of juice and a slice of dry toast was a more typical breakfast for her, Britt ordered the pancakes. After the waiter had gone, she glanced around the room, taking it in for the first time since sitting down.

"This is my first meal in the Polo Lounge," she said.

"I thought it might be appropriate, considering we're here to wheel and deal."

"Somehow I don't think my little screenplay is in the same league with what's going on at the other tables."

Derek looked around himself. "A lot of these folks are strangers to me, as well, but there are at least two network entertainment-division heads who I recognize. I assume they're talking deals."

"For millions, I imagine."

"Many millions."

Britt felt her pulse jump up a beat or two.

"That silver-haired gentleman in the booth with the man and woman is Jack Valenti, head of the Motion Picture Association of America."

"Oh, yes, I recognize him now."

"Care to meet him?" Derek asked, cocking his brow whimsically.

Britt looked at him questioningly. "Do you know him?"

"No, I was just kidding. In fact, if you want to know the truth, this group is out of my league. I'm still triple A, but with major-league potential."

"It's nice you can admit that. There's a lot of pretense in this town and precious little humility."

"Honesty has always felt better to me than trying to be something I'm not. Maybe it's the way I was raised."

His words stabbed at her like a knife.

"So tell me, Allison, how and where did you come to know Miranda?" he asked.

The question was uncannily ironic. She looked into his clear green eyes, and a terrible urge welled up in her to blurt out the truth. The first words—"I'm not Allison O'Donnell. My name is Britt Kingsley and I've deceived you"—were forming on her lips when she swallowed them, choking them off.

"I met her through a friend," she said shamefully. "Somebody who knew someone who worked for one of the other agents at C.A."

Derek nodded. "Miranda's an interesting lady, isn't she?"

Britt's cheeks had to have turned a blistering red. The worst part was knowing she had nobody to blame but herself. "Yes, very interesting," she replied.

"So you haven't known her long, then?"

"I've only seen her a few times," she said, agonizing with each additional lie.

The trouble was, if she stopped now, before the deal was done, everything could go down the drain. Just a few more hours and it would be over. Once it was safe to come out in the open, she'd find a way to make amends and clear her conscience; she promised herself that.

"Have you met with Miranda at C.A.?" Derek asked. "Or somewhere else?"

His tone was nonchalant, his manner conversational, but even so, the question struck her as curious. Could he be suspicious? A tremor went through her at the thought. "Not in the office," she told him, sensing it was the thing to say. "Why do you ask?"

He shrugged. "I was curious. I haven't met Miranda face-to-face yet, but I hope to soon. Naturally, she's the one I'll have to work out the deal with."

Britt managed to smile, covering the horror she felt. "I don't imagine I could relay any messages or anything."

"No, you don't want to get involved in the messy stuff. The reason you have an agent is to protect you. Besides, she'd kill me if I tried to cut her out of the loop."

"I'm sure that's not true."

"Well, it's your first deal, so let's do it by the book."

Britt groaned inwardly. "Whatever you think."

The waiter came with two enormous glasses of orange juice. Although it was eight-thirty in the morning, Britt almost wished there was a shot of vodka in it. She could have used something to settle her nerves.

"Ah," Derek said, "my favorite beverage."

He picked up his glass and extended it, offering to touch it to hers. Britt took hers, suddenly so shaky she was afraid she'd drop it.

"To *Dream Girl*," he toasted. "And to you, Allison. Here's hoping you're the dream writer I've been looking for."

Britt managed to return his smile, but it was all she could do to keep from bursting into tears. The weight of every bad deed she'd ever done pressed down on her.

Lowering her glass, she scooted to the edge of the banquette. "Will you excuse me, Derek," she said. "I'll be back in just a minute."

He started to get up, but she motioned for him to stay seated. He reached out and grasped her hand, stopping her from leaving.

"Allison," he said, "I'm going to give Miranda a buzz on my cellular phone and tell her to draw up an option agreement. I've decided there's no need to drag this out. You and I are going to do *Dream Girl,* and it's going to be one of the biggest hits of the year."

Britt's heart soared. But her guilty conscience brought it right back down. Tears bubbled from her eyes. She mouthed the words, "Thank you," and turned, practically running from the room.

6

————►◄————

Derek watched Allison O'Donnell leave. He had no idea what to make of her or the situation. But one thing was certain—he found her fascinating. She was damned attractive. The heads she turned were evidence of that. Yet more than the physical beauty, he found himself attracted to her as a person. Things had really clicked between them. He'd never experienced that before—at least not so dramatically, and not in the same way.

Of course, there was still the matter of the hoax involving Miranda Maxwell. He assumed that Allison was involved in some way. He had briefly considered the possibility that she too was a victim, but it was hard to believe that a third party would have anything to gain by trying to deceive both Allison and him.

But why they'd resorted to such a grand deception wasn't clear. The screenplay was real enough. He had no doubt that Allison had written it because it would be impossible to fake the conversation they'd just had. Still, something was fishy and he was determined to get to the bottom of it.

He knew he had to be careful. The last thing he

wanted to do was alienate her—he had as much at stake as she. First and foremost, there was *Dream Girl* to consider. He wanted to make it into a movie.

He took his cellular phone from the briefcase and dialed C.A., asking the receptionist for Miranda Maxwell's office.

"Neither Ms. Maxwell nor her assistant are in today," the woman said. "I can connect you to Miranda's voice mail, or if you'd prefer, Mr. Mallik's assistant can help you."

"That's all right. Just have Miranda telephone me as soon as you can, will you, please? This is Derek Redmond."

"Yes, sir."

"Thanks."

He disconnected the call and put away the phone. Then he pondered the situation. It had all the earmarks of some kind of a con game, but the motive eluded him. The key had to be the imitation Miranda Maxwell. That was who he had to get to.

Britt came out of the ladies' room and headed back to the dining room. Passing a pay phone, she suddenly remembered that Derek was going to phone Miranda. She wondered if Tiffany would have put the call through to Sally, and if so, what Sally had said to him. Maybe she should find out before returning to the table.

Britt put a quarter in the telephone and dialed C.A. "Tiffany," she said when the receptionist answered, "this is Britt. Have there been any calls for Miranda?"

"Yes, Derek Redmond called a few minutes ago."

"Did you put him through to Sally?"

"No, he just said he wanted Miranda to call. I thought I'd let you handle it. Will you be in soon?"

"No, I'm going to be tied up a while longer. Would you put me through to Sally, please?"

"Sure."

"Sally," Britt said when her friend came on the line, "I need to get ahold of Derek Redmond for Miranda. Is there a way you can get his cellular number for me?"

"I suppose so, but it'll take me a minute. Want to hold?"

"Yes."

Britt waited, agonizing. Things were getting more and more complicated. She didn't know why that should surprise her. Once you started lying you got sucked in deeper and deeper. The only question was whether she could keep her head above water long enough to get Derek on the dotted line.

As she waited, she pictured his smiling face. The man was incredibly handsome—sexy and intelligent, sensitive and yet strong. She felt one of those intense, physical attractions that she wrote about, the kind that left her heroines numb. That tug in the gut was the most wonderful feeling in the world. What a shame the first guy in years to do that to her should be Derek Redmond, of all people. She was already playing a dangerous game.

"Britt," Sally said, coming back on the line, "I've

got it.'' She read off the number and Britt jotted it down on a scrap of paper she took from her purse.

"Thanks,'' she said. "You're a lifesaver.''

"What's going on, anyway? I thought you were at the doctor's.''

"I am. I just remembered I had to make this call for Miranda. Oh, and Sally…''

"Yes?''

"If Derek should happen to call in and you talk to him, don't mention that Miranda's in England, okay?''

"Why not?''

"Let's just say Miranda didn't want him to know.''

Sally sighed. "All right. I assume you know what you're doing.''

Britt hung up, then glanced around to make sure no one was within hearing. She closed her eyes for a minute to conjure up Miranda. Then she dialed the number Sally had given her. The phone rang several times before he answered.

"Derek, darling, Miranda Maxwell here. I understand you wanted to speak with me.''

"Yes, I did. Thanks for returning the call.''

"What's up?''

"I'm meeting with Allison and we're hitting it off real well. I wanted you to know.''

Britt beamed happily. "That's fabulous, dear. I couldn't be more pleased.''

"I think we'll be able to work together,'' he said. "In fact I'm sure of it. She's bright, engaging. It's love at first sight.''

She almost jumped for joy. "That's smashing, Derek! You've made my day."

"Hold on a second," he said.

Britt waited a few seconds, then he came back on the line.

"Listen, Miranda, can I call you right back? I've got to take care of something here. Are you in your office?"

"No, as a matter of fact I'm out doing breakfast myself."

"Do you have a number where I can reach you? It'll be just a minute or two."

Britt did a quick calculation. "I can wait here a few moments, Derek, but not long."

"Give me the number."

"It's 555-4839," she said, reading the number off the pay phone.

"I'll get right back to you."

Britt hung up, wondering what that was all about. Had somebody come to the table? She considered going to have a look, but was afraid someone might try to use the phone in her absence. She stood waiting and after another thirty seconds the phone rang.

"Hello."

"It's me, Derek," he said.

"Yes, dear."

"Listen, I want to get together with you as soon as possible to discuss *Dream Girl*," he told her. "Do you have plans for dinner this evening?"

"This evening? I'm afraid I do have an engagement. Sorry."

"How does tomorrow look?"

Britt gulped. She knew she couldn't put him off forever and it sounded like he was determined. "My schedule is just rotten this week, love."

"We really need to discuss the option agreement."

Britt felt sick. It wasn't going to be as easy wrapping this up as she'd hoped. "I'd be delighted to sit down with you in good time, Derek, dear, but there's really no reason to hold things up until we do. Why don't I give you a jingle tomorrow, and we can discuss the option. You know, it won't come cheap."

He hesitated before answering. "Yes, there won't be any problem there. I want the film."

"Then let's do a deal, by all means. Will you be in your office in the morning?"

"More likely at home."

"I'll ring you up as soon as the fog lifts, as it were."

"Okay. I look forward to hearing from you, Miranda."

"Until tomorrow, then, dear." Britt hung up, relieved. What if he'd insisted on negotiating in person? That would have been a disaster. Of course, she wasn't off the hook yet. Things could still blow up in her face. She sighed and headed for the dining room. The wages of sin.

Derek was sipping orange juice when he saw Allison enter the room. She walked toward him with the long graceful strides of a model. She was attractive without being flashy. Hollywood was full of gorgeous women, but there was something about this one—the way she moved, the intelligence in her eyes.... It was hard to put his finger on it. They had a lot in common, although it was too early to say he knew her. But he *wanted* to know her. That much was certain.

As she slid into the booth, he noticed the faintest sign of worry on her brow. When she saw that their breakfasts had been served, she protested.

"Derek, you shouldn't have waited for me. Sorry I was so long."

"No problem. I was on the phone, as a matter of fact. Doing a little business."

The waiter, who'd left the plate covers on to keep the pancakes warm, came over and removed them. Derek watched her lean over to inhale the aroma of the food, catching her eye. Her cheeks colored as she smiled.

"Smells good," she said.

There was a mischievousness about her. He liked that. Yet, a part of him wasn't quite sure how far to trust her, considering the hoax. He decided to hold back a bit, at least until he was sure what was going on.

"I spoke to Miranda," he said, as he watched her pour maple syrup over her cakes.

"Oh? What did she have to say?"

"We agreed to work out a deal for *Dream Girl.*"

Britt grinned. "Was she pleased?"

"I think so. But she seems to be having a little trouble finding time to meet with me." He took a sip of coffee.

''Miranda's an odd duck, Derek, and really busy. But I'm sure she's eager to do the deal. She damned well better be!'' She smiled and took a bite of her Dutch apple pancakes.

''You know, you sounded like her just then, the way you said, 'odd duck' and 'damned well better be.'''

Allison blinked, then smoothly said, ''Accents are contagious. We were talking about Miranda and that made me think about her voice, I guess. I just love the way the English talk, don't you?''

''I suppose.'' He studied her face, liking what he saw very much, even if he knew she'd gotten herself mixed up in something fishy.

Color came to her cheeks as he watched her munching. He put some syrup on his cakes. This game they were playing was getting more interesting all the time. He was eager to see what would happen next.

The waiter came with more coffee. Allison picked up her cup, holding it with both hands as she looked across the table at him. He evaluated what he was feeling for her and found it as remarkable as it was simulating.

''What are you doing for lunch, Allison?'' he asked.

''Lunch?'' She blinked. ''I haven't finished breakfast.''

''I know, but I like to plan ahead.''

She threw back her head and laughed. There was a joy about her that he loved.

''You aren't serious,'' she said.

''Of course, I'm serious. I think we should do lunch,

further explore our collaborative relationship.'' He
eyed her, waiting to see her reaction.

''I'm supposed to work today.''

''You get sick days, don't you? Where does your
employer think you are, anyway?''

''I said I had a doctor's appointment.''

''Couldn't the shot he gave you have made you
sick?''

''You're counseling crime, Derek.''

''I feel like playing hooky and would like company.
What would you say to a drive up the coast and having
a leisurely lunch along the way?''

She leaned her elbows on the table, resting her chin
on her hands. ''What exactly did you have in mind?''

''A drive, lunch, conversation.''

''Is that all?''

''Should there be something else?'' he asked.

She shifted uncomfortably. ''I've been in Hollywood long enough to know that sometimes there
are…expectations.''

''I'm not propositioning you, if that's what you're
concerned about. If that's what I had in mind, I'd say
so.''

''Being the supplicant in this situation, I tend to be
a little paranoid.''

''Let me reassure you. I don't make sex a condition
of my professional relationships. My interest in *Dream
Girl* is quite separate from my interest in you. As far
as I'm concerned we're going to do the picture, Allison. Whether we do lunch today or at any other time
is up to you—unconditionally.''

"I like your attitude, Mr. Redmond," she said. "And I appreciate it."

He took a bite of pancake as he regarded her, feeling the energy flow back and forth between them. She wasn't afraid to look him in the eye. He liked that. He took another sip of coffee.

"I don't pretend to be a Boy Scout or a monk, however," he said.

Allison lifted a brow. "Is that a warning?"

"More a disclaimer."

"And what are you disclaiming?"

He smiled, looking her in the eye. "I can't promise not to enjoy your company, even if I manage to behave myself."

"My, all this candor is unexpected."

"Aren't you used to men being straight with you?"

"No, not most of the time."

"Then I'll try not to disappoint you," he said, as he reached across the table and took her hand. "Respect—and by that I mean mutual respect—is an important part of every friendship, Allison."

"Do you mean that, or is it just a fancy line?"

"The proof will be in the pudding."

"What you're saying is that if I want to find out, I'm going to have to take a chance."

"Ultimately every relationship is a matter of trust. You have to trust me. I have to trust you. We both have to trust Miranda."

She flushed. If he didn't know better, he'd have said he was seeing guilt at work. He rubbed the back of her hand with his thumb, noticing that she wasn't looking him in the eye now as she had earlier. He decided they were likely in for a very interesting afternoon.

Britt knew the last thing she ought to be doing was running off with Derek Redmond for a carefree afternoon, but she'd agreed to do just that. He was suspicious, that much she could tell. But what she didn't know was what, exactly, he suspected. Her task for the afternoon would be to put his mind at ease.

Before leaving the Polo Lounge, Britt called Sally and told her she wasn't well and wouldn't be returning to the office. Then she went with Derek in his Porsche, driving west on Sunset Boulevard toward the coast.

From time to time she glanced over at him, watching the breeze from the sunroof flutter his ebony hair. Derek was the perfect Hollywood Lothario—good-looking, a successful filmmaker who drove a sports car and probably had a nice house in the West Los Angeles hills. He'd have his pick of starlets, that was obvious. There was no shortage of girls who'd hop in his bed in hope of furthering their careers.

Yet there was something about him that said he wasn't like that. Or was it simply wishful thinking on her part?

"You don't do the Hollywood social scene, do you, Derek?" she asked when he'd been silent for a while.

He glanced her way. "No, that is, no more than the requirements of the business. A certain amount is done in almost any profession. Even college professors have to schmooze the dean."

"How is it you haven't been seduced?" she asked.

"Probably the same reason you haven't."

"I haven't had the opportunity. I didn't make it as an actress and I'm only getting started as a writer. But you've been in the middle of the action for some time."

Derek stared ahead at the road, not saying anything for a moment. "I take my work seriously and don't want distractions."

"You're hardly a puritan."

He laughed. "No, I like to think I'm just a regular guy. My dad is a college professor, my mom a child psychologist."

"How did you get into films?"

"My girlfriend in high school was an actress and she got me into theater. The acting side didn't appeal, but the behind-the-scenes aspects did. I wrote plays and worked with the director. When I went to U.C.L.A., I decided to major in film arts. I put in my time learning the business, had a couple of lucky breaks. One thing led to another, as they say, and here I am, courting a most promising screenwriter."

Britt chuckled. "Somewhere along the way you learned to flatter."

He took her hand and squeezed it. "Creative people have vivid and lively imaginations, Allison."

He had an easy, natural way of expressing himself, inspiring such confidence and trust that she wanted to throw off her cloak of deception and confess her fraud. His obvious honesty made her feel all the more guilty, the worst being whenever he called her "Allison."

Eventually she would tell him the truth, but she couldn't just yet.

For that reason, if for no other, it had probably been a mistake to agree to spend the day with him. She'd simply given in to the temptation of the moment.

"You're passionate about your writing, aren't you?" Derek said.

Britt looked over at him. "Yes. Maybe too passionate. Maybe more possessed and driven than I should be."

"Why do you say that?"

Britt wanted to say, "Because of what I've let it do to me, because of the lie I'm living. And most of all because I'm not true to myself when that should be more important than anything." Instead, she simply said, "Maybe a person can want something too much."

They came to a traffic light and Derek brought the Porsche to a stop. He turned to her. "I've got a hunch this is going to work out fine."

Britt wondered what he meant by that. When he saw the questioning look in her eye, he reached over and pinched her cheek in an affectionate, friendly way.

"All we have to do is trust each other," he said.

The light changed and the car started up. Britt glanced out at the lush green of West L.A., suddenly afraid that by going off with Derek Redmond, she'd made a dreadful mistake.

7

As they drove through Brentwood and Pacific Palisades, Derek chatted about the film he'd just wrapped and the battles at the studio with the publicity department and the way they planned to position the film for the market. Derek was treating her like a colleague and she loved it. For the first time ever, she felt like an insider, someone whose opinion mattered. It was a heady experience.

"I can't wait to see how they try to position *Dream Girl*," he said. "Unfortunately, the way a film is marketed is nearly as important as the way it's made."

Britt had to remind herself that this was actually her baby they were talking about, not someone else's project. Derek spoke so matter-of-factly. Would the day ever come when she could talk about the success of her work so casually? "I'm sort of curious what they would do myself," she said ironically. "It's hard to imagine that it could really happen."

"First-time nerves?" he asked, understanding her anxiety.

"Yes."

Derek patted her knee. "It'll all be old hat to you soon, Allison. But enjoy it while you can."

"Before I get jaded, you mean?"

"Let's say, before you lose your innocence." He gave her a wink.

When they got to the coast, he turned west and they drove though Topanga Beach and Malibu. They talked about the movie business the whole time. When they got to Corral Beach, he pulled off the highway.

"I guess you aren't exactly dressed for a walk on the beach," he said.

"No."

"If I spring for a new pair of panty hose, will you go for a stroll with me?"

"I suppose I could take them off and spare you the expense."

"Shall I close my eyes?" he asked.

"Why don't you take a little walk instead?"

"Aren't used to getting undressed in a car with a man, huh?"

"I'm a preacher's daughter, Derek. There's got to be at least a pretense of propriety."

"A preacher's kid, eh?"

"I may not seem like it on the surface, but I am and the influences run deep, believe me."

"I won't hold that against you, Allison."

"And I won't hold it against you that you won't," she quipped.

He laughed and climbed out of the Porsche, then strolled off toward the water. Britt watched him looking out to sea as the wind tossed his dark hair. His hands were thrust into his pants pockets. She was more than intrigued by Derek. She liked him. She liked him a lot.

After glancing around the mostly empty parking lot to make sure the coast was clear, she kicked off her shoes, pulled up her skirt and wriggled out of her panty hose. She stuffed them in her purse, then got out of the car. Derek turned when he heard the door slam.

"Are you decent?" he asked, sauntering toward her, a big smile on his face.

"Definitely PG."

Derek chuckled and took her hand. They made their way toward the distant breakers across the broad expanse of sand. It was a pleasant day, but the wind had a nip to it.

"Will you be warm enough?" he asked.

"I'm okay for now, but I may try to talk you out of your jacket later."

"Fair enough."

Britt liked the feel of the sand between her toes. Her big beach experience as a child growing up was at the shore of Lake Michigan. The Pacific was a whole other thing. She had only been to the ocean half-a-dozen times since coming to California, so she could hardly be considered a connoisseur of beach life.

"Don't tell me you were a surfer," Britt said, as they strolled along at water's edge.

"I tried it a few times, but mostly I've sailed."

They talked about their college years. He told her that a turning point in his life had come during the

year he'd bummed around Europe following graduation. It was then he'd grown up. In answer to her question, he admitted that there'd been a girl involved in
the equation, an English girl who'd been the first serious love of his life.

"So that's what's behind your passion for my
screenplay," she observed, tossing her hair in the
wind. "An English girl from your past."

"Art reflects life," he said.

"A philosopher, I see."

He laughed. "You know, you're the second person
who's said that to me recently. I had lunch with Oliver
Wheatley the other day and he said the same thing.
Maybe I'm too ponderous. What do you think?"

Britt's ears had pricked up when he mentioned Oliver Wheatley and the rest of what he'd said sailed
right over her head. "When was that?"

"When was what?"

"When you had lunch with Oliver Wheatley."

"I don't know, a few days ago," he replied.
"Why?"

"I was just curious." Britt was thinking fast, trying
to figure out if there was any chance her screenplay
or Miranda might have come up in the conversation.
She glanced at him, but saw no sign of secret knowledge, no giveaway smile or smirk.

"Oliver's an interesting guy," Derek said as a gust
of wind blew hard against them, rippling their clothing. "He was up to his ears in a big film deal when I
saw him."

Britt decided there hadn't been anything said that

compromised her or the story she'd spun. But it did show she was sailing in very dangerous waters.

"Have you met Oliver?" Derek asked.

She shook her head. "No. You're the first director who's said more to me than 'Thanks for the reading, we'll get back to you.'"

"Directors aren't at their best during casting calls."

"Well, those days are behind me."

"Now you're the genius behind the words, instead of the beauty in front of the camera."

"You keep talking that way, Derek, and I'm going to start believing it. Then I'll become insufferable."

He grinned and put his arm around her shoulders, hugging her. "No, Allison. I can tell you're a lady with her feet firmly on the ground."

They soon came to the end of the beach and turned back toward the car. Britt started getting chilly and asked Derek if he'd be willing to give up his jacket. He promptly slipped it off and put it around her shoulders. She savored the warmth, liking the feeling, the intimacy.

On the way back they watched windsurfers beyond the breakers. Britt waded ankle-deep into the water. The wind was getting stronger, pushing frothy globs of foam across the sand. She clutched the lapels of his jacket together at her throat and skipped ahead.

After a while she stopped and looked back. Derek strolled along unhurriedly, his smile signaling that he was as happy as she. It was nice that they could be like this with each other. Britt almost regretted they had business dealings, that he was the key to getting her writing career off the ground.

"What do you say, Allison, shall we run off to Hawaii?"

"*Hawaii?* I thought you were taking me to *lunch?*"

"Why not both?" he asked, catching up with her.

"You're joking, of course."

He shrugged.

"I think breakfast and lunch is enough for a first date, Derek, but thanks for thinking of me."

He put his arm around her again, intentionally bumping his hip against hers. "I guess I'm just a wild and crazy guy."

"I take it you aren't like this often."

"Not for years, at any rate." He reached over and pulled a strand of windblown hair from her face, smiling. "Maybe it's you."

"Spontaneity is nice and all, but…"

"As a preacher's daughter, you intend to keep me on the straight and narrow—is that what you mean?"

She laughed. "Yes. And get you on the dotted line."

"So that's all you're interested in, eh—selling your script at any cost?" He gave her a bemused smile.

"Not at *any* cost, Derek."

He chuckled. "It's nice to know you've got your limits."

The gentle teasing made her consider her true motives for coming to the beach with him. She *did* want to sell her script; Derek was right about that. After all, that's what had brought them together in the first place. But the truth was, she was enjoying his company, their conversation about the film business. In fact, she liked being with him, period.

"If I didn't know better, I'd say you're blushing," he said, interrupting her thoughts.

Britt gave him a sideward glance. "Must be all the fresh air."

He looked disappointed. "I'd rather think it was me."

She felt a sudden, uncontrollable urge to get away from him, to hide her emotions. On an impulse, she whipped his jacket off and handed it back to him.

"There's something about the seashore that makes me want to run. You don't mind if I jog up the beach, do you?"

"Nope. I love athletic women."

Britt arched a brow. "Maybe you just love women, Derek."

With that she hitched up her skirt and took off at a full run. After a hundred yards she stopped and turned around, her chest heaving. Derek continued walking at the same deliberate pace. She ambled back toward him. Her heart was pounding, but the surge of adrenaline in her blood was spent.

She caught her breath before they met, tossing her hair in the wind. She laughed. "That felt good."

"You're a regular gazelle," he said, peeling off his jacket again and putting it around her. He straightened the shoulders on her slender frame. They stood facing each other. "What other secret talents do you have?"

"You've pretty much seen my repertoire," she replied.

"You weren't Indiana state chess champion?"

"Chinese checkers is my game."

"You were probably Phi Beta Kappa."

"No," she said, "but I did win the seventh-grade spelling bee."

Derek took her face in his hands and looked into her eyes. "I knew you were talented. Now I discover you're an athlete and a scholar to boot. Am I in store for any more surprises?"

Britt shook her head, wishing things had been different. If only she hadn't started this damned charade. It would have been nice to hear the sound of her real name on his lips. "No," she murmured miserably. "What you see is what you get."

"I'd say I got a hell of a bargain." With that he lowered his head and lightly kissed her.

They were frozen in that pose when a wave washed over their feet. Britt jumped from the shock of the cold and Derek looked down at his shoes. They were soaked, as were his socks and pant cuffs.

"Hmm," he said, his hands settling on his hips. "What do you think? We're already wet. Shall we flick it in and go for a swim?"

"Derek, this is a two-hundred-dollar dress! I know that doesn't sound like much to you, but to me it's a whole lot. Anyway, you're the one who's wet. I've got bare feet."

He swooped her into his arms without warning and started walking toward the water.

"Derek! Don't you dare! Put me down!"

"What the hell, I already owe you a pair of panty hose. Why not a new dress?"

Britt tried to wiggle from his arms as another wave came toward them. "If you throw me in the water I'll never speak to you again. And I *won't* sell you my screenplay!"

He stopped dead in his tracks as the wave came swirling up around his ankles, rising to his calves and knees. "You really don't want to go for a swim, do you?"

"I'm impetuous, but not that impetuous."

"Where's your sense of romance? Remember Burt Lancaster and Deborah Kerr in that beach scene in *From Here to Eternity?*"

"They had swimsuits on."

Another wave came in, swirling about his feet. "You're robbing this sparkling moment of its poetry," he lamented wryly.

"I'd rather be dry, thank you."

"Where's your sense of adventure?"

"I left it in your Porsche. Shall we go get it?"

He threw back his head and laughed. "Come on, Allison, tell the truth. In your heart of hearts, what do you want? What is your adventurous spirit crying out for?"

"Lunch."

Shaking his head with amusement, he turned and began trudging out of the surf. "You're a woman who knows her mind."

"That's better than the reverse, isn't it?"

When they got to dry land he put her down. Then he looked at his soaked pant legs. "I either take you to Taco Bell for lunch or we run down to my place so I can change. I'm just down the road a piece."

Britt couldn't help wondering if that was coincidental, or if his spontaneous dip in the Pacific was a ploy to take her to his place. She decided not to make an issue of it. "I'm sure you're not very comfortable, soaked that way."

Derek offered his arm and they marched through the sand back toward the parking lot. "I haven't felt this carefree—or been this silly—in months," he said, "maybe years. Thanks for indulging me."

"I feel pretty good myself, Derek."

He looked up at the clear blue sky. "It's easy enough to understand my euphoria. It's a wonderful fall day. The salt air is invigorating. I'm in the company of a beautiful woman. A new project is spinning around in my head." He gave her a joyful smile. "What's your excuse?"

Britt shrugged. "You like my screenplay and want to turn it into a movie. What could be more exciting to a beginner than that?"

He reached over and gave her a playful cuff on the chin. "You're a tough one, Miss O'Donnell. But I'll do what I can to loosen you up a bit."

"I hope that's not a threat," she said.

Derek grinned. "No, it's a promise."

His place in Brentwood was on a street of stately homes—not magnificent mansions, but substantial residences, many walled and protected by security gates, all opulently landscaped. It was a neighborhood where prominent doctors, lawyers, executives and other well-heeled citizens resided. These were not people who mowed their own lawns.

Britt suspected a few Hollywood types might be scattered about the area, but it wasn't the sort of place tour buses would frequent. They pulled into Derek's circular drive and he stopped.

"You're looking at *Code Red*," he said. "I was fortunate enough to have a piece of the action."

"Before that you were just one of us, I suppose."

"I had a condo in Santa Monica."

"That still puts you a step above us plebeians."

"Where do you live, Allison?"

"I've got an apartment in West Hollywood. It's musty and furnished in 'early student,' but it's home."

He smiled. "I think I was a previous tenant."

"You were one of Horatio Alger's boys?"

Derek chuckled. "It's nice to be with someone who knows there was life before Edwin Porter and *The Great Train Robbery*."

"You sound more like an old warhorse than one of Hollywood's young lions, Derek. Next thing you'll be telling me is that you remember the Beatles."

He laughed. "Touché. But you're right, Allison. This town can corrupt a guy. I make a couple of films and I think I know everything."

Britt touched his arm. "That's not what I meant."

"But it's what *I* meant," he said, giving her a wink. "Come on, let's go inside. I'll get out of these wet pants and we'll have lunch."

8

———→ ←———

Britt gazed in the guest-bath mirror and had the oddest feeling that the woman who stared back at her was a stranger. All morning she'd been playing Allison O'Donnell, screenwriter. All morning she'd allowed herself to be charmed by Derek Redmond. It had been a crazy, wonderful, exciting day, but a false one. That was the problem.

When she went back out to the sparsely furnished front room there was no sign of Derek. Through the sliding-glass door she could see the pool and the trees and shrubs beyond. The garden had the look of a glade. The living room had two cream leather sofas, an easy chair and a walnut wall-unit. There was an Oriental carpet on the hardwood floor but the decor was clearly of an interim nature. Derek had said he intended to have the place professionally decorated when he could afford it. *Code Red* had been successful, but it hadn't made him a millionaire.

Britt went to the window and watched the pool sweep moving like a robot across the surface of the water. She had to remind herself she was in the home of the director of *Code Red*. Being there seemed too good to be true, and in a way it was, because it was happening under false pretenses.

"Pleasant out there, isn't it?"

Britt turned at the sound of Derek's voice. He was in jeans and a black turtleneck, looking relaxed and much more comfortable than when they'd arrived.

"Yes," she said, "you have a lovely home."

"Why don't we grab a bite? Then, if you like, maybe we can talk about *Dream Girl* a little."

Britt's ears perked up at the mention of her screenplay. Funny that she should have to remind herself that was the point of all this.

Derek took her to the kitchen where they decided on a deli lunch. He kept his refrigerator stocked with meats and cheeses because he wasn't much of a cook and didn't like eating out of a can. Britt offered to help, but he insisted she was his guest.

She watched him bustling about, not exactly looking like he was in his natural environment, but not looking like a fish out of water, either. He was chatting away, making small talk. She responded to his comments, but mostly she was focused on Derek. His casual, natural manner put her at ease. He treated her like a friend, a confidante, which Britt found very disarming. Whenever she found herself relaxing and starting to let her guard down, she had to remind herself where she was and what was going on.

Derek let her take the sandwich fixings to the table while he carried over a couple of different deli salads and two beers. Britt discovered that the ocean air had given her an appetite and she dug in enthusiastically.

They munched away contentedly for a while before he spoke.

"*Dream Girl* has a nice, light romantic touch," he said, taking a big bite of his sandwich. "Have you ever been in love the way Casey was in your script?"

Britt considered the question. "Never."

"She's very sympathetic." He took another bite and studied her. "As I get to know you better, Allison, I see her in you."

"Oh?"

"I suppose it's the vulnerability. Her struggle, the fact that she's trying so hard against such formidable odds."

"That's descriptive of my life, too." She took a swig of beer. "Maybe you have a point."

"So, how have the romantic tussles in your life been like Casey's?"

She smiled, giving him a look. "Aren't you the subtle one. I've heard of innovative ways to ask personal questions, but that's the most clever yet."

"That was too personal?"

She nodded. "Maybe."

"Casey is such a fascinating character that it made me curious about you."

"As you well know, Derek, real life is not like fiction." Britt took a bite and chewed. "But I'm glad you liked Casey."

"I fell in love with her, if you want the honest truth." He grinned. "So my curiosity about you is understandable, right?"

She shifted uneasily. "But I'm not Casey."

"Are you sure?"

They looked at each other for a long moment. The tug of energy flowing back and forth between them was strong. Britt knew she was blushing, but she also knew there was no easy way to hide it.

"If I'm embarrassing you, I'm sorry," he said. "I didn't mean to make you uncomfortable."

She wiped the corner of her mouth with one of the paper napkins he'd put on the table. "I've heard of directors getting emotionally caught up with their stars, but I assumed writers were safe from that sort of thing."

"For starters, most screenwriters don't look like you. But that's not the point. It's the soul, the inner spirit revealed in your work, I find myself so attracted to."

She looked into his terribly sincere eyes and couldn't help but be affected by his words, whatever their secret intent. "I don't know what to say, Derek. I'm flattered."

He contemplated her. "Maybe I should confess something else."

Britt's heart skipped a beat. His comments had caught her off guard. She was torn between the joy his flattery brought and her instinct to be cautious.

"When I first saw you," he began, "I wondered if you'd really written *Dream Girl,* or if you were some sort of shill."

Her eyes widened. "A shill?"

"Don't worry, I became convinced you're the real McCoy soon enough. But the idea crossed my mind."

A little wave of trepidation went through her. "Why?"

Derek smiled. "Let's just say you seemed too good to be true." He drank some more beer. "Odd comment from a guy who makes his living by creating illusions, I know."

"I hope you're satisfied now," she ventured.

He nodded. "You're real, all right. Seeing Casey in you is one of the things that convinced me. That and the fact that you know your stuff."

Britt gave a secret sigh of relief.

"It's my job to entertain the public." he said. "But I can't be any better than the material I work with. Therein lies the power of the written word, Allison. If you can make me love Casey, then I can make the people in the movie theaters love her. This magic we work with can be a very powerful thing."

Britt looked at him in awe. Maybe her mouth was even hanging open. She didn't care. She thought she understood her craft, perhaps she even loved it to the point of obsession, but nothing had given her such a sense of pride as the words Derek Redmond had just uttered. "That's a lovely thing to say," she murmured.

"It's from the heart," he said, his eyes shimmering. "And it's a hundred-percent honest. That's important for people who work together, to be completely straight with each other."

A lump formed in her throat. Britt swallowed hard, trying to control her emotion. The euphoria of one moment became the shame of the next. It was all she could do to keep from breaking into tears. The urge to blurt out the truth welled in her again. Her lip trembled.

"It'd be okay to say you feel good about me, too," he prompted.

"Oh, I do! I'm terribly grateful. It's just that I...I..."

"What?"

"Feel so...unworthy."

Derek laughed. "That's a natural rookie reaction. I felt the same way when *Code Red* was finally in the can. I wanted to drive down to the beach and fling all the reels in the ocean. And I might have done it if it weren't for all those investors who'd put millions into it."

Britt bit her lip and a tear actually did overflow her lid. She wiped it away, then dabbed her eye with her napkin. "Thanks for telling me that."

"Hey, I had my mentors, Allison. I hope to be one of yours."

They both smiled and he reached across the table and patted her hand. Britt sighed. She felt tremendous gratitude, but more than that, there was a sense of kinship that was hard to describe.

She recalled one evening while she was in college when she'd had a father-daughter conversation about romance and love. "It's not easy to explain love to somebody who has never felt it," he'd said. "It's the sort of thing a person has to learn about on their own. But I can tell you this, the best is love that's built on friendship, mutual respect, common values and common purpose."

At the time Thomas Kingsley had said that, the words had sounded an awful lot like the sorts of things he'd said from the pulpit—great-sounding ideas, but not always easy to apply to life. Over the years, though, whenever she was with a guy, she would think about what her father had said. But try as she might, she'd never been able to internalize them—until now, anyway. She'd only met Derek that morning, but he, more than anybody she'd ever known, gave her father's words meaning.

"Assuming you'd allow me, of course," he said.

"Huh?"

"To be your mentor."

Britt gave a little laugh. "Are you kidding? I'd be honored. Who wouldn't be?"

He looked pleased. "Finish your sandwich," he told her. "Then I'd like to show you something."

Britt insisted on helping to put away the leftovers. Then Derek led her into the front room and sat her down on one of the leather sofas. He went over to a table, got a ringed binder and dropped down beside her so that their hips and shoulders touched. She liked his proximity, his body warmth. Since their walk on the beach she'd craved his touch. She leaned against him.

"What's that?" she asked, gesturing toward the binder resting on his knees.

"*Dream Girl.* I did some work on it last night— until two in the morning, as a matter of fact—and I wanted to share some of my thoughts. If you don't mind.''

"Of course, I don't mind.''

Derek toyed with the cover of the binder. She squirmed nervously, waiting.

"Don't be alarmed at the extent of my notes and the comments in the margin,'' he said. "Believe it or not, what I've done is a sign of love.''

"That certainly sounds provocative,'' she said, lifting an eyebrow.

He gave her a crooked grin. "Yeah, it sort of does, doesn't it?''

Britt looked at him from the corner of her eye and he looked at her. *Dream Girl,* the things they'd been discussing, faded and suddenly there was just the two of them. Derek leaned toward her, kissing the end of her nose. Then he kissed her lips.

It seemed so natural, and yet it was surprising in a way. Having him kiss her was what she'd wanted, even if it made no sense.

"I hope you won't always be this distracting,'' he murmured. "It might be difficult to get anything done.''

"*You're* the director.''

"In other words, it's my problem,'' he said with a laugh.

"I guess you could say that.''

Derek gave her a chiding look and flipped open the binder. He let it lie open on their laps. "I went through your script line by line, scene by scene. I thought we could walk through it together and do a little fine-tuning.''

Britt was thrilled.

For the next two hours they evaluated the script, getting into Casey's head. Derek had diagrammed the plot to look at the structure. Writing, Britt knew from experience, was a lonely business. To delve into it with someone else, to hear another person talking about Casey and her other characters as though they were real, was profoundly moving for her.

Their conversation was animated on occasion, even passionate. A few times Britt got really upset and they snapped at each other. But mostly they were in harmony.

When they finally finished, Derek closed the binder and laid his head back on the sofa, sighing deeply. ''I think we just did something very important,'' he said.

''You think so?''

''Yes. I knew we had to do this together. It's like good sex, when you think about it.''

Britt gave him a sideward glance. ''I've never quite thought of my writing quite that way.''

He laughed and rolled his head toward her. ''Maybe it's you, Allison. Maybe you bring it out of me.''

Britt leaned away from him. ''If you're a pervert, don't try and blame it on me.''

Derek turned her face toward him and kissed her again. This was a more passionate kiss. Whatever hesitation or restraint had been there before dropped away and the next thing she knew they were stretched out on the sofa in each other's arms.

Excitement swept over her. Soon they were half undressed, panting, undoing each other's clothes. They rolled off the sofa and onto the floor. Britt landed on top of Derek. She pulled her head back to look at him. There was desire in his eyes. She struggled to catch her breath.

"How did this get into the script?" she asked.

"I think it's been there from the start. We're just discovering it, Allison, that's all."

When he called her Allison, everything suddenly snapped into perspective. She rolled off him and sat up, straightening her dress.

Derek looked perplexed. He propped himself up on his elbow, studying her. "What's the matter?"

"Is this routine?" she asked.

"If you mean do I do this with all my writers, the answer is no."

"Then what happened?"

"I think we're attracted to each other. Or maybe I should say I'm attracted to you."

Britt furrowed her brow. "I'd hate to think this is just a routine step in the filmmaking process."

He laughed. "It's not. If you need an explanation, it's that we share a zeal for our work and for each other. It's actually kind of nice, in my opinion. Both is better." He gave her an inquiring look. "Don't you think?"

She thought for a moment. "So what happens next?"

Derek took her hand. "Well...how about dinner?

We can rustle up something here, or I can take you out.''

"Derek, we've already eaten breakfast and lunch together. Wouldn't dinner be overdoing it? I mean, I've heard of extended first dates, but this is ridiculous.''

"Hell, if I'd had my way, we'd have headed for Hawaii.''

"I thought that was a joke.''

"I was more serious than not. I admit, though, it wasn't a very practical idea.''

Britt shook her head. "You know what? You're crazy.''

He shrugged. "Like I told you at the beach, I'm in a spontaneous mood. I don't get this way often, and I thought I ought to go with it.'' He pulled her hand to his lips and kissed her fingers. "So what will it be, my darling? Dinner in or out, this evening?''

She couldn't help laughing. "You really are crazy.''

"Well, what do you want to do?''

"I want you to take me back to the Beverly Hills Hotel so I can get my car and go home.''

He frowned, looking unhappy. "Does this mean you're rejecting me?''

"It means I think we should proceed at a slower pace.''

"I've been too forward for a first date, is that it?''

"Yes, and for a first picture.''

Derek gave her a wink. "Touché.'' He toyed with her fingers. "Sure I can't convince you to have dinner with me?''

Britt was sorely tempted, but she needed to get her priorities straight. She was here because of her career, not to find romance. That meant she had to get Derek on the dotted line. Unfortunately, that was shaping up to be more difficult than she'd thought. It wasn't easy to say no to him. Reaching out, she touched his face.

"I think we should save something for act two."

"You're definitely a writer, Allison O'Donnell. There's no disputing that!"

9

Britt climbed the stairs to her apartment. She felt totally wrung out. She'd spent a glorious day with Derek. In fact, if she hadn't been under the strain of pretending to be someone she wasn't, it would have been one of the best days of her life. But the guilt she felt over her grand deception just wouldn't go away.

And if that wasn't bad enough, when Derek drove her back to the Beverly Hills Hotel to pick up her car, he'd dropped a bomb. After kissing her sweetly—so sweetly that she'd wished she'd stayed with him—he'd said, "I want you to know I'm going to put the muscle on Miranda, so if you hear about some unhappiness on my part, you won't be surprised."

She'd blinked. "What's the matter?"

"I'm going to insist she meet with me tomorrow. I'm not going to let her put me off again. If she tries to, there'll be fireworks. I wanted you to know in advance so you won't be alarmed."

Britt had thanked him, but the comment had put her into a blue funk. Driving back to her apartment, she'd agonized over what to do. When she got to the third floor Britt went right to Allison's door. Her friend had gotten home a few minutes earlier and was still in her work clothes.

"Britt, what's wrong? You look like you've been hit by a truck."

"I have, Ms. O'Donnell. And in a way you have, too. We've got to talk."

Allison invited her in and Britt went to an easy chair and dropped down in it like a rock. Allison went to the kitchen and returned a moment later with a glass of wine for each of them. Handing one to Britt, she pulled up an ottoman and said, "Okay, what happened?"

Britt gave her a two-minute summary, ending with Derek's intention to have it out with Miranda. "What am I going to do? Not only is my screenplay at stake, but so's my—"

"Future happiness?" Allison said, finishing the sentence for her.

"That might be a little strong."

Allison gave her a skeptical look. "When you were talking about him, I could hear the bells ringing myself. You think you might have found Mr. Wonderful, don't you?"

"Lord, I don't know, Allison. To be honest, I'm so confused I'm not even sure who I am, let alone how I feel about anybody else."

Allison pondered the situation. "Well, you've got yourself a double-barreled problem, kiddo—a professional and a personal one."

"Don't forget you're in this, too. It was your idea."

"*My* idea?"

''Well, *our* idea. Let's not quibble over details.'' Britt took a slug of wine. ''The question is, what am I going to do? Do I turn myself in and cheerfully await execution?''

''Maybe he'd take pity on you.''

''Maybe he'd kill me. I would if I was in his shoes. He thinks I'm this wonderful, virtuous, straight-shooting virgin saint.''

''Virgin? My, this was quite a first date, wasn't it?''

''Quiet, bitch.'' Britt sighed woefully. ''Seriously, what am I to do? How can I get the deal signed before I do my mea culpa. After everything I've gone through, I can't see giving up at the eleventh hour. On the other hand, Derek's determined. I don't think he'll sign anything without meeting Miranda face-to-face.''

''Then maybe he *should* meet with Miranda.''

''Are you crazy? If she heard about this, she'd kill me before Derek had a chance.''

''I'm not talking about the *real* Miranda. I mean you!''

''Me?''

''You've played her on the phone,'' Allison said. ''Why not play her in person?''

''How am I going to do that? He's already seen me in my Allison O'Donnell role.''

''Then you'll have to meet with him in disguise.''

''Disguised as what? A bank robber with a ski mask over my face?'' Britt took another gulp of wine—a very large one.

Allison was thinking. She had that evil look on her

face that Britt had seen before—like when they were hatching her Continental Artists plot.

"I guess I'm somewhat responsible for the pickle you're in," Allison said, "so here's what I'm going to do. I have a friend at the studio, a makeup artist. Lucien owes me a favor anyway, and he's a genius. He'll transform you into a thirty-five-year-old English-woman. Trust me, when Lucien's finished, Derek won't have the slightest idea that Miranda Maxwell and Allison O'Donnell are the same woman."

"You're crazier than I am."

"You don't want to tell him the truth, so what other choice do you have?" Allison asked.

"It's not that I don't *want* to tell him the truth, it's that I *can't*."

"Don't split hairs, kiddo, we don't have the time. When does he want to meet Miranda?"

"Tomorrow."

"Make it for dinner. That will give us time. I'll have Lucien here after work—say, at six," Allison said. "He'll turn you into Miranda Maxwell for your dinner date. You work out the arrangements with Derek as to the time and place, but you might want to consider someplace dark. What you say and how you handle the negotiation is up to you, Britt. Once I have you in costume, you're on your own."

"Allison, that's the nuttiest idea I've ever heard. It would never work."

"You convinced him you were Miranda over the phone, didn't you?"

"Yes, but..."

''You're trying to tell me Hollywood can turn Dustin Hoffman into Tootsie and Robin Williams into Mrs. Doubtfire, but it can't turn you into Miranda Maxwell?''

''But this is real life!''

''Men never look below the surface, you know that. All Lucien really has to do is make you look unrecognizable, because Derek doesn't know what the real Miranda looks like, does he?''

''No, I guess not. They've never met.''

''There you go, then! Piece of cake!''

''Oh, God. I'm going straight to hell. I know I am.''

Allison laughed. ''It'll be a hell of a trip, though, kiddo.''

Britt rolled her eyes. ''All right, I guess I'll give it a try. Even if I blow it, I won't be any worse off than I am now.''

''Think of it as the role of a lifetime! A final chance to do something with that acting talent of yours.''

Allison began laughing. Britt wanted to smack her, but the situation was so absurd that she was soon laughing, too. After a minute they were both practically rolling on the floor.

''The only thing better,'' Allison said through her tears, ''would be if you had to go disguised as a man.''

Britt laughed until her sides hurt. Finally she got control of herself. ''Glad you're having such a good time with this. I'm the one who's probably going to end up looking like a fool.''

''But if you pull it off, Derek Redmond will have to marry you just to shut you up. He couldn't afford having you running around town telling this story at cocktail parties!''

Britt wiped her eyes. ''And I couldn't afford having him running around town telling the story on me.''

''Guess your mission is clear, Ms. Maxwell. First you get an option agreement signed for your client's screenplay, then you marry the guy.''

''But which one of us is he supposed to marry— you or Miranda or me?''

Allison scratched her head, then a wicked smile crossed her face. ''Know what, kiddo? There may be a movie in this!''

The next day, just before noon, Derek Redmond sat in his black Porsche on Santa Monica Boulevard. He was parked outside the building where Continental Artists was located. Drumming his fingers on the steering wheel, he looked toward the entrance, which was set some distance back from the street. He drew a long breath and stared vacantly through the windshield, curious about what, if anything, Oliver Wheatley would turn up.

Derek was more confused than ever. He'd had a surprising call early that morning from Miranda. The call had actually awakened him.

''Darling, why didn't you tell me you were upset? If I'd known you wanted to meet with me *that* badly, I'd have agreed in a flash. I feel dreadful. You must think me an absolute dollybird. I do hope you'll forgive me. Here I am, trying so hard to be the matchmaker and get you two young people together and I do it all wrong.

"Derek, I promise you on my honor, my sole intent was to let nature take its course, see what would happen when the creative juices started flowing. I wanted you and Allison to feel the match was right. But what happens? I get you all in a rage."

"Miranda, I'm not in a rage," he'd said. "I was concerned because you didn't seem that eager to meet with me to do this deal."

"Nothing could be further from the truth. I miscalculated, that's all. But I've canceled my dinner plans just so that you and I can dine together and discuss *Dream Girl* to your heart's content. I thought perhaps Musso & Frank Grill on Hollywood Boulevard at, say, seven this evening. Would that work for you, love?"

"Sure."

"Oh, and by the way, Allison told me she was terribly impressed with you. She'd previously confided her concern that you might play games with her, but you seem to have allayed her fears in that area. I do hope you're sincere."

"Completely," he'd replied. "I couldn't be more pleased with the way things went yesterday. What I want now is to meet with you and get the deal wrapped up."

"And so we shall, love. Tonight."

"I can't wait."

They'd hung up then. Derek had lain in bed, musing. Miranda—or whoever she really was—had caught him off guard, which was probably her intent. But at least she'd agreed to meet with him, which, he decided, would be interesting if nothing else.

He slept badly, not having fallen asleep until the small hours. All he could think about was Allison. Even *Dream Girl* paled beside his preoccupation with her. In fact, the screenplay seemed almost inconsequential in the greater scheme of things.

He'd teased Allison about whisking her off to Hawaii, but in truth he couldn't think of anything he'd have enjoyed more. It was easy to imagine himself holed up with her in a villa on some isolated, romantic beach. She was one woman he could talk with for a week, a month—maybe a lifetime—without getting bored. He'd never felt that kind of rapport with a woman before. Never.

But the call from Miranda had brought back the issue he'd halfway swept under the carpet. All morning he'd thought about her and Allison, trying to decide what the hell was going on. His best guess was that Allison had hired or cajoled an Englishwoman into posing as Miranda Maxwell. But it had to be either someone with connections at C.A. or someone who actually worked there.

After breakfast he'd given Oliver Wheatley a call to discuss the matter. Oliver had told him he had business at C.A. that morning and would be glad to poke around and see what he could find out. Derek had asked him to be discreet. God knows, he didn't want to upset the applecart before he signed the deal—he badly wanted to make *Dream Girl* his next film. In

the end, they decided Derek would drive him to C.A.
and they'd do lunch afterward to consider the matter.

Derek glanced toward the building just as Oliver,
resplendent in a Harris-tweed sports coat with ascot
and matching floppy silk handkerchief, ambled toward
the car. He climbed in and sighed.

"Well, old boy, I'm not quite sure what to say. I
spoke with Miranda's assistant and got the truth from
her. Miranda is in England, I was told, which is what
I knew from the beginning. The young lady even had
a message for me from her."

"Hmm. Miranda's assistant. Let's see, her name
is…Britt, I believe."

"Yes. Miss Kingsley."

"I spoke with her on the phone once or twice. She
was the one who initially told me about the script, as
a matter of fact." Derek stroked his chin.

"I wonder if you might have spoken with an im-
postor, Derek. The young lady I spoke with was forthcoming, not the least bit dissembling. Bright and engaging, and most attractive."

"I only spoke with her on the phone so I don't
know what she looks like. I was impressed with the
way she pitched the script, though. I thought to myself
that Miranda had her well trained. It was like she really wanted me to…"

Derek and Oliver looked at each other, the identical
thought probably going through their minds.

"You don't suppose this Britt is somehow involved," Derek said.

"An avenue to be pursued, I'd say. Oh, and another

point of interest,'' Oliver went on. ''I chatted with Gordon Mallik—he's looking after things for Miranda in her absence.''

''And?''

''As you requested, I was discreet. I asked if there were any of my countrymen in the firm, apart from Miranda. The only one was a lad in the mailroom, but I should think he'd be innocent of this involvement.''

''Unless he can do a mighty convincing falsetto.''

''Quite.'' Oliver smiled. ''I did inquire about your Allison O'Donnell and learned that there's no such person in the firm. The name meant nothing to Gordon.''

Derek stroked his chin again, pondering. ''You know, I'd have sworn Miranda—the fake one, that is—said something about having gotten the script from one of the other agents at C.A. and it seemed to me she'd said it was Gordon. I remember being struck by the way he'd described it, a Generation X *Bridges of Madison County*.''

''How tantalizing.''

''Yes, the whole business is tantalizing. And the plot seems to be thickening.''

''Maybe you should go in and have a word with Miss Kingsley yourself. She seems to be the only individual in this melodrama we've been able to put flesh to.''

''Yes, but I'm not sure a confrontation is called for at this point.''

''Hold on!'' the Englishman exclaimed. ''There's our young lady now!''

Derek looked toward the building. Two women had come out and were strolling past the fountain on a tangent walkway, headed toward the corner. One was a short plump brunette with a head of unruly dark curls. The other was a beautiful tall blonde—Allison O'Donnell. Derek watched them proceed up the street, his mouth agape.

"I take it you've had some sort of enlightenment," Oliver said ironically.

"You might say so."

"Must I drag it out of you?"

"Oliver," he said, turning to his friend, "the woman I met yesterday…the woman I'm halfway in love with…apparently isn't who she claimed to be."

"Bloody inconvenient. I take it we're talking about Miss Kingsley?"

"Or Allison O'Donnell. I guess it depends on which story you wish to buy."

Oliver shook his head. "I must say, you Yanks have a novel approach to life. Is it the culture or the climate?"

"I don't know. But whatever it is, Hollywood's got it in spades."

They sat musing. "I should think you're going to have a rather interesting dinner engagement with Miranda this evening, Derek."

"You can say that again, Oliver. You can say that again."

10

B ritt stared at herself in the mirror of Allison's dressing table as Lucien fussed with the dark brown wig. The face she saw looking back at her was no longer hers. She'd been transformed into someone she didn't know.

"This is scary," she said.

Allison, who was standing behind them, her arms folded, had been nursing a big glass of wine throughout the entire operation. "Why scary?" she asked. "Think of it as just another part. The role of your lifetime—if you play your cards right."

"First, I never got that many parts. I was a singularly unsuccessful actress, don't forget. And second, this isn't a play or a film. This is real life."

"Fiddlesticks," Lucien said as he teased a wisp of hair. "Life is just a stage and all the men and women on it actors. Didn't Macbeth or Othello or somebody say that?"

"Right playwright, wrong play."

"Well, I can tell you that with some of the people I work on it's hard to tell whether they're more phony as themselves, or as their characters. In this town, honey, there ain't no real life. That's why nobody lives here anymore but us peons.'' Lucien was a small, very thin, delicate man of thirty, with an assured manner. ''Think of this as Halloween.''

''I personally think you look smashing,'' Allison said, affecting a less-than-convincing British accent.

Britt glanced at the photograph of Miranda she'd brought back with her from the office. She knew Lucien couldn't make her look like the same woman, but she wanted him to capture Miranda's type. The most important thing, though, was that he disguised her well enough so that Derek wouldn't recognize her.

When Allison had hatched this scheme, Britt hadn't thought it would work. But Lucien was a genius. In addition to the dark wig, he'd changed the shape of her nose and the contour of her face, making it appear rounder with thin layers of latex and a careful application of makeup. She also wore false eyelashes and extra-long nails that were painted a pale pink. The final touch to the disguise was a pair of lightly tinted glasses.

When the transformation was complete, Lucien stepped back. Both he and Allison examined Britt carefully. His arms folded, Lucien placed a long thin finger against his cheek. ''I wouldn't recognize her as the same person, would you?''

Allison shook her head. ''No. You've done a masterful job, Lucien. Really super. She could probably rob a bank and never be identified.''

Britt turned around, putting her hands on her hips. ''Isn't it enough that you've turned me into a con artist? You want me on the FBI's Most Wanted list now, too?''

Allison laughed. ''You know what they say, kiddo. Once you've started a life of crime, there's no turning back.''

Britt rolled her eyes. ''If my father could only see me now.''

Britt ended up parking her ancient Toyota in front of the post office on Wilcox Avenue. Then she walked up to Hollywood Boulevard, crossed the street, and headed west toward Musso & Frank Grill. That stretch of the boulevard had gotten fairly tacky over the years and the sidewalks were sprinkled with weird-looking characters. Still, the restaurant was a perfect choice, under the circumstances.

The Grill was the only celebrity hangout Britt had been in. Six months earlier she and Allison had gone there for lunch. The two of them had sat at the counter, eating soup, as they watched the cooks at work. It had been Allison's treat.

''Every writer should eat where Ernest Hemingway and F. Scott Fitzgerald used to hang out in the old glory days of Hollywood,'' she'd said. Their agreement was that Britt would take her to Musso & Frank when she sold her first screenplay.

But it was not only her familiarity with the place that made it desirable. Musso & Frank tended to be dark. And the darker it was, the better she'd like it.

Nearing the entrance, Britt got increasingly nervous. She'd been running Miranda's voice through her mind, but even so, she knew this would be tougher than the telephone act. Derek was a director, used to working with actors—not to mention the fact that he'd gotten to know her as Allison O'Donnell.

God, what if he saw through her act? As she reached for the door handle, she was struck by a crisis of confidence. Had not a group of five or six people come up behind her, virtually pushing her inside, she might have turned on her heel and left. Once in the doorway, she stepped aside to gather herself. Her heart was pounding like crazy. She took a couple of deep breaths, then strode toward the reception desk.

Britt had tried to create a distinctive walk for Miranda, one different from her own. She'd also developed idiosyncratic gestures and mannerisms—some actually borrowed from Miranda, others made up from whole cloth. The idea was to make Britt's two personas as distinctive and unalike as possible.

She was wearing a dark gray gabardine suit she'd borrowed from Allison and a plain white silk blouse. The suit was well made and expensive, but a little out of style. The skirt was long on her. The effect bordered on frumpy, but not overly so. Miranda was understated in her dress and certainly not stylish. Britt had approximated the look.

The heavyset maître d' was on the phone, probably taking a reservation, as she waited. Britt was running Miranda's persona through her mind when she suddenly wondered if she'd remembered to stick the option agreement form Sally Farland had given her into her purse. Rummaging through her bag, she was re-

lieved to discover the contract was there. Britt sighed.
She intended to get Derek Redmond on the dotted line
that evening. God knew, she wouldn't go through this
again.

"Yes, ma'am?" the maître d' said.

Britt looked up at him as another crisis of confidence struck. "I'm…meeting someone," she stammered. "Derek Redmond."

"Oh, yes. Mr. Redmond is expecting you. I'll show
you to his table. This way, please."

They made their way into the huge dining room that
hadn't been redecorated since the 1930s. Hardly anyone glanced her way, but Britt felt that her every step
was under scrutiny.

They went to the far corner. Britt couldn't see past
the maître d', but when they arrived at the table, she
found herself face-to-face with Derek. He was in a
charcoal gray sport coat and black turtleneck and
looked devastatingly handsome. Seeing him, she froze.
Her mouth went dry. A lump formed in her throat. She
felt nauseous and even thought for a moment she
might faint.

Derek had an expectant look on his face, but there
was no telltale sign of recognition, thank God. He got
to his feet.

"Miranda," he said warmly, as he stepped around
the table, extending his hand, "how good to meet you
at last."

Britt gave him a brittle smile. "It is so lovely to be
here," she chirped, mercifully falling right into the
role. "I'm delighted."

He pressed his cheek to hers and Britt stiffened, sure that the latex on her face would shift, or her nose would crack. But it didn't. Derek smiled pleasantly, so she assumed she was still intact.

"You seem to have forgiven me," she said, looking up into his clear green eyes.

"I'm relieved that we've finally gotten together," he replied, helping her with her chair. "Let me put it that way."

He returned to his place. They gazed at each other. She was glad the dining room was relatively dark. Still, she could see him clearly, which meant that he could see her. Of course, he wouldn't be suspecting anything and that was in her favor. Britt tried her best to be nonchalant as she favored him with a little smile.

"So," she began, "you're taken with both my client and her work."

"'Taken' is a real understatement, Miranda," he said. "The screenplay is terrific and I love Allison. She's a wonderful, wonderful person."

He smiled into her eyes and Britt felt herself flush under the latex mask. "Then I guess there's nothing left but to do the paperwork at this point," she said decisively.

He picked up his water glass and took a sip. "Well, that and to celebrate," he added. "I thought it might be nice if the three of got together to toast the success of *Dream Girl*."

"That would be lovely, Derek. Let's plan on it sometime in the future. On the weekend, perhaps."

"Why put it off? In fact, I thought I might ask Oliver to join us. After all, if he hadn't thought so highly of you in the first place, I never would have given your office a call, and I'd never have heard about *Dream Girl*."

"Yes, well…bloody fortunate, that."

"And you know what," Derek continued, "while we're at it, we really ought to include your assistant, Britt. I mean, she's the one responsible for us all getting together. Besides, Oliver tells me she's quite a charming young lady. Attractive, too."

"Yes, well, Britt has her moments, I must say. But I don't know that she'd be all that interested."

Derek grinned. "Been in Hollywood so long she's become jaded, eh? Seen one director, seen 'em all."

"Well, no, certainly not that…. It's just that—"

"Tell her for me I'd like very much to meet her and express my personal thanks."

Britt swallowed hard. "I shall, Derek. I'm sure she'd be pleased."

The waiter came to take their drink orders. Britt was thankful for the respite. She ordered a vodka martini— something she never did. Usually the extent of her drinking was a glass of wine or two, but tonight she felt she needed all the help she could get.

She watched Derek as he spoke with the waiter, admiring his cool, confident manner. Of course, *he* wasn't playing a role. It was easy for him. She, on the other hand, was a nervous wreck. She was sweating profusely and was scared to death that the latex would start to slide off her face.

"So, you've spoken to Allison," he said when the

waiter had gone off to fill their drink order, "and she's pleased with the way things are going?"

"Positively delighted. Allison feels a real rapport with you. Creatively speaking, I mean."

"Only creatively?"

Britt blushed deeply and for the first time that night was glad to have the mask and all the makeup on. "She seemed to find you charming. Let me put it that way."

"I find her charming, as well," he said. "I like her a lot, in fact. Maybe too much."

Britt smothered a self-satisfied grin. "Too much? How so?"

"Well, you know how distracting personal attraction can be in a professional relationship." He fiddled with the silverware on the table. "Tell me, Miranda, do you think it would be a mistake for me to get involved with her?"

Britt swallowed hard. "Well…do you want to get involved with her?"

"I was taken by her. She certainly seemed interested in me, too. But in the back of my mind I couldn't help…wondering."

"Wondering what?"

"If her…friendliness, shall we say…was calculated to get me on the dotted line."

"I'm sure not, Derek. I don't know Allison awfully well, mind, but I think she's perfectly sincere. Don't forget, you'd decided you liked her screenplay before you'd even laid eyes on her."

"Yes, that's true. But the price hasn't been agreed

upon yet. And there's the future to consider. Maybe I'm paranoid, Miranda, but a guy always wonders when a woman comes on to him that way.''

Britt bristled. ''I... You mean, *she* came on to you? You're saying she was the one—''

Derek was looking off, reflecting. Britt was livid. What a pompous, hypocritical bastard he was! What did he mean, *she* had come on to him? *He'd* tried to seduce *her!* And he'd seemed like such a gentleman when they were together.

''It could be she misunderstood me,'' he said thoughtfully.

''And it could be you misunderstood *her,* love. How do you know Allison's feelings for you aren't entirely professional? Perhaps you misconstrued her enthusiasm for the project as enthusiasm for you!''

Derek considered that. ''Now that would be unfortunate, wouldn't it? I sort of enjoyed the flattery of thinking it was me who interested her most.''

Britt had all she could do to keep from leaning across the table and slapping his face. She clenched her fists, hating the man's arrogance.

Their drinks arrived and Britt lost no time in picking up her glass. She would have taken a slug immediately if Derek hadn't extended his own glass, proffering a toast.

''To you, Miranda, who made this possible. To *Dream Girl,* the next big romantic-comedy hit, and to Allison O'Donnell, the creative genius behind it all.''

Britt took a healthy gulp. ''I'm surprised you'd want

to drink to her,'' she said, sounding more miffed than she'd intended.

"Oh, but of course I want to drink to her. I love Allison. Her mind, her talent, her beauty, her body—you name it.''

"Really? A minute ago you practically said she was a conniving opportunist.'' Her eyes narrowed and she gave him a long, penetrating look. "Or did I misconstrue your remarks?''

"No, that isn't what I meant at all. I was simply concerned that her feelings for me weren't genuine, that doing the deal was more important than…well, the relationship.''

"She might wonder the same thing about you, mightn't she?''

He fiddled with his drink glass as he considered that. "I certainly hope that's not the case. I was completely taken with her, but…''

"But what?''

"Underneath I sensed something was wrong—not quite…how shall I put it? Not what it was represented to be. Naturally I wondered if she was deceiving me. If maybe her feelings weren't genuine.''

"I should think that would become obvious one way or the other in time. A person can't be ingenuine forever—if they are at all,'' she finished, clearing her throat.

He gave her a wry smile. "So I should go ahead with the deal and see what happens? Is that what you're saying? Forgive me, Miranda, but that sounds like an agent talking to me. This is not just another picture, it's my professional and personal life we're talking about.''

Britt sighed with exasperation. "Why don't you just tell me what it is you want, then?''

"I want to do *Dream Girl* and I want an honest, sincere and—shall we say, meaningful?—relationship with Allison O'Donnell.''

Britt reached down and took her purse. "That's what I want, Derek, and I believe it's what Allison wants." She removed the option agreement she'd drawn up that afternoon with Sally's help and handed it to him. "I think the time has come to stop talking and be done with it. Once we've signed this, everything will fall into place, I'm sure.''

Derek looked at the paper and Britt picked up her glass, taking another healthy gulp of the martini. She watched him reading the agreement.

"You've left the price blank," he said.

"I discussed it with Allison, and she and I are of the mind that you should propose a figure based on your feelings about the project.''

"My feelings about the project or my feelings about her?''

"The project, Derek.''

He looked at the contract again. "You've left off the names of the parties, too, I see. Is that an oversight?''

Britt's stomach tightened. She knew she'd have to finesse the author's name because she couldn't write in Allison O'Donnell when Britt Kingsley was legally the contracting party. "I wasn't sure if you did your deals individually or if you have a production company,'' she ventured.

''I option projects in my own name,'' he replied.

''Then you can enter your name, darling. I'll fill in the author's portion when I get Allison's signature.

''I see,'' Derek said.

Britt took a pen from her purse. ''So, what figure shall we put in?''

Derek stroked his chin. ''It's her first screenplay, so Guild minimum plus, say, twenty-five percent is fair, don't you think?''

Britt was thrilled. That was a lot of money. Of course, Derek would have to get financing before he exercised the option, but it was a start. A good start. And somehow she was certain they'd make the picture.

It was all she could do to keep from bouncing in her chair, but she knew she had to hold herself together until everything was properly signed. She took a calming breath and looked Derek in the eye. ''I'm sure that would be acceptable. What about the option price?''

Derek studied her. Britt felt the perspiration running down her back.

''How about twenty-five thousand?'' he prompted.

''Agreed.''

''Shall I write the figure in?''

Britt handed him the pen and watched him fill in the blanks. Her heart was racing and once again she felt light-headed. But she reached down inside herself, summoning her willpower. Just a bit longer, and she could get out of there.

"Go ahead and sign it, love," she said jauntily. "Once I've gotten Allison's signature, I'll have the agreement delivered to you. On receipt of your copy you can issue the check."

Sally had explained the procedure to her, so she spoke with some assurance on the point. Derek's pen moved to the bottom of the page, where it hovered. After a short hesitation, he looked up at her.

"You know, this is a big moment for Allison. I really think she ought to be present so she can enjoy it with us. It would be nice if we both signed at the same time. Why don't I give her a buzz and see if she can come over here?"

Britt's heart practically stopped as Derek reached down, got his briefcase and removed his cellular phone. "Can you tell me her number?"

"Well…uh, do you really think this is necessary? I mean, it would be jolly fun, but Allison is not anticipating—"

"Oh, come, Miranda. Her first film deal. Of course, she'd want to be here. She lives in West Hollywood, so she could probably get here in twenty minutes."

The knot in Britt's stomach was so big that she wondered if she might get sick. Hold on! she told herself. You've come this far!

Her mind spinning, Britt reached for Derek's phone, taking it from his hand. "Here, love, let me ring her up and see if she can drop by for the ceremony."

Britt forced a tight smile, but she was furious with

Derek for putting her through this. But she told herself that he could not have done it intentionally. He undoubtedly thought Allison would be thrilled.

Britt dialed Allison's number, figuring she could alert her friend to what was happening and maybe get some help in the process. Allison answered after a couple of rings.

"Allison, dear, Miranda here. Derek and I are having a delightful meeting. We've negotiated all the messy details, but Derek, being the dear, thoughtful boy he is, suggested you come by and have a drink with us while we sign. Can you pop into Musso & Frank Grill and finalize the contract with us?"

"Britt, you're in trouble, aren't you?" Allison replied.

"Not really, love. We just want your participation."

"You need a suggestion," Allison said, sounding every bit as panicky as Britt was feeling.

"That would be lovely, dear—if you can figure a way," Britt said, smiling at Derek.

"Put him off," Allison said. "Tell him I'm—I mean, you're…sick or something."

"But darling, this must be done tonight. We've all waited long enough. Poor, dear Derek is so eager to get this done and I know you are, as well. Can't you find a way?"

"Uh…uh…tell him I—I mean you—will meet him later. Then you can sign the contract after you've gotten out of your Miranda costume."

"Capital idea! I'll arrange it." Britt punched the Off button and handed the phone back to Derek.

"Is she coming?"

"She is indisposed, and it would be a hour or more at best before she could make it down here. But she shares your enthusiasm for signing this evening. She proposed she'd drive by your place in two hours' time so you can do the honors there. Surely that would do, wouldn't it?"

Derek rolled the question through his mind. "I guess that would work. We can drive over after we've finished dinner and wait for Allison."

"I'd love to, honestly. But I've got a rendezvous of my own later this evening," she said, flickering her eyebrow. "If you know what I mean, darling."

"Ah, yes, of course, Miranda." He folded up the contract and stuck it in his jacket pocket, then handed Britt back her pen.

She watched, realizing he had the option agreement and it was still unsigned. Britt suddenly hated her life and every lie she'd ever told, especially those of the past several days. God was getting even with her, she was certain.

"Well," Derek said, signaling the waiter, "we might as well go ahead and have dinner. How about another drink while we wait for our meals?"

Britt looked at her mostly empty glass. She had the good sense not to accept the offer, knowing that after another drink she'd be speaking English with a Polish accent. "Thank you, darling, but I'll decline," she said. "In fact, I'm considering doing something horribly impolite. I'm thinking about begging off dinner and asking you if sharing a drink as we have won't be sufficient for our first meeting.''

"You want to leave?''

"The gentleman I'm seeing later is very special and…well, what truly matters is you and Allison." She gave him a broad smile. "I've done my part by setting the wheel of fate in motion. Won't you allow me to bow out?''

Derek reached over and patted her hand. "If that's what you want, Miranda.''

"Smashing!'' she said. "I'll take my leave of you, then. It has been oh-so-delightful, Derek. It positively has.''

She got up and so did he. Britt gave him a quick peck on the cheek. "Give my love to Allison, darling. And by all means don't give the girl a hard time. Ta-ta!'' she said with a smile, then turned and walked from the room. It took all the restraint she had to keep from running, but she made it out of the dining room and to the entrance without incident. A moment later she was outside, sprinting up the street, headed for home.

Britt paced back and forth in her bedroom as Allison sat watching her. She was wearing her bathrobe now and she was livid.

"Damn him, anyway," she said. "Derek had the pen in his hand, the contract was lying right in front of him, and he didn't sign it. I could have killed him!"

"He was just thinking of you, Britt—I mean, you in the guise of me."

"Well, then, I wish he wasn't so damn considerate."

Allison laughed.

"It's not funny," Britt insisted. "It's tragic. I can't tell you how much I want this behind me."

"But even after it's finished, you'll have the problem of explaining who you really are."

"Yes, but I'll have my deal. And if Derek or Miranda or both of them want to kill me at that point, at least I won't have to die in vain. The worst would be if I lost the deal, Derek's friendship and respect, and got fired by Miranda, to boot—all of which seems to be getting more probable by the hour."

"Not necessarily," Allison said. "Derek still

doesn't know what's going on. He's got the contract in his pocket and all you need to do is go to his place, bat your eyelashes a little, get his signature, and come home."

"Granted, it sounds simple, but I've learned from experience that nothing works like it's supposed to. Each step I've taken was supposed to be the last, and each time it's ended up leading to another one. This is like one of those nightmares about being chased— you don't get caught, but you can't escape, either."

"At least you still have a chance to pull it off."

"Yeah, but only because I've become the biggest fraud in Hollywood."

"An hour or so from now it will be over," Allison reminded. "Hang in there."

Britt dropped down on the bed and sighed. Allison went over and sat next to her, putting her arms around her shoulders.

"You know," Britt said, "the worst part is I'm not even sure what I want anymore. I really do care about Derek and that makes everything especially painful. If it wasn't for my damned screenplay I'd be on the beach with him in Hawaii right now."

"If it wasn't for your damned screenplay, you'd never even have met him."

Britt chuckled, shaking her head. "The classic case of good news, bad news."

"So what are you going to do?"

"Finish what I started, I guess. I've gone through hell, the past few days. I can't quit now, Allison."

"I know how important *Dream Girl* is to you."

It *was* important. To give up now would be tanta-mount to discounting everything she'd gone through over the past few years. How could she turn her back on it when victory was within her grasp? The problem was she had a lot of guilt, which made the prospect of getting caught with her hand in the cookie jar so painful.

Britt looked at her watch. "Well, I'd better drive over to Derek's and get this over with."

She went to her closet and got out a pair of freshly pressed jeans. Then she got the fisherman's-knit sweater her father had given her for Christmas from her chest of drawers. Allison watched her.

"Regardless of how things turn out," she said, "I want you to know I admire you for your guts. There aren't many people who could do what you've done."

"There aren't many people this stupid," Britt answered ruefully.

Allison gave her a big hug. "Having fire in the belly is worth a lot in this town. People respect determination. I know it'll work out." She went to the door, where she stopped. "It's the last act, kiddo. Break a leg."

Britt nodded. "I'll do my best."

Derek poured himself a glass of orange juice, then strolled through the house, drinking it. He checked his watch as he went into the front room. Allison—Britt, that is—was due at any time. He hardly knew what to expect.

Miranda—or whoever the hell the woman at Musso

& Frank's was—had left the restaurant so abruptly he hadn't had time to react. He found that behavior strange. In fact, he'd found the woman herself strange, a difficult person to peg.

On the whole she was credible, although he'd detected a minor lapse in her accent—enough to suggest that she might not even be a Brit. He'd rather liked her, though. She was quirky and a hell of a con.

Truth be known, he found the hoax and everybody involved in it rather amusing. What a charming band of hustlers he'd gotten tied up with—Allison/Britt and the putative Miranda. It would make a good movie—something worth keeping in mind.

Derek stared out the sliding-glass door at the brightly lit pool, gleaming in the darkness of his backyard. He took a long drink and wondered what sort of line Britt would give him this time. He couldn't decide whether he should confront her or not. He was inclined to play along with her game, if only to see what she was going to do next.

Just then Derek heard a car outside. He finished his juice, took the glass to the kitchen and headed for the front door. The doorbell rang as he reached the entry hall.

Opening the door he found her on the porch. She was wearing tight jeans and a bulky, white fisherman's-knit sweater. She'd slung a black leather purse over her shoulder. She looked so inviting—wholesome and well scrubbed—not at all like the sophisticated woman he'd met at the Polo Lounge. This, he judged, was the down-to-earth side of Allison—or Britt. The girl from a small town in Indiana. The innocent.

"Good evening, Allison," he said, giving her a welcoming smile.

"Hi."

"Come on in."

She stepped inside. He closed the door and they stood looking at each other.

"Thanks for coming over," he said.

"Thanks for inviting me. Miranda told me you thought I should be present for the signing of the contract since it's such a big occasion for me. That was very thoughtful of you."

He shrugged. "It was an excuse as much as anything else."

"An excuse for what?"

"For seeing you, being able to share the moment."

She gave him a faint smile. "You're a romantic, aren't you, Derek?"

"You gotta have feelings of some kind to make films, especially relationship films."

She seemed uncomfortable, more circumspect than he'd have expected, given the way things had gone between them last time. He leaned against the door, appraising her.

"I hope I didn't tear you away from anything important."

"Oh, no, I...was just having dinner with someone, a friend. He understood."

Derek was a little taken aback. "Oh. I'm sorry. I didn't realize. I mean, Miranda didn't say anything."

He felt a pang of jealousy, something he wasn't accustomed to. "Had I known, I wouldn't have insisted that—"

"No, it's all right," she said. "Really."

"You're sure?"

"Honest. I wouldn't have missed this for anything."

He was glad she'd said that. God knows, he wanted it to be true. But the fact remained that she'd deceived him once already by assuming a false identity. That sort of made him question her feelings now. About the only thing Derek was absolutely certain of was that she was the author of *Dream Girl*.

He stepped over and took her hands. She gave him her first real smile and he embraced her. When she was in his arms, he felt the oddest desire. He wanted to say, "Look, I know you're a phony. But it doesn't matter. I don't care because I like you just the way you are." But try as he might, he couldn't get the words out.

So he stood there silently, holding her, inhaling her clean, fresh scent as he stroked her head. He had another desire then....

"Why do I like this so much?" he asked, running his hand through the silky hair at the back of her neck.

She looked up at him. "Do you?"

He noticed there were tears running down her cheeks and he was surprised. "Allison, what's the matter?"

She half laughed through her tears. "I guess I'm feeling emotional."

"*Happy* emotional?"

She wiped her face with her sleeve and nodded. It wasn't a very convincing response.

"You must cry all the time at weddings," he said, giving her his handkerchief.

Britt dabbed her eyes and gave it back to him. "Not really. I don't know what overcame me. I'm sorry."

"No need to apologize," he replied. "I'm ready to cry myself."

She gave him a skeptical look. "Because you're happy?"

He shrugged. "Because you are."

She searched his eyes and the tears welled again. "Give me that handkerchief back," she mumbled.

He did. She wiped her eyes again. Then he led her toward the front room. "I think it's time we put on our happy faces," he said. "After all, this *is* a celebration." When they entered the room, he gestured toward the stereo system. "Why don't you pick out some music, whatever meets your fancy, and I'll get the champagne?"

"Champagne?"

"We're celebrating, aren't we?" He gave her a wink and headed for the kitchen, feeling as emotional as she.

Britt flipped through the CDs, hardly seeing the discs. Instead, she was thinking about Derek, how sweet he was being. Her annoyance for him having put her through an ordeal at the restaurant had dissipated—after all, there was no way he could have known the consequences of what he was putting her through, so it was hardly fair to blame him for that. And if he'd bent the truth when he'd told Miranda that *she'd* come on to *him* the day before, instead of the other way around, well, his white lie was nothing compared to her black ones!

On the drive over, Britt had decided to make the evening short and sweet. Now that she was here, she felt sentimental; she no longer wanted to pressure Derek into signing just so that she could get her confession out of the way. She'd let him sign the contract at his own pace.

She heard the pop of a champagne cork in the other room. Moments later Derek returned with an ice bucket, a bottle of champagne and two flutes. He put everything on the end table next to the sofa.

"Find something you like?" he asked.

Britt hadn't paid much attention to what she was looking at, except to note that most of the recordings were jazz piano. "These all look good. Who's your favorite?"

"I like both George Shearing and Marian McPartland," he replied, taking the bottle from the ice bucket. "I have several recordings by each of them."

Britt snatched a couple of compact discs from the tray. "I'll let you put them on."

Derek finished pouring some champagne into each of their flutes and carried them to the stereo, where she was waiting. He handed Britt one. "To *Dream Girl*," he said, gazing into her eyes. "And to us. May we have a long and fruitful collaboration. I hope this is only the beginning.''

Britt's eyes filled. She was making a habit of wearing her emotions on her sleeve. Derek could hardly say a thing without her getting misty.

She blinked back her tears. ''Thank you for appreciating my work,'' she said softly.

They touched glasses and each took a sip. Britt watched as he set down his flute and put the CDs on. It was hard for her to accept that it had only been twenty-four hours since she'd first come to this house—it seemed like she'd known Derek for weeks, if not months. That old cliché about meeting someone and feeling as if you'd known them forever now made sense. She'd gone out with some guys half-a-dozen times or more, and still hadn't had a clear idea what they were like as human beings.

Derek was different. He wasn't afraid to expose his vulnerabilities. Artists, she'd learned, often did that. They had to risk themselves if they wanted to reach their audience in a profound way. This was true of filmmaking and writing, both. They had that in common.

''So, what are you thinking?'' he asked.

''You heard the wheels turning, huh?''

''It was making a terrible racket,'' he teased.

Britt leaned back, reflecting. ''I guess I'm savoring the moment. Enjoying the chance to relax.''

In truth, now that she'd let herself slow down for the first time in hours, she realized that she felt spent, just like she had after a tough performance back in her old acting days. God knows, that night, as Miranda Maxwell, she'd given one of her most demanding performances ever, although she could hardly claim it as one of her prouder moments.

When she thought about it, though, she was still acting. She had to be Allison for a little bit longer. But at least she was out of costume and able to be herself in all but name. For that, she was grateful. She hungered to be honest—dead honest—more than anything.

"The day I signed on to direct my first picture I was bouncing off the walls," he said. "I guess we each deal with our triumphs in our own unique way."

"I'm having trouble putting it all in perspective, if you want to know the truth," she told him.

Derek, who was sitting close to her, took her hand. "The important thing is that you're happy."

Britt leaned against him, liking the feel of his body. "You've been very good to me. I'd like to…"

"To what, Allison?"

"I don't know. Feel more deserving, maybe."

"Don't be silly. Relax and enjoy yourself."

Britt wished she could. She wished it more than anything in the world. But it wouldn't happen—not until this lie she was living was behind her.

They drank champagne and talked about *Dream Girl*. She liked it when they discussed their work. Ironically, it was at these moments that she was most herself, and felt closest to Derek.

Soon, between the chanpagne and Derek's comfortable manner, she felt mellow. By the time he'd drained the last of the champagne into her glass, she was starting to enjoy herself.

Derek had been toying with her hair. As they talked, he'd kissed her temple a time or two. Each time she'd felt his warm breath on her ear, she'd shivered, but she'd managed to keep the conversation rolling anyway. Now the talk about their work sort of faded and her awareness of him took center stage.

Her inhibitions gone, Britt had no trouble following her desires. She put her hand on Derek's thigh, even knowing it was forward, a suggestive thing to do. It was Dutch courage, but it was working.

Britt was conscious of the lean firmness of his leg. She gave it a little squeeze. "You know what, Mr. Redmond?" she said.

"What, Miss O'Donnell?"

Britt shivered, coming very close to telling him that wasn't her name and she didn't want to be called Allison O'Donnell anymore. "It's occurred to me that we're celebrating and we still haven't signed the contract."

He gave her an ornery smile. "You noticed."

"I noticed."

He stroked her cheek with his finger. "But if we don't sign it now, then we'll have an excuse to celebrate again tomorrow—when we do sign."

"Tomorrow?"

Derek shrugged. "Why not?"

"Why wait?"

He pushed a strand of hair off her temple and leaned close. "There's nice soft jazz on the stereo, I'm feeling good, and I've got the most beautiful screenwriter in North America and maybe the world, right here beside me. A contract's the furthest thing from my mind.''

Britt sat up straight and pulled away from him. What did he mean? That he wanted her to come over here to seduce her, not because he was serious about a deal?

''Allison,'' he said, drawing her back into his embrace, ''is something wrong?''

She looked him in the eye. ''I'm not sure where I stand, all of a sudden. Are you saying the deal isn't important to you but seducing me is?''

''*Am* I seducing you?'' he asked.

She sighed. ''You aren't playing tiddledywinks, Derek.''

''Would you rather I sit across the room?'' he asked. But as he spoke, the tip of his index finger moved lightly over her cheekbone.

She gave him a look. ''Dirty pool.''

''Better than tiddledywinks,'' he said with a laugh.

She took his hand and put it on his lap. Then she folded her arms over her chest. ''I'm not going to bed with you to get you to sign that contract.''

''Did I say that's what I wanted?''

''I feel it's implied.''

''I certainly wouldn't want you thinking that. I'll get the contract now,'' he said matter-of-factly. ''Then we won't have to discuss it anymore.''

He got up and left the room. Britt pondered the situation. She'd resolved not to press him about the contract, but she had not felt right about the way things were going. Her chain of lies was the problem. But until Derek signed the agreement and she told him the truth, she'd have to live with the consequences of her actions.

Derek returned. He had a pen in his hand and the form that she'd given him earlier that evening. After plopping down on the sofa, he leaned forward and put the contract on the coffee table. He took the pen, filled in his name in the appropriate place and signed. Then he handed her the contract and the pen. "There you are, my dear. You've got me on the dotted line. You can sign and leave if that's what you wish."

Britt looked at the form. This was what she'd been working for. This was what she'd all but sold her soul to the devil to have. She stared at the blank space where she had to insert her name. All she had to do was write in "Britt Kingsley" and tell him what she'd done. She didn't even have to go into any detail if she didn't want to.

"What's the matter?" Derek asked, when she'd sat for a minute without moving.

Britt put the form down on the coffee table. "Thank you for signing that, Derek. I'm sorry I doubted your motives."

"Aren't you going to sign it?"

"Yes. Later." She took his hand and looked into his clear green eyes. "But there's some nice jazz playing, I'm feeling good and I've got the most dashing film director in North America and maybe the world, right here beside me. The contract's the last thing on my mind right now.''

Derek smiled. ''You're one crazy lady. Has anyone ever told you that?''

''Not quite so romantically.''

Smiling, he leaned over and kissed her. Britt put her arms around his neck and they fell back on his sofa. Soon they were kissing passionately. She wanted him. She wanted him badly. Right then, he was all she cared about, all that mattered.

Within moments Derek was pulling off her sweater and she was unbuttoning his shirt. Her jeans went flying, then her bra. Britt sat astride him, looking into his eyes. She put her hands on the dark mat of hair on his chest as he caressed the tips of her nipples with his thumbs.

She moaned. If it felt like she'd known him forever, it also seemed like she'd wanted him forever, too. He pulled her down on top of him, crushing her against his chest, taking her mouth and kissing her deeply.

Her head was spinning. She couldn't tell how much of it was the champagne, and how much was the dizzy excitement of his kiss. After a while she pulled back to catch her breath and stare into his eyes.

''I understand now where Casey got her fire,'' he mumbled.

''Is this why you loved her?''

''It's *how* I would have loved her.''

''I'm not my character, Derek.''

''And this is not a movie.'' He kissed her again.

Derek was holding her, stroking her head. She felt

the pounding of her heart. He gazed into her eyes. Britt knew it was time.

"Shall I carry you to the bedroom?" he whispered.

"Men actually do that in real life?"

He smiled as George Shearing's piano music tinkled softly in the background. "They do in Hollywood, my darling."

_12_

➤ ◀

Britt awoke early. The sun was up and the soft morning air was coming in the partly open sliding-glass door of Derek's bedroom. He was sleeping peacefully.

Britt smiled, recalling how wonderful it had been, making love with Derek. After he'd carried her to the bedroom, they had slowed down, each of them wanting to savor the experience, drag it out. When Derek had put her on the bed he'd said that there could only be one first time for them, and he wanted to make it last.

He'd seduced her slowly, kissing her everywhere, making her tremble with desire. The sheets had felt cool when he'd laid her on the bed, but soon her skin was hot. She felt warm and creamy, ready. And yet, she didn't mind waiting. The anticipation was sweet.

Derek had taken his time, licking and kissing her from her toes and ankles to her upper thighs. He ran his tongue up the inside of each leg. His tongue felt hot, but when the balmy air flowing in the sliding-glass door hit the moist patches of her skin, Britt shivered. It was incredibly erotic.

Best of all was when he'd stopped the teasing and

parted her curls to kiss her center. Britt inched closer
to him and clutched the sheets in her fists as he stroked
her. The joy was exquisite and for a moment she
thought she would come that way. But Derek pulled
back, apparently sensing she was on the edge.

By the time he'd finally entered her, she was more
than ready. Never had sex been so fulfilling. Holding
her afterward, he'd whispered that he never used the
word *love* lightly, but his feelings for her were special.
He'd never gone to bed with one of his actresses—
and certainly not one of his screenwriters—but it
seemed entirely natural to be making love with her.

Britt had cried after he'd said that. He'd asked her
what was wrong and she'd almost told him the truth.
But she didn't want the evening to end with a tearful
confession. If this was to be their one and only time
together, she wanted it to be perfect. Morning would
come soon enough. She would tell him then.

They'd made love one more time in the middle of
the night. For Britt it had been bittersweet, in part
because she was less carried away by the passion of
the moment. She desired him—wanted to be a part of
him—but she'd had time to put things into perspective. She could no longer pretend that she could avoid
facing up to reality.

Now it was time for her mea culpa.

Britt looked over at Derek, hoping he wouldn't hate
her afterward. Even if he was angry with her, perhaps
in time he would forgive her.

She crawled out of bed and headed for the shower.
When she'd finished dressing, she returned to the bedroom. Derek was still asleep. Not wanting to awaken

him, she padded off to the kitchen and got some orange juice. Then she went to the front room and found the contract where they'd left it.

Taking the pen, she filled in her real name and signed at the bottom, next to Derek's signature. She'd already decided that was how she'd tell him. She would show him the form and explain why she'd signed as Britt Kingsley instead of Allison O'Donnell. And then, if he didn't strangle her on the spot, she would tell him the whole sordid tale.

The pool was beautiful in the morning sun. Britt picked up her glass of juice and the contract, opened the sliding-glass door, and then stepped onto the patio. Although it was early, the air temperature was pleasant. She strolled over to the pool and sat down at the umbrella table at the far end. She would drink her juice and enjoy the setting while waiting for Derek to awaken.

There were some beautiful flowering shrubs around her. Birds were singing in the trees. Britt watched a calico cat slink along a fence at the far end of the yard. She inhaled the soft air, savoring the moment. If she didn't have that damned confession hanging over her head, this would be a perfect morning.

The telephone rang, jolting him awake. It took a moment for Derek to realize he was in bed alone. He stared groggily at the offending instrument before snatching up the receiver.

"Yeah?"

"Oliver Wheatley here, mate."

"Oh, Oliver, hi… Good morning… It is morning, isn't it?"

"I've rung up a wee early, haven't I?" he said with a laugh. "Sorry."

"It's all right. I had a long night that didn't include much sleep," Derek said.

"Lucky you. Well, sorry to wake you, but I shan't take all the blame for disturbing you so early," Oliver said. "Actually, I'm ringing you up at Miranda Maxwell's request.

"You're kidding?"

"Not at all. She arrived early this morning from London. My sodding three-pic package is in trouble and the love was good enough to fly in to help me sort things out. Anyway, we've been chatting over our cornflakes, as it were, and Miranda was most interested to hear she'd negotiated a deal with you over the past few days."

"I can imagine she was."

"In a word, Miranda's distraught about everything that's happened and she wants to set things right. I tried to tell her the problem's not urgent, but she's determined, old man."

"Gee, Oliver, I appreciate her concern, but you're right, there's no particular rush."

Derek sat on the edge of the bed, pulling his thoughts together. As he listened to Oliver he glanced out the window and saw Britt out by the pool, the morning sun gleaming in her blond hair. He was struck by the image, and also relieved to know she hadn't gotten up early and sneaked off.

"Miranda's here at my side now," Oliver said.

"Will you chat with her, or shall I have her ring you up later?"

Derek was getting an idea. "Oliver, is there any chance the two of you could come to my place right away? Now that I think about it, there may be something that Miranda could do."

"She'd be delighted, I'm sure. We aren't more than fifteen minutes from there."

"Good. Come on over, then. Tell Miranda I'd like to teach our Miss Kingsley a lesson. Maybe have a little fun of our own while we're at it. After the merry chase she's led us on, she deserves to be the victim of a prank herself."

Oliver chuckled. "Knowing Miranda, it won't take any convincing."

Derek hung up, then glanced out at Britt once more. He rubbed his hands together, anticipating their meeting. Payback time was almost at hand, and he intended to enjoy every blessed moment of it.

It was fifteen minutes after the phone had rung before Derek showed up at the door of the patio. Britt watched him approach. He was wearing jeans and a white cotton turtleneck and he looked absolutely delicious. As he made his way around the pool, bits and snatches of the previous evening filtered through her mind. What agony it was to jeopardize the memory of that! How would she ever be to able to endure it if he wound up hating her for her deceit?

"Up with the birds, I see," Derek said, arriving at the umbrella table.

"Early bird gets the juice," she replied, pointing to her empty glass.

Derek leaned down and kissed her neck, nuzzling her. He smelled wonderful, sending twinges through her as she recalled the feel of his naked body against hers.

"Glad you didn't sneak off without saying good-bye," he said.

"Why would I do that?"

"I don't know. You're full of surprises, Allison. For an innocent, you can be fairly unpredictable." He picked up her empty juice glass. "How about some more?"

Before she could answer, they heard the sound of a doorbell ringing through the open sliding-glass door.

"I wonder who that could be. Excuse me, I'll be back in a sec." He headed for the house. "How about a pastry with some more juice?" he called over his shoulder.

"No, thanks."

As Derek went back inside the house, Britt glanced down at the contract. It was too bad they'd been interrupted before she could get to what she wanted to say. Now she'd have to screw up her courage all over again. She sighed.

Several minutes passed. She began wondering what was going on. What kind of caller would be dropping by this early?

Just then someone came out of the house, but it wasn't Derek. It was Oliver Wheatley and he was carrying a glass of juice. Britt nearly jumped to her feet at the sight of him. What was *he* doing here?

Oliver lumbered toward her, squinting in the bright morning sunlight. As he came around the pool, he saw her plainly. A shocked expression crossed his face.

"Britt? Britt Kingsley, isn't it? From Miranda's office. What on earth are *you* doing here?" Oliver was several feet away. He stopped and gazed around the yard. "I was given to understand Miss O'Donnell was out here, Derek's new screenwriter."

Britt slumped in her chair and groaned. Why didn't the earth just open up and swallow her? It would have been so much kinder.

Oliver continued on, looking very perplexed. "I would have sworn Derek said it was his young lady out here, the lass who did the screenplay." He put the glass of juice down in front of her and scratched his head.

"I'm afraid there's been some confusion, Mr. Wheatley," she said lamely.

"I should think so...." His words trailed off as Derek came out of the house. He was carrying a tray of pastries, a pitcher of juice and a couple of empty glasses. "Ah, here's the man who can clear up the mystery," Oliver said, as Derek approached the table.

Britt closed her eyes, certain at that moment that she'd be better off dead.

"I hope you two managed to introduce yourselves," Derek began cheerfully, setting the tray on the table. "I apologize for not being here, Allison, but one of the great directors of our time hardly needs an introduction." He slapped Oliver on the back. "And Oliver, mark my words, the name Allison O'Donnell will soon be in lights along with the other great writing talents of Hollywood.''

Britt put her face into her hand.

"Derek," Oliver said, "we have a wee problem."

"What sort of a problem?"

"I believe you're under a misapprehension, old bean."

Britt looked up at Derek, her face the model of misery. He seemed thoroughly perplexed. He turned to Oliver, then back to her.

"What are you talking about?" Derek asked.

Britt and Oliver exchanged looks.

"I defer to you, my dear," Oliver said.

"Derek," Britt faltered, her voice so shaky she could barely speak, "I'm afraid I've done something absolutely unforgivable." She picked up the contract. "I intended to tell you first thing this morning, but—"

"Tell me what?"

She agonized. "First, let me say that last night— wanting to be with you—was real. There wasn't a thing phony about it." She glanced at Oliver, embarrassed to have him listening to this, but she had to go on. "If you believe nothing else, please believe that."

"Allison, what are you talking about? Why is this sounding like a funeral oration?"

Britt glanced at Oliver, who was sitting there silently. He seemed oddly bemused. She turned back to Derek, who was waiting for her to explain. She opened her mouth to say how sorry she was that she'd lied, how much she regretted it, but it was hard to speak.

"This is awfully embarrassing," she said finally.

"Especially considering Mr. Wheatley knows who I really am. The fact is, I've lied to you, Derek. I'm not the person I said I was. I'm a phony. A fraud."

She slid the contract across the table. Derek picked it up. She watched him read it. When he got to the bottom, where she'd signed her name, he glanced up at her. Britt's heart rocked.

"The signature says Britt Kingsley," he said.

She watched his face, hoping to get a hint of what he was thinking. But she couldn't tell a thing. "That's my real name. Allison O'Donnell is a friend of mine. I borrowed her name to hide my true identity because, as Mr. Wheatley here already knows, I work at C.A., as Miranda's assistant."

Derek turned to Oliver, who nodded.

"You can't imagine how shocked I was to come out here and find Miss Kingsley sitting by your pool, old bean."

"I had to use a pseudonym," Britt explained, "because when you called the office that first time, asking for Miranda, I told you my name was Britt...and you made a little joke about it, Derek. Remember?"

He nodded, putting down the contract. "Yes. But that was no reason to put another name on your screenplay. Unless you're saying you didn't write *Dream Girl*."

"Oh, I wrote it, all right. That's the problem. C.A. doesn't allow self-dealing. That's a big rule. I took my job there under false pretenses. It was wrong, but I was desperate. I knew I could write, but I couldn't get anyone to read my work. I even sent you something once but you sent it back unread.

"So I got the idea that if I worked at C.A. I might make some contacts, have a chance to tell someone about my work. You were my first opportunity. When you called, saying you were in the market for a project, it was like a dream come true."

"And when I showed interest in the script, you sent it off under another name. Allison O'Donnell."

She nodded, biting her lip.

"And I bought it—hook, line and sinker." He glanced over at Oliver, shaking his head. "I guess there's a sucker born every minute."

"If you say so, old man. But I wouldn't be too hard on myself, if I were you. Our Miss Kingsley is a clever girl."

"I really didn't mean to hurt anyone," Britt pleaded. "I had no idea things would get so complicated. In fact, I was hoping it could all be done by mail."

Derek and Oliver exchanged long looks.

"This ever happen to you, Oliver?" Derek asked.

"Can't say that it has, old man."

Derek shook his head. "I'm not quite sure what a guy's supposed to do in a situation like this. It's sort of the equivalent of being seduced under false pretense."

"Rather dicey, all right," Oliver agreed.

"They'll be joking about this at the Polo Lounge for years," Derek said woefully.

Britt knew she was being the made the butt of their black humor, but she was hardly in a position to complain. "You have every right to hate me, Derek. I can't blame you. My mistake was wanting to sell my screenplay too badly. I realize now that what you think of me is much more important than making a sale. So I'm going to make it easy for you."

She reached across the table, picked up the contract, and tore it in half, then tore it in half again.

Derek watched her, surprise on his face. "Why did you do that?"

"Because honesty, integrity, and my own self-respect demand it."

Derek and Oliver looked at each other again.

"The lady understands drama," Oliver declared. "That much is real."

"No, this is her and she's speaking from the heart. I can tell," Derek said.

Britt eyes filled. "Thank you."

Derek reached over and patted her hand.

Just then, she saw movement out of the corner of her eye. The iron gate at the side yard opened and a woman came though it. When Britt saw that it was Miranda Maxwell, she just about died all over again.

"Well, here you are!" Miranda called as the men turned. "I've been ringing the bloody chimes for five minutes."

Derek and Oliver got to their feet. Britt sat frozen like the proverbial deer caught in the headlights of a car.

"Jolly glad to see you made it, Miranda," Oliver called to her.

"Miranda?" Derek said.

"Oh, Lord," Britt muttered. She scrunched down in her chair, wishing she'd never been born.

"I had a call from her this morning, shortly before

heading this way,'' Oliver explained. ''She's just in from London to help me sort out my bloody three-pic package that's gone awry. I told her to pop by and join us. Hope you don't mind, old man.''

Britt groaned the groan of the dying as Miranda, in a crisp blue suit and Liberty scarf, approached them. She couldn't bear to watch. She buried her face in her hands.

''This is not Miranda Maxwell,'' she heard Derek mumble to Oliver.

''What's that, mate?''

''Hello and good morning!'' Miranda said cheerily. She gave Oliver a kiss. ''And you, dear boy, must be the illustrious Derek Redmond!'' she added, turning to Derek. ''I'm so terribly pleased to meet you!''

They shook hands. Derek appeared to be stunned.

''I say,'' Miranda said, leaning around him, ''is that you, Britt? What in heaven's name are you doing here?''

''Odd,'' Oliver said. ''I asked the same question.''

Miranda regarded them all quizzically.

''You are not the woman I had a drink with last night at Musso & Frank Grill,'' Derek announced.

Miranda blinked. ''I should hope not, love. I spent the night in an airplane flying in from London.''

''We seem to have another mystery on our hands,'' Oliver observed, rubbing his hands together with glee.

Derek grabbed a chair for Miranda and they all sat down. Britt couldn't have felt any worse if she were Marie Antoinette on her way to the guillotine. In fact, it might have been better.

"Would somebody care to explain the mystery bit?" Miranda requested airily.

There was a brief silence, then Derek spoke. "For the past several days you and I have been negotiating an option agreement for Allison O'Donnell's screenplay."

"How terribly fascinating," Miranda replied. "I do hope I squeezed every penny out of you I could. By the way, who's Allison O'Donnell?"

Derek and Oliver looked at each other. Britt closed her eyes.

"Your assistant, Miranda."

"My assistant, you say? Allison O'Donnell? Heavens, I do seem to have developed a mild case of amnesia, don't I?"

Britt couldn't bear it anymore. All her chickens were coming home to roost at once. "What they're trying to say, Miranda, is that I've deceived you as well as Derek."

Her eyes widened. "Pray, do go on."

"I assumed the name Allison O'Donnell to sell my screenplay to Derek."

"*Your* screenplay?"

"Yes. I used your office and name to promote my interests while you were in England. It was very foolish. I've already tried to apologize to Derek for the embarrassment I've caused him. I owe you an apology, as well. I meant no harm, but I screwed up badly just the same."

Miranda seemed stunned. She blinked, opened her mouth to speak, shut it, then finally said, "Quite a homecoming, I must say."

"You warned me about self-dealing," Britt went on, "but in your absence, I promoted myself anyway. I have no choice but to resign, I know. I've breached your trust and I'm very sorry for any embarrassment I've caused you."

"I appreciate that, Britt. It isn't the first time I've been taken advantage of and, I dare say, it won't be the last. But it doesn't explain how I managed to have a drink with Mr. Redmond last evening while to the best of my knowledge I was somewhere over the North Pole about then."

"I've been curious about that, myself," Derek said.

The three of them—Derek, Miranda and Oliver— all turned to her.

Britt's insides turned to Jell-O. She swallowed hard. They waited. She summoned her courage for the final mea culpa. "Bloody hell," she said in her best Miranda accent, "I'd rather die than admit this, especially with Miranda sitting here, but the awful truth is, you're looking at her, ducks."

There was a brief silence. Then Miranda began laughing hysterically. Oliver joined her. They were soon red in the face. Derek was incredulous.

"You mean...you..."

Britt nodded.

"I've been in Hollywood for three years now," Miranda said, "but this is the dottiest charade I've yet to encounter. Good Lord, Britt, you're priceless!"

She went off again into gales of laughter. Oliver wiped his eyes.

But Derek was just shaking his head. "But how...did you manage to..."

"The real Allison O'Donnell helped me pull it off," Britt explained. "She knows a makeup artist at Paramount who has the ability to completely transform people. I know it was crazy of me to do it, Derek, but I was desperate."

He could hardly speak. "That woman last night at Musso & Frank...was really *you?*"

"Yes, and it was me you spoke with on the phone all those times."

"But what about that call at the Polo Lounge? *I* phoned her."

"No, you called the office and *she* called you back." Britt chewed on her lip. "That was me—calling from a pay phone by the rest rooms."

Miranda and Oliver both dabbed their eyes as they listened. Miranda touched Derek's arm. "Darling, if you don't have the rights to this story, you must get them immediately."

Derek shook his head, a reluctant smile filling his face. "This is unbelievable. I had a drink with this woman and hadn't the slightest idea."

"I'm not proud of it," Britt said. "I didn't even want to do it. But I kept getting sucked in deeper and deeper. All I wanted was for you to read my screenplay and like it."

"You certainly accomplished that."

She searched his eyes. "Do you hate me?" she asked. "Or are you just disgusted?"

He drew a long breath. "I'm more shocked than anything."

"I know what I did was wrong, but I didn't mean

to harm either of you," she added, glancing Miranda's way. "I just wanted you to love *Dream Girl,* Derek."

"Lord," Miranda said as she looked back and forth between them. "I don't know whether to laugh again or cry. Perhaps you can help, Derek. Is this the moment for us to tearfully embrace? Or do we ring up our solicitors?"

"I'm not into guilt and blame, Miranda."

"You're suggesting we should let her off the hook? No hanging her by her thumbs or fifty lashes with a cat-o'-nine-tails?"

"The issue, the only issue as far as I'm concerned," Derek said, "is whether I get that script."

"I thought I—that is, my alter ego—already negotiated an option agreement with you for the screenplay."

Derek picked up the torn pieces of the option form and arranged them in front of Miranda. "Miss Kingsley has opted to rescind the contract."

"Oh, dear. You mean I haven't earned a commission, after all?"

Miranda and Oliver chuckled.

"I consider this an urgent matter," Derek said. "You're her agent, Miranda. What are we going to do?"

Miranda looked Britt in the eye. "All joking aside, you did intend that I represent you."

"Well...I..."

"We can draw up the agency agreement later, dear. A verbal arrangement will do for now." Miranda studied the form arrayed before her. "With all due respect,

Britt, in future you should keep to your writing and leave the agenting to me.''

''Is there something wrong?'' Derek asked.

''You took advantage of the girl.'' She paused, and looked up at Britt. ''Not that she didn't deserve it, mind you. But I'd never let a client of mine sign anything like this. You do like the script, don't you?''

''It's potential Oscar material.''

''In that case, I'd say we start negotiations at triple the figure you've listed here.''

''What?''

''You want the project, don't you?''

''I thought we already had a deal,'' he protested.

''It was negotiated under false pretenses. I'm afraid you're dealing with me now, darling. You'll have to do better if you want this script.''

Derek glanced at Britt. ''I never should have let you tear that up.''

Britt didn't know if they were putting her on—getting their pound of flesh—or if it was for real. ''This is a joke, right? You're just getting even with me?''

''I can't force you to accept me as your agent,'' Miranda answered blandly, ''but I do hate to see you being taken advantage of. We can do better than this, assuming they're right about the caliber of your work. And if Derek won't talk turkey, as you Yanks say, then we'll have to look elsewhere.''

''Hey,'' Derek protested, ''I'm the innocent victim here.''

''Not so innocent as you'd have us believe,'' Miranda replied. ''Fun's fun, but it's time to get down to business. You've heard our price, love. Do you want Britt's screenplay, or not?''

"All right, it's a deal.''

"And twenty-five for option money is far too little,'' Miranda declared. "We want fifty and not a penny less.''

He grimaced. "I think I liked the other Miranda better.''

Miranda regaled him with bemused laughter, then checked her watch. "Heavens, we're late, Oliver. We must tend to your problem.''

She rose, as did Oliver.

"Derek, I'll have a new agreement drawn up and delivered to you by this afternoon. We must be on our way now, however. The time's gotten on.''

Oliver, who'd been taking it all in with a look of utter fascination, said, "This has been delightfully zany, I must say—more amusing, even, than a few of the pictures I've made. I'd almost rather stay.''

"Sorry, Oliver. I think our friends would rather be alone,'' Miranda said. "Am I right, Derek?''

"It might not be a bad idea if you did leave,'' he replied, "while I've still got a shirt on my back.''

"Oh, nonsense.'' Miranda took Oliver's arm. "You've enjoyed every minute of this.'' She glanced at Britt. "It might be a good idea if you come by the office and clean out your desk, love. I'll have a client agreement ready for you to sign. I'm not cheap, but you'll end up making more with me handling your affairs—and you staying out of mine.''

"I don't remember ever being screwed and enjoying it so much,'' Derek muttered dryly.

"Britt," Miranda said, "when we've gone, do console the man." She led Oliver toward the house. "Come along, dear, let's get your deal back on track so I can get on a bloody plane back to England."

Oliver gave Britt and Derek a wink. "I love this town. If it didn't exist, somebody would have to invent it."

Britt and Derek stared at each other for a long time after Miranda and Oliver left.

"Come on, love," he said, pulling her to her feet, "let's go inside and have some breakfast."

Britt stopped him, holding both his hands. "Do you really forgive me? You don't hate me for what I did?"

"Oh, don't worry, I'm going to rub your nose in it every once in a while. But no, I don't hate you. Truth be known, I think I've fallen in love with you."

"Really?" She looked into his eyes.

"Yes."

"I love you, too."

He gave her a penetrating look. "I can trust that?"

"Oh, definitely. I'll never lie to you again, Derek. I promise. I've learned my lesson. I truly have."

He folded her arm over his and started toward the house. Britt stopped him.

"Wait! I have to know. Did all that last bit at the end really happen? Are you going to buy my screenplay? It's not a hoax, is it? Revenge for what I did?"

He grinned. "Hell, no. I kid about a lot of things, Britt, but money isn't one of them. Do you have any idea what *Dream Girl* will cost me now? Miranda just made you a very wealthy woman—at *my* expense."

She put her arms around his waist. "Aren't I worth it?"

He held her face in his hands, then leaned over and kissed her lightly on the lips. "I guess we'll have to wait and see."

"You mean until the box-office receipts come in?"

He nodded.

"What if it flops?"

"Then let's hope we've had a hell of a lot of fun getting from here to there."

He kissed her again. They smiled into each other's eyes.

"Something else just occurred to me," he said.

"What's that?"

"You're unemployed. You told Miranda you'd resign and she told you to clean out your desk."

"So?"

"So, you don't have anything to do today—except drop by C.A. later to sign your agreement."

"So?"

"So you might as well spend the rest of the morning here with me."

"Doing what?" she asked.

"I thought maybe we could research some love scenes."

Britt gave him a look. "Which love scenes are we talking about, Mr. Redmond? Mine? Or the ones in my screenplay?"

Derek grinned at her. "Funny how the lines between fact and fiction get blurred, isn't it?"

"Are you going to tease me forever for what I did?" she asked.

He gathered her close. "I guess not. It would hardly be fair, considering…"

Britt pulled away a bit and looked him straight in the eye. "Considering what?"

"That I knew you were a fake almost from the beginning."

She blanched. "No. You didn't. You're just saying that to make me suffer a little more."

Derek shook his head. "No. After we spoke the first time, I had lunch with Oliver and he happened to mention that Miranda was in England. When I didn't believe him, he even called her there to prove it to me. I spoke with her housekeeper."

Britt was dumbfounded. "Then you knew all along?"

"I knew Miranda was fake. I figured you were, too, until we talked about the script. I didn't discover that you were Britt Kingsley until I drove Oliver to C.A. and we saw you come out of the building. I knew you as Allison, and Oliver pointed you out as Miranda's assistant."

"You mean Oliver and Miranda were in on everything that just happened? The three of you put on that little drama to embarrass and humiliate me?"

"No, it was actually to teach you a lesson."

"Teach me a lesson!"

He gave her a look. "You aren't suggesting you didn't deserve it?"

She lowered her eyes. "No, you're right, I did."

"I'll tell you this, Britt. Nobody will ever match your performance of the past few days. I'd never have guessed that the woman at Musso & Frank Grill was the one I slept with last night.'' He playfully cuffed her chin. "Perhaps you ought to revive your acting career, my love. You might have missed a bet."

She shook her head. "No, thanks. I never want to be anyone but myself again. No more acting and no more lies. I've reformed."

Derek gave her another long, lingering kiss. When the caress ended, he pulled back, looked into her eyes, and said, "That's fine by me, because the woman I made love with last night is the one I want."

"It was me, Derek. Honest."

"Never change," he said, holding her. "Because I love you just the way you are."

* * * * *

Irresistible?

STEPHANIE BOND

Dedication

Many thanks to Natalie Patrick and Beth Harbison
for giving me a leg up;

To Rita Herron, Hillary Bergeron and Mary Barfield
for the weekly cheerleading;

And to Chris Hauck, for providing a constant
source of comedic inspiration—our marriage.

1

ELLIE SUTHERLAND opened her mouth to speak, but the sound that emerged was more like a croak. "I'm fired?"

Her supervisor, Joan Wright, coughed lightly, then leaned forward to rest her elbows on the desk. "Not fired. With the new budget cuts, I'm afraid we have no choice but to let you go. In one week," she added sorrowfully. "Please don't take it personally."

"I don't believe this," Ellie mumbled, shaking her head. *How am I going to make the rent?*

"Ellie, yours is not exactly a dream job."

"Oh, great," Ellie said. "I'm fired from a job that sucks, and that's supposed to make me feel better." *Credit cards. Food.*

"You know what I mean, Ellie. You're overqualified to be a gofer in a dumpy little federally funded arts center. You're too talented."

"Yeah, that's why gallery owners are beating down my apartment door." *Utilities. Painting supplies.*

"You'll get your break. Just hang in there. You know as well as I do it takes talent, luck and perseverance to make it in the art industry. And since you have incredible talent, you only need one of the other two qualities."

Tears pricked the back of Ellie's eyelids. "I had a feeling when I woke up this morning I should just stay in bed." She sighed. "I'd hoped to make some contacts at this job."

Joan brightened. "You did—me. I'll see what I can do about throwing some commissions your way."

Ellie raised her head to look over at the woman who'd become a friend in the short time they'd worked together. She could tell Joan felt bad about the turn of events. Ellie summoned her best what-the-hell smile, rose to her feet and said, "I'd appreciate it."

"Let me buy you lunch," Joan offered, glancing at her watch.

Ellie shook her head. "Thanks, but I'll be poring over the want ads." She trudged toward her tiny cubicle and grabbed her purse. She couldn't afford it, but she'd go out for lunch today and save the bagged egg-salad sandwich for dinner. Right now she needed the time to think.

She walked half a block to her favorite gourmet deli, then admired the handsome order taker as she waited her turn. The hunky guy in the apron was no small part of the reason this was her preferred lunch stop. When she stepped up to the counter, she took her time ordering a salad. The guy scribbled her order on a pad, then studied her intently. Ellie smiled demurely, enjoying the unexpected attention.

"You've been in here before," he stated simply.

"Several times," Ellie confirmed, sucking in her stomach and turning at a more flattering angle. She saw his nostrils flare as he leaned toward her slightly and inhaled.

"May I ask what kind of perfume you're wearing?"

Ellie fought to suppress the smirk that teased the corners of her mouth. Maybe this day wouldn't be a total loss, after all. "It's my own special blend. I worked on it for months to get it just right."

The attractive man smiled wryly and scratched his temple. "I just realized I get a migraine every time you come in here. I figure it must be the perfume."

She stood stock-still, her eyes darting sideways to see how many people were privy to the remark. Several customers snorted to cover their laughter and the buxom, vacant-eyed blonde behind her looked downright triumphant.

Ellie paid for the salad as quickly as possible and slunk to a table by the door. *Will this day ever end?*

She sighed as she sipped her diet cola and skimmed the wedding announcements. Starting with the life-style section had seemed like a good way to cushion her journey to the classifieds. But rather than enjoy the snippets about impending weddings, Ellie miserably counted off the handsome men with straight teeth who were now officially out of circulation in the city of Atlanta. She conceded the pictures also proved a little less female competition existed, but a new crop of coeds graduated every spring to catch the eyes of marriageable men. And spring commencements were upon the city.

She winced. Twenty-nine and dating wasn't so bad. But twenty-nine without a prospect in sight was downright depressing.

The bell on the door tinkled, announcing another customer. A stiff gust of unusually warm May air rushed over Ellie's table, lifted the page she'd been reading and wrapped it around her head. She clawed at the sheet with her hands, battling the breeze. After a few seconds of flailing, she tore her way clear, sneaking a glimpse at the person who'd just entered.

Her pulse jumped in appreciation of his profile. His dark head was down, alternately consulting his watch and a day calendar spread on his palm as he joined the long line snaking toward the counter. Ellie frowned at the expensive drape of the olive-colored Italian suit and turned back to her mangled paper.

Why do the cute ones always look as if they were just stamped out with a Donald Trump cookie cutter? Give me a great-looking guy who doesn't own a beeper and I'll give him lots of imperfect little kids. Where are all the good men, anyway?

A sudden jolt to Ellie's elbow sent her cola flying, dousing the paper, her salad and her lap. The icy liquid sluiced down her legs, stealing her breath. Ellie raised her arms, helplessly watching bubbly pools gather and run over the sides of the tiny café table to plip-plop onto the white tile floor. She squeezed her eyes shut and mourned the short life of the white linen skirt she'd scrimped for two months to buy. Then she stood and furiously spun to face the klutz who had ruined her lunch and her outfit.

Mr. Italian Suit had wedged himself between her table and another one, presumably to take a cellular phone call in peace, away from the din at the counter. He held one finger to his ear and stood with his back to Ellie. The big palooka hadn't even noticed his errant rump had wreaked so much havoc. Or worse, he didn't care.

"Hey!" Ellie yelled, reaching up to poke the man none too gently on his shoulder blade.

The man was just ending the call and turned toward her, his chocolate-colored eyebrows lifted in question. Ellie caught her breath. *Mamma mia.* He was gorgeous. Light brown hair, with green eyes framed by those wonderful dark, dark eyebrows and lashes.

"Yes?" he asked, apparently still unaware of the soda puddling around Ellie's shoes.

Ellie opened her mouth to speak, and the phone started ringing again. The man muttered, "Excuse me," then flipped down the mouthpiece and said, "Hello? Yeah, Ray, what's up?" He glanced at Ellie and shrugged apologetically. Ellie stood, arms akimbo, and glared.

Of all the nerve! A few diners around her tittered and shook their heads. The hunky guy in the apron cast worried glances toward the spill. Well, Armani-man had picked the wrong day to mess with Ellie Sutherland.

She marched around to face him and jerked the phone from his unsuspecting hand. "Ray," Ellie spoke into the phone, "he'll have to call you back, sweetie." She snapped the mouthpiece closed, but held the phone out of reach when the red-faced man lunged for it.

"What are you, some kind of lunatic?" he thundered. "That was my boss—give me my phone!"

"No," Ellie said sweetly. "Not until you pay me for damages."

"Damages?" Confusion cluttered his handsome face. "What on earth are you talking about?"

Ellie swept her arm down dramatically to indicate her skirt.

The man stared blankly. "You're saying I did that?"

"That's right." Ellie smiled tightly. "And I have witnesses," she added, gesturing to the diners close by.

The man looked flustered, then sighed, withdrew a gold

business-card holder, flicked out a card and extended it to her. "Send me the cleaning bill."

Ellie pushed his hand away. "No cleaning bill, mister. A new skirt. You can't get cola out of white linen."

The man looked briefly at her skirt and made a sound as if he didn't deem the garment worth saving. He ran his fingers through his hair, obviously out of his element dealing with a pint-size irate woman. "How much?" he asked finally, taking out his money clip.

Ellie couldn't help doing a double take at the wad of bills stacked there. "Geez, mister, what are you doing carrying that much cash around? You got a mugging fantasy?"

Every eye in the diner turned to the money in his hand. The man looked around, then shook his head and leaned forward. "Great," he whispered angrily in Ellie's face. "That's just great! Why don't you go out and tell everyone on the sidewalk, too?"

Ellie balked and swallowed. "Sorry."

"How much?" he asked through clenched teeth.

"Let's see..." Ellie frowned. "The skirt was brand-new. This is the first time I've worn it."

"How much?" he demanded, counting off bills. "Fifty?"

"Well, then there's my salad and drink."

"Sixty?"

"And my panty hose are sticky."

The man inhaled a mighty breath and expelled it noisily. "Here's seventy-five, and we're even, okay?"

"Okay." She took the money, grinning. "Thanks."

"Do you think I could possibly have my phone back now?"

"Oh, sure," she conceded with a generous smile, handing him the unit.

He snatched the phone out of her hand and gave her a final glare, then strode out of the deli without ordering. Immediately, he began punching numbers as he walked by the window and out of sight.

"Yuppie scum," Ellie murmured, counting the bills. "What a waste of good looks," she continued to herself, stuffing the bills into her wallet. She mopped up the table and herself as much as possible, ordered another soda, then begrudgingly turned to the want ads.

Jobs were plentiful on the north side of town, in Alpharetta. But Ellie didn't own a car and public transportation hadn't yet caught up with the economic explosion in that area. She narrowed her job search to the few-mile radius surrounding her Little Five Points apartment. She could ride her bike if necessary, or take the train. The pickings were slim, and the artistic opportunities were nil. She had resigned herself to the waitressing section, when a blocked ad caught her eye.

Wanted: Single women of any age with no current romantic attachments to take part in a four-week clinical study. Minimal time commitment. Above-average compensation. Must be willing to keep daily journal.

Ellie frowned. No current romantic attachment. She scanned the bottom of the ad to see if she was mentioned specifically by name. No, but it looked, sounded and smelled like her. She wondered briefly if it could be a scam to target unsuspecting women, but she recognized the address as a reputable clinic. Shrugging, she circled the ad with a red felt-tip pen. It was worth a phone call. A glance at her watch told her she'd be better off to make the call from her desk.

The rest of the afternoon passed mercifully fast. Everyone had heard Ellie would be leaving, so in between expressing their heartfelt regret, co-workers piled last-minute remedial tasks on her desk. Somehow between photocopying, filing, and delivering mail, she managed to call the clinic to obtain a few vague details about the study.

The woman who answered prescreened her with several lengthy general questions. Ellie had to interrupt the interviewer twice to answer other calls. After paging Joan over the intercom, Ellie feverishly punched a button to retrieve the woman she'd been talking to.

"Sorry—I'm back. Now, where were we?"

"Are you heterosexual, bisexual or homosexual?"

"Hetero."

"And are you currently romantically involved with anyone?"

"No."

"When was the last time you had sexual relations with a man?"

Ellie coughed. "Um, about a year."

"Can you be more specific?"

Ellie sighed. "Fourteen months, five days, and—" she checked her watch "—two hours."

"Very good."

Indignation flashed through her. "If you must know, no, it wasn't very good."

"That wasn't a question, ma'am," the bored screener replied.

Her cheeks burned. "Oh."

"There will be an information meeting tomorrow evening." The woman gave her the time and place, and the compensation rate.

Impressed, Ellie counted the days on her fingers until her rent was due, then asked, "When will the study begin?"

"As soon as enough participants register," the woman told her. "And you're the most ideally suited caller we've had today," she added cheerfully.

Ellie's eyes rolled. "I'm thrilled for us both," she said, then slammed down the phone just as Joan walked around the corner.

"We're thrilled for you too, Ellie," she said, fighting a grin.

"How much of that did you hear?" she asked, embarrassed.

Joan started to respond, but was interrupted by a yell from John, the accountant who sat two cubicles over from Ellie. "No more than anyone else, Miss Fourteen Months, Five Days and Two Hours." Choruses of hoots and cheers all over the department backed up his belly laugh.

Her eyes darted to Joan. "The intercom?" she whispered.

Joan bit her lower lip and nodded sympathetically.

DESPITE THE FRIGHTFUL DAY, Ellie's spirits rose on the walk home. Yes, it was incredibly expensive to live in downtown

Atlanta. Yes, traffic was a nightmare. And yes, in summer the humidity was unbearable. But it was worth every inconvenience to be part of the supercharged atmosphere. Ellie loved the outdoor cafés, the street musicians, the colorful murals, the unique shops. People-watching was one of her favorite pastimes, and the eclectic mix of residents that made up the artistic and somewhat affluent area of Little Five Points always provided a treat for the eyes. Atlanta was a wonderful place to live. Now if she could just find a decent job.

Ellie pulled her keys from her purse as she walked down the hall to her apartment. When a motion in front of the door caught her eye, she gasped. "Esmerelda, what are you doing outside?"

The tabby meowed an indignant reply, and Ellie scooped her up, hurriedly glancing down the hall. Her landlord would probably evict her if he discovered she was breaking the no-pet rule.

"It's me," Ellie yelled as she walked in. She could hear Manny in the kitchen. Dumping the cat on the couch, she said, "Esmerelda must have gotten out when I left this morning." She headed in the direction of enticing aromas, her pet pouncing off the sofa to follow her.

"Naughty puss," Manny chided, shaking a long finger at the cat. "Bad day?" he asked when Ellie flung her purse on the table.

Ellie suddenly felt close to tears. "Would being fired and having my new skirt ruined qualify?"

Her roommate clucked and came over to give her a hug. "You'll find another job," he said soothingly. "And that skirt—" he examined it with a thoughtful eye "—we'll dye it black and no one will ever know."

Ellie laughed. "You're an incurable optimist. Can't you let me be depressed for even a little while?"

He shook his blond head. "No. Now go change. I'm trying something new for dinner."

Ellie stopped long enough to unwrap her uneaten egg-salad sandwich for Esmerelda, then walked the few steps through the living room and down the hall to her bedroom. Manny

Oliver was a gem. They'd been friends for three years—in fact, his friendship with Joan Wright had landed Ellie the job at the arts center in the first place.

He made his living doing cabaret shows in drag. Ellie had seen him perform many times, and stood in awe of his singing, dancing and his killer legs. Her male roommate looked better in stockings and heels than she did. And if that wasn't bad enough, the man could cook, too.

After Ellie had changed, and joined Manny in the kitchen, she recounted her day over a scrumptious meal of Italian potato dumplings.

"Men are dogs," he supplied when she described the deli disaster.

"He gave me seventy-five bucks," she said, grinning.

"But rich dogs can be housebroken," he amended, and they both laughed. "Was he divine?"

She nodded, the image of the man's face forming in her mind. "Definite model material."

"Nice dresser?"

"Immaculate."

"Straight?"

Ellie shrugged. "I think so, but who knows these days?"

"*Tell* me you got his name," Manny pleaded.

"No, he offered me his card, but I smacked it away."

He shook his head. "Ellie, how many times do I have to remind you, the game is *hard* to get, not *impossible*."

She laughed. "He wasn't my type at all, Manny. A real stuffed shirt. I'll bet you couldn't get a toothpick up his—"

"Ellie!"

"Well, you know what I mean. Except for his obviously better taste in suits, he reminded me of the way my dad used to be—a corporate robot."

"People change, Ellie. Look at your dad. The man sees more naked people than a doctor."

"Yeah," she said with a short laugh. "Imagine my mom and dad retiring next to a nudist colony. It *was* by accident, you know."

"Oh, sure, Ellie, what would you expect them to tell their

daughter? If they didn't know about the nudist colony when they moved there, why haven't they posted a For Sale sign in the two years since?"

"I don't want to think about it. The whole situation brings to mind pictures I'd rather not see."

"The point is, your dad finally mellowed out."

Ellie snorted. "After thirty years of missing family dinners and undergoing two bypass surgeries." She stabbed another dumpling. "My mom should have left him decades ago."

"He's a good man, Ellie, you said so yourself."

"He neglected his family."

"But your mom was always there for you."

Angry tears welled in her eyes. "But who was there for her?"

Manny reached over and laid a hand on her shoulder, giving her a light shake. "They're happy now, Ellie. Save it for your therapist." He took a sip of wine, then asked, "So what are you going to do about rent money?"

Leave it to Manny not to mince words. "I called about an ad for participants in a clinical study. The money sounds good—I'm going to find out more about it tomorrow night." She told him about her conversation with the screener. Manny laughed and agreed it sounded promising.

"You've got a guardian angel on your shoulder, Ellie. How else can you explain losing a job, then finding a want ad for desperate women on the same day? A toast!" He lifted his wineglass to hers.

Ellie stuck out her tongue at him, then good-naturedly clinked her glass to his.

THE MEETING ROOM WAS more crowded than Ellie had expected. Based on the cramped accommodations, the crowd had apparently surpassed the clinic's expectations, as well. The room resembled a college classroom: no windows except the tiny one in the door, fairly new, dense low-grade carpet in a speckled gray, and filled with more folding chairs than the fire marshal would probably care to know about. A large blackboard covered the entire front wall. The side walls were adorned with various-size corkboards bearing dozens of multicolored sheets on topics ranging from sleep disorders to impotence.

Ellie lowered her dark glasses and, as inconspicuously as possible, peered at the other women in the room. She judged her appearance to be somewhat better than the room's average, and the observation depressed her even more. She pulled down her floppy hat and slumped in the hard metal chair.

Opening her pocket sketchbook, Ellie flipped through to find a clean page, always ready to draw the face of the person nearest her for a few minutes' practice. Her hands stilled at the page where she had sketched a caricature last night. Mr. Italian Suit with the gooey dark eyebrows smirked back at her, a cellular phone clutched in his cartoon hand. His athletic body strained at the savvy suit, miniature in comparison to his big, good-looking head. Ellie studied the rendition of his eyebrows and nose and wondered how close she'd come to capturing his true expression. If she remembered when she got home, she'd add a smudge of green to highlight those brooding eyes.

At that moment, a bespectacled, lab-coated woman walked to the front of the room and raised her arms to hush the chatter.

"My name is Dr. Cheryl Larkin. I'm a medical doctor, and a professor of human behavior, and it is my privilege to oversee this clinical study. Each of you has been prescreened to a certain extent to qualify for a four-week experiment using pheromones, chemicals produced in animals which attract other animals of the same species."

Ellie sat up. Her own experiments in perfume making had overlapped into the area of aromatherapy. She had become intrigued with the idea that certain scents could be aphrodisiacs. Supposedly, pheromones went even further.

The doctor continued. "Pheromones are subtle but powerful secretions. Some people say they explain the elusive chemistry that attracts a specific man to a specific woman, and vice versa. The objective of this study is to see what effect, if any, oral pheromones have on your ability to attract and meet a romantic interest."

Ellie glanced around and saw that Dr. Larkin had the undivided attention of every woman in the room. Hope shimmered in the eyes of the shy, the overweight, the very short and the very tall. She swallowed because she knew her own baby blues reflected the same emotion.

"It will be necessary for participants to answer a lengthy and somewhat personal questionnaire, and to keep a daily journal detailing encounters, or absence of encounters, for each day." A spirited buzz broke out in the room as applicants whispered excitedly to strangers next to them. Ellie ignored the gleeful exclamation of the middle-aged woman beside her.

"The dosage is two pills first thing in the morning, around midday, and again at bedtime. Besides the aforementioned hypothesis," the doctor said, finally smiling, "there are no proven side effects with this particular formula. We will ask, however, that participants be especially aware of and record any changes in your energy level or in your eating and sleeping patterns."

An arm shot up near the front. "Let's say I take these pills and meet a great guy. You're telling me after four weeks the rug gets jerked out from under me?" Everyone laughed and the doctor joined in, then raised her hands defensively.

"Wait a minute—we can't guarantee you'll meet even one eligible man during the course of this study. If that were true, we wouldn't need the experiment at all."

Intrigued, Ellie nodded. This could be fun. After the doctor had finished her talk, Ellie stayed to fill out the necessary paperwork and wait for a counselor to administer the dreaded questionnaire. Three hours later, she emerged with a week's worth of pills and a small blank journal in her purse, feeling as if she'd just been to confession. But she noticed a new spring in her step. She believed in the powers of aroma. Pulling off the hat and dark glasses, she tossed her short blond locks.

Unsuspecting men of Atlanta, beware!

"WELL, Marcus, if you're not going to get married, you're going to have to learn to cook," Gloria admonished her son as she held a dripping whisk.

Mark Blackwell plucked a green olive from the tray on the kitchen counter and popped it into his mouth, smiling. ''I like to eat out.''

The plump woman turned back to her bubbling red sauce. ''It's beyond me how, out of all those women you've dated, not one of them could find her way around a kitchen.''

''I don't—'' he walked over and took the whisk from her hand ''—date women for their culinary skills.'' He flashed a grin in his mother's direction.

''Oh, you,'' she snorted, rapping him playfully on the arm. Then her tone grew more threatening. ''If you're not careful, you're going to grow old all by yourself.''

''I'll hire a comely young nurse,'' he teased. ''Besides, you'd be bored if you couldn't fret over my state of bachelorhood all day.''

''Not if I had grandchildren,'' she replied with a twinkle in her eye.

Mark didn't miss a beat in the familiar exchange. ''You're much too young to be a grandmother.''

''And you're much too young to be working yourself to death in that law firm,'' she chided.

Mark grabbed two plates and settled them onto his arm, waiter-style. ''That's what I came to talk to you about,'' he said, smiling. He dished up a hearty helping of lasagne for each of them, and spooned on the rich homemade sauce. When he set the laden plates on the table, he struck a cocky pose and said, ''Say hello to the newest partner of Ivan, Grant, Beecham, and...Blackwell.'' He bowed slightly, rewarded with enthusiastic applause from his seated mother.

''How wonderful, Marcus!'' She beamed and brought his hand to her mouth for a long kiss. ''I'm so proud of you, son. I wish your father were here.'' Tears sprang to her eyes immediately, but she blinked them away.

Mark swallowed the lump of emotion that lodged in his throat. He knew his father would be proud of him at this moment, even if Mark *had* ''caved to the corporate philosophy,'' as his flighty father was fond of saying. Ever the softheart, his dad had been struck by a car three years ago when he'd stopped to help a stranded motorist. Mark patted his mother's hand. "I wish he were here, too," he said simply, then smiled. "Now, let's eat."

During dinner, they chatted about his long-awaited promotion, but Mark had a feeling he wouldn't escape without at least one more lecture on the importance of finding a good woman. Especially now that he'd made partner. He was right. As he helped his mother clean the dishes, she said in an innocent voice, "You know, the family reunion is this weekend. Are you coming?"

"Yes," he said patiently. "Don't I always?"

"Hmm," she agreed, then asked, "Are you bringing a date? Your cousin Albert will be there with his new bride and baby. And Claire with her newborn—this is her third, you know. Her husband is such a dear man."

"I can't wait," Mark said, inwardly wincing. He considered these get-togethers his penance for bucking the long family tradition of having a houseful of kids before having a house. He would endure one whole day of shaking hands and exchanging cheek kisses with new family members. And dutifully praising and holding everyone else's kids while his mother drank wine in a corner and her sisters tsk-tsked over her woeful lack of grandchildren.

"So, are you bringing a date?" she asked hopefully.

"I'm definitely bringing a change of clothes in case Mickey's little one has the runs again."

Gloria covered her mouth and shook with laughter. "The video he took of you two is just precious."

Mark rolled his eyes heavenward. "I'm awaiting my debut on one of those home-video shows."

"Stop changing the subject. Are you bringing a date or not?"

His thoughts shifted to Shelia, the woman who'd last graced his bed. She hadn't struck him as a woman who'd appreciate the rural pleasures of pitching horseshoes and doing the hokey-pokey. Neither did Vicki, Connie or Valerie, come to think of it. "I'll see what I can do," he said. It was as close to a promise as he could make. Suddenly, a vision of short blond hair and flashing blue eyes came to mind, and he frowned. "I'm not really seeing anyone right now."

Gloria clasped her hands together gleefully. "Stella's niece is in town for the Sunday-school teachers' convention—shall I give her a call?"

"No," Mark said quickly, then recovered. "I have a lot to do at work this week, you know, rearranging my office and all that. I'll be working late every night."

His mother shrugged, clearly disappointed. "Suit yourself."

Later, Mark squashed down guilty feelings which threatened to surface as he drove home. He knew his mother wanted to see him properly settled with a nice, quiet girl, but he truly liked being single. He'd sacrificed his social life during law school and the first few years after joining his firm in order to get a foothold. Now at thirty-six and established in his career, he was enjoying his unattached status. Life was good.

He almost managed to drive by the interstate exit to his office, but he merged onto the ramp at the last second. Just a few minutes to go over some paperwork, he told himself.

After he unlocked the office suite, he walked across the glossy inlaid wood floor not without a measure of pride. He considered the law office tastefully furnished, with just the right amount of opulence. His new office space had been achieved by removing a supply room adjacent to his existing office. He had been asked to select additional furniture, and he was pleased with his pecan wood and cream marble choices.

The Piedmont Park painting had been hung, and he approved of the location. One of his favorite pieces of art in the law office, he'd requested it for his own work area when the move began. He flipped on a floor lamp near his desk, and settled into his familiar tan leather chair to shuffle through the stack of papers on his desk.

Congratulatory memos comprised the top layer of paper. A box of cigars and an expensive leather-covered pen set were gifts from thoughtful colleagues. He smiled in satisfaction. Everything he'd worked for had finally been realized. He would never have to struggle like his father just to make ends meet.

Clasping his hands behind his head, he leaned back in the swivel chair to prop his feet on the corner of his desk, basking for a moment in the recognition of his hard-won achievement.

Partner.

At a sound from the doorway, Mark turned his head. Patrick Beecham stood there, holding the hand of Patrick, Junior. "Hi, Mark," Patrick said, his voice full of surprise. "Pretty late to be working."

Mark rearranged himself into a position more appropriate for talking. "I could say the same," he said to his partner with a smile.

"I just stopped by to get a fax," Patrick said. The small boy pulled on his father's pant leg. "This is Pat, Junior," he added.

"I remember," Mark said. "He's growing like a weed. How're you doing, buddy?" he asked the boy.

"Okay," the child ventured, half hiding behind his father.

"Say, Mark," Patrick said, "Lucy and I would love to have you over for dinner sometime. Do you have a lady friend?"

"You sound like my mother," Mark said. "Are you two in on a conspiracy to get me settled down?"

Patrick laughed. "No, but I must admit it helps to have someone presentable when socializing with the other partners and clients. I'll warn you—Ivan kind of expects it."

Mark felt a sudden swell of anger that anything would be expected of him other than top-notch work. "I like being un-attached," he said evenly.

"So did I," Patrick admitted. "But there comes a time when we all have to grow up. Luckily for me, Lucy was there when I came to my senses." He swung the little boy into his arms. "Just food for thought, friend," he said absently, tickling the little boy until he squealed. "Don't work all night, and let me know about dinner, okay?"

"Sure," Mark said. "Sounds great."

Mark listened to the footsteps fading down the hall, and pounded his fist lightly on his desk in frustration. What idiot had said behind every successful man was a good woman? He'd made it this far on his own, and he wasn't about to share the fruits of his labor with some money-hungry man-eater. He'd seen the way women's eyes lit up when they discovered he practiced law. He'd seen them peruse every stick of furniture in his home as if assessing its worth. He bought nice things because it made him happy, not to impress women. And he resented the females who thought he'd be all too eager to turn over his possessions to their care. Demanding, all of them. Take that little chiseler in the deli the other day—seventy-five bucks for a scrap of fabric!

Where could he find a woman who'd settle for a no-strings-attached arrangement to be his escort, in return for a few nights on the town and an occasional romp? Oh, sure, they all said they weren't looking for a commitment, but after a few dates, whammo! Feminine toiletries and articles of clothing started to appear in his house, and every jewelry commercial seemed too clever for her to let pass without a remark. Where was it written every man was supposed to settle down with one woman and be content for the remainder of his days?

He resumed his propped position and nodded his head in silent determination. *Bully for the poor schmucks who fall for it, but count me out.*

2

"WHAT DO YOU THINK?" Ellie asked, peering at the two shell-pink tablets in her palm.

Manny leaned forward, sniffed at the pills, then said, "I think if these little pills can make you irresistible to men, then I want in on the action."

Ellie scoffed. Manny was tall and slim, with a handsome face. On more than one occasion, female acquaintances of Ellie's had offered to try to "convert" him. "Manny, you've got more dates now than you know what to do with."

"But none of them are keepers," he said, sighing dramatically.

"What do you consider a keeper?"

"Anything below eight inches gets thrown back," he declared, making an over-the-shoulder motion.

Ellie shook her head, grinning, and pulled a clean glass from the dishwasher.

Manny's forehead knitted. "This is what—the fourth day you've been taking those things?"

"Uh-huh," she said, tossing the pills into her mouth and downing them with a swallow of fruit juice.

"Shouldn't something be happening by now?" he asked, watching her face carefully. Suddenly his eyes widened, and he covered his mouth to muffle a scream.

"What?" Ellie yelled, shoving past him to run to the hall mirror.

"Gotcha," he called, doubled over laughing.

"Oh, very funny," she said after a reassuring glance in the mirror. "You're a regular comedian, Manny."

"Gotta run," he said, heading for the door. "Good luck on your last day at the Smithsonian," he joked.

Ellie pantomimed a drumroll. "Ba-dump-bum."

Friday at last. When she walked to her overflowing closet, she toyed with the thought of wearing something ratty—what did it matter? Then she spotted her pink-and-black-checked mini. Why not go out with a bang instead?

With renewed vigor, she pulled on black hose, clunky-heeled pumps and a long, white knit cardigan. She buttoned up the lightweight sweater so she could omit a blouse, then added large earrings, funky bangles and a handful of gold chains around her neck. She slicked back her pale hair with gel, then traded her regular beat-up canvas bag for a soft shoulder-strap briefcase and a small silver purse. At the last second, she remembered to skip perfume, lest it interfere with the pheromones. When she stopped in front of the mirror on the way out, she nodded. Not bad for a gal down on her luck.

She held her head higher than usual when she stepped onto the sidewalk. Not quite seven o'clock on a beautiful May morning, and suited pedestrians already clogged the walkways. A few well-trained individuals even read the morning paper while their feet moved and stopped automatically at cross-walks. Ellie shook her head in determination. She would never get caught up in a seven-to-seven job like a lot of people she knew, like her father.

It had taken two bypasses to convince him to change his workaholic ways. He'd wasted so much of his life cranking out numbers for a big-eight accounting firm. If not for her mother's patience and virtue, their marriage would never have survived. And less than a year of the bureaucracy at the hole-in-the-wall arts center where Ellie worked convinced her she wanted no part of a rigid office setting on a long-term basis. Still, the regular, if small, paycheck had paid her rent.

An oncoming dark-suited banker type lowered his stock quotes long enough to admire Ellie's legs and whistle. Her spirits rose and she shrugged guiltily. Okay, it didn't hurt her feelings to be *appreciated* by the well-heeled.

With the money from the study to tie her over for a few

weeks, she planned to spend her free time updating her portfolio, and pestering gallery managers to take a peek. Being fired might turn out to be the best career move she'd ever made.

The aroma of bagels and cream cheese reached her, prompting her to dig in her bag for loose change. "Ellie!" old Mr. Pompano exclaimed. "You look good enough to have for breakfast, yourself. Did you get a promotion?"

"No," she said smugly to the popular street vendor, pointing to a chocolate bagel. "I got fired."

"Well, it suits you." He smiled, handing her the dark bread. "You are especially—" he made a corkscrew gesture in the air "—appealing today."

"Why, thank you, kind sir who wants my money." She curtsied.

He grinned and bowed slightly, then patted his right knee. "Something good will happen to you today—I can feel it in my gimp leg."

Ellie winked. "Can your bursitis tell me if he'll be a blond, a brunette or a redhead?"

"The way you look today, *Cara,* you might get all three."

Ellie flipped him a quarter tip, and munched her bagel the rest of the walk to the musty office building where she worked. Several men's heads turned, eyes lingering, and she felt her body unconsciously adjust to the attention. Her short stride lengthened to show off her legs. She thrust her shoulders back and her small breasts out, and clenched her buttocks with each step to add a powerful sway to her back view. It worked. She'd heard two wolf whistles by the time she reached her office, where a handsome co-worker, Steve Willis, who'd never even glanced her way before, held the door open.

"Ellie, isn't it?" he asked, his pale eyebrows arching attractively over his tortoiseshell-rimmed glasses.

"Yes, but I'm afraid I don't know your name," she lied.

"Steve," he said, straightening the knot of his tie. "Steve Willis. I was thinking, maybe I could call you sometime?"

"Sure," she said nonchalantly over her shoulder.

"What's your number?" he called behind her.

Ellie turned to eye the man who'd gone out of his way to ignore her when she'd delivered his mail every day for the past year. She almost felt sorry for him—he didn't stand a chance against the pheromones. "I'm in the book," she said simply, and left him standing. Once she got around the corner, she brought her fist to her chest in a triumphant gesture. "Yes!" There was something to these pills, after all.

The flowers on her desk were a nice surprise. She knew they were from Joan even before she opened the card. But before she had a chance to thank her boss, the phones started ringing, and the day began.

Later, a few co-workers took her to lunch, and Steve Willis appeared out of nowhere to sit beside her. He even managed to knee her a couple of times under the table. Feeling generous, Ellie humored him with a smile. He really wasn't bad. Maybe Mr. Pompano's gimpy prediction had been right.

Joan stopped by Ellie's desk an hour before closing. Ellie smiled, gesturing to the flowers. "I meant to swing by to say thank you."

"You're welcome. I wanted to talk to you before you left."

Ellie turned her swivel chair toward Joan. "What's up?"

"A commission, if you're interested." Joan leaned against the cubicle wall.

Ellie nodded enthusiastically. "Sure."

"It's a corporate portrait for a law firm—pretty boring stuff, but good money."

"Suit-and-tie picture?"

"Yeah."

"How did you hear about it?"

"I know the wife of one of the partners. I've acquired a few paintings and a couple of sculptures for their office. It's the same company that bought your Piedmont Park scene, by the way."

Landscapes were Ellie's forte. Although she enjoyed painting portraits, as well, she preferred a little creativity with the subject's presentation. Still, it was a job. She smiled and nodded to Joan. "Sounds great."

Joan handed her a card. "Here's the name of the firm and the address. I've written the agreed fee on the back."

Ellie turned over the card and her eyes bulged. "I get to keep this?"

"Less the ten percent cut for the center, yeah," Joan said. "Consider it a severance bonus."

"Gee, thanks."

Joan glanced at her watch. "If you leave now, you can get over there before they close."

The women said their goodbyes and Ellie promised to let Joan know how the commissioned painting progressed. Stopping by the apartment, she dropped off a box of accumulated desk junk and her briefcase. After taking a few minutes to freshen up, she walked to the street to hail a taxi.

"Where to?" the heavyset man yelled, looking her up and down with appreciation.

Ellie told him the address and climbed into the back seat. During the ride, the talkative driver hinted at his single status. Ellie, enjoying the attention but not wanting to encourage the man, simply smiled and said, "That's nice."

He screeched to a halt in front of the building, and she got out. He leaned out the window and said, "Miss, do you mind telling me what kind of perfume you're wearing?"

Ellie rolled her eyes. "Let me guess—it gives you a migraine?"

The man looked confused. "No, I'm serious."

Ellie opened her mouth to tell him about her own special blend, then stopped short. "I'm not wearing any," she said, suddenly remembering.

"Yeah, sure, lady," he said. "Whatever it is, I hope my date is wearing it tonight when I pick her up." The man tipped his hat, waved away her fare and drove off.

Ellie stood on the sidewalk, perplexed. She raised her wrist to her nose and sniffed. Nothing, just skin. She shrugged, glanced up at the towering building, then walked in.

When she exited the elevator onto the appropriate floor, Marcus Blackwell's name was being gilded onto the double glass doors. The graphic artist seemed to be having a heck of a time repositioning the firm's name on the door to work in all the letters. If they added another partner in the future, they'd have to install a third door, she thought wryly.

Ellie sighed, wondering how much money would be squandered by the firm to herald the addition of Mr. Blackwell. A new sign, new company stationery, an expensive portrait. Must be nice.

His secretary was beautiful. More like gorgeous, really. The woman's nameplate said Monica Reems.

"May I help you?" she asked.

Ellie frowned. Nice, too—how despicable. "I'm Ellie Sutherland. I'm here to see Marcus Blackwell about painting his business portrait."

"Is he expecting you?"

"No, I'm sorry, he isn't. I received the assignment only a half hour ago and I was hoping to catch him before he left for the day."

The woman smiled, displaying—what else?—model teeth. "He's in a meeting, but he should be out any minute. Have a seat and I'll make sure he knows you're here as soon as he gets back."

Ellie sat down and studied her surroundings. Ivan, Grant and Beecham were doing very well for themselves. And of course, Mr. Blackwell, the latest rising star of the firm. She tried to picture him—early fifties, salt-and-pepper hair. Eyeglasses, probably, which were always a pain to paint because of the glare and because they made the eyes seem flat. Dark suit, no doubt. Small gray teeth. Or bright white dentures. And one or two prestigious rings—Harvard perhaps, or Michigan. Very ho-hum, but relatively easy.

Begrudgingly, she conceded the office decor was impeccable. A little stodgy, but first-class leather furniture and textured wallpaper. And honest-to-goodness artwork. Ellie wondered where they'd hung her Piedmont Park painting, and prayed it wasn't in the men's room. She'd heard those things happened. From her position, she could see the door to the men's room at the end of the hall. As minutes clicked by and boredom threatened to settle in, she became convinced her painting adorned the wall. Over the urinals.

She sneaked a peek at Monica, who had her back turned and the phone crooked between her shoulder and ear. It would take only a few seconds to check, and she hadn't seen anyone go in the entire time she'd been seated. After one last glance at the busy secretary, Ellie sidled down the hall, then pushed open the heavy door, straining to hear voices or other sounds of activity. Silence. She stepped inside.

The outer room was a lounge of sorts with inappropriately elegant furniture. Ellie began a hurried search of the walls. There were several framed prints, most of them architectural, but she didn't see her painting. She sighed in satisfaction. An arched doorway led into a tiled room of more predictable sterile-looking gray Formica stalls. Three individual urinals lined an adjacent wall, and Ellie eyed them curiously. "I've always wondered," she muttered. Her voice echoed, and she jumped. Then another sound reached her, approaching footsteps from the outside hall. Sweat immediately broke out on her upper lip.

Searching frantically for cover, Ellie dived into a stall and slammed the door behind her. Then she realized her pump-clad feet would be a dead giveaway because the door didn't extend all the way to the floor. She jumped up and straddled the black seat of the commode, crouching so her head couldn't be seen.

The man who entered whistled tunelessly, probably celebrating the forthcoming weekend. When he stopped in front of her stall, Ellie held her breath. She could see the shadows of his feet and legs. At last, he walked away from her hiding place and stopped near the urinals, she deduced. Sure enough, she heard the slide of a zipper and the sound of urine splashing against porcelain. Ellie grimaced and prayed he had a small bladder.

What if someone else came in? What if a whole crowd came in at once? She'd be trapped listening to a herd of men relieving themselves!

The man peed. And peed. Ellie rolled her eyes. This guy

belonged in the record books. And just when she thought he'd stopped, he started again with the same gusto. Her arms began to ache from balancing herself between the slick walls. She repositioned herself slightly forward to relieve her shoulder pain, and caught a glimpse of the marathoner's back through a tiny slit in the closed door. Her hand slipped and she caught herself, thumping lightly against the stall. She jerked back and held her breath, then relaxed. He seemed to be conjuring up a grand finale, too occupied to hear her.

Finally, the man zipped his pants and flushed the urinal. Ellie listened as he washed his hands slowly and seemed to dry them just as slowly. He walked by her stall on the way out, and she grew weak with relief.

Then she dropped her purse.

Most of the contents were emptied on the first bounce, then the silver bag rolled out of sight. Makeup, coupons, pens and miscellaneous items scattered everywhere. She watched a tampon slide until it stopped by a leg of the stall. She closed her eyes and waited.

At first there was no sound at all. Then the man took three slow steps back to stand in front of her door. And he knocked.

Ellie swallowed. "Y-yes?" she managed to get out.

"The ladies' room is down the hall." His voice vibrated deep, distorted with echoes.

"I, uh, I didn't know this was the men's room," she improvised.

"Are you standing on the toilet?" he asked, incredulous.

She carefully stepped down and straightened her shoulders, then addressed the man through the closed door. "No," she said, and bent to retrieve the strewn articles within her reach.

He'd bent to pick up the purse and the items laying outside the stall. He wore nice shoes, soft black leather loafers with perfect tight little tassels. On feet big enough to make Manny salivate.

After a few seconds, he asked, "Are you coming out?"

"I'd rather not," she confessed.

"Okay," he said, his voice booming. He sounded close to laughter. "I'll put your purse on the counter and leave."

Ellie waited several seconds after the outer door closed before she moved. She opened the door and scooped up her purse, quickly checking the floor for wayward keys or coins. Then, praying fervently the man wasn't waiting outside, she swung the door open and stuck her head out.

No one in sight. Uttering her thanks, she trotted down the hall and reclaimed her seat near the still-distracted Monica. When the secretary ended her phone call, Ellie stood and asked, "Has Mr. Blackwell returned?"

Monica shook her head. "Any minute now, I'm positive." The phone rang again and she answered it quickly.

Ellie sighed. Then, hearing someone approach, she turned, and inhaled sharply. Mr. Italian Suit. The yuppie who'd ruined her skirt! What was *he* doing here?

Still several feet away, the man slowed, his head tilted in question. Suddenly, his eyes widened in recognition, and he strode toward her, his forehead knitted. "Look," he said, making chopping gestures in the air, "I don't know how you found me, but I'm not giving you another red cent for that overpriced skirt you said I damaged."

Fury gripped her. Ellie drew herself up to her full height of five foot two inches and leaned toward the fool, ready to…to…muss his hair. "For your information, you big klutz, I have no idea who you are and I haven't been looking for you." She lowered her voice to a hiss. "I'm here to see a client and I hope you scram before he gets here because I'd like to make a good impression."

Blue eyes blazed into green ones as the silence mounted. Behind them, Monica hung up the phone and coughed politely. "Excuse me, Mr. Blackwell."

Ellie heard the name and the pieces fell into place. She felt the blood drain from her face. "You?" she whispered.

"Me, what?" he asked impatiently.

"You're Marcus Blackwell?"

"Mark Blackwell," he corrected. Turning to Monica, he asked, "What's going on here?"

"This is Ellie Sutherland, sir. She's here about your portrait."

He frowned and threw up his hands in a gesture of frustration. "I'm lost."

"Didn't Mr. Ivan tell you? Your portrait will go up in the boardroom beside the other partners'."

Mark Blackwell glanced from Ellie to his secretary. Ellie relaxed her stance and offered him an exaggerated shrug, smiling wryly.

"I'm not prepared for this," he said finally, in a guarded tone.

Ellie gave him a shaky smile. "This isn't litigation—there's nothing to prepare for."

He looked at her, chewing his lip. Obviously Mark Blackwell stood in unfamiliar territory, and didn't like it one bit. His eyes narrowed. "And how, may I ask, did you get involved?"

Ellie smiled brightly. "I'm an artist."

Mark rolled his eyes and sighed mightily. "Why doesn't that surprise me?"

She glared. "What's that supposed to mean?"

He waved dismissively. "Forget it, um—what did you say your name was?"

"Ellie," she said with growing impatience. "Ellie Sutherland."

He ran his fingers through his hair, a gesture she recognized from the deli incident. "Well, Ms. Sutherland, perhaps we can discuss this, er, project in my office." He swept his arm toward a door a few steps away and motioned for Ellie to precede him.

She stood her ground. "After you."

He pursed his lips, then turned and walked toward the door.

Ellie noticed the painting as soon as she entered the huge masculine room. She walked over to it, soaking up the familiar shapes and colors. An afternoon in the park. A cliché, really, but her first truly good piece. There had been others since, additional impressionistic renditions of city landmarks, but she had been especially proud of Piedmont Park and the price it had brought. She lifted a finger, and almost touched the canvas. "Nice picture," she murmured.

"Nice purse," he said sarcastically.

Ellie's hand flew to her bag as her eyes swung across the room to his feet. They were big feet, wearing nice black leather loafers with tight little tassels.

"Do you make a practice of skulking in men's washrooms, Ms. Sutherland?"

She felt a blush start at her knees and work its way up. She raised her scorching chin indignantly. "Certainly not. I told you, I didn't know it was the men's room."

"Sure." He smiled a disbelieving smile, then leaned on the front of his desk. "Now then, what do you need from me?"

Ellie turned and took a step toward him. Their eyes locked. And just like that, something passed between them. At least she felt it.

A shiver ran up her back, and a low hum sounded in her ears. Looking at him, she realized she'd done a shamefully good job of capturing his features for the caricature. His eyes reminded her of a length of dark green velvet she'd once bought just because she liked it. She'd hesitated to cut it, to tamper with the natural drape of the lush fabric. She'd ended up folding it across the footboard of her bed, unhemmed. Now every night when she went to bed, she'd be thinking about Mark Blackwell's eyes.

"Hmm?" she asked, completely oblivious to the reason she'd come here.

Mark shook his head, as if to clear it. "Um, I asked, what do you need from me?"

This time, his words were slow and coated with fresh meaning. Need from him? A hundred images galloped through Ellie's mind, and Mark Blackwell loomed naked in all of them. She could see the surprise in his eyes, the slight confusion lurking there. Then she remembered. Of course, the pheromones.

For an instant, disappointment fluttered in her chest. Then she recovered and walked closer to his desk, conjuring up a natural smile. "Just a few hours of your time, really." She paused for a moment, then said, "Do you have a favorite suit?"

"I never thought about it," he answered slowly.

"One you reach for when you have a very important meeting?" she coaxed.

He pondered for a few seconds, seeming embarrassed. "My olive one, I suppose."

"I've seen it," Ellie said, nodding her approval. "It's a good choice."

"Is this a new look?" he asked, eyeing her avant-garde hair and outfit.

Ellie recognized a diversionary tactic when she saw it. She looked down at her trendy, chic clothes. "Don't get out much, do you?"

His left eyebrow rose a fraction of an inch.

She blinked purposely and continued. "Wear the olive suit to the first sitting. Bring both a solid white shirt and an off-white shirt. And a handful of ties."

"First sitting? I'm afraid this is all new to me."

"I'll need you to sit for me for a total of about fifteen hours."

His eyes widened. "Fifteen hours?"

Ellie laughed and raised her hands in defense. "Not all at once. One or two hours at a time—whatever you feel up to. I'll take photographs to work from at home."

He scowled and folded his arms. "I'm not comfortable with this."

The toothpick remark she'd made to Manny came to her lips, but she bit it back. Instead, she said, "Just relax—I'm not painting you in your mallard-print boxers."

Mark studied her for a minute, the tiniest hint of a smile lifting the corners of his mouth. "I don't wear mallard-print boxers, but then I thought you'd know from your earlier vantage point in the men's room."

Ellie swallowed. Maybe he wasn't as uptight as she'd thought. "Briefs, then."

He shook his head. "Wrong again."

"Bikinis?" she squeaked.

Mark extended a finger and beckoned her to come closer.

Ellie did, and leaned forward for him to whisper in her ear. "Bare-assed."

Ellie jerked up and took a step back before she realized he was laughing at her.

"That wasn't very nice," she retorted.

"You fished for it," he said matter-of-factly.

"Where were we?" she asked, trying to reassume a professional stance.

"I was sitting for you."

"Shall we do it here in your office?"

His eyes raked over her body. "It would be a first, but sure."

Her pulse leaped. The image of them vibrating his desk across the room came to mind, but she stifled it. The chemicals she emitted triggered his reaction and she'd do well to remember that. She forced a serious face, refusing to verbally acknowledge his innuendo. "Fine. When?"

He still smiled, his eyes dancing. "Tomorrow morning at nine?"

"I'll be here with my camera," she said, already walking toward the door.

"You bring your equipment," he called to her. "And I'll bring mine."

Mark caught the flash of her silver purse being slung over her shoulder as she closed the door. Where had that idiotic comment come from? He jumped up and clutched his head with both hands, pacing. He'd never made suggestive comments to women he'd worked with. Willing women were plentiful, he'd never had to worry about mixing business with pleasure and risking a ruinous outcome. He cursed, rubbed his eyes, and walked the length of his office to his liquor cabinet. Appraising the newly stocked shelves, he selected a fine Kentucky bourbon, and poured himself a shot.

Tomorrow he'd conduct himself like the professional he was. He'd refuse to rise to her bait, no matter how enticing. The last thing he needed was for a nut like Ellie Sutherland to complicate his life.

3

"YOU'RE JOKING," Manny said, his eyes wide.

"Nope," Ellie declared, swallowing a bite of cheese omelette. "It was him, in the flesh."

"Was he as dreamy as you remembered?"

She nodded enthusiastically. "Absolutely."

"And single?"

Ellie frowned. "I didn't notice a wedding ring, and he was kind of…flirtatious. But that doesn't mean anything these days."

"You said it, girlfriend."

"He's too stuffy, and way out of my league. He probably has a black book full of women named Muffy and Phoebe."

Manny touched her forearm. "You're probably right." Then he grinned. "So why don't you introduce him to *me?*"

"Sorry," Ellie said, and pulled a sympathetic face, "but I don't think Mark Blackwell is your type, either."

"I can put on a skirt if he insists," Manny said, pouting.

"I'll see if I can work it into the conversation today," she offered sarcastically.

Manny lifted a sausage link to his mouth and bit off an end suggestively.

"You're a kook," she said, laughing.

"Me?" he asked. "Who's the one who sneaked into the men's room and listened to him pee?"

"I didn't see anything."

"Oh, so you did look?"

"No!" She grinned sheepishly. "Okay, I peeked, but I only saw a sliver of his back. Cut the wisecracks for a minute. I have to tell you the strange things that happened yesterday."

"I'm all ears."

Ellie told him about the incidents with men on the street, with Steve Willis, her co-worker, the taxi driver and some of the things Mark Blackwell had said to her. "And when I got home, Steve Willis had left a message on my machine. I haven't had *that* many men flirt with me in my lifetime," she asserted, reaching for the bottle of pink tablets. "It has to be these pheromones working."

"Well, aren't you glad they're working? What's the name of the manufacturer? I'm buying stock." He reached down to stroke Esmerelda's ears.

"Do you think I'm imagining things?"

"I think you're horny. You haven't had a relationship since…Drew, wasn't it? That was ages ago. I've forgotten, why did you end it?"

"His penis had attention deficit disorder."

"Oh, yeah, right." Manny nodded. "Well, if you want to see if the pheromones are causing all the hullabaloo, don't doll up today and see if you get the same results."

Ellie snapped her fingers. "Good idea."

THE LAW OFFICES of Ivan, Grant, Beecham and Blackwell were several blocks away, but easily accessible by bicycle. Ellie pulled on a neon green helmet that matched her bike, strapped on her backpack of supplies and jumped on to begin pedaling away her breakfast calories. No man could possibly flirt with her at this speed.

It was another beautiful day, too nice to be cooped up inside. She figured she'd be through with Mark Blackwell by noon, then she could spend the day sketching crowds at Underground Atlanta in preparation for her next portfolio painting. She stopped at a traffic light and waited for a police officer to wave her through the dense jam.

The police officer was within touching distance. And, she noticed, cute beneath his half helmet. He waved the traffic by on the side street, but his eyes stayed on Ellie the entire time, a whistle clasped between white teeth. She smiled at him and he smiled back. He waved through more traffic and studied her legs. She smiled. He waved through more traffic and winked at her. She winked back. Suddenly horns began to sound behind her from commuters impatient with the lengthy amount of attention the officer paid to the cars on the side street. Finally, he pulled his eyes away from Ellie and blew his whistle to halt the line of cars whizzing by. When she pedaled by, he lifted his hand to his helmet in a friendly gesture. Definitely the pheromones, she thought.

When she reached Mark's building, she took the elevator to his floor. The law offices were much quieter than the previous day, but still busier than Ellie imagined they would be for a weekend. On the other hand, Mark Blackwell probably worked Saturday, Sunday and holidays. To her surprise, more than one set of male eyebrows raised appreciatively when she made eye contact in the halls. Of course, she did look a little out of place wearing her cycling togs.

Monica's station sat neat and unoccupied, so Ellie stepped to Mark's office door and knocked.

"Come in," he called.

He sat at his desk, pen in hand. He glanced at his watch and said, "I was getting ready to check the men's room."

"Sorry," she said. "I had a flat this morning." She patted her bike, walked it over to the side wall and lowered the kickstand.

She pulled off her gloves and realized he was staring quizzically at the bike. "No place to chain it up out front," she said cheerfully. "I can't afford to have it stolen."

He pointed to the bags of dried herbs she'd picked up from a street vendor on the way. "I hope you don't plan to smoke that stuff."

Ellie glanced at the ingredients she'd purchased for a new perfume recipe. "Not here," she said, grinning wryly.

"Is that your night gear?" he asked, smirking, and indicated her neon clothing.

Ellie looked down at her pink bike shorts and bright yellow tank top. She had certainly dressed down today, complete with running shoes. She pulled off her helmet and ran a hand through her short waves. "You can't be too safe in this traffic."

He stood, tossing the pen on a stack of documents, and tugged gently at his waistband. Ellie caught her breath. Mark Blackwell looked deadly in pleated olive slacks and an off-white shirt, open at the collar and revealing a shadow of dark hair. *Easy, girl. This is just a job.* His jacket hung from a light-colored wooden valet in the corner behind his desk. Several ties hung there, as well as a white shirt, still under the dry cleaner's plastic.

"I see you brought the things I suggested," she said, nodding her approval.

His eyes locked with hers. "I'm nothing if not obedient," he said in a tone which indicated that wasn't the case at all.

The undigested omelette flipped over in her stomach. "Well," Ellie said nervously, "let's get started, shall we?" She unstrapped her backpack and pulled out a folder. "I've taken the liberty of drawing up an employment contract."

Mark poked his tongue in his cheek as if he was amused, but said nothing.

"Pretty simple stuffy, really," she continued. "It mentions the materials used, the fee and the delivery time frame of the portrait."

Mark reached for the document and read it quickly. His eyes swung up to her. "I would never have imagined painting to be so lucrative."

Ellie set her jaw and took two deep breaths. "It isn't. Jobs like this are few and far between. And I'm buying all the supplies, which includes framing the finished portrait."

"Still, it's a lot of money. You must be very good." He sounded doubtful.

Ellie bit her tongue, tempted to mention the Piedmont Park scene hanging ten feet from her, but the thought suddenly struck her that maybe he didn't even like the picture and had merely inherited it with the office. Instead of leaving herself open, she raised her chin, gave him a small smile and said, "I am *very* good."

Mark Blackwell chewed on his tongue for a moment. Then

cleared his throat. "What is a 'kill fee'?" he said, looking back to the document.

Ellie shrugged. "My protection. I do freelance photography for magazines, and I've been burned on last-minute publishing cancellations. This protects me if you—" She stopped and bit her bottom lip.

"If I'm run down by a beer truck?" he finished.

"You could say that, although I doubt if the term has ever been applied quite so literally."

"What if I don't like the painting?" he asked, laying aside the contract and folding his arms.

Ellie opened her pack and pulled out miscellaneous supplies, including a camera. "Satisfaction guaranteed," she said, smiling wryly.

He opened his mouth to speak, but a knock on the door stopped him. "Yes?" he called.

The door opened and a handsome, wiry, black-haired man stepped in. "Blackwell, about the Morrison deal—" He stopped when he spied Ellie, a blatant admiring look crossing his face. Glancing back to Mark, he said, "Maybe we can discuss this some other time."

Mark's face hardened. "After our conversation yesterday, Specklemeyer, I thought there was nothing left to discuss."

The tension between the two men hung in the air, almost palpable. "Perhaps I should wait outside," Ellie offered, starting for the door.

Mark stopped her, holding up his hand. "No." He glared at the younger man. "This won't take long."

Specklemeyer's shoulders went back and anger diffused his smooth skin. "Morrison is my client, and I intend to do what the man asked me to do."

Mark's voice hummed low and deadly. "You work for this firm, and you will do what you're instructed to do. If not, there won't be anyone here to cover you when the IRS comes calling for you."

The man's face contorted in a sneer. "Being partner has gone to your head already, hasn't it, Blackwell? Last week you were just a flunky like the rest of us, and now you think you have veto power.''

''You're wrong,'' Mark said calmly, refolding his arms. ''I *know* I have veto power.''

The other man's eyes narrowed, his fists balling at his sides. Convinced they were going to fight, Ellie moved her supplies back a few feet to the perimeter of the office, but when she glanced up, the younger man was stalking toward the door. He closed it with a resounding slam.

''Sorry for the interruption,'' Mark said into the ensuing silence. ''Tell me how this works,'' he said, waving an arm to encompass Ellie and her things.

''First I need to see the other portraits yours will be displayed with so I can maintain the corporate mood, so to speak. Your secretary mentioned it will be hung in the boardroom— is it close by?''

''Right this way.'' He led her out of his office and down a wide hallway. The boardroom sat dim and deserted this weekend morning. It reeked of old books. The overhead lights did little to brighten the dark paneled room, so Ellie opened all the blinds. Then she walked around the room, perusing the five large somber portraits adorning the walls. Two partners had apparently retired—or worse.

''Pretty standard stuff,'' she acknowledged, pulling a tape measure from her pocket and recording the size of the canvasses and frames. She glanced at the towering man beside her. ''Wouldn't you at least like to smile in your portrait? Remember, it'll be your legacy.''

Mark frowned. ''My legacy will not be a vanity painting on a wall.''

His vehemence surprised Ellie. ''You have children?'' It hurt more than a little to know he was married, after all.

The frown deepened. ''No, I don't have any children— yet.''

''But you're married?''

''No,'' he said, a bit flustered, then added, ''not yet.''

''Engaged?''

''Not yet.''

"Oh, you're one of *those*," she said knowingly, then turned her eyes back to the painting in front of her, immensely relieved.

"One of those what?" he said defensively.

"You're a Peter Pan man. No wonder green suits you," she said, indicating his slacks.

His mouth opened, then closed. Pointing with his index finger, he said, "I don't believe this—*you* are psychoanalyzing *me?* And what is all this Peter Pan nonsense? Let me guess— *Cosmo's* feature this month, right?"

"There have been volumes written on men like you," she said, sashaying past him into the hall.

He caught up with her in a few seconds. She thought he'd be angry, but surprisingly, he seemed to concede defeat. "Do you by chance know my mother?" he asked. "Gloria Blackwell sent you here to torment me, didn't she?"

Ellie laughed as she reentered his office. "No, I don't know her, but I know someone just like her in Florida—Gladys Sutherland." She shrugged. "It's universal. It's what mothers *do.*"

One corner of his mouth went up. "Is your mother a matchmaker?"

Ellie snorted. "She's Chuck Woolery in a girdle."

He laughed. "Mine, too. The last woman she set me up with brought a book along to read."

Ellie threw her head back and laughed. "The last guy my mom set me up with informed me over a fast-food dinner that women were getting way out of hand and needed to be put in their place."

"Oooh," he said. "A real charmer." Their laughter peaked, then petered out as they looked at each other and realized they'd just shared a friendly moment.

"Well." Ellie cleared her throat, and moved toward her supplies. "I guess I'd better get to work."

"Just tell me where you want me," he said, hands on hips.

Ellie looked up and saw the implication in his eyes. He was tempting, all right. She measured her response. "How about in that straight-back chair by the table?'' *Which has always been a personal fantasy of mine.*

"Suits me," he drawled.

To her horror, a stab of desire knifed through her as she watched him swing his coat on, grab a tie and walk to the chair. She stood mesmerized as he efficiently tied a tiny knot at his throat. Watching his nimble fingers move was suddenly the most sensual thing she'd ever seen. Ellie moistened her lips with the tip of her shaking tongue. Few men could be this sexy *putting on* clothes.

The celibacy was making her behave this way. She'd gone too long without a man's body next to hers. And now, the first time a man with the physique of an exotic dancer came along, she fell to pieces. She wiped beads of perspiration from her forehead. "Turn the chair sideways, and have a seat." She picked up the camera and busied herself attaching the lens, willing her pulse to slow.

At this rate, she'd be jumping his bones by lunch.

Mark eased into the chair and exhaled deeply. She was doing it again, throwing him sexual crumbs—and he was gobbling them up like a starved man. He clenched a fist to steady his nerves, but his traitorous eyes sought her out. How was it possible this woman could turn screwing on a camera lens into foreplay?

He had steeled himself against her this morning, but he hadn't counted on her wearing skintight elastic neon clothes. And little white crew socks with pom-poms on the heels. And for her hair to be so...mussed. He groaned.

"Are you okay?" Ellie asked, walking toward him, concern on her pert little face.

"Uh, sure," he said, sitting straighter.

"First I'm going to rape you," he heard her say matter-of-factly.

Lights burst behind his eyes. "Excuse me?" he croaked.

"Drape you," she repeated. "I'm going to drape you." She held several different-colored cloths over her arm and, picking up a navy one, shook it in front of him for emphasis. "See?

I need to decide what color background would be the most flattering.''

Disappointment shot through him and he fingered his collar a fraction looser. ''Whatever you say,'' he said, laughing nervously. *Get a grip, man.*

Using small, capable-looking hands, she placed the navy fabric over his right shoulder. Her fingernails lightly nipped the back of his neck, and a gray swatch suddenly appeared over his left shoulder. Ellie stepped back to observe him, stepped forward to adjust the drapes, and back again, studying. She reached for her camera and snapped five or six pictures at lightning speed.

With eyes narrowed, she walked toward him and leaned forward. Suddenly her face was mere inches from his. He could see a freckle centered perfectly on the end of her nose, and for one crazy second, he thought she might kiss him. He parted his lips and waited. She grabbed his chin and adjusted his head, sharply, to the right. ''Don't move,'' she ordered, then started snapping more pictures.

''I can't,'' he said testily. ''I have whiplash.''

If she heard him, she didn't acknowledge it. If fact, her next adjustment to his head was even more severe than the first. ''Ow!'' he yelped. But she was busy focusing and clicking. More drapes appeared, this time red and burgundy, then dark green and gold. To pass the time, he'd been halfheartedly keeping track of the number of rolls of film she'd used. But as she draped him in a deep plum color, he'd gotten a chinful of soft breast, and the blood rushed from his brain to more urgent parts of his body. She reloaded. Did that make twelve rolls? Or twenty-one?

Ellie Sutherland turned into a different person when she worked. She was a study in concentration, utterly efficient.

''Smile,'' she ordered.

And she was devastatingly beautiful. He could imagine sliding those bike pants off and pulling her onto his lap, her straddling him wearing those delightful pom-pom socks.

''There's a good smile,'' she said. Click, click. ''Whatever it is you're thinking, keep thinking it.'' Click, click, click.

He could reach under that ridiculous yellow tank top and push it up to expose her to him. She'd have great tan lines, her breasts outlined perfectly, surrounded by sun-kissed skin. And her nipples—

"Hey," she said, lowering the camera. "The lurid grin suits you, but I don't think it's what you want for posterity, is it?"

Mark recovered with a start, and reined in his wayward thoughts. "Are you almost finished?" he asked somewhat brusquely.

"Just a few more," she said, bending down on one knee for a different angle. When she stood up a few seconds later, Mark breathed a sigh of relief. Finished at last, he hoped. Then she would leave. Out of sight, out of mind.

Ellie, however, reloaded again. "Now, let's try the white shirt and a different tie," she said without looking up.

Mark gritted his teeth. How much longer was he going to have to put up with her incessant teasing? He stood and walked past her to the valet, loosening his tie along the way. With his back to her, he unbuttoned his cuffs, then the front, and slid the shirt off his shoulders. As he lifted the plastic from the white shirt, he distinctly heard the camera go off. He swung his head, but Ellie was wrestling with the camera, pointing it at the floor. Her head was down.

Mark turned back to his new shirt, and heard two more clicks. Again he swung around and her face looked downward, contorted from her strenuous efforts with the suddenly temperamental camera. This time, when he resumed his task of removing the shirt from the hanger, he kept her in his vision in a mirror to his right. While he appeared to be absorbed in undoing buttons, she glanced at him over her shoulder, then turned, focused on his naked back and snapped two quick pictures.

Why the little voyeur! Then a thought occurred to him, and he grinned to himself. "Don't turn around," he said over his shoulder, rehanging the new shirt. "I must have sat down in talcum powder before I left this morning. Give me a minute to remove my pants and dust them off." In the mirror, he saw the back of her head jerk up. He unzipped his pants and made other noises of undressing, but left his slacks buttoned. Her head moved slightly side to side as if she was contemplating her next move. Just as she raised the camera and turned, so did he.

He heard two clicks before Ellie realized she'd been had. She straightened, her face flushing to a most becoming shade of deep rose.

"Are these for your personal collection?" he asked, crossing his arms over his bare chest.

Busted taking pictures of the man changing clothes! Ellie's mind raced faster than the heat growing in her cheeks.

Mark Blackwell stood completely still, except for a muscle that twitched beneath his left pec. God, the man was gorgeous. His shoulders were broad, his arms athletically defined, but not overly so. A tangle of dark hair covered his chest, his dark nipples slanted on firmly uplifted muscle. His waist was sectioned in flat planes of taut skin, which narrowed into his waistband. Ellie felt a single drop of sweat trickle between her breasts as she moistened her dry lips.

With an effort, she shrugged into a relaxed posture, then threw one arm up in what she hoped resembled a casual gesture. "It's not what you're thinking. Some people are more relaxed when they don't know their picture's being taken," she said in her most authoritative voice, bobbing her head for emphasis.

Seconds passed. Then a full minute. She willed her head to stop bobbing, but it jerked up and down of its own volition.

"If you'd gotten the picture you wanted," he said quietly, "you'd know just how *un*relaxed I am at the moment."

"I don't know what you mean. Can we get on with this, please? I do have other plans for today."

He eyed her for a few seconds longer, then a strange look came over his face. Reaching to tug on the white shirt, he said, "Sure." His face once again melded into a serious, professional mask.

Ellie frowned while he concentrated on his buttons. No wonder this guy was still single. Who wants a moody man? Up then down, hot then cold in a matter of a few seconds.

Then it hit her and she almost slapped her forehead in revelation. She kept forgetting about the pheromones. The poor guy didn't know what was going on. It all made sense now—his early teasing, and now suddenly pulling back, as if he'd just regained his senses.

She busied her hands with the camera, but kept one eye on him. His hands were slow on his buttons, and he seemed almost thoughtful. So intent was she on analyzing his silence, his voice startled her.

"Do you mind telling me what kind of perfume you're wearing?"

Bingo! "I'm not wearing perfume," she said.

Mark looked up and frowned slightly. "Scented lotion? Shampoo?"

Ellie shook her head.

"Are you sure, because I could swear…" His voice trailed off, and he shook his head in uncertainty.

"What does it smell like?" she asked. She could record his observations in her journal. The counselor stressed the importance of noting details.

"I don't know," he said. "It's hard to explain. Like…fresh air." He glanced at her, seeming embarrassed.

Ellie grinned nervously. "In downtown Atlanta? Your schnoz must be playing tricks on you."

"Right," he said, sliding on a tie and stepping to the mirror to complete the knot.

His phone trilled, causing Ellie to jump. Mark strode to his desk, glanced at the tiny number-display screen, then groaned.

"What?" Ellie asked.

"It's my mother," he explained, picking up the receiver. "Hi, Mom…yes, I saw your number come up on the screen." He looked at Ellie and smiled. "Yes, it's an expensive feature, but all the office phones have it…no, I don't know how much it costs, but it's worth it…yes, if I think of it, I'll ask Monica…yes, I promise."

Ellie giggled and motioned she was leaving to give him privacy. Mark shook his head and waved her toward a chair, holding up a finger to indicate he'd wind up the call in a minute or so.

"No, the name of the person calling doesn't appear, just the number...uh-huh...no, it wouldn't be possible for you to know if Stella was calling from Gert's house, Gert's number would still appear." He rubbed his eyes with index finger and thumb, clearly trying to remain patient.

Ellie enjoyed eavesdropping on his conversation. Even a senior partner could be reduced to childlike politeness around his mother.

"Mom, did you call just to talk about my telephone?" He frowned. "Oh. Sure you can ride with me and my date." He turned slightly away from Ellie and she couldn't see his face.

Ellie felt a tiny pang of jealousy. Which was ridiculous, she thought. It was only reasonable to assume a man like Mark Blackwell dated, whenever his hectic schedule allowed, that is.

"No, you don't know her...uh, a couple of weeks now... yes, she's nice...no, no children...no, I don't think she's ever been married, but the subject hasn't really come up...yes, I agree that's very important, but it just hasn't come up...you'll meet her tomorrow, okay? Look, I've got someone in my office, so I'll call you later, okay? I love you, too, Mom. Bye."

He hung up the phone with a heavy sigh, then turned a wry grin toward Ellie. "That was the infamous Gloria Blackwell."

"She sounds persistent."

"The IRS should hire her," Mark agreed. Suddenly his face brightened. "Hey, are you busy tomorrow?"

Ellie's heart skipped a beat. A date? In an instant she remembered the woman in the clinic who had asked about the chances of meeting a great guy and then having the rug pulled out from under her when the pills wore off. It would be too easy to lose her heart to Mark Blackwell. Plus, she wasn't about to get involved with a man whose arteries were probably already clogged with stress. And he'd only made the offer because he was under the influence of the pheromones. Self-preservation kicked in. "I'm busy every Sunday," she said.

"Working or playing?" he asked in a teasing voice.

"A little of both," she admitted. "I usually go to Underground and set up an easel to draw caricatures." Gathering courage, she stood and attempted to clarify the situation. "Look," she said earnestly, "you're not exactly my type and I'm probably not yours, either, so—"

"Whoa," he said, raising his hands. "It's just a family picnic. I'm in a bind and I really need a date."

"And I really need the money I'll earn at the mall," she said sincerely. *And you scare me to death.*

He leaned against his desk and drummed his index finger against his chin. "How about a business proposition?"

"What do you have in mind?" Ellie ventured cautiously.

"How much money will you make drawing at Underground?"

Ellie averaged her earnings from the last few times she'd worked there and added twenty percent. "About two hundred fifty dollars."

Mark whistled. "Two fifty? Okay, I'll give you three hundred to go to the picnic with me."

"Why?" Ellie asked, suddenly suspicious. "You could probably get a date just by picking up the phone."

"How good an actress are you?" he asked, smiling.

"I made a pretty convincing artichoke in my fifth-grade play. Why?"

"Because," Mark said, now grinning broadly, "I want you to be the epitome of my mother's worst nightmare."

Hurt speared through Ellie. "Excuse me?"

He stood up and walked toward her. "Don't take this wrong. But if we could convince my mom you're my new girlfriend and that we're completely wrong for each other, she might ease up a little and realize my being a bachelor isn't so bad, after all. Come on, it'll be fun."

Ellie balked. "I'm not sure if I'm flattered or insulted."

Mark took a step toward her with his arms extended. "You said yourself I'm not your type. Think about it. We seem to get along okay—"

Ellie snorted.

"Sort of, plus, I need a date with no strings attached, and you need the money," he finished triumphantly.

Ellie frowned. "I'm not for sale."

"Three hundred fifty."

"Shall I bring baked beans or potato salad?"

"UNBELIEVABLE! This man is actually paying you to go out with him?" Manny exclaimed, counting the bills Ellie handed him. "Do you realize two out of the three times you've seen this man, he's handed you a fistful of cash?"

"Oh, for heaven's sake, Manny, you make it sound sordid," Ellie said. "It's a simple business arrangement, that's all."

"Sure. And I guess you're naive enough to think this man is going to shell out money like this and be satisfied with a peck on the cheek at the end of the day?"

Ellie frowned. It hadn't occurred to her that Mark would expect anything other than a convincing performance.

"Ellie," Manny continued in her silence, "you already think this man and several other strangers you've encountered are affected by those pills you're taking. Did you ever think it might be dangerous if the pheromones push someone to, you know, take liberties with you?"

"I can take care of myself, Manny," Ellie countered, then she softened. "But I appreciate the concern."

Her roommate touched her arm, his face serious. "I want to meet this guy, to check him out and see if he's safe, okay?"

"You just want to check him out, period." Ellie poked a finger in his side, lightening the mood. "I told you, he's not your type."

Later, when she picked up the developed film from the photo shoot with Mark, Manny's warning of Mark's physical interest resurfaced to send Ellie's heart pounding. She flipped through dozens of photos of his handsome face, and groaned. Not only was the man good-looking, but photogenic, too.

Her breathing became shallow when she came to the photo of Mark shirtless, arms crossed, his eyes haughty from tricking her. Recalling their light, fussy banter, Ellie realized uneasily she could get used to his company. But the memory of the

deal they'd struck sobered her immediately. He needed someone his mother would object to, and he'd chosen her for the
part. How much clearer could he have made it that he would
never be interested in her romantically?

4

"SPARE SOME CHANGE, buddy?" The ragged man's dead tone and tired eyes told Mark he fully expected to take no for an answer.

Mark hesitated outside Ellie's building, then withdrew a five-dollar bill from his wallet and placed it in the man's trembling hand. The man thanked him profusely, then trotted down the street. He wasn't in the habit of giving handouts, but he'd felt a stir when he'd looked into the man's lost eyes. Mark shook his head sadly. His old man had given away and loaned out enough money to save an entire generation. And look where it had gotten Rudy Blackwell.

Mark shook off the somber thoughts of his father and looked around the neat, trendy area. Panhandlers knew Little Five Points inhabitants were liberals, for the most part, with a social conscience and lots of spare change to back it up. Mark knew this because he'd rented an apartment not far from Ellie's building before he'd signed a hefty mortgage and moved north to Dunwoody.

At only eleven-thirty, the sun already hung high and scorching. He pulled a finger around the collar of his golf shirt and felt relieved he'd worn khaki shorts. He'd arrived at Ellie's a few minutes early, but his mother wanted to get to the picnic shelter at Stone Mountain before anyone else so she could prevent relatives from setting green-bean salad next to strawberry pie, or some similar unforgivable act. He chuckled, thinking about Ellie Sutherland and Gloria Blackwell mixing for an entire day. He couldn't imagine the surprises Ellie had in store. This might be the most fun he'd ever had at a family gathering. And it would very likely get his marriage-happy mother off his back.

As he climbed the steps to her second-floor apartment, Mark tried to ignore the anticipation he felt at seeing her again. Many times during the previous sleepless night he'd reminded himself she'd managed to extort a good chunk of cash from him in the one week he'd known her. She was just like the others, he told himself. So why had he tripped twice in his haste to get to her door?

He knocked twice before he heard footsteps approaching. When the door swung open, a tall, handsome blond man stood before him with a questioning look on his face.

"Excuse me," Mark said abruptly. "I must have the wrong apartment."

The man extended his hand in a firm grip. "You must be Mark," he said. "Ellie's almost ready. I'm Manny, Ellie's roommate. Come in."

Mark blinked. A ridiculous stab of jealousy jolted through him. Ellie hadn't mentioned she lived with a man—a very good-looking man, to boot. He followed her roommate through a shallow entryway and halted to stand on the black-and-white kitchen floor, grimacing at the screeching voice that reached his ears. Ellie stood at the stove with headphones on, her back to them, stirring a fragrant concoction in a saucepan and belting out a horrid rendition of Patsy Cline's "Crazy."

Manny turned to him and shrugged apologetically. "It's country this week, next week—who knows?" He walked over and tapped Ellie on the shoulder. She jumped several inches, her hand to her chest, and the shrieking stopped. She saw Mark and smiled, tearing off the headphones.

"Hi," she said, picking up a towel to wipe her hands.

"Hi, yourself," he said, annoyed at the rush of pleasure he felt. "Is that your contribution to the potluck?" he asked, pointing to the gooey liquid in the pan.

Ellie laughed and reached around to untie her frilly cotton apron. A vintage garment, he suspected, noting the pleasantly faded fabric. "That," she said, nodding to the pan, "is twenty-five thousand dollars."

"What?"

"I'm entering a homemade-perfume contest. The entry fee is one hundred dollars, which I'm working off today." She smiled at him impishly. "Top prize is twenty-five thousand, and I want it."

Intrigued, Mark walked over to the pot and sniffed. A sultry blend of musk, fruit and flowers assailed his nostrils. "Hmm," he said, nodding. "Very nice. I've never smelled anything like it. A woman's fragrance, I assume?"

"Of course."

"What's in it?"

"Oh, this and that. Chamomile, marjoram and juniper for relaxation, ylang-ylang as an aphrodi—" She stopped and cleared her throat loudly. "Plus vanilla, and a little cocoa."

"It's colorful," he said, noting the muddy brown hue.

"I haven't worked out all the kinks yet, but my idea is to launch a whole line of perfume products based on foods."

"Pizza perfume?" he asked, teasing.

She smiled. "More like orange marmalade or peach pie."

When she pulled the apron over her head, Mark inhaled sharply at the sight of her in a full-skirted, floral minidress and flat cloth tennis shoes. No bra either, which was not unbecoming. She looked all of sixteen. He swallowed. "What do you call the perfume?"

"I've decided to call it Irresistible You."

Bull's-eye. Mark nodded. "Very appropriate."

She turned off the flame and said, "I see you've met Manny. Let me grab a couple of things and we'll go." She swept by him in a cloud of homemade fragrance, the pompoms on her socks bouncing up and down as she strode away.

Mark watched her, then turned when he felt Manny watching him. As the man waved him toward a purple-and-gold velour chair in the tiny living room, Mark again wondered about his relationship to Ellie. They were both blond, perhaps he was her brother. "Are you related to Ellie?" he asked when they were seated.

"No," Manny said, tapping a cigarette from a pack and rolling it between his fingers. "Ellie and I go way back."

His tone implied intimacy, and Mark didn't really want to delve further.

"She's a great gal," Manny continued. He lit the cigarette, inhaled deeply and turned his head to release a stream of white smoke from his mouth. His voice and bearing suggested a challenge.

Mark nodded his agreement, but said nothing. His nose itched ferociously, and he ran a knuckle over it.

"She has men falling all over her."

It seemed like a strange thing for her roommate to say, but Mark smiled amicably. A savage sneeze seized him, and he dragged a handkerchief from his back pocket. Wiping at watery eyes, he sniffed. "I can see why," he finally managed to say.

"Is the smoke bothering you?" Manny asked, cupping his hand over the cigarette.

Mark shook his head. "Smoke never bothers me." On cue, he sneezed into the handkerchief three times, each more powerful than the last. "I don't know what's wrong." Mark felt a sudden soft weight land in his lap, and he looked down into the green eyes of a very hairy orange cat. One inhale solved the mystery as Mark dissolved into a sneezing fit, which did nothing to spook the arrogant feline.

"Allergic, huh?" Manny said, stubbing out his cigarette in a nearby ashtray. "Come, Esmerelda." He removed the feline from Mark's knee and disappeared down the same hallway Ellie had taken.

By the time he returned, minus the cat, Mark felt much better.

"Sorry about that," Manny said unconvincingly. "Ellie loves the puss." When he sat down, Manny leaned forward in his chair. "Do you find yourself drawn to her?" he asked.

Mark frowned and drew his shoulders back a couple of inches. "Who?"

"Ellie," Manny said.

"Drawn?"

"Yeah, you know." Manny toyed with another cigarette, but didn't light it. "Like *compelled* to be around her?"

Mark glanced from side to side. *Is this guy for real?* "I don't know if I'd use that word exactly," Mark said slowly, "but she does seem to have an effect on me."

Manny's sandy eyebrows shot up and he leaned back, nodding and contemplating. Mark glanced toward the hall. "Ellie?" he called, standing.

To his relief, she appeared with a huge canvas bag over her shoulder. A floppy denim hat nearly hid her cropped wavy hair and made her appear even younger. She smiled and shaved off another couple of years.

"Just how old are you?" he asked.

"Twenty-nine," she said cheerfully. "Did I go overboard?" she asked, looking down at her outfit. Silver earrings brushed the tops of her shoulders. "Your mom will hate it, won't she?" Concern pulled down the corners of her eyes and mouth.

Mark grinned. "Yes."

Ellie grinned, too. "Then let's go." She leaned forward to study his face, undoubtedly red from the sneezing. "Sorry about Esmerelda. She's a hairy thing, isn't she?"

He waved off the incident and reached for her bulging bag, then playfully buckled under its weight. "Let me guess—you brought books to read, didn't you?"

Ellie laughed. "No, just a few necessities for a picnic." She picked up a small bottle from the kitchen counter, shook two pink tablets into her palm and filled a glass with water from the tap.

"Headache?" Mark asked, suddenly concerned.

"Hmm?" Ellie asked. Apprehension crossed her face, then disappeared. "These are just, um...vitamins." She stuck the bottle into the weighted canvas bag. "I have to take them throughout the day," she explained. "Woman stuff," she added in a whisper.

Mark had figured as much and nodded curtly, and he hoped, sympathetically.

When Ellie pulled a huge chocolate layer cake from the fridge, he shot her a questioning look. The last thing he needed was for his mom to think he'd snared a domestic dream.

"Well, I can't go completely empty-handed," she said defensively.

"Okay," Mark relented. "But it'd better not taste *too* good." For a few seconds, he experienced misgivings. What if she did hit it off with his family? If they pestered him to bring her around again, his plan would backfire in his face.

"SO TELL ME, what kind of woman does your mother expect you to marry?" Ellie hoped setting the stage for her performance would soothe her jangled nerves.

Mark pursed his lips and glanced back at the road in front of him. He looked relaxed and athletic in his casual clothes. The muscles in his legs bunched when he shifted gears, sending shocks of awareness through Ellie's body.

"Someone demure and domestic, I suppose. Like her." He smiled wryly. "She thinks I need someone to be a hostess in my home and help me entertain to further my career."

"And you don't?" she asked.

"No," he said flatly.

"Why not?" she persisted.

He sighed. "Because I've seen too many of my friends get rooked into marriage only to find themselves digging out from under a divorce settlement within a couple of years. I worked my tail off to get where I am. I have no intention of starting over."

Ellie sat still, heat burning her neck and cheeks. Mark was convinced that women were fortune seekers. And she'd given him ammunition by lowering his bank account by more than four hundred dollars since she'd met him a week ago. "So," she said, trying to cover her embarrassment, "you've never been married?"

"Nope." Then he shot her a worried glance. "Have you?"

"No," she said quickly, not that it mattered to him anyway.

"Who's Manny?"

For a split second, Ellie felt pleased he even cared, but his concentration on the road and casual tone indicated he was just making conversation. "Just an old friend," she said and

Mark nodded lazily, clearly uninterested. Her heart sank. "Is your mother a widow?"

"Yes," Mark said, frowning slightly. "Dad died three years ago."

"I'm sorry," Ellie said. "Were you close to him?"

"As close as you can be to someone with whom you have nothing in common."

Ellie felt a stirring of kinship. "My father was never around when I was growing up, either."

Mark's low laugh held no humor. "Mine was always around. Couldn't seem to keep a job. He was a great man, but a lousy provider."

"Where do you live?" Ellie asked, searching for firmer ground.

She thought she saw his lips tighten. "Dunwoody," he said.

He didn't have to add "in a big, expensive home." The one word said it all. "Do you have a large yard?" Ellie asked.

Mark glanced at her sideways. "I suppose so."

"Trees?"

"Uh-huh."

"What kinds of plants and flowers?"

Mark shrugged. "The usual stuff—azaleas, forsythia, a few bulb flowers and lots of ground cover. I might build a gazebo this fall."

"That sounds nice," Ellie said, and meant it. Room for a large herb garden was the only thing she yearned for that apartment living couldn't give her.

"I like it," Mark said, his voice tight.

From his manner, Ellie concluded he probably didn't want her discussing domestic things like gardens and homes with his mother.

"How exactly do you want me to act?" Ellie asked. "And what should I talk about?"

Mark smiled again, and she felt a rush of pleasure. "You've got a mom," he said. "You'll know what to say and how to act."

"Don't you feel guilty about lying to your mother?"

Mark shook his head. "I know my mom. It's only when

I'm *not* seeing anyone that she panics and puts me on a guilt trip because she doesn't have grandchildren. The minute I *do* meet someone, she scolds me for neglecting my career and says I've got plenty of time to get married." He relaxed his hands lower on the wheel. "I'd rather not have to stage this little charade, but no one's getting hurt."

Ellie bit her tongue, and a little sliver of disappointment shook her heart. *Speak for yourself, Mark Blackwell.* She'd promised him a wacky performance for his money, but deep down she wished today could be different. It was easy to imagine herself as Mark's girlfriend, on her way to meet his family at a picnic. But, a deal was a deal, and today she'd be everything Mark Blackwell wouldn't want in a partner. The bad thing about it was, she wouldn't have to do much of an acting job. She realized, for the most part, just being herself would be suitably unsuitable.

Gloria Blackwell strutted out to the car exactly as Ellie had envisioned. Buxom and conservatively dressed in a shapeless jumper. Neat hair in a low bun. Plump elbows and arms full of pot holders and steaming casserole dishes.

Gloria gave Ellie's outfit a long glance, then offered a shaky smile. Introductions were cheery and forced. Gloria asked Ellie to move to the back seat of Mark's sedan, citing her perpetual car sickness as the reason she needed the front passenger seat. As Ellie moved to oblige, she heard the woman whisper to Mark, "Isn't she going to miss her prom?"

"Be nice," Mark whispered back.

Ellie smiled wryly. This would be the easiest money she'd ever made. The thought did not ease her conscience.

"Ellie, dear," Gloria asked when they were on their way, "what do you do for a living?"

Ellie hesitated a split second, then said, "I was laid off from a secretarial job a few days ago." She saw Mark frown at the news, then his face cleared, as if in understanding. He winked at Ellie in the mirror. He thought she was making it up to get under his mother's skin!

"So you're unemployed?" his mother asked, her disapproval thinly veiled.

Ellie ground her teeth, but maintained a sweet and pleasant voice. ''Well, I'm really an artist, working on my portfolio and doing commissions on the side—like painting your son's portrait.''

''An unemployed artist,'' Gloria chirped. ''How interesting.'' She addressed Ellie by looking at her in the side-door mirror. ''My late husband dabbled in paint—it never earned him a penny.''

Ellie sat back in her seat, biting off a defensive retort. Gloria Blackwell had disliked her on sight. That fact might have bothered her if she thought this thing with Mark was going anywhere. But since he'd made it clear he wasn't interested in pursuing a relationship, she could relax. So what if his mother pooh-poohed her occupation and clothes? Mark said he wanted to go for shock value. For three hundred and fifty dollars, she'd be Madonna for a day.

''So how did you meet my son?''

''The first time we met, he dumped a cola in my lap and paid me off to avoid a scene.''

''And…the next time?'' Gloria ventured.

''In the men's room at his law office. Your son has an enormous—''

''I don't think—'' Gloria tried to interrupt.

''—bladder,'' Ellie finished.

Gloria fanned herself. ''Do your parents live in Atlanta?''

''No, Florida.''

Mark's mother breathed an audible sigh of relief at finding a safe subject. ''That's nice. Are they retired?''

''Semi-retired,'' Ellie said pleasantly. ''They run a restaurant.''

''How lovely!''

''At a nudist colony.''

Gloria gasped and a sudden fit of coughing seized Mark. Ellie bit back a wry smile.

For the rest of the drive, Gloria conversed with Mark, making general comments about the picnic and who would be there. Ellie guessed Mark's mother would not be directing any more questions her way, so she relaxed into the soft leather seat and listened to the woman's chatter.

"Did I tell you your uncle Jerome will be there? I know you're not fond of him, Marcus, but he *is* your grandmother's only brother. He's married again, did you know?"

Ellie smiled as Mark made a big show of counting off on his fingers. "Is this the fourth wife, or the fifth?"

"Fifth. You know the second Julia was really a gem—we all wish he'd kept her."

"I don't remember his second wife."

"No, I'm talking about Julia, his third wife. His second wife was also Julia, but we didn't care for her. She sniffed all her food before eating it. Always sniffing, it was very annoying. But his third wife, Julia—the second Julia, we always called her—now *there* was a nice girl. Real Southern manners, and a proper wife she was."

Ellie couldn't resist. "If she was such a proper wife, why did he get rid of her?"

Gloria jerked her head around quickly, as if she'd forgotten about their passenger. She adjusted the mirror so she could see Ellie. "I really wouldn't know," she said airily, as if gossiping was beneath her, then adjusted the mirror back with a snap.

"Here we are," Mark said cheerfully, shoving the gearshift into Park and turning off the ignition.

"How am I doing?" Ellie whispered as they walked to the back of the car.

"Great," he said, smiling. "I think she hates you."

Ellie frowned, then nodded agreeably. She was earning her pay, wasn't she?

She spied several shelters within walking distance, but a sign bearing the name "Blackwell" led them to one off to the right and up a small incline.

"I thought this was your mother's family," Ellie said to Mark as they unpacked the food.

He smiled. "It's both, really. Without getting too complicated, my dad and four of his brothers married mom and four of her sisters."

"Is that legal?" Ellie asked.

This time he laughed. "It's legal, but sometimes I don't think it was very smart. All of their children are double first cousins. It makes for a pretty tight-knit group." He pulled a huge cooler from the trunk of his car, and led the way up the path. Gloria hurried ahead, visibly crestfallen that one of her sisters had beaten her to the punch and, having arrived first, was already spreading vinyl tablecloths over the ten or so picnic tables in the shelter.

Within a few minutes, several carloads had arrived, and Ellie's head spun from the names and faces she'd tried to commit to memory. Everyone, including Gloria, seemed impressed with the chocolate cake she'd made. "It's low-fat, too," she said to Gloria.

"Well," harrumphed Mark's mother, giving Ellie a sweeping glance, "not everyone was meant to look like a stick." The cake was thereby relegated to the lowly salad table, to occupy a spot beside a plate of unpopular celery and carrot sticks.

After an hour, Ellie decided to take a break from the adults and mix with Mark's young cousins. Delighted to discover several of them had brought in-line skates, she retrieved hers from her bag and joined them on the paved parking lot, ignoring disparaging looks from Mark's mother. She taught the more experienced skaters a few moves and was soon enjoying herself very much, laughing in spite of the sick feeling building in her stomach. She felt like a fraud, but it was equally disheartening to know that even when she was being herself, Mark's mother disapproved.

As unobtrusively as possible, Ellie watched Mark mix with the odd collection of relatives. The fussy aunts, the crying babies, the joke-telling men were so different from the stoic manner he put on. Ellie wondered how he'd metamorphosed into the polished, articulate executive he'd become. He was obviously everyone's favorite. It was gratifying to see he'd originated from homespun people—good, decent people with simple wants and needs whom he seemed to care about. This was a side of him she hadn't expected to discover, and it caused an unsettling shift in the characteristics she'd assigned to him.

It bothered her, too, that his family was so different from hers. He'd mentioned he was an only child, like Ellie, but Mark's extended family was large and varied, warm and comfortable around each other. She tried to conjure up images of long-forgotten aunts and uncles from faded photographs she'd seen in family albums. Both sets of grandparents had died before she was a toddler. Ellie's mother had been the youngest of her three siblings by nearly a generation—she wasn't close to them at all. Her father had one brother left, living somewhere on the West Coast, she recalled. She wondered how many unknown cousins she had all over the country, and made a mental note to pump her mother for more information the next time they talked on the phone.

She stole a glance at Mark, and felt a zing go through her at the sight of him, his head thrown back, laughing. She envied Mark Blackwell and his rowdy relatives. Ellie sighed. A big, close, loving family was all she'd ever wanted, and all she'd never gotten.

Mark slapped his cousin Mickey on the back, enjoying a shared joke. His gaze slid to Ellie, an annoying habit he'd adopted in the last hour, along with every male relative at the picnic over the age of ten. His smile died and his mouth went dry as she whirled on the skates, causing her skirt to billow alarmingly high.

"Where did you snag *her?*" Mickey whispered hoarsely, admiration tinting his voice.

Mark jerked his head around to find the eyes of his balding, chunky cousin riveted on Ellie. A strange feeling of possessiveness descended over him. "She's an artist and my office commissioned her to do a painting."

"An artist, huh? That explains it."

"That explains what?"

"Why she's not like every corporate female clone I've ever seen you with."

Mark frowned. "What's that supposed to mean?"

"Not that you haven't dated some beauties, cuz," Mickey

hastened to add. "It's just that my tastes lean toward *warm*-blooded creatures." He exhaled heavily. "And that woman is hot."

Mark's frown deepened. He hadn't hired her to be hot. Guilt stabbed him in the gut when he remembered the money he'd paid her. The thought struck him that it might be nice if Ellie Sutherland had accompanied him of her own volition, instead of having to be bribed. Then she could have acted naturally and his family could have fallen in love with her...wait a minute—what was he thinking?

His cousin let out a low whistle through his small teeth. Mark joined him in holding his breath when a particularly risky move revealed every square inch of her rock-hard thighs and the barest glimpse of white cotton undies. Mark licked his lips nervously and Mickey dragged a handkerchief out of his back pocket to mop his forehead.

"I don't think she hit it off with Mom," Mark said carefully, attempting to plant a seed of dissent.

"That settles it," Mickey said, nodding confidently. "Marry her."

Someone rang a bell to signal the meal being served. Ellie removed her skates and rejoined the adults, dutifully giving disappointing, but true, answers to repeated questions from Gloria's sisters about what she did for a living and how she'd met Mark. Mark hovered close by, as if to verify she was doing what he'd asked of her. Every infant at the gathering squalled when she held them, and soon the new mothers were keeping their babies to themselves. Ellie slipped her camera from the bag and snapped two rolls of pictures, the women politely rigid when she focused on them, the men curiously hamming for the camera.

Indeed, it seemed the chilly reception extended to her by the Blackwell women wasn't a feeling shared by the Blackwell men. They buzzed around Ellie continually, laughing and flirting, elbowing appreciation to a silent Mark. Uncle Jerome, the marrying man, shadowed her every move, offering her lively, if suggestive, conversation throughout the afternoon. Even beating the men at horseshoes didn't banish their smiles and winks. When it looked as if the female relatives were about to descend on her with tar and feathers, she rejoined the children. This time, she pulled out her sketchbook and drew caricatures of the ones who could sit still long enough for her to render a pastel drawing. The children gleefully took the sketches to their parents, and before long, an audience had gathered.

The sudden attention made Ellie nervous and she noticed a frown on Mark's face. He wasn't paying her to make a favorable impression. She glanced at her tablet. "One sheet of paper left," she said. "Gloria, how about it?"

Mark's mother suddenly turned shy and blushing, but smiling, she nodded and sat before Ellie, striking a regal pose.

Ellie scanned the woman in front of her for a few seconds. The phrase *queen bee* kept going through her mind. Ellie looked at Mark, who gave her a slight nod. "Go ahead," he seemed to say. "One last nail in the coffin."

Hurriedly, Ellie sketched, hardly looking up. Once finished, she swallowed, amazed at how unkind the picture had turned out. With a bemused smile, Gloria reached for the drawing as everyone gathered around. Instantly her smile dissolved and her face reddened, then she handed it back to Ellie and huffed away amid choruses of laughter from her family.

Mark stepped forward to look at the sketch, a buxom insect with a tiara on her head, wielding a giant-size stinger. He pursed his lips. "Queen bee," he said, studying the drawing with a tight smile. "So true. You're very good."

Ellie watched people drift away to the dessert table and said, "It was hurtful to her, and I should apologize."

Mark shook his head. "You're doing just what I asked you to do," he said, handing the sketch back to her and looking into her eyes. "Everyone got a chuckle out of it. Mom's just not very good at laughing at herself."

"Still, I feel so mean," she said, biting her lower lip.

He extended his hand to her and pulled her up. "Let's get dessert." His first touch sent charges of electricity through her fingers. She quickly withdrew her hand once she got to her feet.

When everyone discovered Ellie's cake was low-fat, most of the women relented and served themselves portions ranging from polite to generous. Uncle Jerome even teased Gloria into having a chunk, pointing out it wouldn't hurt her to start counting her fat grams. Gloria begrudgingly ate every crumb. The men deferred to more fattening fare. Mark declined, saying he wasn't big on sweets, and Ellie declined as well so someone else could have the remaining piece. To her surprise, it was Gloria.

"Are you sure this is low in fat?" she asked Ellie, shoveling in the second piece. "It's surprisingly good."

Ellie beamed, glad she would leave with one redeeming mark. "The guy I live with gave me the recipe." When she saw Gloria's eyes widen in response to the remark about her roommate, Ellie hurried on, "This is the first time I've made it. I'm glad it's as good as he said it would be."

"You know," Gloria said thickly through a mouthful, "Marcus needs a good cook in his kitchen."

Ellie's smile froze, wondering if Mark had overheard the comment. She nodded woodenly, surprised at the concession his mother had made, but more surprised at how good the idea sounded, her cooking in Mark's kitchen. Of course, they'd have to eat chocolate cake every night since it was the first and only thing she'd ever made that had turned out well enough to actually serve. Avoiding Mark's eyes, Ellie enjoyed the slight lifting of her heart.

About halfway through the hokey-pokey, the Blackwell women started dropping like flies. Clutching their stomachs, they ran for the nearest bathroom, several yards away. Gloria seemed to be the most violently ill. When they emerged an hour later, wiping sweat from their clammy foreheads, they'd determined the culprit must be Ellie's cake since no one else had been afflicted.

White as a sheet and mad as a hornet, Gloria demanded, "What did you put in that cake?"

Ellie backed up a step and tried to keep the shakiness out of her voice. "The normal stuff—flour, eggs, cocoa, prune juice—"

"Prune juice?" Gloria screeched. "Who puts prune juice in chocolate cake?"

"It replaces the oil and m-makes the cake low f-fat," Ellie stammered.

"How much did you put in?" Gloria asked, her eyes bulging.

"A b-bottle of concentrated—" She stopped at the horrified looks around her. "A s-small bottle," she added weakly, holding up her thumb and index finger.

"A whole bottle? Lord, we'll be purging for a week—" Gloria stopped, grabbed her stomach and trotted back up the hill to the rest room, followed by six others.

Ellie closed her eyes and took a deep breath. When she opened them, Mark stood before her, a wry smile on his face. "That really wasn't necessary, Ellie—" he took her hand "—but it certainly cinched you a spot on my mother's least-likely-to-be-a-good-daughter-in-law list."

Her senses leaped when he touched her, her mouth instantly parched. She swallowed miserably. He'd never believe her if she told him none of it had been planned. Ellie fought back tears of frustration.

This day had proved one thing to her. She was inherently wrong for Mark Blackwell.

MARK SWUNG his glance from the road ahead to Ellie's profile and tried to guess what she was thinking. The day was an unqualified success as far as his original plan was concerned, but he hadn't counted on his feelings shifting somewhere between the time he'd picked her up and the time he dropped her off. Away from her, he seemed able to logically dismiss her. But once in her presence, some undefined feeling took control.

"Your pictures turned out well," she said, breaking the silence and, thankfully, his train of thought.

"Did they?"

"Yes." She still stared straight ahead, her voice unreadable. "I think the dark gold background will be the best, if that's okay with you."

"You're the artist," he said.

"Yes, and I'm very proud of what I do," she said, a note of defensiveness in her voice.

"As well you should be," he said quickly, once again speaking to her profile. Suddenly he remembered the disparaging remark he'd made about her being an artist when she first came to his office. And, the raised eyebrows and rolling eyes of his mother and her sisters had not escaped him today. Apparently, they hadn't escaped Ellie, either. "I admire your talent," he said sincerely.

She didn't respond, but her head shifted slightly toward him.

"It was a nice day," he said lightly.

Ellie's dry laugh rang out. "Sure it was," she said miserably. "I gave enemas to your mother and all of your aunts."

"Most of them have been constipated all their lives." He chuckled, but at the look on Ellie's face, he bit his lip to stem his laughter. "It's okay—no one was hurt." Actually, he couldn't remember enjoying a family gathering more than he had today. His family's bout with diarrhea aside, he'd enjoyed watching Ellie skate and mix with his young cousins. And cut up with his uncles. And her drawing ability was truly special. She was a very unusual woman, and damned attractive, at that. Another peek at her in the semidarkness of the car revealed a long expanse of lean, tanned leg. His right hand itched to reach over and rub the smooth length of skin.

"When can you sit for your portrait again?" she asked.

"How about Saturday morning? That is," he added quickly, "if you don't mind spending another Saturday with me." He held his breath for her response. Could he wait another six days to see Ellie again?

"Saturday morning is fine," she said, finally swinging her head around to meet his gaze.

"Fine," he said, feeling the breath leave his lungs. God, she was beautiful. "Fine," he heard himself repeat. His groin tightened uncomfortably and he dragged his eyes away from hers. Her apartment building loomed ahead on the left.

"Thanks," Ellie said quickly, hopping out as soon as he pulled to a stop.

"Wait," he said to the closed door. He cut the ignition and jumped out of the car. "Wait," he called, and she turned back, struggling under the weight of that ridiculous bag. "I'll walk you to your door." He strode toward her, his knees suddenly rubbery. Would she let him kiss her? Would a kiss be appropriate under the circumstances? And when was the last time he had ever worried about whether or not to kiss a woman good-night?

She waited until he'd caught up and taken her bag, but remained a couple of steps ahead of him, walking into the apartment building and up to her door on the second floor.

"Thanks," she said, sounding a little breathless.

"You did me the favor," he said, referring to the picnic.

She smiled. "I meant, thanks for walking up with me. It wasn't necessary, but nice."

He could barely see her eyes for the brim of her hat, which sat slightly askew. New freckles glowed across her cheeks from the afternoon's sunshine. Her lips held the frosty remnants of pink lipstick long since faded. She hadn't bothered to renew it. How refreshing to be with a woman who was content to be her natural self sometimes. He wet his lips. "Ellie?"

She raised wide, innocent eyes to his. "Yes?" She didn't have a clue he wanted to kiss her. And why should she? He'd hired her to go on a picnic with him. The whole arrangement seemed very impersonal at the moment. Did he dare?

"Ellie?" he repeated.

"What is it, Mark?" she asked, her head slightly angled.

"This," he breathed, lowering his mouth to hers. Her lips were silken, parting to accept his fully, her tongue tentatively offered. Desire shot through his body. He dropped the canvas bag with a loud thud and took her into his arms to draw her deeper into the kiss. Suddenly, the apartment door swung open.

Mark and Ellie parted and turned their heads to see a questioning Manny, holding a half-eaten apple. "I heard a thump," he explained, leaning on the door frame and taking a large bite.

Mark straightened. *What is the deal with this roommate man, anyway?*

Everyone stared at everyone else, the silence broken only by Manny's loud chewing. After a few seconds, Mark cleared his throat. "Well, I'd better be going."

Manny reached inside the door to retrieve a light jacket from a hook. "I was on my way out myself—just wanted to make sure you got home safely, El." He flashed her a tight smile. "I'll walk out with Mr. Blackwell." He took a last bite out of the apple for punctuation and tossed it into a trash can beside the door. Then he stepped squarely between them in the hall, struggling into his jacket with exaggerated movements that obstructed Mark's view of Ellie.

Mark frowned slightly, then said, "I'll see you Saturday, Ellie." He peeked around Manny's breadth as the man took his time pulling on the jacket. Ellie said nothing, but he saw—reproachfulness?—flicker in her eyes. Had his kiss been unwelcome? It hadn't seemed so, but then again she hadn't counted on her roommate/boyfriend/whatever catching them.

Mark walked side by side with Manny down the stairs and out into the dusk. They stopped on the sidewalk and Mark withdrew his car keys. "So," he said casually, "what's your relationship with Ellie?" He pressed a button on his key ring and his car interior light came on a few feet away. Mark swung his attention back to her roommate.

Manny stood with his hands in his jacket pockets, studying Mark silently with narrowed eyes. Finally, the tall blond man spoke quietly, "Ellie means more to me than anyone else in this world. Don't break her heart, mister." With that, he turned and walked away, pulling a cigarette from his pocket and poking it in his mouth.

Driving away, Mark decided it had been one of the most unsettling days of his life. The picnic had been unexpectedly

enjoyable, and Ellie's good-night kiss unexpectedly flamma-
ble. Feelings nagged at him, annoying him like radio static.
Just exactly what did Ellie Sutherland mean to him, other than
a guaranteed end to his orderly life?

5

"YOU DIDN'T!" Manny looked horrified.

"I did." Ellie nodded solemnly, slathering jelly on a plain bagel. Breakfast was the first chance they'd had to talk. "You should have seen those big women running for the john. And we had to stop three times on the way home for his mom to go."

"I always said you were going to poison someone with your cooking one of these days," he chided. "You've got to remember, preparing food is not the same as whipping up one of your perfume batches."

Ellie brightened. "Which reminds me, I'm sending a vial of Irresistible You to the contest today." She pointed to a small bottle of reddish-brown liquid beside a gummy saucepan. The recipe I came up with yesterday turned out just right, after all."

Manny shook his head. "You can kiss that hundred-dollar entry fee goodbye. It's a scam, El."

"No, it isn't," she insisted. "I know someone whose cousin's girlfriend won the contest two years ago. And my proposal for a line of fragrances is a great idea."

"Who wants to go around smelling like food?"

"For your information, studies show men are more turned on by the smell of pumpkin pie than by most expensive store-bought fragrances."

"Makes you wonder what Betty Crocker wears under her apron, eh?"

"Go ahead, make fun, but I'll get the last laugh. That twenty-five grand is mine." She rubbed her thumb against her fingers to emphasize her quest for big money.

"You'd better hope so," he said. "It doesn't sound as if you're in danger of marrying into the Blackwell bank account."

Ellie stiffened. "Very funny."

"Hey," he said, laughing gently, "I was kidding, okay? Don't look so wounded. I thought you weren't impressed with this guy."

"I'm not." Ellie studied Esmerelda's paw, refusing to look at her roommate. "He's too much like my father, you know...corporate. I want a man who worships the ground I walk on, who isn't tied to his desk, who would play hooky just to spend the day with his kids. My mother never had that, but I intend to, one of these days."

Manny groaned. "Despite your wish list, you've fallen for him, haven't you?"

Ellie opened her mouth, but Manny held up his hands to ward off her protest. "Before you say anything, Ellie, let's look at this in black and white. The guy hired you to make a bad impression on his family—this is not the sign of a marrying man. Why on earth would you put yourself through the agony of going after someone who's made it perfectly clear he doesn't want to be caught?"

Ellie tried to speak, but once again he stopped her. "But," he said in a singsongy voice, "it's nothing to me." Manny stooped to pick up the cat. "Not to change the subject, but we have other problems more imminent than your love life. Have you noticed anything different about Esmerelda?"

"No," Ellie murmured, popping the pinks pills into her mouth with a grapefruit-juice chaser. "Why do you ask?"

"Here," he said, handing Ellie the furry package.

She abandoned her glass to juggle the struggling feline. "She's heavier," Ellie said immediately, shifting the cat slightly for confirmation. "We should have put you on a diet weeks ago," she said, snuggling the cat's face to her own.

"We should have put her on a *leash*," Manny amended, arms crossed and lips tight.

"What do you mean?"

"Esmerelda is knocked up."

Ellie's eyes widened. "Kittens? Are you sure?" She held the cat up to scrutinize her rounded tummy, grinning. "It must've happened on one of those days she escaped."

"Must have," Manny chirped. "You realize, don't you, this means your cat has a better sex life than you do?"

She shot him an exasperated look. "Oh, Manny, do you have to be so…so…"

"The word is *truthful,*" he supplied. He plucked a piece of paper from the counter and waved it in front of her. "It gets worse. This was under our door when I got up this morning."

Ellie reached for the paper and gasped at the words in large print across the top of the page. "Eviction notice? Why?" She began reading the sheet in earnest, but Manny cut in.

"It's the cat, El. She got out one too many times and someone complained. According to the notice, we have one week to find a home for her or we'll have to find a new home for ourselves."

"I'll find someone to take her in," she said, gently setting Esmerelda on the floor, then reaching for the phone.

Two hours later Ellie had called every person in both her address book and Manny's, but no one could shelter her precious cat. She sighed, explaining to Manny, "Denise has a new baby, the Worths have a dog, and Robin just bought a bird. Everyone else already has too many cats or kids, or lives in a no-pet unit." Ellie pulled Esmerelda to her and relished the deep purr of the mother-to-be. "What am I going to do?"

"YOUR MOTHER CALLED TWICE," Monica said, handing Mark the message sheets. "She asked me to tell you to call her back as soon as you get a minute."

Mark nodded absently and laid the notes aside.

Looking over his shoulder, Monica asked, "What's so important about Saturday?"

Mark glanced up at her and frowned in confusion.

She pointed to his calendar. "It's circled. Do I need to add something to my schedule?"

Mark realized with a start he'd circled the day while thinking about Ellie. "No," he said quickly, then added, "just another sitting for the portrait."

Monica's left eyebrow rose a fraction and she smiled. "Oh, yes, the cute little painter. Are sparks still flying between the two of you?"

He feigned innocence. "What do you mean?"

Monica brought her steno pad to her chest and crossed her arms. "What I mean is, when she came to meet you that first day, you were at each other's throats. I haven't mentioned it, but you two have got me curious."

Mark felt his neck grow moist beneath his collar. "A simple misunderstanding in a delicatessen, that's all."

His assistant leaned forward slightly, as if eager for more details, but Mark picked up a memo on his desk and began reading to signal an end to the subject. Monica took the hint and walked toward the door.

"Hey," his partner Patrick said as he strolled in after a perfunctory knock.

"Hey, yourself."

"Clear your calendar Friday evening."

"Okay. Mind telling me why?"

"Lucy's organizing a dinner party and my instructions are to make sure you come." He grinned at Mark apologetically. "Can you scrounge up a date? Ivan will be there, too," he added in explanation.

Ellie's face rose to float in Mark's mind, but he squashed down the image. "Is an escort mandatory?"

Patrick shrugged. "I have my orders." He turned to leave Mark's office and added over his shoulder, "Come stag at your own risk."

"It might be safer than the alternative," Mark muttered as Ellie's face stubbornly reappeared to taunt him. Absurdly happy for a reason to call her, his fingers itched to punch her number. Then, furious with himself, he deliberately dialed Valerie's work number instead. He'd managed to keep from getting emotionally involved with a woman for this long, and he wasn't about to start with someone who was obviously so wrong for him.

But when Valerie responded with such clinging enthusiasm at the sound of his voice, he winced and manufactured a vague excuse for calling. Within seconds of hanging up, his traitorous fingers dialed Ellie's number from memory. Instantly nervous, he wondered if he'd have to bribe her again, or if she'd go freely this time. Too late, the thought surfaced that she might feel obligated to buy a new dress. And he suspected she couldn't afford it.

"Hello." She sounded breathless, and he imagined her in her work apron, wiping her hands after working on some creative project.

"Hi, it's Mark," he said, then added, "Blackwell."

"Oh, hi," she said with a slight question in her voice.

Mark felt awkward and fished for conversation. "Are you busy?"

"As a matter of fact, I was preparing the canvas for your portrait." Animation exuded from her voice. He liked the musical quality of it, not throaty and superficial like most of the women he knew.

"I don't have a clue as to what that entails. Is it difficult?"

Ellie laughed lightly, a tinkling sound. "No, I tack canvas over a wooden frame, then paint over it with gesso, a white substance that makes the canvas stiff when it dries."

"Ah, I see," Mark murmured.

The silence stretched for thirty seconds, then they both started talking at once.

"What's up—"

"The reason I called—"

They both laughed and then Mark started again. "The reason I called is to see if you're busy Friday night. I'm in another bind—are you up for a dinner party at the home of one of my partners?"

Ellie's heart had just stopped thudding from the initial shock of hearing his voice. Now it began pounding anew, followed by a sharp barb of disappointment. Apparently, he needed another date for hire. Or maybe not. Maybe this would be a real date. "I, uh, that is…what did you have in mind?"

Mark hesitated for an instant. "Same terms as before?"

Ellie's heart sank, then she panicked. Oh, God, did he think she was trying to wangle a higher price? "Look," she said finally, "I'm caught up on all my bills, so thanks, but I really don't need... Wait a minute." Her mind raced furiously. "How about a business proposition?"

"Go on." This time, *he* sounded cautious.

"My cat needs a home for a few weeks."

"Impossible," he began. "I'm allergic—"

"And I'm desperate," Ellie interrupted, pleading. "She's pregnant and my landlord won't let me keep her—"

"I really can't—"

"Please? Just until the kittens are born and I find homes for them? That's only four or five weeks—eight at the most. Once Esmerelda's gone, he'll get off my back. Then I'll be able to sneak her in again later."

Mark exhaled heavily. "I really can't...believe I'm doing this," he finished, with wonder in his voice. "Okay, it's a deal."

Ellie grinned into the phone. "Great! I'll get a cab to your house Friday night and bring Esmerelda with me." She scribbled down the address. "What should I wear?"

"I'll have something sent over," he said, surprising her.

"I *do* have clothes, *Mr.* Blackwell."

"Why is everything an argument with you? Let me do this, okay?"

He obviously didn't trust her judgment. Or perhaps he wanted her to make another bad impression. Either way, the ball bounced in his court. "Okay," she agreed hesitantly.

"I'll see you Friday," he said, then hung up.

Ellie sat holding the phone and listened to the dial tone. Her scalp tingled. Every day it seemed her life became more enmeshed with Mark Blackwell's. The memory of his kiss had kept her up late last night. She felt warm now just remembering how she'd pulled the length of green velvet from the foot of her bed and slept with it cuddled against her cheek.

She touched her lips, her mouth watering at the thought of his taste. For a brief moment, he'd pulled her to him and she'd felt his arousal for her. Desire stabbed her even now and she allowed herself the luxury of wondering what it would be like to lie beneath him. She knew the pheromones were getting to him—he'd probably bed her willingly enough, she mused. But was her heart durable enough to withstand the letdown once the chemical reaction fizzled out?

The following day, Tuesday, marked exactly one week since Ellie had begun taking the pills. She dutifully collected her journal and walked the few blocks to the clinic.

The unadorned white two-story building squatted on Parish Street between a parking garage and a vintage clothing store. Ellie waited politely while two women entered the door in front of her, wrinkling her nose appreciatively when the smell of paint wafted out. The old structure was getting a face-lift.

Two giant stepladders flanked the wide entryway, supporting slow painters with big paint buckets and tiny brushes. Ellie tilted her head back to check their pace and progress. They'd be there at least a decade, she decided, then turned toward the empty waiting room, relieved she wouldn't have to wait.

A cold, slimy dollop of something plopped onto her head. Ellie closed her eyes and lifted her shoulders in a deep shrug, instinctively wanting to touch the stuff oozing down behind both ears, but already knowing it was off-white wall paint.

"Sorry," came a muffled voice many feet above her. "Nice buns, though."

"Thanks," Ellie mumbled without looking up.

Thirty minutes later she sourly joined a large cluster of people waiting to speak to the harried receptionist standing behind the tall white counter. The clinic was a busy little place. Apparently, a crowd had arrived during her attempt to remove most of the paint from her hair in the rusty old bathroom.

After a long wait, she was directed to one of the cracking vinyl-upholstered chairs lining the perimeter of the waiting room. Ellie passed the time leafing through an ancient copy of *Museum Art,* her hair dripping milky water on the curled pages.

At last her name was called, and she followed a gray-haired, stocky, somber-faced woman to a tiny closet of a room. "I'm

Freda,'' the woman said defensively, as if Ellie was going to make something of it.

She didn't. "Pleased to meet you."

Freda looked more like a prison guard than a clinical assistant. After a perfunctory glance over her chart, the woman snatched Ellie's journal and perused the contents with tight lips. After a few moments, her eyes swung up to meet Ellie's. "Impressive," the woman muttered. "All true?"

Ellie nodded patiently.

"Are you taking the pills exactly as directed?"

"Yes."

"Any physical symptoms? Changes in energy level or diet?"

Ellie thought for a moment. "My concentration seems diminished, and my appetite has been depressed." She grinned and patted her stomach. "I've lost two pounds."

"How about your exercise level?"

Ellie shook her head. "About average—no change."

The woman noted Ellie's answers on a form. "Have you become sexually active with any of the men you've mentioned in the journal?"

Ellie squirmed. "No."

"Have you developed an emotional attachment to any of them?" She skimmed the last journal page with her index finger. "I see the name Mark mentioned quite often." She peered over her glasses at Ellie.

Clearing her throat, Ellie said, "N-no. Well, maybe."

"I don't have a checkbox for 'maybe,'" said Freda. "Do you like the man or don't you?"

"Yes, I do."

"And do you have reason to think he likes you?"

"I'm not sure *like* is the right word. He looks at me in this certain way…"

"Do you feel the pheromone pills have in any way influenced this, er, watchfulness?"

"Yes, I do."

"In what way?"

Ellie hesitated, then tried to put the situation in words. "He seems to be attracted to me, but confused by it all—like he doesn't understand why he would be. I've seen him shake his head as if trying to clear it. He told my roommate I have 'an effect' on him. And, he and other men keep asking me what kind of perfume I'm wearing. I think I'm emitting some kind of odor.''

Freda leaned toward her, sniffed mightily, then shrugged. ''Hmm.'' She scribbled notes on the form and turned it over. ''Keep omitting any commercial body fragrances like we instructed. Here's a new supply of pills, and your payment for the week.'' She pushed the items toward Ellie and resumed writing.

''I mean, it's nothing serious,'' Ellie rambled. ''I wouldn't even call it a relationship, really. It would never work between us because he's allergic to my cat and his mother hates me. Of course, I did ruin her family reunion, but that was purely by accident. Besides, if he ever settles down, it'll be with some classy woman, not an unemployed artist. No, it would never work, not in a million years.'' Ellie frowned at the woman's silence. ''Any advice?'' she asked.

Freda didn't bother to look up. ''Practice safe sex.''

MANNY LET OUT a long whistle. ''Damn, you look good, girl.''

Ellie grinned and smoothed a hand over the short black crepe dress. ''Think so?'' A froth of pearl-studded cream chiffon floated around the low neckline and spilled over her shoulders. The formfitting dress would have been an impossibility two pounds ago.

''Fabulous,'' Manny said cloyingly, then he frowned. ''If only we wore the same size.''

''I'll let you borrow the earrings,'' she promised, fastening the dangling pearls.

''He must have spent a mint,'' he said, picking up the Parmond's garment bag.

Ellie nodded. ''What are you doing tonight?''

''I have to do an early show, then Joan's picking me up. We're going to swing by a friend's house for cocktails, then downtown for some real fun. By the way, El, she feels terrible for having to let you go.''

She shrugged. "It was just a job. So tell me, does Joan like men or women?''

"Neither, as far as I can tell—or maybe both. You know how outrageous Joan can be—I think she likes to keep everyone guessing.''

"Well, tell her hello for me, and that the commission is going well. Will you help me gather Esmerelda's things? The cab should be here any minute.''

The cabbie appeared daunted when he saw the cat and all her feline paraphernalia, but when Ellie smiled at him, he softened and began loading the trunk of the car.

"'Bye, Cinderella,'' Manny said to Ellie before she stepped into the back seat. "Have a good time at the party. But remember to take your pills or you'll turn into my cousin Betty at midnight.''

ELLIE HAD TRIED to visualize Mark's house, but two blocks away from his address, she realized his home would surpass all her expectations. The cabbie pulled up to a two-story, taupe-colored stucco house with elaborate arches and pale cornerstones. The sloping yard was a paradise, the lawn all but completely sacrificed to tall trees, enormous mulch beds and lush leafy plants. Mounds of blooms flowed downhill. A fountain of stacked stone bubbled a stream of water, which fed an aquamarine goldfish pond. Ellie had never seen a more beautiful sight.

"Are you sure this is the place?'' she breathed.

"Sure as shootin'.'' The driver nodded. "Nice spread, eh? Friend of yours?''

"Yes,'' she said absently, unable to take her eyes from the house.

"Some guys have all the luck,'' he said dismally. "But if you get bored with Richie Rich, my name's Cal, and I get off at ten.'' He swung out of the cab and opened her door before she had a chance to respond.

The front door of the house opened. Mark came out and

descended the steps to the walkway. He wore dark slacks, a crisp off-white shirt and a mustard-colored tie. He looked absolutely devastating. Ellie alighted from the cab and smiled toward him. She could detect the clean scent of his cologne as he neared her. Esmerelda struggled for release to inspect the fish, but Ellie held on tight. "Hi," she said.

"Hi." He smiled, and held his hands at his sides, swinging them slightly as if not knowing what to do next.

"Nice house."

"Thanks. Nice dress."

"Thanks."

"Nice bill," the cabbie spoke up, motioning to Mark.

Mark reached for his wallet and counted off several bills, folded them, then handed them to the man.

The cabbie thanked him and opened the trunk. Mark's eyebrows shot up. "What's all this?"

Ellie stepped to the back of the car. "Esmerelda's things."

Mark passed a hand over his face. "You've got to be kidding."

"No," Ellie said, pointing. "Her bed, litter box, kitty litter, food bowl, water bowl, food, brush, play gym, scratch pole, toys, videos—"

"Videos?"

"Sure—one shows birds flying around, the other is of fish swimming and splashing. They keep her entertained for hours."

Mark nodded and pursed his lips. "I see."

The cabbie started pulling things out and setting them on the sidewalk.

"I wrote down her schedule for you." Ellie pulled a sheet of paper from her tiny evening bag. "She's got a bladder infection right now, so you'll need to give her medication once a day." She looked up and recognized impatience on Mark's face. Suddenly he sneezed violently. "We can go over this later," she said with a weak smile, refolding the sheet.

While Mark made several trips to bring in the cat's accessories, Ellie stood in the two-story slate foyer of his home and stretched her neck to see as much as possible from her vantage point. The open layout and cool colors stole her breath. A large living room stretched to her left, an expansive dining room to her right. His furniture was fairly traditional in design, but light fabrics and colors lifted and extended the rooms.

"Wow," Ellie said out loud. If she hadn't been sure before that she and Mark Blackwell existed in different worlds, she was convinced now.

Esmerelda yowled and jumped from Ellie's arms, bounding up the stairs. "Esmerelda!" she yelled, then took off after her.

When Mark entered the house with the last armload, he found the foyer empty. "Ellie," he called, setting the things down on the stairs. He sneezed, and pulled a handkerchief from his pocket to blow his nose. "This is unbelievable," he muttered. "Why did I agree to this?" An implausible answer skated across his mind, but he dismissed it.

When she didn't respond, he walked around the first floor, thinking she might have gone to the bathroom. When he found the door to the downstairs bath ajar, however, he assumed she'd gone upstairs to look around. One of the things that had impressed him the most when she'd asked about his home was that she'd seemed much more interested in his yard than in the grandeur of the house. Mark felt a slight pang of disappointment that she'd been so anxious to check out his digs that she'd helped herself to a tour.

He climbed the stairs, calling her name as he walked room to room. He heard a muffled sound coming from his bedroom and frowned. Not that he hadn't entertained ideas of Ellie seeing the inside of his bedroom, but her forwardness annoyed him slightly.

When he entered his bedroom, he covered his mouth to smother a chuckle, then decided she couldn't hear him, so he laughed out loud, anyway. Ellie Sutherland's very fine-looking rear end stuck straight up in the air, the points of her high heels following suit. He'd pictured her in his bed many times, but never under it. Her head and shoulders were hidden beneath the dust ruffle of his black bed, and she seemed to be saying something, he surmised, to the cat.

After enjoying a full minute of the delectable view, he spoke loudly. "Ellie?"

She raised her head quickly and he heard bone collide with metal. "Darnit!" she yelled, her voice still muffled by all the fabric surrounding her.

Mark laughed again, this time more quietly.

She inched her way backward, out from under the bed, and Mark felt his groin tighten as her hips tested the strength of the dress's seams. He couldn't remember when he'd ever found a woman more appealing than at that very moment.

Her head appeared, her hair wonderfully mussed. She dragged her fingers through it and stood awkwardly, brushing the front of her dress. "I'm sorry," she said. "Esmerelda jumped out of my arms and ran up here and under your bed. I didn't mean to snoop." She chewed on her bottom lip, her glorious blue eyes wide with worry. "I think she's scared."

Her beauty slammed into him with enough power to stagger his senses. *I think I know how the cat feels.* "I'll put her things in the guest room down the hall. Will she come out and look for her bed later?"

Ellie nodded. "Probably."

"Then leave her. How about a drink before we go?"

Ellie smiled at him and his breath caught. "Can I use your bathroom for some repair work first?"

"Sure." He pointed to the master bath. "I'll meet you downstairs."

Ellie took a few seconds to glance around his bedroom, impressed at the sheer size of the bed. King-size and sleekly modern, the elevated bed reigned over a huge room lit by a bay window encompassing an entire wall.

She walked into the spacious bathroom and flipped on the light. "Mmm," she murmured, taking in the tiled floor and large sunken tub. Gold fixtures winked at her from the long double vanity and porcelain sinks. The fragrance of his aftershave lingered. A razor drained on a folded hand towel. Frosted doors encased a shower large enough for a quartet. She could picture Mark showering, soap running down his slick body. She bit her bottom lip and shook her head at the image, then turned to fix her hair.

She gasped at her reflection. Besides her explosive hair, the expensive dress he'd bought her was covered with long cat hairs and carpet fibers. And her lipstick smeared down the corner of her mouth. She groaned, opening her purse and spilling its contents across the counter in her haste. Ellie tugged a brush through her hair, yelping when it skated over the lump fast forming from her encounter with the bed rail. Tears of frustration gathered in her eyes.

"Look at you," she said miserably. "You're a nobody going nowhere. What business do you have falling in love with Mark Blackwell?" Gasping at her own words, Ellie covered her mouth with her hand. Taking a shaky deep breath, she straightened her shoulders, and set about making herself presentable again. All the while, she hummed to herself, taking great pains not to talk to the crazy woman in the mirror.

6

ELLIE FELT SPARKLY from the two rum drinks she'd downed to alleviate her nervousness before they left. Too late, she realized she should have had a nonalcoholic beer with Mark. She could feel her body pulling toward him in the darkness of the car. His cologne, the soothing music, the special dress, all of it combined to make her feel languid and sexy. A shiver of premonition traveled the nape of her neck and she trembled. Trying to shake the feeling, she turned to Mark as they exited the expressway and said, "Any last-minute instructions?"

Mark looked at her, eyebrows lifted and said, "Such as?"

Ellie shrugged. "Such as, is there anybody in particular I'm supposed to make dislike me?"

Mark stared at her for a moment, then quietly said, "No, just be yourself."

A pretty scary prospect in itself, she thought. "Will your partners be there?"

Mark nodded. "Ray Ivan will be the one with the pipe. His wife passed away only a year ago, so I suspect he'll be alone. The other partners and their wives will be there, and various guests, I suppose."

When he maneuvered the sedan into a luxurious neighborhood, Ellie's shoulders tensed.

"Hey," he said, reaching over to cover her hand with his. "Relax. You look wonderful."

His touch electrified her hand. Ellie swelled under his praise. "Any woman would in this dress."

He pulled the car behind a long string of vehicles in a semi-dark driveway, then cut the engine. He unfastened his seat belt, turned toward her and leaned forward until his lips were mere inches from her face. "Not true," he said, then dipped his head to sweep a quick kiss on her jawbone. "Trust me." His voice reverberated in her ear, flaming her senses. Ellie swallowed hard at the rush of desire flooding her body.

Mark looked into her eyes. "We were rudely interrupted last weekend outside your door," he whispered.

Ellie tried to smile. "Oh, that M-Manny. He's always looking out f-for me."

He smiled, his eyes crinkling at the corners. "You're not scared of me, are you?"

Terrified. "N-no, of course not. That's not what I meant—"

He silenced her words with his mouth, his lips hungrily descending upon hers. Her throat constricted for want of much-needed moisture and oxygen, then she finally remembered to breathe. His tongue parlayed hers in a sensual battle she gladly forfeited. He twined his hands firmly around her waist, she lifted her arms to his neck and wrested sideways to deepen the embrace.

Something restrained her, prevented her from meeting him fully. She reached down to fumble with the seat belt and it snapped loose, tangling in his arms, then hers as they struggled to free themselves. Gasping for breath, they dived at each other again. This time Mark lifted her, putting his hands beneath her hips to pull her up and against his chest. She could sense his mounting frustration at the awkward angle. Suddenly he pulled her over the low console to straddle his lap. Her hair brushed the ceiling of the car and the steering wheel pressed into her back as she settled around his arousal, her dress hiked up to expose the garter belt she wore. Somewhere along the way she'd lost her shoes, but she didn't care. All that mattered was Mark Blackwell touching her, wanting her.

Mark thought he might climax on the spot when his hands discovered the snaps of her garter belt. This woman was killing him. "Ellie," he whispered against her neck. She arched her breasts against his chin and he buried his face in her cleavage. She rained kisses over his forehead as she wrapped her arms around his head to pull him closer. He bit lightly at her hardened nipples through the fabric of her dress and bra. His hands rode her waist, pushing her down on his arousal. The blood pounded in his brain as it exited, rushing to his midsection. Her breathing rasped as ragged as his as she moaned her pleasure.

"Hey!" a voice shouted outside the window. Mark jerked his head up and panic seized him. One glance confirmed his worst fear. Ray Ivan stood there, crouched and peering into the window. "Blackwell? Is that you? Get a room, son!" Then his partner turned and walked toward their host's home.

They were still for a few seconds as the realization of their indiscretion sunk in. Mark laid his head back and groaned. His arousal wilted. He opened his eyes and looked into Ellie's, wide with concern.

"That was bad, wasn't it?" she asked, biting her lip.

Mark stared at her for a few seconds, then burst out laughing at the incongruity of the situation. And the more he laughed, the harder he laughed. Soon, Ellie joined him as she climbed from his lap and fell into her own seat.

Slapping her knee, Ellie laughed and laughed, until she realized Mark had fallen silent. Looking at his suddenly somber profile, she emitted a final, weak giggle, then cleared her throat.

"What is it about you?" he asked, still staring straight ahead. His rumpled hair and slack mouth were in startling contrast to his dressy attire and normally regal bearing.

Uneasiness crept over Ellie as she fished for her shoes under the seat. "What do you mean?"

He looked over at her with an exasperated expression. "I mean, you drive me to do crazy things like make out in the front seat of my car at a business dinner!"

Anger flashed through Ellie and she pointed her index finger at him. "I didn't exactly fly over there and land on your lap, buster!"

He turned back to stare ahead, then raised his hands in a questioning gesture. "I'm a normal, red-blooded guy, but I've never done anything this stupid before." He spoke quietly, as if to himself, his hands animated. "After all these years of busting my butt and keeping my nose clean, my partner now thinks I'm Mr. Happy Pants.''

Ellie sat up, and snapped open her purse to retrieve a comb. The pheromone pills fell into her lap, and she froze. She straightened her dress and asked, "Are we still going in?''

"If you're up to it, I am. I'm sorry I put you in this situation—''

"It's all right, Mark," Ellie assured him guiltily. If not for those magic pills of hers, the whole incident would never have happened. "Let's just make the best of it.''

"You're right," he said, adjusting his tie. "It'll look worse if we don't go in. Thanks for being a sport.''

They spent a few minutes righting their clothes, then stepped out into the cool early-June night air. Ellie took several deep breaths to clear her head, and took the arm he offered her to walk up the steps.

Mark rang the doorbell, then smiled at her as they waited. "I'll have to admit," he said, turning back to stare straight ahead, "the garter belt was a nice surprise.'' He rocked back on his heels casually, confident.

Ellie couldn't resist knocking him off balance again. "Then I can't imagine what you would've thought of my tattoo.'' The look on his face was priceless as the front door swung open and a man who identified himself as Patrick pulled her into his home with a friendly handshake.

It appeared they were among the last of about seventy-five to arrive. Cocktails and finger food circulated the room. Laughter and spirited conversation buzzed around them.

"Ellie?" A familiar female voice spoke behind her, and Ellie turned to see her former boss, Joan Wright, walking toward her.

"Joan," Ellie said, delighted, stepping forward to hug the woman.

"How wonderful to see you!" the older woman said. "What brings you to the Beechams'?''

"I do," Mark said, stepping in to introduce himself.

Joan shot an amused glance at Ellie, then said, "Ah, you

must be the new partner.'' She shook his hand, then frowned slightly. ''Is something wrong with your forehead?''

Ellie's eyes and Mark's hand traveled upward. Lipstick kisses dotted his hairline. She made a frantic wiping motion with her hand, then turned to draw Joan into a conversation about the arts center.

''And the commission is going well?'' Joan's eyes asked more questions than her lips.

Ellie nodded. ''The preliminary work on the painting is done. I hope to get down to business tomorrow.''

''I'll let you ladies talk,'' Mark said, inclining his just-cleaned head. ''Excuse me.'' Ellie felt a curious sense of loss as he walked away. Darn, she was getting much too used to having this man around.

''Hi.''

Ellie turned to see Mark's secretary, Monica, standing next to her and Joan. Ellie made the introductions.

''So,'' Monica said, her tone silky with innuendo, ''how's it going with you and Mark?''

''Oh, we're just friends,'' Ellie assured her.

''Mark is quite a catch,'' she said.

Ellie smiled. ''I'm not fishing,'' she said, then steered the conversation in a safer direction. ''Joan, I thought you and Manny were going someplace tonight.''

Joan's eyes twinkled mischievously, then she moved her head slightly to indicate someone across the room.

Ellie turned to look and nearly swallowed her tongue. Manny, looking feminine and elegant in a brunette wig and long navy dress, stood chatting with none other than Ray Ivan, senior partner. He glanced up and caught her eye, then gave her a tiny shrug of bewilderment. She beckoned him frantically, but even as Manny tried to break away, Ivan followed him with a hand at his elbow. A finger of fear nudged Ellie's stomach.

While Ray and Joan exchanged greetings, Ellie pulled Manny down and whispered furiously, ''What are you doing here dressed like that?''

He grinned. ''I look fabulous, don't I?''

"Manny!"

He pouted prettily. "Relax, would you? It's a joke—Joan thought it would be hilarious to crash a stuffy gig. I had no idea it was the same party you were going to." He grinned and lowered his voice. "I love fooling the straight ones, and I think this Ivan guy is loaded."

"He's Mark's partner, you idiot!"

Manny looked hurt. "But he likes me."

"He likes *Molly,*" she said, using his stage name. "There's a big difference."

"Joan and I are splitting in a few minutes, anyway."

"Don't do anything foolish—Ray just caught us practically naked in the car. Mark is worried to death."

Joan and Monica slipped away. Ray Ivan stepped to Manny's side and smiled at Ellie. "Are you a friend of Molly's?"

"Ellie's my roommate," Manny purred in a low, silky voice. "She's here with Mark Blackwell."

Ellie smiled tightly. *Gee, thanks, friend.*

"Blackwell?" Ivan's eyebrows shot up. "I gather you are, er, close."

Embarrassment flooded over her and she floundered for something to say.

"They're practically married," Manny assured him, patting his arm.

MARK WANDERED OVER to a drink tray and picked up a martini, then scanned the room for Ivan. He needed to extend an apology for what had happened, and he wanted to get it over with. Not sure what he'd say when he did find him, Mark just prayed the right words would come to him. He removed the lipstick-stained handkerchief from his pocket. Between cat allergies and various mishaps, he'd have to remember to carry two hankies with him when Ellie was around. He used the soiled cloth to wipe the sweat from his forehead.

Raising his glass to take another sip, he glanced back to Ellie and choked on the liquid in his throat. Ray Ivan stood talking to her and an attractive brunette. He hurried over to the group as unobtrusively as possible.

"Blackwell!" Ivan boomed. "Glad to see you finally came—I mean, made it—er, good to see you, son." Mark felt the heat climb up his neck as he shook the senior partner's hand.

"Good to see you, sir."

Ivan gestured to the striking woman at his side. "I assume you've met Molly since she's your lovely fiancée's roommate."

So, she had another roommate. "No, I haven't had the pleasure—" His hand stopped in midair. "Did you say fiancée, sir?"

Mark and Ellie exchanged panicked glances, then spoke at the same time.

"I'm not really—"

"She's not really—"

Ivan raised his eyebrows. "What's that, Mark?"

Mark thought about the picture they'd presented earlier to his conservative partner who'd been married for forty years. Mark reached over to put an arm around Ellie's shoulders and squeezed her against him. "Yes, she is lovely, isn't she? Could I have a word with you in private, sir?"

"Certainly."

Mark loosened his grip on Ellie and steered the senior partner to a quiet doorway. "Sir, I want to apologize for what you saw—"

Ivan raised his hand and waved Mark's words away. "Perfectly natural for a man and his bride-to-be, son. When's the big day?"

Mark's mind raced. "Well, we really haven't discussed a day, sir."

"Molly told me you and Miss Sutherland met when she came to the office to paint your portrait a few days ago. Love at first sight, eh?" The older man chuckled. "You're a lucky man, Mark, with good taste. I like to see my partners settle down, become family men. It's important to the firm's image, you know." He winked at Mark, then turned to the room at large and stepped forward. "Everyone," he called, "may I have your attention?"

Dread ballooned in the pit of Mark's stomach as the room quieted.

"I'd like to propose a toast. To our new partner, Mr. Mark Blackwell, who has two reasons to celebrate tonight."

Mark's bowels twisted.

"Raise your glasses with me to honor him and his bride-to-be, Ms. Ellie Sutherland."

The room erupted into gasps and applause. Mark swayed, but caught himself on the door frame, then swung his gaze to Ellie. He pleaded for forgiveness with his eyes. A bewildered smile froze on her face as she nodded to those around her.

Mark soon found himself engulfed by well-wishers. Patrick seemed especially surprised and elbowed him. "You sly dog, what was all that nonsense the other day about remaining single?"

"What can I say?" Mark said, conjuring up a tight smile, his stomach cramping.

"Dinner's served," Patrick's wife announced.

Ellie watched Ray Ivan walk Manny to the door, and to her horror, plant a kiss on her roomie's smooth cheek. Manny waved to her gaily, and she raised her hand halfheartedly in response. Her mind still reeled when Mark took her arm. As they walked toward their table, she whispered, "An engagement wasn't part of the deal. What's going on?"

"I'll explain later," he muttered. "Just remember, I've got your cat."

Ellie reached for another rum and cola as they passed a drink tray and finished it before they were seated. He held out a chair for her at one of the six-person, cloth-covered tables and took the adjacent seat on the end. His leg nudging hers when he spread his napkin across his knee sent tremors through her body.

She knew the alcohol had affected her, but the events of the evening were taking their toll, as well. First, his assault on her senses in the car, then Manny showing up, and now everyone thought they were engaged. She nearly laughed out loud at the irony. She wondered what he would do if she stood on the table and announced that he'd hired her to make his mother hate her, and that a pregnant cat was the only reason she'd come with him tonight?

Well, not the only reason, she conceded, choosing a skewered scallop from a platter on the table. She studied his face as he talked to the man on his right. Mark was one great-looking man, and right now the pheromones were running in her favor. So what if his interest in her was short-lived? There were worse things than having a raging three-week affair with a gorgeous wealthy man.

Time to have some fun.

She slipped off her shoe and snaked her foot around his ankle. Mark jerked his head toward her a fraction, and seemed to stumble on his words, but continued speaking to his companion. Ellie smiled seductively, then worried his shin and calf with her traveling toes. Mark shot her a sharp glance, obviously trying to concentrate on his conversation. Popping the scallop into her mouth, she rolled it on her tongue suggestively. Mark swallowed visibly and shook his head as if in warning, then turned back to the man.

Smothering a giggle, she extended her left leg farther over her right and nudged his knee open. She ran her foot down the inside of his thigh. Suddenly, he jerked again, his hand grabbing her foot to halt its progress. She tried to pull away, but he held her steadfast, and suddenly his other hand claimed her foot, as well. His face was averted from her and he remained deep in conversation.

Teasingly, he swept his finger across the pad of her stockinged foot, sending shudders up Ellie's spine. Her toes crinkled in response, but he slowly and sensuously inserted a large finger between her big toe and its neighbor. Rhythmically, he explored the shallow valley, running the length of his finger in, then out, in, then out.

The ability, as well as the desire, to withdraw her plundered foot vanished. Ellie relaxed into her chair as much as possible without drawing attention to herself, then began squeezing her toes together, clasping his finger harder and harder. As the minutes passed, she grew moist between her thighs, imagining his strong fingers dipping elsewhere. As his finger became more forceful, she increased the pressure. Faster and faster he plunged. Ellie could feel her body pulse inside in tune with his finger's song. The tension mounted, mounted…

"OOOOoooooHHHHhhhhhhh!" she screamed, bringing her hand down upon the table with a solid smack. Every eye in the room turned to her, and even Mark seemed surprised, his ministrations halting momentarily.

"Are you all right, dear?" the woman next to her asked, leaning closer.

Ellie recovered, sitting ramrod straight. "Oh!" she repeated, slapping the table again, "Oh, boy, are these scallops good!" She popped several into her mouth to illustrate, smiling and nodding to everyone at her table, then waving assurance to Patrick's wife across the room. Every woman at the table lunged for a portion.

Afraid to look at Mark, Ellie kept her eyes turned away. What would he think of her now? She withdrew her ravaged foot from his relaxed hands and stretched her cramped toes. Who could have guessed learning to pick up pencils with her toes would come in handy one day?

When at last she chanced a glance at him, his eyes were still on her, slightly widened with an expression that asked, "Was that what I think it was?" She chewed on her bottom lip and nodded ever so slightly.

At her affirmation, amazement washed over Mark. He, too, had become aroused during their little game under the table, but he couldn't believe she'd really—

"As I was saying." The man to his right laid a hand on Mark's arm to resume their conversation. Mark frowned at him, and in the few seconds he broke eye contact with Ellie, she disappeared from sight. Confused, Mark craned his head to search the room, then noticed the tablecloth moving at her place setting. Then he felt her crawl over his feet. Mark stiffened in disbelief, then noticed other people at the table jump, then frown and shift in their seats. She was obviously traveling the length of the table.

He excused himself once again from the man bending his ear. With a quick glance around, Mark swallowed and, as inconspicuously as possible, bent over, then cautiously pulled up the white tablecloth.

For the second time tonight, he was treated to a mouthwatering view of Ellie's rump, but Mark didn't have time to stop and ponder his good fortune. "Ellie!" he whispered sharply. She had to back up, her rear coming very close to his face, in order to twist around and look over her shoulder.

"What?" she retorted, clearly inconvenienced.

"What the hell are you doing?" he whispered.

"Looking for my shoe," she said simply, slurring her words slightly.

"Get out from under there and I'll find it for you," he said, trying to remain patient.

Suddenly, two other heads joined them under the table, both male. "Is there a problem?" asked one fellow who had been paying rapt attention to Ellie all evening.

"No!" Mark barked.

"I can't find my shoe," Ellie said, pouting.

"Well, now," said the other man, tsk-tsking at Ellie, "that will never do."

Mark sighed in exasperation. "For God's sake, Ellie, get out from under there!"

But now nearly everyone at the table was peering beneath the cloth and asking if something was wrong.

Mark reached forward and grabbed Ellie by her upper arm, then steered her out backward. When she stood up and plopped down in her seat, her hairstyle a little worse for wear, Mark ground his teeth in frustration. Their table companions were slow in rejoining them topside, as if Ellie had found something wonderful under the table and they wanted to experience it, too.

"Is this what you're looking for?" The chatty fellow to his right held up a black pump. Sex appeal fairly dripped off the stiletto heel.

"Oh, thank you," Ellie said, grinning, then she reached across the china and crystal to retrieve it. The man looked curiously pleased, until his wife elbowed him sharply in the ribs.

Mark closed his eyes and counted to ten. When he opened them, Ellie was walking away from the table, presumably to find a bathroom, but wearing both shoes, thank goodness. He watched her hips sway, then suddenly realized nearly every man in the room feasted on the same sight. This woman packed a powerful punch.

Mark felt a ridiculous urge to follow her, lock the bathroom door, lift her onto a porcelain sink and wrap her legs around his waist. If a little foot flirting sent her into orbit, what kind of reaction could he elicit with no holds barred? And where would he find her tattoo? Shoulder? Hip? He swallowed. Bikini line?

A tap on his right shoulder startled him. A smiling waiter set a plate of exquisitely arranged salad in front of him, and he was glad to have his attention diverted for the time being. That woman was going to be the death of him, or at least his career. He would eventually need a wife who could entertain a group on this scale, but not one who could double as the entertainment.

Ellie returned a few minutes later, looking refreshed. She nodded at him when she took her seat, smiling brightly. He noticed the color in her cheeks seemed high, and he assumed it had something to do with the amount of rum she'd ingested since they'd arrived. Not that he blamed her, with everything that had happened. Engaged. How on earth was he going to get out of this mess?

She seemed a little flustered still, making small talk with the ladies at the table, one of them his secretary, Monica. He felt a sharp pang of guilt at the questions she had to answer. Yes, she was so proud of her fiancé for making partner. She patted his hand. No, they hadn't shopped for a ring yet. Yes, they planned to have several children. Mark choked on a cherry tomato, but was saved by the gabby man who pounded him hard between the shoulder blades.

Children? Mark patted his mouth with a linen napkin. Would he make a good father? Would Ellie make a good mother? He studied her profile as she spoke to someone across the table, nodding and smiling. She was a beauty, no doubt. Her features were elfin, small and chiseled. Her blond hair was cropped in short layers, a style only a woman with exquisite features could wear with panache. With her outgoing nature and easy smile, Mark suddenly knew she would be a wonderful mother—romping with her children, singing and dancing to keep them entertained, finger painting the walls if necessary. He smiled and Ellie turned to him at that instant, coming up short at something she read in his eyes. Mark blinked to clear his head and she visibly relaxed.

For the rest of the meal, Mark tried desperately to concentrate on anything but the woman beside him. He puzzled over the power she seemed to wield on his senses. This attraction—it seemed almost supernatural. Not one single aspect of Ellie Sutherland set her apart from any number of beautiful women he'd met, but in totality, she was sensational. Ellie defied science because her whole far outweighed the sum of her parts. The woman was walking synergy.

And he was completely taken by her.

Mark's hands shook slightly as alarms went off in his ears. He'd read about this in men's magazines—and it didn't bode well for his future as a bachelor. No sir, he wasn't about to don the albatross of commitment when he'd just reached a zenith in his career. Yet even as he nodded his head resolutely, Mark's chest clogged with dread when he thought about taking Ellie home and being alone with her. The answer? Stall as long as possible, of course.

"HOW MUCH LONGER?" Ellie whispered a few hours later, trying to smile. Only a few guests lingered over coffee. She could feel her eyelids dragging, threatening to close for good. She'd had no chance to talk to Mark about their abrupt engagement, and she wanted to be somewhat awake on the ride home.

Mark squinted at his watch. "You're right," he said. "We should be going."

They said their goodbyes to their hosts, and a few minutes later they were off.

She waited until they had driven a couple of miles in silence before she cleared her throat. "Well?" she asked.

Mark glanced sideways. "Well what?"

Ellie sighed. "Well, what the heck is going on?"

He passed a hand over his face and pinched the bridge of his nose, squinting. "Believe me, I was as surprised as you were at Ivan's announcement. He's old-fashioned and, after witnessing our little, er, display, he must have arrived at his own conclusion."

Manny's offhand comment to Ivan about she and Mark being "practically married" crossed Ellie's mind, but she didn't mention it. She angled her body toward him. "Why didn't you correct him?"

In the dim interior, she saw his shoulders fall in defeat. "He started telling me how important it was to him that all his partners be settled down, you know—family men—and I couldn't tell him the truth. Next thing I knew, he was toasting our engagement."

Ellie's heart drooped. Mark Blackwell's career meant more to him than anything else in the world. Maybe she'd caught his eye, or rather, his crotch, for a few days because of these pheromones, but she was fooling herself if she thought she'd ever be able to compete with his first love—his job. He had no room for a woman in his life, least of all a woman like her.

"I'm sorry you got dragged into this," he said, reaching over to grasp her hand. "It'll die down in a few weeks, and I'll simply say we broke it off." He squeezed her fingers. "By the way, Ivan seemed taken with your roommate Molly. Why haven't you mentioned her before?"

His hand was so warm, his touch so welcome. Ellie said nothing and just stared at his fingers. "It never came up," she mumbled distractedly. Just a few hours ago she'd told herself to seize the moment. And that was before she knew he could induce her to orgasm, fully dressed and in a crowded room. She felt heat travel up her face. Would he kiss her good-night, or had she scared him off completely? Surely he'd guessed how long she'd been celibate if toe sex sent her over the edge.

When he parked in front of her building, he hesitated slightly. "It's okay," Ellie rushed to assure him. "You don't have to walk me up." She scrambled to loosen her seat belt and find her purse.

"No," he said, turning off the ignition. "I want to."

They walked quickly and quietly into her building and up the stairs. Ellie's heart pounded furiously as she fumbled with the key. Mark took it from her, then unlocked the door easily. The door swung inward, creaking, and darkness stretched before them. Was it her imagination, or had her bed suddenly become a living, breathing entity, palpitating and calling to them from down the hall and behind a closed door?

"Coffee?" she squeaked, flipping on the kitchen light.

"Sure," Mark answered. "A shot of caffeine for the drive home won't hurt." He smiled at her, lowering himself into a kitchen chair. She rummaged nervously for a filter, and managed to get the coffeemaker going within a few tense minutes. "Well," she said brightly, turning to face Mark. "What an interesting evening." She bent to remove her shoes, nudging them under a chair as she rubbed one throbbing arch.

"Yes," Mark agreed in a choked voice. She glanced up to see his eyes riveted on her stockinged feet, and she immediately realized her mistake. She watched as Mark moved in slow motion, standing and reaching for her, pulling her into his arms. Lifting her face to his, she offered her lips to him. His mouth descended on hers, his lips moving hungrily, as if he were a starved man and she a bountiful fare.

Ellie's knees weakened and she swayed into him, twining her arms around his neck for support. He groaned and his voice vibrated inside her mouth, inciting her to respond in kind. Drawing her against him, he lifted her off the ground to settle fully against his arousal. Wild barbs of desire knifed through her as Ellie inhaled the scent of his skin, felt his need for her pushing against her stomach. Mark's hands slid over her back and waist, gripping, massaging, caressing. She felt her nipples bud and bloom against his chest, and raised one leg to hook around his thigh. Immediately, his hands sought her lace-covered rear, exposed by her movement. His breathing became more ragged, until he finally raised his head.

"Ellie," he whispered hoarsely. "I'd like to see that tattoo."

She smiled languidly, desire and...love?...expanding her heart. She might regret this tomorrow, but tomorrow lay a world away, and tonight she needed to live. "I can't walk unless you put me down," she said, referring to her dangling toes.

In response, he swung her up into his arms. "Where's your bedroom?" he asked, his eyes dark with passion. Ellie directed him, her arms still around his neck, her pulse beating out of control during their brief journey. Mark lay her on the bed, then left her long enough to close the door. The only light came from a small window. She watched him move across the room, his movements unhurried. When he returned, he was removing his tie.

"Let me," she said, reaching for him. She sat up, and with deft fingers, made short work of his shirt buttons, then stripped the garment from his back. How many times had she thought of him standing before her like this, bare-chested, the way he looked in his office when she'd taken his picture? He was breathtaking. His hands stilled her when she moved to his waistband.

"I want to see you," he breathed. "I have to see you." Blazing a trail across her skin, his hands enveloped her, moving around to find the zipper at her back. Ellie heard the slide of the enclosure giving way, and felt the fabric fall from her shoulders. Mark leaned toward her, easing her onto the soft comforter, and slipped the dress to her waist. Instantly he found her lace-covered breasts, kissing and suckling through the fabric. Ellie moaned and arched her back, thrusting the small peaks up for his onslaught. Without taking his mouth from her, he lifted her hips and eased the dress down her legs. She heard the whoosh of the fabric as it landed somewhere on the floor.

When Mark drew back long enough to take in the sight of

Ellie lying before him in black bra, panties, garter belt and stockings, he had to clench his teeth in resolve. *Hold on, man, hold on.* The fact that his body had been in a near-perpetual state of arousal throughout the evening convinced him his present control bordered on tenuous, at best. Slender and smooth, she was beautifully arched to reveal endless valleys and peaks to explore. From her shapely collarbone to the divot in her flat stomach, to the valley between her thighs hidden by her raised knees. Where to begin? Hours seemed woefully inadequate to sample Ellie's gifts, yet his body told him he had scant minutes left.

A loud groan escaped him as he stretched out beside her, capturing her mouth in a kiss that threatened to be his undoing when she wriggled against him. She turned in his arms and he managed to undo her bra, sending her small, full breasts tumbling into his hands. He dipped his head to taste their richness and grew heady from the overwhelming desire flooding his body. The intoxicating scent of her skin took him near the brink. Such exquisite torture he'd never had to endure before, and Mark knew he couldn't take much more.

Her small fingers splayed across his back then down to his waist, struggling briefly with his zipper, then helping him drag the pants down with her feet. He kicked them off, his breath leaving him when Ellie reached to clasp his stiff manhood. She stroked him within milliseconds of exploding. He grabbed her hand to still her movements.

"I'm not superhuman," he groaned, rolling over to lie between her legs. Mark took a few deep breaths to steady himself, then undid her garter belt. Thoughts of slowly rolling her thigh-high stockings down and off her pretty feet flickered through his mind, but he knew he'd be lucky to remove her panties in one piece. Hot need billowed in him, and he tugged her underwear down hurriedly, raising her knees to speed the process. A glimpse of dense dark blond curls registered in his mind before he returned to the cradle between her legs. His heat-seeking member rushed to her entrance.

"Mark," she whispered, "I'm not protected."

Sanity flashed and he lowered his head. "Of course," he

said, then gritted his teeth. Sighing, he gently rolled off her and lay still, fighting to gain control. "I'm sorry," he said. "I lost my head."

Ellie sat up and reached to open a drawer in her nightstand. "I have regular and extra-large," she announced, rummaging through its contents.

Mark bounced upright. "Whichever you think."

She peered at him, a smile playing on her lips. "Extra-large."

It seemed to take hours for her to roll the condom into place, and Mark shook with his need to make love to her. At last, she lay back and pulled him to her, her neck arched, leaving it exposed for his kisses. He licked at the hollow beneath her chin, then found an earlobe to nuzzle as he eased himself into her warmth. Their moans mingled as he stilled, taking a few seconds to experience her. She tightened around him and Mark tensed to hold on a little longer. Just long enough for her to—

A long scream escaped her lips and she clawed his back in the throes of her passion. Amazement registered for an instant, but quickly gave way to gratitude as he began to move within her, feeling free now to expend himself. The mewling sounds she moaned into his ear urged him on. He felt his senses soar, his body tense in preparation for release, then shuddered again and again as ecstasy delivered him from his suffering.

Not until minutes later, as he lay nuzzling a pert nipple and feeling her heart beat against his cheek, did Mark realize he still hadn't noticed a tattoo.

MARK OPENED HIS EYES, disoriented at first. Then he remembered he slept in Ellie's bed. He turned his head to see the clock. Three in the morning.

Usually he lingered with a lover until morning, but now he had an overwhelming need to go home. Or more to the point, to get out of Ellie's bed. The walls of her bedroom, covered with eclectic groupings of prints and various bric-a-brac, suddenly seemed to close in on him. As noiselessly as possible, he got up, gathered his clothing and dressed. He winced at the sight of the wadded pile he'd made of the dress in which she'd bewitched him and every man at the party. Carefully, he picked it up and folded it neatly, placing it on the dressing table.

Mark walked back to the bed, planning to kiss her, but instead stopped to watch her sleep, her breasts easing up and down with her deep, even breathing. A tingling sensation settled in his chest and made his own breathing difficult. After a last glance, he opened her bedroom door, stepped into the hall and closed it behind him.

Silently, he retraced his steps to the front door, then stopped when he realized someone was unlocking the door from the hallway. His heart raced. A burglar? Then Mark relaxed. It was probably just one of Ellie's roommates.

Molly stepped inside, then her eyes widened in fear, a key dangling from a manicured hand raised to defend herself.

Mark rushed to explain in a loud whisper, "I'm Mark Blackwell, Ellie's, uh, friend. We met earlier this evening." He smiled apologetically and pointed to the door. "I was just leaving." He stepped into the hall and closed the door behind him.

The short drive north seemed interminable, not just because Mark fought falling asleep, but because his big lonely bed no longer seemed so inviting. Ellie's sleep-softened face came to him, and her plump nipples sitting atop her breasts like puffs of pink whipped cream. He moistened his lips involuntarily, and nearly ran off the shoulder of the highway. Loud music from his stereo and a full-blast air conditioner got him home safely.

The clock on his nightstand read ten minutes past four. Mark began to strip off his clothes again, then grimaced as his shirt raked across his uncomfortably tender back. One glance in the mirror showed why, and his mouth fell open. Bright red welts and a few tiny drops of dried blood marked his back where Ellie had clawed him in her passion. Too tired to register more than passing astonishment, Mark climbed into bed. He had just closed his eyes, when his nose began to itch. He rubbed a knuckle over it, annoyed. At the same time, something warm and furry touched his foot. Mark shouted and sat up in the bed, scrambling for the light.

A muffled yowl sounded under the covers. Mark jumped out of the bed and watched the lump travel beneath the covers to the pillow where his head had rested. Esmerelda poked her orange head out to peer at him angrily.

''Scat,'' Mark barked, buck-naked and waving his arms. The cat blinked. A fit of sneezing seized him, sending him in search of a handkerchief. ''Get out of my bed,'' he commanded, gesturing again. Esmerelda yawned. When Mark reached for her, she flattened her ears against her head, and flung an evil hiss toward him. He jumped back, wondering if the beast had been declawed. Deciding he'd rather not find out tonight, Mark tramped noisily down the hall to a guest room, sneezing the entire way.

As he punched down a lumpy pillow, Mark cursed sourly. He'd left one unsettling she-cat only to come home to another.

7

ELLIE AWOKE with the most delicious feeling in her bones. Her hazy mind struggled to remember what event had triggered this languid, buoyant state. She'd won the lottery...no. Her paintings were being offered at an exclusive auction...no. She'd slept with Mark Blackwell...

Ellie's eyes popped open. Yes! A tentative lifting of her knee triggered soreness in several little-used muscles, and she grimaced. Sitting up and pulling the sheet around her breasts, she scanned the room for evidence of Mark's presence. Her dress had been folded neatly. The indention in the pillow next to hers felt cold.

A foreign scent assailed her nostrils. Sex. Their fragrances lingered on the morning air. Ellie pulled her pillow higher against the headboard, and reclined against it with a sigh. On impulse, she pulled the other pillow over her face and inhaled his aroma, then settled it across her stomach. Her heart raced. Now what?

A knock at her door stymied her rising panic. "Ellie, are you up?" Manny's voice was soft but insistent.

"Just a minute," she called, reaching to pull a short terry robe from its home on the bedpost. She still wore her stockings and loosened garter belt, although the garments had twisted uncomfortably. She tied the frayed robe belt around her waist and tucked the ends under her hips, then straightened the covers around her. "You can come in."

"Breakfast in bed," Manny announced grandly, entering with a laden bed tray.

Ellie grinned. "And what, may I ask, is the occasion?"

Manny smiled wide, his eyes knowing, as he set the tray

on her lap. "Your introduction back into a morally bankrupt society."

"What makes you think—"

"Don't bother denying it." Manny held up his hand. "I passed Mark on his way out this morning." He smiled, triumphant. "So?" he prompted, settling in cross-legged at the foot of the bed.

"So what?" she said, taking a bite of toast.

"For heaven's sake, give me the details."

As Ellie chewed, the events of the entire evening began to resurface in florid detail. She winced.

"Come on, 'fess up," Manny urged. "You set Ray Ivan straight about your engagement, right?"

Ellie bit into her bottom lip.

Manny's eyes rolled back. "You didn't?"

"There didn't seem to be a good time to mention it."

"Unbelievable," he said, shaking his head. "Your life is better than a soap opera. So tell me, how did you go from being a fake fiancée—" he leaned over to retrieve a stray earring from the floor "—to a genuine seductress?" He dangled the bauble for emphasis.

The quick sip of juice did not lessen the heat that rushed to Ellie's face. "He brought me home, then I asked him in for coffee, and the next thing I knew, he was carrying me in here." She shrugged.

"Well, that explains the full pot of cold coffee," Manny said sarcastically, then he brightened. "Was it earth-shattering?"

Ellie tried to hold back a grin, but couldn't. "I can't remember having two really great orgasms in one night."

"Two? I'm impressed. Didn't think Mr. Republican had it in him."

"Well, one occurred at the dinner party—"

"What?"

"It's not what you think. We were fully clothed, and sitting down. After you left, I got a little tipsy and started playing footsie with his...well, anyway, he grabbed my foot and the next thing I know, I'm screaming like a banshee in the middle of the appetizer course.''

"You got off on him playing with your *feet?* You were in worse shape than I thought, woman.'' He howled with laughter, pounding his knees with his fists. Wiping his eyes, he suddenly sobered. "Has anything like that ever happened before? I mean, do you think the pheromones had something to do with your reaction?''

Ellie took another drink. "No, it's never happened before, and yes, I think it has everything to do with the pills.'' She hadn't meant to sound so glum.

"Did Ray Ivan ask about me?''

"Manny, you're playing with fire.''

"I think it's fun.''

"He's a sweet, *straight* old widower. If you took off your skirt, he'd probably have heart failure.''

He waved off her concern. "It doesn't matter, El, I'll never see the man again. By the way—'' he wagged his eyebrows ''—when will you see Mark?''

Ellie gasped and looked at the clock. "I have to be at his office for a sitting in forty-five minutes! What am I going to say to him after last night?''

"Hmm.'' Manny tapped his cheek in mock deep thought. "How about 'thank you'?''

"THANK YOU,'' Ellie said as Mark held the door to the office building open wide enough to allow her to wheel in her bike. They'd arrived at the same time, Mark rounding the corner from the parking garage just in time to see Ellie ride up in front of the building.

He smiled stiffly at her, feeling awkward. She certainly looked chipper today in pink bike shorts and a glove-fitting zebra-print tank top. But then, she didn't have to apply salve to her battle wounds, then don a starched dress shirt for a sitting. Her dangling black claw earrings were a staunch reminder of the injuries she'd inflicted last night. Still, he had to admit it was the greatest sex he'd experienced. He rolled his shoulders, trying to ease his taut skin as they walked through the reception area to the elevators. Neither of them spoke on the ride up. She looked completely at ease, and he didn't have a clue what to say about last night. Finally, she broke the silence.

"How's Esmerelda?" she asked, reaching over to extract a long orange hair from his shirtsleeve.

Mark frowned and brushed his sleeve with his hand, dislodging more hairs. He promptly sneezed. "Your cat has taken up residence in my bedroom. In my bed, to be more precise."

"Really? She hardly ever leaves her bed at night. She must be under a lot of stress, being in new surroundings. Or there could be something wrong with the room where you put her bed."

A flash of annoyance surfaced, but he forced patience into his voice. "Your feline already has the run of my house. What could possibly be wrong?" The bell sounded and the doors slid open.

Ellie stepped off the elevator and guided her bicycle toward his office. "The room where you put her bed, what color is it?"

"Blue."

Ellie smacked her handlebars with one hand and nodded. "That's it—she hates blue."

Mark took a mighty breath and rubbed one temple. His aggravated allergies were giving him a headache. And now the allergen didn't approve of his decor.

"Hey, you two," Patrick called, walking toward them, smiling.

"Oh, damn," Mark muttered, then donned an appropriate smile. "Hey, yourself," he said as Patrick drew nearer. "Nice party."

"You two were the spotlight," Patrick insisted, then turned to Ellie. "And I can't tell you what a pleasure it is to meet the woman who's tamed this maverick. I never thought I'd see the day Mark Blackwell settled down."

Ellie shrugged and nodded, her expression one of agreeable shock. "Amazing, isn't it?"

"Actually, Patrick—" Mark began.

"Good morning, all!" Ray Ivan boomed from down the hall. "Well, if it isn't the happy couple." He walked up and patted Ellie's arm, then clapped Mark on his raw back, sending spasms of pain down his spine.

Mark inhaled sharply. "Good morning, sir."

Ivan pointed to the canvas and paint-stained tackle box strapped to the panniers of Ellie's bike. "Working on the portrait, today, are we?"

She smiled wide, her eyes bright. "We sure are."

Mark's partner nodded agreeably, then said. "Listen, kids, let me know as soon as you set a wedding date, because it's been my policy to start a brokerage account for my married employees as a college fund for their children. Right, Patrick?"

"Right," Beecham said.

"Children?" Mark and Ellie said in unison.

"Monica told me last night that you plan to have a big family," Ivan said.

Mark remembered Ellie's words at the dinner table and felt his underarms grow moist. They'd very nearly started a family last night. He looked at Ellie, and she looked back, eyes wide.

Ivan laughed, slapping Mark's back again, twice. "Didn't mean to put you on the spot. Just let me know, Blackwell. And congratulations again, you picked a beauty." He winked at Ellie, then engaged Patrick in a conversation as they walked away.

"I need some aspirin," Mark said, moving toward his office.

Once the door closed behind them, Ellie took a deep breath. Trying to sound casual as she lowered her kickstand, she said, "Why did you leave in the middle of the night?"

"Huh?" Mark swallowed the pills he'd shaken into his palm. "Oh, well, I knew I had to come in here this morning, and there were some papers at home I wanted to go over." His voice sounded vague. "And don't forget about the cat," he added, his eyes darting around the room. "I had to check on her."

Ellie frowned slightly. He wasn't very convincing. Obviously he preferred hurrying home to handle work details to dawdling in her bed. A career man, through and through.

"By the way," he said, "I ran into Molly while I was leaving your apartment. I didn't see a third bedroom. Where does she stay?"

Ellie's mind raced. "Uh, she stays in Manny's room."

"Ivan will be heartbroken," he said.

"Oh, they have an open relationship," she improvised. "You never see them together." She swallowed, then scrambled to change the subject. "This session shouldn't take too long. All I really need to do is a composition sketch."

"Sure," he said in a distracted tone. "Where do you want me?"

They locked gazes. Ellie's heart pounded as snatches of their lovemaking spun through her mind.

Mark cleared his throat. "We really should talk—"

The phone rang, breaking the spell.

"I'll get set up," she explained, gesturing to her supplies. She kicked herself mentally. Mark Blackwell was the epitome of her father in his younger days. Hadn't she always promised herself she deserved more than her mother had put up with? So why on earth was she entertaining thoughts of a future with him? It had to be the pheromones.

She heard Mark push a button. "Mark Blackwell," he said, all business.

"Marcus!" his mother's voice screeched over the speaker-phone.

Ellie watched as Mark rounded his desk to sit down, worry in his face. "Mom? Where are you calling from? Is everything all right?"

"No!" she continued more shrilly than before. "How can everything be all right when I arrive at Stella's house for bridge and she announces to me that my own son is getting married?"

"Mom—"

"And *please* don't tell me it's to that fruitcake you brought to the reunion. I lived in the bathroom for three days—"

Mark stabbed the intercom button and picked up the receiver, then spun around in the chair, his back to Ellie, murmuring low into the phone.

Oh, great, Ellie thought, the woman *does* hate me. And the only thing she needed in her life less than a workaholic boyfriend was a workaholic mama's boy.

"Mom, don't worry," she heard him say. "It's all a big mistake that got way out of hand." He paused. "Mom, if I were getting married, don't you think you'd be the first to know?"

Probably even before the bride, Ellie mused as she unpacked her supplies.

"Yeah, you can reassure Stella she doesn't have to buy an expensive wedding gift, after all. I have to go, Mom. I'll call you later." He hung up and sighed. "Sorry about that." He stood and walked toward her, shrugging sheepishly. "Mom is a little excitable, if you hadn't noticed."

"Oh, really?" Ellie said, injecting a hint of sarcasm into her voice. "Did you set her straight about our little pretend engagement?"

He did have the good grace to blush. "I told her it was all a mistake."

"She didn't sound like the same woman who's desperate for you to get married."

He smiled wryly, shrugging again. "I guess when it comes right down to it, she doesn't want another woman in my life."

"More to the point, she doesn't want *me* in your life."

Mark pursed his lips. "That's my fault. I shouldn't have asked you to pull all those stunts at the reunion. I guess my behavior was childish." He looked into her eyes, and reached over to touch her hand. "I'm sorry, Ellie."

His voice and expression were genuine. Ellie blinked furiously to stem her welling tears. "All those stunts" were natural events.

"Where were we?" he asked. Restlessly, he shoved a hand through his light brown hair, leaving it disheveled. For a few seconds, she felt sorry for him. His life had been turned upside down inside a week of meeting her. But then, so had hers.

"You messed it up," she said, reaching up to smooth the

errant strands. His hair felt silky and thick, fresh from a recent shower, she guessed. Memories of twining her hands through it last night came to her, but she brushed them aside. He stood perfectly still, his eyes locked with hers while she fussed with his hair. Desire lurked in the depths of his forest green eyes. And what else? Affection? What might her traitorous eyes be revealing to him? "There," she said, giving his hair a final pat and easing the moment.

"I think we should talk about last night," he said.

"Well, I am curious about the blood on the sheet."

Mark gestured loosely over his shoulder. "I didn't realize your nails were so long." He smiled and added, "Or so effective."

Embarrassment sent heat rushing to her face. Ellie gasped, covering her mouth. "I did that?"

He nodded. "You were the only other person in the bed."

"I'm so sorry, are you okay?"

Now he laughed. "I only regret I won't be in senior gym class tomorrow to gloat in the locker room." He reached for her, and she went to him, her kiss a peace offering.

The phone rang again. They parted. Mark glanced at the display, and reached for the handset. "It's Ray," he said. "Hello, sir." He paused. "Yes, she's still here."

Ellie's eyebrows shot up.

Mark listened for a few seconds, then surprise registered on his face. "Hold on and I'll ask." Mark pushed a button to mute the sound and said, "He wants to take Molly to dinner. Can you arrange it?"

Ellie's stomach dipped. "But Manny—"

"I thought you said they had an open relationship."

"I, uh…Molly's not exactly your partner's type, Mark."

"Okay, she's younger than Ray by a couple of decades, but you have to admit she's showing a little wear herself. He's a young and wealthy sixty-two. She could do worse."

She floundered. "But she hardly knows him…I don't think she'd be comfortable."

"So we'll double."

Her heart pounded. "As in a double date?"

"Sure. It would give me a chance to get to know Ray more informally. And maybe we can find a way to explain away our pseudo-engagement."

"I'm not sure—"

"Help me out, Ellie. I need to redeem myself for that little car-necking incident, which was really your fault, by the way."

"*My* fault?"

He leaned toward her and nuzzled her earlobe. "It wouldn't have happened if you weren't so damned irresistible."

Ellie's pulse jumped erratically. He was right—the episode before the party *had* been her fault. All roads led back to the pheromone pills. "Well…"

He pushed a button to retrieve his partner. "How about the four of us going to dinner? The Lexington Diner? Tonight?" Mark looked at Ellie for affirmation and she nodded resolutely. "Ellie will talk to Molly and get it all set up. I'll pick up the girls and we'll meet you there around seven."

"Thanks," he said to Ellie after he'd hung up. "Ivan hasn't dated at all since his wife passed away. This is a big step for him."

If he only knew how big. Ellie coughed. "I have to go to Underground this afternoon to stand in for an artist friend," she said apologetically. "I guess I'd better get started here."

"Explain to me again what you'll be doing today," he said distractedly.

The Puritan-white canvas she withdrew begged for paint. She loved the faintly pungent odor of newly dried gesso. "I'll be applying a base coat of thin oil paint to develop a working composition—what objects are placed where in the painting." She gestured to the canvas with a dry paintbrush for emphasis.

"I thought it was just me in the painting," he said, grinning.

That smile of his threatened to be her undoing. "It *is* just you, but the background will also have its place in the painting. And the size of your shoulders, face, etcetera, is very important."

His grin deepened. "How low are you going?"

Ellie rolled her eyes. "Just to your chest, Mark." Not that

she wouldn't enjoy painting a full-length portrait of him, and nude, at that. In art school she'd drawn professional nude models who cut a less impressive figure than Mark Blackwell.

"Anyway, the important thing today is to sort out the colors and placement. Then I can begin the detailed work. By the way, the thinned-down paint I'll use now will dry quickly, but once I start layering in color, I'll be using long-drying oils. At that point, it's going to be difficult to transport the canvas," she smiled, suddenly fidgety. "Especially on a bike."

He looked confused. "So?"

Ellie sighed. She hated doing this, it would seem as if she was trying to get him back to her place. "So, since I don't have a studio to work in, I'll have to set up the easel in my apartment and ask you to come there when I need you to, uh…sit." Her face burned, but the situation couldn't be helped.

"And how often would I get to come and…sit?" he asked, leaning close. His dark green eyes danced merrily.

"Not much at first, but then about every other d-day."

His face fell. "Is that all? I've got a better idea. Why don't you set up at my place? I've got plenty of room, and you could take care of—I mean, check in on your cat." He stopped for a moment, concern on his face. "Is it a problem getting to my house that often? I'd hate for you to have to take a taxi every time."

"No," Ellie said slowly, thoughtfully. "I could ride my bike to the train, take the train to the Dunwoody station, then ride the short distance to your house. It's only a couple of blocks." Ellie's mind spun. It did seem like the perfect solution. And she missed Esmerelda terribly.

Mark nodded. "Good, then it's settled."

"But I'd have to be there during the day," Ellie warned.

"I'll give you a key," he said simply. "No big deal."

Sure, Ellie thought miserably. Obviously he didn't perceive their working together in an intimate setting as a big deal. And why would he? He didn't intend for their "relationship" to go anywhere.

Of course, she had more immediate problems to deal with. Like matchmaking between Mark's partner and her transvestite roommate.

8

"*This* I'm not sure about," Manny said, drumming his painted fingernails on the kitchen table.

"Me, neither," Ellie admitted, sorting through the junk mail. "But you owe me one for leading Ray Ivan to believe Mark and I are engaged."

Manny threw his hands in the air. "I was only trying to save your reputation. He jumped to his own conclusion."

"Okay, okay. Go to dinner as Molly and you can help us explain the misunderstanding. Then you can make excuses the next time Ray Ivan calls." She lifted a finger in warning. "But no funny stuff."

Manny reached over to toy with a rose petal that had dropped onto the table's surface from the bouquet of a dozen in the delivered vase. "The man does have class," he said, fingering the card with "Molly" written on it. "I take it you haven't told Mark about the real me?"

Ellie chewed the corner of her lip. "No."

His mouth tightened. "I can't blame you. He'd die if he knew he'd come within a hundred feet of a drag queen."

"Manny, Mark's a big boy raised in a big city—he's not *that* naive. But I didn't want to divulge details about your life to a man who was a stranger little more than a week ago." She stood and tossed a handful of envelopes in the trash can. "And once the painting is finished and I'm out of pills, he'll be a stranger again."

"Why do I feel a Barry Manilow song coming on?"

"Look," Ellie said in exasperation. "I need to know if you can pull this off tonight."

"*Moi?* I've been a woman nearly as long as you have, El.

Of course I can pull this off.'' He brightened at the challenge. "It'll be fun."

Warning bells sounded in her ears at his exuberance. Manny loved nothing better than performing—she hoped he didn't outdo himself.

Indeed, when Mark picked them up, a bewigged Manny looked a picture of cool, tall, slender femininity in a short wrap skirt and fitted jacket. Ellie, on the other hand, was sweating profusely in her red silk shift by the time they reached the restaurant. She hadn't expected Mark to recognize Manny— she sometimes had to look closely herself to believe the meta- morphosis—but still she was a nervous wreck.

The Lexington Diner enjoyed the reputation of being one of the swankiest eateries in the upscale area of Phipps Plaza. Not only was the menu famous, but the establishment also boasted a celebrated orchestra that played big-band tunes be- hind a large dance floor. According to Mark, all the attorneys at his firm held memberships.

Ray Ivan sat waiting for the group at a secluded table. Everyone exchanged pleasantries. "You look stunning, my dear,'' he crooned to Manny, standing to pull out his chair. The older man looked flushed and excited. Ellie noted the half- empty wine bottle on the table with a shiver of premonition.

"Thank you," Manny responded, his voice honeyed.

The waiter brought more wine posthaste, and Mark ordered appetizers. Ellie didn't take her eyes off the couple across from her, and concentrated hard to hear every word.

"Molly, what do you do for a living?'' Ray asked.

Manny smiled coquettishly. "I'm a performer."

"A singer?'' He seemed quite pleased.

"And a dancer," Manny confirmed.

Ray leaned in to Manny's ear. Ellie leaned forward to listen. "I should have known by those legs," she heard him say, his words slightly slurred.

"Oh, my!'' Manny jumped, slapping playfully at Ray's hand beneath the table.

"Ellie,'' Mark whispered, "didn't your mother ever tell you

not to eavesdrop? Let's dance and leave them alone for a few minutes.''

''But—''

''Come on.'' He stood and tugged her along behind him.

Thoughts of a masquerading Manny were swept away when Mark pulled her to him in a slow, close waltz. She fused her curves to his hollows, tucking her head beneath his chin, and gave herself up to his liquid movements. He was a wonderful dancer, graceful and strong. She loved the feel of his muscles moving against her, his hips melded to hers, guiding her to the low throb of the music. His hand stroked her lower back, stirring volcanic reactions in her midsection.

''You smell wonderful,'' he breathed into her ear. ''Can I take you home with me?''

Ellie winced. She was oozing pheromones again. *There's nothing quite so romantic as an old-fashioned synthetic chemical reaction.* She lifted her head. ''What about Molly?''

''If things go well, and it looks like they will, I suspect Ray will want to see her home.''

Worry pooled in her stomach. ''I didn't expect Ray to be so…taken with her so quickly.''

''Why not? He's lonely, and she's a striking woman. Let's just let nature take its course.''

Right now at that table, nature is being stood on its ear. Ellie bit her tongue hard.

''So you'll sleep in my bed tonight?'' he murmured.

Ellie lowered her chin to hide her eyes. She was falling for this man, and setting herself up for a fantastic tailspin. ''Let's just let nature take its course,'' she said, settling into his broad chest.

When she opened her eyes a few seconds later, she saw that Manny and Ray had joined the dancers on the floor. Manny held himself rigidly, but Ray's hands were roaming freely. When he grabbed a handful of Manny's rear end, Ellie missed a beat and stepped on Mark's foot.

''Ow,'' he said, chuckling.

''Sorry. We'd better get back to our table—I'm starved.''

She tugged him back to their chairs, and, thankfully, Manny and Ray followed suit.

The waiter came around to take their entrée orders and delivered yet another bottle of wine on the house. Ellie lost count of the glasses Mark's partner downed. When the saucers of escargot arrived, everyone dug in but Ray, who appeared to be well on his way to becoming smashed.

Mark leaned over to whisper to Ellie. "I've never seen Ivan drink like this—he must be nervous."

Ellie nodded, glanced at Manny and swallowed a snail whole. His left eyelash was coming unglued and flapped precariously when he blinked. She looked over at Mark. He, too, had noticed and was studying Manny closely.

"Um, Molly," Ellie said, trying to keep alarm out of her voice.

Manny looked up and Ellie winked hard at him several times, then wagged her eyebrows.

"Is something wrong, Ellie?" Ray asked, exaggerated concern evident in his blurry eyes.

"I, uh…" Ellie's mind raced. "I need to go to the bathroom, and I need Molly to come with me." She jumped up, grabbed Manny by the forearm and dragged him away from the table.

"What is it now?" Manny demanded.

"You're losing an eyelash," she hissed, herding him toward the lounge.

He reached up to finish yanking it off. "Damn, you can't find good adhesive anymore. I've got more in my purse—it'll just take a minute."

They shuffled into the bathroom where Ellie wet a towel to hold to her perspiring face.

Manny leaned into the mirror, carefully reapplying the lash. "Gee, El, Mark's partner is as horny as the brass section of the Atlanta Symphony."

She threw him a sarcastic look. "And you're complaining?"

"Let's just say what little appeal the man *had* evaporated

a vineyard ago. And I don't know how I'm going to get rid of him.''

"Maybe our best strategy would be to wait for him to pass out.''

"And when do we get to the part about your engagement being a farce?''

"Even if we tell him, he won't remember tomorrow.''

"You're right, which is why I'm going to tell him to kiss off.''

Ellie's eyes bulged. "You can't! You have to let him down easy so he won't hold it against Mark. You and I got Mark into this mess, we have to see it through.''

Manny pointed a long nail at her. "Let's get this straight—I'm doing this for you, not Mark. And believe me, you can't be gentle with men like Ray Ivan. He'll have to be hit over his balding head, or he'll be calling me from now on. This has gone too far. I think we need to tell Mark the truth.''

Ellie's throat constricted. "You mean, about you?'' Manny's occupation and alter identity would not be within Mark Blackwell's scope of understanding. And she didn't want Manny to be offended by a confrontation.

His face fell. "Are you ashamed of me?''

"Oh, no, Manny,'' she rushed to assure him. "But Mark is pretty conservative. He might not be very accepting.''

"Then let's get Ray away from the table and broaden Mr. Blackwell's horizons.''

Ellie felt faint as they left the ladies' room. The only guaranteed outcome of this evening would be a retraction of Mark's invitation to share his bed tonight. Manny stopped at a pay phone outside the lounge and dialed the restaurant's number, asked for Ray Ivan to be paged, then left the handset lying on its side.

"We're back,'' Manny said brightly as they approached the table.

"Are you okay?'' Mark asked Ellie when she claimed her seat. "You look a little pale.''

She mumbled she was fine, and took a long drink of wine for courage.

The maître d' appeared. "Mr. Ivan, a phone call for you. Right this way."

Ray straightened his suit, and managed to walk away with only a slight stagger.

The entrées had arrived during their stint in the bathroom. Ellie let a few seconds of silence pass watching Mark eat two bites of rare steak. Her salmon sat untouched.

Manny cleared his throat violently and frowned at her, nodding toward Mark's bent head.

"Mark," Ellie said, moistening her lips. "We have something to tell you."

"What?" he asked, taking a swallow of wine, then proceeding to carve off another cube of prime rib.

She looked at Manny, and he nodded encouragement. Ellie gripped the napkin in her lap into tight fists. "Well, the truth is—"

"The truth is," said Manny in his own voice, "looks can be deceiving."

Mark stared at Manny and blinked, his lips parting slowly. He leaned forward, squinting, then his eyes bulged. "M-Manny?"

Manny lifted a manicured hand in a small wave. "How's it hanging, Mark?"

Mark dropped his silverware with a loud clatter, and felt the blood drain from his face. "Oh…my…God." He gripped the chair arms and gaped at them for interminable seconds. "You're telling me—" His voice was high and shaky. He stopped and looked around, then cleared his throat and began again, this time speaking low and deliberately. "You're telling me I set my partner up with a *man?*"

Ellie winced and Manny nodded.

Mark gripped his head with both hands. "This can't be happening." He looked around hopefully. "Am I on 'Candid Camera'? Please tell me I am." Blood pounded in his ears and he felt faint. He jerked his head around to look at Ellie. "Why the devil didn't you *tell* me?"

"I tried, but you said you needed to make amends for us being naked in the car—"

"*I* wasn't naked—"

"Technically, neither was I—"

"Kids," Manny snarled, "we don't have time for this. Here he comes, and he already asked me to go home with him." Their heads pivoted to see Ray striding toward the table, having eyes only for Manny.

"You have to get out of here," Mark hissed to Manny. "Right now!"

"That won't keep him from calling me and sending flowers," Manny insisted. "I'll have to hurt his feelings sooner or later. We have to nip this in the bud. I've got an idea—work with me."

Ray slid into his seat and flashed them a bleary smile. "False alarm." He moved his chair closer to his date, looping an arm around the back of Manny's chair. "Now, where were we?"

Mark's career flashed before his eyes. Sweat popped out on his forehead, and he downed the glass of wine. Manny leaned forward to whisper something to Ellie, and she nodded in response, her eyes darting to Mark. *What are they up to now?*

"Mr. Ivan," Ellie said sweetly. "Would you like to dance?"

"Well, of course, dear." Ray tore himself away from Manny and accompanied Ellie to the dance floor.

Mark narrowed his eyes at Manny. "Don't even think about asking me to dance."

Manny waved him off, exasperated. "Don't be ridiculous— you're not my type at all. But I do need for you to go to the men's room with me."

"Excuse me?"

"I need to borrow your pants."

"*What?*"

"Look, for both our sakes, I've got to shake this guy once and for all. Are you with me?"

Cornered and out of options, he gestured toward the rest room and relented stiffly. "This is against my better judgment."

"I'll go first, and you follow in a few minutes."

Manny escaped and Mark played with his empty wineglass for a few seconds, then whistled tunelessly while he watched the second hand on his watch. When exactly one minute had passed, he strolled toward the men's room.

He breathed a sigh of relief to find the room empty. Perhaps Manny had gone home. He'd make excuses to Ray and somehow convince him not to call her, uh, him again.

"Pssst!"

Mark jerked his head toward the sound. One of the stall doors was closed, but no legs or feet were visible.

"Pssst, over here, Mark!"

Mark walked over to the stall and said, "What the hell are you doing?"

"I'm getting undressed."

"Are you suspended in midair?"

"I'm standing on the toilet."

Mark put his hands on his hips. "Did Ellie teach you that trick?"

A man entered the bathroom and walked to the sink, eyeing a large red stain on his lapel. He nodded to Mark and reached for a towel.

"Would you stop clowning around and take off your pants?" Manny whispered loudly.

Mark groaned inwardly. The man's head snapped up. He made wide eye contact with Mark, then turned and bolted out the door.

"Great," Mark said, walking into the adjacent stall. "We just scared a customer to death. He's probably reporting us right now. What are you doing, anyway?"

"I'm going to get Ray off Molly's back. Hurry up—I need your shirt, pants, socks and shoes."

"And what am I supposed to wear in the meantime?"

"Oh, that's right—Ellie says you don't wear undies."

"Does she tell you everything?" Mark sputtered.

"*Every*thing—you can hang on to your jacket for security."

Mark began stripping off his clothes and handed them over the top of the stall. "This had better work."

"Trust me."

"Oh, yeah," Mark said sarcastically. "The man wearing the WonderBra says 'trust me.'"

"Don't knock it till you've tried it."

Why hadn't he worn boxers tonight? Mark felt utterly ridiculous standing naked in his suit jacket and holding his tie in front of his crotch while Manny dressed in his clothes. He wondered briefly if he could be disbarred for public nudity. Probably.

A couple of minutes later, a wad of clothing sailed over the top of the stall. Mark dodged panty hose, girdle, a set of fake boobs, wig, high heels and other mysterious items, watching them settle onto the tiled floor around him. "What's all this crap?" he demanded.

"All that crap is my wardrobe," Manny said hotly. I can't leave it in here—someone might take it. Keep it with you until I get back."

Mark crossed his arms and shook his head in defeat. "I saw this once in a movie. If you leave me stranded with nothing to wear out of here but women's clothes, I'll track you down and kick your butt. You've got ten minutes."

"I'll be back," was Manny's acid response. Mark heard the stall door open and close, then lots of water splashing, then finally Manny exiting the outer door.

A few seconds later, the outer door opened again, this time admitting someone with a slow lazy stride. Mark looked down at his hairy legs and bare feet and imagined how it would look from the other side. He quickly stooped to snatch Manny's clothing from the floor and out of sight. Sweat beaded on his forehead.

"Having problems in there?" the man asked haughtily, walking over to stop in front of the stall.

Mark's heart stopped. He knew that voice.

"Hey, buddy." The man knocked, and raised his voice in a challenge. "I said, are you having problems in there?"

His co-worker, Tony Specklemeyer. The little hotshot who'd come to his office for a showdown over cheating on a client's tax forms. Mark cursed silently, scalding the air. The ambitious little jackass would hang him out to dry if he saw him like this. A drop of sweat dripped off his nose.

Mark pictured the headlines: Partner of Prestigious Atlanta Law Firm Found Buck-Naked In Men's-Room Stall Amidst Pile of Women's Underthings. He could visualize himself saying, "Honest, Officer, I was just loaning my clothes to my fake fiancée's transvestite roommate so the senior partner of my law firm wouldn't find out I'd set him up with a man."

Specklemeyer's feet had disappeared, and Mark prayed the man would simply leave. He nearly had a stroke when he heard a gasp above him. Mark turned and looked straight up into his co-worker's astonished face hanging over the top of the stall.

"Blackwell?" he screeched, his voice incredulous.

Mark reached up to grab him by the throat, dropping most of the clothing he held. "Listen, you jackass, this isn't what you think, and if you so much as breathe a word of this to anyone, I'll rip out your spleen, got it?"

But Specklemeyer wasn't shaken. "Gee, Blackwell, you're much more intimidating when you're not wielding a pair of size eleven turquoise pumps."

Mark looked down at the shoe in his other hand. His fury exploded, and he shook the man until his head rattled. His voice was low and deadly. "I mean it, Specklemeyer. You did not see this."

Tony held up his hands in surrender and rolled a smile around on his lips. "Sure, man, sure. Whatever you say." He jerked loose from Mark's grip, and Mark heard him step down from the toilet seat and leave the rest room.

Mark sank to the toilet and put his face in his hands. *My career is definitely over.* Next week, being partner would be a distant memory.

He clasped his hands together. "Please, God, let me get out of here alive so I can wring Ellie Sutherland's neck!"

ELLIE HELPED an unsteady Ray into his seat before she slid into hers. She glanced around frantically for Manny and Mark. They'd been gone for several minutes.

"I need to visit the men's room," Ray announced, half standing.

"No!" Ellie yelled, drawing the attention of patrons around her.

Ray looked at her, startled.

"I mean, not yet," she said, laughing nervously. "Can you wait until Mark or Molly get back so I won't be here by myself?"

Ray sat back down obligingly. "Where *are* those two?"

Good question.

"Ellie!" Manny's voice exclaimed behind her. She turned to see Manny, clad in Mark's clothing, striding toward her. Despite her panic, she had to suppress a giggle. His feet were swimming in the bigger man's shoes, and he'd rolled up the cuff of the dress pants to keep them from dragging.

"Where's Molly?" Manny asked dramatically.

"I think she's in the ladies' room, Manny."

"Is this a friend of yours, Ellie?" Ray asked cautiously.

"Ray Ivan, meet Manny Oliver."

Ray stuck out his hand, perplexed. "Pleased to meet you."

Manny didn't shake his hand, and instead cried, "Are you the man who's trying to steal my Molly?"

"What?" the older man exclaimed.

Manny swooped down on one knee and clasped Ray's hands. "Don't do it, sir. If you have a heart, don't do it."

"Don't do what?" Concern lined Ray's face.

"Don't take my Molly." Big tears filled Manny's eyes. "I love her, but she keeps a flock of men on the side. She's so beautiful, I can't compete with them all. You understand, don't you, sir?"

"I guess so," Ray said dubiously.

Ellie hid a smile behind her napkin. Manny hadn't removed his eyelashes, and his long fingernails were still blood red, but the sodden Ray didn't seem to notice.

The maître d' approached the table with a worried look on his face. He addressed Ray. "Is everything all right here, sir?"

Manny's sobs increased, his head bent over Ray's hands.

"I think so," Ray said in confusion.

Manny raised his head. "So you'll give me your word to not see her, no matter how tempting she is."

Ray looked at Ellie, then back to Manny. "I guess so."

"Oh, thank you, sir." Manny's sobs began anew. "You've made me a new man. But please, when she comes back out, let her down gently. I love her so much, I couldn't stand for her to be hurt."

Ray nodded rapidly. "Sure."

Manny kissed the man's hands, then made a tearful exit.

"I'm so sorry, Ray," Ellie said, patting his hand. "Perhaps it really is for the best."

He nodded wisely. "Better to have loved and lost..." His voice faded as he lifted his wineglass to his lips for the hundredth time.

A few minutes later, Mark came walking hurriedly back to the table, glancing around the room and tugging at his tie.

"Where've you been?" Ray slurred. "We've been worried about you, son."

Mark glared murderously at Ellie, but turned a smile on Ray. "The snails didn't agree with me, sir."

"Have you seen Molly?" Ellie asked, her eyebrows raised.

"I believe she'll be here any minute," he said through clenched teeth.

"Hello, all," Manny said in his sugary Molly voice, swinging into his seat.

He looked slightly worse for wear, his wig askew and lipstick hastily applied. He turned a smile on Ray. "Miss me?"

"Yes," Ray admitted, his voice sad. "But I'm afraid I must call it an evening."

"But why?" Manny's eyebrows furrowed dramatically.

Ray took Manny's hand in his. "Well, the truth is, Molly, you're too much of a woman for me, and I don't think this is going to work out."

"Oh, no." Manny pouted prettily.

Mark rolled his eyes, and Ellie kicked him under the table.

"Shush, my dear," Ray said gently. "It's for the best. You've been a lovely dinner companion, and I thank you very much."

"Well, if you're sure," Manny said cautiously.

Ray waved for the maître d' and asked him to hail a taxi, then signed for the meal, folded a fifty into the man's hand and bid everyone good-night.

When he was out of sight, Ellie sank into her chair in relief. "Whew!"

Manny snapped his fingers. "Told you it would work."

"Except," she added glumly, "he still thinks we're engaged."

Mark scanned the room again, obviously agitated. His scowl was black and ugly when it landed on Ellie. "Although being engaged to you is a harrowing prospect, believe me, it's the least of my problems right now."

FREDA ESCORTED ELLIE to the first available closet-room. "So," the clinical assistant said in a tired voice. "How's it going?" She sat down heavily in a creaking metal chair and flipped through Ellie's journal, stopping occasionally to scratch at her temple with the end of a pen.

"Fine," Ellie replied nervously, sitting on a stool wedged between a trash can and a Formica desk. Absolutely nothing in her life was fine.

Freda had stopped on one page to read intently. "Well, I can see things have progressed nicely with Mr. Mark."

"Keep reading," Ellie said dryly.

Freda squinted, bringing the book closer. "Try to remember to print your entries next time."

"But I printed them *this* time."

"Well, it's hard to make out what you've written. You had 'toy' sex? Is that something new?"

Ellie felt her skin redden. She coughed lightly. "Mmm, that would be 'toe' sex."

"*Toe* sex? Okay, you had, er…*toe* sex once and regular sex once?"

"That's right."

Freda studied a form on her desk, pen poised, then shook her head. "I never seem to have the right checkboxes for your answers."

"Being categorized under 'other' is the story of my life."

"Do you see this moving toward a long-term relationship?"

"Definitely not."

Freda kept writing. "How often do you see him?"

"For the next few weeks, possibly every day—I work out of his home now, but it's temporary, and partly so I can look after my cat."

"He's keeping your cat?"

"Uh-huh."

"But last week you told me he's allergic to your cat."

"He is, but we made this deal he'd look after her until she had kittens if I would go to a swanky work dinner party as his date. Except it didn't go very well because his partner caught us making out in the car and then announced to everyone that we're engaged."

Freda's eyes widened. "You're engaged?"

"No, but everyone thinks so. Except his mom—he told her the truth because she nearly had a heart attack when she heard it through the grapevine. She hates me because I—"

"Ruined the family reunion," Freda cut in. "You told me."

"It was an accident," Ellie insisted. "Then we double-dated with his partner and my roommate, only Mark didn't know my roommate is a transvestite—"

"Wait," Freda said, holding her palm stop-sign fashion. "That's a whole different study. Let's get back to the pheromones. Have you had sex since you started working in his home?"

"He's not speaking to me."

"Because of the roommate?"

Ellie nodded. "It's a long story, but a co-worker of Mark's saw him in the bathroom naked and holding a bunch of women's clothes—"

"Wait, I thought your roommate was the cross-dresser."

"He is."

Freda looked at her questioningly. "Then why was Mark naked in the bathroom holding women's clothes?"

"He had to loan *his* clothes to my roommate to convince

his partner that the woman he thought he was with had a boyfriend.''

Freda looked totally confused. "And that boyfriend would be...?"

"My roommate."

Pursing her lips, Freda said, "Okay."

"Anyway, Mark hasn't spoken to me since he dropped me and my roommate off Saturday night."

"I thought you said you were working in his home."

"But I only started yesterday. He worked late, probably on purpose, and I left before he got home."

"Why don't you stick around one night until he comes home and see what happens?" She winked, surprising Ellie. "See how long he can resist you."

"The problem is, these pheromones seem to be working both ways."

"What do you mean?"

"Why else would I be so drawn to a man who is everything I would hate in a partner? It has to be these pills."

"Probably," Freda agreed, nodding. Spreading her hands, she added, "Think of it as one big science project."

"Oh, no," Ellie groaned.

"What?"

"I blew up the science lab my junior year in college."

9

WHY, oh, why had he ever thought he'd be able to resist her, and in his own home, no less? Purposely working late each night, Mark half hoped she'd be gone when he arrived, half prayed she wouldn't be. Tonight was Friday and his prayers had been answered. Classic rock thumped through his centralized stereo system when he stepped into the entryway. He inhaled, filling his lungs with her fresh-air skin scent that had permeated his home.

"Ellie," he called, and although he knew she couldn't hear him above Lynyrd Skynyrd, he added, "I'm home." For a few foolish seconds, the image of an aproned June Cleaver flashed through his mind, coming to the door to welcome Ward home from a hard day's work.

"Mark, is that you?" Ellie bawled, coming to the top of the stairs to peer over the railing.

Except June had never worn an apron like that, he mused, admiring the way the short work smock emphasized Ellie's breasts and small waist. And Mrs. Cleaver would have been holding a spatula instead of a paintbrush.

Mark waved, deciding not to yell over the music. He hated himself for being so glad to see her. She held up a finger to indicate she'd be back, then disappeared. Mark set his briefcase by the bottom step and loosened his tie. Walking toward the kitchen, he bellowed, "How have you been?" His last two words reverberated through the house because the music abruptly ended. Then he heard the sound of Ellie's feet descending the stairs lightly and rhythmically.

"Oh, fine," she said cheerfully.

When he turned to her, he noticed immediately she'd lost

the smock. Black hip-hugger shorts and a ribbed lime green turtleneck would have been unforgivable on most women, but Ellie, as usual, looked delightful. Right down to the smudge of gold paint on her chin. Then he realized her cheer had been forced. Her wide smile could not hide her bright, panicked eyes. He slowly placed the two bottles of beer he'd withdrawn from the refrigerator on the counter. "What?" he asked, alarm setting in.

"You might want to have something stronger than a beer," she warned.

Mark bit his lip and summoned patience. "What?" he repeated quietly.

Ellie's face took on a pleading look. "She's just a sweet little kitty, Mark, please don't be mad."

Mark snorted and twisted off the beer cap. "What did Sheba do today? Pee on another blue cushion?"

He lifted the bottle to his mouth, but stopped at the look of dread on Ellie's face. Obviously this was much worse than a couple of throw pillows. "What did she break?"

"She didn't break anything, exactly."

"What the hell did she do, *exactly?*" Suddenly Mark realized the buzz from his fish-tank filter was absent. His head jerked around. "Oh, no. Not my fish?"

Ellie stood wringing her hands. "I guess the fish video got her wound up—"

Anger bubbled inside his stomach. "Your cat *ate* my fish?"

She bit her bottom lip, then said, "Well, she didn't eat *all* of them, mostly just batted them around—"

Mark strode through the kitchen into the den to stare at the fifty-gallon tank of serene, still water. Artificial sea grass drifted up from the bottom. A labyrinth of elaborate ceramic sand castles sat vacant. A single black severed fish tail floated on the surface.

"I turned off the filter," she offered. "And sang 'The Circle of Life' when I flushed them down the john."

"At that point, I'm sure they were glad to be dead," Mark retorted, remembering her singing voice. "What happened to the lid?"

"The veterinarian says Esmerelda has an above average IQ—"

Mark cut her off. "If that were the case, the animal would be smart enough to know not to devour seven hundred dollars' worth of exotic fish!"

Ellie blanched. "Seven hundred dollars? Are you crazy? That's two months' rent."

Mark narrowed his eyes.

Smiling nervously, Ellie quietly stammered, "Well, you certainly can't f-fault her good taste."

Irritation triggered a finger twitch. Soon his hands were jumping at his sides. "I'm filling it up with piranhas tomorrow." He strode back to the kitchen, gulped half the beer, then added, "Big, smart piranhas that say, 'Here, kitty, kitty.'"

"I'm sorry, Mark, really I am, and I know Esmerelda is sorry, too, if only she could tell you," she pleaded, hot on his heels.

"Oh, so *that's* what she's trying to say when she bares her fangs and runs me out of my own bed."

"Please, Mark," Ellie begged softly. When he turned, she slipped inside the circle of his arms. Desire bolted through him against his will. Wrapping her arms around his waist, she turned huge blue eyes up to him, batting her lashes shamelessly. "She's going to be a mother in a couple of weeks," she said earnestly, as if that explained everything.

"Meow," Esmerelda announced, walking regally into the room, tail held high. She glanced toward the den and licked her lips, then blinked at Mark.

"Long live the queen," Mark grumbled, but set his beer down to draw Ellie closer to him.

Ellie inhaled sharply when he tightened his hold. Her breasts, without the protection of a bra, responded immediately. Mark's voice was low as he lowered his mouth to her ear. "If you think kissing up to me is going to make up for that murdering cat of yours, well, then—"

She moved her lips to his and drew his breath into her mouth with a slow, deep kiss.

When she withdrew, he simply stared down at her. "Well, then...you're much smarter than your pussycat." He shook his head in wonder. "Between last weekend and my empty aquarium, I should be furious with you."

"But?" she asked hopefully.

"But...there's something about you that makes me forget what I was feeling or saying before you walked into the room," he said, hearing the wonder in his own voice.

Ellie's smile was tremulous. "I'm sorry. I should have told you about Manny. Does his cross-dressing bother you?"

Mark thought about it for a few seconds. "No. I mean, it takes a little getting used to, but he seems like an okay guy." He smiled wryly. "I just didn't want to be the one who paired him up with the man who respected me enough to make me a partner."

She played with a buttonhole in his jacket. "So did you get in trouble for...you know."

"For my stint as a naked clothes rack for your friend?"

She giggled and nodded.

He loosened his grip on her waist, took a drink of his beer and leaned against the counter. "Specklemeyer hasn't come out and said anything, but he's flirting with disaster."

"How so?"

"We had a meeting this morning with an old client, and Ray told him I was engaged." He watched her expression, curious for a reaction, perplexed by his own curiosity. Her face remained unreadable, and he continued, "I opened my mouth to set the record straight, but Tony sat gloating across the table. He really thinks I'm covering up some kind of kinky life-style. I figured telling everyone we're not engaged would only add fuel to his fire. I'm sorry to keep prolonging this."

She shrugged, a smile on her lips. "Do you think he'll say anything?"

"If I know Specklemeyer, he'll wait until he needs my support for something big, then he'll threaten to tell what he thinks he saw."

"Is he that vicious?"

"He's so blinded by ambition, I wouldn't put anything past

him. The man has a vanity license plate that says 'HUN-GRY.'"

"Would they really fire you?"

"Of course not—even if I were a cross-dresser, it would be illegal to fire me. But it's a label I'd rather not have to defend." God, she smelled wonderful. He pulled her to him and kissed her neck. She felt dangerously good and his body hardened in need. No, his mind screamed, a thousand times no. "Do you have dinner plans?" he asked, nuzzling her ear.

She pressed her breasts against him, moaning slightly. "Nothing I can't get out of," she whispered. "What did you have in mind?"

"Getting you out of something," he murmured, ignoring the warning bells in his head. "Do you think Esmerelda would let us borrow my room for the night? I still haven't seen that darn tattoo."

ELLIE SAT UP GINGERLY so as not to disturb Mark, her heart catching at the sight of him sprawled in the tangled sheets. They'd made love, then ordered Ellie's favorite ham and pineapple pizza, washed it down with beer and made love again. He'd asked her to accompany him to a regatta today in Savannah, and she was looking forward to spending the day together. It seemed he did have time for rest and relaxation, after all. Maybe he wasn't the work machine she had imagined.

At the moment, she sincerely doubted if even Esmerelda could rouse the man. Mark's soft snores attested to his deep state of sleep, but it was his state of undress that mesmerized Ellie. She studied the proportion of his torso, the hard planes of his stomach and the length of his semihard sex with an artist's trained eye. On impulse, she began to frame a composition with her joined thumbs and extended index fingers. Some scenes were meant to be captured on paper. Mark Blackwell in the buff was an artist's dream.

Silently, Ellie rose and lifted his blue-and-white-striped pajama top from the bedpost, then pulled it over her head. She rolled up the sleeves and padded to Esmerelda's room where she had set up an easel and paints.

The corporate portrait was progressing nicely. Mark was coming alive on the canvas surface, devastatingly masculine and authoritative in his olive suit. She'd coaxed him into sitting for her last night in the few minutes between their love-making sessions, and had taken advantage of the time to render his eyes. This most important feature was most accurately portrayed if painted directly from the model in order to capture light and expression. They glistened back at her, serious, but with a teasing twinkle at the edges. Volumes of dark leather-bound reference books made up the background, the books' gilded accents a perfect foil for the green in his suit and eyes.

Ellie snatched her large sketch pad and flipped past the quick sketches of Esmerelda until she found a clean sheet. Then she reentered Mark's bedroom, sighing when Esmerelda dashed through the door before she could close it. Mark remained deep in slumber. She'd bet he hadn't so much as twitched since she'd left.

Sinking into an overstuffed chair in front of the bay window, Ellie propped her feet on an ottoman and spent a few seconds drinking in the sight of Mark's glorious body. The thick charcoal pencil in her hand began to move almost involuntarily. Within minutes she'd scrawled a rough sketch of him across the page. On the second pass, she worked more slowly, blocking in shadows to delineate limbs and muscles. Finally, she added more detail, like body hair and facial features. Taking particular care, she rendered his privates in precise proportion on the paper. Not hard, yet not soft, his current state of semiarousal would aptly reflect his size, yet not come across as vulgar.

The sketch turned out so well, Ellie decided a painting must be done. She grinned. It would be her unique thank-you to Mark for taking care of Esmerelda. He'd probably get a big kick out of it. What man hadn't fantasized about being immortalized in the nude at the peak of health? She'd work on the new painting at her apartment to keep it a secret.

She closed the sketchbook and put it aside to crawl back into bed. Mark grunted contentedly when she spooned up next to him. *I can't believe I'm so stupid. I fell in love with him*

*knowing full well he's devoted to his job. I promised myself
I'd never get tied to a man who thought being with his family
was an option. Besides, the study ends in two weeks, along
with my sex appeal.*

The phone rang, jarring Mark awake. Ellie reached for the
handset on the nightstand and gave it to him. He pulled himself up, rubbing the sleep from his eyes, and spoke into the
phone. "Hello? Yeah, Patrick…no, I'm fine, what's up?"
Mark reached for the pen and pad beside the phone and began
to jot down notes. "No, I'll be glad to take care of it." He
glanced at Ellie and frowned apologetically. "Have Monica
make the arrangements and clear my calendar for next week.
I'll be at the airport in forty-five minutes." He was already
standing when he hung up the phone.

"Sorry about today," he said simply, tearing off the sheet
of paper. "Something came up—I have to go to Chicago with
Beecham and Ivan for a week or so." He bent over and kissed
her quickly.

Déjà vu. How many times had her father missed planned
outings with the family because his boss had called at the last
minute? "Oh, come on, can't you wait until this afternoon?"
Ellie cajoled.

Mark shook his head. "Sorry, I have a plane to catch. Grant
was supposed to go but had to cancel at the last minute. That
leaves me."

"Can't we at least have breakfast?" Ellie pleaded, hating
herself for sounding like her mother.

"Sorry," he repeated. "I'll make it up to you when I get
home. I promise." Then he walked toward the bathroom. After
he closed the door and the shower spray started, Ellie frowned
and pounded her fist on the mattress.

Sorry, sorry, sorry. Her father had had an endless supply of
apologies. Rising from the bed, she scooped her clothing from
the floor. She cursed under her breath, and shook her head.
She had no one to blame but herself. She'd seen the train
coming, but had barreled past the warning signals to straddle
the tracks, welcoming the light with open arms.

SATURDAY AND SUNDAY NIGHT had both been late work nights in Chicago. And since what little sleep time he'd had left he'd spent thinking about Ellie, Mark arrived at the hotel's continental breakfast Monday morning in a less-than-rested mood.

He couldn't get the woman off his mind. Of course, the irritating rash he'd developed from the foamy whipped cream she'd covered his privates with served as a constant reminder of their romps. Granted, she had removed it in a most satisfying way. *It's just a strong physical attraction.* Unfortunately, the one area in which they seemed to be most compatible was in bed.

He purposely hadn't called her since he'd left. Somehow, calling long distance to check in just seemed too…relationship-y. Still, the idea of spending a lot of time with Ellie had begun to sound appealing. The mere thought of the tiny pink mouse tattoo, apparently barely concealed by her garter belt that first night, sent the blood rushing to his groin. Ellie was beautiful, sexy, funny, and he craved her company. He could do much worse, he knew. He might give this novel idea of a committed, monogamous relationship some serious thought.

"How's Ellie?" Patrick asked, breaking into his thoughts.

Mark glanced at Ray, who also seemed interested in his answer. For an instant, Mark wondered if Specklemeyer had leaked the information, after all. Maybe they knew his engagement was a charade and were calling him on it. Shifting in his seat, he replied, "Fine, thanks for asking."

Patrick looked sympathetic. "Big step, isn't it?"

Mark nodded, swallowing a dry bite of bagel.

"Of course it's a big step," Ray declared, snapping open a newspaper. "The last woman you'll sleep with for the rest of your life, the one woman you'll wake up to every day for the next fifty years, God willing."

Patrick nodded solemnly. "Of course, the bedroom gets a little chilly once kids come along, but you get used to it."

Ray grunted his agreement. "Bone-cold."

Mark pursed his lips and shook his head, smiling wryly.

"So why don't married men reveal this stuff to single men *before* the engagement?"

Ray chuckled. "We're not trying to talk you out of it, son. Marriage has its good points. If the right woman came along, I'd do it again." He rattled the newspaper. "Probably." Mark thought about Manny and winced.

"Yeah," Patrick said, "Lucy is fabulous, it's her mother I can't stomach. By the way, how's your mother taking this?"

"She's not ecstatic, but—"

"Uh-oh," Ivan announced from behind the paper. "Not a good sign, but it's to be expected. Don't worry, things will probably work out before one of your parents has to move in."

"Move in?" Mark parroted.

"Sure," Patrick said. "After Lucy's father passed away, her mother was so heavily medicated, she came to stay with us for a couple of weeks. She's been living with us going on two years now."

Mark swallowed. He doubted he could live with his *own* mother, and he didn't know the first thing about Ellie's family. Except that her dad had been a workaholic. But hadn't she said something about a nudist colony? His collar grew warmer and tighter.

"That's nothing," said Ray, bending down a corner of a page to peer at them. "My mother came to live with us back in 1970. She and my poor wife argued so much, the police were at my house three times the first week because the neighbors complained."

Mark imagined his mother and Ellie in the same house. Not in a million years. He pushed his plate away and grabbed a glass of water. He'd never experienced heartburn before, but it didn't take a medical degree to perform a quick diagnosis. His previous notion of entering a relationship with Ellie ended along with his appetite.

10

ELLIE WAVED at the messy painters as she ducked through the entryway of the clinic. She was almost sorry she wouldn't be around to see the finished product.

Freda stood behind the receptionist's counter when Ellie walked in. "Well, if it isn't the woman with the experienced toes." The woman's eyes were actually twinkling. She led Ellie back to a tiny room and asked, "So, what's the latest?"

"Nothing kinky this week," Ellie informed her as she took a seat and handed her the journal. "I consider whipped cream to be pretty standard stuff."

"Oh?"

"We were together Friday night, then he left town Saturday."

"Sounds like he came around."

Ellie grinned sheepishly. "Around and around and upside down."

Showing uncharacteristic concern, Freda asked, "Have you heard from him?"

Ellie shook her head sadly. "It's the pheromones, isn't it? He's not near me to be affected by them, so he's not interested."

"Is that what you think?" Freda asked, her pen poised.

Ellie nodded.

"Could be," Freda admitted, making notes. "But haven't you heard the saying 'Absence makes the heart grow fonder'?"

"I thought it was 'Absence make the heart wonder.' Or is it 'wander'?"

"You don't have much confidence in your relationship, do you?"

Ellie's laugh was short and dry. "Relationship? What Mark and I have is a physical attraction brought about by these…these fake love-inducers." She pointed to the bottle of pills sitting in front of Freda. "It's not fair—they mess with a person's mind—they make you think something's there that really isn't." She blinked away tears and tried to smile at Freda. "Tennyson was wrong—it's better *not* to have loved at all than to have loved and lost."

"You haven't lost him yet," Freda said.

"Yeah," Ellie said miserably, gesturing to her final supply. "This should delay the inevitable by about one week."

"Have you considered the possibility you might feel differently about *him* once you quit taking the pills?"

Elation zigged, then zagged through Ellie's heart. She lifted her chin and flashed a genuine smile in Freda's direction. "You're right!" A burden the size of Mark's cellular phone bill rolled off her back. Since it was a chemically induced fluke she'd fallen for the very type of man she'd sworn to avoid, this attraction would probably disappear as quickly as it had surfaced.

"Anyway," Freda said, "it'll be interesting to see what happens when he returns." She handed Ellie the final week's supply of pheromones.

Ellie fingered the bottle, the pills suddenly weighing heavily in her palm. The honeymoon was almost over, and she was happy to see the end in sight.

Wasn't she?

"WHERE HAVE YOU been keeping yourself?" Manny asked, dumping his bags of groceries on the counter. "As if I didn't know," he added.

Ellie angled her head at him across the room. She'd set up an easel in a corner of the breakfast nook by the window. After wiping a brush on a turpentine-soaked rag, she stretched her cramped fingers. Sometimes, a picture practically painted itself. This was one of those times when once she started painting, she couldn't bring herself to stop. She checked her watch. Three hours, nonstop.

Manny walked over to peek at the painting and gasped, his hand to his chest. "My, my." Mark Blackwell lay slumbering on the canvas, his sleek and muscled nude body accented, not covered, by the twisted sheets. "Now I know where the phrase *too big for his britches* originated."

"Manny," Ellie warned, "if you let on you've seen this painting, I swear I'll burn your gowns."

With his hand, Manny made a zipping motion across his mouth, then turned back to the painting. "It's divine, El," he said with sincerity in his voice.

"One of my best," she agreed. "A shame no one will ever see it."

"Then why on earth did you paint it?"

"It's a surprise gift to Mark for taking care of Esmerelda." Manny looked incredulous. "He doesn't know about it?"

"Nope."

"Well, that explains a few things. I thought it was rather loose of Mr. A. Retentive. How's the other painting going?"

"Almost finished. Mark's in Chicago."

"When did he leave?"

"Saturday morning."

"This is Tuesday. You've been at his house three entire days by yourself?"

"Esmerelda was there," Ellie said defensively.

"What have you been doing?"

"Working on the other portrait, weeding his flowers—"

"Sleeping in his bed. Did you rearrange the furniture, too, Goldilocks?"

"No! Although the couch in his den *would* look better under the window."

"You're getting too comfortable at this house," Manny warned. "What's going on with the two of you?"

"That's a very good question."

"And?"

"And I intend to pursue an answer once he returns from his trip."

"Which will be?"

"Soon, I think."

By Friday, when she still hadn't heard from Mark, Ellie was decidedly depressed. Pride kept her from calling his office to see when they expected him to return. She'd put the final touches on the business portrait still drying at his home. The finished nude, drying on an easel in her bedroom, no longer seemed like such a grand idea.

Mark Blackwell was firmly entrenched in his career, and had made it crystal clear this week he didn't care enough about her to spare five minutes of his busy schedule to call. For all she knew, he could be flitting around the Windy City with a busty woman on each arm. In fact, the more she dwelled on it, the more convinced she became he was doing just that. Misery wallowed in her stomach.

Saturday afternoon, Ellie returned home with new sketches for two more Atlanta landmark paintings she intended to add to her portfolio. A quick glance at her answering machine told her there was one message. Her heart lifted. Mark? She rushed over to the machine and pushed the play button.

"Ellie, this is Monica. I wanted to let you know in case Mark hasn't called that he'll be back Wednesday morning." So, she'd been relegated to receiving messages through his secretary, and probably only because Monica had taken it upon herself to forward the information. She knew the routine—some weeks her mother had talked to her husband's secretary more than she'd spoken to her own husband.

Ellie's heart crumbled in disappointment. She deserved more than a philandering businessman who slept with his briefcase. More than a man who would fly off for weeks at a time and never check in. She refused to expose herself to it, she refused to expose her children to it. Ellie made a painful decision. If Mark Blackwell ever came home, she wouldn't be seeing him anymore. Which was just as well, she noted. The end of the study loomed in plain sight.

She went to the Dunwoody house that afternoon to check on Esmerelda, and decided from the looks of her cat's bulging tummy, she'd better start spending the nights again, at least until Mark came home. To soothe her guilty pangs, Ellie slept in a guest room and bought groceries, then puttered around the yard, weeding, watering, trimming, even transplanting. She found a tiny vacant mulch bed which would have made a perfect herb garden, but she swept the thought aside. Better to concentrate on reality, such as finding a job.

So the next morning, she and Esmerelda pored over Mark's Sunday-paper classified ads. She would receive the last check from the study on Tuesday when she turned in her final journal, which was practically blank this week, except for the occasional street admirer. She'd be able to collect the largest and final installment on Mark's portrait from the law firm in a couple of weeks. But she needed to look for something steady and, preferably, with insurance.

Ellie sighed, circling possibilities, tears filling her eyes when she remembered the last time she'd done this. It had been the day Mark Blackwell had bumbled his way into her life. Only this time, tears, not displaced soda, wet the paper. Ellie wished she'd never heard of pheromones, because if not for those darned pills, she wouldn't have lost her heart to Mark. She put her head down and cried in earnest. Esmerelda licked Ellie's hand.

IF ELLIE HAD ANY DOUBTS about whether she wore her heart on her sleeve, Freda put them to rest Tuesday morning.

"I take it he's still in Chicago?"

Ellie nodded forlornly.

"And you haven't heard from him?"

She shook her head, just as forlornly.

"When is he due back?"

"His secretary left me a message he'll be back tomorrow."

"And you'll be taking your last two pills this evening, right?"

Ellie nodded again.

Freda sighed. "Don't fret about it—you'll just make yourself sick." She smiled and patted Ellie's hand. "Good luck."

"WHAT'S THE PROBLEM?" Mark grumbled to Patrick. They'd been sitting on a runway at O'Hare for over forty minutes waiting for their plane to take off.

Patrick looked up from his magazine. "Relax, man, this is typical."

"You think they could at least serve us a beer while we wait."

Patrick raised an eyebrow. "Are you cranky for a particular reason or can I look forward to this every time we fly together?"

Mark frowned. "Sorry."

His partner laughed. "Hey, I miss Lucy, too. You'll be home before you know it. And reunion sex is the best, don't you think? It's the only time I can get near Lucy anymore." He went back to his reading, leaving Mark to brood.

He'd decided earlier in the week he wouldn't be seeing Ellie anymore. That is, he wouldn't be *dating* her anymore. She'd still be at his house occasionally during the next few weeks until that darn cat dropped her kittens and weaned them. Come to think of it, he and Ellie hadn't really dated much, when he subtracted the dates he'd bartered for and the disastrous double date with Ray and Manny.

Okay, so he wouldn't be *sleeping* with her anymore. That thought sent a pang of regret through his midsection, but he remained determined. He was too young to settle down and when he did, it would be to someone better suited for him. He hadn't figured out the hold she seemed to have over him, but if staying away from Ellie and her powerful sex appeal held the answer, he'd do it. He'd made sacrifices before. He'd be happier in the long run. So how to break the news to her? The way men had been delivering bad news for decades. In the gentlest, safest way possible.

By telephone.

ELLIE'S HEART LEAPED involuntarily at the sound of the ringing phone. Manny's eyes shot up in question as he reached for the handset. She motioned for him to answer it.

"Hello? Yes, she is. May I ask who's calling? Well, Mark,

how nice of you to call. We thought you'd died. Hold on, please.''

Ellie rolled her eyes.

Manny covered the mouthpiece and said unnecessarily, ''It's him.''

After taking several deep breaths to calm herself, Ellie picked up the handset and said, ''Hello?''

''Hi, it's Mark.''

She couldn't read anything into the tone of his voice. But he didn't sound especially glad to be talking to her. ''Oh, hi. Are you home?''

''Yeah.''

''How was your trip?'' She tried to shoo Manny from the room with her hand, but he smiled and shook his head, plopping down on the couch within hearing distance.

''I had a busy week,'' Mark said distractedly. ''And long. It'll be nice to sleep in my own bed tonight.''

The silence hung heavy after his loaded offhand comment.

Ellie cleared her throat. ''Well, hopefully Esmerelda won't bother you.''

''I see she still hasn't had her kittens.''

''No, but she should any day. I hope you don't mind—I stayed over there the last few nights in case she needed me.''

''So you're the one who replenished my beer.''

''Yeah, I figured it was the least I could do. I can't tell you how much I appreciate your letting her stay.'' She was rambling, she knew, but she wasn't sure where they stood anymore.

''A deal's a deal,'' he said simply. ''The portrait looks finished.'' He seemed to be grasping at conversational straws, too.

''It is. As soon as the paint is dry enough, I'll bring it home to frame.''

''Would it sound conceited if I said it looked great?''

''A little, but I know what you mean. Thanks.''

''Sure.'' He cleared his throat. ''Look, Ellie, I've been thinking now would be a good time to let everyone at work know our engagement is, well…off.''

Ellie bit her bottom lip to stem her tears. Although she'd been entertaining the same thoughts, it just sounded so final coming from his mouth. Manny leaned forward on the couch, looking ready to pounce on the phone. She took a deep, steadying breath. "Uh, sure, my thoughts exactly. I'm sure no one will be surprised. We're not really each other's type, you know."

"Right." He sounded relieved. "But, hey, don't let that keep you away. I know you'll be wanting to check on Esmerelda, so hang on to that key, okay?"

"Okay," she said, forcing brightness into her voice.

"I'll see you soon, then?"

"Soon," she promised, and hung up slowly. When she turned, Manny was already by her side. He pulled her into his arms, rocking her and shushing her tears.

AFTER UNPACKING and showering, Mark went to the office for a few hours, but couldn't seem to concentrate. *I'm tired,* he rationalized. He toyed with the idea of calling Valerie, but an early evening and a long night's rest sounded more appealing. He carefully kept at bay the words and emotions of this morning's stilted phone conversation with Ellie. In a few weeks, he'd forget about her. He'd probably run into her one day with a rumpled poet on her arm. He frowned, then pushed all thoughts of Ellie Sutherland from his mind.

After pulling into the garage, Mark walked back down his short driveway to check the mailbox. While idly flipping through bills and junk mail, he scrutinized his landscaping. Something seemed different, but he couldn't put his finger on it. Not one thing, but maybe everything. He stopped. The gardens were neater, perhaps. Which was odd, since the landscaping company wasn't scheduled to come out for another month. He examined the bushes and flowers more closely. Completely weed free. And showing evidence of recent pruning. Frowning, he reentered the garage, then noticed his gardening gloves were hung in a different spot. As were some of his tools. Ellie? He shook his head, a small smile curving his lips.

All was quiet when he entered the house. For a split second, he craved Lynyrd Skynyrd, but settled on a shot of bourbon. After he poured the drink, he stopped to study the expensive crystal decanter, heavy and cool in his hands. Very elegant, like all his possessions. Given the chance, how would Ellie spend his money? Leopard-skin-upholstered furniture? Baubles for the cat?

Trudging upstairs to change, Mark registered the fact that Esmerelda hadn't made her normal snooty appearance. Probably lying in wait somewhere to pounce on him, he decided. He walked into his bedroom, flipping on the light. He reached for the remote and tuned in a sports channel, then stripped off his clothes as he walked through the bathroom and into his walk-in closet to retrieve a pair of sweats. A slow, low growl sounded beneath the spot his long coats were hanging.

"Out of here, Esmerelda," Mark said sternly, moving the coats aside to shoo her away. A pungent, sweet odor reached his nostrils an instant before his first sneeze. Never fond of seeing blood, Mark noted it seemed especially graphic against the light camel of his best cashmere coat. "Nope, can't fault your good taste," he muttered, allowing the coats to fall gently back into place as he backed out of the closet, and trotted to the phone.

Manny answered it on the second ring.

"Hello?"

"Is Ellie there?"

"She's not feeling very well. Who's this?"

Mark sighed in frustration. "It's Mark. I need to talk to Ellie about her cat. There's blood everywhere."

"SHE'LL BE FINE, you'll see," Manny assured her. He'd insisted on accompanying Ellie because she felt so ill.

The rhythm of the train threatened to lull Ellie's mind to numbness. She knew she looked like hell. Passengers averted their eyes. Between the crying jags and a head cold she'd succumbed to this evening, she felt as if she'd been trampled. Her eyes were red and puffy, her nose the size of W. C.

Fields's. She sneezed savagely into a large crumpled handkerchief.

"Your immunity is down," Manny chided. "All that worrying over a straight man, for heaven's sake."

Ellie felt too miserable to respond. Her chest ached. And to cap off this rotten day, Mark would see her at her absolute worst. Then he'd be kicking his heels he'd broken it off.

"You shouldn't have come," Manny mumbled.

"Esmerelda needs me," she managed to get out between parched lips. It hurt to breathe.

"*You* need you. That cat can take care of herself."

"Manny—"

"Okay, okay, I'll hush."

Mark stood waiting for her when they stepped off the train. She tried to calm the beating of her heart, but it raced at the sight of him. A look of concern came over him when she drew nearer.

"Are you okay?" he asked.

"No," Manny snapped. "I couldn't talk her out of coming."

"It's just a cold," Ellie assured them, blowing her nose noisily. "How's Esmerelda?"

"In labor, as far as I could tell," Mark said, studying her. "Maybe you should go home."

"No, I want to see her. Manny offered to meet me here in two hours, if you don't mind bringing me back."

He touched her elbow and steered her in the direction of his car. "You'll stay at my place tonight," he said firmly. Then at the look of challenge on Manny's face, he added, "In a guest room."

"El?" Manny asked, apparently not ready to relinquish her to Mark's care.

"I'll call you later," she promised.

The short trip to Mark's home was silent, punctuated only by Ellie's occasional sneeze or cough. Her arms ached to touch him, or just plain ached, she couldn't tell which. When they arrived, Ellie asked, "Where is she?"

"In my closet."

She made her way up the stairs as quickly as her complaining joints would allow, Mark following her wordlessly. Esmerelda's deep purr could be heard at the top of the stairs. Ellie rushed to the closet and gently pushed back the coats. In the dim light from the bathroom, the proud mother lay on her side with her new kittens gathered around.

"Oh, Esmerelda," she said softly. "You're a mother, five times over." The cat raised her head weakly at Ellie's voice, then closed her eyes to rest. "Look at them," Ellie whispered in awe. The tiny wet balls of fur resembled hamsters, wriggling next to their mama.

"Tiny, aren't they?" Mark asked over her shoulder. Ellie stood and turned to him. "I'm sorry about your coat. I'll pay for it, and the fish, too, out of my commission."

Mark waved his hand. "Forget it."

"The kittens are just minutes old. She'll be nursing them soon, and grooming them. Would it be all right to move her bed in here? She'll need somewhere clean to take the kittens when she's up to it. We'll put the bed back in her room later."

"Sure."

Ellie conjured up a shaky smile in gratitude. Her head started spinning, and she leaned against the door frame for support.

"I'll take care of moving the bed," he said gently. "You need some rest."

She allowed him to guide her in the direction of the guest room. He turned the covers back, an odd expression on his face. "Do you need anything?"

Her head ached too much to keep her eyes open. "Can you spare a T-shirt?" she asked. "I hadn't planned on staying over."

Mark returned in a few minutes with the shirt over his arm, but Ellie lay sound asleep on top of the covers, fully dressed. He shook his head, reaching forward to touch her smooth cheek, flushed from fever. As gently as possible, so as not to disturb her, Mark undressed her down to her panties. Stopping only long enough to caress the mouse tattoo just above her bikini line, he then pulled his baggy T-shirt over her tousled head. She murmured his name groggily, then turned on her side and curled into a sleeping ball. When the temptation to stay and cuddle her became overwhelming, Mark rose quickly and left, closing the door behind him.

After moving the cat's bed to the closet a few feet away from the birthing nest, Mark dialed Ellie's apartment and assured a wary Manny that both patients were resting. Then he climbed into his own bed as he'd meant to hours ago. But the sleep he craved eluded him. The vibes radiating from Ellie in the room down the hall beckoned him, and Mark couldn't remember ever having to exert so much control just to lie still.

11

"ELLIE." Mark was shaking her awake, gently calling her name from a distance. She moved forward through the fog until at last she managed to open her eyes. She blinked, trying to adjust to the daylight, and attempted to raise her head. A splitting pain shot through her ears, and she groaned, resting back against the pillow.

"Ellie," he repeated, his voice slightly muffled. "I think something's wrong with Esmerelda. Who is your vet?"

She licked her dry lips with her thick tongue. "Dr. Doolittle," she croaked.

"Here, have some ice." He held ice chips to her mouth and she took them with her tongue, the wetness pure heaven in her sandy mouth. "Ellie, I'm serious, I need the name of your veterinarian."

"Dr. Doolittle," she repeated. "Dr. Edmund Doolittle. His office is in Midtown. What's wrong?"

His green eyes were full of worry. "I'm not sure, but Esmerelda's acting funny. She's sneezing. Do you think she could be allergic to *me* all of a sudden?"

Smiling, Ellie shook her head painfully. She tried to sit up, but he pressed her back. "Wait until I call the vet, then I'll help you up." With a start, Ellie realized he'd tied a white handkerchief over his mouth and nose. No wonder he sounded so far away. She pointed, giggling weakly.

He shrugged. "Between the cold germs and cat hair, I figured I'd be safer this way. Someone has to take care of the rest of you." His statement seeped into her, drenching every dehydrated pore. Watching him dial directory assistance from the phone in her room, a myriad of feelings assaulted Ellie, ranging from euphoria that this was the way life was supposed to be, to sorrow that it wasn't reality.

Ever so slowly, so as not to trigger the bolting headache, Ellie inched her way up to a semireclining position on the pillow. After a series of transfers, Mark got through to the doctor. Still talking through the handkerchief, he explained the situation of Esmerelda being in his care, then described the cat's condition.

"The kittens are clean. Five of them. Esmerelda is sneezing and wheezing a lot, plus her nose and eyes are runny."

Ellie bit her bottom lip to keep from smiling at his concerned, serious tone. As if he were talking about a child.

"Yeah, she moved them to the clean bed. They've been trying to nurse, but I don't see any liquid coming out, and they're wearing her out, I think. Yeah, I put a bowl of water and some food next to the new bed, but she hasn't touched it."

After a minute, he covered the mouthpiece with his hand, still listening to the doctor. "He thinks she might have a respiratory infection. She won't be able to nurse for a while."

Alarm shot through Ellie. Would the kittens live?

Mark scribbled on a notepad. "Thanks, Doc. I'll let you know. Sure thing."

He hung up and turned to Ellie. "He says it's probably a virus and it'll have to run its course. Just in case, he says to refill the antibiotic she was taking for the bladder infection. And I'll need to pick up a bottle and a week's worth of formula for the kittens. I called my own doctor earlier for advice on what to do for you, so I'll go get everything we need and be back in a little while, okay?"

"I thought you went to law school, not med school," she whispered.

He leaned over as if to peck her on the cheek, then remembered the hankie and straightened abruptly, saying, "I won't be long. Try to get some rest."

But Ellie's eyelids were already floating down and Mark's voice fading away.

"OPEN WIDE, Esmerelda," Mark pleaded. The tablet had been easy enough to hide in her food before, but how could he get her to swallow it if she wasn't interested in eating? Following the vet's orders, he held her head with one hand, then tickled her chin to get her to open her mouth. Once he saw her pink tongue, he pushed the capsule into her mouth. "Ow!" he yelped when her teeth caught his skin as he pulled his finger out. Then he held the struggling cat's mouth shut until she swallowed. "Sorry about that, old girl," Mark mumbled through his mask. Then before he let her go, he wiped her eyes and nose with a clean handkerchief. "Now, let's see to your kittens."

He'd scrubbed his arms raw with antibacterial soap. Now he reached for the first tiny animal next to Esmerelda and cupped it in his large hand. He smiled. Its eyes were still tightly closed, its face and front paws snowy white, the rest of its sleek fur as orange as its mother's. "Boots," he dubbed it, not sure of the sex. "Open up, Boots." Mark moved the tiny nipple of the bottle to its lips. At first it resisted, but when he drizzled a few drops of the warm formula over the kitten's mouth, the seeking tongue licked it up, finally seeking the nipple. Astonishment struck Mark as the tiny animal nursed, its miniature paws kneading his hand. A strange paternal feeling crept over him. He held the kitten within Esmerelda's sight the entire time, but scant minutes passed before the tiny stomach filled and the suckling stopped.

He named the solid black one EightBall, the solid orange one, Juice, the black and white one, Jersey, and the white one with a splash of orange under its chin, BowTie. Each of them caught on as quickly as their first sibling, and were soon sleeping contentedly next to their mother. Mark even coaxed Esmerelda to take a few bites of her food, and to drink her fill of water. Then he removed the food as the vet suggested.

That done, he checked in on his other patient, pleased to see her rousing from her nap at the sound of the guest-room door opening. She was a mess, her hair limp and matted, her eyes still red and puffy. But she was beautiful. "Hey," he said, his voice filtering through the ever-present mask.

"How is she?" Ellie asked weakly.

"The doctor says she'll be fine. I got her to take the medicine, then fed the kittens."

Ellie smiled. "I wish I could've seen that."

"How are you feeling?"

"Like I've been run over by that beer truck of yours."

I'm starting to feel that way, too. "Are you hungry?"

She paused, as if checking with her stomach. "Yeah."

"Then let's get you up for a shower, and I'll fix you some soup."

"I kind of like being horizontal."

"But you'll feel so much better," he encouraged. "I'll get the water hot, then come back for you."

As he adjusted the spray of water, Mark had the distinct feeling he teetered on some kind of threshold: seeing an attractive woman in a near state of undress and not acting upon an urge. It struck him as very domestic, and not sexy at all. Perhaps this was what he needed to work through his lust for Ellie, to see her in an unsexy light.

"Are you ready?" he asked, walking into the room.

"I rather like it here," she insisted again, obviously not looking forward to the effort.

"Up you go," he said, placing a hand on her shoulder and easing her up slowly.

"Oh, my head," she said, grimacing.

"Sit on the edge of the bed for a moment to gather your strength," he instructed.

"You look ridiculous with that handkerchief tied over your mouth."

"You don't want to know how you look. Come on, try to stand up."

After a few false starts, Ellie made it to her feet, leaning heavily on Mark's arm for support. "I feel so weak," she moaned. "My teeth hurt."

Mark guided her into the guest bath toward the large shower stall. He'd set a stool beneath the spray so she wouldn't have to stand. The hot water had moistened the air, steam rising and swirling toward the ceiling.

"Oh, my God," Ellie said when she caught a glimpse of herself in the mirror. "Who is that?"

Mark chuckled and walked her to the shower door. "Here's your towel and some sweats. Do you need anything else?"

"While you're here, I might as well humiliate myself completely and ask you to help me with this shirt. I don't think I can lift my arms and pull at the same time."

Taking a deep breath, Mark nodded. She raised her arms slowly, then Mark slid the flimsy cotton shirt up her body and over her head. At the sight of her tan lines and skimpy undies, his body overheated immediately. *Unsexy. Yeah, right.*

"Thanks, sheik," she mumbled, obviously still amused by his makeshift mask. She rolled down her panties and kicked them off, then opened the shower door and collapsed onto the stool. Ellie leaned forward to let the warm water run over her head. "Come back in about an hour," she gurgled.

Mark exited gratefully.

BY VISUALIZING Mitzi Gaynor singing "I'm Gonna Wash That Man Right Outta My Hair," Ellie managed to give most of herself a once-over with the soapy sponge. Then she must have dozed off for a while, because she was jarred awake by a blast of cool water from the showerhead. "Mighty scrawny water heater for such a big house," she grumbled. Only the freezing air from the ceiling fan spurred her into putting forth enough effort to leave the shower and wrap the towel loosely around her chilling body. But within another few steps, she felt lightheaded. Reaching for the wall, Ellie slid down to rest on the floor, leaning forward to put her head between her knees.

She heard the tap at the door, but her neck refused to raise her head. Taking a shallow breath, she mumbled a response into the towel cave she'd created for herself. Suddenly Mark was by her side, worry evident in his voice.

"Ellie, are you all right? I should have stayed."

"I'm fine," she said into the thick terry cloth. "Just lightheaded."

"Light-headed? You're probably dehydrated." He tugged

on her arm to pull her body up a few inches, then swung her gently into his arms, and carried her.

Even through the haze of sickness, Ellie remembered when he'd last carried her to bed, it was to make love to her for the first time. That had happened last year sometime. Or was it yesterday? She couldn't be sure. She only knew she felt much better lying down on the fresh, cool sheets. Mark must have changed them. She opened her eyes and smiled at him. "You were right. The shower did make me feel better."

Mark pulled the wet towel from her body and helped her tug the covers up to her neck. Then he disappeared for a few minutes, returning with a tray of soup, crackers and two glasses of water. The smell alone revived her enough to sit up. And she was able to feed herself. She felt her strength returning a little with each bite. "I'm sorry, Mark, I should have stayed home. Now you'll probably be sick, too."

He smiled behind his hankie and pointed to it. "Besides," he added, "I had a flu shot in the spring."

"Is that what I've got?"

"My doctor said it sounded like the flu." He handed her two tablets. "For body aches," he said.

Got anything for heartaches? she wondered. "I want to see the kittens. Are they adorable?"

His cheekbones rose above the handkerchief and his eyes danced. "Yeah. Finish eating and then see how you feel."

"How's Esmerelda?"

"Relieved, I think, that the kittens are fed."

"She'll love you for it," Ellie said, quickly taking another spoonful of soup. When she glanced up, he was staring at her, his eyes unreadable. Suddenly her stomach rolled. "Oh, God." She brought her hand to her mouth.

"What?" Mark asked, his voice anxious.

"I'm going to throw up."

Mark jumped to his feet, searching for a container, then thrust a small trash can in front of her, not a second too soon. Between every retch, Ellie prayed a time warp would open and swallow her into another dimension. Could she be any more humiliated in front of this man?

Yes, she decided an hour later when her menstrual cramps began. Fortified with a smaller second helping of broth, Ellie dragged herself to the edge of the bed and stared in horror at her reflection in the mirror. Her hair had dried pasted to her head in the back, then straight up on end all around. "I look like the Statue of Liberty," she moaned, trying to smooth down the spikes. She struggled into the sweats Mark had laid at the foot of the bed, then stumbled into the bathroom to splash water on her blotchy face and comb her high hair.

"You're up," Mark said, his voice cheerful. He leaned against the door of the bedroom, but could see her standing through the open door of the bathroom.

"Yeah," said Ellie, embarrassment flooding her body. "And so is my hair."

He grinned. "Feeling better?"

"Uh, well, no, as a matter of fact, things have taken a turn for the worse. Is there a convenience store close by?"

"Just down a couple of blocks." He stepped into her room, concern in his eyes. What do you need?"

"Could you drive me?"

"No way you're getting out in your condition. Look at you."

"Thanks."

"I mean, look how sick you are. You're hanging on to the vanity to stand up, for Pete's sake. I'll get whatever you need."

"Okay. I need tampons."

He blinked. "T-tampons?"

Ellie raised her hands. "Forget it, I'll go."

"No," Mark said hurriedly. "That's all right, I'll be glad to." He started to leave, then turned back. "Anything else?" he asked, swallowing.

"While you're in that section, could you grab some panty shields?"

MARK SAT IN HIS CAR, scoping out the parking lot of the convenience store. He'd run into neighbors and colleagues here on more than one occasion. He closed his eyes and tried to remember which aisle held feminine-hygiene products. He'd bought painkillers once in the middle aisle and figured those two things should be pretty close. After all, it was all kind of…medical, wasn't it?

The object was to get in, get the goods and get out. If he waited until the cashier's line dwindled to one or two people, he figured he could buy what he needed and be safely back in his car within three minutes.

He watched two people pump gas and then walk in to pay for it. They were the only two customers in the store. He pulled a ball cap low over his forehead, and entered the store. He kept his eyes focused on the medicine aisle, but came face-to-face with a rack of picnic supplies. He glanced over at the beer case and saw milk instead. They'd rearranged the entire store.

A woman in a striped smock was sweeping up a spill a few feet away. "Can I help you?"

"Yeah," Mark said. "Can you show me to the aspirin?"

"Follow me, sir."

She walked slowly to aisle two and swept her arm at the array of painkillers as Mark scanned the shelves for the items he'd really come to purchase.

"We have regular, extra strength, buffered, childproof caps, nighttime—"

"Buffered will be fine," he said, then took the bottle she gave him.

The clerk stood with her hands on the broom, looking at him. "Anything else, sir?"

"Uh, I'll just look around."

"Go right ahead." She turned and shuffled toward the front of the store.

Mark walked up and down each of the eight aisles, keeping his eyes peeled for anything that said Personal or Feminine. Nothing. He made a second pass, this time more slowly. Nada.

He glanced around nervously and spotted the same clerk watching him closely, this time from behind a counter. She elbowed the cashier, a sour-looking teenager, and whispered something, nodding toward him. The cashier carefully pushed a button on her console, her eyes glued on him.

Mark grunted in frustration. *They think I'm stealing something.*

Within a few seconds, a jacketed, severe-looking older woman appeared. Her badge said Store Manager. *Great.*

"Can I help you, sir?"

"Uh, yeah," he said, keeping his voice low. "My…wife sent me out to pick up some personal things."

The woman frowned in confusion. "Personal things?"

"You know," he said, making vague gestures with his hands. "Woman stuff."

"Woman stuff?"

He sighed. "You know, *pads* and stuff."

"You're looking for menstruation products?"

He smiled tightly and nodded, admitting defeat.

"Right this way." She took him to an end cap in the front of the store which held a mind-boggling array of colored packages.

"Did you need pads or tampons?" she asked, her face serious, her voice rigid.

"Uh, tampons."

"Will that be deodorant or nondeodorant?"

"The pink box will be fine," Mark mumbled, heat rushing to his face.

"Slim, regular, plus or super-duper?"

"She's snug—I mean, small…she's a small lady." He reached up to rub his hand across his mouth.

"That has no relevance in this case, sir."

"Uh…regular, I guess."

She sighed. "Twelve count or twenty-four?"

"I'm not sure." Mark looked around, then leaned forward and whispered, "And I'm supposed to get some panty things, too."

"Panty shields?" she asked loudly. The clerks giggled openly, as did a few onlookers.

"Yeah," he murmured.

"Regular or winged?"

Mark sighed, pinching the bridge of his nose with forefinger and thumb. "Just give me two of everything."

She stacked his arms full, and carried a couple of packages toward the counter, herself. Except now the cashier's line had grown to about a dozen. Mark swore under his breath and inched his way forward, careful of his cumbersome load.

He maneuvered around a beer display, but his knee accidently nudged the mountain of twelve-pack bottles. The seemingly unending sound of crashing bottles was superseded only by the security alarm triggered from the shattering glass.

By the time the cops arrived, the clerks had most of the mess cleaned up and tallied.

Mark used his credit card to pay for two hundred thirty-eight dollars and fifty-nine cents' worth of "woman stuff" and beer.

"BLACKWELL!"

Mark jarred awake, his eyes flying open, his head jerking back. The men around the table chuckled as Mark shook his head to clear it, then repositioned himself in the conference-room chair. He'd fallen asleep in the middle of a staff meeting!

Ray Ivan frowned. "Are we keeping you up, son?"

"No, sir, sorry." Mark ground his teeth in frustration. Between frequent kitten feedings and Ellie's bouts of vomiting, he wasn't getting much rest. Two sleepless nights in a row had taken their toll.

When the meeting ended, Specklemeyer said, "Keeping late nights, Blackwell? I wonder what you could possibly be doing." He flashed a knowing smile, then trotted out when Mark's hands tightened on the chair arms.

Patrick walked out with him. "Why don't you take the afternoon off, Mark? You look beat."

"Ellie's got the flu," Mark explained, rubbing his eyes. "And the kids—I mean, the kittens…never mind. That's a very good idea. I'll see you tomorrow."

On the drive home, Mark berated himself over the predicament he'd gotten himself into. In just two days, he'd had his fill of domesticity. He breathed a quick prayer of thanks he'd broken it off with Ellie before all this mess. At least she'd been feeling better this morning, so he'd be rid of her and her cats soon. No more sneezing, no more litter boxes, no more heating pads. Good riddance! He'd probably have to take a nap in his car when he got home, just to have some peace and quiet.

Mark wheeled into the driveway and pulled into the garage, already dreading the melee that awaited him inside. He sighed, pushing open the kitchen door, waiting for the scents of cat milk and chicken soup to hit him. His nose wrinkled. Disinfectant?

"Ellie?" he called, walking through the kitchen. A note on the counter stopped him. Ellie's feminine writing curled across the page.

Great news! We have a new landlord who lifted the no-pet rule. Manny and a friend came over to pick us up today and take us home. I took the painting, too. It's not much, but I did a little cleaning to help repay you for all the trouble. We can't thank you enough. Ellie and Esmerelda.

A paw print in—lipstick?—stood out by Esmerelda's name. The extra key lay nearby.

Mark stood stock-still. Not even a goodbye? Who's to know she wouldn't have a relapse once she got home? And she didn't know the kittens' feeding schedule the way he did. Or that BowTie ate better when his little ears were rubbed. The kittens' eyes weren't even open yet, for heaven's sake! What was she thinking?

Wadding the note into a ball, he stomped upstairs. Not a sign of them anywhere. Every room sparkled, smelling clean and fresh. Not a cat hair in sight.

Mark sneezed.

"SAY CHEESE," Ellie said to the furry group squirming on the love seat. She snapped several pictures.

"What are you doing now?" Manny asked, walking into the living room.

"Just finishing up a roll of film. I thought I'd send out birth announcements for Esmerelda."

"I think your fever must have risen higher than anyone realized."

"Oh, stop. It'll be fun," Ellie insisted. "And a great way to find homes for the kittens. I'll send them to everyone we know."

Manny stooped to catch a wriggling kitten before it rolled off the cushion. "How soon can they be weaned?"

"Well, they're not quite two weeks old yet, so maybe another four weeks, possibly five since Esmerelda only started nursing yesterday."

"Have you heard from Papa Blackwell?"

Ellie's heart stirred. "No," she said brightly. "Why?"

"I was hoping I'd underestimated him. Unfortunately, it seems I was right again."

"He did take good care of us," Ellie said, practically to herself. The way he'd watched over them in his home did more to tangle her heartstrings than his previous wild love-making. While he'd held the trash can for her to empty her stomach, she'd felt herself sinking deeper in love with Mark. At that point, she'd vowed to leave as soon as she was physically able. That she'd been able to take the cats with her had been a bonus.

"I suppose you'll see him when you deliver the portrait."

Ellie glanced over at the twin portraits leaning against the wall, waiting to be framed. "I was thinking of having it couriered over when it's ready."

"Why don't you get dolled up and deliver it in person?"

"Manny, do you honestly think a cute outfit is going to erase the memory of him seeing my partially digested food?"

"Okay, I see your point. What are you going to do with the nude?" he asked, his voice wistful.

"Hmm." Ellie frowned. "I'm not sure. Harry will give me a better deal on the framing if I have them done at the same time. Afterward, maybe I can alter the face enough to sell it."

"You're welcome to use mine."

She grinned. "I might take you up on that."

When Ellie rewound the film and put away her camera, she discovered the two undeveloped rolls from the Blackwell picnic. Adding them to her backpack, she then changed into riding togs and grabbed her helmet.

"Back in a few minutes," she yelled.

It was a beautiful day for a ride, and Ellie hadn't been out much since recovering from her bout of the flu. She'd avoided it since she tended to think too much while cycling. And she hadn't been ready to face the sad thoughts until now.

She loved him. With all her heart. She'd seen glimpses of the kind of partner he would be. They could have made things work.

If only he loved her, too.

Mark Blackwell might have been fooled by the pheromones in the beginning, but now that he'd seen her at her worst and without the influence of the love chemicals, she didn't have a chance of moving his heart the way he'd shaken hers. So she'd grieve for a few months, then pick up the pieces and start looking again. Maybe she'd give Steve Willis a call.

Ellie dropped off the film at a one-hour developing center, then went in search of dried fruits and herbs for her latest perfume brainstorm. One good thing about being finished with the pheromones, she could wear her customized fragrances once again.

But, she decided as she rode by the sexy traffic cop without garnering so much as a second glance, it was the *only* good thing about not taking the pills. Her sex appeal had apparently nose-dived to its normal basement level.

She took a few moments to study the photos when she picked them up. She ordered lots of reprints of the best group picture of Esmerelda and the kittens. The photos of the picnic resurrected bittersweet memories. She'd gotten several good candid shots, especially one picture of Mark with his arm around his mother. Gloria was smiling, looking flushed and pretty.

A thought struck Ellie, and she checked her watch, gauging

the distance to Gloria's house. Just far enough for a good ride, she decided, and she'd be back in time to pick up the reprints.

Ellie pumped her legs furiously, enjoying the rush of adrenaline. After several blocks, apartment buildings and commercial property gave way to small older homes, with tiny picturesque yards. She slowed her pedaling to check the street signs, then turned down the road where Gloria Blackwell lived.

Wheeling into the neat driveway, she hopped off her bike and walked it to the sidewalk. After removing her helmet and running her hand through her hair, she took a deep breath, then removed the photos from her pack.

She climbed the steps leading to the pretty white clapboard home, nervousness rattling in her chest. After ringing the bell and waiting a few minutes, Ellie was tempted to leave the package of photos against the door and go, but suddenly the door opened and Gloria stood there, her hair rolled in large lavender curlers.

"Yes?" she said cautiously, her hand going to her hair.

"Hi, Mrs. Blackwell. I'm Ellie Sutherland. We met—"

Recognition dawned on the woman's face. "At the picnic, I remember," she said tartly.

"Yes, well…I brought you the pictures I snapped that afternoon." She extended the envelope to Mark's mother. "There is one of you and Mark I think you'll be especially pleased with."

"Why, thank you," Gloria said quietly. "But why didn't you just give the pictures to Mark?"

Ellie's heart lurched. "We're not seeing each other anymore."

Gloria's eyes brightened a fraction. "Oh?" She flipped through the photos, a small smile playing across her mouth. "My, Audra looks hippy in that flowered dress."

"Well, I guess I'll be going." Ellie started to turn away.

"Would you like to come in?" Gloria asked, obviously uncomfortable but mindful of her manners.

Ellie smiled and shook her head. "Thank you, but I really must be going. I have some other photos to pick up—" She

stopped as an idea struck her. "Mrs. Blackwell, do you share
Mark's allergies?"

Gloria smiled. "Me? Heavens, no. His father was always
the sniffly one. My son inherited it from him, I suppose." She
counted on her fingers. "Marcus is allergic to grass, pollen,
animals, feathers—"

"Whipped cream," Ellie added without thinking. When
Gloria frowned in confusion, Ellie said weakly, "The foamy
kind." Then she cleared her throat noisily. "Well, anyway,
maybe I will come in for just a moment." She flashed her
most persuasive smile. "Do you have any pets?"

"OH," Monica cooed. "Aren't they adorable?"

"Um," Mark murmured, studying the birth announcement
Monica had received. The question "Do you have a home for
one of my babies?" was lettered in bold print across the bottom of the card holding the photo. Written as a letter from
Esmerelda, the announcement doubled as a solicitation to
adopt one of her precious infants. The kittens' eyes were open,
their heads and paws woefully out of proportion to their tiny
bodies. He noted with relief that BowTie, the runt of the litter,
seemed to be holding his own with his rowdy siblings.

"I think I'll take one," Monica said. "Would you tell Ellie
the next time you see her?"

Mark cleared his throat. "We, uh, aren't seeing each other
anymore." He shuffled through a handful of phone messages
she'd handed him a few minutes earlier, hoping one of them
would be from Ellie.

"What? But you were engaged!"

Mark frowned at her wide-eyed expression. "Well, now
we're not."

"Just like that?"

Irritation shot through him. "No, not just like that. We both
agreed we weren't right for each other."

Monica shook her head in disbelief. "Are you blind?
You're perfect for each other."

Mark raised his hands in astonishment. "We're complete
opposites!"

''Like I said, the perfect match.''

Shaking his head, Mark headed toward his office. ''You're not making sense.''

''Well, at least I know why you've been so testy the last few days,'' she called after him.

''I have *not* been testy the last few days!'' Mark yelled as he slammed his door.

12

MARK SPENT a restless Sunday morning doing nothing of significance. It was shaping up to be a blah, overcast day, and he had a mood to match. He sat down heavily on the couch and began flipping through channels. A lump under his hip caught his attention, and he pulled out a toy cloth mouse. One of Esmerelda's less destructive pastimes. The pink mouse resembled Ellie's tattoo, the memory of which had him shifting positions again.

Why couldn't he get the woman out of his mind? Somehow she'd wormed her way into his heart, then sprouted barbs, at once anchoring her image and promising bloodshed if he tried to dislodge it.

He reached over to pick up the cordless phone and dialed his mother's number, thinking he'd probably regret this phone call later. "Hi, Mom," he said.

"Hello, dear, it's so nice to hear from you. Where have you been keeping yourself the last few days?"

He swung Esmerelda's mouse by the tail. "Mostly at the office, you know, working late."

"You're so industrious, Marcus, I suppose you get it from my side of the family." She sighed. "Lord knows, your father never hit a lick at anything, God love him."

Mark frowned and leaned forward to place his elbows on his knees. "Mom, I've never asked you this before, but you and Dad seemed so different, why did you marry him? I'm sure you could have found a better provider."

She was silent for a long moment.

"Mom?"

"I'm here," she whispered.

"I didn't mean to upset you."

"If I'm upset with anyone, it's myself. I guess it's easy to point out a person's shortcomings. To other people, I suppose your father and I seemed somewhat the odd couple. I'm sorry I never took the time to tell you why I fell in love with Rudy."

He sat in silence, afraid to interrupt her train of thought.

"Your father was a wonderful, caring man, Marcus. His heart was ten times bigger than his bank account, and I knew that when he proposed." She laughed softly. "I was a comely woman in my day, and I had a fair amount of suitors, some of them real catches. But not one of them could make me laugh like Rudy."

His mother cleared her throat. "I followed my heart instead of my head. And you know what? I might have wished for your father to be more financially stable, but I never regretted my decision to be his wife."

Mark's eyes clouded and his insides tingled. Ellie's face floated in and out of his mind, taunting him. *Follow your heart, follow your heart...*

"Well, enough about that," Gloria said brightly. "How's the little painter?"

It took a few seconds for Mark to recover from his surprise. "You mean Ellie?"

"Yes, Ellie. She came by the house the other day, you know."

He frowned. "No, I didn't know."

"Brought me pictures she'd taken at the picnic—she got a lovely one of you and me together."

"That's nice." Was that cheeriness in his mother's voice?

"She offered me a kitten, too. She said you'd helped nurse them when the mother couldn't. And got her through a bout with the flu, I hear." Her voice rolled with innuendo. "Is there something you're not telling me, son?"

"What do you mean?"

"You like this girl, don't you?"

"Well, sure I like her—"

"Do you love her?"

Mark snorted. "What kind of question is that?"

"A legitimate one considering you bottle-fed five kittens for her."

She had a point. "I haven't made up my mind how I feel about her."

Gloria clucked. "It's none of my business, but I wouldn't dawdle if I were you."

"What did you two talk about?"

"Lots of things—she's really very nice, Marcus, even if she is a bit quirky. She found me a fourth for Sunday bridge tomorrow."

"She plays bridge?"

"No, but she knew that Ray Ivan plays and she called him right up."

"My partner is playing bridge with you tomorrow?"

"Stella is making coffee cake and we thought we might splurge on a bottle of sherry."

Mark smiled and shook his head. "Sounds like a day."

"Oh, look at the time," she exclaimed. "I have an appointment to get my hair done."

He laughed and injected suggestion into his voice. "Go, Mom."

"Oh, you." She giggled, clearly pleased at the prospect of having a beau.

"Uh, Mom, I was wondering…did Ellie have anything to say about, well, you know…me and her?"

"Hmm." He could picture her squinting at the ceiling. "I recall her saying something about…" She paused.

"Yeah?" he prompted.

"No," she said suddenly, "come to think of it, I don't think she said a word about the two of you."

"Oh," he said, frowning. Disappointment squeezed his heart.

"I'll call you tomorrow when I get back from bridge," his mother promised. "Bye now."

Mark hung up the phone, then stood and grabbed his keys, fully planning to drive to the office for a few hours. Instead, he drove around in circles before he finally parked at the train station and caught the line speeding toward Underground Atlanta. Maybe she would be there, drawing caricatures. And what if she is? his conscience probed. I'll think of something brilliant to say, he promised himself.

Underground Atlanta, located in the center of downtown, boasted nearly a hundred shops in its restored multilevel structure. The lower level, abandoned early in the century when the entire city was elevated, now resembled a town street, with shops on either side, the ceiling stretching far above the foot traffic. The quaint atmosphere and curbside entertainers combined to make it a favorite place for locals and tourists.

Mark strolled the length of the cobbled main street, moving with the crowd, stopping to watch a humorous puppeteer, tossing a dollar into the man's hat at the conclusion of the show. The small knot of people gathered at the end of the indoor street might have gone unnoticed by him, except for the glimpse of a floppy hat. He walked closer, carefully staying out of Ellie's line of vision. His heart pounded at the sight of her smile as she invited a young woman to pose for a caricature. Stepping close enough to watch her sketch, Mark marveled once again over her talent, and her ability to banter with the audience as she drew.

She must have inquired into the woman's hobbies because the finished drawing showed the woman holding a flute. The woman thanked her and paid for her drawing, then Ellie glanced around for another customer. Suddenly her eyes landed on Mark, and she stopped in obvious surprise. He tingled in response to her expression. He'd been too rash in suggesting they stop seeing each other. Perhaps she would go to dinner with him this evening.

"Sir," she called to him, "would you like to have your picture drawn?"

The crowd turned for his response, and he nodded, happily stepping up and taking a seat in front of her.

She frowned, studying him in an exaggerated fashion before beginning the sketch. Mark remembered the queen-bee drawing of his mother and wondered how Ellie would portray him.

"Tell me about yourself," she said, obviously for the crowd's sake.

"I'm an attorney," he said simply.

She smiled, and spoke to the crowd. "Shall I draw him as a shark?" The audience tittered.

He shrugged good-naturedly. Ellie picked up a pastel crayon and began drawing on her sketch pad. Mark couldn't see the picture from where he sat. She looked beautiful in a pink denim jacket buttoned up to her chin over a long flowered skirt. She was multifaceted: Ellie the artist, Ellie the perfume maker, Ellie the wild lover. He smiled. And all of her personas made him happy, made him laugh. *"But not one of them could make me laugh like Rudy…"*

As she sketched, she asked him questions she already knew the answers to.

"Are you a visitor?"

Mark played along. "No, a native."

"Are you married?"

"Single."

"Do you like cats?"

"I'm allergic."

The audience watched, their faces splitting into grins as Mark's drawing progressed. He squirmed. Would she put him in his sports car? A briefcase in one hand and a phone in the other? A fancy suit and harried expression? He wouldn't blame her if she did. Work had always been his top priority. Could it be his values were beginning to shift toward settling down? Mark felt an odd sensation settle in his stomach. What good were all his possessions if he had no one to share them with? And not just anyone. He wanted Ellie.

"There," Ellie exclaimed, finishing with a flourish. The crowd laughed outright when she shifted the easel toward him for his reaction. Mark swallowed, then smiled. She'd drawn him standing, a white handkerchief tied around his mouth, concentrating intently, a squirming kitten in one hand, a bottle in the other. Four other kittens climbed his jeans legs.

"It's great," he said, looking into Ellie's bright eyes. "How are they?"

"The kittens? I still haven't found homes for Jersey, EightBall or BowTie, but I'm hopeful."

"Mom said you'd talked her into adopting one. By the way, thanks for taking her the pictures."

Ellie shrugged and nodded. "No problem."

"And for arranging the bridge matchup."

Another shrug. "I owed your mother one—and Ray, too."

He fished around for any scrap of conversation. "Monica said she'd take a kitten."

"Great," she said, her smile jarring his heart. "Three down and two to go."

Listen to your heart...do you love her?...don't dawdle... "Ellie—"

"Hey," a fair-haired man exclaimed, walking up to Ellie. "How much longer?"

"This was my last drawing, Steve," Ellie said, smiling up at the man. Her face flushed a becoming rose at his appearance—she was obviously pleased to see him.

Mark's gut twisted at the man's familiarity with Ellie. She tore his drawing off her pad and handed it to him. Instantly, Mark reached for his wallet.

Ellie stopped him, holding up a hand. "It's on the house." She stood and turned to the crowd. "Thank you, everyone, I'll be back next Sunday."

The Steve guy began to gather up her supplies, and Mark stood awkwardly. Ellie folded her easel, then glanced at him with a half smile. "See you around," she said, lifting her hand in a friendly wave, then walked off with the man's hand at her elbow.

Mark stood like a statue, his eyes riveted on the couple. At the end of the indoor street, Ellie stopped in front of a bag lady who sat sprawled on the curb, her possessions huddled around her. He saw Ellie reach into her purse and extract a couple of bills, then hand them to the woman, smiling and saying a few words before she went on her way.

Ellie, already on a tight budget, giving away her hard-earned money to a needy person. *Just like Dad...Rudy would have been crazy about Ellie.* He watched helplessly as the blond man put his arm around her shoulder and kissed her hair.

Mark wondered if he'd caught a lingering flu bug, after all. He suddenly felt very sick to his stomach.

"THE PAINTINGS turned out great," Harry said, emerging from the back of the framing shop with one in each arm.

Desire washed over Ellie as Mark's face leaped from one picture, his body from the other. An ornate cherry-wood frame lent more formality to his business portrait, a simple black wood frame set off the nude perfectly.

"Great," she agreed with a forced smile. "I'll take the nude with me. Courier the bust to this address and add it to my bill." She handed the framer a slip of paper.

"Wait and I'll wrap them both," he said, winking. "Else you might have a trail of women following you home wanting this guy's number."

In the few minutes Ellie waited, she changed her mind a dozen times about having the painting delivered. Maybe she should take it herself, to gauge Mark's reaction to her. He'd come to Underground a few days ago, presumably to see her, although she couldn't be sure. Maybe he did care for her, after all. But without the pheromones, how long could she keep his interest? And she couldn't bear going through another breakup.

Harry appeared with the wrapped nude a few minutes later. "My driver was leaving with a delivery, so I gave him the bust. It's already on its way."

Ellie nodded. It was for the best.

But on the walk home, doubts nagged at Ellie. She'd never felt toward any man what she felt with Mark. Steve Willis was a nice man, but no feelings surfaced when he kissed her. What if Mark Blackwell was the one great love of her life, and she let him slip through her fingers because he reminded her of her father? Mark wasn't Joe Sutherland. In his early years, her dad would never have nursed kittens and gone shopping for feminine-hygiene articles.

Ellie took a deep breath and turned in the direction of the clinic. After a few minutes' walk, she pushed open the door and asked a receptionist to page Freda. Soon, Freda emerged, her face folding with puzzlement when she saw Ellie.

"What brings you here?" the woman asked.

"Kittens," Ellie said, extending one of Esmerelda's birth announcements. "I'm trying to find homes for them and wondered if you'd be interested."

It was the first genuinely happy smile she'd seen on the woman's face. "My tabby passed on two months ago. I've been meaning to go to the shelter to find another, but I couldn't bring myself to replace her just yet."

"The black female is still unspoken for."

Freda nodded, satisfied. "I'll take her."

"Great," Ellie said, smiling. Then she glanced side to side, shifting slightly. "Uh, Freda, can we talk?"

The gray-haired woman checked the watch on her wrist. "I've got about ten minutes, come on back."

Ellie chewed her bottom lip nervously, wondering how the woman would react to her request.

"I've been wondering about you and your fellow," Freda said, glancing over her shoulder at Ellie as they entered her small office. "How did you make out?"

Ellie shut the door. "That's what I wanted to talk to you about."

Freda's eyebrows went up. "Oh?"

"I need more pills."

After a few seconds of hesitation, Freda replied, "I can't do that."

"Please?" Ellie pleaded, folding her hands together. Tears welled and spilled over her cheeks. "I've never been so miserable in my life. I love him."

Freda shook her head. "It's impossible—"

"I'll pay you," Ellie said through her tears. "Whatever it takes, just a few weeks' supply, just long enough to regain his attention and show him how really good we can be together."

"The pills are controlled, I can't distribute them outside the study."

Ellie sniffled loudly. "Then put me back in the study."

Handing her a tissue, Freda said, "You've already been

through one cycle of pills, you wouldn't be a pure study subject again so soon."

"You've got to help me." Ellie sobbed. "What am I going
to do?" She blew her nose noisily, beseeching Freda.

The lab-coated woman sat back in her chair and sighed, then
rose and crossed to a file cabinet. Opening the drawer, she
fingered through several folders, finally stopping to extract
one. Ellie saw her name on it. She hiccuped.

Freda studied the file, flipping through several pages
quickly, obviously looking for a particular piece of information. At last she found it, because understanding dawned on
her face. "Just what I suspected," she muttered thoughtfully

Ellie held her breath. When she could wait no longer, she
asked, "Can you help me?"

Lifting her head to study Ellie, Freda's eyes narrowed
"What I'm about to tell you could cost me my job, so you
have to swear to keep this quiet."

Her heart pounded. "What is it?" Ellie asked, her tears now
dry from fear.

"Promise?" Freda asked.

"I promise," Ellie agreed, crossing her heart solemnly.

Her new friend took a deep breath, then exhaled it roughly
"In the pheromones study we conducted…"

"Yes?" Ellie prompted, making a rolling motion with her
hand. "What?"

"You were in the placebo group."

Confusion washed over her. "The placebo group?"

"That's right—you were taking sugar tablets. Any so-called
effects of the pills you took were self-induced."

Ellie's arms and shoulders grew weak. She lifted her wobbly hands in question. "How can that be? Men kept smelling
something."

"Maybe the extra sugar you were ingesting, maybe your
natural scent—who knows? The power of suggestion is not to
be underestimated." Freda sat back in her chair and crossed
her arms. "Tell a woman she has the ability to attract any man
she wants and watch her throw her shoulders back and begin
to exude self-confidence." She leaned forward, waving a hand

at Ellie. "Look at you—you have all the tools, you're pretty and funny and nice. What makes you think you need some silly old pills to make this man fall in love with you? If he's that blind, honey, then he can't be the one for you."

Ellie walked home, fighting back tears. Despite Freda's pep talk, her heart dragged heavily in the wake of the woman's revelation. If Mark had never been under the influence of pheromones, then he *had* been physically attracted to her, at least in the beginning. But it also meant whatever feelings he'd developed had waned naturally, and not because she'd suddenly run out of pills.

She'd been trying to make a mountain of commitment out of a molehill of lust.

The many tiny balls of fur that came running for her when she stepped into the apartment lifted her spirits somewhat. She grabbed a cold cola from the fridge and one for Manny as he came sauntering through the hall.

"Hey, girl."

"Hey."

He wrinkled his nose. "Are you going to be in a blue funk over Mark Blackwell forever?"

"Maybe," she said defiantly, cracking open the soda can and lifting it to her mouth.

He did the same. "Well, I for one get a boost every time I think about him getting caught in the bathroom at that restaurant." He laughed. "You've got to admit it's hilarious, El."

She smiled, begrudgingly lifted from her bad mood. "He could still get in worlds of trouble if Tony Specklemeyer decides to make an issue of it."

Manny stopped. "Is that the guy's name? Specklemeyer... Why does that name sound familiar?" He walked around the kitchen absently. "I can't think...wait a minute!" He snapped his fingers. "Does he drive a black Jaguar?"

Ellie shrugged. "Beats me. I do remember Mark saying he had a vanity license plate that says—"

"'HUNGRY,' in capital letters," Manny finished.

"How did you know that?"

He leaned against the counter, a cunning smile warming his

face. "Because that vile man circles the club where I work every other night, trying to pick up the performers as they leave." Manny shuddered. "He says the most disgusting things."

Ellie's mouth dropped open. "You're kidding?"

"Nope."

"Well, that's no crime."

"No," Manny agreed, "but you'd think the pot wouldn't be so anxious to call the kettle black if he could be thrown into the same dishwater."

She grinned. "You're right. I'll call Mark later and let him in on the news. I'll bet if he just drops a hint to this guy, he'll back off."

"If Mark hadn't been stupid enough to let you go, he wouldn't have to worry about any silly old rumors."

Ellie walked over and gave him a bear hug. "You're so good for me."

He pulled back in sudden recollection. "El, I forgot to tell you—you got a letter back from the perfume-making contest." He flipped through the mail on the counter and handed her an envelope.

Ripping it open, she scanned the letterhead, and read out loud. "Dear Ms. Sutherland, we are pleased to announce your formula, Irresistible You, has been chosen the winner—" Ellie screamed, then grabbed Manny and jumped up and down. "I won, I won, I won!" After a few moments of elation in which she kissed him and every cat within arm's reach, she continued reading. "Please contact us as soon as possible to arrange to collect your winnings, and to discuss your ideas for an entire product line. We look forward to hearing from you." She threw back her head and squealed in delight, dancing around the kitchen. In her exuberance, she knocked against the painting, the resulting tear in the wrapping paper exposing a glimpse of dark cherry wood.

Cherry? A tiny seed of dread sprouted in her stomach, then mushroomed when she ripped the paper farther and stared at Mark's business portrait.

"Oh, my God," she breathed. "Harry delivered the nude

to Mark's office by mistake!'' Her eyes locked with Manny's. Thirty seconds later she pounded down the stairs, carrying the portrait under her arm. Running into the street, she hailed the first taxi she saw with a loud, ear-piercing whistle.

13

MONICA TAPPED on the door, then opened it a few inches. "Mark," she said, holding up a letter and a bulky package. "Two things—Habitat for Humanity sent a thank-you letter for your donation, and a work schedule for the next home being built."

He reached for it. "Thanks."

"If I may say so," she began tentatively.

"Yes?"

"Your donation was very generous, Mark. And for you to volunteer to help build a home for a needy family, well, it's a side of you I didn't know, but one I'm very impressed with." She smiled and sincerity shone in her eyes.

"Thank you," he said softly, placing the letter on his desk.

She held the large package toward him. "And your portrait just arrived."

His pulse leaped. Ellie was here! Mark craned his neck to look around Monica. "Where is she?"

"Who?" Monica asked, confused.

"Ellie."

"I don't know. A courier delivered the painting."

"Oh." Mark tried to keep the dejection out of his voice, but he knew he failed miserably. "Leave it, please."

Monica leaned it against his desk and made a hasty exit. Mark turned back to the work spread across his desk and forced himself to concentrate. After a few minutes, he gave up, tossed the pen straight up in the air, then watched it bounce off a corner of his desk, disappearing over the edge.

He turned to look at the package. Even after all that work, she didn't want to hand-deliver it. She didn't want to see him

Not that he blamed her. He'd made it coldly clear on the phone when he returned from Chicago that he didn't want to see her anymore. What an ass he'd been. Mark slammed his fist on his desk, but it only brought Monica back to the door.

"Mark? Are you okay?" she asked, concern written on her face.

"Fine," he said through clenched teeth. When she retreated, he massaged his throbbing hand, then reached for the painting. He fingered the wrapping for several seconds as sadness welled in him. He didn't want to see the portrait right now. He didn't want another painful reminder of Ellie and his foolish behavior.

He pushed a button on his phone. "Monica, please have maintenance come to pick up the painting and hang it." Within minutes, she entered his office again and retrieved the picture. Then Mark heard her give explicit directions to the man as to where it was to be hung.

Walking the length of his office, Mark rubbed his temples. He wished a headache would erupt, because then he'd at least have a reason for feeling lousy. This gnawing in his stomach and this heaviness in his chest were becoming unbearable. Damn! He never thought he'd let a woman get to him. Maybe he needed a vacation. That's it, he decided. *I'll go to some paradise for a couple of weeks and get Ellie out of my system. After all, she's just a woman.*

The Piedmont Park painting beckoned to him and he smiled. The picture never failed to lift his spirits. He walked over to and absorbed the artist's impression of a day in the sun and wind. The colors, the movement, everything about it made him feel the way he did when his father took him to the park as a child. He could almost feel the grass between his toes and see his dad doing card tricks for a crowd of kids. They'd eat a cheese-sandwich picnic and fly kites, then roll up their pants and wade in the kiddie-pool. Back then, the days seemed to last forever, and every hour brought new and wonderful pleasures. He'd loved his father fiercely. He loved him still.

I really should contact the artist someday and tell him how much I enjoy this painting. He'd never before thought about the artist, and for the first time, his eyes searched the bottom-right corner for a name. There it was, in white, but very small and not quite clear. "E. Sutherland," he muttered slowly, then froze. Could it be? He double-checked the signature. A dim memory surfaced of the first day she'd walked into his office. Nice picture, she'd said.

"Ellie," he murmured. A wondrous feeling began in his chest and slowly radiated to his extremities. "I might have known it was yours." Then he threw back his head and laughed. She had brought joy into his life even before he'd known her. Mark laughed until he had to lean against the wall for support.

Another knock sounded, and Monica stuck her head in warily. "Mark? Are you okay? I'm worried about you."

But Mark just grinned and chuckled, waving away her concern. "Never better, Monica." She exited with a reluctant expression, then Mark slid down the wall to sit on the floor as he dissolved in laughter once again. When he'd finally regained control, he shook his head at his own stupidity. He loved Ellie, he had from the beginning. But would she give him another chance?

"I'm not letting her go without a fight," he said, pulling himself to his feet and crossing to his desk. He hadn't felt this good in days. Mark punched in Ellie's number and waited nervously to hear her voice.

"Hi, this is Ellie and Manny's place. You know the drill." Then a beep sounded.

He frowned, but began to speak. "Ellie, it's Mark. If you're there, please pick up, I need to talk to you right away." He hesitated a few seconds then said, "I l-l-lo—" He stuttered over the words, then tried again. "I l-l-lo—" Darnit, it was harder to say than he'd imagined. Mark took a deep breath. "I l-l-love you, Ellie. Please call me." He hung up slowly.

"I love you, too," Ellie said.

Mark spun around and his heart vaulted at the sight of her standing in his doorway with a package, a beaming Monica pushing her inside, closing the door.

Ellie swallowed tears that welled in her throat. He did love her.

He leaped to his feet and rushed toward her. Ellie leaned the wrapped painting against the wall, then met his embrace. He kissed her, lifting her off the ground and spinning her around. "Where did you come from?" he asked, grinning.

"Iowa," Ellie said, laughing through her tears.

"You were born in Iowa?"

Ellie nodded. "We have a lot of catching up to do."

Mark reached behind her to lock the door, then stepped to his desk and cleared the top with one sweep of his arm. He grinned. "We can start right here." Papers swirled to the ground at their feet.

Ellie's heart swelled as she allowed him to pull her to his desk. How she loved this man.

He lowered his head to hers and drew her into a deep kiss, his hands cupping her rear, pulling her against his arousal. They grabbed at each other's clothing, Ellie's skirt ending up around her waist, her panties on the ceiling fan. Mark's pants sagged around his ankles. Buttons from his shirt missiled against the wall as she yanked the front open.

"I don't have any protection," he whispered.

"I'd like to start a family as soon as possible," she replied throatily, positioning herself for his entry.

"Lots of kids?" he asked, sounding pleased.

"Five or so."

He plunged into her and Ellie stiffened with overwhelming desire.

"I feel like I could plant at least that many right now," he warned, moving inside her. They rocked together for a few seconds, then Ellie felt her ecstasy ballooning. "Mark," she whispered urgently. "Oh, Mark." He covered her mouth with his to absorb her scream of release. She heard, rather than felt, his shirt rip as she clawed his back. Suddenly he tensed and moaned low into her mouth, his body jerking in relief.

"I've missed you," he breathed.

After a few seconds, her pulse slowed. "I missed you, and so has Esmerelda."

Mark's eyes rolled heavenward. "I guess this means I'll have to paint my bedroom blue if we're ever going to have any privacy."

A loud commotion outside caught their attention. Mark frowned, pulled away, and started righting his clothes. "What's going on? It sounds like it's coming from down the hall."

Beads of perspiration popped out on Ellie's upper lip. "Mark," she said. "Do you really love me?"

His face softened. "I really do." Pulling a chair over to the fan, he retrieved her lace panties and handed them to her.

Ellie began to dress, biting her lower lip. "Do you really, *really* love me?"

Mark's smile widened even as he surveyed his shredded shirt in the mirror. "You know I do. Remind me to buy you a pair of gloves right away."

The commotion was getting louder, the sound of many voices raised. Mark pulled on his jacket, straightened his tie and walked toward the door. "Something's going on."

"Mark!" Ellie grabbed his hand and fought to keep the desperation out of her voice. "Please tell me there's nothing I could do to make you stop loving me."

He turned toward her again, taking her face in his hands. "Sweetheart, there's nothing you could do to make me stop loving you." He lowered his mouth to hers for a quick, loving kiss.

A knock sounded at the door. "Mark?" Monica asked from the other side, her voice urgent.

"Promise?" Ellie asked, gripping his hands.

"Yes, I promise, Ellie." He turned to open the door, then noticed the wrapped portrait Ellie had brought. "What's that?"

Ellie just shrugged her shoulders, smiling wide.

"The last time I saw that look, Esmerelda had gone fishing."

"Mark?" Monica's voice was insistent, her knocking louder.

He opened the door. "What's all the noise, Monica?"

His secretary wore an unreadable expression, her eyes wide. "You're needed in the boardroom. *Right away.*"

"Is something wrong?" he asked, concern written on his face.

Monica glanced at Ellie, and Ellie saw raw admiration on the woman's face. "Not everyone would think so."

Mark walked out the door and strode down the hall toward the boardroom. Ellie hesitated, but Monica grabbed her arm and pulled her along. Ellie's mind raced. How was she going to explain this one?

She stepped into the crowded room a split second behind Mark, in time to see his eyes land on the nearly life-size sprawling nude. A roomful of suited men and women roared, Ray and Patrick both bent double, tears streaming down their faces.

Mark's jaw fell, and his mouth worked up and down, but no sound came out. He turned his head slowly to look at Ellie, and she winced, taking a half step back. This was going to be an interesting relationship.

His eyes were round in disbelief, his hands clenched in fists at his sides. "Ellie," he said, his voice ominously low. "What the hell is that?"

All eyes turned to Ellie and the room quieted, poised for her answer. Swallowing, Ellie tried to gather her courage. She lifted her chin and smiled nervously at her glowering husband-to-be.

"That, as everyone can see," she said brightly, sweeping her arm in a grand gesture, "is one well-hung portrait."

Our hottest *Temptation*®
authors bring you...

BLAZE

Three sizzling love stories available in one volume
in September 1999.

Midnight Heat
JoAnn Ross

A Lark in the Dark
Heather MacAllister

Night Fire
Elda Minger

Turn the page now for a sneak preview of the first
story *Midnight Heat* by JoAnn Ross...

Midnight Heat
by
JoAnn Ross

What If I Said

"SO, WHAT ARE YOU going to do?" RaeAnn asked
as she sat in the kitchen of the Montgomery ranch,
staring at the single ticket in the middle of the table.

"I really don't have much choice," Erin said.
The curt note accompanying the ticket had informed her that she could either come to see Jace
after his show at the fairgrounds, or he'd be coming out to the ranch to see her. "I'm going to have
to go."

"Well, I realize that no one's asked me," Julia
Martin Montgomery said as she rolled out pie
dough on the counter, "but I think it's about time
you and C.J.'s father had a serious talk about the
future." The nurse who'd at first visited the ranch
to keep a professional eye on Erin's father after his
successful surgery, had stayed on to become his
wife. Erin had been delighted when, after all those
years of being a widower, her father had married
again. And lately, the couple had professed a desire

to buy a motor home and see the country. Finances, always tight, had precluded such an adventure.

"The boy's got a right to know his father," John Montgomery seconded his wife.

"I know." Erin sighed again. "It's just so difficult."

"It's not difficult at all," RaeAnn argued. "For heaven's sake, Erin, those of us who know the situation can tell that Jace has been writing all those songs about you, which means that he was wild about you back then."

"And furious at me now," Erin said glumly. The dark album entitled *Promises in the Wind* hadn't left any doubt as to how he'd felt when she'd refused to see him after the European tour.

"What happened is in the past. And granted, it can't be changed, but even though some could argue that you may have used poor judgment, that's no reason why you and Jace can't have a second chance," Julia said sensibly.

"And whatever happens, at least C.J. won't be the only kid in kindergarten next year who doesn't know who his father is," her father added, returning to the argument he'd been making since the FedEx man had brought the concert ticket to the ranch.

"I'm going to tell him," Erin assured them all. She'd come to realize, even before receiving Jace's note, that she owed both him and C.J. the truth. "After the concert."

RaeAnn stood. ''Now that we've got that settled, let's go into town and get you a dynamite new dress—one that'll knock his socks off and make him forget what he was angry about.''

Erin opened her mouth to argue that she didn't need a new dress just to tell Jace he was a father. But some deep-seated feminine instinct she thought she'd put away when she'd made the decision to have her child alone, stirred in her.

Was it so wrong of her to want him to find her attractive—to look at her the way he had that long-ago, unforgettable night? Short of finding a time machine in Whiskey River that would transport her back to that fateful morning five years ago, when she'd rejected Jace's offer to take her to Las Vegas with him, Erin decided that a new dress might be exactly what she needed.

THIS TIME THEY'D SPELLED his name right. This time he was at the top of the marquee, above the demolition derby and the little wranglers' goat-roping competition. This time the audience had come to see him. And this time Jace was more nervous than he'd ever been before in his life.

Fortunately, he managed to click onto autopilot the moment he stepped onstage to the screams of his fans. Somehow he made it through the entire show without screwing up once, even though afterward, he couldn't recall having sung a single note.

THE DRESSING ROOM, which was really just an eight-by-ten Airstream trailer parked behind the rodeo grounds, had finally emptied, leaving him alone, wondering if she was going to come—and what the hell he was going to do if she didn't.

A hesitant knock answered that nagging question. "Come on in. It's open." Deciding not to make it easy on her, he didn't bother to open the door himself.

As she paused in the doorway, backlit by the setting sun, Jace realized that his memory hadn't failed him. Five years ago she'd been lovely. But she'd been a girl, only a few years out of her teens. The woman who looked as if she was prepared to bolt at any moment had matured into the most stunning female he'd ever seen.

"Hello, Jace." Her voice, which hadn't changed, slipped beneath his skin. The scent he'd not been able to get out of his mind engulfed him. And Jace knew he was sunk.

"Erin." He pushed himself out of the chair and took the few steps toward her. "It's good of you to come."

His voice was distant. His chocolate-dark eyes were not. Erin decided to focus on them. "I didn't have all that much choice," she reminded him as she forced herself to enter the trailer and shut the door behind her.

"We always have choices."

He was close, too close. She could smell the

musky scent of sweat from his energetic performance, feel the warmth radiating from his body. It could have been that night five years ago, were it not for the anger surrounding him—anger she had to admit he was entitled to. If he was furious with her now, she worried, how was he going to react when he learned she'd kept the existence of his son from him for all these years?

Without warning, his hand fisted in her hair and he pulled her against him, as close as they'd been when they'd danced together by the river that night. The air became so charged, Erin could practically hear the electricity crackling around them.

"One question." His harsh voice might have frightened her if it hadn't stirred so many feminine chords. "Are you married?"

He'd pulled her head back, forcing her to look a long, long way up at him. Her breath tumbled out from between lips that had gone painfully dry. "No."

"Thank God."

Midnight Heat is one of three stories in

BLAZE on sale in September.

Don't miss it!

MILLS & BOON®

*M*akes
any time
special

Copyright © Harlequin Enterprises Limited 1997
All rights reserved

Enjoy a romantic novel from
Mills & Boon®

Presents™ *Enchanted™* *Temptation*®

Historical Romance™ *Medical Romance™*

Our hottest *Temptation*® authors bring you…

BLAZE

**Three sizzling love stories available in
one volume in September 1999.**

Midnight Heat
JoAnn Ross

A Lark in the Dark
Heather MacAllister

Night Fire
Elda Minger

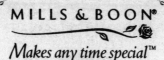

MILLS & BOON®

Makes any time special™

*Bestselling themed romances brought
back to you by popular demand*

Each month By Request brings you three
full-length novels in one beautiful volume
featuring the best of the best.

So if you missed a favourite Romance
the first time around, here is your chance
to relive the magic from some of our
most popular authors.

**Look out for
Her Baby Secret in June 1999
featuring Lynne Graham,
Jacqueline Baird and Day Leclaire**

*Available at most branches of WH Smith, Tesco,
Asda, Martins, Borders, Easons,
Volume One/James Thin
and most good paperback bookshops*

MILLS & BOON®

Makes any time special™

THE

Regency

COLLECTION

Where rogues find romance

Mills & Boon® is delighted to bring back, for a limited period, 12 of our favourite Regency Romances for you to enjoy.

These special books will be available for you to collect each month from May, and with two full-length Historical Romance™ novels in each volume they are great value.

ONLY £4.99.

Volume One available from 7th May

Available at most branches of WH Smith, Tesco, Asda, Martins, Borders, Easons, Volume One / James Thin and most good paperback bookshops

Available from bestselling author of _Random Acts_

TAYLOR SMITH

WHO WOULD YOU TRUST
WITH YOUR LIFE?

THINK AGAIN.

THE BEST OF ENEMIES

MIRA®

Published 18th June

Bestselling author

LAURA VAN WORMER

DOWNTOWN
Tonight

WEST END

where the people who report the news...
are the news

From its broadcast centre in Manhattan,
DBS—TV's newest network—is making
headlines. Beyond the cameras, the
careers of the industry's brightest stars
are being built.

MIRA®

Published 18th June 1999

When winning is everything... losing can be deadly.

HIGH
STAKES
Rebecca Brandewyne

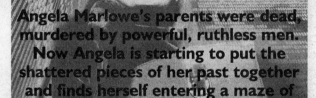

Angela Marlowe's parents were dead, murdered by powerful, ruthless men. Now Angela is starting to put the shattered pieces of her past together and finds herself entering a maze of danger and corruption. But she is not alone.

MIRA®

Available from July

Full Circle
KAREN YOUNG

Thirty three years ago, five-year-old Kate lost
her father in a tragic boating accident.

Now Kate, an E.R. doctor, is experiencing
disturbing flashbacks. Is is burnout?
Or something more sinister?

Kate is looking for answers. But, somebody
doesn't want the past stirred up, and is
prepared to kill to keep it that way.

Available from 21st May

Jennifer
BLAKE

LUKE

Luke Benedict figures he's the only one in
Turn-Coupe, Louisiana, who can save novelist
April Halstead from someone intent on revenge.
If only he could get April to cooperate.

Down in Louisiana, a man'll do whatever it takes…

MIRA®

Available from 21st May